Myself, Christopher Wren

A

Myself, Christopher Wren

by

DAVID WEISS

HODDER AND STOUGHTON
LONDON SYDNEY AUCKLAND TORONTO

Dedication

To London
For all that you are
to all those who return to you

London what are you

It is not what you were
that you are

It is not what you are
that you are

It is not what you will be yet
that you are

It is all that you are
to all those who return to you

that you are

Stymean Karlen

Contents

I Wonder What God Calls Himself

I wonder what God calls Himself
It is only our name for Him
And if we knew
Would we call Him that too
Or would we presume
And tell Him what His name is

Stymean Karlen

A*

I Wonder What God Calls Himself

THE FIRST THING THE FOUR-YEAR-OLD CHRISTOPHER REMEMBERED was his father telling him that his playmate, Prince Charles, was different from him. Until then, the child enjoyed being with his six-year-old playmate. But now, after his father's admonition, he was uncomfortable.

The next day when Charles pushed him, he didn't push back. They were playing in his father's quadrangle, which was attached to the Deanery of Windsor Castle where Christopher, his sister, Susan, and his father lived, but Charles stated authoritatively, "It is mine!"

"No, it isn't," replied Christopher. "It is my father's."

"My father's!" retorted Charles, "And mine! Everything here is mine!"

The six-year-old wanted to wrestle, but the four-year-old hesitated. Christopher didn't know what the word Prince meant, except that it must be something important, for whenever anyone addressed his playmate as Prince they bowed, although Charles was a child like himself and not much bigger or stronger. No one bowed to him. Did everything really belong to Charles? He must ask his father. This didn't seem fair.

He wondered if he should bow to Charles the next time his playmate pushed him. Or push back? He knew that his father was important, too, for everybody was polite to him, and yet in Charles' presence his own father was humble and soft spoken and not only looked shorter but walked shorter. This puzzled the diminutive Christopher. If he were tall, he would act tall.

He was even more upset when his father gave him a small wooden sword to wear and Charles wanted it. Christopher refused to surrender the sword, it was such a splendid object and it made him feel taller, and his playmate grabbed it. They were struggling over possession of the sword when Charles' father appeared.

Christopher's father, who was fond of God, the child noticed, for he was always referring to Him, exclaimed, "My God, child, this is a terrible mistake! Give the sword to Prince Charles. The King is approaching."

Christopher looked up and in this instant he didn't like his father, for in this moment of distraction, Charles wrested the sword away from him. He saw a short, stern man striding towards them with an uncompromising expression, moving through the quadrangle of the Deanery of Windsor Castle as if he owned it. And his playmate, carrying the wooden sword triumphantly, ran up to this man and bowed.

Was this a game, the four-year-old wondered. If it was, he thought, it was an unpleasant one. He wanted to cry. His playmate was wearing his sword. He could no longer share things with Charles. His toy belonged to him, everything belonged to him. Christopher could tell by the way his playmate wore his sword. Did he have to be so greedy?

Yet his father must approve of the way Charles behaved. He ignored the tears in his eyes and whispered, "Christopher, it is good for you to be exposed to the King. Bow to him, child."

Christopher tried, imitating Charles, but he didn't like the feeling. It wasn't natural and he slipped on the wet grass.

But the King smiled, which was a relief to the child, even though it was directed at him, for the King looked so strict until now. And he said to Christopher's father, with a slight stammer and a trace of a Scottish accent, "Dean Wren, your son has virtuous manners."

"Your Majesty, Prince Charles has been quite kind to Christopher."

"He should be," Charles I said patronisingly. "He is a Stuart."

Christopher didn't agree with his father that Charles had been kind; his playmate had not returned the sword.

His father said, "Your Majesty, it is gracious of you to allow Christopher to play with Prince Charles."

The King shrugged as if it were a matter of little consequence and said, "Your son is very small."

Christopher thought, so was the King; he only came up to his father's shoulder and his legs were slightly bowed, but perhaps this did not matter, for his father had such reverence for the King—as he did for God. Yet he did not like his father saying, "Sir, Christopher is very frail and delicate." That sounded as if there was something wrong with him.

His father continued, "Your Majesty, for quite a while I didn't think he would live. Only Christopher and his sister, Susan, have survived, although I sought to follow our Lord's admonition to multiply. I have lost five other children at birth and my dear deceased wife, Mary, departed this life two years ago, with our daughter, Elizabeth."

The King frowned, as if he had no wish to hear anything unpleasant, and his stammer increased as he stated, "God's will, Dean Wren."

"Yes, Your Majesty. He giveth and He taketh away."

"Has your son acquired any learning yet?"

"He is only four, sir. Just four."

"Would you like him to be tutored with the heir-apparent? While my son is in residence at Windsor? His tutor is worldly, yet pious."

Christopher thought his father would burst with pride as he replied, "It would be a great honour, Your Majesty." Now he was stuttering.

Charles I's Scottish accent was more pronounced but his stammer lessened as he declared, "Your brother, Bishop Matthew Wren of Norwich, who preceded you in the post of Dean of Windsor, has given me many valuable services throughout the years, I am happy to say."

Christopher wondered why the King looked so weary and remote.

"Of course," added Charles I, "My son has a large establishment, so your boy, Dean Wren, will have to accommodate himself in his learning to the duties and pleasures of Prince Charles' day."

"God bless you, sir!"

"These lessons will commence when the Prince's tutor and governor, the Earl of Newcastle, arrives. I expect him at Windsor any day now."

"Thank you, Your Majesty. I shall be eternally grateful."

Charles tugged at his father's sleeve.

"What is it?" the King asked angrily. He hated to be touched, even by his children. He could be intimate only with his Queen. And his son was being undignified, and thus behaving unlike a Prince.

"Sir, I have to make water and there is no closet within sight."

For a moment the King forgot himself. Gone was his carefully composed gravity. He snapped testily, "Charles, this is not the sort of thing to discuss in public. You must be more fastidious, behave with constraint."

"It is the physic," whimpered the child. "It works at the wrong end and the apothecary gives it to me even when I don't need it."

"Tell that to Lord Newcastle. When he comes."

But when Charles looked so uncomfortable he seemed about to use the quadrangle to relieve himself, despite his father's scorn and disapproval, Dean Wren remembered there was a water closet nearby and assured the King that it was fit for a king.

Even so, Charles didn't move until the King gave his permission, although he felt a burning pain in his loins.

After the King dismissed the Wrens, Christopher was not sure he agreed with his father about the King's generosity. Although his father continued to talk about His Majesty's benevolence, the child felt that Charles I did not really care about him one way or another.

Dean Wren congratulated himself on his wisdom. As soon as he returned to the privacy of the Deanery, although he disliked vanity, he permitted himself a smile of satisfaction. Now he was certain he had been wise to bring his son here when he had been appointed Dean of Windsor, so that Christopher would be within sight and sound of the royal family. Dean Wren was a devout and passionate monarchist and recent events convinced him of the correctness of his faith.

The kingdom was at peace despite religious differences among the populace this year of 1636. Since the King had dismissed Parliament in 1629 and had ruled the country without it, there had been less open discontent. Dean Wren was hopeful this relative calm would continue in spite of the Puritans and Papists who, in his view, still afflicted the country. He possessed confidence in the ability of his brother, Bishop Matthew Wren, who had been assigned by Charles I and William Laud, the Archbishop of Canterbury, to root out the Dissenters.

To play and to study with the heir-apparent could be of inestimable value to his son. God surely must have listened to his prayers. Not for nothing had he named Christopher after himself. If the King could do it, so could he. Only one thing worried Dean Wren. Charles I's word was not always to be trusted.

But the King kept his word. Early one morning, earlier than the Dean expected, the Prince's favourite page, Pierre Ravic, called at the Deanery with orders from the King for young Christopher Wren to appear immediately at the Prince's apartments to meet the tutor. The ten-year-old page was tall for his age, fair and slim, which was the fashion, and with a fine pair of legs and a splendid posture which he expected to carry him far. Pierre Ravic was very sure of himself.

Christopher was still in bed, but this was a command. His father awoke him and after giving him a hurried breakfast of buttermilk and a boiled egg—consoling himself with the thought it would be better for his son to be abstemious rather than a greedy schoolboy—sent him off with the impatient page, after warning him, "Mind your manners, child, and only speak when spoken to."

The page was so talkative this wasn't difficult, the child realised.

As they crossed the ditch which separated the Upper Ward of

Windsor Castle from the Lower Ward, the page proudly informed Christopher, "We are entering the royal residences, the state apartments."

Christopher had been in this part of the grounds before, although never in the state apartments, but this morning the page seemed determined to give this journey a special significance.

"Prince Charles has his own household. Many people, hundreds, serve him. But I am one of his favourites. I am French."

"What is French?"

The page regarded Christopher with contempt. He wondered why they were allowing this child to study with the Prince; Wren was hardly more than a baby, so small and fragile. Yet something in Pierre had to impress—everyone around the royal family was always trying to—and he rushed on, "I go everywhere the Prince goes. To Whitehall, Richmond, Greenwich, whatever palace he prefers. Even to Windsor, although he doesn't like it much. Windsor is so run down." He stared irritably at his charge. This child wasn't saying a word. Wren must be too young to impress.

Christopher didn't know what a palace was. He was trying to absorb his new impressions and they were many, for they were entering a part of the castle in which he had never been. He was in a high state of excitement, but he was taken aback by the tutor's forbidding façade.

The Earl of Newcastle looked about the same age as his father and was almost as tall, with a ruddy complexion, a neat body and a brisk manner, but he greeted Christopher curtly and the child felt unwelcome.

He was seated at the end of the long table, below everybody else, although he was not the youngest or the smallest. Charles sat at the head, his chair elevated above the rest, and Christopher was introduced to the other children. James, the Duke of York, was Charles' younger brother, a fair, blue-eyed baby of three. The other two boys were older than Charles and were brothers: the eight-year-old George Villiers, the Duke of Buckingham, a handsome, rosy-cheeked youth with light brown hair and grey eyes, and the seven-year-old Lord Francis Villiers, whose fine skin and blue eyes possessed the same radiant colouring as his brother and which made Charles look even more swarthy than he was.

Christopher noticed that George and Francis Villiers were quite possessive with Charles, who seemed to admire them very much.

Then James started to cry almost at once and had to be removed.

Christopher felt like an outsider, although Charles greeted him. The grandeur of the royal apartments overwhelmed him even though his playmate's sneer conveyed an open distaste for these rooms. Yet his rooms were the largest and most elaborately furnished that Christopher had ever seen, particularly the study in which the lessons were starting, and Charles' servants were everywhere. Christopher was surprised that his playmate needed so many people to wait on him. He had only two, a cook and a housekeeper. However, he tried to smile and to feel at home, even when he saw that Charles was still wearing his sword. But he remained uncomfortable, for as soon as Charles was seated the Earl of Newcastle called for attention.

The Earl thought of himself as a governor; he despised the title of tutor. He felt it was fit only for theologians, an occupation he also disliked; he believed it led to bigotry. Now, worse luck, he had to teach a theologian's son. But he was proud of his competence. He knew he was a man of many interests, clever and learned, who had risen at court because his manners and taste did not offend the King. He was a devoted monarchist. Yet he realised that his greatest virtue in Charles I's eyes was that he was an accomplished horseman. He was aware that once the King was on horseback all sense of inferiority because of his smallness, stammer, and Scottish accent disappeared, and then Charles I felt superior to anyone in his kingdom. And the Earl of Newcastle knew that his most vital assignment was to give the heir-apparent the same skill and sense of superiority.

But first his pupils must learn their catechism. He ordered all his pupils, but Christopher in particular, since he was the commoner, to memorise the following words, although the child could not yet read or write:

"Our monarchy is the foundation, the strength, the greatness of our country, and the King is its anointed head, chosen by God to rule. Our religion has to be constructed for the support of the Throne. Our Church must maintain the same order and obedience to the Crown we give to God. Our King, God, and Church are one and inseparable."

Christopher was puzzled. The Earl was saying his father served first the King, then God, but that was confusing; until now he thought his father served God first. He wished he understood better.

The Earl persisted until Christopher was able to repeat these words by heart. He didn't correct Charles, who made several mistakes, and he accepted the Villiers' enthusiasm as a substitute for exactness.

He declared, "Now we will divide your learning into bodily pursuits, courtly pursuits, and mental pursuits. A sound body leads to a sound mind and both must be suitably adorned with proper and virtuous manners."

Instruction followed in dancing, fencing, tennis, and riding. But when Christopher joined the older boys, he was halted by the Earl who informed him, "Wren, you are too slight for dancing, too frail for fencing, too small to play tennis and too young to ride."

Christopher didn't mind about dancing or fencing, and he wasn't sure about tennis, but he passionately yearned to learn to ride. He was allowed to watch the others but that was all. James, the three-year-old Duke of York, was brought back to the class by his nurse for the riding and when he was too small and weak to sit on a pony alone, even when it just walked, Christopher noted critically, Charles' Master of the Horse accompanied him and held him in an upright position on the pony.

The older boys rode horses which made them very proud and superior. At length Christopher's patience wore out and he appealed directly to the governor, "Please, sir, can I try to ride? I won't fall off."

The governor retorted, "You are behaving childishly and selfishly."

"My Lord, when can I start my learning?"

"Tomorrow, when we turn to manners and pedantry. You need the first, child, and no doubt will succeed at the second."

However, the following day the Earl concentrated on the duties and pleasures of a monarch. Christopher was ignored again and even George and Francis Villiers were relegated to a secondary place, while there was no sign of the three-year-old James, the Duke of York.

The Earl stood in front of the heir-apparent, not asking any questions nor encouraging discussion, yet Christopher sensed this was a test for Charles, and a code of conduct. For in a way, the child thought, the governor was telling his playmate not to misbehave.

The Earl stated to Charles:

"*A ruler must always be courteous even when he is bored. He can never be too civil to his subjects, and he must always be considerate of women, especially great ladies. Yet he must not allow them to educate him or he will be enervated. His tongue must not flutter or trill over words but be employed distinctly. He must not be extreme in anything. Especially not in matters of learning and religion. Too much study clogs the brain and too much piety causes rigidity. It is good to know a little Latin so the ruler will be thought learned, but an excess can sound pompous. Too much reading leads to a surfeit of contemplation and hinders action. A happy monarch is one who rules without appearing to, who can be gracious even when he is the master, who knows when a smile at the right moment will be to his advantage, who has a good seat on a horse so the populace will be impressed, and who appreciates the arts without applying himself to them. Application to the arts can lead a monarch to careless and indiscriminate judgments. It is always better for a ruler to be opportune rather than fixed. To know when to be opportune is more sensible than all the book learning in the world. A ruler's true learning is in his understanding of the behaviour of those around him. Many will try to flatter and humour him, but he must not be deceived. Charles, never allow yourself to be deceived, it is the worst sin of all."*

Christopher saw the Villiers brothers listening carefully now, as if they were memorising these precepts, and Charles, often restless when ideas were being expressed, had not stirred but was regarding the governor intently. He wished he could be included, these words sounded so important, even if he didn't comprehend everything that was being said. He felt at such a disadvantage, not being able to read or write. When he learned, he thought, what a happy and exciting day that would be.

Suddenly, when the governor paused to take breath, Christopher blurted out, "Please, sir, can I learn words soon? Like the others?"

This child was being troublesome, Newcastle thought angrily, and instead of reassuring Christopher, he snapped, "We are not concerned with that here. Things matter, not words."

"I will study hard, sir."

"Each of my pupils studies hard. It is the least they can do."

Yet all he really cared about, thought the child, was Prince Charles.

Pedantry was the curriculum the next day and the child began to learn to read and write. Newcastle continued to devote more time to bodily and courtly pursuits but each week some attention was devoted to words. They became Christopher's new enthusiasm and as his learning grew he was happy again. When he was able to put words on paper with other words they took on a life of their own. He still yearned to ride, which was still the most vital activity in the classes, and he resented that he was not taught while the others became quite skilful.

But with reading and writing he felt their equal. He learned with ease and speed, while they resisted this instruction. Soon Christopher was as good as Charles and better than George and Francis Villiers. Charles liked to read for entertainment, but he was bored by facts and ideas; he was interested in people and things and outdoor pursuits, but he was a poor hand with a pen; while the brothers were disdainful of such laborious activities. They saw no need to read or write expertly, since they could always hire someone to do it for them—a view that Charles was inclined to share.

What pleased Christopher most about words was that they gave so many things, hitherto shadowy and unsubstantial, meaning and memory. This caused him to feel stronger, even a little taller—although he remained much smaller than the other boys—and when he learned to ride, he assured himself, he would feel wonderful and be as clever as his fellow students. Meanwhile, he resolved to practise words every chance he got.

Christopher adjusted himself with loving exactitude at his father's long table in the study of the Deanery. The first thing he did was to put cushions on the leather seat of the great oak chair so that his arms could comfortably reach the top of the table. Then he sat in front of his carefully arranged paper, pen, ink, and blotter. He wanted to feel natural. He formed O's, other letters, all sorts of figures, as straight as he could, until they became easy to write. He sought to avoid any blots, for he knew his father would be angry if he dropped any ink on the wood itself. He could write his own name now, but after writing it out several times that became tedious. Next he fell in love with circles and wrote endless ovals, fascinated by the circular movement of the lines. Determined to write a perfect O, he was so absorbed in what he was doing he didn't hear his father enter.

Dean Wren was preoccupied. The King had ordered him to design a building at Windsor for the Queen and to submit an estimate of its cost. Although he was flattered by the commission, he was troubled by its nature. He was certain Queen Henrietta Maria wanted this building so she could turn it into a chapel and she was a fanatical Catholic. This could put an intolerable strain on him. He could not in good conscience design a Roman church, and yet he felt sure that the Queen would not accept any other kind.

Then he was concerned about the physical deterioration of St. George's Chapel. He was the Registrar of the Order of the Garter and in less than two years he would be responsible for the ceremony held in the chapel when Charles, as the heir-apparent, would be installed as a "Companion of the Garter". Yet by that time the building could be in a deplorable condition. The fabric of the chapel was defective, the roof was leaky, several walls were cracked, some of the stained glass was shaky, and there were loose stones. All in all, he reflected, in desperate need of an architect. When it was rainy and chilly, which was often, the chapel became damp, cold, and draughty, and Prince Charles would only be eight at the time and could catch his death of cold.

Dean Wren remembered that at his previous church in East Knoyle, when the roof had collapsed he had built a new roof, but even so, as an architect he was just a gentleman and an amateur.

If only Matthew were here now. His brother would know what to do.

Matthew was very good at such matters and loved to build. When his brother had been Master of Peterhouse at Cambridge he had reconstructed the college. He had built a new chapel in a Renaissance style and ornamented it with a window which was a copy of a picture by Rubens.

Matthew was an ingenious man even when he was most authoritarian. He must write to him and ask his advice. Where was his pen and ink? It wasn't on his desk. Then he saw his son. "What are you doing?" Dean Wren exclaimed. "You are not supposed to use the great table!"

"Writing, father, When was I born?"

Dean Wren felt uncomfortable. He knew he should chide his son, but the child had been neat and there were no blots on the table. Moreover, as he glanced at what his son was writing, he thought, his son was remarkable, Christopher was forming a perfect O and his writing was straight, as if done on a line, although there were no lines on the paper.

"I had to learn when Charles was born. May 29th, 1630."

"Prince Charles. You were born October 20th, 1632. It is in the parish records in East Knoyle where you were born. How is your learning progressing?"

"They ride a good deal. Will you teach me to ride?"

Dean Wren shrugged.

"Can you ride, father?"

"A little. Enough for my needs."

"Charles loves to ride."

"So does the King. Do you like to read and write, Christopher?"

"Most of the time."

Dean Wren felt hopeful again. His son should become educated and the best educated men, the true university men, entered the clergy as he and Matthew had done from Oxford and Cambridge. The thought of his only son becoming a clergyman heartened him. With the proper ecclesiastical training and Matthew's influence, Christopher could become a bishop, too, or perhaps, even an archbishop like William Laud. It was useful for a bishop to write skilfully; it was one of Matthew's virtues.

"How old am I now, father?" asked Christopher.

"Four, going on five." As the Dean embraced his son his anger and anxiety vanished. He would go ahead with the estimate for the Queen's chapel and subtly convert it into a lodgings or something for her pleasure. She loved pleasure. Like the King, she preferred a well turned leg and flattery far more than contemplation and study.

Christopher was surprised by his father's emotion. All he was doing was writing straight and evenly. But it was fun to fill space.

After his son said his prayers Dean Wren put him to bed and added his own. Then he wrote to Matthew for guidance.

One day the King visited the class accompanied by two young men who were introduced as: "Sir Anthony Van Dyck, Principal Painter in Ordinary to their Majesties," and "Wenceslaus Hollar, formerly of Prague and newly appointed Drawing Master to the Prince of Wales".

Everybody stood up at the entrance of the King. But what interested Christopher was the differences in the two artists. The Dutchman was slim, elegant, suave, while the Bohemian was stocky, awkward, and plainly dressed. Van Dyck walked by the side of the King and was greeted with deference by Newcastle, while Hollar trailed behind and was regarded by the Earl as a servant. Van Dyck's apparel was as fashionable as the King's, who looked as if he had just come from a sitting.

Charles wore a beautiful white satin jacket, light yellow leather jack-boots, with a broad-brimmed black hat on his long hair, while the painter's high-waisted brown doublet stressed his fine figure, and his green silk stockings suggested the quality of his leg and his situation.

When all the proper formalities were observed the King spoke first. "Master Hollar will give Prince Charles drawing lessons, and if the Prince so disposes, the others may be included, too."

Christopher wondered why the King was so reserved with his own son, but Charles replied, "Sir, I would like to include the others."

"As you wish," the King said coldly, obviously disapproving of his son's decision. "But my Lord Newcastle, no instruction in face painting. That is for ladies and experts like Sir Anthony."

Charles asked, "Sir, may I sit for Sir Anthony soon?"

"It is being planned."

Van Dyck said, "Your Majesty, I would be very pleased to paint these children. It would be an attractive grouping."

The King said, his stammer increasing, "It could be arranged."

"All of them, sir?" Newcastle asked questioningly.

"Of course not. Buckingham and Lord Francis will suffice."

The King's tone indicated that the idea of including young Wren was unthinkable and the child wanted to flee. But as he started to leave the chamber, forgetting it was forbidden without the King's permission, Charles stopped him and as Christopher looked desolate he whispered, "Don't be disappointed. You can draw with me. You will like to draw. It is much like writing."

"Don't whisper, Charles!" the King said reprovingly. "If you have any questions ask Lord Newcastle or Sir Anthony."

The children stood like statues. Christopher's heart was hammering in his throat. He felt, somehow, as if he were loathsome.

Van Dyck said, "I hope all of you will listen to Master Hollar."

But Christopher noticed there was lassitude in his manner as if he were tired. Van Dyck began to cough, so violently he had to spit into his silk handkerchief to hide his discomfort. The King looked irritated at such behaviour, as if the painter had violated an idyllic illusion.

Hollar said worriedly, "Sir Anthony, you should stop working so hard. Before it is too late."

Van Dyck shrugged as if to say, One could not refuse commissions. The King turned on his heel and left abruptly.

His son thought, "So anything unpleasant must be avoided."

Van Dyck said in his most conciliatory tone, "Drawing can be sociable. Model for each other and then you can model for me."

Hollar agreed with the Dutch painter. As soon as his instruction started, he added, "Draw anything. Even the face of each other."

However, Charles didn't want to draw anybody else's face and when Hollar said, "A firm hand on the pencil is essential," he told himself this was true of riding but he didn't fancy what the teacher suggested.

Buckingham decided that if he wanted anything drawn it would be easier to pay someone else to do it, while Lord Francis was afraid they would laugh at his efforts and so he pretended, like his brother, that it was an occupation fit only for those in service.

Christopher felt that drawing was another form of play. Charles was complaining, "He is giving me too much paper," which was his playmate's way of refusing to draw any more, but he wished Charles would take his hand away from his face so he could draw it better. Hollar was praising his long fingers and the instant he saw paper he longed to put something on it.

Newcastle watched disdainfully; he knew this drawing was a waste of time, but no sensible courtier contradicted the King.

A month after the drawing class began the King returned to observe his son's progress. He brought Van Dyck with him so his favourite painter could agree with his wisdom in arranging for his son to learn to draw, and to judge his son's work, and Hollar had nothing to show him. Only Christopher was drawing and the King was offended.

He angrily asked Hollar, "Hasn't Prince Charles drawn anything?"

"Your Majesty, whatever he draws he tears up."

He turned to his son. "Is this true, Charles?"

"Sir, it is like a physic. It works at the wrong end and I don't need it."

"What about the others?" asked the King. "You, Buckingham?"

"Your Majesty, I was told this is not an occupation for a gentleman."

"And you, Lord Francis? Do you agree with your brother?"

"Sir, I tried, but it is not easy and as my brother said . . ."

The King cut him off impatiently.

Christopher spoke up, "Sir, I can draw."

"Quite well, Your Majesty," volunteered Hollar.

"Let me see."

Christopher proudly handed Charles I the face he was drawing.

"Who is this, child?"

"Charles, sir."

"Who?"

"The Prince, sir," said Hollar. "It is not a bad likeness, is it?"

Van Dyck asked, "May I see it, Your Majesty?"

"No."

"But perhaps, sir, the child has some ability."

"Yes, Your Majesty," said Hollar. "Young Christopher draws with a firm hand and with some consequence. He is a good pupil."

"I said no face painting." The King tore up the drawing.

Christopher cried out, "Sir, was it that bad?"

Charles I turned to Newcastle and said, "The child has no manners."

Newcastle nodded; he was against including this child from the beginning. But he didn't remind the King whose decision that was, that could be disastrous.

Van Dyck asked, "Your Majesty, was there any virtue to the likeness? Did it bear any resemblance to Prince Charles?"

"I didn't look at it," the King said stiffly. "This child is presumptuous. It may have been a mistake to have included him."

No one spoke. Then as Christopher bent over to pick up the pieces of his drawing in the hope he could patch it together, Buckingham—who stood next to him—put his foot on the child's hand and whispered, "Don't."

"Why not?"

"You don't belong here."

Christopher had to struggle to hold back his tears and Charles saw this and said, "Father, I have affection for him."

The King stared angrily at his son as if he had violated a basic rule of sovereignty, but Van Dyck said, "Your Majesty, you respect his uncle."

"Matthew Wren is not a child. And he knows his place."

"Begging your pardon, sir," said Hollar, "But this child is a bit unusual. He already has a sense of topography."

"Master Hollar, when I want advice, I will ask for it."

"My Lord," Charles said, "he has good posture."

"That is enough, Charles," the King said severely. "Hollar, you were recommended to me as an expert on drawing maps. You should have interested the Prince in such matters. Has he seen your views of London?"

"Yes, Your Majesty. Prince Charles seems to enjoy them, his only visible difficulty is his lack of interest."

Newcastle agreed, but the King ended any further discussion. He knew what he had decided; the other opinions didn't concern him. He declared, "I will settle this situation myself." Young Wren's suspicious pale looks were a presumption of guilt. Charles held out his hand to be kissed, and then, this completed in the proper order by the children, he departed.

Van Dyck didn't immediately follow the King, although that was expected. Curious about Christopher, for Hollar was not one to praise idly, he asked, "Do you have anything else the child has drawn?"

"Sir, the Earl of Newcastle ordered them destroyed."

Van Dyck turned to the governor and asked, "Why my Lord, Why?"

Newcastle bowed slightly to indicate his respect for the Dutch painter and replied, "If I wished to preserve any drawings, Sir Anthony, they would be yours. But these were scraps of paper. My duty is to instruct the Prince, not to collect the scribblings of a child."

Van Dyck sighed. These great lords knew so much, he reflected, they often knew nothing. His eyes met Hollar's and he was relieved to find that the Bohemian and he could communicate. Good art broke down all language barriers, perhaps not only language either. He wanted to bow to Hollar in deference. Hollar could do many artful things skilfully, etch, draw, paint, and the Bohemian tried his hand at everything, maps, portraits, landscapes, book plates, etchings, drawings, even surveys of towns and buildings; while he, Sir Anthony Van Dyck, he said to himself contemptuously, was so tired, although he was only thirty-seven, just seven years older than the Bohemian. Yet everything had happened as he had hoped since he had settled in England at the King's invitation. He earned more than any other painter; he painted more than any other painter; so much that now he needed a group of assistants to complete his commissions. But when he was tired, which was becoming frequent lately, and he was racked by his persistent cough, he wondered if all of his activity was worth the effort. Depressed then, he felt he was just prettifying his subjects even though they were flattered and pleased. In his most fatigued moments he was not even sure he was particularising. He was supposed to be Rubens' successor, he reflected ruefully, but when he was exhausted he felt he was using Rubens' flamboyance without his fire, although he was living far better than he had ever expected to. One shilling for meat, two shillings for a servant, and apothecary bills growing larger and larger. Yet the King liked to compare him to Raphael, only Raphael had died young, and he shivered at that prospect. And now his thoughts returned to the chamber, for the others were waiting for him to speak, even Newcastle, who gave him a respect the Earl accorded very few others. Van Dyck said, more politely than he felt, "I'm sure, my Lord Newcastle, you did what you considered correct. But it might have been intriguing to see if Master Hollar was right."

Newcastle said, "Our Drawing Master is an ingenious craftsman, but as a judge of character he should leave that to his superiors. Now if they were your drawings, Sir Anthony, I would preserve them with my life."

Van Dyck bowed and said, "You are gracious, sir." As he started out Newcastle accompanied him as a sign of his favour. Perhaps it was better after all, Van Dyck decided, to keep affairs orderly and polite; Newcastle had considerable influence with the King.

Hollar wanted to console Christopher, but Prince Charles was speaking.

"I'm sorry, Christopher, but my father is like a physic, he is always doing something for my health."

"Are you sick?"

"Not at all. And at a suitable time he will forget that you draw better than I do."

"Anyway," interrupted Buckingham, who took liberties with Charles no one else did, "It is not important. Drawing will be of no advantage to us. Your father only wants us to do this to keep us out of mischief."

"That is not so," Hollar denied indignantly.

Buckingham ignored him, addressing only Charles, "You know you prefer our entertainments. They're fun."

Charles grinned but he said, "You must not say that to my father."

Buckingham said disdainfully, "He will forgive me as he forgave my father."

No one had answered the question which troubled Christopher. He asked Charles, "Do you think there will be a drawing class tomorrow?"

Before Charles could reply, Buckingham said, "We are riding tomorrow."

The following morning the French page called at the Deanery

and informed Dean Wren that the tutoring of his son was over.

Stunned, the Dean asked—he was counting so much on this situation—"Why? What's wrong?"

Pierre Ravic replied, "Prince Charles and his entire establishment are returning to his palace in London."

"I thought the Prince liked Windsor."

"The King prefers Whitehall. Particularly now."

But something in the page's tone disturbed the Dean. "Did my son offend?" He had not heard about a royal departure.

Pierre shrugged. "No one is perfect."

"I will punish him if he offended. What sins did he commit?"

Suddenly the page felt sorry for his charge. He had grown fond of the child, for Christopher had never imposed on him, and he blurted out, "He learns too fast. He outdid the Prince."

"How could he? He is younger. He is . . ."

Pierre interrupted, stricken by his own temerity, "You won't tell anybody what I said? Please, sir. The King could send me back to Paris or to the Tower for gossiping."

Dean Wren muttered to himself, "I didn't know a love of learning could be a defect of character. And I was so proud of him."

"You will be yet, sir. He is very smart for his age."

"But not in everything. He must learn better manners."

Christopher looked so sad on hearing that the class had ended, the Dean didn't have the heart to scold his son. Instead, when the child asked him what he should do, the Dean said, "Play in the garden."

"Who with? Susan is helping cook in the kitchen, the housekeeper is busy elsewhere, and Charles doesn't want to play with me any more."

"It isn't that. He can't. Prince Charles has to return to London."

"Will you go to London, too? For the King?"

"I have work to do here." There had been no reply from Matthew as yet, and he had received word—privately—that the King was waiting impatiently for his estimate of the cost of the Queen's building. He must create some figures, reasonable figures, even if they were not actually accurate. "Now go into the garden and amuse yourself. And when I'm finished I'll tell your sister to play with you."

"Susan won't play with me. She says I'm too young."

"It won't do you any good to argue. I must finish my work."

After he gave Christopher a gentle push in the direction of the garden his son obeyed him. If only the child had paid the Prince the compliments due him, he thought, the present situation would not have arisen. He sighed and instead of remaining at his huge oak table and compiling reasonable figures he rose and stared in his glass. He must be practical as well as pious, he decided. The glass reflected what he wished to see: a tall, grave divine dressed in a spotless white collar and neat black robes, his face severe, but not as severe as his brother's, his nose long and narrow, his chin sharp and pointed, his brown eyes large and steady. But his son was so slight, so delicate it was a miracle the child had survived. Marriage had been one childbirth after another and one death after another except for Susan, who was nine now, and Christopher; and finally, on the seventh birth his wife, too, had departed this earthly life. He was afraid that Christopher would always be frail. But when he saw his son skipping about the garden he felt less anxious and he was able to return to his work.

Now the child was forced to play alone and to keep himself company ne invented many games. He watched himself grow and he felt that his height changed so rapidly these days that when he went to bed he was taller by morning. His curiosity about this was so active it was as if growing was something he invented. The size of objects took on great importance. His clothing and shoes needed to be changed and he became aware of the smallness of the Deanery gate in contrast to the massive gates at the entrances to the Castle. He felt that his house was dwarfed by the huge stone walls of Windsor. Everything that belonged to Charles was enormous while whatever belonged to his father was insignificant. How cramped the Deanery garden was! While Charles' gardens were glorious parks that never seemed to end! The Castle ceilings were so lofty but his father's ceilings were low. The Castle doors were so high and wide while theirs were no taller than his father and narrow enough to span with one arm; not yet his, he thought, but soon.

He developed his own language in which the Castle people were *Those*, his father was *Him*, and he was *Myself*.

One morning in his need for a new excitement he ran into the study when no one was there and invented a new game. He moved three chairs together and the largest one he called *Those*, the next in size he named *Him*, and the smallest he addressed as *Myself*. While he was preparing a contest to see which of the three was the strongest the housekeeper entered and shouted, "Christopher, why have you rearranged my chairs? Your father will be very angry."

He thought, "She wouldn't understand." Miss Smyth was middle-aged, unmarried, and of large proportions, with a loud voice and a florid complexion. But she expected an answer and so he said, "I just want to see how they grew since yesterday."

"And I'm so busy," she complained, as she put the chairs back in the order the Dean preferred. She felt overworked as it was. "What's wrong now?" The child was staring at her as if she were the silly one.

"You are so busy you don't notice anything. Did you notice how different I am? Look at my fingers, this middle one is taller than the others. And my big toe never stops growing. Do you want me to show you?"

"No. You go and say your prayers before the Dean starts looking for you. I'm too busy to play with you."

"You are so busy all you see is the dust and dirt. Go on, be busy." He moved the chairs together again and sat down in the one called *Myself.*"

"What are you doing now, child?"

"I'm sitting down on *Myself*," he said, forgetting it was his secret. In her confusion she struck back angrily, declaring, "You keep it up and you will stop growing altogether and your tall finger will shrivel up and your big toe will just walk away by itself and leave you behind."

Upset, he shouted back, "You are too busy to know anything!" He ran into the garden and counted cobbles, telling himself that he must call her *The Busy*, not Miss Smyth, which didn't mean anything anyhow. And he felt better when he was able to jump from cobble to cobble without touching any of the cracks. He had spent many hours learning this.

When Alice Smyth told the Dean how his son had misbehaved, he decided it was time he took a hand in educating his son himself. It was a propitious moment, for on the advice of his brother he had prepared an estimate for the building at Windsor to be used by the Queen. Matthew, knowing the Queen's extravagant tastes, assumed the building would be of considerable size and he provided for a chapel, banqueting hall, and chambers for a large entourage, and he wrote the Dean an amount which should cover every detail. On Matthew's instructions the Dean submitted this figure, £13,305 —the exactness of the estimate should prove to the King how thorough he was—and the plans to the Surveyor of the King's Works, Inigo Jones, as well as to the King. Nothing was built by the King without consulting his Surveyor, who was easily offended. Now all he could do was wait and devote himself to Christopher.

Lessons began the following day in the study and the Dean taught his son regularly. Since his son could read and write already, he was able to concentrate on arithmetic, the other immediate necessity. Accounts would have to be kept, letters of business, gossip, and affection exchanged, and if Christopher travelled or consorted with the great lords and ladies his son might even want to keep a diary.

The Dean was good at arithmetic and he was pleased with the child's interest. Christopher was enchanted with numbers and he learned them the way other children learned the alphabet. What pleased his father even more was his son's love of learning. Instead of having to force him to study, the child's desire to know was as natural as breathing.

Soon he was able to teach Christopher the rudiments of Latin and Greek, which pleased the Dean most of all, for these subjects were essential to an educated man, particularly an ecclesiastic.

But Christopher—although he absorbed the knowledge his father bestowed on him as if he were a sponge—glowed when he drew. He became so excited his father was jealous. Then Christopher's curiosity was spontaneous, especially about the natural world. The instant the child saw a piece of white paper he had to put something on it.

This worried Dean Wren. It was fine to become well grounded in Latin and Greek, but he was disturbed by Christopher's taste for drawing and designing. The King liked only Dutch painters such as Rubens and Van Dyck, who were already famous, and the Dean felt it was an unreliable occupation, without any sense of duty or dedication to God.

Yet his son said happily, "I'm a good drawer, father."

"That doesn't make it right. Or important."

"I can draw animals, birds, castles, walls, gardens, trees."

"So can I. But I don't do it all the time."

"Will you teach me to ride?"

"Christopher, I gave you my answer. You're too young."

"Charles can ride. And he isn't much older than I am."

Dean Wren intended to reprimand his son then, but the child looked so wretched he said instead, "Would you like a drawing board?"

"That would be wonderful!"

"But if I get you one you mustn't think it is all you're fit for."

"I promise." Then suddenly he exclaimed, "Do we have the means?"

"What are you talking about, child?"

"Can we afford a drawing board? A pony?"

"We have more important work to do than discuss such matters."

But Christopher persisted in spite of his father's frown. If he could have a drawing board, maybe he could have a pony, too. "Charles has many ponies, and horses, too."

"Prince Charles is the heir-apparent," Dean Wren stated.

"You told me. But Susan says we keep a good house."

"Susan's education is different. Work with the needle and wheel are a necessary part of a well bred lady's education. We are not in easy circumstances like some churchmen I know, but by careful house-keeping and judicious expenditures we are able to live consistent with our position. Yet we are not rich and we must be remunerated for our services." The Dean wasn't sure his son understood him, but the child was listening so attentively he asked suddenly, "Do you remember your mother?"

"I remember crying and everybody in black and a long coffin."

"Do you remember any more?" Dean Wren's tone grew imploring.

"No more. What was my mother like?" No one ever gave him a clear picture, he thought, not even his father. He talked about her virtue and piety but they were only words. "Do I look like her?"

"You have her light brown hair, grey eyes, and good colouring. She was such a good woman. And died so young."

"Where is she now?"

"She is with God. We must show the noble virtues of resignation and acceptance." He returned to the lessons. He couldn't tell his son that his wife, Mary, the only child of Robert Cox of Fonthill Abbey, had been an heiress and had brought him a substantial dowry.

"Father, are you in service?"

Dean Wren was puzzled. He didn't answer.

"Like the page and Lord Newcastle?"

"Yes. In a way. Certainly in the King's service."

"Charles doesn't draw as well as I do. But he can ride."

"That's enough questions," Dean Wren said curtly. "You have a streak of impertinence in you. You need more instruction on manners." But even as he taught his son to be more subservient, and he was still anxious about Christopher's health, for the child was still delicate and very small, he was proud of his son's wit. He reflected, 'The excuse that Christopher was too young and small to study with Prince Charles was wrong; his son was too intelligent and responsive. The heir-apparent was quick-witted, too, but indifferent to the learning that absorbed his son. And perhaps that was fitting,' the Dean decided: 'Charles was a born prince while Christopher was a born scholar.'

Christopher felt he was entering a new and exciting world. No matter how often his curiosity was gratified, there was more to learn. He was fascinated by the stars and he started to study them in a book he found in his father's library. He marvelled there was so much to discover in the world; he could play so many more games with what he was learning.

Numbers were such fun, and there were other books to read, mostly religious tracts which he didn't understand much of the time, but he liked learning new words, and his father gave him all the paper he needed for drawing. Susan still wouldn't play with him and he was still alone most of the day, but he no longer felt lonely with his numbers, stars, drawing, and books. And when his father gave him a drawing board he hugged it to his chest and felt wonderful.

There was no reply to Dean Wren's estimate for the Queen's building and he decided it had been rejected. He pretended it didn't matter and he continued to devote himself to his sermons and to the education of his son. But a letter from Matthew troubled him. His brother wrote:

"The more I root out the Dissenters, the more these weeds spring up. Here in Norwich our faith is assailed on many sides. Some of the most powerful peers are Papists with a secret allegiance to Rome, while many of the merchants and workers insist on conducting the congregations in their own fashion and infecting them with Dissenter dogma. They protest so loudly against my strictures they could wake the dead. Sometimes my head spins so from the noise it is hard to know which way to turn. But our Lord and Primate, Archbishop Laud, advises me that he has the King's absolute approval and support and that I must, however painful the task, disperse these rebels. I have to rid our land of these impious Dissenters who, in many ways, are even worse than the Papists. The law is on my side. The King has stated clearly and unequivocally that every one of his subjects must worship according to our Anglican ritual. But I fear that if I am not strong and resolute, if these Dissenters are allowed to flourish wherever they spring up, we are in for harsh times, even perhaps, a civil war."

The Dean paused in his reading. A cold sweat broke out on his back. The possibility of armed rebellion shook him profoundly. Yet he agreed with Matthew that the Calvinists were becoming more of a difficulty than the Catholics. And now there was the affair of Prynne, the most fanatical pamphleteer of the Dissenter cause, who regarded Matthew as his chief enemy. Because of Prynne's attacks on the King and the Church, the pamphleteer had been fined £5,000 and had been placed in the pillory, where he had been branded and had his ears cut off.

According to Archbishop Laud, who stated it publicly at Prynne's trial, the official charge was *"sedition against the State and an incendiary attack on the Church"*.

That inseparably interwove the Crown and the Church, thought the Dean, and added to the desperation of the Dissenters. And Prynne, now the martyr, now was also a hero to most of dissenting

London and much of England, too. Worse, almost everyone believed that the extreme severity of Prynne's punishment was because of his hostility to Matthew.

Had his brother been too authoritarian, the Dean wondered. Wishing Matthew's letter was more cheerful, he read on.

"So, I cannot waste time. As Bishop of Norwich I have to put many questions to the congregations. Not only have I investigated the condition of the churches, which in most instances is deplorable, I have questioned the looseness of the services, the careless dress of the clergy. I have searched out those blasphemous persons who profanely discourse on the Holy Scriptures without the proper guidance. I am resolved to rid my diocese of anyone who speaks against the King's authority or the Archbishop's. Dear Brother, I must pursue my labours with vigour, whatever befalls me personally. Anyone who does not support our King and Church is, in the final reckoning, a foreigner and a heretic."

Dean Wren stood up—he had been sitting at his great table in the study—and walked across the room and glanced out in the garden.

Christopher was playing with their new gardener, Seth Hale. Dean Wren was glad that he had employed this lean, dark-haired eighteen-year-old native of Windsor, for Seth was efficient and loved the garden, and enjoyed playing with his son and teaching the child the virtues and beauties of the garden. But there was one thing about the gardener that worried him. Despite the young man's industry and cheerfulness, he sensed from his speech and dress that Seth Hale might be a Dissenter.

Then, as he felt the quiet and comfort of the Deanery, dissent seemed far away and Matthew's vehemence unnecessary. Windsor was just a village, he reminded himself, and the Castle that dominated it the King's to obey and respect. A voice whispered to him, 'He must love all men.' He was a priest of God; he must be full of God's love of man; he wished he could love individuals more. And when he saw Seth showing his son the newly planted roses and tulips, he longed to absorb himself in the flower beds with them. At this moment he didn't want to agree with his uncompromising brother. If he could only stand before his congregations with love in his heart. The sight of his son's joy was almost angelic.

By the time Christopher was going on six he could read Latin and draw the Castle so his father could recognise it. He knew the names of the stars; he could add and subtract; and he was learning to garden. But what gave him the greatest happiness was Seth. Now he possessed a playmate, for the gardener was always willing to give his time and attention.

Today, a brilliantly sunlit afternoon in early spring, Seth was discussing improvements in the garden with his father and suggested that Christopher be allowed to participate and the Dean agreed. It gave the child a big, grown up feeling, even though he was smaller than anyone else.

"First, Dr. Christopher," Seth said to his father, "We must raise the land above the flood level by adding loads of muck and dung."

"Where will you get it, lad?" asked the Dean.

"From my father's farm, sir. He has horses, hogs, a cow, and a pony."

"A pony?" Christopher asked with sudden excitement.

"Yes. I learned to ride on him. He is strong. But peaceable."

"Child, you will learn next year," said the Dean, "when you are bigger." Now he felt like a builder again, even if, so far, his estimate for the Queen's work had been ignored. "I agree with Bacon, who declared, '*God Almighty first planted a garden and without one a building is but a gross handiwork.*' I will arrange this garden with rectangles and squares so that it has a proper sense of order, regularity, and proportion."

His son nodded, pleased; he liked things to be even. Each flower possessed its own face and character, each was wonderful in its own way.

Seth followed the Dean's instructions so ably that when he had to get a load of muck and dung from his father's farm, the Dean allowed his son to go with him when the child promised to be obedient and careful.

It was a moderate walk to the farm, which was at the bottom of the hill and just across the Thames River, and the first farm Christopher had seen.

Seth introduced Christopher to his father, Jeremiah Hale, a small, elderly man, with a flushed face and a terse manner, who lived alone and who bowed before the child as if he were a gentleman, yet the child noticed that Jeremiah Hale was quick and curt with his own son.

He was surprised that the Hale house was not stone like the Deanery but wood, and much smaller than his own home, and there were primitive rushes on the floor rather than carpets, and stools to sit on instead of chairs, and a vegetable garden in preference to a flower garden. But Seth took him about the farm proudly, showing him the small crops of rye, barley, and oats, and some beans and peas sown in strips. Hogs pastured in the woods and

B

there was a small forest for firewood. Beyond it, however, was a high stone wall and Seth regarded it fearfully.

"What is it?" Christopher asked, his curiosity aroused.

"It belongs to the King. His hunting park. It is the long valley you see from the Castle, that extends for miles and miles."

"Yes." He saw the pony and nothing mattered now but to ride him.

"Don't encourage him," Jeremiah said to Seth. "This young gentleman, educated in all sorts of useful learning, could be pitched off."

"I won't fall off," the child assured him. "I'm not the biggest tree in the world, but I'll sit on him as if I grew there. What's his name?"

"Monk," grinned Seth, "because he is black and stubborn and was owned once by a Papist." The mention of the pony's name and origin brought a smile to Jeremiah Hale's face, the first friendly expression Christopher had seen. Then Seth helped him on the pony in spite of Jeremiah Hale's disapproval. And while the gardener held the pony, he didn't hold Christopher, which gave the child a good feeling.

"Keep your knees tight," said Seth, "and hold the reins firmly and if he lurches or canters, bring him up quick with the reins."

As Monk moved under Seth's guidance and Christopher stayed on, he didn't feel so little and he longed to shout with joy, but Jeremiah Hale scowled and said, "Seth, the first time you rode you had a stomach ache."

Christopher felt so lucky. The trips to carry the muck and the dung occurred often and each time the child practised riding. After a few rides he was able to start Monk by himself and stay on without help, although Seth remained close to him and watched him carefully. Now he understood why Charles and the King liked to ride so much; he loved the motion, the air in his face, feeling grown up. He wished he could ride every day. Each time he rode it was different, better, faster.

But he was puzzled by Seth's father. Jeremiah Hale rarely spoke, except about God, and then he referred to Him in terms of the utmost familiarity. And then his manner was so different from the Dean's.

One day when Jeremiah Hale thought Christopher couldn't hear him—the child was riding completely alone for the first time and was some distance away from father and son, who were loading muck and dung into a cart—he snapped at Seth, "I don't like you working for the Wrens."

"This clergyman is different," Seth replied. "He's not like his brother. And he gives me a shilling a day and pays extra for the muck."

"These High Churchmen are all alike," muttered Jeremiah. "They stuff our churches with Roman pomp and before you know it we will be Papists again. They have a craving for superstitious popery."

Christopher felt wicked, overhearing someone else's private words, but Monk, as if Seth was calling him, refused to obey his command to move away, and turned toward the cart, which he pulled also.

Jeremiah Hale continued, "I am expected to conform when I know the Book as well as they do. But do they truly fear God? Or their loss of power? Do they match me in holiness, mortification, or fervent prayer?"

Christopher realised that Seth's father didn't expect an answer, which reminded him of his own father, for Jeremiah Hale rushed on: "We must root out their idolatries. I have as much integrity and knowledge as any dean or bishop."

He said that, the child noticed, as if he were impregnable. The child wished Monk wasn't so stubborn; the pony wasn't obeying him at all now.

"These High Churchmen have mighty pretensions. And they hold all the best livings in England. With a grip of iron. The . . ."

The child didn't hear the rest; he kicked Monk to force him to obey and Monk cantered in the opposite direction, and Seth— thinking that he had lost control of the pony—ran after him, afraid the child would fall off.

Nothing bad happened, Christopher demonstrated happily, when Seth caught Monk, for he stayed on. But afterwards, as they carried a new load of muck and dung in the cart behind Monk toward the Deanery garden, he asked, "Seth, is your father a clergyman, too?"

Seth shrugged and said, "In a way."

"What way? Does he preach? On Sunday?"

"Yes."

"But he is not a bishop or a dean?"

"No."

"He does believe in God?"

"Of course."

"My father's God?"

"Christopher, there is only one God!"

The child was surprised at the irritation in Seth's voice. But he was also curious. "Then why does he dislike my father and uncle."

"He doesn't dislike them."

"He sounded angry to me."

"So you did overhear us?"

Seth looked reproachful and Christopher said apologetically, "I'm sorry, but Monk thought you were calling him. Why was your father angry?"

"I'm rather tired."

There was silence now, until they approached the Deanery. Then, just outside the Castle gate, Seth stopped abruptly and said to Christopher, "You won't mention any of this to your father?"

"Why not?"

"It would upset him. Worry him. You don't want to do that, do you?"

"No. Not at all. If that's what you want."

Yet when Seth saw the anxious expression on the child's face, as if he didn't know who to be loyal to, Seth added hurriedly, "My father has a right to his opinions. The Bible is God's word, not man's. My father knows every word of the Holy Scriptures. As much as your father does."

"Then why wasn't he chosen by my father?"

"In our church he doesn't have to be. He has the ministerial call, the inclination and the sufficiency. Remember, I won't tell your father you are riding Monk if you don't tell him about my father's views."

Christopher agreed.

But while he intended to keep his word, Jeremiah Hale's words aroused his intense curiosity about God. So he decided to ask his father about Him, without revealing the farmer's views. Since however, the Dean had taught him to accept God without question, he approached him indirectly.

He waited until his father was alone in the study and then, that night, after supper, while the Dean was preparing a sermon at the long table, he asked, "Father, what is longer? If I'm a friend of yours for the rest of *my* life, or for the rest of *your* life?"

The Dean was startled by his son's unexpected question, but the child was so earnest he tried to be equally thoughtful. "Since I expect you to live a long life and my life should be shorter because of my age, I'll be satisfied if you'll be a friend of mine for the rest of my life."

"Then what's left over from mine will be a friend of yours in heaven. That's where God is. Why do you say for God's sake?"

"Sometimes I say it too quickly. We do everything for God's purpose."

"Everything?" Christopher was surprised. "I can't image what God would do with some of the things I do. They don't even serve my purpose."

"You are a very young philosopher. And you sound like a pessimist."

"What is a pessimist?"

"Wait until you grow up!" His son could ask exasperating questions.

"Does he believe in God?"

"For God's sake, they say that when a child is ready for knowledge he should get it, but I'm not so sure. Go and play or learn your numbers."

"I know all my numbers."

"You need a wash. Has the housekeeper given you your bath?"

"I don't see how a bath helps God's purpose."

"Some people like to think that cleanliness is next to godliness."

"Father, you've told me that before."

"Since your mind is wandering beyond your years, a pessimist is one who has a gloomy outlook. But all this is beyond your understanding."

"I don't know. I like that you call me a young philosopher. I hope I'll be a sensible philosopher when I grow up."

"You will be. With God's help."

"Will God get all the credit for it?"

"For God's sake, you are wearying. I believe you are going to be a sermoniser, but I do hope you will be God's servant at the same time."

"I'll consider it, but I do like God. He never said I was disobedient, as *The Busy* always does. She could never be God's wife."

"Child, go to your room! You sound blasphemous!"

"*Blas-phem-ous*, that's a beautiful word. Will you teach me how to write it? *Blas-phem-ous*. What does it mean. And what is a philosopher?"

"You'll learn when you're older. Who is *The Busy?*"

Christopher felt self-conscious now, not wanting to reveal his secret, and he was silent, not wanting to lie either.

"Child, it is a sin to tell a falsehood."

"Father, is it a sin to believe in God differently than you do?"

"Who has been talking to you?" The Dean was alarmed. And when his son didn't answer he ordered him to go to bed and the child obeyed. Then, while the housekeeper put his son to bed he called Susan.

His daughter was eleven now, and she was supposed to take care of Christopher when no one else did, although she still didn't like to play with him, saying he was too young, too inquisitive. But she might know some things that had escaped his attention.

Susan listened attentively as he suggested this, a slim, brown-eyed and brown-haired girl who resembled her mother, and replied softly, as a lady should, "Cook says Seth's father preaches in the village below."

"But he is not one of my flock," the Dean said, puzzled.

"I think he is what you call a Dissenter. At least Cook says so."

The Dean frowned. Then he asked, "Are you certain?"

"Cook is."

But Cook was a skinny, young woman with a quick, malicious tongue, whose lips moved faster than her hands, and who looked down upon anyone who came from the village. Besides, he needed Seth at the moment. He had just heard that the royal family were returning to Windsor for the installation of Prince Charles as a Companion of the Garter, and since the ceremony was occurring in St. George's Chapel, which was close to the Deanery, his garden must be presented in the most favourable manner. So, deciding to dismiss Seth after the royal visit, he said, "If you learn anything else, Susan, you must keep me informed."

"Tell tales?" Susan looked shocked and she blushed. She was a good girl, even if she didn't want to play with her brother.

"Of course not! But false views must not be circulated in God's own house. Especially when the King is present. That is unthinkable."

"Is Uncle Matthew coming, too, father?"

"Very likely." He wasn't sure, but he didn't like to appear doubtful in front of his children, and it was not in Matthew's nature to miss such an important royal occasion, especially since his brother had been Dean of Windsor before him. "It will be a great moment, the Installation of Prince Charles. I will be officiating personally." If only, he thought, St. George's Chapel would not fall about his ears.

Susan had never seen him look so proud, so she felt proud, too, and she decided to do what her father asked.

Christopher, as he said his prayers in his bedroom, wanted to agree with his father, and yet. . . . There was Seth, whom he liked so much, but Seth saw God differently, whatever the gardener pretended, and he knew that old Jeremiah Hale had a view all of his own. It was very puzzling. He wondered what God called *Himself*. *The Busy* was tucking him in under the blankets, ordering him to be a good boy, and he couldn't ask her, for she would scold him. It wasn't enough to be *Myself*, he thought. He wondered if Charles had such problems. He fell asleep, asking God what he should call Him.

All the Houses Housed All

All the houses housed all
Except those that were left

Those that were left
Stoned all the birds
and slept in their nests

Smell a beautiful flower
And grow a soul, then rise

To the top of everything
Where nothing reigns
As a kingqueen

Not even a house

Stymean Karlen

2

All the Houses Housed All

"You have the advantage over me, brother," Matthew Wren declared. "The office of the Registrar of the Order of the Garter is always to be vested in the Dean of Windsor now. When I was Dean that was not so."

Was Matthew envious, Dean Wren wondered. With all of his power?

The Bishop stood purposefully, but for once not condescendingly.

And nothing was forever in this transitory world, the Dean reflected. He looked up from the great table in the study of the Deanery where he was arranging the records of the Order of the Garter to be sure they were correct and paused as he sought to decide how to answer his authoritative brother. His son sat by his side, wide-eyed and listening intently—it was useful for the child to learn about affairs of state, he thought—even though he doubted that Christopher understood much of what they were discussing, for the child hadn't said a word.

Now, for the first time, Christopher was aware of his uncle as a presence. Although the Bishop was shorter than his father, the Bishop dominated. He wondered if it was because his uncle was a bishop. Or older? He longed to ask but he didn't dare. Yet as his uncle strode up and down the long study while his father continued to sit and put together the papers before him, his inquisitive mind had to compare them. They looked alike, Christopher decided, both faces were severe, but his uncle's was more severe; they possessed the same sharp chin and thin, narrow nose, except that his uncle's was sharper and stronger.

Perhaps that was because his uncle was a bishop, the child thought. He decided to call his Uncle *We*. He wished he had pen and paper like his father to write that down, then he felt his father nudge him—to warn him to stop dreaming and to listen to his uncle.

B*

41

Matthew said, "However, brother, you must not only be a clerk to the King. You will never win his respect that way."

His father answered, "The King does not like errors. He has revived all the splendour and ancient observances of the Order. He is giving the ceremony on the 29th of May a special significance."

"Yes, he has come to Windsor with a vast retinue. The King is determined to stamp out all resistance to his authority. He is saying that once Charles becomes a Knight of the Garter he is the Sovereign-to-be in God's eyes and there is no gainsaying it."

Christopher interrupted, "Father, has Charles come, too?"

"Of course. He is the King's heir."

"Do you think he will notice me?"

Dean Wren doubted that, but he didn't want to hurt his son, so he said, "Children should be seen . . ."

"But not heard," thought Christopher. He knew these words by heart, and he subsided into silence as his uncle frowned at the interruption.

Matthew said, "I hear His Majesty's Surveyor, Inigo Jones, is with him and that they are going to examine St. George's Chapel for possible repairs. It will be an appropriate moment to bring up the Queen's work."

"But you said you doubted that Jones will approve."

"I am not an admirer of his, but he is the King's Surveyor, and has to be consulted. And His Majesty respects me."

"Uncle," asked Christopher, "what is the King's Surveyor?"

"Child!" The father was upset by this new interruption.

But Matthew, who fancied himself as an architect and wanted all Wrens to know how to build—it was useful for a churchman and he was sure that was young Christopher's future—stopped pacing and said, "The King's Surveyor is responsible for all of His Majesty's works and buildings and everything connected with them. Designing them, constructing them, and finishing them."

"Even gardens?"

"Sometimes, even gardens."

"Uncle, why don't you approve of the King's Surveyor, Jones?"

"Child, he is too Italian, too Popish for my taste."

"Does the Surveyor have a good seat on his horse?"

But his uncle was ignoring him as he said to his father, "I believe the Queen still desires the work and she has influence with the King. And she respects me, too, even though I am not a Papist."

His father nodded. May was starting and the weather was turning mild and beautiful after a long, bitter winter, and that improved his own disposition. There was nearly a month to go to the ceremony, which should give him time to get everything in the proper order.

Matthew had arrived this morning, at the same time as the King, although he had come from Norwich while Charles had journeyed from London. And to give Matthew his due, Matthew was usually right, and he said so.

"Possibly," Matthew agreed. "I look back with satisfaction on the affairs I've instigated. Particularly for His Majesty. As you recall ever since he went to Madrid years ago as Prince Charles to woo the Spanish princess, and I was appointed by his father, King James, to accompany him as his chaplain and to display the face of Protestantism to the Papists, he has been attentive to my views. When we returned, after a hazardous voyage, I was given the important living of Bingham in Nottinghamshire, and I was able to resign my fellowship at Pembroke, although I had doubts about leaving Cambridge. But since then I have advanced, except for the post of Bishop of London, which went to Juxon."

"Undeservingly in my view, Matthew."

"Perhaps. But I must not be vain. We must convince the King and Queen of the worth of your building. Are all your new plans ready?"

"Indeed. I'm presenting them as you suggested."

"Good. It will help us circumvent Jones' objections."

"But he has great influence. He is very positive, formidable."

"Because he has made a career out of architecture," Matthew said disdainfully. "That may be extraordinary, but his taste and knowledge of design are not. He believes himself a greater architect than he is. He overbuilds everything he does. Witness his new portico for St. Paul's. He is putting a Roman front on a Gothic cathedral. It is utterly incongruous, a profanation. Is there any sign of the King yet?"

"No. But we will know as soon as he approaches the chapel. I have placed my gardener outside to keep us posted."

"Is he to be trusted?"

"I'm not sure. He may be a Dissenter."

Matthew was shocked. He said, "I would dismiss him at once."

"But Uncle!" Christopher cried. "Seth is a splendid gardener!"

Matthew rushed on as if he hadn't spoken, declaring, "I do not regret anything I did in Norwich. We cannot allow any frivolity in matters of faith. I have taken an oath to God and I cannot break it. Let your conscience be at ease, brother. Harsh measures are necessary."

Christopher was surprised that his father was so humble before *We*. He could hear the thrushes singing in the garden and the blackbirds joining in and Seth had told him that May was a golden time for the garden, but neither his father nor *We* were noticing this or getting the same pleasure from the music of the birds that he was. He wondered if being grown up was like this. But if he asked he would be rebuked. *We* was saying that young Christopher must glorify God by going to church diligently, by reading the Bible daily, but the garden was God's house, too—didn't *We* know that? If he knew that, *We* should.

Seth stood in the doorway, informing his father that the King and the royal party were approaching St. George's Chapel.

Charles had come from Whitehall to Windsor with unusual enthusiasm for him. He stood in front of the high altar of St. George's Chapel and thought, It was fitting that the royal ceremonies were to be held here. This was the third richest ecclesiastical situation in the realm, next only to Westminster Abbey and Canterbury Cathedral in importance, yet free of London's dissenting views and only a minute from his apartments in the Castle. So he had decided to attend personally to the great business of his son's installation to the Order of the Garter, and he was resolved that nothing must block his plans—the effect must be stupendous. To achieve that purpose he had brought his Surveyor to construct the proper setting, one that must be as splendid, elaborate, and knightly as any of Jones' court masques. And he had ordered Van Dyck to depict the royal family during the ceremonies, and Hollar, the engraver, to record the scene.

But as he stood under the soaring Gothic roof it was as if a great weight lay upon his shoulders. The King knew St. George's Chapel was one of the finest medieval churches in England, with a perpendicular stress on space, light, and air, but he thought it was too irregular; he preferred the order of the classical. His right leg ached from a recent fall from a horse, yet he wished he could be in the saddle right now. Charles knew no one in the kingdom rode better than he did; when his hand was on the reins there was no indecision, no need to ask advice; then he was certain of what to do and he did it with skill and vitality. He didn't feel so short in the legs when he was on a horse.

Suddenly the King was annoyed that anyone was taller than he was; it didn't seem fitting. He was relieved when he was joined by the Queen, who was shorter than he was. Then he saw Bishop Wren and Dean Wren standing by the wrought iron gates near the high altar. There was a little boy with them who, he recalled vaguely, was the Dean's son. They were waiting with bared heads for his signal to approach.

He smiled slightly; Bishop Wren had performed a valuable service rooting out the Dissenters in Norwich with a single-minded devotion to the throne. And the Dean was a competent clerk. He frowned however, as he motioned for them to come forward, for the child followed them.

The Dean said, "Sir, I thought you wouldn't mind his presence."

What a small child, he thought, but he said, "It will do no harm."

Christopher noticed that the King was more interested in a large, elderly man who was by his side. He addressed him as Mr. Jones and the child inched closer, for the King was regarding Jones respectfully.

He recognised Sir Anthony and Hollar walking behind Jones, and he saw the Earl of Newcastle escorting Charles into the chapel. Then he became aware of a small, dark lady, whom he would not have noticed except that he realised she must be the Queen, for all the ladies in attendance hovered about her. He was surprised that Sir Anthony looked so much older and tired, and that Charles had grown even more than he had—he wondered if that was a condition of royalty—and was even more swarthy.

Impatient for new impressions, Christopher was curious about the Queen. He thought, Henrietta Maria was not beautiful but she acted as if she were. She was very short and dark, almost as dark as her son, although he heard her complaining about his darkness, as if it were something that distressed her. She stood expecting everybody to look at her and her thick curly black hair, her long nose with a slight bump on it, her heavy, hooded eyes, and her sallow complexion. Yet when the Queen moved she was graceful. And her expression compelled attention, it was so quick to be responsive, animated, and even alluring.

But for Christopher the most interesting person was Jones. All eyes were on him as he surveyed the chapel as if he were a part of it. Jones was the only one not in a court costume except for his father and uncle, yet his presence dominated. He wore a simple livery cloak.

"A sign of his office," Christopher's father whispered to him.

What attracted the child most was the Surveyor's personal appearance. Although he was an old man he was still handsome and hawklike. He wore no wig, which on many of the courtiers came to their waists, but displayed his own hair, wavy and disorderly. His pointed beard and flowing moustache were also slightly untidy, as if he had more vital matters to consider. His eyes were brown, his complexion ruddy, and his long, pointed face was dominated by his strong nose and vigorous chin.

Yet his uncle was regarding the architect severely and his father was uneasy, although all eyes were on Jones as he surveyed the chapel.

When he finished the King said, "This should furnish you with a splendid opportunity for magnificence and elegance. Like your masques."

"Yes, Your Majesty, if this chapel was only more appropriate."

The King frowned as if his own judgment had been questioned and he said coldly, "The chapel has been the scene of many notable ceremonies."

Jones didn't abase himself before the King's critical tone as most people did, but said, "Sir, in my opinion it is not worthy."

"What is worthy, Mr. Jones?"

"St. Paul's, sir, where the Prince's birth was celebrated."

"St. Paul's is little better than a ruin."

"Despite my restoration, Your Majesty?"

"The new west front is well shaped, the work of a virtuoso."

"Sir, it is the only portico on such a scale this side of the Alps."

"No doubt. But it is not suitable." The King turned to Matthew and said, "Bishop Wren, you have some fondness for building."

"Which you have encouraged, sir, through your good offices."

"What do you think of the virtues of the chapel?"

"They are many, Your Majesty," Matthew said emphatically.

The King allowed himself a brief smile.

"But sir, there is a desperate need for repairs. My brother, Dr. Christopher, reports that the roof is leaky, some walls are cracked, parts of the stained glass are shaky, there are loose stones, and the entire fabric is defective. He is very anxious about that."

The King asked, "Why didn't he consult my Chief Surveyor?"

"He did. He sent this report of the chapel with an estimate of the cost of the building for the Queen that you requested."

"Mr. Jones, did you receive these reports?"

"Yes, Your Majesty."

"Why didn't you act upon them?"

Jones paused, as if to consider his reply, while everybody crowded around him and the King, even the Queen and Prince Charles. He thought angrily, He had seen and experienced so much and a bishop was worried about a chapel. Besides, he worked for the King and no one else. He had designed and built so many things and the Bishop and his brother acted as if their single assignment was important. For the moment he loathed all of them. Even the King, who favoured him. Despite that, Charles never asked for or expected affection—only obedience. Jones longed to laugh in their faces, to ridicule them. What did they know? Compared to himself? He, who had known Shakespeare and Elizabeth and many others. He had been thirty when the old Queen had died and only nine years younger than the dramatist. He knew more about Italy than any other man in England; Shakespeare, before he had written "Romeo and Juliet", had consulted him about Italy. And so had Ben Jonson, before they had quarrelled, and Heywood and Webster, Dekker and Middleton, all of whom had been his age. He had outlived so many of his friends and acquaintances—Donne, who had become Dean of St. Paul's, and Raleigh, and Ben Jonson, who had died last year. It was one of the things of which he was proud. These churchmen might think him fragile because of his age, but they were wrong; at sixty-five he was still granite within.

He had to be, he reflected ruefully, there were so many problems to face as Surveyor. In the last year there had been no time to design or build anything, he had been so overwhelmed with the duties of his office. Let the King wait, he decided angrily, when he saw him stirring restlessly.

Jones pretended he was contemplating the chapel, as if that would help him arrive at an answer, while he recalled the time he wasted supervising the maintenance of existing structures, investigating frauds in building materials, in the manufacture, transport, sale, and use of timber, stone, brick, lead, and sand, the pollution of the King's water supply, and the worst difficulty and danger of all, the overcrowding in the city of London. Supposedly, as Surveyor, he possessed the power to condemn any buildings which jeopardised the health and safety of the inhabitants.

But when he sought to remove such houses because they increased the possibilities of plague and fire, he was disregarded, even though he was supported by a royal proclamation. The populace felt at liberty to build just what they liked without regard either to their neighbours or anybody else. Everybody ignored his warnings and used more inflammable timber rather than less, crowded closer together, blocked streets and lanes with confined wooden buildings, and added to the perils of fire and plague.

And the open sewers were even more frightening. Sweepings of houses, streets, and other refuse were piled close to inhabited quarters or thrown into foul streams, while Londoners pretended there was no risk.

Yet when he saw the King's stony expression, he chose his reply carefully. Bishop Wren couldn't be a stupid man with his connection, he thought, and his ecclesiastical situation was strong. He said, "I appreciate the Bishop's concern, but the money is needed elsewhere."

"Where?" asked the King.

"It's a rather difficult matter to bring up here, sir."

But everyone, even the Queen and the Prince, who had become impatient, were listening now. "Speak up," said the King. "What is it?"

"It's your water supply, Your Majesty. For your palace at Whitehall. I have discovered that your drinking water is being polluted."

"By whom?" The King was stern, but also uncomfortable.

"From houses in Piccadilly, sir. The occupants are throwing their garbage into the drainage which supplies the water for Your Majesty's diet and other uses."

"Remove them!"

"I have tried. But they refuse to go."

"I command it!"

"Thank you, sir. But it will be useful if the Privy Council could issue such a proclamation and have it read in the churches. And it will require considerable money to draw your water from other sources."

"It is most depressing," said the King, but he looked apprehensive.

"Thus, you see, sir," said Jones, "any money that can be spared must go to save you from pollution. Then there is another matter."

But the King changed the subject. "Examine the chapel, Mr. Jones. I don't want it to fall upon my head during the ceremonies."

Jones strode about purposefully while the King lingered reluctantly.

As if the King had a watch within himself that was ticking away, thought Christopher, but Jones was so active he became breathless. When he walked he was portly and vulnerable to strenuous activity, the child noticed and felt sympathetic, for Jones grew pale, striding faster than he should, pointing a pudgy finger to indicate his examination, although the child saw that his uncle and father still regarded Jones critically.

The others waited, although the Queen looked fatigued, but no one was able to sit without the King's permission and the King seemed determined to see this affair out, though with distaste. The child wished the bowing, curtseying, taking off the hat, entering a room, standing or sitting down wasn't so strictly regulated. It was graceless, for it didn't encourage his imagination or curiosity, and he felt out of place.

But Charles whispered, "How are you? Have you learned to ride yet?"

"A little. On a pony."

Charles said proudly, "I have my own stables and many horses."

"Are you excited by the ceremonies?"

"If they are not too dull. Do you still draw?"

"Sometimes. Do you?"

"Hollar is still my drawing master and Sir Anthony likes me to sit for him, but I'm too busy. I will have a kingdom to rule."

Jones was back and assuring the King, "The ceremonies in the chapel will not injure anyone and I will adorn them as Your Majesty wishes."

"How will I sit?"

"It will be arranged in a manner to please you, sir."

Matthew asked, "Your Majesty, what about the repairs?"

The King replied curtly, "You heard what my Surveyor said."

"Your Majesty, I hope no one will be hit by the loose stones."

"My compliments, sir," stated Jones, "but there is no such danger. I will see to that. Although these Gothic churches are barbaric."

Christopher saw that his uncle's face was dark with anger while his father's unhappiness had grown, but neither of them said anything.

Jones declared, "Your Majesty, the ceremonies will be all that you wish. I will decorate the chapel and Hollar will record it. Yes, Hollar?"

The engraver agreed.

"And Sir Anthony will paint portraits of the most illustrious persons."

Van Dyck was preoccupied, thinking his accumulating bills were a nuisance. The apothecary demanded ten pounds for his services, two of his chambers required upholstery and hanging which brought that bill to fifteen pounds, there was eighteen pounds owed for a bed, and his expenses for food were rising. But the King expected an answer, so he mumbled, "Sir, it will be all that you expect."

The King was turning to depart, when Matthew said, "Your Majesty, I wonder if you could favour me for one more moment."

"Do you still doubt Mr. Jones? He has a great knowledge of design."

"Sir, it is the Queen's building I am inquiring about."

But the King was prepared to dismiss his uncle without an answer, Christopher realised, when the Queen interrupted, "Charles, you promised me that I could have my own chapel in Windsor."

Matthew said, "And my brother, Dr. Christopher, submitted an estimate to you and Mr. Jones, Your Majesty. At your request, sir."

"Charles!" implored the Queen, "You do remember?"

He didn't, but he never could refuse her anything, so he said, "Yes."

She asked, "Could we discuss it where I could sit down? I'm tired."

Dean Wren said, "Your Majesty, the study of the Deanery is nearby."

"Are there sufficient places to sit comfortably?" the King asked.

"Chairs in abundance, sir. Just through the cloister and the quadrangle."

A few minutes later the King sat at the head of the great table, the Queen by his side and the Prince just below him, while the others still stood. Christopher was pleased that they sat in his chairs, the King in *Him*, the Queen in *Those*, and Charles in *Myself*. The Queen was vivacious again, excited by her prospective chapel. Yet he was scared that the King would not approve of his father's plans and this made him uncomfortable.

The King didn't ask to see the plans but said to Jones, "Why didn't you bring Dr. Christopher's estimate to my attention?"

"Sir, I didn't think you would approve of the cost."

Matthew said, "Your Majesty, it was very carefully estimated."

"Thirteen thousand, five hundred and five pounds," Jones said scornfully. "It is far out of proportion for such a building."

"For Her Majesty!" Matthew retorted just as scornfully.

"For Her Majesty!" Jones repeated in the same tone. "I designed and built the Queen's house at Greenwich for under five thousand pounds."

"Costs have risen," Matthew said. "Times have changed."

"Not that much," Jones said.

"Your Majesty, may I show you the plans? They are skilful."

"First, we must settle this matter of costs. There are many demands on the royal purse these days." Just this morning the Earl of Newcastle had presented a list of his son's expenditures that shocked him. Although he disliked figures and rarely remembered them, he remembered these. For he kept repeating them, he was so annoyed by them: twelve hundred pounds for building, thousands for horses, hawks, and dogs, two thousand six hundred pounds for tennis, dice, and cards, and one particularly irritating item, three hundred and thirteen pounds for tennis balls. What could his son have done with tennis balls? Such a passion for spending was troubling. "Mr. Jones, are you sure about the estimate Dr. Christopher submitted?"

"Positive. Sir, I examined every item."

"But Charles," the Queen reminded him, "you did promise me a chapel at Windsor like the one Mr. Jones finished for me at St. James."

Jones said, "Your Majesty, I am honoured by your regard for that humble building, but it cost only a little more than five thousand pounds."

"Exactly," said the King. "Perhaps, Bishop Wren, the excessive cost is because Dr. Christopher is an amateur."

"Sir, he is a born architect."

The Queen added, "Charles, you did tell me that the Banqueting House cost over fourteen thousand pounds and it is still not done."

"But it is a triumph! The greatest building in England!"

Christopher was wishing he could see it—he had never seen the King so enthusiastic—but his uncle, thinking, sometimes it was easier to be attached to the idea of kingship than the person of the King, said, "Sir, if you could look at the plans, I'm sure the costs could be adjusted."

The King was reaching for them when Jones said, "Your Majesty, there is also the matter of your stables."

The King halted abruptly. "What's wrong with them?" He was alarmed.

"Sir, the royal stables, both in London and in your country palaces, are in such a state of decay that there is no decent accommodation for your horses. Whatever money is spent, aside from that required for the completion of the work on St. Paul's and the remedying of the pollution of your water, must be spent on repairing your stables."

Yet the King hesitated as the Queen still looked at him imploringly.

Jones added, "Sir, the Lord Treasurer informs me that if any money is to be made available for the repair of the royal stables none can be spared for any new buildings at Windsor. So while I would be honoured to design a noble and commodious country seat for Her Majesty, or another chapel, it would be impossible at this time, for there will be no place to house your horses."

The King stood up.

"Your Majesty, should I prepare estimates for the Lord Treasurer?"

"For what?"

"For the royal stables, Your Majesty."

"With all possible speed."

Matthew asked, "Sir, what about the building for the Queen?"

"What about it, Bishop?"

Matthew wavered. The King was formal now, which indicated his disapproval, and yet if he could only remind him about Geoffrey Chaucer, who as Clerk of the Works to Richard II had received instructions to repair St. George's Chapel, which, although only forty years old at the time, had become already unsafe. He even recalled the date: July 12th, 1390. The King liked the poet, even though he didn't like people. But they were discussing the Queen's building, not the chapel, and the King could be harsh with irrelevancies. So Matthew blurted out, angry at his own lack of composure, "Sir, I'm certain a building for the Queen would be regarded favourably by many of the people. Most of your subjects are sincerely devout."

"And you should continue to devote yourself to keeping them that way. You have performed useful services in the north."

Jones smiled victoriously and Matthew thought bitterly, Ben Jonson was right, the Surveyor was vain, arrogant, a *Dominus-do-it-all*, but he said, "Your Majesty, you are gracious to praise my poor services. May God bless your reign as you have blessed us all."

The King nodded and as he turned to go, he said, "Dr. Christopher, I trust you have prepared all your records for the Garter ceremony."

"Your Majesty, I have compiled a record of the members of the Garter from its foundation. Every chapter of the Order is fully recorded, as you requested, with an exact account of all the ceremonies."

"Membership in the Order is the highest honour I bestow."

"I have three registers, sir. All carefully done on this great table."

"It is a magnificent table, Dr. Christopher."

But while Christopher's father beamed with pleasure long after the King and his party were gone, his uncle muttered over and over, "Jones, a *Dominus-do-it-all*, I'll never forgive him for this."

The child wondered why. If he were the King, he would have the best stables, too. And Jones did seem to know what he was talking about. He wished he could see some of the things the Surveyor had built.

The installation of Prince Charles, as a Knight of the Garter, occurred several weeks later. The Dean secreted Christopher in one of the stalls of the chapel where he could see without being seen.

The child was curious about what Jones had done and he observed that under his supervision everything was cleaned but nothing was repaired.

Yet the chapel looked impressive, for it was freshly painted and full of banners, coats-of-arms, enamelled shields, and heraldic armour which were shined so brightly they glowed.

Great effort had been bestowed on the woodwork and the windows and the many treasures of the Garter. And so many nobles crowded into the chapel with their attendants that the King decreed that no knight could have more than fifty at the ceremony, but Christopher had eyes only for Charles, the King and Queen, the Surveyor, Sir Anthony and Hollar, his father and his uncle, and his sister. Susan sat at the rear, since as a girl it was felt she needed less attention and schooling than he did.

The King was in the Sovereign's Stall beneath the Royal Standard. Charles and the Queen and the rest of the royal family were near the King, but a little below and behind him. Christopher's uncle was with his father, who as Dean and Registrar of the Order, was in the upper tier of the choir. Jones was in the next tier with Sir Anthony and Hollar, which was also a place of honour, and the child could see all of them.

He wondered whether Charles was excited. Some of the ceremonies were interminable and several times he almost fell asleep, but when the actual moment of installation came he felt wide awake. As Charles knelt before the King, Christopher was surprised by the amount of ritual. But as his former playmate became a Knight of the Garter, his heart beat faster. If it were happening to him, despite all the ritual, he would feel proud. But while the King appeared as haughty as the child had ever seen him and the Queen smiled with gratification, he sensed that Charles was not taking this ceremony as seriously as his parents. Then he stared at the Surveyor, Sir Anthony, and Hollar, and wondered what they were thinking and feeling.

Jones was remembering he had seen the Sistine Chapel in person, that possibly he was the only one here who had experienced this glory, and that he had sketched Michelangelo's figures from his Last Judgment. He could not be expected to revere these ceremonies. And he was pleased that he had not been servile. Yet the putting of this chapel in order had affected his stomach and given him what he called a vomiting melancholy, then it had gone to his head and he had caught a severe cold which still lingered. Only he couldn't use his favourite remedy—he believed that to sneeze with a feather in his nose relieved the discomfort in his head—but such behaviour would offend the King. Even he, he thought angrily, couldn't afford to do that. But he had put the Bishop in his place, he reminded himself, and now he felt a little better. He was surprised that Van Dyck had such a glazed stare.

The painter was wishing the King had allowed him to sketch the Garter procession as he had requested, instead of having to sit motionless and mute. But the King had stated, "It would be offensive. Do it from memory." But he had no memory, he needed models. He couldn't tell the King that he was really only content when he was working, in spite of all the gossip about his need to be a courtier. He was tired of stupid portraits, where the subjects insisted on being flattered. Some of them were disgusting. Sketching and painting were natural and the more successful he became the less he was independent. Even the Queen, who was not truly attractive, had to be portrayed as beautiful in his work.

All during the ceremonies Hollar was making mental notes. The King had ordered him to engrave the installation from memory and since he didn't have to falsify like Sir Anthony, he didn't worry. And Hollar was pleased to see Christopher again, the child had been his best pupil; he wanted to draw, unlike his noble charges. But as the cremonies began, the engraver concentrated on them, for the King demanded accuracy. From everybody, reflected Hollar, but himself.

The next day all the visitors were gone from Windsor but

Matthew. He remained an extra day to discuss his nephew's future. Christopher discovered this, accidentally approaching the study while his uncle was addressing his father. When he heard his name mentioned and he sensed from his uncle's severe tone that his father was being given advice about himself, he paused in the doorway, and hid behind the drapes so they would not see him. He knew it was naughty, but he was curious.

Then suddenly, his uncle changed the subject. "Brother, I hope you are not too disappointed about the Queen's building. There will be other opportunities if we are patient. And Jones won't live forever."

His father replied, "I'm more concerned about Christopher. It is time he had a better education than I can give him."

"You've given him a fine start. He already knows his Latin primer. It is the best grounding for a clergyman."

"But I think he prefers mathematics. He is very fond of numbers."

"That will pass. You have inculcated him with a decent and proper respect for the authority of the King and the Church. It was wise of you to have him witness the installation. He should be proud of you. Did the King compliment you on how accurately you keep the records?"

"Not a word."

"Nonetheless, he knows he has left his treasures in safe hands."

"Yes. I think so."

For the first time Christopher detected pride in his father's voice.

"I hope the child realises how fortunate he is to witness such events."

"What school do you prefer, Matthew?"

"Westminster. It is a royal school, founded by Elizabeth in its present form and attached to the Abbey, with strict orders that all religious observances be followed. Latin prayers are said at the start and end of every day and each year students are elected to Christ Church and Trinity, and so encouraged into an ecclesiastical career."

"But I'm not sure he should go away from home. He is delicate, Matthew. When Christopher was born I didn't think he would survive, and even now his frailness worries me."

"Your concern is natural. God called all of your children except Christopher and Susan, where four of my sons have survived, and my daughter. But observe him carefully. He has the Wren features, a high forehead, a good nose, a firm mouth and a strong chin. He may surprise you and have the endurance to do even tedious and tiring things. And at Westminster, he will be close to the royal palace of Whitehall. Moreover, it is a Church school with useful ecclesiastical connections. I hear that Dr. Busby, the new headmaster, is the kind of a man who will make many bishops. It will be good for the child."

Christopher saw his father nod, apparently convinced. But he was not. The idea of living in London excited him, yet he felt homesick at the thought of missing Seth, and where would he ride? And he resented being called the child and he wanted to talk to *Myself* about this, but his uncle was sitting in his chair. He ran into the garden to talk to Seth, thinking, His uncle wanted him to be a clergyman like himself, but he didn't want to be like his uncle. His uncle was positive about everything and he wasn't positive about anything. And nothing had been done about the repairs.

Truth And The Lie

Truth and the lie
Are twins
Born of one mother
Each would not
Be known
Without the other

Stymean Karlen

3

Truth And The Lie

CHRISTOPHER WISHED HIS FATHER WOULD STOP THE COACH AT Charing Cross so that he could get out and view the city ahead of him. In his entire life he had never seen such a spectacle. He had eagerly anticipated this journey to London, but what excited and astonished him the most was the diversity of the city. No two buildings were the same. From the smallest lodging to the largest palace, from the Gothic church spires which filled the skyline with artful gestures from the magnificent medieval public buildings to the fine Tudor town houses they delighted Christopher with their variety. And above all of them was the huge, dominating bulk of a cathedral.

He cried out, "Father, it's the biggest thing I've ever seen!"

"It is St. Paul's. It was even taller, until the spire was knocked down by lightning in 1561. Some think it was God's will."

"Do you think so?"

"Perhaps it was malicious gossip, for some wanted it pulled down."

"Why?"

"They claimed that St. Paul's had become profane. But there has been a church here for centuries. This site was destined for divine worship."

"Can we see it closer?" asked Christopher, his curiosity aroused.

His father didn't reply, but he ordered the coach to pause at Charing Cross, as if to decide whether to go down the Strand and into the city or to move toward Westminster. Actually, he was trying to make up his mind.

Should he proceed on to the school or turn back to Windsor?

It was September 1640, and while Christopher was nearly eight now, he had grown very little, although the child's learning had expanded. And the tutor he had hired for his son, Dr. Sheppard, had been unable to keep up with the child's craving for knowledge, and so he had resolved to enrol his son in Westminster School. But he was doing this with many forebodings. Since his son might be at the school for six years, he was worried about London's growing hostility to the King and to the Church.

He had been in London a few months ago when the dispute between the Dissenters and the Church had flared into open rage and violence and made the situation of Archbishop Laud and his brother almost untenable. What had occurred could have grave consequences for Matthew. He recalled the riot at Lambeth vividly. It was the reason he paused.

May day was usually a festive time in London, but Dr. Christopher was meeting with Matthew and other bishops on Archbishop Laud's orders at his palace at Lambeth to discuss how to halt the dissent spreading throughout the kingdom. And he had been invited, although he was not a bishop, because of his post at Windsor and its closeness to the King. But while their opinions would be asked, he knew that the final decision would be Laud's.

The Archbishop was not always likeable, thought the Dean, but he was a man of great learning despite his humble birth. Dr. Christopher had heard even the King, who was a friend of Laud's, blurt out—in a moment of exasperation with Laud's insistence on a uniform ritual even for the Queen—"A little, low, red-faced man!" And then Charles looked embarrassed, as if he had not been responsible for what he had said.

Lambeth Palace was a rambling pile of red brick and ragstone. It was on the south bank of the Thames, directly across from Westminster School, and Dr. Christopher accepted this as a good omen.

Laud said, "We cannot afford to show any weakness to the Dissenters. We must turn them out of the episcopal chapels."

Matthew added, "And charge them, Your Grace, for the damage their changes have wrought to the chapels."

Laud was thinking, what a clever idea! when there was a great roaring noise at the door of the palace. Dr. Christopher glanced out the window and couldn't believe his eyes. Young apprentices from the city, joined by burly men from the docks and seamen, converged by the hundreds on the Archbishop's palace. Then, sacrilege of sacrilege, the Dean thought with horror, one of the seamen, so young he didn't have the trace of a beard, went apparently mad, trying to break down the Archbishop's door with a crowbar, while his companions shouted, "Down with these supporters of the Catholic Queen!"

Dr. Christopher wanted to step outside and order them to halt, but Laud cried, "We are not prepared!" and fled out the back way. Matthew signalled for the others to follow and they did, into a waiting boat and across the Thames to the safety of Whitehall and the King's palace.

After the mob was dispersed the seaman who had tried to break down the door was captured and charged with high treason. A few weeks later he was publicly hanged and quartered and his head spiked on London Bridge.

Suddenly Dr. Christopher couldn't look at the bridge, which was visible in the distance. Now the seaman was a martyr, his death blamed on Laud and Matthew Wren. The young man had been only nineteen.

Suppose these disturbances grew worse? Yet Westminster was where his son belonged, he thought; the child should be safe there. Westminster was a royalist stronghold and close to the King and the King's power.

He ordered the coachman to turn right and toward the school, although his son looked disappointed. To console him, the Dean pointed out the places of structural interest that they were passing.

Christopher was surprised that his father was anxious. As they rode south on Whitehall the King's palace was huge and impressive. But there was a dreadful odour from the river and when he asked, "What is it?" his father replied derisively, "The King's water supply. The Chief Surveyor said it would be fixed two years ago, but he is so busy repairing stables he can't even provide a proper drainage system. The pollution is bad."

The child wondered why his father was pleased; the stench was worse than the manure on Seth's farm. Then Whitehall, which was a very wide thoroughfare, ended at the Holbein Gate, whose two octagonal turrets, Tudor decorations, and arched entrance fascinated him.

His father said, "The Holbein Gate marks the start of the palace grounds, and the upper storey over the gateway is supposed to have been the study of Henry VIII, where he could keep an eye on things. And that building on the left is the Banqueting House, which you asked about."

Christopher stared thoughtfully at the long, lofty building. Automatically he counted the number of storeys and windows. He decided that the two storeys were sensible, but he wasn't certain about the seven windows on each level. Yet Jones must have had a reason, he decided, and the Banqueting House possessed a symmetry that was pleasing and the facade flowed rhythmically. He was startled by the simplicity of the design, so different from the Gothic buildings nearby, and he expressed a wish to see the inside of the Banqueting House.

"Later," his father said. "The Chief Surveyor wants to see my plans for the Queen's building after all. Your uncle must have talked to the King. I am seeing Jones at the Banqueting House tomorrow."

"May I come along, father? I would love to see the inside."

"It depends on what your Head Master says."

Once through the Holbein Gate, they rode on a narrow thoroughfare called The Street, and after a short journey they reached the King Street Gate, which Christopher found dull and over-ornamented after the Holbein Gate, and then they were on King Street and at the school.

His father said, "You will be advantageously placed, next to Westminster Abbey and part of it, and a quick walk to Parliament Hall," and Christopher was homesick. He longed to shout at his father: turn back! He thought irritably, this was his uncle's doing, his fault.

"Archbishop Laud's palace at Lambeth, which I've visited, is just across the river. I'm staying there tonight."

"Could I stay with you, father?"

"Christopher!" Dr. Christopher was shocked.

The child subsided into silence.

Westminster School must have many secret lives, thought Christopher, as his father took him into the Head Master's office, the buildings were so ancient and gloomy. He knew it had been a Benedictine monastery, but he felt it had been built as a fortification against life itself, for the windows were constructed to shut out the sunlight rather than admit any, and the jumble of stone and wood was damp and chilly. It was starting to rain, a heavy mist which gave everything a grey, foggy crust, and he shivered, although it was not that cold. Yet he felt winter in his bones, even though it was September, and he missed Seth so. He even missed Susan, and she was only his sister.

While they waited for the Head Master to arrive, Christopher sought to reassure himself with the knowledge that Seth was still working for his father despite the gardener's dissenting views. Because Seth was such a good gardener, his father said, introducing laburnums and nasturtiums and red maples into their garden. But the child was glad that his father had stood up to his uncle. He felt better, too, remembering that the Dean had been presented with the living of Great Haseley near Oxford, and in addition to being the rector there, his father had retained their home in East Knoyle in Wiltshire, although Christopher had not lived there for years. He decided that his father was richer than he thought. Even if the

Dean didn't have as many homes as the King. he did have more than Seth, who only had two, the garden and the farm. Then Christopher felt funny, feeling better than Seth.

His reverie was interrupted by the entrance of the Head Master. He was surprised by his father's reverence for Dr. Richard Busby, for the Head Master was small, slight, spare, almost scruffy with his gaunt features and austere presence. He wore a canonical black gown and a tight-fitting black skull cap which came down to the back of his neck and he looked more like a monk than a teacher. His eyes were a dark brown, and his hair, heavy eyebrows, and carefully clipped beard were black. He looked old, although Christopher's father had told the child that the Head Master was young for such a post, in his early thirties. But the child wondered if Dr. Busby had ever been young, he was so stern, righteous, and uncompromising.

Yet his father bowed before Dr. Busby, just as he did for the King, and said, solemnly, "Sir, I am honoured that you are admitting my son to Westminster School."

Even so, Dr. Busby seemed surly, replying, "You are late."

But we were kept waiting, Christopher told himself.

"Sir, it was a long journey from Windsor. A test of endurance."

"Many things are. But you do come with good credentials. You and your brother were proteges of my master, the saintly Lancelot Andrews, Dean of Westminster. I understand he was responsible for your rapid advancement. And your brother's."

"Matthew Wren, the Bishop of Ely, is a most capable churchman."

"No doubt. Is that why he was transferred from Norwich to Ely?"

Dean Wren was silent.

"Nonetheless, I approve of his views. If anything, he was not strict enough. Though some say he was transferred because he was too strict."

"Dr. Busby, do you think the mobs in London will attack the Abbey?"

"Not as long as I am here! I will organise the boys if necessary into a regiment. Dean Wren, what else worries you?"

His father hesitated, then said slowly, "I have a meeting with the Chief Surveyor tomorrow and I would like my son to go with me."

"Why?"

Christopher said, "Sir, I've never seen the inside of the Banqueting House and I would like to hear Mr. Jones's views on it."

"The child has some interest in buildings, Dr. Busby, although I hope, under your tutelage, he will be prepared for the Church."

Dr. Busby growled, "I will make many bishops. Despite the Dissenters. Does your son have any knowledge of the classics?"

Christopher said, "I can read Latin. May I go, sir?"

"How old are you?"

"Eight, sir. Almost."

"Either you are or you are not. I trust your Latin is more precise."

He pushed a Latin grammar in front of the child, which he had written himself and said, "Read." When Christopher finished, having read precisely and perfectly, he said, "Your pronunciation could be improved. Dean Wren, your son will waste himself at the Banqueting House."

"At eight, Dr. Busby, a child is excited by anything."

"Not necessarily. But he can go. On one condition."

"What is that, sir?" asked Dr. Christopher.

"He is enrolled after this visit. Once your son is a member of the school, he cannot be withdrawn from class during the day for any reason. It is an inflexible rule. I find this method quite satisfactory."

"My apologies, sir, but that will have to be the day after tomorrow."

"Very well."

But when the Head Master was disdainful, Dean Wren hurried to add, "Sir, my child is a humble petitioner for your favour and protection, and for the honour of being a scholar in your distinguished school, and he hopes that in time, he will have the words and sense to say this."

"Good," agreed Busby. "But he is quite young. Most of our students enter at ten or older. However, I do not mind that too much, as long as he meets our requirements. He must be acquainted with the eight parts of speech, and have the ability to write at least moderately, and possess, above all, piety, and a capacity for Latin. I trust, Dr. Wren, you will provide quarters for your son yourself tonight."

"It might be difficult, sir," said Dean Wren. "If you could change that rule just once, sir, or . . ."

"No!" Busby cut him short abruptly. "I make the rules here. Not anyone else. Not even the King."

That night Christopher was forced to sleep in the same bed with his father at Lambeth Palace, since there were no other accommodations, and then they were put in the attic, for all the comfortable bedrooms were occupied by visiting bishops. There was no one to appeal to, for the Archbishop was absent and these bishops didn't regard Dean Wren as distinguished and learned as his brother said he was.

However, the next day, the child—although he slept very little because his father snored loudly—eagerly entered the Banqueting House. When he saw that Sir Anthony and Hollar were with the

Chief Surveyor, he was sure he would learn much. He stared about him avidly.

He was surprised. He expected to see a number of rooms; instead, the Banqueting House was one enormous room extending the length and height of the building. It was much longer than it was wide, and quite high, and he wished he could measure it to determine the proportions. He liked to understand the boundaries of things, particularly buildings. But if he paced the length and width Jones would assume he was critical, and he was not. With all the grandeur of the Banqueting House, it contained a simplicity that was pleasing and there was a clarity and logic to the design and structure that gratified him.

He wanted to say this to Jones, but he didn't, for it would be considered rude, and Jones was staring at him as the Chief Surveyor spoke to his father. "Your son hasn't grown much. What is he doing here?"

"He wanted to see your work."

"But isn't he going to be a clergyman? Like you and your brother?"

"This is why he is here. He is entering Westminster tomorrow."

"That was Ben Jonson's school. It didn't help him much!"

Dean Wren knew about their quarrel which had developed into open hatred and he changed the subject. He said to his son, "Christopher, the paintings on the ceiling are by Rubens. They are famous, too."

The child wished his father wasn't so obvious in his flattery, and he was more interested in the design of the building than the paintings. Moreover, the only way to see the ceiling was to lie on the floor and that wasn't allowed.

His father was showing his plans for the Queen's house at Windsor to Inigo Jones and the Chief Surveyor was nodding and saying, "Good."

"You will consider them?" his father asked.

"That is why Sir Anthony is here," said Jones. "He wants to paint a ceiling like Rubens. And Hollar will make engravings of it later."

"Despite what you said at Windsor?"

"The past is past. Of course, I may have to change the design."

Christopher felt that Jones had no intention of going ahead with his father's plans, but had another reason for wanting to talk to him. He was shocked by Sir Anthony's appearance. In two years the painter had aged visibly and now he coughed constantly into his handkerchief and the child saw blood.

His father asked, "Mr. Jones, what caused the King to reconsider?" although Christopher, if he was in his place, would not have asked, for the Chief Surveyor was clearly anxious to change the subject.

C

"The Queen wants an edifice with Sir Anthony's paintings on the ceiling. She thinks it will make her famous as an art patron."

Sir Anthony sighed, "I'm not sure I've the strength to complete it."

Hollar said, "You will. You will find it amusing. As soon as you control your cough."

Sir Anthony didn't feel amusing, although this was his reputation at court. Hollar mixed his work without question and appeared content with whatever he did, but the Principal Painter in Ordinary to their Majesties was supposed to be a courtier, too. But he was exhausted from painting familiar faces, rose-cheeked and lamb-featured English ladies, and fathers of the family, although most of them were notoriously unfaithful. Was it worth the effort? Or pure vulgarity? A man was judged by the company he kept and Henrietta Maria had sat for him thirty times and he was tired of trying to make her beautiful. He remembered what Bernini had said about her: "*What an unfortunate countenance!*" But he didn't dare express this. His debts were too large and his health was too uncertain. On the King's insistence he had married a practical wife, but that hadn't improved his fortunes or his cough. Charles had returned his sketches depicting the Garter ceremony, implying that his estimate was exorbitant, and had reduced the price for the heads of his children from twenty pounds to ten. Poor devil, Sir Anthony said to himself, I'm no better than a servant, whatever I pretend. If only my experiments in alchemy had worked. Instead, my cough gets worse every day. And now Jones is pretending interest in the Dean's plans, when the Chief Surveyor has no intention of using them, and is wasting my time by insisting that I be here. Yet he knew he could not refuse. Jones was building a new house for him and he must support the Chief Surveyor or it would never be finished. Or worse, he would be overcharged.

Jones said, "Dean Wren, to be honest, the construction of any more buildings depends on what happens in the kingdom. Do you think your brother could be a little less harsh on the Dissenters? His behaviour could jeopardise all of us. Even the King."

"Matthew is doing only what the King orders."

"But so severely?" questioned Sir Anthony. "He is the most hated churchman in the land, next to Laud. One must compromise if one is to survive."

Jones added, "Dr. Christopher, could you speak to him? Then your building can be reconsidered after all."

"Mr. Hollar, what do you think? You are in the city often."

"Dr. Wren, London believes your brother was responsible for the execution of the seaman and for Prynne's punishment. Anything he does from now on will only inflame the city more. There could be other riots. London may not be a safe city for supporters of the King."

Jones said, "Suggest to your brother to be more moderate."

"I will try, but Matthew may have gone too far." Then Dean Wren was sorry that it had slipped out, but it was too late to remedy that.

Jones didn't notice; Jones was distracted by Christopher, who was listening so attentively it was disconcerting. He tried to ignore him, but he couldn't, the child's concentration fascinated him. Too bad, he thought, forcing the child to be a bishop when young Christopher Wren possessed the potential to become something interesting.

As everybody but himself joined in the conversation, Christopher felt that the three artists were more interested in his uncle's behaviour than the Queen's proposed building and that this was just a ruse to get his father to change his uncle's severity. Why didn't his father see? Was he so blind? Or so eager to build that nothing else mattered? There was silence as his father said, "Let us pray for peace and understanding."

Sir Anthony bent his head, thinking, My work has been shattered by all these threats, perhaps Matthew was right, putting them in their place.

Hollar wished the Dissenters weren't so noisy, they distracted him just as he was reaching the skyline in his sketches.

Dean Wren reflected, What good was Van Dyck's pain if he had no faith?

But Jones had a feeling this meeting had failed, and decided he was right to prefer Michelangelo's God to the God of these churchmen.

At the door Christopher had to say—he had prayed twice already today—"Mr. Surveyor, are you going to build any more Banqueting Houses?"

"Why, child?" He was very intent and respectful.

"It is such a sensible building, spacious and logical. Like numbers."

"I used mathematical principles. How did you know?"

"It's simple, sir, the Banqueting House is so orderly and so are numbers. And the proportions are precise."

"The building is a double cube," said Jones. "One hundred and ten feet long, fifty-five feet wide. And fifty-five feet high."

Christopher exclaimed joyfully, "I thought the height was the same as the width, but I wasn't sure about my eyes, sir."

"Never trust your eyes alone. But don't neglect them either."

"I won't. Father, could I see Mr. Jones' chapel at St. James?"

"No. You are starting school tomorrow."

At five the next morning Christopher was awakened at the school with the shout of *"Surgite!"* It seemed senseless to him that every-thing spoken at Westminster was in Latin, since no one on the street used the language, but it was an inflexible rule at the church school.

He rolled out of bed, alongside many other students in the old, vast dormitory, and he felt bleak. It was dark outside as if it were still night and the air was icy. He was surrounded by a multitude of boys, all of whom looked older and bigger than himself, and he was lonely. No one spoke to him as he donned his school uniform, which was like a monk's robe, except to give him orders in Latin—as if to test him quickly—and he was grateful to his father for having prepared him properly in this language. The dormitory, which once was a granary for the Benedictine monastery, contained two long rows of beds. It was Christopher's first clear view of it—he had been brought here late the previous night by his father, who said, "I will be back in London soon for the King's return," and with a sudden, impulsive kiss left him—and he didn't care for what he saw. Yet the ancient monastic granary was the same size and shape as the Banqueting House, for it was almost similar in width, length, and height, and about twice as long as it was wide and high. After that, however, he noticed sadly, the similarity ceased. Where the Banqueting House was blessed with beauty and stressed its spaciousness, the dormitory was grey and dreary, with many small, square windows that suggested a dungeon and gave no pleasure to his eyes.

When all the boys were dressed, and at the end of five minutes it was assumed that they were, for no dawdling was allowed, a monitor ordered them to kneel and to pray in Latin. The wooden floor was cold and Christopher got a splinter in his knee, but he realised that the discomforts must be disregarded, it was part of the discipline of the school. But he was preoccupied, and as he stood up he bumped into another boy. Hurriedly, afraid he would be punished, he apologised.

"That's all right. I'm not a statue and you didn't break me."

He looked up and saw the boy starting to make the bed next to him.

The boy said, "I'm Daniel Van Doorn. Are you Christopher Wren?"

"Yes." He was glad that this student wasn't much older or bigger than he was, sturdily built, with fair hair, rosy cheeks, and hazel eyes, and speaking to him in English, although with a slight Dutch accent.

"I've been assigned by the Head Master to tell you what to do, since you've been put in the second form with me rather than in the first, like most beginners. Because you know Latin. But you should, your uncle is a bishop, I'm told. My father owns ships. What does your father own?"

"My father is a Dean."

"Oh!"

Daniel looked so disappointed that Christopher hurried to say, "My father is the King's Dean. At Windsor."

"Is that why you are entering the school late?"

Christopher felt he needed an excuse and he wanted to impress Daniel, who sounded friendly, and he replied, "Yes. I was delayed because my father was on the King's business."

Daniel was silent a moment and then he said, "My father serves the King, too, sometimes. But I was born in Amsterdam."

Christopher nodded, not knowing what to say. He had never met anybody who had been born in Amsterdam and he eyed Daniel curiously.

"Most of the students in the dormitory are King's Scholars. But I don't want to be a King's Scholar. Most of them are trained to be bishops and I want to be an artist. My father knew Rubens. He brought his paintings for the Banqueting House to London for the King."

"I saw the Banqueting House. Yesterday. My father showed it to me."

"What did you think of the balcony? I wish we had one here."

Suddenly Christopher blushed with embarrassment as if he had caught himself in an unworthy act. He hadn't even noticed the balcony in the Banqueting House. His mind said to him, Fool, why didn't you go up to the viewing balcony and see the paintings on the ceiling? A balcony built all around the Hall was there for a purpose and that wide, spacious stairway leading to it was meant to suggest that purpose. He was annoyed at himself for not being more observant.

Daniel asked him, "How old are you?"

"Eight. In a couple of weeks."

Daniel said proudly, "I was eight a month ago."

There was silence and then Christopher asked, "What do I do now?"

"Make the bed, sweep, and wash for the Head Master's inspection."

"Is he very strict?"

"Very! Busby always catches somebody. He is a great beater. The greatest beater in the school. Some of the older boys say, in England."

"Is my bed all right?" Christopher fixed his blanket carefully.

"Fair. I was supposed to board with Busby, since most of the boys here are King's Scholars. I was put here to study with them, so I could become one, too. But I don't want to go to Oxford or Cambridge and take Holy Orders. I'm going to return to Amsterdam and study painting."

Christopher had never met anyone his own age who was so assertive, and he was both fascinated and apprehensive, longing to know more about Daniel and yet a little afraid of where this might lead him.

After the boys made their beds and swept under them, Christopher and Daniel, as the youngest and newest boys, were ordered by the monitor—who was much older and in an upper form—to collect the sweepings and to carry them out. Then all of them went two by two to wash.

Daniel whispered to Christopher, "While they mention only the hands, be sure your face and ears are clean or you will be flogged."

When the wash was completed the boys lined up in front of their beds while the Head Master prepared to inspect them, a long rod in his hand.

Just to remind them where they were, however, Busby ordered the dormitory to say grace. The fifty boys knelt, the sentences said by one boy and then the rest. Each of the boys said the first sentence in his turn in Latin. Christopher, when it came to him, was filled with fear, but he made no errors and he was glad again for his father's training.

Then Busby said, "Let us pray!"

Christopher bent his head like the others, but he was so nervous he heard only fragments of the Head Master's words: "Jesus, lift us above our weak flesh . . . for your love of sinners . . . by your strong humility . . . your justice . . . righteous and saving . . . give us your mercy or we'll be damned."

Next they sang a hymn. Very badly, thought Christopher, and glancing behind him he saw that Daniel was smiling slightly.

Busby's prayer was Busby's views, reflected Christopher, as the inspection began, came near him, then paused several boys away. The offending student, who looked about ten, had forgotten to wash his ears.

"Bagshaw, put out your hands!" ordered Busby, deeply concerned.

Bagshaw cringed, but he put out his trembling hands and the Head Master whipped them until Christopher was sure they would bleed.

"Of all people to ignore my precepts!" snapped Busby.

"I didn't ignore them, sir. I forgot."

"Bagshaw, I expected more from you. You are a monitor, too."

"I'm sorry, sir."

"Nothing will ever be perfect," Busby grumbled, "but we must aim for perfection. It is the Westminster standard."

As Busby neared Christopher he became angry. The child turned pale, but it was the boy next to Daniel who had aroused Busby's temper.

The Head Master turned to an under master, a young, fumbling man in his twenties who was following him dutifully and fearfully, and spoke so everyone would hear him, part actor and part orator, and in English so there would not be an excuse to misunderstand him: "The dutys of each master is not only to instruct in tongues, in poets and orators, and to mould morals and manners"—and now his voice became especially stern and forcible—"but to enforce cleanliness of skin and hair and nails. Above all, he is to take care that no *pediculi* are to offend by presence on a boy or by transition to his neighbour. But here we have a case, in young Fotherby's instance, of common *Laus Pediculi*. If I find any more instances I will have a barber shave all the boys' heads. I will do anything, no matter how drastic, to keep Westminster free from *Laus Pediculi*. It is a very serious matter."

Christopher shivered; Busby made it sound like a hanging matter.

The Head Master ordered Fotherby to bend over so that his bare bottom faced him, and then he flogged the boy until his rod broke. Fotherby, plump and round-faced, red-haired and freckled, never said a word, although he whimpered a little under Busby's harsh stroke. Then, when the rod cracked, the Head Master commanded Fotherby to make a new one. And as a final, conclusive punishment to repeat an oration by Cicero.

But I don't know any Cicero, thought Christopher, and he had a moment of terror as the Head Master approached him. The first thing Busby examined was his ears and Christopher was grateful to Daniel for his advice, for he would never have washed them at home. He had a terrible moment of uncertainty however, as Busby stared down upon his head and hair, but apparently the Head Master found nothing offensive, for he asked, "Do you know any Cicero, boy?"

"I'm sorry, sir," mumbled Christopher, "but . . ."

"Speak up, Wren. You are eight, you said. Almost. Do you know Cicero?"

"No sir. My father concentrated on the liturgy."

"Oh yes. He would. Did you like the Banqueting House, boy?"

"Indeed, sir!" Christopher's eyes lit up. "It was beautiful! So pleasing to the eye. Everything was orderly and symmetrical."

"But too Italian to suit my taste. However, you are observant. I wish more of our bishops were. Van Doorn will take you around."

"Thank you, sir."

"What for? You've learned nothing yet. Except a little discipline."
Christopher nodded humbly.

"If you spare the rod, the child suffers. And never becomes a
man." Busby motioned for the classes to begin. "Wren, you will
need all the strength of a man if you want to become a Westminster
boy. And don't fancy yourself ill used. It will be much worse when
you are in the world."

So Many The Many

So many the many
So few the few
So everything everything
So something something
Anything can be anything
except be
one of an Only thing
        Since that is You

Stymean Karlen

4

So Many The Many

THERE WAS NO TIME TO REFLECT ON BUSBY'S WORDS. AS SOON AS HE
left everyone was ordered to study their assignment for the day.

Christopher was relieved that the second form's lesson was to
memorise Aesop in Latin; the text was easy and he learned it
quickly.

At seven his class was called by its monitor to stand in a circle
around an under master and to quote Lily's Latin grammar, with
the stress placed on memorising the meaning, use, and order of the
rules.

At eight there was a hasty breakfast, as if it were an after-thought,
and Christopher, while he was famished, ate very little, for he didn't
like the stale bread, the pudding was tasteless, and the beer turned
his stomach. But Daniel ate avidly, warning him that there would
be nothing more until noon, and he nodded and wished the food
tasted better.

Fires were lit at each end of the dormitory by students in the
first form, but none of this heat reached the part Christopher was in.

"That is for the upper forms," Daniel whispered to him in
English.

By now Christopher was very much aware that no language but
Latin was allowed to be spoken in the school—he had seen two boys
flogged in the past few minutes for lapsing into English when they
were unable to find the right Latin word—and he shivered at
Daniel's temerity.

At nine the students were led into the College Hall. Christopher,
determined to be observant after what he felt was his failure at the
Banqueting House, saw that it was like the dormitory he had just
come from, a spacious but gloomy chamber. The schoolroom was
also much longer than it was wide and quite high, an ancient stone
fabric of Gothic design, with a wooden interior, a lofty pitched

ceiling of oak beams, and three rows of school benches the length of the Long Room.

This hall was also heated by two open fires at each end, but again, Christopher's form—as one of the least learned—was seated far away from the heat. And before he could view the room in detail, there was another prayer, and then there was a two hour session devoted to translating Aesop from Latin into English in writing.

He realised that the entire school was taught under a single roof, that this was considered an essential part of the common life, but there was no time for reflection. There were fifteen students in his form and when the translating was finished, the pupils were ordered to examine each other's work. It was a clever trick, he thought, for the students were harder on each other than the under master and took delight in finding mistakes. Three mistakes meant another flogging, and several students, including Fotherby, were guilty of this delinquency and were beaten, this time by a monitor not much older than themselves.

At eleven the form was ordered to read a chapter of the Gospels in Latin for pronunciation and accuracy. The readings were low, monotonous, and Christopher noticed that Daniel mumbled when his friend read, and with distaste. Yet the under master said nothing, as if he had decided to put up with this, as long as the Head Master wasn't present.

By the time food came at noon the child was weary of the memorising and repetition, but after a pause for porridge, vegetable, and eggs, which he ate ravenously, although the meal was tepid, classes resumed.

From one to three the form read Erasmus' *Colloquies* in Latin.

Then to Christopher's surprise, there were no lessons for an hour.

"Nothing to do?" he whispered to Daniel, who sat next to him.

"Nothing. Except to rest. Busby allows this so we don't fall asleep in class. Too many students were falling asleep at their desks."

"Could we go outside?" asked Christopher. It was relaxing to talk in English after all the Latin, and no one seemed to be listening.

"Not unless Busby gives permission. I'm going to nap. You'll learn, with practice." Daniel put his head on his desk and fell asleep.

At four the second form was assigned the memorising of a page out of a book of rhetorical figures and proverbs collected by Busby. Near the end of the hour Busby appeared to hear the students read.

"Out of respect to the worthiness of this exercise," he said, "and to be certain you learn to pronounce naturally and sweetly, and without vanity or affectation." But he was annoyed by Daniel's Dutch accent.

Fotherby hurried to get Busby's rod and he said, "I will lay on a few strokes so our Dutch friend will show more discretion in his speaking."

Christopher flinched, but Daniel took his flogging in silence.

Busby added, "Tomorrow, Van Doorn, you will be instructed in geography so that you will become better acquainted with countries and learn that Dutch is an inferior language and not worth a beating."

At supper the beef broth was so hot it was steaming, but Busby, a great believer in fresh air, threw open the doors as well as the windows and by the time Christopher ate his soup and mutton, the food was cold and he felt nauseous. But no one seemed to notice or care, for everyone was studying their Latin grammars for tomorrow's lessons.

Yet later that evening he saw Daniel writing in a little book. When he asked him what it was, Daniel replied, "My account book. What my father pays Busby. What does your father pay him?"

"I don't know."

"Only the King's Scholars don't pay. Do you want to be one?"

Christopher shrugged, not sure.

"My father pays Busby twenty guineas a year, and I'm supposed to keep a record of what everything costs. Busby says we must understand the value of a guinea, every penny and shilling of it. Six pence for a comb, one shilling six pence for a geography book, eight pence for a looking glass, a shilling for mending my boots, three pence for a purse, seven pence for candles. Don't you have a light by your bed?"

"No. I came in so late last night." But had it been only last night, he wondered, it seemed a lifetime now.

"Here!" Daniel impulsively gave him one of his candles.

"You've only one left."

"It's enough. I hope you sleep properly."

"Why shouldn't I, Daniel?"

"I didn't, the first few nights. Surrounded by so many strangers."

"You're not a stranger."

Daniel smiled, pleased with Christopher's comment.

"And everything we do here is with so many other people."

"It is one of Busby's favourite precepts." Daniel quoted it: *"No boy liveth by himself, No boy suffereth by himself."*

But while it was inconceivable to Christopher that he had been in Westminster School only twenty-four hours and that he had just met Daniel this morning, he fell asleep easier than he expected. He was exhausted from the labours of the day and he felt comforted by Daniel's company and nearness. His smile was so friendly and relaxing.

The next few weeks Christopher learned that the most important thing at the school was to conform to the rules, to be on time for every activity, and to be obedient. Piety was essential and the boys who prayed the best received the best marks. Vital, too, was a thorough knowledge of Latin, and a pronunciation like Busby's. And for the boys in the upper forms skill in Greek, and in a few instances, Hebrew.

Christopher was disappointed that the teaching of English was ignored, mathematics was neglected, music was avoided except for singing hymns, and drawing was regarded as a profane interest and was scorned.

But household duties were also vital. Fotherby scoured his gown and his hair every week as if it were a religious rite. Daniel memorised his geography until he was able to illustrate Busby's belief in the supremacy of the kingdom of Charles Stuart and his Church over such inferior nations as the Dutch Republic and the Spanish Empire. And Christopher learned that his gown was no mere ornament, but the chief part of his clothing and an essential expression of the school.

Busby was proud of his passion for rules; he was determined his boys would become gentlemen, even if he had to flog them three times a day to convince them. Despite his smallness and his canonical habit, which he always wore—some of the boys said he slept in it, for he was never seen out of it—he was grateful to the Lord for having given him wiry arms and strong hands, to which he attributed his excellent technique with the rod. One of his favourite sayings was, "I don't suffer from a deficiency of muscular strength as some of my under masters do."

Christopher felt Busby flogged as if he were upholding the honour of the school, and that all boys were—whatever they pretended— wicked. Running and skipping were forbidden, each boy's gait was scrutinised and criticised and corrected, and laughter was frowned on, except when Busby joked, which was rare, and usually at someone else's expense.

Yet Busby did know Latin, Christopher learned, and taught it with a devotion that forced most of the students to know it, too, if sometimes unwillingly. Upper form boys—especially King's Scholars—could read Horace, Virgil, Terence, Ovid, and Cicero. And on special occasions some of them could perform exercises in Greek, Hebrew, and Arabic.

What bothered Christopher was the lack of imagination in his classes. Nothing was questioned; to do so was dangerous and led to flogging. Latin was easy and he learned Busby's rules quickly and accurately, and even his pronunciation, and he was surprised that Daniel found Latin troublesome. Most of the time he was ahead of his class, while his friend had to struggle to keep up with them.

But Daniel drew easily and excellently.

Christopher discovered this one morning in class when they were supposed to be studying Church catechism, which he knew and which bored Daniel, and he noticed that his friend was drawing.

"It is a good likeness of the under master," Christopher whispered.

"I wanted to study with Rubens," Daniel whispered back. "But he is dead. My father said he died in June and now Van Dyck has his studios in Antwerp. But I don't like Van Dyck's work, it is too pretty."

Christopher was surprised. He said, "But I saw Sir Anthony at the Banqueting House. The day before I entered Westminster."

"He must have left immediately after."

Christopher felt betrayed. He thought, Jones and Sir Anthony never had intended to accept his father's plans and they should have said so.

"But you have to accept the catechism, with your father and uncle."

Now Christopher drew, too, when he was bored, which was much of the time. He learned to appear attentive, as if always prepared to answer, and since he was the best Latin student in the second form he was rarely called or tested. As long as he didn't fall asleep in class but apparently sat motionless, he found he could draw without being detected. And as protection, whenever one of them drew, the other watched and used a Latin code as warning.

One afternoon while the under master read selections from Erasmus' *Colloquies*, asking the second form to analyse the passages, and Christopher drew while Daniel watched, Busby entered from the rear and neither of them saw him. Christopher handed the drawing of the under master to Daniel for his opinion and Busby took it.

Busby asked harshly, "Wren, is that why your father sent you here?"

Christopher didn't answer.

"You must have worked hard at it, to judge by the likeness."

Christopher was petrified, the Head Master sounded so stern.

"I was considering you as a candidate for a King's scholarship, but I wonder now whether you are worthy."

"But I did it," Daniel mumbled.

Busby snapped, "What did you say? With your ugly Dutch accent?"

"It is my drawing, sir. It fell on the floor and he picked it up."

"Have you gone mad, Van Doorn? You go to school to learn."

Daniel pleaded, "Please, sir, don't tear it up."

Christopher thought his heart would break, for Busby tore the drawing into many pieces. And it was a terrible problem. He didn't want Daniel punished for himself, yet he didn't want to be punished either. But his friend bent over before he could say a word, while Fotherby handed Busby his rod and the Head Master beat Daniel until his buttocks bled.

Afterwards, all he could say to Daniel was, "Did you mind very much?"

"When I sit. And translating Cicero when I have trouble with Aesop."

"I'll do the Cicero for you. What made you take the blame for me?"

"I got you to draw. The under master gave me an ointment for my skin. Would you put it on, Christopher? I am allowed to wash myself down."

As Daniel stood nakedly and Christopher applied the ointment to his wounds, his buttocks bled again and Daniel shivered from the pain. Yet Daniel insisted he continue with a courage he admired and Christopher noticed an odd thing. Daniel's penis was different from his. He had not noticed this before, although they had been naked in front of each other several times the last few weeks, but this afternoon he was seeing his friend differently, for his friend had bled for him.

Daniel knew what he was thinking, although he hadn't said a word.

"Oh, that!" Daniel exclaimed, as Christopher stared at him.

"But nobody knows," as if letting him in on a great secret, "except you."

"Knows what?" Christopher was embarrassed.

"You mean what I pee with."

"It's different from mine."

"I've been circumcised."

Christopher didn't comprehend.

"It's done to you if you are born Jewish."

Christopher was still puzzled. He had never known a Jew, and his father said there weren't any in England and hadn't been for centuries, and he said, "What are you doing here? In a school like Westminster?"

"My father wanted me to come to this church school so I could learn to be a Christian, but I'm not sure I want to be a Christian, they are always fighting among themselves."

"Does Busby know?"

Daniel regarded Christopher as if he were insane. "No one knows."

"Except me?"

Daniel nodded.

"What is your father?"

"He has homes in Amsterdam and London and sometimes I think he wants to be a Christian, but I haven't been baptised yet and neither has he. But everybody thinks we are Dutch, and accepts that as why we are different."

Christopher didn't say a word for a minute, and then he said, irritably for him, "If you don't stop squirming, I won't be able to apply the ointment and you wanted me to, didn't you?"

"Yes." And now Daniel stood motionless and stoically while Christopher applied the ointment until the bleeding stopped. Then he asked, "You have no ill feeling toward me, have you, Christopher?"

"Why? Should I?"

"What you found out. And what I told you."

"No."

"You're certain?"

"You didn't make a fuss over the beating."

"You won't tell anybody? I'm not ashamed, but it could cause trouble."

"And get you expelled from school?" That possibility was more than Christopher could endure and he said, "I won't say a word." He felt excited, keeping Daniel's secret as well as Seth's.

History

History
Has
All the facts

But not
The
  Answers

Having
Lost
Its instinct

And cannot
Feel
The Questions

Stymean Karlen

5

History

SEVERAL DAYS LATER DEAN WREN CAME BACK TO LONDON TO VIEW the King's return to his capital. He was able to take Christopher out of the school when Busby let it be known, as a devout royalist, that it was the duty of all Westminster boys to display their support and devotion to His Majesty by greeting him with their presence and cheers. So the street which led to the King's palace on Whitehall, and which was a short walk from the school, was crowded with Westminsters.

Christopher stood there next to his anxious father and he was surprised by the size of the crowd and the large number of fellow students. He saw Daniel with Fotherby and Bagshaw and he had a tinge of envy and he wished he could be with them. But the crowd was unruly and his father held his hand so tightly he felt like a little boy.

"Some of it is a London crowd," his father whispered apprehensively. "They have a seditious look and could cause a disturbance."

This puzzled his son. The plainly dressed Londoners were quiet; it was the fashionable country gentlemen with their brightly coloured cloaks and fancy scarlet doublets who wore the swords, and who were throwing cushions at each other's head. Yet when he said this to his father, the latter replied, "They only do it for sport and exercise, although it is a little unseemly here. But they will honour the King when he passes. They will give proof of their virtue. This is important. So His Majesty will know that the greatest part of his kingdom is behind him."

Before Christopher could ask why that was so important now, he was distracted by the hawkers behind him. He saw barrows piled high with nuts, gingerbread, and oranges. He could buy anything from a pair of whalebone stays to a clay pipe, from a charm to keep away witches to bottles of scent that perfumed gloves as well as the body. He was particularly attracted by the candy flowers and the plague water. They possessed so many strange and startling ingredients it gave him an urge to experiment. Then his father nudged him—the King was coming.

He couldn't see, he was so small and everybody in front of him was taller, and his father lifted him up and there was the King on a beautiful grey rather than in the royal coach, as if to impress the populace with the royal horsemanship and seat. Yet the King looked remote and he was surrounded by a vast entourage and the pomp and ceremony seemed to awe the crowd for it was silent. Christopher saw Busby on the other side of Whitehall cheering and ordering the boys around him to join in. Their shouts became an ovation which drowned out ominous rumblings from parts of the crowd.

His father said, "An excellent idea. Busby is intelligent."

Christopher was pleased that his father was relieved. The cheering evoked a smile from the King and he even deigned to wave his hand.

"Good. Charles must learn not to be so disdainful."

But Christopher felt that the King, underneath his broadbrimmed hat and long, curled wig, had not changed and still felt contempt for the mob.

As his father was about to say goodbye at the entrance to the school, Christopher asked, "How is Seth?"

"The garden is flourishing. Much of it is still green."

"And Susan? Is she well?"

"She is growing up to be a proper young lady. Soon she will be thinking of marrying. She will be twelve in a few months and she has become very good with the needle and she will have a suitable dowry."

But his father still looked anxious despite the hearty welcome for the King, and so Christopher asked, "Do you expect more trouble, father?"

"The King will have to call Parliament in session, to raise money, and many members are hostile. Sometimes, I wonder whether you should be at Westminster. It may not be safe, it is so close to the palace and Parliament."

"I can see both buildings from the school," Christopher said proudly.

"It is one of the reasons I enrolled you in Westminster. The school is history. With Westminster Hall, the Abbey, Lambeth Palace, and the palace of Whitehall all close by." Dean Wren sighed. "I thought that was important but now I'm not sure."

"What happened with the building for the Queen, father?"

"Sir Anthony went back to Holland. Apparently that ended it."

"Are you disappointed?"

"I think he wanted to get away from Charles and his commissions. He should be grateful for the King's patronage, but he isn't. Are you comfortable in the school?"

"I'm living with the King's Scholars."

"I asked Dr. Busby to put you there. So you could become one, too."

Christopher was silent.

"How is your learning progressing?"

"Dr. Busby beats somebody every day. He says it keeps him warm on cold mornings and keeps our minds on the Scriptures."

"Has he beaten you, child?"

"Not yet. But he would have, if not for Daniel."

"Who?"

"Daniel Van Doorn. A classmate. He took the blame for something I did."

That was Christian of him. Has the Head Master told you about the trouble your uncle is in?"

"No."

"The Dissenter dogs are attacking his Majesty's chief minister, Strafford. If they succeed in destroying him, Matthew will be next."

"Are you afraid, father?"

"For your uncle, yes. There are many things about Strafford I do not admire, but he is a strong man and a genuine supporter of the King."

"What do the Dissenters want to do to Uncle Matthew?"

"There is talk that if Parliament brings Strafford down, they will impeach Laud and your uncle. And I could be the next one attacked."

"Would I have to leave Westminster?"

"I don't know. We could be entering difficult times. The King will strike them down if they oppose him, but he comes in peace."

When Christopher asked Daniel the next day, "What did you think about the King's parade?" his friend replied, "Bagshaw and Fotherby were more interested in the horses than in the King. And Bagshaw, who, I think, is a Dissenter, says the King will have to call Parliament, even though he doesn't want to. There could be a lot of excitement here. And I've found a way to get into Westminster Hall. Bagshaw showed me. It leads from the school into the Abbey, and then into the Hall, through the back way. Besides, there is an old law that says all Wesminsters are allowed into Parliament and no one has ever taken the trouble to change it. Will you watch with me, Christopher?"

He was gratified that Daniel preferred him to Bagshaw or Fotherby, but he had to ask, "What about Busby?"

"That is no problem. The royalists in Parliament will want supporters in the gallery. If your uncle is tried, you will be able to see it."

Parliament opened soon after and within ten days Strafford was arrested and placed in the Tower to await trial. This was done behind locked doors and Daniel was unable to get in. And while Parliament concentrated on proving Strafford's guilt, school went on as if Parliament was far away.

Christopher didn't comprehend all the political struggles, even those involving his uncle, but he could tell from his father's concern—his father was still in London—that the difficulties were not over.

However, Daniel now had to prove that he could slip out of the school undetected. He arranged to do that one afternoon when Busby was away.

Daniel gave the under master in charge of the second form two shillings and they were marked present.

"For Christmas," he whispered to Christopher. "Early."

Then he arranged for a riverman to take them down the Thames to St. Paul's Cathedral for two more shillings. He told a nervous Christopher, "It is the most exciting place in the city. And the river is the best way to see it. You said you wanted to see it closer."

"I do. But if Busby catches us . . . we could be expelled."

"He won't. He is away for the day. Don't you want to go?"

Daniel looked so critical Christopher had to say, "Of course!"

And once they were on the river the minutes went quickly. Daniel was right, Christopher thought excitedly, everyone on the shore was far easier to see from the river.

Daniel ordered, "Dock us at Paul's wharf!" He spoke with such assurance that despite his youth the florid waterman nodded.

He whispered to Christopher, "I've been on the Thames before. My father is in the East Indian trade and the Baltic. His ships bring porcelain and spices from Java and Ceylon and herring out of the Baltic and grain from Danzig. But he will not deal in slaves. He says it is immoral."

But Christopher, while the voyage down the Thames was going smoothly now that the waterman rowed vigorously, was still anxious about the school. He asked, "Are you really sure that we won't be found out?"

"Yes. Our under master, Thomas Ryles, won't say a word. Busby thinks Ryles doesn't give us enough homework, but Ryles gets sick from what he calls our false Latin, with its Busby pronunciation, which he says is more West Country than Roman. And the Head Master says he is stupid, so Ryles fights his battles through us, although Busby is his cross."

"What will the under master do if we are found out?"

"He'll pretend he knows nothing about it. But don't worry, we're not the only ones. Some of the older boys stay out all night."

"Doesn't Busby know?" Christopher noticed that the waterman rowed with great skill and seldom splashed, although the open boat shook.

"A shilling here and there closes eyes and mouths, and the Head Master doesn't know everything, although he acts as if he does."

"You think Ryles dislikes Busby?"

"Very much. He is only twenty, new from Cambridge, who only went there because he was a King's Scholar—he is a poor boy— and Busby never lets him forget it. Then he is overworked and underpaid so whatever he gets from us is needed. He says Busby neglects the school by not providing enough masters to teach the boys, out of greed and to avoid expense, and so there is much playing of truant. And he feels that Busby treats him in an insolent and ignominious manner."

"How did you find out, Daniel?"

"I don't like the school. I thought I would run away at first, but it wouldn't be sensible. My father has a home on Warwick Lane, near St. Paul's, but he is usually in Amsterdam and my mother is dead."

"So is mine. I never knew my mother."

"Neither did I" Daniel said sadly. "Do you miss her?"

"Sometimes," Christopher admitted. "My father says she was beautiful. But I don't really know what she looked like."

"I have a picture of mine," Daniel said proudly, "painted by Rembrandt."

"Who is he?"

"A Dutch painter who lives in Amsterdam."

"Oh, he is like Sir Anthony."

"No. Not at all. Rembrandt is better."

"Like Rubens?" He was the only other Dutch painter Christopher knew.

"His tones are quite different. I want to be a painter, too, you know."

Christopher was surprised by how much his friend knew, but the boat turned the bend of the Thames and he was amazed by the view. As far as he could see there were boats. He was glad he was far sighted, for below London Bridge he saw the high masts and furled sails and proud flags of anchored merchantmen from Amsterdam and Venice, from Lisbon and Cadiz, from Archangel and Constantinople. There were fishing boats and coal colliers and many barges which the waterman rowed hard to avoid. Ferry boats passed them and a large painted barge, moving toward the watergate of a great lord's palace on the Strand.

The waterman paused a moment as he eased them toward the shore and said grandly, "London, most of all, is a seaport. On a good day thousands of boats, great and small, can be seen here."

Christopher wasn't listening. Rowing on the Thames was as exciting as riding on a pony, but dominating the horizon was old St. Paul's.

Daniel was annoyed by his distraction. He liked that it was easy to talk to his friend, Christopher listened so attentively, giving him a feeling what he said was of consequence, but now he was being ignored.

Christopher was seeing so clearly. He got a straight feeling behind his eyes whenever he saw a fine building and St. Paul's, in spite of its greyness, delighted him. He missed that the cathedral didn't have a spire, and he recalled what his father had told him. He wondered why it had been neglected. This building, he thought, taught him far more than reading or writing, or Latin. And the cathedral was so well placed, on top of a hill that was the highest part of the city, so that it was the first object seen, so that it had to be seen. The only things higher than St. Paul's here were the stars, the sun, and the moon, and he decided to investigate them when he got the chance. What a shame, he said to himself, Busby's enthusiasm for memorising made him want to avoid the rod, but it didn't make him want to learn. Perhaps Daniel was right about Busby.

The waterman almost ran on to a mud flat as he docked at Paul's wharf and for a moment Christopher thought they would be swamped. But while he smashed a plank with the violence of his landing, he managed to tie up at the wharf. Then he wanted to know if they wished to be taken back. As Daniel seemed to hesitate, he asked him, "How old are you, boy?"

"Twelve."

"You're very small for twelve and your friend only comes up to your shoulder. I'll take you back to Westminster for a shilling."

"No. My father lives nearby. We're going there. To Warwick Lane."

"That's up the hill. Near Newgate. The prison."

"I know." Daniel scrambled ashore, pulling Christopher with him.

"For another shilling I'll show you the Tower. You can see the famous people waiting trial or execution. Or Newgate prison. Or the brothels, or the remedies for two shillings. I'm a reliable guide, and don't mind the Dissenters, I know how to avoid them. I can tell from your clothes that you're not one of them. Or maybe you want something to eat? Calves' heads, geese, roast pork, or Cheshire cheese?''

"We know where we are going." Daniel pushed the boat off with his foot so that the waterman wouldn't pester him any further.

Daniel knew exactly where he was going, but Christopher kept hearing the waterman shouting, "Oars! Oars! Do you want any oars?" and Christopher kept thinking that the waterman was shouting, "Whores! Whores! Do you want any whores."

Daniel was possessed with London now. He led Christopher up a narrow, winding street to Ludgate Hill. But the walking was difficult, even though they went hand in hand and were the smallest people on the street.

There was mud everywhere, mud in the streets, mud in the houses, mud between the timbers of the houses, and mud in their faces. And the number of carts, drays, and coaches were dangerous. Christopher thought ruefully he must watch every step he took or he would be run down. It were as if the world of London ran on wheels, although he preferred to go on foot. The coaches and carts didn't look where they were going, but drove so their weight and size forced everything else out of their way.

He was upset also by the noise. The vehicles rumbled so loudly the earth beneath them seemed to shake. Hawkers screamed, "Pancakes! Tarts! Dumplings! Pears and pippins!" In reply, tradesmen stood outside of their shops and shouted even louder, to divert the passers-by from the itinerant hawkers. There was no quiet anywhere. And he was disappointed by the look of the city. What appeared impressive from the Thames was oppressive as he approached it. This section of London was a wooden city, he saw. Most of the houses were half timber and half plaster and so badly constructed they could easily be ignited by a fire. Roof tops converged upon roof tops and overhung the narrow streets which often were only alleys, and the aimless crowding added to Christopher's feeling of disappointment. He expected something grand, not this confusion and ugliness. He liked the slant of the roofs and the occasional red bricks and smoking chimney pots, although they were creating a fog, but he was shocked by the lack of sanitation. Some of the smells were petrifying and now he understood why so much scent was sold. And there was such an abundance of church spires. What a pious people, he thought, and then he remembered how critical his father was of the inhabitants of London, and he asked himself, were there so many churches because the Londoners were not good and needed such support? He wondered if Daniel's father was wise to settle here, if it was a fit place to live.

But when Daniel brought him before the west front of St. Paul's, he forgot everything else. Ever since Jones had praised his own portico, he had been eager to see it. There was a great space around St. Paul's and the cathedral was even more conspicuous here, perched on the top of Ludgate Hill, and Daniel said proudly, "You can see this side from our house. My father wanted to be close to the heart of the city. They cleared away many houses on this side, and even changed a church to make room, but we weren't disturbed, although it was uncomfortable for a while."

For a moment Christopher wished he resided here. He was fascinated by the regular proportions and symmetry of Jones' design. He thought, Everyone was compelled to look at the portico, it was the finest, most pleasant view of the cathedral. Like the Banqueting House, he noticed, just about twice as long as it was wide and high, and with much the same kind of columns, used to impress and to suggest grandeur. Instinctively he counted them, eight on the front and three on each side.

By now however, he was also seeing the rest of St. Paul's, and as his eyes strayed past Jones' work he was startled. Although the portico was beautiful and splendid, it was utterly different from the remainder of the cathedral, which was Gothic. He thought Jones' preference for a simpler style caused what was left of St. Paul's, which was most of it, to appear old-fashioned and inferior. It was as if the Chief Surveyor placed the portico as a screen to shut out the Gothic. Or to express his better taste, and that worried Christopher. He preferred Jones' clarity and precision, and yet, in this instance, that struck him as being out of place, wrong, for Jones' portico created a St. Paul's that was without harmony. Was there a kind of stone-blindness in the Chief Surveyor, he asked himself, with his all-absorbing passion for the regular?

Daniel said, "It is the largest building I've seen. Do you like it?"

"I'm not sure. I should, I guess, yet it sprawls so."

"Is that all?"

"I don't know whether the old church is over done or the portico is not done enough. But they don't fit."

Daniel shrugged. "My father says Gothic buildings are considered unworthy now. Yet wait until you see the inside. It's more exciting." He took Christopher by the arm and pushed him into a long promenade.

"It's the middle aisle and it's called Paul's Walk. Seems to go on forever. I measured it once. It took me over a thousand steps and my father told me that it extends about seven hundred feet."

There was such a confusion and babble of tongues and activity on Paul's Walk that the world outside was quiet by comparison. And Christopher's first thought was of the building. He had heard much about the worth of St. Paul's, that the Prince Charles was baptised here and that Guy Fawkes was executed here, and he was amazed by the dilapidated condition of the fabric. Masonry was decaying, statues were crumbling, he expected stones from the roof to fall upon him. But no one else appeared to care.

All sorts were walking elbow to elbow with him and arguing and selling and buying and most were just looking, gallants and soldiers, gentlemen and lawyers, merchants and lords, whores and gulls, and many others, in an excited and fervent state.

Daniel said, "You can buy anything you want here. From a woman to a horse, from a doctor to a cut-throat."

"And your father leaves you go here?" Christopher was frightened, for he saw two burly, scowling seamen eyeing them intently.

"He doesn't know. Oh, don't worry about them," Daniel added, when the two seamen approached them. "They are looking for youngsters to press into the navy as cabin boys. But we're too young."

Nonetheless, Daniel grabbed Christopher by the arm and quickened their pace until they lost the seamen in the crowd.

In the centre of Paul's Walk was a market place, the walls filled with gaudy advertisements selling plague water, witchcraft spells, looking glasses, scents, Flemish wall hangings, shirts and ruffs and doublets, Dutch spectacles. Others announced where bear-baiting and cock-fighting could be witnessed, or prize-fighting if this was preferred.

Christopher thought the roof of the cathedral would fall in from the commotion and he asked, "Isn't any of this forbidden?"

"The King issued a proclamation that no one can shoot a gun or use a dagger within St. Paul's, but even that isn't always obeyed."

A young woman sidled up to them and said, "Have a shilling, lads?"

Daniel blushed, but he said, "What for?"

"Don't be a gull, lad. I won't take any chances, it is only a short walk to Newgate. You won't be abused, I promise." Her dress was tight.

Christopher wanted to run. While the girl looked only about eighteen, her skin was pock-marked, her teeth were bad, and she smelled.

But Daniel was curious and he asked, "Will we have lechery?"

She laughed. "I have a house on Cheapside. What do you want to see?"

Christopher's apprehension grew as Daniel said, "Your breasts."

But when she started to unbutton her dress so they could see her petticoat and then her skin underneath and she said, "Come

along!'' and she reached out to take their hands and the two
shillings Daniel was holding, Christopher said, "I don't like your
fashion," and fled.

Daniel followed, saying, "I just wanted to see how far she would
go."

Christopher declared angrily, "In St. Paul's she is a desecration."

"It happens all the time," Daniel said matter-of-factly, but
wanting his friend to feel comfortable he took him to his home.

Christopher was glad it was a well-designed red brick building.

"In the Dutch fashion," Daniel said, and led him through the
arched entrance of a walled court and into a garden with fine
flowers and a stone fountain spouting out water. "We have four
floors with many large chambers furnished with good tapestry and
damask and some velvet and fireplaces in most of the rooms. And a
spacious hall as you enter."

"Won't your father be angry? Mine would be."

"I'll find a reason." Daniel knocked on the front door.

It was answered by a middle-aged woman with red hair, a big
bosom, and bright blue eyes and she was astonished to see the two
boys standing there. "Master Daniel, what are you doing out of
school?"

"We were allowed out. To celebrate the King's return to
London."

"That was several weeks ago."

"The school is still celebrating."

"Will you be able to get back safely? It will be dark soon."

"I'll hire a coach."

"Who is your friend?"

"Christopher Wren. A classmate."

"He looks so young."

"He is the best student in the form. And he is going on nine."

"Does Master Wren's parents know where he is, Master Daniel?"

"Is my father home, Mistress Stubbs?"

"He is in Amsterdam."

Daniel shrugged and said to Christopher, "Mistress Stubbs is our
housekeeper. She thinks I'm still a child. She is so English."

Before she could reply, he rushed off and he didn't halt until he
and Christopher were on Ludgate Hill again. Then he said, "She
thinks she is like a mother to me, but she is a housekeeper by
nature, always worried about the house instead of my feelings. Do
you have a housekeeper?"

"Yes, but my sister is supposed to be like a mother to me, only
she is just three years older than I am."

It was growing dark and Daniel hailed a hackney coach. The
driver hesitated, but when he saw the two shillings in the boy's

hand he took them back to Westminster, although Daniel didn't pay him until they reached the school. He told Christopher as they slipped into their dormitory by the back way, "You never know what tricks they will play."

No one appeared to notice they had been gone, but Fotherby, who slept on the other side of Christopher now, said, "Busby is very angry."

Christopher was sure they had been found out, but Daniel was composed as he asked, "Is the Head Master back already?"

Fotherby answered, "He returned sooner than expected. He heard that Parliament is talking of taking away our privileges and he rushed back to protect them. Where were you?"

"Next time I'll take you," said Daniel.

Christopher thought this was a day that to be alive was sufficient.

I Know And I Don't Know

I know and I don't know
Together
I know and I don't know
Much more

Stymean Karlen

6

I Know And I Don't Know

The news there was a riot at St. Paul's brought fear to Westminster. Rumours spread in the school that a mob of seamen, apprentices, and shop keepers were occupying St. Paul's in the name of the Dissenters and were stripping it of all ornament and ritual; that Lambeth Palace was to be invaded and crowds were growing in the city crying for the heads of Laud and Matthew Wren, now that Strafford was in the Tower; and that Westminster— as the King's school and Laud's—was to be attacked.

Christopher sat in the College Hall and heard these reports with the other students and didn't know what to believe. It was a November day, a few weeks after the trip down the Thames, and he had not been out of the school since. He was worried by the news about St. Paul's. He felt a loyalty to it now, and the possibility of damage distressed him. And he was concerned about his uncle. Bagshaw said to him, "Your uncle, Matthew Wren, is the most hated churchman in London."

All the under masters were meeting with Busby in his office and the second form, like all the other forms, were supposed to memorise their lessons under the guidance of their monitor who was Bagshaw.

Christopher stared at his grammar and Ovid and the Latin seemed absurd. He had no interest in Rome with so much happening around him. His imagination was attracted by St. Paul's, yet it wasn't an ancient monument to be preserved, even though it was almost a ruin. And Bagshaw was supposed to maintain order, but the monitor was not much older than his classmates and nobody was obeying him.

Several students in an upper form started to fight and a ring formed around them to cheer them on, and Christopher tried to see who was winning, but he was too small, and then he found a stool and stood upon it and saw better until somebody pulled him down. He turned to protest angrily and looked into the scowling countenance of Busby.

The other boys scattered like the wind and he expected the rod.

Busby said, "Boys, you should save your energy for the apprentices, you may need it. Wren, they are trying to humiliate your uncle. You must never allow yourself to be humiliated. Do you know your Ovid?"

"Passably, sir."

"Either you do or . . ." He hesitated, seeing the boys smiling at the expected retort, " . . . or you will not be a King's Scholar. Which is also the intention of some of those in Parliament." He turned so that he addressed the entire school, the under masters standing behind him in a body. "The next few days, weeks, months, even years may be difficult. But we must defend ourselves, even by force if necessary."

Christopher asked, "Sir, what happened at St. Paul's?"

"There was a disturbance at the cathedral."

"Was my uncle there, sir?"

"The mob thought so. That was one of the reasons they attacked it."

"Was any of the cathedral damaged, sir?"

"Some of the mob pulled down benches and stalls."

Daniel interrupted, "Sir, was that all?"

"What else would there be, Van Doorn?"

"I heard that the crowd attacked the High Church Commission who was sitting in St. Paul's and shouted, 'No Bishops—No Commission!' and smashed in several doors and drove out the commissioners."

"Where did you hear this?" Busby asked severely.

"My father told me, sir. He lives nearby."

"I know. That is not extraordinary. Boys, I hope we have no trouble here, but if we do, we must resist like true Westminsters."

After Busby was gone and the students returned to their books, Ryles took Christopher aside to speak to him privately. The slight, dark young man, with his brown eyes and soft features, looked anxious as he warned Christopher, "Your person may be in danger. Be careful if you go out of the school. If anyone asks your name, don't tell them. The name of Wren is much disliked in London."

"Bagshaw said my uncle is the most hated churchman in the city."

"Bagshaw talks too much. But you must be careful. London is on the verge of exploding and there could be more riots in the city."

Christopher wondered what good was it to be an outstanding student if he didn't have the freedom of the streets. Perhaps

Bagshaw and Ryles exaggerated—Bagshaw often did. But when he asked Daniel for his opinion, Daniel said, "Ryles is right. I heard that your uncle's chief enemy, Prynne, has been freed from prison by Parliament and is going to make a grand entrance into London."

Prynne did soon after, but no Westminster was allowed to witness his entry on pain of dismissal. Yet Daniel did, curious about this passionate pamphleteer who had accused Christopher's uncle of Popery. And afterwards he told his friend that the adoring crowd was larger than it was for the King's return and more fervent in its applause. It was frightening, thought Christopher, the man his uncle called a heretic was regarded now by most Londoners as a martyr.

And the students talked more about what was happening outside the school than what was occurring in Westminster, for their fate could be decided in Parliament. It was hard to concentrate on Latin. At this moment that language seemed very dead indeed.

Shortly after Prynne's triumphant return to London, Parliament impeached Laud and charged him with treason. There was deep concern in Westminster when the Archbishop was placed in confinement, for he was the spiritual leader of the school. Christopher was afraid that the school was going to be closed by Parliament. But when Busby learned that Laud was going to be taken from Lambeth Palace to avoid any public demonstrations of support, he decided to respond in his own way. Busby ordered his boys to line the opposite bank of the Thames to express their affection and loyalty for their Archbishop.

As the stocky, red-faced Laud stepped into the barge that was to take him into the official custody of the Usher of the Black Rod, the boys stood bare-headed as an expression of their respect and homage, and on Busby's orders, uttered a silent prayer for his safety. But Christopher was thinking of his uncle. Ryles had told him that if Parliament succeeded in bringing down Laud, his uncle would be next. He noticed that Laud, who was almost seventy, had to hold on to the sides of the barge when he stepped into it to keep from falling. But once in, he stood erectly and proudly as the fading twilight fell on his grey hair and reddish skin. He wondered if his uncle would be so resolute in such a crisis, although his uncle was younger and very active.

The day after Laud was impeached similar charges were brought against Matthew Wren and he was ordered by Parliament to answer in person.

Christopher sat in the gallery of Westminster Hall with Daniel when his uncle appeared before Parliament, and wished he could see better. He could hear the speakers, but the burly man in the row ahead of him blocked his view. Yet Daniel insisted on sitting in the rear of the gallery so they would not be detected. And that was essential, for he glimpsed Busby and his father in the opposite gallery, where the churchmen sat, and he didn't want either of them to see him.

He heard his uncle charged *"with setting up superstition and idolatry in our English Church, and acting the same on his own person"*.

But that was not his uncle, he thought, his uncle was an Anglican. Why did his uncle have to suffer for being righteous?

The next accusation puzzled him even more: *"It is also charged that Wren has tried to escape from England to evade the just punishment of God."*

It was not like his uncle to run away. How could they be so wrong?

He heard Matthew's firm and eloquent voice reply, "If it is the wish of God that I should suffer, it is better that I suffer from doing good rather than evil. I do not repent anything I have done. It was done in the name of our Lord and His ruler on earth, our blessed King. Whatever I did, was done to save souls, with a good conscience."

Then he missed what was happening, for Bagshaw crowded in beside them and exclaimed, "What are you doing here, Wren? It's dangerous."

The burly man in front of them turned around and scowled at the boys as he asked, "Are you one of that scoundrel's brood? A Wren?"

The questioner was dressed with Dissenter severity, all in black, and Christopher started to say, yes, in a way, but he felt afraid, for the man stared at him harshly, as if about to thrash him.

Daniel said hurriedly, "He is my cousin. Dutch. Our name is Van Doorn. We're here because my father is a friend of Mr. Prynne's."

"I trust you speak with a good conscience," the man growled.

"Sir, our consciences are exercised daily in prayer and devotion."

"At Westminster, no doubt, that den of royal iniquity."

"No, sir, we are just visiting London. This fellow mistook us for someone else. Didn't you?" He kicked Bagshaw so hard that Bagshaw nodded in agreement and Daniel sounded convincing. Before the man could say anything further the galleries were ordered cleared.

Busby put a watch on the doors the next day and no boy was able to get out of the school, and when Christopher was called to Busby's office several days later he felt that his truancy was discovered. This feeling increased when he saw his father and uncle there, and his father said, "We are thinking of taking you out of Westminster."

"Have I done anything wrong?" Christopher asked. Suddenly he didn't want to leave. He would miss Daniel, Ryles, even Bagshaw and Fotherby, and so much was happening nearby. "I know Ovid now."

"Your regard for Latin is commendable," said Matthew, "but your father is concerned that our enemies may vent their spite on you."

"Then I haven't done anything wrong," Christopher said with relief.

"Everybody does. But blessed are those who honour the Lord."

"I do, Uncle, I think."

"Of course he does," said Busby. "He is a Westminster boy."

His father said, "But I would neglect my duties if I didn't concern myself with my son's safety. I'm not sure he is safe here."

Busby said angrily, "It would be a pity to take him out of the school. I don't intend to allow any of my boys to be harmed. And he is one of my best students, even if he does stray occasionally."

"Not intentionally, sir." Then Christopher was silent, not sure.

"Bishop, I'm surprised you are worried. You are free on bail."

"Ten thousand pounds. It is a vast sum and shows the will of my enemies. If not for the efforts of my brethren in the Church I would be in the Tower at this moment. With Strafford. I may still be soon. My trials have just begun. That is why I am worried about my nephew."

"But I don't want to leave Westminster," Christopher said suddenly.

Dean Wren bit his lips as if he couldn't make up his mind and his son threw his arms around him and cried out, "I'll be careful!"

"If anything happens to me, you will take care of your sister?"

Matthew said sharply, "Nothing will happen to you. I'm their prey."

"Can I stay, father? I'll take care of Susan. I promise!"

Busby added, "It will be taken as a sign of submission if he leaves."

The Dean looked over to his brother who indicated Yes.

"Thank you, father."

"Then you like the school, son?"

It wasn't that. But he couldn't explain with Busby standing there.

Busby said, "Bishop, I think the King will stop Parliament from attacking you any further. And he will never allow Strafford to die."

"I'm not so sure. Charles is indecisive these days. Even allowing Strafford to be tried. And Laud and myself. He is really permitting himself to be judged. Which, in a ruler, could be unforgivable."

"He will save Strafford. He can't show weakness. It would be fatal."

"If he allows his chief minister to die, we will all suffer for it. Let the Dissenter dogs destroy Strafford, Laud will be next, then myself and the Church. It would be a calamity for England."

What bothered Christopher the most was that his uncle sounded just like his father—or was it that his father sounded like his uncle? They were so sure they were right, and he never was, not even a little.

Strafford's trial a few months later was about to reach a decision when the fifteen-year-old Prince of Orange arrived in London to wed the King's daughter, the nine-year-old Princess Mary, and Matthew, as Dean of the Chapels Royal, was given the honour of marrying them.

Christopher heard the news from his father, who assumed this was open and direct support of Matthew, but Christopher was not so certain.

He remembered his own feelings when his father took him to witness the trial of Strafford in Westminster Hall a week ago.

Busby gave permission, although it was a breaking of his own rules, but he didn't explain why and he was even more brusque than usual.

Christopher sensed that Daniel and Bagshaw envied him when his father called for him at the school, but they bowed humbly before the Dean and asked for his blessing, which he bestowed upon them with warmth.

Christopher was amazed by the crowd outside of Westminster Hall; the line to get in extended as far as his eye could see.

His father said, "They wait for a seat on the public benches. Some have been here all night, but it won't do them any good. The public benches have been filled since dawn, mainly with supporters of Parliament. That is why we must attend, to show we support Strafford and your uncle."

He wondered why his father was optimistic. Laud was in the Tower now, to reinforce Parliament's determination to curb the King's power.

"Child, nothing else is being talked about in London these days but the trial. As if everybody feels that the future of our country depends on the fate of Strafford's head."

He noticed most of those waiting for the public benches were ragged and dirty, but the soldiers who lined the streets were tidy and clean.

"Parliament's troops really," Dean Wren said, "although they wear the royal insignia. Parliament is making sure Strafford will not escape. He is taken daily from the Tower guarded by six barges rowed by fifty pairs of oars and manned by troops. You might think he is a wild beast."

As they sat in the gallery where they could see clearly, Christopher saw Hollar sketching the scene with care and detail.

His father whispered as he leaned over to view the trial better, "Today is the summing up. When Strafford gives his final defence."

He yearned to see as Hollar saw, objectively and accurately. After his failure to observe the Hall on his previous visit because of the need to remain hidden, he was resolved to see everything today. But it was difficult, for a holiday atmosphere pervaded Westminster Hall, there was so much talking, laughing, and sauntering about.

Dr. Christopher, aware of his son's interest in the structure and believing this was the child's first view of it, said admiringly, "It is possibly the most spacious building in Christendom. Certainly it it the largest and longest without pillars."

"It is much longer than the Banqueting Hall," said Christopher, comparing it to what had become his favourite building.

"Over twice as long," said Dr. Christopher, proud of what he knew. "Two hundred and twenty-eight feet in length, ninety feet high, and sixty-six feet in breadth." He had dreamed of constructing a building of this size, but nothing was being done these days with all the difficulties between the King and Parliament. "The original fabric goes back to William Rufus, who built it in the year of our Lord, 1097."

And old-fashioned, thought Christopher, staring critically at the stone floor, the boulder-like walls, the Gothic windows.

"The ceiling is quite unusual," said his father. "No pillars support the roof despite its great height. This is achieved cleverly by buttresses of Irish oak, which are always free from vermin."

He didn't share his father's enthusiasm for the building and his attention turned to the floor below. The head of the Hall was dominated by the chair of state which was shaped like a throne and elevated above everything else on the floor. Behind it was a long, dark cabinet.

"Provided by Parliament for the King and Queen," his father said.

"But the curtain is torn."

"It was done deliberately by the King, so everyone can see him and realise he supports his servant, Strafford, openly and with honour."

Three rows of seats extended the length of the Hall for the Peers, and behind them nine rows for the Commons, and at the

D*

far end was a desk for the prisoner, which was stacked high with documents.

Then the King entered, but nothing changed; Christopher noticed that even the Peers were keeping their hats on. The hubbub didn't cease until Strafford was led in with an armed guard. There was a sudden silence, and everyone took their assigned places: the Peers, Commons, and the officials, clerks, and soldiers, who surrounded Strafford.

Christopher expected Strafford to march in as befitted his position as a chief minister and a renowned general; instead, although he was only forty-eight, he was prematurely aged, his back bent, his once black hair completely grey, and he walked slowly and with effort.

Yet as the proceedings began and his name was announced, "*Thomas Wentworth, Earl of Strafford,*" he lost his stoop and stood tall and straight and his careworn features were brightened by a proud smile.

Bagshaw had said that Strafford was a tyrant, a murderer, who, according to Parliament's indictment for treason, had declared, "*I will make the little finger of the King heavier than the body of the law,*" yet Christopher wasn't sure and he wondered if Parliament was. Then he had a feeling it didn't matter. Strafford was speaking in his own defence, as eloquently as he had heard anyone speak, and many, particularly in the Commons, were not listening. But he wanted to hear every word. Westminster Hall was so crowded there seemed no space even for words, body pushed against body, and the Keeper of the Tower stood by the prisoner while he spoke, as if even here Strafford must be aware of Parliament's authority, and yet his words overrode everything else.

"*My Lords, whatever I have done, I have done according to the laws of our land. To punish me for that, gentlemen, is to make a new law, and that is against every principle of English justice. When I drew my sword, I drew it for the King. My failing, if it was a failure, was to express the King's prerogative with all my vigour. When I defended the King, I defended our beloved England.*"

Then Strafford paused. His children stood beside him and for a moment he could not speak, but suddenly, although the tears were streaming down his cheeks, he resumed. "*My Lords, I have delayed your lordships longer than I should have, but it has been for the interest of these pledges*"—he pointed to his children—"*which a departed saint in heaven has left me.*"

A flood of tears halted him, but once again—and now there wasn't another sound in Westminster Hall and Christopher sensed that everyone, even those with their minds made up, were listening intently—Strafford continued. "*What I forfeit for myself is nothing,* but *I confess, what my indiscretions could forfeit for them, wounds me deeply.*"

There were shouts from the galleries of, "Withdraw! Adjourn!"

Strafford's voice grew firm. "*Now my Lords, I thank God that I have been, by His blessing, sufficiently instructed in the vanity of all temporary enjoyments compared to the importance of our eternal duration. So, with all humility, and tranquility of mind, I submit, clearly and freely, to your judgment. Whether that righteous fate shall be life or death, I shall rest myself, full of gratitude and confidence, in the arms of the great Author of my existence. Te Deum laudamus.*"

As he sat down, his children beside him, the cries of "Withdraw! Adjourn!" increased. Christopher thought Strafford caught the King's eye, who nodded with approval, but he wasn't sure, the King's face so quickly became a mask again. His father looked pleased, as if Strafford's case was unassailable and Matthew's prospects enhanced, but the contour of Parliament appeared unchanged. For while the brief speech that followed from the leader of Parliament, John Pym—a heavy-jowled, high-browed, middle-aged man, with a properly cut moustache and pointed beard and sober black dress—was ordinary and unimpressive, Christopher felt that the majority had no intention of being merciful.

He wished he could put them into a coherent whole, but he had taken a dislike to these deliberations, the accusers who were the judges, the mob eager for revenge, the Commons hungry for self-justification, and the speakers without pity in their voices, even when they drooled.

He heard only a small portion of the prayers that concluded the session: "Teach us, Oh God, give us guidance . . ."

Strafford bowed to the Peers and the Commons as if he were addressing them one by one, and this time he did march out, soldiers on all sides of him, as if, this time, he was going home and not back to the Tower.

Now it was one week later and a few hours after Dean Wren told his son of the new honour and support the King was conferring on his uncle, and he mentioned this to Daniel, and yet Daniel asked, "Will your uncle officiate at the wedding even if Strafford is found guilty?"

"Whatever happens, I was told. But my father thinks he will be freed. What do you think? I understand the verdict is coming tomorrow."

"Yes. My father says Parliament is determined to destroy Strafford. And that this will only be the start of the trouble, not the end."

The next day Matthew was rehearsing the Prince of Orange and the Princess Mary in the marriage ritual and he was pleased with the way it was going, for the King was smiling with approval, when he was interrupted by an urgent messenger. Annoyed, he wanted to protest, he was at the vital part of the ceremony, but the messenger looked stricken, afraid to approach the King, yet having to. Matthew wondered if Strafford was dead already, the King paled so as the messenger spoke to him, and then he heard Charles groan, "Parliament has voted for the Earl's death. I must stop it, somehow. I feel so ill."

Two days later, on Good Friday, when Charles ended his devotions, which were conducted by Matthew, he wrote Strafford: *"Upon the word of your King, he will not permit such a faithful servant to suffer in life, honour, or fortune, for that would be a very mean reward from a master to so faithful and able a servant."* Even a dog deserves better, he thought, I am sick to death of being vilified by so monstrous and cruel behaviour. He knew this attack was really directed against him. Yet after Charles sent his letter to Strafford, he began to seek ways to appease Parliament, or at least, in his view, to find a compromise.

But Christopher felt there was no reconciliation anywhere. The school was so close to Westminster Abbey, Whitehall, and Westminster Hall, the three centres of power—Church, King, and Parliament—that he and his fellow students knew most of what was happening. Or was supposed to happen, he reflected, for the rumours outweighed the facts.

No Westminster was allowed to go out of the school, for the size and vehemence of the mobs roaming the streets increased daily, but Daniel slipped out. He refused to take Christopher, saying it was too dangerous for anyone called Wren, for the mobs continued to cry for the head of Matthew Wren as well as for the heads of Strafford and Laud.

Bagshaw also slipped out to prove his bravery, but Daniel said, it was not perilous for him, he had Dissenter connections.

Charles' letter to Strafford became known and rumours spread like weeds: that he planned to seize the Tower and free Strafford and Laud, that he was going to invade Parliament and dissolve it, that the army was going to mutiny because Parliament had not paid the soldiers, that Pym, as the leader of the Dissenters, was to be given the post of Chief Minister to the King, or possibly, that of Chancellor of the Exchequer.

But each time one of these rumours circulated, so did the mobs. There were riots outside the Tower, Westminster Hall, and talk that the King's palace and family at Whitehall would be next.

Yet when Matthew married Princess Mary to William of Orange

in the royal chapel at Whitehall, he prayed for peace, although Christopher, who stood in the rear with his father, could hear a mob outside the palace windows shouting for Strafford's death.

Someone screamed, *"Soon this building will be for let!"*

Another yelled, *"The Catholics are making their last confessions!"*

Christopher trembled before this violence, but the King ignored it. Whatever he was, thought Christopher, he was not afraid.

After the ceremony Christopher edged closer to the Prince of Wales in the hope that he could talk to his former playmate, but the King was ahead of him. He heard the King say to his son, "Be vigilant. You are the chosen and you cannot turn back. When you follow me, proclaim your word with power, and advance the glory of our realm."

Then the King said, "Bishop Wren, will you pray for us?"

Christopher wondered whether it included Dissenters and Daniel.

At the school afterwards Daniel told him that Pym had discovered a plot by the King to seize the Tower, to be done at the time his daughter was being wed—to avoid suspicion—and that it had failed.

"Now, it is said," Daniel added, "Parliament will not hear any more pleas for mercy, even from the King, and to show they mean this, they have set the date for Strafford's execution."

It was difficult to know what to think. Christopher had been moved by Strafford's summing up and his father and uncle admired him, yet many hated him and Daniel was undecided in his own views.

Several days later Busby appeared as usual for his morning inspection, but for the first time since Christopher had entered Westminster, no one was flogged. Instead, as he ordered all the students and under masters to pray, he added, "for Thomas Wentworth, the Earl of Strafford."

Then he said, "Grave days face our realm. The wolves in Parliament are seeking the blood of the King's greatest supporter and our King is confronted with a terrible decision. Parliament is demanding that he sign the Earl of Strafford's death warrant, and so far, he has refused and he has promised Strafford that he will never sign it. But now the Earl has written to His Majesty releasing him from his promise."

Busby paused to gather strength to continue. Christopher had never seen the Head Master this emotional; he was being quite human.

"So, in place of the hymn after the prayer, I am going to read you a letter you must always remember. It expresses a devotion to our King I expect every Westminster to practise. It is from

Strafford and it is written to the King in answer to his promise to
save him. I will read it in English so even the stupidest among
you will comprehend it."

He halted until the room was absolutely silent and then he read
out:

*"May it please Your Sacred Majesty, I understand the minds of men are
more and more incensed against me, notwithstanding Your Majesty has declared
that, in your princely opinion, I am not guilty of treason, and that you are
not satisfied in your conscience to sign the bill. This brings me to a very
great difficulty: there is before me the ruin of my children and family, hitherto
untouched with any foul crime, and the many ills which may befall your Sacred
Person and the whole Kingdom should yourself and Parliament part less
satisfied one with the other than is necessary for the preservation both of King
and people. And there are before me the things most valued, most feared by
mortal men: Life and Death. To say, Sir, that there has not been strife
in me, were to make me less man than God knows my infirmities make me.
And to call a destruction upon myself and from my young children will find no
easy consent from flesh and blood. Yet to set Your Majesty's conscience at
liberty, I do most humbly beseech Your Majesty, for the prevention of evils
which may happen by your refusal, to pass this bill."*

No one spoke when Busby finished.

And while the school waited for what the King would do, the
many prayers at Westminster were for the life of the Earl of
Strafford.

Charles didn't know what to do. At first, he flatly refused to sign
the death warrant in spite of Strafford's letter; then there were
threats against his family and demonstrations outside the palace of
Whitehall and now he hesitated. Finally, still unable to make up
his mind, he asked the advice of judges on the legality of the death
warrant. They replied that he was the final authority in the
Kingdom, but considering his family's safety . . .

He could think of only one other authority to consult. While
Strafford's letter released him from his promise, it did not release
him from his conscience. And it was against his conscience to sign
the death warrant. So, since that in his opinion, was answerable
only to God, he called in his spiritual advisers.

He didn't consult the Bishop of Ely—he knew *his* views; and
Laud was in the Tower, and his mind was made up already, too;
but asked three other churchmen he considered impartial. The first
said the King should not do anything against his conscience. The
second stated that the question had many sides and required further
deliberation and prayer. And the third declared a King must also
have a public conscience; if he didn't sign much blood would be
spilled.

But the moment Charles signed the death warrant he regretted it, crying out, "My Lord Strafford's condition is happier than mine!"

He couldn't accept what he had done, for his conscience still troubled him. When he heard that Strafford's execution was ordered for noon on May 12th, and that was only two days away, he sent Prince Charles to the Lords to beg for mercy for Strafford—the Peers had been more sympathetic to Strafford than the Commons—and they didn't even read his plea. His letter was returned, unopened.

The day of the execution Busby ordered all classes to be cancelled and that every Westminster must pass the time in prayer for the Earl of Strafford and the safety of the King. But Daniel couldn't resist the public occasion the execution had become, and Christopher was curious, too, although he was apprehensive about venturing on the streets of London. At first Daniel didn't want to take him, but when he promised to be careful, Daniel assented, although still hesitantly. Yet as they trudged down the Strand toward the Tower, for there were no coaches available, everything was very quiet, there were only a few people about and it was like a holiday.

The walk was so long Christopher thought his feet would fall off, but when they neared Tower Hill he realised why the city was so empty of people—most of them were here. He had never seen a space so filled with bodies; the ground around Tower Hill was even more crowded than Westminster Hall was for the trial. He wondered if Hollar was sketching this scene as the engraver had sketched so many others. No one paid any attention to them; they were just two small boys in a mob of thousands.

As the fatal moment approached the people crowded on to platforms built so they could see the scaffold better, on tiptoe, pushing forward, and Daniel whispered, "He's coming, all in black!"

"Can you hear what he is saying?"

"No. We are too far away. But he is standing very erect."

The thousands of people who were chattering and laughing as if they were at a great festive party suddenly hushed. There was an instant of profound silence and then a giant sigh arose.

Christopher whispered, "I couldn't look."

"I couldn't look either," Daniel confessed. "Do you think he is in another life now? They are washing down the blood. He bled a lot."

He didn't reply; he would have given anything for solitude. He could hardly wonder about the execution, let alone accept it. He could hardly live with it, let alone forget it. He felt diminished by it, everything seemed diminished by it. He felt buried deep inside himself.

Daniel pulled him away from the crowd, which was still waiting. "For more excitement and sport, I guess," he said. "I don't like it here."

He didn't either. He must break out. He saw the Tower, dank and inanimate, its mindless stone foreboding and revengeful, and unlovable, and at this instant, unbearable.

"Don't worry. No one will bother us. We're too young."

But he wasn't afraid any more. As they started back to Westminster, he saw a tree, and it was so alive it was miraculous, the trunk grew out of the earth, the branches grew out of the trunk, the stems grew out of the branches, the buds grew of the stems, the leaves grew out of the buds. Everything grew like a man's head grew out of his body.

"I have no choice," Matthew said. "Now that Strafford has been brought down, I must resign as Dean of the Chapel Royal." He strode up and down Busby's study as he had done months ago while his brother and Busby listened, and Christopher wondered why they wanted him here. Then his uncle turned to him and said, "If you see me about, you must ignore me. Not a word must get out that I am staying in the Abbey."

"It could be attacked if the Dissenters learn of your uncle's presence," said Dean Wren, seeing his son's bewilderment. "Matthew, are you sure you should resign? Will the King accept it?"

"He will accept it. As he accepted Strafford's sacrifice. Besides, I've already resigned, on the grounds that my presence at court will only prove an embarrassment, and Charles has accepted it."

"What will you do now, Uncle?" Christopher blurted out.

"Stay in the Abbey until my trial. It does possess the right of sanctuary, although I doubt the Dissenters will honour it."

Busby said suddenly, angrily, "We will not let them harm you."

"You can prevent that?" Matthew looked incredulous.

"I will prevent that. I, and my Westminsters."

The next morning Busby dispensed with all the studies and took the entire school to the rear of the Abbey, where there was an enormous pile of ancient masonry, stone, and rubble. "It is part of the original foundations," he said, "that was unearthed when the Abbey was being renovated several years ago." He ordered the boys to place anything heavy that could be thrown in a chamber near the doors of the Abbey. He also distributed rods to all the older boys and warned the under masters to keep their own rods handy, and his own flogging didn't stop.

If anything, reflected Christopher, it was more vigorous than ever, especially since Strafford had been beheaded. Daniel was curious why all these preparations were being made, but he couldn't tell him, although he felt, somehow, as if he were betraying their friendship.

Then Bagshaw said several mornings later, when the second form was assigned to add bricks and bludgeons to the pile of home-made weapons, "Busby must be hiding somebody Parliament wants."

Christopher sensed that Bagshaw, who secretly favoured the Dissenters, was conniving to find out and he started to talk about the examinations for King's Scholars which were coming soon. "Are you taking them?"

Bagshaw replied, "No. Are you?"

"No. I'm not qualified. Not yet."

"With your family connections? They must impress even Busby."

Daniel said, "You know that Christopher is a good scholar."

"Yes. And with the best royalist connections. Which is what Busby wants. When is your uncle going to be tried by Parliament?"

"I don't know."

"Where is he now?"

"How should I know?"

Daniel interrupted, "Stop pestering him. He said he didn't know."

"I heard the Bishop of Ely has been seen in London. Many people would like to get their hands on him. Especially the apprentice boys."

Yet when their attack occurred Christopher was surprised. Since the death of Strafford the streets of the city and Westminster had been empty of the roaming mobs, as if they were waiting for Parliament to decide on the next victim. The regular routine of school resumed, with many of the students preparing for the coveted yet dreaded examinations of King's Scholars, when the news came one morning that a large group of apprentice boys had learned that the Bishop of Ely was hiding in Westminster Abbey and they were going to seize him and hang him in a public display of Dissenter opinion.

Busby immediately armed all the students with bricks, bludgeons, and rocks, and manned and fastened the doors of Westminster Abbey. "We'll teach them a lesson," he muttered. As he consigned the apprentice boys to limbo, he prepared to crack them on the head.

By now the sound of the approaching mob could be heard, the beat of the drum to keep them in order and to arouse them emotionally, the cries of "For God and Parliament!" and the most frightening noise of all, the shouts of "Give us that damned Bishop of Ely!"

Christopher, put for protection between Daniel and Bagshaw by

Ryles, felt a chill go down his spine as he heard the pounding on the front door of the Abbey and the shouting, "Wren! Wren! We want him now!"

Busby had erected a barricade of stones, masonry, and benches next to the front door of the Abbey, and he placed behind it the Westminster weapons: more stones, chunks of masonry, bricks, rods, and bludgeons. He stationed each form behind a portion of the barricade, with an under master in command, but he was in supreme command as he stood on the high altar where he could see most clearly and dominate.

Rocks smashed windows and ricocheted into the Westminsters kneeling behind the barricade, but no one moved, as if Busby's punishment was worse than any wounds that could be inflicted by the apprentice boys, although glass shattered at their feet.

The front door shook from the assault of the mob, then split and a few apprentices pushed through the door to be met by Busby shouting, "Ignorant hooligans! You are violating the right of sanctuary. You are desecrating the high altar. Westminsters, attack! Attack!"

A shower of bricks and rocks greeted the intruders, who paused, startled and dismayed. Christopher was surprised that most of the apprentices were young, a few not much older than himself, and some were quite small. But their leader was a tall, frantic, well dressed man.

"Sir Richard Wiseman," Daniel said to Christopher. "They say he is a little crazy since he lost his Baronetcy and was fined ten thousand pounds for attacking the King. He is determined to hang your uncle, and anyone who is supposed to be supported by Charles. A fanatic."

There was no time for further talk, for the battle became violent.

Christopher joined in, not because he liked fighting, but because everyone else did, and he was afraid to be left out, sensing that if he didn't join in he would pay for it. A dozen apprentices pushed by the smashed door and as they turned toward the high altar, led by Wiseman, who was determined to strip it of all ornamentation in his pursuit of the Bishop of Ely, they were assailed with a new shower of rocks. As the invaders wavered, shaken by such resolution and fury, Busby gathered the upper forms—who were the oldest, strongest boys in the school—and fell upon the invaders with bludgeons and rods.

Christopher heard both sides cry, "God bless us!" but he saw there were far more Westminsters than apprentices, whose reinforcements were blocked by the growing pile of rubble in the doorway and the hail of stones from the Westminsters still kneeling behind the barricade.

As Busby's charge struck home most of the apprentices in the Abbey retreated outside, but several followed Wiseman who ran to the high altar. And when in his frenzy he tore down hangings and tapestries, Busby pursued him with a number of the older Westminsters. The apprentices with Wiseman, seeing they were outnumbered, fled around the choir while the Westminsters chased them, beating and hacking at them as they ran. But Wiseman stood his ground as another group of students, with Busby in command, hammered at him with their bludgeons.

Christopher felt sick. His schoolmates didn't need any instruction from Busby in the art of flogging—they were doing it with such skill and pleasure, ceaselessly pounding on Wiseman until he fell, while the others lashed at the fleeing apprentices, though they cried for mercy.

When the Abbey was cleared of intruders, except for Wiseman, who lay motionless on the floor below the high altar, Busby—ignoring him—addressed the victorious Westminsters. In the commotion the top of one of the piers had fallen down with the iron and lead fastened to it, and Busby said, "They were trying to steal the iron. English iron is the best in the world." But Christopher thought, It was no mystery why the pier had collapsed; it was of poor construction, like a half-finished kitchen chair, anyone could tell that. Busby added, "Did you see how slovenly they were dressed? They are criminals, with their absence of piety. Ill-mannered, ill-behaved, stupid children! I must say I am pleasantly surprised by the active muscular prowess of my Westminster boys, even some of the King's Scholars."

Suddenly, as a last gesture of defiance, rocks were flung through the door at Busby by the retreating apprentices. Busby never faltered in his speech or his stance, but Christopher shivered. One of the rocks brushed against his head and hit the barricade from which he had emerged. It did not break, but shattered part of the stone barricade. As he picked it up he shuddered; he could have been killed. He was sorry he had thrown any rocks; the risk was too great. But as he fingered the rock and another that lay at his feet, he remembered that these stones came from the original fabric of Westminster Abbey. The rock that had almost hit him was centuries old.

He was glad he hadn't thrown it back, even though some of his schoolmates hurled rocks after the fleeing apprentice boys. Stones were not made to throw, but to build with. Didn't any of them understand? Even Daniel, standing by his side, looked at him queerly when he saw him fondling the rocks. Yet he couldn't help it. He loved their shape and feel.

Ryles, assigned by Busby to examine the damage done to

the Abbey, said, "Sir, very little was damaged, but Wiseman is dead."

Ryles sounded shaken as he announced this, but Busby's tone was cold as he replied, "Dissenter dog. Let him lie there."

"But, sir . . ."

"Ryles, who began it?"

The under master was silent.

"He will be an object lesson. He bumped his head against the altar."

And God struck him dead, Busby assumed, thought Christopher, but he couldn't look at the dead man. When no one was watching he hid the two stones he had fallen in love with under his surplice and put them beneath his bed where he could gaze at them without being caught. They were so well shaped even after the centuries of wear. One of them was almost a perfect rectangle.

Who would know where they came from? He asked Ryles and the under master replied, "England is well supplied with building stone. There is anger in the Parliament about the attack on the Abbey."

"Because of Wiseman's death?"

"No. They didn't like him either. And most of them think Busby was right, defending the Abbey as a religious institution, and admire him for winning. I blame myself for Wiseman's death. I could have stopped his pursuers and I didn't. Why are you so interested in old stones?"

A voice inside of him said, "Because I respect stone, you can build with it," but he replied, "Have you heard anything about my uncle?"

"He is to be tried soon. The attack on the Abbey hastened that."

Christopher was puzzled by his uncle's trial. He sat in the gallery of Westminster Hall with his father and Parliament treated Matthew as a monster who preyed upon people, but they weren't talking about his uncle at all, not the man he knew. Yet the attack gathered venom as the articles of impeachment were increased to twenty-four and Widdrington, the Recorder of York, stated: "*The Bishop of Ely is not a true Christian, but a wolf devouring his flock; an extinguisher of light; a Noah who sent out doves from the ark and refused to receive them back until they returned as ravens . . .*"

Christopher tried to stop listening, but it was impossible, the accusations were so loud. "*. . . and the Bishop raised fines for his own profit, he is a great robber, a mirror of superstition, popery . . .*"

Widdrington brought no proof, thought Christopher, yet he spoke as if what he said was gospel.

"Why doesn't uncle answer?" he asked his father.

The Dean, staring sorrowfully at Matthew, sitting impassively in the same place Strafford had faced his accusers, said, "It will do no good. Parliament has its mind made up."

"Then why are they having the trial?"

"To prove they are right."

Prynne took the floor. He wore a long quilt cap that came over his eyes and which served as an umbrella to defend himself from the light, and he munched on some bread and swayed back and forth as he spoke, but his words were as relentless as the rods beating on Wiseman's head and Christopher listened, for Prynne's intensity was hypnotic.

Prynne said, "I challenge anyone to equal my labours in the study of theology and ecclesiastical practices."

This man was deadly, reflected Christopher, he wanted to kill.

Prynne continued, "*We must reform our age. Our fashions are full of follies and vices. Drinking healths are sinful, and it is most unseemly for men to wear their hair long, unseemly and unlawful and unchristian. While it is mannish, unnatural, and impudent and unchristian for women to cut it short. Brethren, we commit many sins these days. We profane our stages with plays which are incentives to immorality, and are the means to return to our realm the evil of Popery. We have a church with a torso and legs, but no head, no heart, no . . .*"

Matthew interrupted, "Whatever I did, I did for God."

"And made it the devil's work," muttered Prynne.

Everyone was listening intently as if this was what they had been waiting for, and Dean Wren said, "He is setting a trap for Matthew."

Prynne stated, "You drove three thousand Christians out of Norwich."

"I only drove unbelievers out of the house of God."

"With an iron hand and tread."

"I did not intend to tread lightly. Not in the service of God."

"Neither do I," retorted Prynne. "You and the King are fellow workers in the design of introducing Popery into England."

"Because my hair is longer than yours?" Matthew said unexpectedly.

"Much longer!" Prynne snatched his quilt hat off his head and revealed that his hair was so closely cropped it brought a gasp of astonishment even from his supporters.

Matthew asked contemptuously, "Does that make you more pure?"

"More Puritan!" Prynne snarled back.

"With your round head?"

Indeed, it was, Christopher thought, and he smiled, but there was no humour in Prynne, for Prynne's response was deadly serious.

"Bishop, I am proud to be a Roundhead, a Puritan. Not for me your Cavalier ways, the fancy dress of the court, the most extravagant and ostentatious and overbearing abuse of humility our country has known. God's judgment will fall upon you for these monstrous vanities."

But his uncle was wearing black, Christopher wanted to shout, a dress almost as simple and sober as Prynne's.

"It will not help," his father whispered, as if he read his mind. "It might comfort your uncle, but it will not change any minds."

Matthew ignored Prynne as he turned to the members of Parliament who sat around him in judgment and said, "I do not think the question of whether a man wears silk or not determines his piety. Or his devotion to God. What I am really charged with is obedience to the King. But I would be a poor creature if I changed my faith and fidelity to save myself from further persecution."

Matthew spoke with such fervour, it was clear he knew God was on his side, thought Christopher, and yet Prynne was equally sure. Whose side was the stone on? The stone that could have split his head open. Or lain in the sun. Or built Westminster Abbey. At this moment he yearned so to build something, anything that would halt this endless fighting.

Prynne shouted at his uncle, "Confess!" and Matthew dropped to his knees and prayed, "Dear God, I come to You in faith and trust, forgive us our trespasses as I forgive those who trespass against us. I will not waver in my duty to You, whose gracious love and mercy fillest all . . ."

Yet as Matthew lifted his head as if God would give him peace, even if no one else would, Christopher was thinking that the chunks of rock under his bed possessed more of love and mercy than any of these men in Westminster Hall.

Time Is Not The Passing Of Itself

Time is not the passing of itself
but its content
    As a clock is not creation

Stymean Karlen

7

Time Is Not The Passing Of Itself

PARLIAMENT FOUND MATTHEW GUILTY OF TREASON AND PUT HIM IN the Tower.

Christopher feared his father would be next and that his uncle would follow Strafford to the block, but Parliament turned on Inigo Jones.

The King's Surveyor was ordered to appear before the House of Lords to answer charges brought by the House of Commons, and the day of the hearing Christopher and Daniel tiptoed into Westminster Hall. No one noticed them. Only a few people were present. But the charges were read with severity: "*The defendant tore down part of the ancient and holy church of St. Gregory, which adjoins the cathedral of St. Paul, in order to establish more space for his profane renovations of the cathedral. And he threatened the parishioners, if they tried to stop him, to tear down the entire fabric of St. Gregory and to throw it into the Thames.*"

Jones had aged since Christopher had seen him last and his large, heavy body sagged when he stood up to reply, but his voice was firm as he said, "Whatever I did, I did on the authority of His Majesty."

Prynne spoke then, "And desecrated a worthy church, St. Gregory."

"It was essential to strengthen the foundations of the cathedral."

"Laud's toy. Which he intended to convert into a Roman church, until we halted him. Look at the portico, it is an imitation of St. Peter's."

This was stupid, thought Christopher, Jones was his own man. But Daniel wasn't listening, and when he asked him why, Daniel answered, "They have made up their minds. Jones' arrogance offended many peers."

Prynne added, "You are a Jesuit at heart with your love of Italy."

Jones said, "I want to restore St. Paul's to its former dignity."

Prynne snarled, "We should pull it down to the ground. All of its impious ornamentation and as a warning to those who wish to return Popery to England. Before it becomes an instrument of the devil."

Jones thought there was nothing worse than a man who was sure he was good. But he said, "I declined any reward for my repairs on St. Paul."

"No wonder. It is a monument to idolatry, without virtue. Like the masques you designed, infected with the most licentious implications."

Prynne was as spiteful as Ben Jonson, Jones realised angrily, Jonson who had berated him for his bad Latin and who felt superior because the dramatist had gone to Westminster while he had gone only to Italy. As if Latin influenced his designs, he said to himself bitterly—how absurd! Yet the Puritan hated the entertainments he created for the court because they were sensual with Jonson's sensuality and learning.

Christopher waited eagerly for Jones to reply, but he didn't, deciding it was futile. None of these Dissenters knew a thing about architecture, Jones thought, and Prynne pursued anybody who disagreed with him with a relentless animosity. Yet in his heart his portico was more alive than all of them judging him and he would not alter one stone for any of them, not even to save himself from the axe.

But as Prynne added savagely, "We intend to tear down the scaffolding around the cathedral, where you are altering the roof of the south transept," Jones' heart sank, and he had a dismal feeling that this was the end of his work. For a moment he almost went to his knees, to plead for mercy. Then as he saw the triumph in the Puritan's eyes he stood straighter. But he felt so old. He, who had set out to purify English architecture, who had to endure long arrears of pay without grumbling, had to listen to these savages. If he could only express his defiance. In some ways this was the heaviest cross of all to bear.

By the time the House of Lords reached their verdict Christopher was embarrassed. They were treating Jones like a child; there must be more to life than this. Jones was led to the bar, looking very old now despite his effort to maintain his composure. The day was over, the light was gone, and the lanterns flickered in the wind and nearly went out.

There was a great rage in the Chief Surveyor, yet he couldn't say a word—it had been all said in his work—but he longed to shout, I don't shiver from fear but because I have the ague and these winter days do not warm the heart. He stood motionless while he waited for the verdict, recalling when no one would have ventured to do this to him, not even the Lord Chancellor, and thought, How dare they judge my work!

The chief judge stated solemnly, *"We cannot mete out justice to you differently from that applied to insignificant persons. For the time being, we will allow your west portico to stand, but you are hereby ordered to return all the stone taken from St. Gregory to that worthy church, to see that all the scaffolding within St. Paul is removed, and to pay all the costs out of your own pocket."*

As Jones stepped out of Westminster Hall into the darkness of the street, tired and depressed, he didn't see the men waiting for him.

Parishioners from St. Gregory picked up rubble that remained from the battle of the Abbey and threw it at him and several of the stones almost hit him. Instead of fleeing, he halted, sick at heart. He could hardly endure any more. Wouldn't they leave anything of his standing?

Christopher watched this attack in horror. He had followed the Chief Surveyor in the hope of telling him how much he admired his work, but now he was afraid to approach him—the elderly, black-coated parishioners were just as bloodthirsty as the apprentice boys—and Jones looked shattered, on the verge of collapse. Christopher sighed. So much malice. Perhaps this was the plague that people were always talking about. It made him ill. Jones laboriously entered his sumptuous carriage and drove away, but it moved like a hearse. Christopher felt he was witnessing the Surveyor's funeral, although Jones was not dead.

Then Van Dyck died.

Sir Anthony knew he was not supposed to die. He lay on his huge curtained bed, of such substantial proportions he felt lost in it, his delicate, feminine head against the panelled headboard, fondling lovingly and sensually the rich velvet drapes with his fingers stained from paint—so much paint! the soul of his existence!—such nimble fingers! he loved them so!—and stared at the massive foot-posts and their bulbous knobs, and thought, He could not die, he must not die, he possessed everything a painter could desire. He who was precocious beyond almost any other painter, with his own studio, income, pupils, and reputation at the age of seventeen. He who attracted such attention with his paintings that even the great, the omnipotent Rubens appointed him *the* favourite protege. He who was known throughout Europe for his portraits by the time he was twenty-one. He who in the next ten years became first in the art of portraiture. Rubens was more fleshy but he was more refined. He who was now the *preux chevalier* of portraiture. There was hardly an eminent personage in Europe or England he had not painted.

These sheets could not be his shroud. Jones, on the order of the King, had designed this magnificent mansion for him on the old monastic grounds of the Black Friars. The King and Queen were frequent visitors here. The Surveyor had constructed a handsome landing so they could go directly from the river to his studio in the utmost comfort.

Where was His Majesty now? In Scotland, Ireland, the north of England? It was difficult to remember, Charles was so uncertain in his movements these days. Perhaps it was deliberate, to confuse Parliament. But his painting from the very beginning was always infused with certainty.

Stricken with a fit of coughing, he felt dreadful. He longed to kneel and pray, but he couldn't; he was so weak he felt strapped to the bed. He couldn't even lift his head; it took a supreme effort to turn his eyes. On the verge of weeping, but that required more strength than he had, he wondered if he was all alone and he saw his physician standing nearby, his apothecary behind him. They looked like ravens; Dr. Greene wore black and had a long beak of a nose and a chin as sharp as an axe, and the apothecary, black-haired and black-eyed, also arranged funerals.

As Dr. Greene sponged his burning head he asked, "Where is my wife?"

"She is with your daughter. She gave birth a few days ago. Remember?"

He didn't, but he couldn't admit it. "What day is this?"

"December 9th, Sir Anthony," volunteered the apothecary.

No wonder he was cold, he thought, as an icy chill went through him.

"Your daughter is being baptised today, sir."

Now he knew he was dying. Or they would have waited. They must wait. He intended to live. If he had dissipated more than most, if he had been very suspectible to women, if he felt broken in spirit, still shaken by having his wish to decorate the Louvre rejected, there was still some fire in him. He was not ready for the Bills of Mortality.

"Dr. Greene, why can't I see my wife and daughter?"

"It is not advisable."

As he turned over with a desperate effort, for his buttocks were sore from so much lying, he realised what the physician was thinking. At the sight of his sores and emaciated body Dr. Greene's eyes lit up.

He wasn't sure whether the physician thought it was the French disease or the plague, but Dr. Greene ordered the bedchamber to be fumigated with acid vapours and the burning of brimstone and he thought he was in hell. He yearned to cry out, It is consumption that has rendered me helpless, not the plague or syphilis, but they were fumigating so their lungs would not be injured or irritated by the sulphurous vapour, and yet they would escape the infection themselves, and they were destroying him.

Dear God, he prayed, I am dying of women and mistakes.

But no one seemed to hear him.

The physician and the apothecary retreated a safe distance from him.

Would God and all His blessed angels want him to paint their portraits? He laid his cheek against his beloved, precious fingers, then he felt he was holding a paint brush, only it was slipping through his fingers, they were splitting in two, and he thought, I am not a man any more.

Christopher was saddened by the news of Sir Anthony's death, even if he hadn't painted his portrait as he had Prince Charles'. It was no consolation to hear that the painter was buried in St. Paul's, for that didn't seem permanent either these confusing days.

Westminster was rife with rumours about what the King was going to do next, and everybody expected open warfare to erupt at any moment.

Then, on a cold afternoon early in January, when Ryles sent Bagshaw, Daniel, and Christopher outside to collect firewood and Christopher noticed that Bagshaw was able only to find twigs while they picked up logs, they heard a great tumult coming from the direction of Whitehall. Curious, they dropped what they were carrying and hid their surplices under their doublets so they would not be recognised as Westminsters, and hurried toward the commotion. They saw the King approaching Westminster Hall in a coach, escorted by many soldiers and followed by a growing mob.

Daniel said, "He must be coming to capture Parliament."

"With so much noise," said Christopher, "he will scare them away."

"Perhaps that is his intention. Or to dissolve Parliament."

"No," Bagshaw said positively. "He is after the leaders of Parliament. There have been rumours that the King was going to arrest them. He has already had five of the leaders, including Pym, impeached."

"How do you know?" asked Christopher. He was aware that Bagshaw was sympathetic to the Dissenters, but the monitor was being very assured.

Bagshaw smiled knowingly, but didn't answer.

Daniel said, "The King expects to win. The curtains of his coach are open and he looks sure of himself. I think he honestly believes he will catch the birds before they fly away. Maybe he has the exits blocked. Come, let us go in the back way, before the King enters."

By the time Charles dismounted from his coach, which was delayed by the need to have all the proper ceremonies observed, and thus he lost the advantage of whatever surprise still existed, the boys were in the gallery of Westminster Hall, unnoticed because of the excitement below.

Pym was asking permission of the Speaker for himself and his friends to depart, and as the Speaker nodded, three of them followed him to the rear door, but one, William Strode, declared angrily, "We must face the tyrant. To flee is to admit defeat. We cannot afford to show fear."

Pym replied, "He will have lost already—if we are gone. London will be furious at him for making the attempt, but if he succeeds they might forgive him, or, at least, respect him. But if he loses, he loses London."

Someone was at the front door, shouting, "The King is coming, he is in the lobby," and Pym and his three followers pulled the obdurate Strode out of the Hall by the cloak, although he still protested and resisted them.

A moment later the King entered while his soldiers framed the door and cocked their pistols so all the members could see their intention.

To Christopher's surprise, the King didn't hurry but was leisurely —as if to show impatience or eagerness was improper—and when he approached the Speaker he took off his hat as a sign of his respect for Parliament and stood bareheaded as he said, "Mr. Lenthall, I must possess the chair."

The members of Parliament were bareheaded now, too, but silent.

The Speaker left his chair without a word and as the King sat in it Christopher remembered when Charles had occupied his chairs in the Deanery and Prince Charles had sat in *Myself*. He had a sudden yearning for the Deanery then, and his three favourite chairs, *Myself, Him,* and *Those,* and felt closer to them than all these people, except Daniel. He wondered if the King cared for *his* chairs the way he did. As he saw the King's back stiffen as Charles stared at Pym's seat in the Hall and became aware that it was empty, Christopher thought, The King sits in the House of Commons as if it were *his* home now; but there was no love in his gaze.

The King asked, "Is Mr. Pym present?"

No one answered.

"Mr. Speaker, where is he?"

The Speaker dropped to his knees and mumbled, "I cannot talk except as Parliament wishes. I have neither eyes to see nor tongue to speak in this place but as the House is prepared to direct me."

"It doesn't matter. I know my eyes are as suitable as necessary." The King didn't move from the Speaker's chair, but examined the members of Parliament, row after row, while they sat silently and motionless.

There was no welcome here, thought Christopher, or surrender. They were not servants now, but enemies. People could be as fickle as the weather.

Suddenly the King stood up, announced, "All my birds have flown!"

Daniel whispered, "He has lost."

"Yes," Bagshaw gloated, "London will never forgive him now."

Christopher was quiet; he felt sorry for the King. He knew that was not fitting and he had never cared for Charles, but Charles was *his* King, and the King of England, *his* England, and Charles favoured his family and if the King lost his father would suffer and his uncle could lose his head, and he didn't like the lack of respect he saw on so many members' faces.

Charles addressed the whole House, looking irate despite his efforts to keep everything well-ordered, "Gentlemen, you will regret this day."

"So will he," Bagshaw said under his breath, but loud enough so that Christopher and Daniel could hear him. "So will he."

As Charles turned to go, his soldiers cried, "God Save the King!"

But hardly anyone from Parliament joined in.

Charles said contemptuously, "Has no one the courage to speak out?"

Shouts of "Privilege! Privilege!" rose from the members and most of them put on their hats and stood as the King did to indicate their defiance and when he lost his prized composure and snapped, "Insolence!" the shouts of "Privilege!" increased and for the first time Christopher saw Charles look shaken. Instead of the King leaving Parliament victorious as he anticipated upon his entrance, his departure became a retreat and the mob which cheered his arrival jeered his withdrawal.

After the boys returned to the school with the firewood, if Ryles noticed that they were slower than they were supposed to be, the under master didn't say anything. Daniel put two shillings into his hand with the logs, which was more than he was paid for a whole day.

Pym and his men stepped into the barge waiting by the Westminster Hall landing and they were safely down the Thames before any of the King's soldiers could reach them, and an hour later they were hiding in the city. And as Pym expected, Charles' failure turned London against him.

Crowds grew in the city, shouting they would be willing to fight and die for Parliament. Barricades were erected across the streets of the city where Pym and his men were hidden, and the supporters of Parliament organised themselves into trained bands and prepared for Charles' Cavaliers to attack. Instead, he hesitated as he had hesitated with Strafford. Only now there was no one that competent to turn to for aid. He knew it would be fatal to show fear, but when the defiant cries of "Privilege!" reached his ears in the palace of Whitehall, he put the Queen and his three eldest children in the same coach he had ridden to Parliament as a would-be conqueror and fled from London to Hampton Court.

He arrived so late and unexpectedly that all of them—King, Queen, and their three children—were forced to sleep in the same, small bed. It was just one week after he had failed to capture Pym.

The next day Pym and his four followers stepped into the same barge that had taken them from Westminster Hall to return to their seats in Parliament. The largest crowd Pym had ever seen, even larger than the mob which had assembled for the execution of Strafford, acclaimed him as he started up the Thames. And as they were rowed past the palace of Whitehall and Pym saw that it was deserted, he knew that Parliament were the conquerors—they possessed the city of London.

But he was puzzled. He knew he was more clever than Charles— he always made sure to display civility and humility no matter how much power he acquired, so no one would suspect him of wanting to become a tyrant—but he hadn't expected the King to relinquish London so quickly and easily. Without London, the country was like a body without a head.

Yet only a few years ago their cause had seemed so hopeless, he and his friend, Oliver Cromwell, had planned to embark on the western voyage to America and to settle in the new England.

Pym was proud he had planned his escape from Charles' clutches so cunningly it had discredited the King completely, and he was pleased that even Strode admitted this, although he simply bent his head piously and mumbled, "It was God's will." When Strode added admiringly, "And your craftiness, Pym," he blushed, as if such praise was impious. But when several of his followers looked irresolute, he stated, "Our success is the King's doing. We are fortunate in our enemy; whenever he is on the verge of winning, he manages to do the wrong thing."

He didn't add what he was also thinking. While he had hoped to win, to assert the rights of Parliament, even its supremacy, particularly of the House of Commons, he had not expected to become sovereign. But as he entered Westminster Hall many were shouting for "*King Pym!*"

Studying became difficult for Christopher. He watched what was happening apprehensively, for without the protection of the King there might not be any Westminster. Classes were lax now. Everybody seemed preoccupied with other matters. And Busby was absent often the next few months. Some said it was on the King's business, others declared it was to negotiate with Parliament to save the school—there were Westminsters in both Houses—and the under masters obeyed his rules without his severity and certainty and the examinations for the coveted posts of Kings' Scholars were put off indefinitely.

Christopher thought, There was no certainty anywhere. The country teetered on the edge of civil war and he felt on a see-saw.

Then, four months after Charles had left London, Matthew was released from the Tower and Dean Wren hurried into London to welcome him at Westminster Abbey. Busby allowed Christopher to join them, as if to indicate his own support, and the boy was glad to see that his uncle hadn't changed much; a little thinner perhaps, but that was all.

He could tell his father had the same sense of relief, for just a few weeks ago a Catholic priest had been confined to the Tower for preaching a mass, and then was hanged, drawn, and quartered. And one of the charges against Matthew was that he intended to introduce Papist rites into the Protestant ritual. By now, Christopher realised, the one thing neither side could be guilty of was tolerance.

But as his uncle embraced him and his father and he sensed that in spite of Matthew's sternness, his uncle was glad to see him, he cried.

"You must not," Matthew said abruptly, almost harshly. "A Wren must never show weakness to anyone."

His father dried his eyes and said, "He is still young. A child."

"Going on ten? These days that is not a child. These days he cannot afford to be a child." Yet as he gazed at Christopher's gentle features, his brown hair, his grey eyes, his high cheekbones and wide forehead, his plain black doublet and dark grey stockings, so that whatever happened, he would have this memory to cherish, he added, "Christopher could be a Puritan by his appearance, but no matter what happens to us he must remain steadfast in his faith."

"I will, Uncle. I heard Prynne when he attacked you and there was no mercy in him. None at all."

"There is none in any of the Puritans."

But about this Christopher wasn't so certain.

"They only released me as a gesture to the King. To show him that they will give a little if he will. But he won't. If Strafford was not worth saving, Charles won't lift a finger for me either."

"Yet you will support him, Uncle," Christopher blurted out.

E

"He is our anointed ruler and the support of our Church."

His father added, "And the attacks on him are attacks on us."

Christopher asked, "Did they treat you badly, Uncle?"

"I was deprived of fresh air and exercise and a long stay could bring on consumption. I spent most of my time comforted only by my writing and my books, except they tried to force me to read their filthy Puritan tracts, infected with their prophecies and profanities, and enemies to piety. But they will not convert me. Not even if my life is the price. And, brother, you must promise me one thing."

Dean Wren looked puzzled as he asked, "What is that, Matthew?"

"If I'm put back in the Tower, take Christopher out of Westminster."

"But when I wanted to do that last year you stopped me."

"Charles had a chance to control the city then. Now, however, London is a Puritan city. And if I'm imprisoned again it means all attempts at conciliation have failed."

"Don't you think there are any chances for peace?"

"The King thinks so. He has just had two Roman priests executed to demonstrate that he is a devout Protestant. But I doubt it will convince the Puritans. Both were harmless and one of them was almost ninety."

"Are you worried about the scaffold?"

"Brother, you mustn't ask so many questions!"

"I'm sorry, Matthew."

Christopher rarely had seen his father so abject and he spoke up in his defence. "Uncle, it is only because we care."

"I've never enjoyed these public executions. Those who cannot wait to go to these spectacles are creatures of the devil. The few it has been my misfortune to see, I have considered a calamity, and I have stood as far away as possible and at the final stroke I closed my eyes."

"So did I!" exclaimed Christopher, without thinking, glad he wasn't the only one. Then he felt guilty as even his father stared at him reprovingly.

"Whose execution, child?" Matthew demanded to know.

"Strafford. But I didn't look! I couldn't look!" Misery filled his eyes. Why did he have to experience such things if he didn't want to?

His uncle said, "Besides, the executions are always held so early, as if the axe cannot wait but must move with the dawn. One is forced to rise before it is their habit and to look their best when it is the most difficult time to appear that way. Or to face God. A man needs some preparations to meet his Maker. It is not easy to think of God at such moments. But let us be thankful, I am free and perhaps it will last."

"Yes," said his father, "God willing."

Matthew bowed his head in prayer.

"I am sure He will bestow upon us His infinite mercy."

Very fitting, reflected Matthew.

But Christopher could tell that his father was not certain. For his father's arms trembled as they embraced him protectively, and he could feel his father shiver, and then he shivered, too, and prayed that Parliament would be as merciful as God. After what he had seen since he had entered Westminster, he had no faith in the King. And not much more in Parliament.

"If anything happens to me," said Matthew, "do not look."

If You Want To Be Somewhere

If you want to be somewhere
but not here
go there

by getting closer not further
from that little creative park
in the middle of your mind

where moving paths will take you
to the most unexpected sunlit river
and there

you will find a little raft
with a sunlit lifetime chart
and all the little crossed marks

are where
the little great raft will take you
and everywhere is on there

Stymean Karlen

8

If You Want To Be Somewhere

WHEN CHARLES RAISED HIS STANDARD AT NOTTINGHAM ON AUGUST 22nd, 1642, as an act of war against Parliament, Matthew was put back in the Tower and Dean Wren took Christopher out of Westminster, although Busby still ruled the school, and brought his son home to Windsor. Christopher didn't like leaving London or Daniel, but he was glad to see Seth and Susan again.

But Seth was sombre, as if he wasn't sure he should welcome his return, while Susan, although she dutifully kissed him, was preoccupied.

He asked Seth about the pony in the hope that he could ride Monk again, and the gardener replied, "We no longer have him, he is being used elsewhere," and excused himself to tend the garden.

Only the garden was even more orderly than before, everything as neat and well-kept and logical as any Head Master could ask, reflected the boy, but before he could congratulate Seth the gardener was gone.

His father arranged a party for his tenth birthday in October, and invited William Holder, a twenty-six-year-old protege of his uncle, and when he saw his sister's eyes light up as the graceful, handsome rector of Bletchington entered the Deanery, he understood why she was preoccupied. But he was also confused. She looked grown up, yet she was only thirteen. Then he recalled this was a suitable age for a girl to be courted and many were wed at thirteen. And she was pretty in her new dress, a russet brocaded cloth which illuminated her brown hair and eyes and gave her a vivacity he hadn't realised she possessed. Yet while Holder seemed pleased to see Susan, he was equally attentive to him.

Dean Wren said to his son, "Our guest is quite learned in science and mathematics and already is given to much contemplation."

"You are very kind, sir," said Holder, "but I trust Christopher will regard me as a brother and address me as William, as I hope you will."

But when Holder discussed geometry with her brother, Susan frowned. No one considered her worthy of learning such a profound subject, and she assumed an air of calculated indifference to Holder.

Christopher was glad he could speak freely to William, like a friend. Whatever he asked about arithmetic, which was neglected at Westminster, the rector answered. William possessed the same respect for numbers he did and for their value in the order of things. He was annoyed when their discussion of the importance of mathematics was interrupted by the entrance of his uncle's son, Matthew. He wasn't sure whether his cousin had come to celebrate his birthday or to bring news of his uncle.

Miss Smyth, the housekeeper, lit the candles, for it was dark early in October, and his cousin, who was the same age as Susan, was usually self-possessed, but tonight the stocky, dark-haired boy was quite excited.

After he kissed Dean Wren, Susan, and Christopher, and shook Holder's hand, he said, "The Puritans control the Tower now. Until yesterday, my father was able to smuggle out messages, but no longer."

"How is he?" asked Dean Wren.

"As well as can be expected," said Matthew. "Father is suffering from rheumatism of the face and they won't even give him kindling for a fire to heat his cell. And he still complains about the lack of exercise and the books they allow him to read, and his last message said he was being taken from the Cradle Tower where, at least, he could see the river, to the Salt Tower, which is smaller and where there is no view at all."

"Is he able to talk to Archbishop Laud, child?"

"No. They are being kept apart. Laud is in the White Tower."

Holder said reassuringly, "The fact that the Bishop is not in the White Tower, where the most hated prisoners are kept, is hopeful."

Dean Wren sighed. "William, it is a small blessing. Child, have you any other news? Has there been fighting in London?"

"None. It seems securely held by Pym and Parliament."

Christopher cut in, although it was not his nature to do so, "Father, Matthew is allowed to go everywhere, yet you took me out of school."

"Your cousin is older, more experienced in the ways of the world."

"He is only three years older than I am."

Matthew said proudly, "The Puritans do not suspect me because of my youth. I can go everywhere as long as I dress as they do, in sober black, and tell them that my father has been a Dissenter since the days of Elizabeth. But I'm in the royal service. I've learned much."

Dean Wren asked, "How does the King's cause go outside of London?"

"No one is sure, he hesitates so. But there is much fighting."

He recalled what his brother had said, *The King does not always inspire devotion, only fidelity,* but he said, "I thought when he raised his flag at Nottingham most of the country would flock to his side."

"Many did, uncle, but there is much superstition. The evening the King placed his flag in the ground at Nottingham was wet and windy, and instead of a great multitude witnessing this solemn occasion, the weather was so bleak hardly anyone attended and the wind was so strong it blew down his flag. Many consider this a bad omen and the work of the devil."

Christopher wanted to resume his discussion with William, but even he looked disturbed by his cousin's news. Then his father asked, "Matthew, do you have any written message from the Bishop?"

"Only this."

He took the folded note from his nephew and read to himself: *"Be careful. Or all could be lost."* He crumpled the paper into a small ball and tossed it into the fire and tried to hide his fear from the others.

Miss Smyth announced that supper was ready in the dining chamber and Christopher noticed that the housekeeper kept down her loud voice in the presence of his father, and that she had scrubbed her florid face so her complexion shone as brightly as a polished red apple. And when he saw that the great oak table from the study had been moved into the dining chamber to eat upon, and with it his favourite chairs, *Myself, Those,* and *Him,* he hoped he would be able to sit in *Myself,* and yet next to William.

Dean Wren was pleased that Holder took Susan's arm to escort her into the dining room and that she was smiling again. They would be a good match, he thought, in another year. Next to providing for his son's future was the importance of finding a suitable husband for his daughter. She was sufficiently meek and obedient to accept his choice, but it was better if she liked her future husband—as he had cared for his wife. He didn't want Susan to wed with a feeling of resignation. Now he felt sensible that he had dressed her in a fitted bodice which showed off her slimness, for Holder was charmed by her prettiness. Marriage was essential for a young lady and the rector was already building up a reputation as a scholar. Moreover the Bishop recommended

E*

him as a man of industry, character, and yet with enough ambition not to be a plod.

He was also gratified by his wit when Holder commented favourably on the large number of genuine glass windows in the dining chamber, and was attracted by the gold and silver plate that was usually on the mantel to impress but which was being used on the table as if it were a matter of course, the carpets on the floor, and the great oak table itself.

He said, "The Deanery was rebuilt when my brother, who was Dean of Windsor before me, made extensive renovations. If he hadn't heeded the call of the Church, I think he would have been a fine builder."

"Your garden is quite symmetrical. Did he build that, too, sir?"

"Our gardener did. Seth has faults, but he is not afraid of labour."

"It is beautiful, sir," Holder said enthusiastically.

"I love it, too!" burst out Christopher. "Seth is a fine builder, too!"

His father changed the subject and sat Holder between himself and Susan, and put his son—to the boy's disappointment—next to Matthew.

But at least, thought Christopher, he was able to sit in *Myself*, for no one else wanted to, since it was the smallest chair. And he was allowed to sit at the same table with the grown-ups—generally children ate separately—and his father had dressed him as a copy of himself.

Dr. Christopher, who was roly-poly now when he sat, his son noticed, beamed when William admired his claret; he was fond of food and wine.

He said, "The wine glasses were imported from Venice and were a wedding gift from my wife's father. William, I hope you are not shy with claret, it is useful to settle the stomach in times of stress."

"No, I'm not, sir. But you are not drinking any, Susan?"

I am not allowed, she thought, but she didn't know what to say.

Her father said, "I wanted her to wait for the proper occasion."

Holder proposed a toast, "To my charming hostess, Susan Wren!"

But he wished he could steady her hand, she came so close to spilling her drink on him from nervousness.

Christopher noticed there were many courses of meat and fowl, and that his father took great pride and pleasure in carving the joint.

And when Dean Wren apologised for the humble meal, William replied, "It is a noble repast," and because he felt uneasy to be eating so lavishly he talked about religion as if this would be more fitting and to ease his guilt. "I'm not sure we should regard

Romanism as much of a threat to our Church as such errors as Puritanism. What do you think, Dr. Wren?"

"You could be right," said Dean Wren, struggling to hold back a belch. "Our Church must steer a middle way between the pomp of a superstitious tyranny and a fanatical anarchy. That is why I want my son to become a King's Scholar and to enter the Church when this troubled business ends."

"Sir, you are sure the King will win?"

"Of course! When people come to their senses. Don't you agree?"

"I want him to win, sir, but there is so much confusion in his ranks. And he doesn't seem sure of what to do, which adds to the confusion."

"William, a war cannot be fought as a mathematical proposition."

"I wish it could be. It would have more logic then."

"You are a great believer in the sciences, aren't you?"

"Sir, they do not have to be incompatible with theology."

"That depends, William. Busby doesn't teach mathematics or science."

"When I graduated from Cambridge and Pembroke Hall, the Bishop's school, sir, I was offered a post as under master at Westminster, but I turned it down. I respect Busby's stress on Latin and theology, but science and mathematics should also be taught. I believe this firmly."

Christopher longed to applaud these views, and William had such good manners—he didn't belch or pick his teeth as his father did—but Seth was at the door, distraught and shouting, "Dr. Wren, you must flee!"

He wondered why his father didn't respond.

"Dr. Wren, Parliament has ordered its soldiers to seize the castle!"

When his father still didn't reply, Christopher cried out, "Father, listen to him! Please! You can trust Seth!"

"As my brother trusted Prynne?" The Dean still didn't move.

"Dr. Wren, they are coming up the hill from the village."

"Why should they seize the castle?"

"Windsor commands the countryside. And there are other reasons."

"How do you know?"

"I'm not supposed to warn you, it could mean my life, but I want you to be prepared. You have been kind to me and you have good children."

"But we are not soldiers."

"You represent the King, which is enough. And this will be another act of defiance against him, since he values Windsor."

Christopher asked hurriedly, for his father was wasting time,

"What else brings them here? The Deanery is not part of the fortifications."

"They are after the treasures of the Garter. The plate, the armour, the sword. And the jewels, especially the diamonds of the George."

William asked, "How much time do we have?"

"Ten–Twenty minutes, probably. It is foggy outside and they will have trouble finding their way. And some of them are drunk, for there was much drinking to strengthen their resolution."

"What do you think, William?" asked Dean Wren. "Should we ignore them or flee? Or hide the children in the water closet?"

"I don't think they will harm anyone if we don't resist them."

"Do you think we should stay?"

Christopher volunteered, "Father, there are loose floorboards in the Treasury where you could bury the sword and the jewels. They are what the King values most of the treasures of the Garter." He was surprised at himself, telling his father what to do, but he was right, he thought, although he expected to be reprimanded.

But when William said, "Christopher is right, sir," his father nodded.

Seth added, "Everybody talks about the sword, even in the village. They say that if they capture it and use it against the King, it will give them special powers and impress those who are wavering."

Dean Wren stood up hastily, saying, "Seth, why are you helping us?"

"I told you, sir. And you are not a devil, no matter what they say. Or even your brother, although he is too stern for my taste. Often he sounds like my father. You must be ready for them when they arrive."

William interrupted, "But first, as Christopher said, we must hide what we can of the Order of the Garter. Particularly the sword and the jewels. Christopher, where are the loose floorboards?"

The boy was glad he was observant as he led them to the Treasury, a short distance away. He knew intimately this ancient vaulted chamber with its heavy oak door, for his father stored most of the treasures of the Garter here and often compiled his records on the massive table in the centre of the room. All of them were puzzled, for there seemed no place to hide anything, but when, led by Christopher, they pushed the table into a corner they saw the loose floorboards that had been under it, and he said, "Father, I noticed them when you examined the chapel for repairs."

Dean Wren stared at the hole in the floor with disapproval and replied, "This should have been repaired years ago. What good will it do us now?"

"If we push back the table after we hide the treasures in the hole the soldiers will not think of searching for them there."

"I'm not so positive, child."

"They won't look. They won't expect anything to be hidden in such an obvious place. No one discovered the loose floorboards until I did."

"Besides," said William, "we have no choice if we're to hide anything."

"It will do," said Seth. "We will be able to get some things into it if we dig deep enough. I will get a shovel from the garden."

"No, I'll get it," said Christopher. "I know where it is, and you must watch for the soldiers so you can warn us when they approach."

When his father repeated, "How can we trust him?" he answered, enjoying his feeling of responsibility and decisiveness, "He warned us. And he is the only one who will recognise the soldiers. And, perhaps, delay them."

Dean Wren ordered Seth to watch at the Henry VIII gateway, with Susan to act as his courier. But as Christopher got the shovel, Seth whispered to him, "Don't question the soldiers, that could make them violent."

By the time he returned with the shovel his father decided that the most vital treasure of the Garter—as he had suggested—was the huge two-handed sword of Edward III which hung over that sovereign's stall in the chapel of the Order of the Garter. This was the most famous sword in the realm. Edward III had wielded it at Crécy and he was the founder of the Garter.

No wonder Edward III's vigour was a legend, thought the boy, it took the combined strength of William, his cousin, and himself to carry the giant sword. It was six feet eight inches long, far longer than any of them, and even his father regarded it with awe as he directed them. There wasn't enough space for the sword and William dug frantically, for precious time had passed in transporting this treasure. Finally, when the hole still wasn't large enough, Christopher—noticing that the ground was soft under the floorboards—suggested they plunge the blade into the earth so the weapon itself would create the space. They did so with a mighty thrust, all of them stepping on the two handed hilt until it rudely ripped the bowels of the earth and the entire sword was submerged beneath the floor.

In great haste now, but with as much pomp as if they were honouring a king, Dean Wren buried the diamond George, the royal insignia of the Order, and the Garter of Gustavus Adolphus, which was of special importance to him, for it was set also in diamonds, and was the first treasure to be given into his care when he had become Registrar of the Order.

Christopher and William swept up the dirt and put the floorboards back in place, but they needed help from Matthew and the Dean to push the massive table back to the centre of the Treasury. They were just finishing when Susan ran in with the news that the soldiers were approaching.

Dean Wren motioned for them to return to the dining chamber to allay suspicion, but Christopher paused to scatter a number of books on the table, including the Book of Common Prayer and the Authorised Version of the Bible, both of which had been compiled here.

"Carelessly, father, with the pages open, as if this is being used as a scholar's study and nothing else," said Christopher, as he did just that. "And so it appears as if the table hasn't been moved for years. Susan, did Seth escape?"

"Yes. As soon as he warned me, he vanished." She was surprised by her brother's resolution—had Westminster changed him that much?

"Father, is the Treasury door locked?"

Dean Wren said, "In a moment!" But he would have forgotten if his son hadn't reminded him, and he was annoyed at himself for having forgotten and at his son for being more alert than he was. And because of this he had to stress the virtues of his lock, adding, "This Elizabethan lock is built with such skill they will never break it. It is as sturdy as when it was installed a hundred years ago. We don't have such workmanship today." But while he locked the great oak door he was thinking about his son: half child, half boy, undergrown but very observant, disguising in a small body a large, developed mind, already smarter than many men. They couldn't take that away from him, whatever else the soldiers stole.

He was hurrying through the garden when William suggested, "Sir, I think it would be helpful if you could hide the keys to the Treasury."

As he hesitated his son said, "I know just the place. In the garden."

"I'll do it myself." He couldn't allow his son to decide everything; it wasn't fitting or flattering. "What part of the garden is darkest?"

"Under the hedge, father. They are thick and have brambles."

This done, although he cut his fingers on the brambles, the party was just seated at the dining table when a burly figure stood silhouetted in the doorway and announced, "I am Captain Fogg, Gentlemen."

Dean Wren said sternly, "How dare you break in?"

"I want the keys to the Treasury."

"On whose authority?"

"I have a warrant from the King."

"I do not believe you. He would never approve of such behaviour."

"If you do not give me the keys, Wren, I will pull the chapel down about your ears. I'm occupying Windsor in the name of the Commonwealth."

"Don't move," Dean Wren said to those sitting around him. "This man is an intruder. Fogg, you will leave my premises immediately."

Instead, the dark, heavy-set, middle-aged man motioned behind him and an oddly clad troop, carrying muskets and pikes and some of them wearing breastplates like their captain, filed into the room and formed a wall of brass. Christopher counted ten men bearing arms, but he was relieved, for there was no sign of Seth, who, apparently, had escaped.

Dean Wren asked indignantly, "Aren't any of you loyal to the King?"

Captain Fogg replied, "Windsor has already adopted Puritan doctrines and we have occupied the town, the borough, and the hunting park, which is to be used to train our soldiers, and now we are taking over the castle."

"You will pay for this," Dean Wren said angrily.

"But you will pay first," a voice retorted from the ranks. "Let us hang him and show him just how high an opinion we have of his character."

For an instant it looked as if the other soldiers agreed with this threat, but Fogg said, "If you co-operate, Wren, no one will be hurt."

William said, "Don't you think the chamber is already too crowded?"

Fogg motioned for most of the soldiers to leave, but several remained, including the young, fair-haired one who had spoken, who declared now, "I'm Arthur Vertue. One of my ancestors, William Vertue, was the mason responsible for building the vault of St. George's Chapel. I know more about the castle than anyone here. I'll make sure you don't fool us."

"But you are only a carpenter," said Dean Wren, "and not a very good one. I remember you. You did some work on the Deanery. Indifferently."

Christopher thought Arthur Vertue was going to strike his father then, but Fogg restrained him, saying, "We have more pressing matters. At the moment. Parliament has passed an Act sequestering the property of all ecclesiastical bodies, including Windsor. Wren, where are the keys?"

"I've lost them."

"I don't believe you."

"Search me," said Dean Wren. "Although no gentleman would."

There was such contempt in his father's voice Christopher was afraid Fogg would attack him. But as the Dean's lips tightened and he stared stubbornly at the Puritans, Arthur Vertue said, sober now, "Why waste the time? I can get into the Treasury. I know it well."

Fogg nodded, but added, "Wren, if we do not get in, I will not be able to exercise forbearance any longer." He ordered the occupants of the dining chamber to follow him to the Treasury as hostages and the soldiers surrounded them to make sure he would be obeyed.

No matter what Vertue tried, he could not budge the great oak door. Finally, furious at the delay, Fogg forced the stone jambs of the doorway with crowbars and burst into the Treasury followed by Vertue and his hostages. His eyes lit up at the sight of the gold and silver plate, but his pleasure turned to rage when his soldiers informed him that the sword and the jewels were missing. He banged on the table in his anger and demanded to know where they were. But none of the hostages answered.

"They must be in this room," Fogg muttered. "But where?"

Vertue, who was leaning on the table, suddenly grew excited and exclaimed, "This table! It is a treasure!"

Christopher said, "It is oak."

"I know. I can tell good wood when I see it. You could cut down a forest before you could find oak as good as this." He bent down and examined the legs and added, "It is Tudor. About 1600."

Christopher sat on it then, and as he hoped, he distracted Vertue. The carpenter cried out, "You mustn't! You'll scratch it!"

Fogg asked, "What about the sword? The jewels of the Garter?"

"Captain, if furniture is taken for granted it loses its dignity."

"And value, Mr. Vertue," said Christopher. The carpenter had stopped looking at the table and was glaring at his father.

"Wren," he stated, "I'm a better carpenter than you give me credit for. If this was my table, I would take better care of it."

Fogg cut in impatiently, his face red with anger. "I will question the children." He turned to Matthew, then stopped abruptly, and asked, "Aren't you one of the bishop's brood? You bear a strong resemblance."

"No!" declared Christopher, remembering what Daniel had done. "Bagshaw is a friend of mine from Westminster."

"A good Commonwealth name," said Fogg. "Are you related, Bagshaw?"

"Distantly," said Matthew. "On my mother's side."

"Many families are on both sides. Where is the sword hidden, boy?"

"What sword, sir?"

Matthew looked so blankly Fogg addressed Susan. "You are his duaghter, you should know where the sword is."

"But I've been in the kitchen all night, sir, helping with the meal."

"And you were also, no doubt?" Fogg said sarcastically to Christopher.

"No, sir."

Fogg smiled triumphantly.

"I was in the garden. Perhaps the sword is lost, sir."

Vertue said, "What about the table, Captain? It is very valuable. Could I have help moving it out of here? I cannot do it alone."

Fogg said disdainfully, "We have more precious objects to acquire. In the name of the Commonwealth," he added, as Dean Wren protested. "The gold and silver plate of the Garter, the candlesticks, the altar tables, all these various forms of idolatry that profane this church."

The soldiers started to collect the plate of the Garter and Dean Wren could no longer restrain himself. He sought to wrest it from them, only to be knocked to the ground by one of the troop, who grinned proudly. William and the children wanted to go to his assistance, but he cried out, "It's nothing. God will punish them in His own way!"

Fogg paused, insisting, "I bow to no man in piety. Wren, you must take an oath of allegiance to Parliament or you will be named a traitor."

"Suppose I refuse to take your oath?"

"You could join your brother in the Tower."

Dean Wren didn't answer and Susan saw that her father bled from the blow he had received on the forehead. She knelt at his side and told Christopher to obtain a poultice so she could apply it to the bruise.

Fogg stated, "Wren, you have twenty-four hours to vacate the Deanery."

"That is impossible."

"Then you will become prisoners. As Captain in the Parliamentary Army I am converting Windsor into a Commonwealth fortress and jail."

"What about the table?" pleaded Vertue. "I will never have another chance to possess such noble oak. Help me move it, please!"

"It is worth little compared to the plate. No more than these books," snapped Fogg, tossing aside the Bible and the Book of Common Prayer. "We are going to rewrite them anyway. These churchmen read the gospel looking both ways, but our Church will teach them the only true faith."

Christopher returned with the poultice and as Susan's gentle touch eased Dean Wren's pain he said to Fogg, "I will pray for your soul."

"Pray for your own if you and your brood are not out of here by tomorrow," retorted Fogg. "My men will camp in the chapel tonight." He marched out of the Treasury followed by his soldiers.

Vertue trailed him reluctantly, still regarding the massive oak table lovingly as he left and mumbling, "Christ was a carpenter, too," and Christopher wondered why Vertue couldn't feel the same way about people.

His father said, "The Lord will chastise them as I was unable to do."

"We must be merciful," said William.

"Yes, but only up to a point." And when the Dean saw how the soldiers had ravaged the Treasury he wept. They had ransacked every corner of it. Except the space under the table.

Christopher was badly shaken. He had never seen his father cry.

He didn't sleep that night and early the next morning, before anyone else was awake, he slipped out of the Deanery and started for the chapel to find out what had happened. The Puritans wouldn't hurt him, he decided, he was too small to be dangerous. The sun had just risen and as he stood at the entrance to St. George's Chapel, he thought Windsor commanded one of the loveliest views he had seen, but on this bright and cold October dawn this wasn't consoling.

The guard stationed at the entrance to the chapel was asleep and he tiptoed into the nave undetected and he was shocked to find that the Puritans had stabled their horses here. Several neighed and he saw soldiers dozing nearby. There had been much drinking and the chapel smelled like a brew house. Plate was everywhere, altar tables, and some statues that had been destroyed to demonstrate their religious fervour.

He counted twenty-two men and asleep they looked more like farmers, shopkeepers and butchers than soldiers. Then Vertue awoke and immediately roused the others so he could conduct morning prayers, repeating, "Christ was a carpenter, too," and Christopher hid in a choir stall.

He thought, Now that they had drunk heartily and gorged themselves they were unusually fervent in their fasting and prayer.

There was venison on the floor that they had poached from the hunting park of the King, and after their services they chanted as one: "*We are fighting for the freedom of the gospel and for the law of the land. We are not galley slaves yet, to take orders from a Catholic Queen.*"

Christopher saw, too, that they had smashed part of the church glass, torn down hangings, ripped the illuminated prayer books, and slashed the tapestries, but he was grateful that they had left the fabric untouched.

He was reporting all this a few minutes later to his father and the others, who were gathered in the study of the Deanery to await the Dean's instructions, when Fogg and Vertue entered. He halted, not wanting the Puritans to know where he had been, but they ignored him.

Fogg said, "I'm offering you a kindness I doubt your King would allow us. There is a coach outside which will take you where you want to go."

Dean Wren didn't reply, determined not to give him any satisfaction.

"As you wish," said Fogg. "But if you are not gone within the hour I will put you in jail. In your precious Treasury."

"What about the table, Fogg?" asked Vertue.

"I'm not going to waste my soldiers' strength on removing it."

William asked, "What about the plate?"

"It will suffice for my troop's pay. There is no more a Registrar of the Garter. We now have a government that is *great, good,* and *just.*"

Vertue paused a moment, however, after Fogg was gone. And when he was certain he could not be overheard he addressed Dean Wren, "I am the one who persuaded the captain to furnish a coach. I trust you will remember this should fortune favour the King."

"You should be ashamed of yourself," Dean Wren retorted.

"Why?" Vertue shrugged. "My brother is with the King's forces at Oxford. We are a sensible family as well as a virtuous one."

After the carpenter departed Dean Wren ordered William to conduct the children to the coach outside, saying, "We will journey to Oxford where I hear the King, has established his court. The university will be behind him solidly, especially the students."

But as Christopher turned to take a last look at the study and the chairs he loved, particularly *Myself,* wishing he could take it with him as a raft for the stormy seas, he saw his father scratch above the fireplace: "*homo homini lupus*".

He was glad he knew his Latin, for he was able to translate it: "*man is a wolf to his fellow man*".

He hoped the Puritans' Latin was as good.

What Is Most Telling

What is most telling
That it happened
That it happened to you
That it happened between you
and you
Or what it came from

Or the void
fertile or grassless
if it had not happened if

Stymean Karlen

9

What Is Most Telling

OXFORD WAS IN SUCH A STATE OF WAR AND SIEGE, PART GARRISON
and part fortress because of the presence of the King and his court,
Dean Wren decided his family would be safer elsewhere. He sought
refuge in his second living at his rectory at Great Haseley, which
was near Oxford.

Then he returned his son to school when Busby informed him
that no Westminster would be harmed, that Parliament was allowing
the school to remain open, and there was little likelihood of any
fighting in London since the city was held securely by the Puritan
forces.

Daniel greeted him with such warmth Christopher realised his
friend had been afraid he would not see him again. Bagshaw
bragged that the Puritans were winning, although Ryles, whom
he respected, said no one was, so far, adding, "You look well, but
older, more thoughtful. Both sides are unsure, as if they don't know
what to do next."

Most likely, reflected Christopher, they had stumbled into war
because neither side believed the other was serious in their purpose.
Each taking up arms on the assumption their opponents would
yield at the first sight of blood. But now that blood was shed they
were too proud to give in. For the King knew he was right while
Parliament was just as determined to prove itself infallible. So
affairs moved faster and further than either side anticipated, and
now they must stand ready to kill or to be killed.

He wondered why they didn't see the foolishness of this;
he did.

Did they have such a need to be right? To be mad, he thought
wryly, to leave their wits elsewhere, to make such a show of truth
because they couldn't see it, even though it was in front of their
eyes?

What concerned him more immediately, however, was his father's goodbye.

He embraced him so emotionally it was like a final farewell. A cold rain fell as the Dean stood at the steps of the school, preparing to enter his waiting coach, and he blurted out, "For God's sake, as you love me, be careful of your person. The name of Wren is even less regarded in London than before, and you and your sister are my chief comfort."

Suddenly his father was gone, as if he could not endure this parting any longer, and before Christopher could return his father's feelings.

To rectify this he wrote him in his best Busby Latin:

> *"Reverend Father:*
> *"There is a common saying among the ancients which I remember to have had from your mouth: there is no equivalent that can be given back to parents. For their cares and perpetual labours concerning their children are the evidence of immeasurable love. Now these precepts so often repeated, which have impelled my soul towards all that is highest in man, and to virtue, have superseded in me all other affections. What is in me I will perform, as much as I am able, lest these gifts should have been bestowed on an un- grateful soul. May the good God Almighty be with me in my undertakings and make good to you all that you most desire in the tenderness of your fatherly love. So prays your son, most devoted to you in all obedience.*
> *Christopher Wren"*

His father was so proud of Christopher's letter he stored it with his most precious possessions, and prayed that he would be properly remembered by his only son, should God will that they never see each other again. The King, after several quick, early victories, had suffered some defeats, and Matthew's house had been sacked, too, and his brother's appeal for a new trial had been rejected. He hoped these misfortunes would not turn his son's heart against the Church, when, with all his promise, he might grow into a noble divine. Yet he sensed that Christopher was not one to be a martyr; his son was reasonable in his thinking. If only he could pen a book of instructions to support him in the times of trial ahead, to remind him to serve God in faith and obedience no matter what happened. But as he wrote this, as an answer to his son's letter, his eyes filled with tears once again.

Dean Wren's pessimism lessened when William married Susan the following year and they settled in his son-in-law's rectory at Bletchington, not far from Great Haseley. One child, at least, was in the Church still, which was some comfort, and Matthew's head was still on, and his son was well.

He re-read the letter to bring his son closer to him and he frowned. Now that his emotion was less, he noticed there were several errors in the Latin. It was Busby's fault, he decided, with his stress on his own grammar. He liked William's Latin better; it was almost as good as his own. But he didn't reprimand Christopher; as it was, his son preferred too many subjects to Latin. Instead, Dean Wren wrote his son asking him when he was going to take the examinations for King's Scholar, to ease the entrance into Christ Church at Oxford when the rebellion was over, and added, feeling a little bit like Matthew, "Practise your Latin. It was good, but it could be better."

Child If You Speak A Word

Child if you speak a word
that weighs an ounce Child
will you know what weight
word should follow Child

Child do not sink the earth
with the overweight of words
as all children do Child
Meaning is weightless Child

Yes My Elder
    You Just Taught Me

Stymean Karlen

10

Child If You Speak A Word

CHRISTOPHER HEARD THE NEWS OF SUSAN'S MARRIAGE WITH DELIGHT. Now he should see more of William and be able to pursue their inquiries into mathematics. But, as he wrote his father, factually this time: "At the moment the elections for King's Scholar are banned by Parliament, whose visitors have placed a watch on the school, although they have left the classes in Busby's hands and they have not caused any other changes, except to forbid the wearing of surplices."

His father replied, "Persevere, child. Busby informs me there will be King's Scholars again, as soon as the present rebellion ends."

The more Dr. Christopher felt deprived of the rich living and golden stall of Windsor, the more he resolved that his son would achieve the highest place in the Church of England. Not for his son to go to school just to become a doctor, apothecary, or merchant. Christopher was destined for a learned profession and the hierarchy of the Church was the most learned and beneficent. He must have a trustworthy living.

So, although the conditions at the school didn't alter the next year, Christopher devoted himself to preparations for the postponed elections. While he doubted he wanted to enter Christ Church or Trinity and be a divine, he didn't tell his father. Indeed, he studied harder. He learned to read the Old Testament in Hebrew, the New in Arabic, Homer in Greek, and Cicero and Virgil in Latin, which was easy.

"Always the classics," stressed Busby, who taught him Latin personally now. "Then you will not grow up ignorant or foolish."

Christopher obeyed, although many nights numbers danced in his head and he yearned to investigate them and he couldn't sleep. He wished Busby possessed a genuine interest in mathematics. In the upper forms arithmetic was taught and the Head Master even joked about discovering another Euclid, as if the older students might be trusted with numbers, although Busby himself added inaccurately and multiplied badly, and Christopher felt arithmetic was taught without feeling or substance.

One night in October he sat on his bed and felt disconsolate. Two years ago he had celebrated his birthday and now he had another and there was no word from his father or sister. Had they forgotten? But they couldn't have, he assured himself, it must be because the Parliamentary visitors halted all letters. Yet that didn't improve his mood. He had no desire to study, to learn by rote. Moreover, he had seen very little of Daniel lately, as if his friend was avoiding him, too. Everyone was getting ready for bed, as he was supposed to do, and it was the last thing he wanted to do. It was early, only about eight o'clock, and he felt grown up, so much had happened to him, and he had an intense craving for new worlds, for change; almost any change would be better than the discontent afflicting him. He examined the wall where he measured himself nightly, but that didn't improve his spirits; he had not grown much and he was still the shortest boy in his form.

The candles were put out, but he was still sitting on his bed, not undressed, when Daniel sat down beside him and whispered, "We are journeying into London. Do you want to come with us?"

"What about the monitor?"

"Bagshaw is going with us. Actually, it is his idea."

"Isn't he afraid to risk his opportunity to become a King's Scholar?"

"He has friends in Parliament. He cannot lose. Even though he is not an angel, like you."

This was no compliment, thought Christopher, and he said, "If your intention is to irk me . . . ?"

"You are studying too hard. You never have any fun these days. We are under-staffed because Busby wants to save money, many students slip out of the school, even all night, and you never go out a minute."

His father had warned him not to, but Christopher could not admit this, as if this made him less grown up, less worthy to be in an upper form.

"But we have it all arranged, Christopher." Daniel grew excited. "Busby is away again, Ryles will look the other way—he still needs the shillings—and Bagshaw has the key to the rear door."

"Who else is going?"

"Fotherby, and two new boys from a lower form, Hooke and Dryden. They have not been out at night and they have paid Bagshaw a shilling each, and he cannot resist bribery and flattery.

You are not going to allow them to outdo you? Hooke and Dryden are only in the second form."

"Why is Bagshaw including me? With my royalist connections?"

"He may need them some day. He likes to be protected on both sides."

The discussion was cut short by Bagshaw. "Daniel, if you are going to come, we have to go now, while the door is free."

Daniel took Christopher by the arm and led him outside. The touch of his friend eased his discontent and the stars were bright. He heard a frog croak in the fields behind the school and he discerned four other boys in the darkness and he asked, "Daniel, where are we going?"

"To Charing Cross where Bagshaw knows of a theatrical performance."

"I thought all the theatres were closed by an act of Parliament."

"All public theatres. But this is a private performance, Bagshaw says, for Dissenters who still like to celebrate acting and singing."

Christopher was surprised that the streets were quiet and empty. There were no lights or sign of occupancy in Whitehall Palace or in the Banqueting House, although it was only a little after eight o'clock.

Daniel said, "The Puritans closed them. Almost everything is closed. They insist that entertainment is ungodly, except what they like."

Near Charing Cross there was a street light and Christopher was introduced to the newcomers. John Dryden looked his own age, a plump, red-cheeked, self-assured boy, but Robert Hooke appeared to be only about nine and was even shorter than himself, but with an unusually large head, and grey eyes that almost popped out of his head from enthusiasm.

He wondered why they were taking such a child along, until Hooke said, "It would be easier to fly than to walk," and he sensed there was a quick, inventive mind here, while Dryden quoted Ovid to show that he belonged with the upper form boys, but Christopher was not impressed, although Dryden added, "I learned Ovid by myself. Without any instructions."

Bagshaw interrupted impatiently, "I will do the talking if anyone approaches us. Groups are not allowed to assemble unless they have permission and I have a pass." He proudly pulled it out of his doublet and read: "*This is to permit the bearer thereof, Edward Bagshaw, to transport himself, and other necessaries, unto any part of London, without let or molestation. Given by act of Parliament, at Westminster.*" He reminded them ostentatiously, "I have relatives in Parliament, and my uncle owns the tavern we are going to, the Bear and Boar."

Fotherby and Dryden were impressed, as Bagshaw desired, but

Daniel said, "You told me Christopher would not be harmed, if his name is discovered."

"He won't be. I'll say he is my cousin. No one will recognise him as a Wren. Unless he is afraid."

He was, but he said, "You are the one we are waiting for." He felt that Bagshaw wasn't his friend, whatever his schoolmate professed.

They reached Charing Cross quickly, although Fotherby fell into a ditch and Dryden farted from anxiety and over-eating. The tavern was close to the square and from the outside Christopher couldn't tell whether it was an ale house, an eating house, or a lodging house. Inside, however, the main room, which was spacious and built with solid oak timber, was arranged for a performance, with a raised platform for a stage and ten rows of benches to seat a hundred people. A small, spry, wizened man stood at the entrance and greeted Bagshaw, who said, "My uncle," but he did not introduce his companions except to say, "My friends from school."

His uncle replied, "And good friends of the Commonwealth, I trust?"

"Yes, sir. Where should we sit, Uncle Thomas?"

"In the rear. You can stand if you can't see."

All the benches but the first and last rows were occupied and Christopher was wedged in between Bagshaw and Dryden, although he would have preferred to sit next to Daniel and Hooke, who were on the end. Dryden was eager to court him, while Bagshaw intended to lord it over him. But the audience's attention was on the two men who entered and placed themselves in the first row, followed by a dozen soldiers. The tall, strongly built man, who looked about forty, was clearly the leader, thought Christopher— his companion was slight, younger, and almost womanly in his appearance—and he wondered if it was the first man's air of strength and command that focussed all eyes on him.

Bagshaw whispered, "It is Oliver Cromwell."

"Who?" He had heard the name before, but he didn't remember where.

"He is Parliament's most successful commander of horse soldiers."

Is that all? Christopher wanted to say, but instead he nodded, aware this was not a time to be critical. Cromwell's shoulders were massive and blocked out much of the stage, and the commander possessed one of the largest heads he had seen, but his thick brown hair fell below his collar, and Christopher couldn't resist asking Bagshaw, "How can he be a Roundhead with all that hair? After Prynne denounced such long hair?"

"Sssh," said Bagshaw. "You must not call anyone a Roundhead or they will know you are a Royalist."

"Who is the man with him? He doesn't look like a soldier."

"He isn't," Bagshaw said contemptuously, "He is a pamphleteer and poet. John Milton. But Cromwell evidently thinks he might be useful."

"What has he written?"

"A tract on divorce, supporting it, which was ignored, and something called *Areopagitica,* against censorship, which Parliament won't read."

"If his tracts are unpopular, why is he allowed to write them?"

"Cromwell likes the way he writes, and Parliament doesn't want to offend him. There is a box on the stage, where the audience can take one of Milton's pamphlets if they wish, but nobody will, you see."

Nobody did while Christopher watched. Then his attention was attracted to the stage, for the entertainment was starting. It was conducted by Signor Lupino and his daughter, and this puzzled him, for females were not allowed on stage and Lupino crossed himself as he bowed to his audience.

When he mentioned this to Bagshaw, the latter shrugged and said, "It doesn't matter. He is a foreigner. An Italian. A puppet-player, who has a booth at Charing Cross, and likes to perform an odd novelty called Punch. But he and his daughter have good voices, and Cromwell and Milton delight in music.

The first entertainment was a two-character play—"with just enough music to make it acceptable," Bagshaw whispered—"called *The Death of Raleigh.*" It told of Raleigh coming back from the block to haunt James I, as a Stuart, for having betrayed him, and it was plain to Christopher this was meant as a warning to Charles. Only, he thought, what good will it do? The King was elsewhere and all those watching were supposed to be supporters of Parliament, whose minds were already convinced of the King's perfidy. But Bagshaw said to him, "Raleigh is a favourite of Cromwell's. He likes Raleigh's *History of the World* very much."

Christopher didn't care for the play, it lacked imagination and wit, but he wished he knew more about Raleigh. He liked Signor Lupino's singing better, and when his daughter joined him the duet had an endearing quality. She was a pert, pretty, black-haired sixteen and Christopher had a sudden yearning for her. He wished he was full grown, and able to choose as he pleased. The audience liked her, too, he noticed, for the applause for her was loud and Cromwell and Milton congratulated her personally. The poet's compliments brought a blush to her cheeks.

Fotherby asked Bagshaw, "Is he Cromwell's sword-bearer?"

"A poet. My uncle is introducing me. Come along, if you want."

Christopher felt that he shouldn't, but the others followed

F

Bagshaw, so he walked forward, too. Milton was annoyed when
Thomas Bagshaw introduced his nephew, for it interrupted his conversation with the girl enough to permit her to withdraw, but
Cromwell stood and listened without expression. Then the cavalry
commander asked, "Bagshaw, what about the other boys? Are they
our friends, too?"

"My nephew assures me, sir . . ."

"Your nephew has no choice, but these other boys may be a
different breed." He turned to Christopher. "You are very small
to be here, child?"

"I am twelve."

"Sir," interrupted Bagshaw.

"Never mind the formalities," said Cromwell. "Time enough for
that. What brought you here, child, idle curiosity or love of a
spectacle?"

"I wondered why it is permissible to have an entertainment here
since it is forbidden everywhere else in London."

"We are just outside of London," Bagshaw said hurriedly. "The
city limits are down the Strand."

"But the child is right," said Cromwell. "Isn't he, Milton?"

Milton, thinking of the pretty girl, shrugged indifferently.

Daniel, uncomfortable with the way Cromwell was staring at
Christopher, volunteered, "I wondered, too, sir. But i enjoyed the
music."

Cromwell tightened the thick leather sword belt around his sober
black uniform and said, still addressing Christopher, "Do you ride,
child?"

"When I can, sir. I love it."

"So does Charles. It is one of the few things we have in common.
Milton, there is a look about this child I've seen before. What is
your name?" When Christopher hesitated, he said, "We do not
make war on children."

"Christopher, Mr. Cromwell, Christopher Wren."

Cromwell asked, "A son of the bishop?"

"His nephew," said Bagshaw.

Cromwell paused, and even Milton listened now. Then he asked,
"And you, Bagshaw, brought him here to convert him?"

"Yes, sir! Yes, sir! Of course, sir!"

"Christopher Wren, do you feel the same way?"

Cromwell was intimidating, but Christopher said, "No, sir."

"Why did you come, boy?"

"Because I was afraid not to."

"And not to do reverence to the Commonwealth cause?"

"Here, sir? Did you, Mr. Cromwell?"

He didn't answer Christopher. Instead he turned to Bagshaw and said, "You should convert this boy. We could use his logic and honesty."

Milton asked, "Bagshaw, what about the others?"

Fotherby said hurriedly, "I agree with Bagshaw, sir."

"So do I!" exclaimed Dryden, "Although my grandfather was a baronet!"

But Daniel and Hooke were silent, until Milton spoke to them directly.

Daniel said, "Christopher is my friend. You must not harm him."

"No, you mustn't," said Hooke. "He has done nothing wrong."

Christopher couldn't tell from Milton's expression what he felt, although the poet's fair skin was flushed and his slight frame was like lacework against the oaken structure of Cromwell's body. He sensed their minds' clocks varied, even though both seemed sure they possessed the future, yet their imaginations must be different, it was in the way they spoke, Cromwell was slow and measured, Milton quick and impulsive; no wonder one was a poet while the other was a commander of horse soldiers.

Cromwell motioned for his guard to depart and as they marched out—the best trained troops Christopher had seen—he addressed the boys as if he were addressing himself. "God is not always where we expect to find Him. But comes where each person has to find Him. Yes, Milton?"

Milton nodded, but that didn't matter, thought Christopher, Cromwell's mind was decided as he stated, "It is the interference of the established Church and the Church of Rome with our consciences that I object to."

When Cromwell and Milton were gone, Bagshaw's uncle said woefully and apologetically, "A dangerous and difficult man, Cromwell. He is not really a Puritan or even a Presbyterian, but an Independent. And Milton's grandfather was a Catholic. Some people don't know who they are."

The next day he was called into Busby's study. He was sure the Head Master had discovered he had been out of the school, but Busby told him to be seated, which was unusual, and said, "You are a good student."

"Thank you, sir."

"You have much to learn, no one will mistake your Greek for Homer, but you memorise easily and you are not afraid to study. What worries me is your lack of dexterity in the world. You must be able to weather whatever storms afflict you, no matter what the political changes."

"What have I done wrong, sir?"

"You must learn to bend a little, Wren, when it is necessary."

Busby's tone was so sombre he asked, "Is it about Cromwell, sir?"

"He is their best soldier. You must avoid him. Wren, a petition has been presented to the Commons by the London mob, asking for the heads of Laud and your uncle." He didn't wait for a reply, satisfied with the look of shock that appeared, but continued, "That is why I've been away, to try to win support for them; the Archbishop is the ecclesiastical head of Westminster and your uncle is a brave and honourable churchman."

"Will they be executed because someone else is in power?"

"No one knows yet. But I've been asked to dismiss you from the school."

Busby waited until the child's response was what he expected—fear at the possibility of leaving Westminster—and then he said, "But I won't. Unless you give the Parliamentary visitors a real excuse. Have you been out of the school lately?" When he saw Christopher's surprise, he added, "Child, I know that students slip out sometimes. It is no secret. I cannot be everywhere all the time and under masters are easily bribed."

Christopher hesitated; he didn't want to lie.

"If you have, it could go hard with you."

"No, sir." Now that it was out, he discovered some lies were possible.

"Do you know Inigo Jones, child?"

"Yes, sir. Remember, when I first entered Westminster, you allowed me to go with my father to meet him at the Banqueting House which he built."

Busby nodded, although he didn't remember, and said, "The King's Surveyor was also Justice of the Peace for Westminster when I became Head Master. He took those duties conscientiously. Whenever Westminsters came before him, for disturbing the peace, he reported them to me." Busby sighed, "And now he has been dismissed by Parliament, as he has been dismissed from all his duties because he is the King's man."

"But he is such a good architect, sir!"

"That is a matter more disputable, child. I preferred him as a Justice of the Peace. Then he was not so Italian in his ideas."

"Where is he now, sir?"

"With the King, I believe. As your father is."

So that was why he hadn't heard from him, thought Christopher, and his attention was attracted by Busby's library, for prominent was Raleigh's *History of the World*, and prompted by his curiosity he asked, "Is this a book I should read, sir? I have not seen it in our classes."

"It is only Raleigh's opinions. But he had an interesting mind."

"May I read it, sir?"

"No. It is better to stick to your Latin and Greek. What is known."

The next few weeks Christopher felt the King's cause must be failing, for he learned that Pym, who had died last year, was buried in Westminster Abbey, and soldiers were quartered in the church and they broke down the altar rails and burned them, smashed the organ into shreds and pawned the pipes at ale houses for pots of ale. He was even more troubled when Laud was brought to trial; he was not relieved that, for the moment, his uncle was spared. He could not explain, even to Daniel, that the fate of Laud mattered as much to him as his uncle's.

Christopher heard that Prynne was Laud's main prosecutor, pursuing him with a vindictive lust for revenge; that the Archbishop had no chance; Parliament was resolved to execute him, whatever his defence.

But Laud won one victory. After Parliament, again led by Prynne, declared they had the right to decide any crime they wished treasonable and ordered the Archbishop to be executed by the usual means—which meant the hanging, disembowelling and quartering of traitors—Laud asked for mercy. And just two days before his execution it was granted. Parliament agreed that his sentence be commuted to beheading.

The day of the execution became a holiday in London. A huge crowd, bored because there was nothing to do in Puritan London with all the amusements closed, turned out to witness the spectacle on Tower Hill.

Christopher felt full of shame and could not bring himself to attend, although some of his schoolmates did, and he heard about the execution from Bagshaw. The older boy was proud that he remembered every detail.

After the spectacle he told Christopher gloatingly, "The mob was so thick that Laud, who had owned a barge as grand as the King's, was forced to push through the spectators that lined the way from the Traitor's Gate of the Tower to the scaffold. I thought they might tear him apart on the spot, but he was protected by many soldiers.

"He kept saying, as if he had to recall it even if no one else did, *'Whatever I did, I did for the King and England. Our Majesty is as honest a Protestant as any in the realm, and I have always lived in the Protestant faith as created in our kingdom and in that I shall die.'*"

Christopher tried to halt Bagshaw, sick from what he was hearing, but Bagshaw ignored his plea; Bagshaw was having too good a time.

"He was a stubborn old fool. A Puritan minister followed him, ordering him to recant, and on the scaffold, Sir John Clotworthy, a Puritan member of Parliament, accused him of having heard mass before leaving his cell in the Tower, but Laud turned to the executioner and said, '*You are the gentler of the two, who alone can put an end to the argument.*'

"Wren, I heard every word, I was so close.

"The crowd jeered him as if he were a mountebank, and he could see us as he knelt and prayed, a mumble-humble-jumble, and then he put his head on the block and the shout that rose could be heard all over London."

But what Christopher remembered were Laud's last words, which were now part of the school's history: "*Lord, I am coming as fast as I can.*"

He was pondering why men petty and ignoble in living behaved so courageously in death like Laud and Strafford—Would his uncle act the same way if he faced the axe? Or would he himself, should he ever face the axe as so many had?—when Busby wanted to see him again in his study.

Busby was direct. "Child, in a few weeks we are resuming the election for King's Scholars. Parliament feels safe now that Laud is gone as well as Strafford, and they are winning in the field with Cromwell." But before he could express pleasure about the elections as he was supposed to, for he didn't feel as gratified as he should, Busby added, "You cannot take them. Parliament has to approve and they never will, not with a name like Wren. I'm sorry, but it is the only way I can keep the school open." His mouth hardened, sorry he had revealed this much.

Soon after, the Parliamentary visitors announced that Dryden, Bagshaw, and Fotherby were elected to be King's Scholars and admission to Oxford and Cambridge would resume when both universities were in Commonwealth hands; at the moment Oxford was still the King's capital.

Dean Wren was stricken by the news, but powerless to do anything. His rectory at Great Haseley was sacked and he was deprived of his living there, and he was forced to move to East Knoyle, his one remaining parish. And no matter how devoutely he prayed, the King continued to lose.

The Puritan forces possessed a new commander-in-chief, Lieutenant-General Oliver Cromwell, and led by his New Model Army, they decisively defeated Charles at Naseby, destroying his guns, infantry, and the Cavalier will to resist. A year later the King surrendered to the Scots and when Oxford followed, all effective resistance to Parliament ceased.

The summer of 1646 was unusually hot and Christopher prepared to say goodbye to Westminster with mixed feelings. He was joining his father at East Knoyle, for the Parliamentary visitors controlled Oxford now, and potent among them was Prynne, remorseless still in his pursuit of heretics—which meant anyone who disagreed with him—and it was too risky for a Wren to seek to be admitted. And no one knew whether Oxford would open in the autumn; there was talk of closing it permanently, since the university had been such a strong supporter of the King.

Busby's goodbye was curt, but as Christopher was about to leave, he gave him a copy of Raleigh's *History of the World,* and said, "It is not a child's book, but no one will punish you now for reading it," and then he added, as a final present, his own Latin grammar. "Wren, concentrate on Cicero, it should keep you from being a soldier."

Christopher wanted to thank him, but Busby cut him short. "Boy, you are interested in buildings, aren't you?"

He was surprised; the Head Master was the first grown up to discern that craving. And, at least, he was no longer a child.

Before he could reply, Busby said, "It is a ruined and scorned work. Your friend, Jones, I know you admire him, Wren, it is not a sin and he had some taste. More than his enemies, the Puritans, who captured him at Basing House last year and treated him scandalously. The Surveyor was in bed when they arrived and they took him out naked, stripped to the bone, a fat, aged, shivering seventy-two, who could hardly walk from fear and the gout, clad only in a blanket, humiliated beyond repair. No sane man would be a Surveyor. Whatever you build, they will tear down."

Somehow, however, he managed to say, "Thank you," before Busby ushered him out. He realised the Head Master was protecting himself, that Busby could not endure the goodbyes and each year there were many.

Yet when it came time to bid Daniel farewell, Christopher didn't know what to do. Daniel was graduating, too, but he had no intention of going on to a university. "Ever," he announced as he packed. "My father is allowing me to return to Amsterdam and to study with Rembrandt. There is too much blood shed in England for my taste. You are barbarians."

"Even me, Daniel?" asked Christopher, wishing he had something to denounce, at least it would be diverting.

"There are exceptions!" Daniel growled and looked away.

Christopher stared at his friend. Daniel had grown far more than he had, and at fourteen was tall and strongly constructed, and his light hair and complexion had deepened in colour and yet he still had his slight Dutch accent, and the only other boy at Westminster he liked almost as much was Robert Hooke, who possessed a lively and inventive mind. But Daniel was as difficult as Busby now in his effort to avoid the embarrassment of emotion. Christopher could not endure that any longer and he threw his arms around Daniel and he knew what was wrong, Daniel had not trusted his feelings. But now Daniel was weeping and so was he, and then they both tried to laugh, to show they were grown up.

"We'll see each other again," Christopher murmured.

"But Amsterdam is far away and you are destined for the Church."

"No, Daniel, not the Church. I am determined about that."

"Won't your father object? Force you to be a churchman?"

"I can't be a churchman. Not after the way they are cut up, like worms."

"What will you be? I know I must be a painter, but you are clever at so many things. Latin, mathematics, the study of the stars, common sense."

"I'm not sure. I like numbers and if I were going to Oxford . . ."

"You should have been a King's Scholar. More than any of them. Bagshaw was the price for keeping the school open."

"Probably." The coach his father had sent for him was at the door and there was no more lingering, and he thought, Living was a succession of farewells. "Daniel, I hope you become as fine a painter as you desire."

"I want to be another Rembrandt, but that is foolish, isn't it?"

"No."

"Why not?"

"Because you cannot help yourself."

"Or you, either, Christopher."

There were no more words to say and Christopher's last memory of Westminster was Daniel gazing after him and he wondered if his friend had the same thought he did: Would they ever see each other again?

He rode by the dark and empty Banqueting House and wished Parliament would open it, even if they had won, for after all, an architect like Inigo Jones built for use. And as he felt the wind in his face, he was glad to be getting away from the heat of London, and the air dried his tears.

The Only Thing My Neighbour Doesn't Shoot At

The only thing my neighbour doesn't shoot at
is a flower

When it comes to pass and my neighbour
aims at a rose

I will know
the final disgrace is man's

The only thing I know about my neighbour
is that

Even though he is a neighbour of God's

Stymean Karlen

F*

11

The Only Thing My Neighbour Doesn't Shoot At

DEAN WREN LEARNED THAT NO RECTORY SUPPORTING THE KING WAS safe from the persecution of the Puritans. Although they deprived him of his living at Windsor and Great Haseley, they were not satisfied.

Soon after his son arrived at East Knoyle, John Niffen, a Parliamentary visitor, charged: "*Dr. Wren, of that malignant family and name, has committed the grievous sin of idolatry and exhibited Popish affections. He has allowed suspicious pictures of Christ and the four Evangelists to be painted in his chancel, and most shocking of all, for a man reputed to be a practising Christian, Dr. Wren comes every day to view the works and to give direction for their completion.*"

Within days of these charges the pictures were removed from the chancel, Dean Wren was rudely stripped of his ministry, and forbidden to practise it anywhere in the Commonwealth. His living quarters were ransacked and despoiled by Parliamentary soldiers from the village and most of his personal possessions were stolen. But the final blow, the one he could least endure, was when Parliament appointed William Clifford, a Dissenting minister, to take his place in the pulpit of East Knoyle.

Devastated, unable to accept such an unhappy situation, he retired with Christopher to his son-in-law's residence at Bletchington. William Holder's rectory was closed by the Parliamentary visitors, too, but at least, he consoled himself, no one—yet—had robbed his son-in-law.

Shortly after Dean Wren reached Bletchington a mysterious package arrived for him. When he opened it, he almost felt hopeful again. It was evident what the books were; they were the registers of the Order of the Garter, known from the colours of the velvet in which they were bound as the Black, the Blue, and the Red Books. They contained the records of the Order, and he visualised gathering together the Knights of the Garter, despite the Puritan distaste for the Order and its ceremonies.

No one knew who had left the package. It was on the doorstep when Susan opened the door that morning. Christopher was positive Seth was responsible, but there was no name on the package or any indication of who had delivered it, and his father didn't share his views.

He said, "Seth is a Dissenter, and a Dissenter wouldn't dare."

But Christopher cherished the possibility, whatever anyone else felt.

His father sat at a small desk, absorbed for the first time since his pictures had been removed, planning how to assemble the Knights of the Garter, and while Christopher had little hope this would succeed, he was pleased by his father's animation. He stood in the ancient doorway of the small house in which they were living, uneasy about his father's health, for Dean Wren had aged since the dismissal from all the parishes.

Susan joined him and he saw she shared his anxiety; their father's face was much thinner, his hair greyer, the deep lines of age more marked.

But when Dean Wren noticed his children he exclaimed, "The Lord be praised! The records are undamaged! God bless you, children!"

Dean Wren never wore his ruff now, as if it reminded him of another time, but a simple white collar, for he could not abide the black of the Puritans. He had grown a small goatee and moustache in the fashion of Charles, to declare he was still a supporter of the King, whatever happened. His son longed to embrace him, but he didn't; he was grown up now; he was going on fifteen; it would not be fitting.

Instead, he said, "May I help you, father?"

"I wanted you admitted to Holy Orders, but it is too dangerous these days. Child, do you realise Laud is the fifth Archbishop of Canterbury to be murdered?" He enumerated, "Laud, Becket, Cramer . . ."

"Father, you mustn't worry so."

"Why shouldn't I? Your uncle is still in the Tower, your cousin is a refugee in France, and I am reviled, molested, and silenced. And deprived of my living. If I hadn't saved some plate, we would starve. Like some of my colleagues have. But the Puritans like to own silver and gold plate, even if they say it is unseemly and ungodly to use it."

Susan said, "William can support us with his teaching. Even the Puritans have a passion for education, if not for learning."

"He is a fine teacher. He has worked wonders with your brother.

The child multiplies so cleverly, as if born to it. But the Puritans multiply, too. Did you know Laud appointed your uncle his executor?"

"No, father," said Susan, while Christopher listened in silence.

"Yes." It is a great honour, but a great peril, and a new excuse for the Dissenters to persecute us. And Laud left nothing, for Parliament confiscated all his lands and belongings. As they did with me. I wish I didn't have such a stiffness in my joints. I would stand up to them."

Christopher suggested, "We will yet, in our way and in our own time."

"With mathematics?" his father asked critically.

"With learning. William tells me of a body of men who are meeting in London to promote knowledge. If I could join them, father, and . . ."

"You are too young! Did I ever tell you, children, that your grandfather, Francis Wren, a mercer and a citizen of London, was steward to Mary Queen of Scots during her captivity in England?"

Christopher started to say Yes, but Susan shook her head No.

"I wonder if that is why they are persecuting us with such virulence."

Susan asked, "Why should they use that reason?"

"Once Mary was executed, she became a Catholic martyr. It may be why the Puritans accuse Matthew and myself of Popish affections."

Christopher didn't like going back into the past. Somewhere, somehow, there must be a search which would find him a total and absorbing interest such as the Banqueting House or Daniel's need to draw; that would truly give him a private life, whatever the pleasure and the pain.

The next year he searched for it in his studies with William. But there came a time when his teacher said to his father, "I cannot instruct him any more. He has advanced to the limits of my learning. He should go to London and study with my friend, Dr. Scarburgh, the physician."

Dean Wren said, "I don't want him to be a doctor."

Christopher said, "I don't want to be, either," but he also didn't wish to be his father's secretary, pursuing the fruitless search for the Knights of the Garter. "William says he has a cousin in London I could reside with while I continue my studies with Dr. Scarburgh."

"What does your cousin do, William?"

"Samuel Taunton is associated with Gresham College."

"Does he teach?"

"In a way. He assists the professors at Gresham College. He attended Cambridge with me, and studied with your brother."

"That could be useful. Where does he reside?"

"On Fetter Lane. In the centre of London."

"I know where it is! Is your cousin a pious man?"

"He attended services at St. Paul's until the Puritans seized it."

"Why do you suggest Dr. Scarburgh as a teacher for my son?"

"He has a most inventive mind, he is curious about many things, and he is a protege of Dr. Harvey, who discovered that the blood circulates."

"Not everybody agrees with Harvey about the blood. He has no proof."

"William Harvey is also Charles' physician."

"Are you saying he is safe because he is a devoted Royalist?"

"Yes. And I will come up to London each week to attend their meetings."

And, Christopher thought resentfully, to keep an eye on me.

"Dr. Harvey and Dr. Scarburgh are part of a group who call themselves 'The Invisible College'. They meet each week at Gresham College, informally, to pursue the New Learning and to perform experiments."

"I hope nothing so impious as dissections?"

"Of course not, sir. Dr. Harvey and Dr. Scarburgh **are** reputable physicians, very contemplative, pious, and understand Latin excellently."

Christopher asked urgently, "Please, Father, let me go to London!"

"But how can I be sure I can trust these men?"

William declared, "They are the most learned scholars in the Kingdom."

"And the name of Wren? Won't that be a danger?"

"Not if Christopher is careful. And I'm sure he will be. The country is at peace now that the Scots have surrendered the King to Parliament."

Dean Wren's face flushed and he looked on the verge of apoplexy as he shouted, "Our country will never be at peace as long as our lawful and anointed King doesn't rule! But you think he has lost."

"I think he has to negotiate."

"It is too late for that. Parliament will never do that. They will do to him what they did to Strafford and Laud. You will see."

Even William was shocked by this and he exclaimed, "They wouldn't dare!"

"Men will dare anything, if they have the power. Chop down a tree, shoot a flower, deny God. But I won't take the oath of loyalty to Parliament, whatever they do. My conscience isn't that elastic.

And you mustn't either, Christopher, whatever happens. Promise?"

Christopher promised.

His father still looked troubled and as Susan entered, he said, "I'm afraid both my children will be delicate all their lives."

Christopher remembered his sister telling him that their father had not been well since the ejection from Windsor.

"You, at least, William, will protect Susan. But who will protect Christopher in London?"

"I can take care of myself, father."

"At fifteen, child?"

Yet Susan had wed at thirteen, reflected Christopher, although she was given an inadequate education: she had studied only the horn-books, which contained the Lord's Prayer, the alphabet, and numbers; their father had taught her some Latin, so she could translate for him; and she had learned to plan a garden and to supervise a kitchen. And to please her husband and to distinguish his bed from another's, although it was never said. But she had blossomed since she had wed William, and seemed happy.

His father said, "It is not easy to see your only son leave you. Child, I hope you are aware of the sacrifice I am making?"

"Yes, sir." He was tired of being treated like a child, he hadn't been one for years and his father should know that.

But when it came time to say goodbye, he listened to his father's advice, even the portions he didn't intend to heed. William was taking him to London by coach and was going to stay with him until he was settled and was introduced to Dr. Scarburgh. He was surprised that Susan looked uneasy at the thought of William entering London; the city was at peace since the King had surrendered.

Dean Wren stared sadly at his son, thinking, however confident he is, he is still only half a man, and said as his farewell: "*We must not expect much happiness on earth. It is promised to us only in the world to come.*"

Christopher didn't agree. There was so much in this world to learn and London was the place to do so. Westminster was out of the city, but Fetter Lane was next to Chancery Lane, the Temple, near the Strand, between Covent Garden and St. Paul's, within walking distance of so much he wanted to see: Cheapside, High Holborn, Gresham College; and ran into Fleet Street. The best and most interesting brains were in his reach. Whatever happened to Charles and the Cavalier cause, whatever learning crammed the chambers of his brain, it was nothing to what he could learn now. He had read *The History of the World* and he was disappointed by

Raleigh's stress on war—he was tired of war and it didn't matter to him who had won in ancient Rome or Nineveh, and he didn't share Raleigh's view that *"death was eloquent, just, and mighty"*. More often, he told himself, it was stupid and wasteful. Then he remembered that Raleigh was a soldier, courtier, and adventurer, and could not face death without a justification. And one fact about *The History of the World* mattered deeply to Christopher—that Raleigh had written this book while confined to the Tower. It revealed that Raleigh's greatest strength lay in his own mind and imagination. Some men travelled the entire world, Christopher reflected, and never emerged from one room; Raleigh had been imprisoned in one room and had encompassed the universe. No matter what had happened to Raleigh, he had retained his own mind. Nothing and no one had been able to take that away from him. Not even death. Of that, Christopher said to himself, Raleigh should be proud.

Fetter Lane flowed with life and Christopher was delighted with the neighbourhood. It was not a muddy rut of a road as he feared, but paved with cobblestones, and far enough above the river to be free of flooding and less damp and foggy than he expected. There were many more dwellings on it than alehouses and taverns and while it was busy with people, it was quieter than most crowded London streets.

"Quieter since the Puritans control London," said William. "It is not a street where you are likely to be waylaid with sword or dagger or murdered with pistols, and that is one of the reasons I suggested it as a residence."

Yet it should be more exciting than the rectory at Bletchington, Christopher thought hopefully, and he was surprised and disappointed that the neighbourhood was so peaceful. Everything appeared so normal it was difficult to believe that a bloody civil war had occurred.

Samuel Taunton lived in a three-storey house on Fleur-de-lys Court, and Christopher saw that it was an old mixture of brick and timber, but with evenly spaced windows on each floor that were cleverly situated to capture the sunlight, and with an entrance wide enough for comfortable walking. Whoever had designed this house had possessed an eye for the symmetrical, he noted approvingly. And while the houses on Fetter Lane were crowded together, a number of them were on pleasant courts.

He was startled by the old man who answered the door. William said, "Simon Taunton, Samuel's father," but the tall, gaunt man regarded them suspiciously, then morosely as he recognised William, and did not bother to guide them, but shuffled to the nearest chair in the parlour, muttered, "It is a dull day," and buried his chin in his chest sombrely.

Samuel was short and plump, friendly and talkative. He took the newcomer by the hand to guide him through the house and said, "You must be hungry. Can I get you something to eat? A mutton chop, rump steak, veal cutlet, or fowl? Which do you prefer— roast or boiled?"

His father was paying Samuel five shillings a week for his room and board—money Dean Wren had saved from the sale of silver and gold plate to the Puritans—but Samuel seemed so eager to feed him, he wondered if there would be any profit for his landlord.

He said, "Later, thank you, sir. I would like to see my room first."

"Sam, my boy, Sam. Everybody calls me Sam. Your room is upstairs." He led Christopher and William to a simple, but clean room in the rear of the third floor and stated beneficently, "It looks out on both a court and a garden and you have both shade and sunlight. The chair is padded and the mattress is firm, not straw. And the ceiling is plastered like a nobleman's house. We have a direct passage to the garden and the stairs are easy. The floor is strewn with fresh rushes and they are scented with herbs. To lighten the air. And you have a table to work on."

By the time Sam finished showing Christopher his quarters it was time for the evening meal. He was proud that he owned chairs rather than the usual stools and he considered this a remarkable innovation. He was even prouder that his house contained a dining room. "No eating in the kitchen for us. It is the one luxury I allow myself. I may not be able to afford silver, which has become the fashion, but I will some day, and meanwhile I have enough dishes to suffice, nothing has to pass by hand."

Christopher noticed the wooden dishes and utensils were carved with loving skill and were decorative as well as useful. Then his attention was diverted as Sam introduced him to the rest of the family: Sam's wife, Katherine, and her two sisters, Mistress Anne and Lucy Beaufort.

He felt Sam did this in such a way that he would know these two young women were unwed, and Sam placed him between them, while Sam sat at the head of the table, and put William by his side, and Katherine served.

Sam ate with relish, as if everything on the table was part of a feast, and heaped Christopher's plate with roast chicken, mutton, fruit, and cheese, and the youth, who was a small eater, was embarrassed by what Sam regarded as an abundance of riches, for he had no wish to gorge himself as Sam was doing. All of the sisters were attractive and he was surprised that Sam's wife was so young, she looked only eighteen; then he remembered his own sister was the same age, and Katherine was handsome with her black hair, dark eyes, and features as firm as if they had been cut by a chisel. Yet she possessed no appeal for him, for there was a coldness about her that repelled him. After a short conversation with Lucy, who resembled Katherine with her olive skin, brown eyes, and black hair, he realised she was just a child, although Sam whispered, "She is fourteen."

He liked Anne better, for she spoke intelligently, looked about sixteen, and he was attracted by the softness of her voice and skin. Her complexion was clear and white and rosy-cheeked, and while her features were regular like her sister's, they were also delicate and he felt struck dumb. He yearned to caress her thick red hair which fell down to her waist, and while she wore a simple grey and white dress, the plainness, cunningly, compounded her beauty. He wondered why some great lord had not seized this flower, and then he realised that the Puritans ruled and perhaps she possessed a mind of her own.

Anne was amused by the sudden stammer in Christopher's conversation. Sam had warned her to be polite, that their new boarder came from an influential and well-to-do family, temporarily out of favour with the Puritans, but that could alter, and it was vital to the household economy that he remain with them, but she hadn't expected him to be so short—she must be at least three inches taller than him. And he appeared younger than fifteen, particularly when he was embarrassed. Yet, as his features gathered animation, he was interesting to look at: his grey eyes sparkled and he had fine, high cheekbones, a broad forehead, and a sharp and decisive chin for one so gentle spoken, and lovely manners, which had nothing to do with fashion but were as natural as breathing.

They were both brought out of their reverie by Sam saying, "Will, consider my dear girls, they have no portions, so they must remedy the deficences of their fortune by their charm and wit. Of course, the proper use of learning is beyond the knowledge or character of experience of women, mere schooling will not help, but each of them can read and write as well as comfort the afflicted and provide for our stomachs."

William replied, "You are wise, cousin. My own dear wife has great skill in physic and cooking and can read Latin like a man."

"You are even wiser, cousin," Sam said. "You have wedded a companion in addition to a wife. But Katherine does not like learning."

Katherine, who had just finished serving and was eating for the first time, said, "When would I have time, Sam?"

"Lucy helps you in the kitchen and Anne takes care of the house."

"When they are not fussing with their hair or toilet, which is rare."

Christopher was glad Anne's luxurious hair hung to her waist and was loose, yet carefully combed, for it was more enticing this way.

Anne said, "Sam says we must always look our best."

"For the Puritan swains who frequent our streets these days?" Katherine questioned contemptuously. "They don't really approve of women. Any of us who prettify are regarded with suspicion and distrusted."

Sam said, "The Puritans won't last forever."

"I hope not. But they rule our city now. And our fashions."

"Yes," said Sam. "And I'm glad, Christopher, you dressed sensibly. Not in silk and satin as befits your station, that is too dangerous, but quietly, in a doublet and hose of a practical serviceable brown. And while your hair is longer than the abominable ugly cropped shortness of the Roundheads, it is not the shoulder length of the Cavaliers. No one should be able to judge your worthy birth by your appearance."

Simon Taunton said abruptly, "Many Puritans live on Fetter Lane now."

"Why do you object, father?" said Sam. "You share many of their views."

"Because I didn't like Laud. Why should I? The only religion the Archbishop approved of was his own."

"You are not any more tolerant than he was."

"Because I say that no one but a fool would take a wife whose bread must be earned solely by his own labours, but my son did."

"Christopher, their parents died. I couldn't put the girls into an orphan asylum for deserted girls. Or Bedlam or Newgate."

Simon said, "They could work as serving girls, like all the others do."

"Please, father, you are embarrassing our guests."

"Will is no guest, but a drinking companion from Cambridge, and this Christopher Wren will stay here only as long as his father wishes."

William protested, "Sir, he will stay for several years if his studies progress, and if my cousin desires."

William was different with Sam, thought Christopher, quick-spoken and happy-faced, as if he put off his clerical clothes in Sam's presence. Cousin was more an expression of friendship than a relationship; their feeling toward each other was so natural. He wondered why Sam had really married Katherine; they did seem ill-suited to each other.

Sam stated, "Father, I do not intend that my wife's sisters hire

out as domestic servants, and I don't want the subject mentioned
again."

His father grumbled, but subsided.

Sam added apologetically to Christopher, "My father would be a
Puritan, if he could only endure their prayers, clothes, and surly
manners."

When Christopher went to bed that night he felt like anything
but a Puritan. He knew they believed that women by virtue of their
sex were depraved, but he could not get Anne out of his mind. So
much in his room reminded him of her. The soft linen cloth of his
pillow, the fragrance of rosemary and violets in his room, the soap
sweetened with rosewater—Sam had whispered that Anne had prepared his quarters, was Sam trying to arrange something?—
conspired to keep her vividly before him. He snuffed out his candle
and lay back on his pillow and stared out the window at the
sky, and he saw the beauty of her complexion, the neatness of her
dress, the graceful vivacity of her movements, and her delicate
features, as if, even now, they were face to face.

He left with William and Sam the next morning to meet
Scarburgh, and the streets were even more crowded than when he
had first seen the city with Daniel. The noise was still overwhelming; London still ran upon wheels that spoke with a
thunderous voice; the buildings were even closer together.

Sam said, "London continues to expand at an amazing speed. In
a hundred years the population has increased from ninety thousand
to nearly three hundred and fifty thousand. No matter who rules,
London grows. It is now the largest and most powerful city in the
world."

Christopher thought, Sam probably exaggerates, but not much.

"Yet the city never really seems to be content with itself."

Wherever Christopher looked there was destroying and repairing,
digging and hammering, demolishing and rebuilding, a fermenting,
bubbling, bursting overflow, and building materials galore that
widened his eyes and filled him with a desire for the curve and
shape of wood and stone.

Then there was a terrible stench and William said sadly, "With
due respect to you, Sam, London also stinks more than any place
I've been. Without the rosemary and jasmine the putrid smells
would be impossible."

Sam said, "There are things about the city I don't like. After
dark, I wouldn't venture on the streets without a guard. There are
many ruffians about and the watch is seldom close enough to dispel
them."

Christopher wasn't listening. Once more he saw St. Paul's at the top of Ludgate Hill, and he longed to put a dome on top of the burnt-out steeple. Without a head the cathedral was a dead thing, whatever the pious declared. But as they walked on, very carefully, to avoid being run down, he also noticed again that the buildings converged so closely across the narrow streets they almost touched each other, and he thought, It was miraculous that the city had escaped a fatal fire. Didn't the inhabitants know their danger?

Sam said, "Everybody wants to build here. Ludgate Hill is the busiest spot in the city. They all want to see St. Paul's and Paul's Walk."

"So do I, but they should repair St. Paul's, whoever rules."

"The Puritans don't approve of the cathedral," said William. "They would tear it down, except it would cost too much. As it is, they have tried to pull down Jones' scaffolding, only they don't know how."

"Is the Chief Surveyor still alive?"

"Yes, but his duties ended in 1645. When Cromwell won at Naseby."

Everything looked unfinished to Christopher. Now, as he stood before the West Portico, he didn't stare at Jones' Italian restoration which had fascinated yet repelled him, but at the huge scaffolding that surrounded the exterior of the cathedral. "What do they intend to do with it?"

Sam said, "No one seems to know."

"Why don't they try to repair the fabric?"

William said, "And show their approval of Laud, who persuaded Charles to assign Jones to that task? They would consider that impious."

"Then I would take down the scaffolding."

"How?"

"I'm not sure. But I would find a way."

"Without damaging the fabric? And killing the workmen?" William regarded Christopher sceptically. "I doubt you could."

"I could. And the fabric is so dirty."

Sam said, "That is from the sea coal which is becoming the fashion in London instead of wood. It makes for more heat, and more dirt and fog."

"The cathedral should be cleaned." Then Christopher saw a worse profanation. The Puritans were using Jones' West Portico as a market place with stalls that were selling merchandise of all kinds.

His companions' attention was elsewhere. While they had experienced Paul's Walk many times, it never ceased to attract them. They led him into the great central aisle of the cathedral and he found himself one of a huge throng of Paul Walkers. He was

surprised by the amount of business being transacted and that
brought a smile to Sam.

He said, "The Puritans are the last people in the world to stop
a man from earning money, as long as he is pious, fears God, and
is a Puritan."

"Besides," said William, "If they can't pull it down, they must
use it."

The Puritan dictum in Paul's Walk, "*Put money in thy purse,*"
echoed in Christopher's ears as loud as any sermon he had heard.
The market place in the centre of Paul's Walk was more active
than ever. There were no whores about or advertisements for
entertainments, but there were many things to buy: herbs and
scents, pewter and plate, plain hats and Puritan collars, and ruffs
without lace, untrimmed coats and breeches, and candles, tobacco,
and coffee, and wax effigies of Charles, Laud, and Strafford, of
which there was a lively sale, and Christopher wanted to flee. He
hated this place and what was being done to it.

Sam said, "You must see the booksellers. They are one of the
sights of London."

William said, "It may make us late for Dr. Scarburgh."

"The booksellers will only take a minute," pleaded Sam, "and it
will help Christopher appreciate his studies with The Invisible
College."

William nodded, and Sam led them to the open stalls on Paul's
Walk, but Christopher was disappointed that the only books and
pamphlets available were those approved by the Puritans, and
most of them were religious tracts. He looked for Milton, but he
didn't find him, and William said, "The Puritans regard poetry as
sensual, and thus, profane." He did find Raleigh, but edited. There
were many bibles, and *Lessons in Diligence and Thrift, Instructions in
Domestic Relations,* and *Guides to Godliness.*

"Do not despair," said William. "Gresham owns other books."

Sam said, "The Puritans smell Popery in any reading that is for
entertainment. Such as poetry, romances, and plays. But many ways
to piety are offered by these booksellers. If you don't buy one of
these religious tracts, you are wicked. You don't have to worry
about the theology, the author knows it. All you have to do is be
governed by your prejudices."

Christopher wondered if Sam was a freethinker.

William looked annoyed, but he didn't say anything.

Sam said, "The Puritans believe they won because Cromwell
provided for common prayer twice a day while the Cavaliers only
prayed once each day."

William retorted, "No man should dispute theology, but seek out
a clergyman. It is not fit for the unlearned to argue such matters. I

promised Dean Wren I would not allow Christopher's soul to be corrupted."

But while William and Sam argued about what was permissible to discuss, Christopher bought a popular pamphlet for a penny, a romantic ballad which wooed a maid. And as they neared Gresham, he wondered if William was a clergyman as a way of pursuing education. Except for the one outburst, the rector was not concerned with theology, but with the New Learning.

Gresham was on Bishopgate Street, just beyond the old Roman wall, and Christopher was excited by the grandeur of the great Elizabethan town house. The two-storey rectangular mansion was as large as a castle, and while it was in the heart of London, it was so spacious it possessed a life and solitude of its own. His eyes widened as Sam took him through an arched medieval gate and into a vast quadrangle and said, "This is like an Oxford college. But Gresham, who was Elizabeth's merchant, willed this school should be more practical, that there should be professors of Civil Law, Divinity, Astronomy, Physic, Geometry, Rhetoric, and Music. And that these subjects must be taught in English, not Latin, and be made available to those citizens who cannot attend the universities."

They walked up a great marble staircase to the second floor and into a grand hall, which was the entrance to the rooms used by The Invisible College. The marble staircase, the panelled ceiling, the fine windows were so tasteful Christopher wished he knew which surveyor was responsible.

Sam said, "Several, probably. These houses were usually done by a number of artisans. And it has many Flemish touches. But this formal kind of town house is rare, for it was built as if space was no consideration."

"So I see," said Christopher. "Sam, are you interested in building?"

William replied, "Sam is interested in everything. It is the heart of The Invisible College and part of the New Learning."

"What about politics and theology?"

"They are never discussed. We have a wide diversity of opinions."

"Is Dr. Scarburgh a professor at Gresham or Oxford?"

"No, he is a physician. But, as a member of The Invisible College, he is allowed to use a room at Gresham. His purpose, like all of us, is the satisfaction of breathing free air, and of experimenting in quiet, without being engaged in the passions and madness of this dismal age."

Christopher was willing to exclude politics and theology. He wasn't happy with the way many things were being shot at, even flowers.

He was startled by Charles Scarburgh's appearance. The physician was tall, lean, attractive, with sharp features and a fair skin, but now his face was fierce with outrage. They had interrupted him in the middle of an experiment, which he had laboured on all night, and now he didn't remember where he was in his work. There was a small bed in a corner and partially eaten fruit, which he had forgotten about, but the room looked like an apothecary shop with the many drugs, powders, and herbs that surrounded him, and he cried out, "All these preparations cannot stop one hungry flea or louse from killing us! Why is it that a drop of blood knows more about how to cure our diseases than our entire College of Physicians?" He didn't wait for a reply, but turned back to his work.

William said, "Excuse me, but you suggested . . ."

"I suggested nothing. How can I suggest when I do not know!"

"You did say you would be willing to include young Christopher Wren in our studies and experiments."

"I said I would give him a trial. That was all." He glared at the prescription he was mixing and shouted, "I cannot find a cure for the ague or the gout, let alone a simple cold, and you bother me with children!"

William said, "Christopher is going on sixteen."

"He looks twelve. Wren, do you know anatomy?"

"No, sir."

"Astronomy?"

"A little, sir."

"Physic?"

Christopher shrugged.

"What do you know?"

"Mathematics and Latin."

Scarburgh growled, "They are not my speciality!"

William explained, "He is a graduate of Westminster."

"I've had some of them try to help me. They are almost illiterate. They know only Latin thoroughly, and that is just the start of learning, although they act as if it is the end. And Busby is a time server, ploughing with the Parliamentary farmers to protect his own skin."

Christopher wanted to reply, If Busby did, it was to save the school—Busby would do anything to save Westminster—but he didn't, for Scarburgh ignored him, returning to his experiment.

When he saw Christopher looking helpless he growled, "I thought you were supposed to help me. Not one in a hundred who pass through Westminster knows anything about the New Learning!"

"What do you want me to do, sir?"

"And don't call me sir. Everybody here is equal, at least, in work. Everybody here works. Sam, why are you late?"

Sam mumbled, "I had to get Christopher ready."

"What for? He doesn't know anything yet. And probably never will."

William asked, "Charles, what experiment are you conducting?"

"I am looking for a cure for the plague. But one cannot even dissect its victims. Dissection is forbidden by the Puritans and everyone is so terrified of the plague they will not come close to one who has died of it."

Christopher felt this was a good time to withdraw, yet Scarburgh regarded him so critically he said, "I will try to help you, sir."

"Without a knowledge of anatomy? No! You must not act out of vanity. But perhaps you could learn a little." He returned to his work as if no one was there, yet spoke so all of them could hear him. "The plague will strike even more severely than before. The more crowded London gets, the worse it will get." Unable to find what he was looking for, he snapped, "I work here only because of the convenience of mixing drugs. Wren, the only time to learn is from ten to fifteen. After that, Cupid dominates."

William said, "He is devoted to his studies. And the son of a Dean."

"But not a eunuch?"

"I hope not, sir," said Christopher, and blushed.

"No matter. You will find your whores when you need them. We would never have any patients if they realised how little we know."

After helping Scarburgh a week, Wren was grudgingly allowed to assist him a little while longer—if Dr. Harvey approved. William returned to Bletchington and Sam came with the boy to Gresham, but otherwise, they seldom saw each other, Sam had so many clerical duties. The young doctor, who was the same age as William, continued to complain about Christopher's ignorance of anatomy; he was still unreconciled to his Westminster education; but he thought it useful that the boy wrote a good Latin, since his was bad, and everything had to be written in Latin, for that was a custom that no learned man, even the most enlightened, dared deny.

Then Dr. Harvey joined them to advise his protégé on his progress.

William Harvey was the only person Scarburgh praised, and so Christopher was surprised by this physician's appearance. He was as choleric as his protégé who, the boy realised now, was imitating him, and he was short, sharp-faced, with a ruddy complexion, dark eyes, white hair, and he walked awkwardly as if he had the gout.

"He is seventy," Scarburgh whispered to Christopher. "Get him a chair, not so he notices, but so he can sit in it if he desires."

Harvey saw Christopher move the straight back oak chair to the table where Scarburgh was working on his experiment and he snapped, "A stool would do! I'm not ready for the grave. Any progress, Charles?"

"Not much, sir. These drugs are full of lies. I agree with you that nature is the true and real physician, and yet, without some help . . .?"

Harvey muffled Scarburgh's anger with a laugh. "Of course, and our need is to give Nature what she needs for her battles." He took off his stockings and sat with his legs bare and when they still ached, he ordered Christopher to bring him a pail of cold water, and to heat the stove. Then, while Christopher watched with wonder, Harvey put his feet into the water, saying, "I must do this until they are almost dead from the cold, it is the only way to cure the gout." And when his feet were nearly numb he put them next to the stove and said, after a few minutes, and with a great sigh of relief, "The pain is gone. Wren, do you have any pretty wenches?"

"No, sir. I came to London to study and learn. William Holder says learning is the key to advancement."

"And a pretty wench is an obstruction to that?" When Christopher didn't reply, Harvey added, "You are like so many young men, especially these Puritans, repulsively moral. But chastity is one of the chief impediments to the advancement of learning. Besides, man is but a great, mischievous baboon."

Scarburgh said apologetically, "Dr. Harvey expects very little from men."

"Even kings," muttered Harvey. "I was Charles' body physician. If I could only have helped His Majesty. But he does not even believe the blood circulates. Charles is not a man to accept a new idea."

"How can I learn, sir?"

"Study anatomy, young man. Study Vesalius. I will lend you my copy if no other is available. You do read Latin, don't you?"

Scarburgh said, "Correctly. It's the one thing Westminster taught him."

"And use your own eyes. Even when someone else's hand is on the dagger."

Christopher noticed that Harvey wore one and fondled it as he spoke.

"Most of all, observe carefully. Whether you lie next to a pretty wench or observe a hanging at Tyburn. Or dissect a toad or survey a tree or plant. Or observe the moon like our friends Wilkins and Ward. A man does not have to be a physician to be an excellent anatomist. In anatomy, as in astronomy and the other natural sciences, there is much to be learned about many things from observation, even the shape of this building."

Christopher felt most at home with Dr. John Wilkins, whom he met several days later. This chaplain, and learned doctor of divinity, said to him, "Everybody has the right to be wrong."

This was a startling admission and yet Wilkins stated it as if he meant it. He was a little older than Scarburgh, a comely man of middle stature, friendly and pleasant, with a clear, eloquent voice.

"A good scholar," said Scarburgh, "if sometimes too much a supporter of the Parliamentary visitors. But, at least, he protects us from them. As long as he is a member of The Invisible College, we are considered safe."

What Christopher liked best about Wilkins, in addition to his encouragement, was his lively imagination. Although he was trained to be a professor of divinity, he was far more interested in astronomy.

When he saw that this new member shared his interest—and he was the only one not to question Christopher's youth, but to treat him as an adult and as an equal—he gave him the book he had written about the moon.

The Discovery of a New World fascinated Christopher. He didn't agree with everything Wilkins wrote, but several portions of this book excited him and he memorised them, he thought they were so important.

I affirm that the moon may be habitable, and thus, upon good grounds, I believe it possible to make a Flying Chariot, in which a man may sit, and give such motion unto it as shall convey him through the air. And this perhaps be made large enough to carry divers men at the same time, together with food for their visit, and commodities for traffic. It is not the bigness of anything in this kind that can hinder motion, if the motive faculty be answerable thereunto.

Christopher constructed a model showing the moon, sun, and earth in their periodic relationships and he was pleased when Wilkins said it followed accurately the teachings of Copernicus, Kepler, and Galileo.

He sought to think of nothing else but his pursuit of the New Learning, but every time he saw Anne, and he saw her nightly at supper, he yearned to caress her. Sitting next to her at the table, he wondered if the exploration of her innocence would be any less a brave step into the unknown and his yearnings grew. He felt very vulnerable, and he studied harder.

Mathematics became a source of much exploration when The Invisible College was joined by Seth Ward, another young divine, who was a close friend of Scarburgh. Ward even persuaded the physician to leave his medical experiments and to pursue inquiries into mathematics.

They were surprised when he gave the others William Oughtred's famed *Clavis Mathematica*, which he taught at Cambridge, and Christopher mastered it more quickly than anybody else. In this work Oughtred had invented the multiplication table and sign, with which Christopher was already skilful. Then Scarburgh and the quick-tongued, pleasant-faced Ward, who could be satirical, fell into a dispute on how to use the sign, and Christopher thought they were both wrong. They persuaded the elderly mathematician— who was in his seventies and a refugee from the Puritans—to seek shelter with them at The Invisible College, so he could solve their dispute. But he declared in favour of Christopher.

The members of The Invisible College who gathered to hear the renowned mathematician—Scarburgh, Ward, Harvey, Wilkins, and Holder—were stunned by this verdict. They sat around a long table, draped with Flemish tapestry for the occasion, for Oughtred was much esteemed by virtue of his age as well as his learning, and no one said a word.

Oughtred, dressed in an old russet cloth cassock that Christopher thought must have been black originally, tightened his old leather girdle, which looked like it dated from the time of Elizabeth, and said, staring at the Latin translation of *Clavis Mathematica*, "Who did this?"

No one spoke up until Christopher whispered, "I did."

Oughtred had begun his discourse by saying he could not endure a scholar who wrote with an ill hand, and the mathematician looked very severe.

"Boy, you write with a clear hand. And multiply well. Did I ever tell you that I learned to multiply and divide in bed?"

"No, sir. I learned from you."

"So did I." The wizened, stooped, elderly Oughtred chuckled at his own joke. "When I was so troubled I could not sleep, I drew lines on my thigh and my sheet to distract me, and thus, learned how to multiply."

But I already know how to multiply, Christopher thought, and the thighs that matter are elsewhere, and perhaps, spread for someone else.

Oughtred said sorrowfully, "I hear that Parliament is proposing to try the King. May I have a glass of wine to drink to His Majesty's health?"

There was a solemn pause, as if for an instant the mathematician had committed a sacrilege, expressing a political point of view, and then Wilkins, the strongest supporter of Parliament, said, "Of course. I have some fine Flemish wine to celebrate our distinguished visitor's presence. Sam, would you mind getting it?" he asked, for Sam was attending them.

When Christopher discussed this at the supper table, Sam said, "Dr. Wilkins is a sensible man. While he always attaches himself to persons of influence, he would do almost anything to avoid ill-feeling. Even the most ardent Royalist likes him. How are your experiments progressing?"

"Fine." Between studying anatomy with Scarburgh, mathematics with Ward, and astronomy with Wilkins he had no energy to think of anything else. Yet when Anne sat down near him, having just combed her hair and washed her face so her complexion shone, he could not take his eyes off her.

What availed all his learning, he thought mournfully, if his blood circulated toward her and he could not enjoy it.

What mattered any of his learning if he was always to feel so unhappy?

As she leaned toward him, he saw the shape of her breasts, and he wondered, *How could he approach her?*

"Play your cards right . . ."

Christopher thought he was hearing things as he lay in bed that night, but it was Sam's voice and Sam was standing in the doorway.

"You covet, Anne. Now don't deny it. I can see it in your eyes."

"But she is your sister . . ."

" . . . in-law."

Was Sam saying, Help yourself? He sat up, asked, "What do you mean?"

"I am warning you. Seek her out if you must, but be careful."

"Why are you telling me this?"

"I don't want you to make the mistake I did. The Beaufort girls are tempting morsels until you marry them and have to digest them."

"Didn't you want to marry Katherine?"

"Would you expect her to be the wife of the Reverend William Holder's best friend? Of an honours student at Cambridge?"

"No. But . . ." Christopher didn't like the course the conversation was taking and he shifted uneasily and said, "She is quite pretty."

"All the Beaufort girls are. It is nature's trap to snare unwary men."

"Then why did you marry Katherine?"

"She was working in Cambridge trying to support herself and her two sisters, and I fell in love with her. While she was cleaning my chambers. A few weeks later she told me she was pregnant and I, soft-hearted, unable to give birth to a bastard, agreed to wed her and to give the child my name."

Sam sounded so disgusted Christopher wanted to console him and he said, "But she is attractive, a good cook, housekeeper, and sews cleverly."

"And beneath my station. Not a gentlewoman. Without a penny of her own."

So that was why Simon was so sullen, thought Christopher, but he sensed this was not all that was afflicting Sam with self-pity.

"When the university discovered I was married, I was dismissed. I was studying to be a divine like William and Wilkins and Ward, and marriage was not allowed. Although Cambridge had broken away from the Church of Rome, celibacy was still considered essential for an undergraduate. You could have your whores, but a wife was an obvious display of sensuality."

Christopher said, "I don't intend to be a divine."

"I know. But you could have a future. I have none. The best situation that is allowed me is to be a clerk to men I studied with, and was the equal of, until I fell from grace."

"Sam, you do interesting work."

"But always, as a servant. My name will never go on any of the conclusions reached, whatever I contribute."

Christopher was quiet, for what Sam said was true.

"Yet I am supposed to feel grateful for this position. Which I obtained because I knew William and Ward and Wilkins at Cambridge, and also know Latin and Greek. Indeed, better than they do, even your brother-in-law."

Christopher wasn't sure Sam did, for while Sam was a good scholar he was inclined to be hasty and careless in his conclusions.

"And I am paid just enough for food. If you didn't board with me, I wouldn't have enough to pay for the rent of this house."

"Then why did you take in the sisters?"

"Should I let them starve? Or become whores?"

"Yet you suggested that I . . ."

"I suggested that you be careful. But that wouldn't make Anne a whore."

"I don't understand."

"One affair doesn't make a whore. And you wouldn't do it for money."

Christopher wasn't sure whether Sam was being sarcastic and he declared, "I do respect her. I have the highest regard for her."

"Love her if you have to, but wed a rich lady, one befitting your father's station. There will come a time when this madness will end, and then your name could be favourably regarded in England again. Do not marry beneath you, it is folly."

Sam was so bitter Christopher asked, "Why are you really warning me?"

"Because your desire demands that you loosen your breeches. And I like you too much to stand by while you make the mistake I did."

"But why are you so critical of marriage? Is it Katherine?"

Sam wavered, as if what he was feeling was difficult to say, then whispered, "I had one good reason for marrying her. I desired a son as much as Henry VIII did. But I married unnecessarily. Her child was still born. And so soon after we wed, I doubt it was mine."

"And . . ." Christopher checked what he was going to say.

"Express it. I was a cuckold. It is likely. I can never be sure, but as long as I wonder our marriage is no good. And now she cannot have any more children."

"Perhaps she did tell you the truth."

"Christopher, you are already a splendid scholar, but like so many of them, dreadfully ignorant of this world."

"Couldn't you get a divorce? I was told that Milton, Cromwell's favourite pamphleteer, and a Puritan, advocated it."

"Milton wanted to be free of his own wife. But Parliament ignored him and he returned to her. And I am not Henry to behead my wife when I am tired of her. In our lives marriage is a Gordian knot, which may not be loosened except by death. It's the price paid to women for being inferior, that permits them to accept their lower station. You must be resolute."

But how could he feel high minded or resolute when he felt so locked within his body he could hardly breathe.

Sam was leaving and suddenly, as if he had to do it quickly before he changed his mind, he handed Christopher a small package and said, "It is a new invention. Linen sheaths. A protection against syphilis, they say, and unwanted children. It is sold by barbers, bawds, and a few apothecaries. An invention of Fallopio. You can trust it. Harvey studied this anatomist's work and he must have used it himself. I wish I had. At least, if you must have her, have her with some chance of safety."

Confused, Christopher sought to submerge his craving for Anne in his studies, but he held on to the sheaths. And while he worked hard with Scarburgh and his studies progressed the next few weeks, he couldn't stop desiring Anne. He wanted to ask Harvey about the efficacy of the sheaths—there were six in the package Sam had given him—but Scarburgh told him Harvey was away, and he suspected it was on Royalist business, Scarburgh was so secretive. He considered asking Scarburgh for advice, then didn't. The doctor still said Christopher was on trial, and the boy was afraid he would regard his interest in Anne as frivolous.

So he sought to make The Invisible College the best of all possible worlds and he lost his appetite, and even when he studied astronomy with Wilkins and anatomy with Scarburgh and mathematics with Ward, he continued to see Anne in front of him, and her image was the most vivid object in his mind.

One evening, deciding he could no longer endure the torture of seeing her without possessing her, he skipped supper. He had no appetite anyhow, and he concentrated on his studies to drive her out of his mind.

Night had come and it was raining, so hard the rain sluiced down his window in rivulets, and he lit a log in his fireplace to give him warmth, but he still felt chilled. Propped up on pillows, he was trying to absorb himself in Copernicus and Galileo when he realised his bed was different. It was softer and comfortable, and someone had sweetened the sheets with fresh herbs and jasmine.

He was still wondering why when there was a knock on his door.

"Who is it?" he asked, startled. Who was going to distract him now?

"Anne. I brought you some supper. Sam said you weren't feeling well."

He reached for the door, then hesitated and said, "I'm not hungry."

"You must be. Sam tells me that you haven't eaten all day."

"Leave it at the door."

"It will attract mice."

There was still time to say No, and yet . . .?

"The mutton and fowl will get cold. And I cooked it myself."

"Very well. Bring it in. The door is unlocked." Then he felt guilty, for he had left it so purposely, but should he have?

Before he could ask himself any more questions, Anne entered, carrying a tray filled with mutton, fowl, fruit, and wine. She placed it on the bed by his side, then she stood so self-consciously he felt he had to ask her to sit down. But she didn't until he insisted, and she looked awkward and vulnerable as she sat some distance away from him.

He wasn't sure what to do or say. One moment she seemed inviting, the next shy and withdrawn. He mumbled, "Thanks for the food."

"It was the least I could do. Good food can be solace, Sam says."

Had Sam put her up to this, he wondered, after all his warnings?

She suggested a cup of wine as she apologised for the cup being wooden. "I know you are accustomed to better." As he sipped the wine, she handed him sweets. "Candied oranges and lemons. I know you like them."

He did, even more now that she had thought of them. He felt warmer inside and he said, "It is nice of you to go to all this trouble for me."

She blushed and he saw that her face was painted—although this was forbidden by the Puritans—and she was perfumed like a lady. And she was not wearing a starched collar as was the fashion, but a low necked blouse and he could see her breasts and their bulge made him swell with desire.

She said, upset that he was not eating the supper she had carefully prepared, "You mustn't waste food, Sam always says."

He said apologetically, "I'm not hungry. There's much on my mind."

"Your studies at The Invisible College?"

"Yes. And other things."

"The Church?"

"No. The Church is not my vocation."

"I thought . . ."

"Because of William Holder and my father?"

She nodded, and said, "And you are so polite."

And proper, he thought, and as she stood close to him and his manhood stood up straight and firm as a pike, he asked, "Why did you move away?"

"I don't want to distract you from eating."

"But it is not food I need, Anne."

"What do you need, Christopher?"

"Perhaps I do have a fever."

She put her hand on his forehead and he felt his blood pounding at her touch and he clutched her hand and pulled her close to him. She didn't resist and her blouse fell off her shoulders, and he knew he would not be content until he brought her to bed, and he tried to undress her. Anne didn't try to stop him, but he was so clumsy, he thought angrily, he wasn't accomplishing anything, and finally she whispered, "I'll do it."

They arrived at their nakedness together and he cried to himself joyfully: How fair she is! How young, beautiful, and enticing!

When she saw him staring at her, she snuffed out the candles, upset that he saw her naked, thinking, I want love and respect, not vanity and lust.

As the time came for him to enter her, she cried, "I'm afraid," and he realised it was her first time, too, and she whispered, "My gentle lord, be good to me." But he was just sixteen and so was she, he remembered, although at this moment he felt older. Once

G

his manhood was within her, still as firm and straight as a pike, she responded passionately. He was grateful there was as much yearning in her as there was in him. When they were fully joined together nothing mattered but to consummate.

Afterwards, they lay quietly next to each other until she said she was very warm, and he opened the window. It was still raining, but the last few minutes he had not noticed. He returned to her side and he wondered whether Anne was as happy and fulfilled as he was. He longed to say, Thank you! but there was nothing which could express the exhilaration that had flooded his body at the moment of consummation. He was pleased that he hadn't lied to her; he hadn't uttered any fervent protestations of love. While there had been awkwardness, he desired her even more passionately now, but he recalled what Sam had said and he knew he must not commit himself. And when he turned to possess her again, she was gone. She was dressing and she said, "They will miss me if I stay away any longer."

"Will I see you later?"

She didn't answer.

"Tomorrow evening?"

"I don't know." She picked up the tray as she left.

Suddenly he was relieved that he had remembered to use the sheath.

He stayed away from supper the next night, hoping she would repeat what had happened. But she didn't appear and he slept poorly. When he didn't see her the following night, he felt he must have failed her. And when she avoided him at supper the third night, he was sure he had.

After Christopher didn't appear for supper the night after their joining, Anne assumed he was dissatisfied, or that he had realised she was beneath his station, and she couldn't approach him twice in a row. She wasn't a whore, and he hadn't even said he loved her. By the time he did come to supper, she was determined to deny him. Yet she painted and perfumed herself and wore a dress cut so low her breasts were visible.

He tried to remove her from his mind by working harder with Scarburgh, but he ate even less and slept hardly at all. His attitude was: Where can I be of service? When he repeated this a week after his encounter with Anne, Scarburgh asked, "Christopher, are you serious?"

It was the first time the physician had called him by his first name and he replied quickly and positively, "Yes, sir."

"Whatever I am doing?"

Scarburgh's tone was sombre now and Christopher hesitated.

Then, seeing the sceptical look in Scarburgh's eyes, he said, "Whatever it is."

Scarburgh whispered like a conspirator, "I am going to perform a post-mortem examination on a plague victim. It could be dangerous. Some of the infection probably remains. No one is certain. But something has to be done, or one of these days the plague could destroy London."

"Doesn't it have something to do with sanitation? It . . ."

Scarburgh cut him short. "That is what I'm trying to find out. But until we know we must not speculate. You can still change your mind. The contagion may still prevail. I cannot answer for the consequences."

He was apprehensive but he couldn't retreat now that he had committed himself. "If you think the experiment is essential, I'm sure it is."

"I'm not sure of anything." Scarburgh grumbled, "but I must try."

Scarburgh led him secretively into the cellar of Gresham, taking a back passage so no one would see them, and muttered, "If we are found out, we could be persecuted and punished. This is forbidden by law." He unlocked a heavy oak door, lit some candles, and entered a long, dark stone chamber without windows or any other connection with the outside world.

Christopher felt he was in a house of the dead, one foot already in the grave. The candles burned erratically, as if there wasn't enough air in this dank, black underground chamber to sustain him.

But nothing was halting Scarburgh, as if, once he had gathered the courage to venture this far, he had to plunge ahead. He removed a wooden screen from a corner and Christopher saw a small coffin on a table.

He shivered as the physician removed the lid and pointed to the corpse inside and declared, "This may be our ransom against death."

"There is no linen around the body, which is the custom."

"The corpse is freshly dead. I had it delivered as soon as it died. Before it could decompose and decay. For two guineas. A small fortune."

"What was his name?" He could tell it was male, but from a distance little else, and it was unbearable to think of it without an identity.

"Stephen Pennywaite. He was only fifteen. But full grown."

"He looks so small."

"They say the plague shrivels the body. But no one can be sure, for as far as I know, no doctor has ever examined a plague corpse.

The custom is to bury them at once, so no one will catch the contagion."

He wanted to shut his eyes, but he couldn't take them off Pennywaite. Then the stench was so horrible he felt he was fainting. He clutched the coffin for support, but if Scarburgh hadn't held him he would have fallen.

"What's wrong?" the physician asked irritably. "There's nothing to be afraid of." But he laughed uncertainly, as if he wasn't sure.

Chills assailed Christopher and he said, "I don't feel well."

"It must be because you've never seen a corpse before."

"I've never seen a plague victim."

"Notice how the skin is so beset with black, pestilential spots it has lost its normal colour." But as the boy grew pale, he cried out, "I know what is wrong! I forgot to take the proper precautions!" Ignoring him, he fumigated the chamber with acid vapours by burning brimstone in the fireplace. Then he put a lozenge in his mouth and handed one to Christopher. "It is an anti-pestilential pill. These prophylactic measures will help, but don't breathe deeply or the sulphurous vapours will irritate your lungs."

There was no fresh air in the cellar, for Scarburgh had closed the door behind them, and the burning brimstone added to Christopher's discomfort, and when he tried to look at the corpse he felt sicker, and he had just one impulse, to reach the safety of his bed.

As he groped toward the door Scarburgh said, "I should have given you a glass of sack. It warms the stomach, refreshes the spirits, and dissipates any lodgement of the infection. Can you find your way?"

"I don't know, sir." He felt two-thirds dead, not sure what was real.

Scarburgh took him to the door of Gresham and Christopher felt a little better in the air and said so, and the doctor replied, "Of course. It must have been the sulphur fumes that made you ill. After you walk a bit, you will feel better. I must examine the body before it is too late."

The walk to Fetter Lane was a blank to Christopher. He found his way, but he didn't know how. No one saw him as he climbed to his room. He was not sure he would reach it, and when he did, he felt so weak he couldn't undress and he fell into bed with all his clothes on. Chills and fever saturated his body and there wasn't any strength in his legs. He was afraid to look into the mirror, sure he would see the dreaded black spots of the plague and he wanted to cry for help but he was ashamed. Never had he felt so awful. His body was rejecting all of his self.

Nothing was thought of his absence from supper that evening, for that happened frequently now, but when he didn't appear at Gresham the next morning Scarburgh was alarmed. The possibility that Wren might truly be ill gave him a feeling of guilt, for he had been brusque with the boy.

He told Sam, "It is the first time Wren hasn't come to study with me. Did you see him this morning?"

"No, sir. Lately he has been walking to Gresham alone."

"He said he didn't feel well, but I dismissed it as a childish vagary."

"If he said so, it is true. He never complains."

Scarburgh had rid himself of the corpse after Christopher's attack of chills and vertigo, afraid the boy had caught the contagion, although he couldn't admit this possibility to anyone, not even to himself. But now he stopped everything he was doing, and insisted on seeing Christopher at once, saying to Sam, "I'm concerned. The symptoms were strange."

"The French disease, sir? Syphilis?"

"I wasn't thinking of that. Do you think it is possible?"

"He is young. Inexperienced. Impulsive."

The symptoms puzzled Scarburgh. He stood by the boy's side an hour later and the patient's pulse was regular, but chills continued to afflict the boy and an unnatural feeling of fear and horror, accompanied by shaking and trembling, which were indications of the plague. There was also nausea, but no vomiting or black spots. Scarburgh wasn't sure what was wrong, for several symptoms suggested syphilis. Yet he decided not to gamble. He prescribed for the plague. Since the chills became worse after he examined Christopher, he sought to induce sweating by heaping blankets on him and filling him with drugs. He poured into the patient a mixture of veronica, balm, angelica, pimpernel, and ivy berries.

His patient grew sicker and vomited. Feeling desperate himself, the doctor took the ultimate precaution—he fumigated the bedroom as he had done to the cellar. He didn't tell Sam, who was helping him, that this was as much to protect himself as the patient. And before he began this examination he fortified himself with cardamon seeds, filled his stomach with bitters and aromatics, and indulged freely in the smoking of tobacco.

In Scarburgh's effort to kill the plague Christopher felt he was being killed. The mixture of herbs and drugs inside him, the stench of sulphur and tobacco were as disagreeable as the stench of the corpse, and he felt horrible and finally he cried out, "Stop, please Doctor! I would rather die than take any more of this treatment!"

Now Scarburgh was certain the boy was grievously ill and he

whispered to Sam, "His depression is another symptom. I must consult Harvey."

After the doctor left, Christopher felt a little better, for once he was alone he opened his window which cleared out most of the noxious fumes. Then, a few minutes later, Sam brought him food he could digest: eggs, a clear broth, and a simple wine. Sam said, "We are very concerned. Anne wants to nurse you, but I thought it best to see what the doctors advise."

However, her solicitude helped, and when Sam was gone he fell into his first sound sleep in days. But Sam, who locked his door so the sick boy could not infect the rest of the house, also sent a messenger to Dean Wren in Bletchington to inform him that Christopher was seriously ill.

Scarburgh didn't return for several days, and then he was with Harvey. His reason was that it generally took two to four days' progress of the plague before the black spots appeared, but actually he felt helpless without the older doctor and needed his advice desperately.

Christopher felt better, now that he didn't have to smell the sulphur and had eaten and slept properly for the first time in several weeks, and didn't feel so hopeless about Anne. And he was glad to see the doctors, for Sam had refused to allow him out of bed or to leave the room.

Harvey was unusually tidy in his knee breeches, long coat, cravat, thick wig, and gold-headed cane and when Christopher admired it, he said, "It was a present from the King. What is troubling you, young man?"

"Chills, fever, some nausea and faintness earlier."

"I meant what is troubling your disposition."

Christopher was silent.

Scarburgh asked impatiently, "Don't you think it is the plague?"

"After four days? Did you fumigate?"

"Twice. When I opened the coffin and here, several days ago."

"That alone, could have made him sick. And added to a previous distemper may have contributed to his illness. What happened to the body?"

"I removed it and had it burned. I was afraid."

"You were wise. The penalties are severe. He doesn't have the plague."

Before Christopher could feel relieved, Scarburgh blurted out, "But Harvey, he did have many symptoms!"

"Which are from different things. What other ailments do you suspect?"

Scarburgh took Harvey aside so that Christopher couldn't hear him and whispered, "*Lues venerea.* Syphilis, possibly."

Harvey turned to Christopher and asked guessing, "Did you find the girl pleasant?"

Christopher didn't reply.

"Don't deny it. It would be unnatural if you didn't. Was she?"

"Very pleasant. She has a most delicate complexion." As he sensed what Scarburgh was thinking, he added hurriedly, "But I used a sheath."

"You were well advised." Now Harvey did examine him and when he finished he said, "There is no sign of a rash, or scabies, or any trace of the itch. Nothing is ulcerated. There are no pustules, no indication of an impure coitus in his private parts. No blemishes anywhere on him."

Scarburgh declared, "Yet he was very sick! Weren't you, Christopher?"

Christopher nodded.

Harvey suggested, "Full of vapours, nauseous, and faint?"

Christopher added, wanting to be accurate, "Chills and fever mostly. Dr. Harvey, I only got faint when I smelled the corpse, and nauseous after the fumigation and the drugs."

"Precisely. How do you feel now that you have had rest and food?"

"Much better, sir. Almost normal."

"You don't need enemas or blood-letting to get vapours out of the system."

Scarburgh, feeling attacked, said, "Harvey, I didn't use those methods."

"You fumigated, which added to his nausea, and gave him drugs which made that worse. What the stench didn't accomplish, the sour taste did. Drugs should be sweet tasting, even when they are useful, which is seldom. But despite what we did, or in spite of it perhaps, he is better."

"God helped me!" cried Christopher.

"God may have helped you, but nature certainly did. One hair on the back of your head knows more about your health than all the theologians and doctors."

Scarburgh said defiantly, "Nonetheless, he was sick! Quite sick!"

"Wouldn't you be, with all the day-by-day news of war, plague, fire, theft, murder, shipwreck, massacre, foolishness and betrayal?"

"What was wrong with me, sir? There were moments I felt awful."

"Naturally. You were suffering from an excess of melancholy."

"I have been in low spirits, sir. What is the cure?"

"Nature. Fresh air, plenty of rest, good but simple food, and a girl."

"But that is a sin."

"The only sin is to go against nature. And nature created your need for a female. As long as she isn't unhealthy, she is as essential as breathing."

Harvey was turning to depart, when they heard Dean Wren stating outside of the door—every word was plain with their own silence—"William, I'm not sure I agree with your judgment, allowing that little doctor, Harvey, *the Circulator*, to attend my son. He has many strange ideas."

Christopher blushed; his father had used *the Circulator* in the Latin sense, which meant quack. But Harvey preserved a polite silence when Dean Wren entered, which added to Christopher's admiration of him. William and Susan followed Dean Wren into the bedroom and after everyone was introduced, Scarburgh said, "Dr. Wren, I am the physician in attendance. I am responsible for your son. Dr. Harvey was kind enough to agree to join me in a consultative capacity. He is the King's doctor."

"Is he with the King now?" Dean Wren asked pointedly.

Scarburgh said, "It would be useless, sir. The King is in prison now."

William added, "And he was with Charles at the battle of Edgehill."

Harvey smiled as he said, "For which I deserve no praise. I slew no one. Not even as a doctor. While they shot at each other, I sat under a hedge and read. It was the only sensible course for a reasonable man."

"Perhaps. However, I doubt that is what cured my son."

So his father knew, Christopher thought with relief, but he had to ask, "Father, how do you know I am better?"

"Your complexion is good. It is the first thing that fades when you are ill. But I'm sure you should still stay in bed. You were born delicate."

"Yes, Dean Wren," said Scarburgh, "It would be advisable."

"What was wrong with my son? The message sounded as if he were dying."

"He was run-down from overwork and under-eating and lack of sleep."

"I knew this Invisible College was too much for him. I will take him back to Bletchington with me."

"Please, Father, No!" Christopher would have gotten out of bed if Susan and William hadn't restrained him. Indeed, his father looked much worse than he did, he thought, having aged perceptibly, but if he suggested that it would only anger him more. "I love my studies here!"

"But if they make you ill they cannot be continued."

"They didn't make me ill. It was my own fault. But I won't neglect my diet or sleep any more. I promise."

William said, "Sam Taunton's sister-in-law, Anne Beaufort, has offered to nurse Christopher back to good health. She has a healing touch."

Dean Wren hesitated, then asked, "But she is unwed, isn't she?"

"Yes," said William. "She is only sixteen."

"No," said Dean Wren. "It would be improper. Susan will stay with him until he is well. She is very good with physic and can be trusted."

Christopher felt so much better now, however, despite his disappointment that Anne would not be his nurse, for she did care; he had fallen ill and melancholy unnecessarily, but perhaps it had been essential to find out. He said, "Father, I have learned a great deal at The Invisible College."

"Mathematics? Astronomy? What use are they in the Church?"

"I am not going into the Church." Now that it was out he felt relieved. His father was shocked, but he had to continue, while he had the courage. "I am not going to be a divine. It is not my vocation."

"My only son is going to reject his father's principles?"

"I do not reject them, but I prefer mathematics and astronomy."

William said, "Perhaps, Dr. Christopher, they do suit his nature more."

Dean Wren, sensing he wouldn't get any support here, even from his family, for Susan nodded in agreement with William, changed the subject. "Harvey, as the King's physician, you should know his mind. What do you think he will do in his present peril? Stand firm or give in?"

"His is not an easy mind to know. Charles keeps his thoughts very much to himself. But I doubt that Parliament is in a merciful mood now, especially Cromwell and his faction, who are in command these days. And they are easily provoked, and Charles has provoked them."

"But they wouldn't dare violate the person of the King!"

"They would dare anything. Even shoot at a flower if it stood in their way."

G*

The Tree Surgeon Was

The tree surgeon was
cutting
the dying branches
from the oak tree

as though he knew
exactly at which point
the tree would not feel
one stab of pain

I feared for his soul
when my fingers fell off
and my whole body ached
but even worse my mind

Stymean Karlen

The Tree Surgeon Was

THE PATIENT BECAME THE CENTRE OF ATTENTION. AFTER DEAN Wren departed, Sam ordered Katherine and her sisters to help Susan. But Christopher would have preferred Anne to be his sole nurse. Susan and Anne were friendly, but Katherine behaved as if his sister had invaded her home, while Lucy was self-involved. Even when she brought food and wine, she prettified herself, infected with self-love. Then, after a few days, Lucy and Katherine were needed elsewhere, for William was staying in London as long as Susan was there and until Christopher was fully recovered, and he required attention, too. And Susan and Anne knew that Christopher was feeling almost normal when he asked for paper and pencil to draw. Although Susan was still in charge, they were nursing him together.

It was happening without his trying to make it happen. His imagination was devoting itself to the design of St. Paul's. Now that he felt strong enough to draw, he was able to admit to himself there had been moments during his illness he had thought he was dying. At those lapses into melancholy he had promised himself that if he recovered, he must not waste anything, not time, energy, thought, or imagination. He sat up in bed, propped by the pillows Susan arranged for him, while Anne prepared a simple broth for him, not noticing that it was raining, that the girls were in an animated conversation with each other; he was seeking to visualise a completely repaired cathedral, or possibly a new, different one. He mustn't squander what he had imagined. But first, he had to draw St. Paul's as it was. He wished he possessed Hollar's skill and experience, and Daniel's hand—Daniel had such a steady, accurate hand—and he desired accuracy more than anything else; Daniel was almost as precise as the engraver. He searched his memory for an exact remembrance of St. Paul's; he recalled the sky above it, as blue as Anne's eyes; the dents and scratches on many of the columns—had they shifted with time?

All of a sudden he wondered what was wrong with him. Instead of the cathedral, he was remembering a long ago, the fragrance of Seth's garden, the arch of St. George's Chapel, so calm and serene and noble, his beloved chair, *Myself*, and there was no chair here that was as comfortable and friendly and reassuring, and the night he climbed to the roof to stare at the stars and how eagerly he sought to reach up and touch them.

But he had never told *anyone. Anyone* would laugh at him.

Yet he must be able to touch the mountain top, a dome on St. Paul's. If he could only reach up! But he couldn't reveal that he was falling in love. No sensible person fell in love with a building. Yet, as his imagination designed repairs for the cathedral, he was. He craved a better St. Paul's with every fibre of his being. He hoped Inigo Jones wouldn't mind. And as he drew he speculated on the kind of cathedral he would design if he were planning a new St. Paul's. If he painted the dome, he decided, it would be splendid to have Daniel do it; he must be prepared to deviate from the original structure of the fabric; once it had been so severely damaged by lightning and fire—it could suffer again. Another storm could wreck it totally. A dome was more practical than a spire.

So, even as he tried to represent St. Paul's as it was, he continued to alter the design with an impulse he couldn't resist. This gave him a more comfortable feeling. Then he was depressed. He was drawing the columns before he had examined them, which was wrong. The next time he passed through St. Paul's he must survey the columns exactly. Even from memory, he was certain they were off several inches, that the stone towers no longer rested equally on those supporting pillars. Moreover, the sky possessed one expression, the buildings around the cathedral another expression, and St. Paul's wore still a different expression.

Then the girls' conversation distracted him.

"He suffers from too much study. But it is not incurable."

Susan was addressing Anne, but he heard every word. Disgusted with his failure to concentrate, he crumpled up the paper he was drawing on and threw it into the fireplace. He must start again, he must exercise his imagination more thoroughly, but not when he was weary, and suddenly he was very weary. He didn't want to waste what he had visualised, only he wasn't sure what form a new cathedral should possess. He felt ambushed by fatigue and his lack of knowledge and inability to observe.

Anne, perceiving his look of disgust, asked, "Did we disturb you?"

"No. If I just had more time."

His sister said, "You're not seventeen yet. You have plenty of time."

He wished Susan wouldn't stress his youth to Anne. He didn't reply.

Susan sensed his interest in Anne and she was sorry about it, for she liked Anne. Yet, she thought, Anne was not a girl he could wed or even afford to like. She was pleasantly surprised that Anne could read and write, and knew some Latin, and she mentioned this.

Anne answered, "My father believed his daughters should be educated. Then they wouldn't be quite so helpless. I can even read Ovid."

"But the Puritans say that women's reading should be confined to works of divinity and books of physic."

"My father was not a Puritan. But I know physic."

"Every educated woman should. I am very good at it."

Christopher said, "So is Anne."

"Then you shouldn't let my broth get cold. You haven't touched it."

"I'm not hungry." But when she looked unhappy, he sipped the soup.

Anne, having to justify herself, said to Susan but so he could hear her, too, "My father diligently taught us all the rules to be a good wife."

"What were they?" Susan asked curiously, yet sceptically.

"A gentle countenance not given to angry glances, a suitable modesty, a quiet voice, skill with a needle and herbs, a good hand on the stove, the wish to keep a home in order, and, most important, the knowledge that her first duty is to please God and her husband. With all her zeal."

"But she must not seek to rise above her estate and station."

Anne was so distressed at Susan's admonition Christopher hurried to add, "There are exceptions. What did your father do?"

"He worked at Cambridge in the service of gentlemen commoners like the Reverend Holder and Sam, and gained his education from them."

However, Christopher recalled, William had told him that her father had been a porter, hardly better than a common drudge, and he felt guilty that he knew yet pretended that he didn't, and so did Susan, who glanced at him knowingly. To appease his guilt, he asked, "When did your father die?"

"A few years ago. Just before Sam wed Katherine."

"And your mother?"

"When Lucy was born. I was two. I never knew her."

"Neither did I. My mother died when I was about the same age."

Anne looked gratified, as if this gave them something in common, but Susan said severely, "You mustn't be too ambitious. One has to be careful where they give their heart. Given wrongly, it could be disastrous."

But when Susan and Christopher weren't looking, Anne took his crumpled-up drawing from the fireplace. It had escaped the flames without them noticing and it could be a public expression of her existence. She was disappointed to discover it was not a portrait of her as she expected, but of a building. This puzzled her. She knew of his devotion to anatomy and astronomy, but he didn't discuss architecture. She didn't throw away his drawing; he might like that she valued even his discarded work.

It was midnight, hours after Anne had served him, and still she couldn't sleep. She lay in her bed on the floor beneath his, and wondered: was Susan right? But what other way could a poor girl, orphaned early, without a dowry, advance herself? She reasoned that she was only putting to good use what she had learned about human nature. There were moments when she was amazed at herself for so quickly and easily allowing him to possess her, but perhaps it was the sensible way to behave, for he still seemed to crave her—he watched her every move. Lucy had accepted their father's instructions indifferently, too young and selfish to know better, and Katherine hadn't liked them, not having any taste for learning, and yet, if Katherine hadn't been able to read and write, Sam would never have spoken to her. As Anne recalled this, she told herself an attachment to a sensitive young gentleman like Christopher, especially as his first love, could greatly aid her situation. Her intuition indicated he had sound prospects. Sam had told her that his charm and intelligence appealed to the influential men at The Invisible College. And she liked Christopher. He was pleasant looking and possessed such lovely manners. No matter what the circumstances, he always treated her like a lady. Considering his youth and smallness, he was passionate. Only one thing was missing: he hadn't said he loved her. When he indicated that, she would be sure she had acted wisely. He had defended her so earnestly to his sister, he must care for her. She was glad she had not put saltpetre into his broth or mortified her own flesh with harsh, cold baths. She drifted into sleep, thinking the Puritans shouldn't last forever and she could wait.

After Susan returned to Bletchington a week later and Christopher was fully recovered, Anne arranged to be in the garden at the same time he was.

It was a fine May morning, and he was drawing, sitting on a bench, but when he saw her enter he rose instantly and said, "I am honoured."

She said, "I thought you might like some broth. Or fruit."

"It is a little early for me. But you were such a nice nurse."

"I'm always happy to serve you. What are you drawing?"

"St. Paul's. Or how it should look. When it is repaired or redone."

"The Puritans will never allow that to happen."

"True enough, but others might."

"May I see it?"

He hesitated, yet she looked so interested and appealing and she had some education. He said, "It is just a sketch. Indifferently done."

"You do nothing indifferently. I have your other drawing."

"But it was so poorly done I threw it away."

She produced it triumphantly and declared, although she hadn't been certain, "I recognised that it was the cathedral."

This pleased him and he liked that her voice was gentle and modulated.

"Christopher, whatever you do, you do well. Because you care!"

How splendidly she understood him! She was not interested in flirting, but in things that mattered. "Do you really like this sketch?"

"Yes." But unconsciously she frowned.

"What's wrong?"

"You have put a dome on the cathedral!"

He shrugged, then asked, "You think it is not fitting?"

There was such an intent, questioning look in his eyes she realised that much could depend on her answer. She was very thoughtful as she replied, "It is fitting as long as they do not take it for a Roman church."

Startled, he stared at her in wonder. He hadn't thought of that. She was a clever one. Her father hadn't wasted his efforts. Yet she didn't try to flatter him, but was honest. He exclaimed, "That never occurred to me! Yet you could be right!"

"My father showed me drawings of St. Peter's in Rome. But I'm sure you weren't thinking of that church. Since you've never been there."

Jones had. And he had seen drawings of many buildings. Strange reconciliations of the mind. Was he seeking to bring two separate roots together? A church that could perform such a mission could be a mighty noble oak indeed. Desire and belief, and his own signature, and the various schisms no longer feeding upon each other like cannibals. But he was dreaming. Although the King was still a prisoner of Parliament, his supporters had risen in Scotland and East Anglia and the North and the civil war had resumed with more fury and rancour, and each side was certain it would win and the executioners sharpened their axes for the losers.

"Christopher, as long as you care, you must design it your way."

"I will! I do care for my designs! I care for you!" Now that it was out he felt better and he had avoided saying *love*. "You're clever, sweet . . ."

She put her finger to his lips and he would have embraced her in the garden if she hadn't warned him that they might be seen. He suggested she come to his room that night and she blushed, and replied it would be more fitting if he came to her. He wasn't sure Anne was right, but he agreed to her proposal. He would agree to almost anything to possess her again.

That night, joined together easily and quickly, he hoped it wouldn't end. When it did, just before dawn—he left her room at her request so they wouldn't be discovered—she refused to agree to another meeting, saying it must be when they were in the mood, it would be best that way.

Anne was positive her calculations were correct. She felt that as long as their meetings were not regular, he would crave her and not regard her as a whore. Desire had worked for Katherine, it could work for her. She was relieved that he was not suspicious of her motives; he believed she cared as much as he did. And perhaps she did, she told herself, if he said he loved her or made their relationship more permanent.

Sam was curious why Christopher was so cheerful as he accompanied him to Gresham the next morning for his return to The Invisible College; he was not sure how Scarburgh would greet his long absent pupil. Then, as they approached St. Paul's, Christopher wanted to enter the dilapidated cathedral and examine its columns for possible flaws and he would have done so if Sam hadn't halted him and said, "Your concern is commendable, but a waste. The Puritans won't allow it, and you will be late for Scarburgh and you know how angry he can get. Did you use the sheaths?"

Christopher was embarrassed and he didn't reply.

"If you did, you have nothing to worry about." But when he saw that Christopher was unhappy because he had stopped him from entering St. Paul's, he added, "As the son and nephew of two of Charles' favourite clergymen, you could be rudely treated by the Puritans, should they find that out, especially since there is a new civil war now and you are entering an established church they are disestablishing." Sam took Christopher by the arm and led him down Warwick Lane, into Paternoster Row and past the cathedral to Cheapside. "We compromise too much, even in fornication."

Christopher replied indignantly, "I've not indulged in that!"

"What should I call it? Love? Sex can be a glutton, but I expect Anne to wed. You must avoid whores. Do you need any more sheaths?"

He couldn't tell whether Sam was trying to encourage him with Anne, or warning him. He changed the subject. "I received an outrageous apothecary bill for six shillings that Scarburgh charged to me."

"You were the patient. And Scarburgh was very angry with you. He felt you were betraying him, falling ill while working with him. What happened with Anne? I won't tell anyone. She is not a whore."

Christopher was silent.

"As long as you used the sheaths, you have nothing to worry about."

Scarburgh was not at Gresham when they arrived, but Wilkins was working on an invention to determine the weather with a clock, and he was delighted to see Christopher looking well and he greeted him affectionately.

But when Wilkins left the laboratory for a moment to get paper and pencil for Christopher to draw the model—for in his opinion Christopher had the steadiest hand in The Invisible College and drew the most accurate models—Sam whispered, "I don't want him to hear me, he supports Parliament, but the porter told me that Scarburgh is away on the King's business."

"Spying? Raising money? Carrying secret dispatches like my cousin?"

"I believe he is carrying letters from the King for the army. To promote an agreement between them. There are rumours that the army, led by Cromwell, will overthrow Parliament if they win this second civil war."

"Do you really think they can agree?"

"Only if the King wins. And I doubt he will, for the Puritans have the best soldiers and generals. Especially in Cromwell. Sssh . . ."

Wilkins was returning and as he gave the paper and pencil to Christopher, he said, "Your designs are remarkable for their fitness and beauty. You possess an inventive mind, curious, eager, open, determined. Our emotional survival depends on our capacity for experiment and invention. It is the one thing in which we can share a common love and faith."

Wilkins' broad, resolute features glowed as he spoke, and Sam, feeling he was in a good humour—but then, thought Christopher, Wilkins almost always was—took this opportunity to say, "Sir, I understand you have been appointed Warden of Wadham. My heartiest congratulations."

"Thank you, but it is no great achievement. It is one of the newer colleges at Oxford. Created in 1610 by the will of Nicholas Wadham, a wealthy gentleman. Christopher, have you thought of attending Oxford?"

"My father wanted me to enter Christ Church, but with the rebellion that became impossible."

"It is almost resolved. I would be honoured to have you at Wadham."

"It is kind of you to suggest that, but with my royalist background I doubt I would be admitted."

"You are a fine scholar. That is all that matters. I will see to that."

Before Wilkins could pursue this further, he was called away to assume his duties at Wadham. Then Scarburgh returned, not saying why he had been absent, but he plunged into his studies of anatomy with renewed interest.

The next few months Christopher constructed many pasteboard models and drew numerous human bodies for Scarburgh. The physician was particularly interested in whether blood could be transferred from one body to another. Harvey thought this could be done, but Oughtred and Ward disagreed, and said Harvey was too visionary, that the blood could not be trusted.

Christopher believed Harvey, but other matters absorbed him. While Scarburgh pondered how to perform that experiment, he laboured on his own inventions. Much of this year he was alone, for Scarburgh was absent frequently, as were the older men who were deeply involved in the new civil war, and he often taught himself.

He invented a reflecting dial on the ceiling of a room which told the time, a weather clock which used a revolving cylinder to keep a record through the night, a diplographic instrument for writing with two pens, and he reflected on better ways of observing the moon and the stars.

None of this lessened his desire for Anne. He felt she held back some of herself and their love making was irregular, usually spaced several weeks apart, but when they consummated, which was most of the time, he felt indestructible. No one else seemed aware of their liaison, although he found sheaths in his room each month and he assumed they were left by Sam. He didn't discuss Anne with anyone. Sometimes he thought she used tricks to heighten his desire for her, pushing him away more quickly than he liked, never arranging another meeting until she was ready, and always appearing to be reluctant no matter how eager he was, but his impatience was always satisfied eventually, if not as fully and often as he wished.

Despite his interest in St. Paul's, he didn't enter the cathedral,

The Tree Surgeon Was

although he passed it on his way to Gresham. He heard the Puritans continued to ravage the church and he didn't have the heart to see what they had done. And Sam's warning remained vividly in his mind.

He didn't know which way to turn. The Royalist risings were put down and this civil war ended with an even more complete defeat of Charles' followers. He feared there would be new reprisals against his father and uncle, who was still in the Tower, yet Scarburgh, Harvey, and Oughtred—the staunch supporters of the King—said his duty was to his inventions, that the most he could do for his family was not to weaken. But no one explained what that meant. He was shaken when the army seized the person of the King, and demanded that Charles be tried, and if found guilty, punished. He realised the army was deadly serious, for several weeks later they also seized London, and to prove their determination to rule, Parliament. Two regiments of the army surrounded Westminster Hall and purged Parliament of members that didn't share their views, refusing to allow any such opponents to enter the building.

Christopher felt trapped. He had no sympathy for the purged members, but where did order begin? Folly after folly was being perpetrated and giving birth to more folly. He thought, unhappily, Not even the army could build the country with a crumbling wall. No one could construct without interior designs. Anyone convicted by the army was judged guilty without redress. He couldn't listen to such a voice.

While he was still trying to decide what to do, Sam told him The Invisible College were giving a party at Gresham for Wilkins and Scarburgh and he was invited. He was surprised anyone could be festive with all the destruction around them, but Sam added, aware of his mood, "It is the only way they can console themselves for what is happening. They are celebrating Scarburgh's admission as a member of the College of Physicians and as an anatomical reader by the Barber-Surgeons' company, and Wilkins' appointment to be one of the commissioners who will rule Oxford, although that is still tentative and subject to Cromwell's approval."

"But this is justifying the Puritan domination of the university. Wilkins has adhered to the Parliamentary side."

"Isn't it better to have a friend in control than an enemy?"

Christopher gulped. He liked Wilkins better than anyone else at The Invisible College and yet . . .? He mumbled, "I don't know."

"Aren't you coming? There will be beer, bisket, cakes, and wine."

"Why am I invited?"

"You are a member."

"At my age?"

"That is their way of indicating you are."

"What about yourself?"

Sam's usually cheerful countenance assumed an air of melancholy. "I'm to serve. To make sure everybody's appetite is encouraged."

Holder was at the party and he assured Christopher that his father was as well as could be expected and desired him to continue his studies at The Invisible College. And the others were not mountebanks, reflected Christopher, but the best brains in the kingdom, and as they formed a circle around him at the table he no longer felt like a student, but like an equal. Even Oughtred, old enough to be his grandfather, asked him about his newest invention and before he could reply, Wilkins said, "We must not be deceived by his youth, he is as capable as any of us."

Oughtred nodded, but they must have been drinking, Christopher decided. Oughtred and Wilkins were embracing each other, although they were on opposite sides politically. Then they did fall into a dispute.

He was disappointed to discover it was about witchcraft. Oughtred believed in it and Christopher discovered, to his surprise, that most of the others agreed with Oughtred who stated proudly, "I am an excellent astrologer. I have foretold so much by the stars many people think I can conjure."

Holder asked, "Can you, sir?"

Oughtred looked mysterious and adjusted his wig but he didn't reply.

Christopher asked, "William, do you believe in witchcraft?"

"Many do."

That was no answer but before Christopher could say so, they were interrupted by four soldiers who marched in and assumed positions at the doorway and stood without a word. Were they being seized, too, he wondered? Even Wilkins was upset. Then Cromwell entered.

When he saw the look of distress on Wilkins' face, he said, "The soldiers have mismanaged. They have orders from the army to protect me wherever I go. They didn't realise you are scholars." He ordered the soldiers to withdraw out of sight, yet not from the building.

Wilkins stood up to greet him, but none of the others did.

Cromwell said, "May I join you, gentlemen?"

Oughtred blurted out, "Do we have any choice?" but Wilkins added loudly, "We are honoured, Oliver. Do you know everybody here?"

Cromwell nodded until his eyes fell on Christopher. He frowned and Wilkins hurried to introduce them. "Lieutenant-General Cromwell."

Christopher said, "I know."

"Oliver, my very good friend and estimable scholar, Christopher Wren."

"The Bishop's son?" asked Cromwell, his tone growing ominous.

"His nephew," Holder answered nervously.

"We met before," Christopher said, determined to be calm even if no one else was. Victories had altered Cromwell, he noticed, the soldier had grown sterner and more assured. Yet he was clad in plain grey clothes and grey worsted stockings and showed no sign of military authority except for the sword he wore at his side. "Some years ago. At the Bear and Boar tavern. It was an entertainment. You were with the poet, Milton."

"It was a musical evening," Cromwell said apologetically. "I do not approve of the theatre but music often speaks with the voice of God."

"Yet you said, *'God is not always where we expect to find him.'*"

"That is right, boy. I remember you now. You were not afraid."

Christopher sought to continue as a man, "'*But comes where each person has to find Him.*' I memorised what you said, it sounded so sensible."

Cromwell paused to answer Christopher more carefully. This Wren was personable, with his light brown hair, inquiring grey eyes, high cheekbones and sharply cut features, but things had changed. Now he could not afford to be charitable. Great power was too close. The fate of his cause could depend on what happened the next few weeks. God must tell him what to do, even if these scholars didn't. Yet they might still be useful.

Wilkins asked, "Oliver, what is your pleasure?"

"Grave decisions face us."

Oughtred cried out, "Are you going to try the King?"

"It hasn't been decided yet."

"It would be blasphemy!" Oughtred declared with horror.

Cromwell said solemnly, "God will try him. We are only His instrument."

Christopher whispered, "Then it is decided."

"Nothing is until God speaks."

Wilkins suggested gently, "I trust He will be merciful."

"He is always merciful," Cromwell stated, "And just."

But God was not Cromwell, thought Christopher, although Cromwell acted as if he were God. He wondered why the more power a man possessed, the more the man felt possessed by God.

Wilkins said, "Oliver, I am sure you will do only what is necessary."

"Precisely. If Charles is punished, it will be because it is necessary.

To prevent bloodshed from being needlessly prolonged. As long as he opposes us, we have no choice. He may make it a *necessity, a cruel necessity. And God's will.* Parliament is in God's hands now. Harvey, you were the King's physician. You know how strange his moods can be."

"I know that he is my King."

"If you could testify to his mental difficulties it would be a great service to the Commonwealth and God."

"In return for what?"

"You are a great scholar as well as a fine physician. Many would believe you and I would be honoured to have you as my body physician."

"Are you ailing, General?"

"No. But the country wants my health protected. And your protégé, Dr. Scarburgh, could be your assistant."

Scarburgh said abruptly, "I am too inexperienced."

Harvey added quickly, "And I am too old."

Cromwell exploded, "But I cannot trust Charles!"

Harvey asked quietly, "Can you trust yourself, General?"

Cromwell said stiffly, "I do not comprehend. You talk in riddles."

"Or in parables, perhaps."

"God will determine who is right, Harvey. As He brought us our victories on the battlefield. Wilkins, it will not be easy for me to convince Parliament to allow these heresies to continue here."

"Do you want to be remembered as the man who stopped learning?"

No unseemly haste. He must not act from passion but from careful calculation. And be certain of God's support. But Charles was another matter. Soon he would know what to do with him. Wilkins would humble himself to preserve his precious learning, always the Moderator, but he lacked common sense with all his charm, lucid brain, and great learning. His course of action was clear, once God settled his mind.

"Oliver, we owe much to your regard for knowledge."

"Possibly." He had forgotten these men were scholars, and so, not practical. It had been a mistake to approach Harvey; he probably wouldn't need his testimony now that Parliament was in God's hands.

As he turned to go, Christopher asked, "General, what about my uncle?"

"He is where he belongs. He brought us close to popery."

"He isn't a soldier. He intends no harm. He shouldn't be in the Tower."

"I do not trust the competence of the Bishop."

"He does his duty as you do yours. You did say, *'God comes where each person has to find him.'*" Cromwell looked reflective, and he added, "If you freed him, it might heal many wounds. And show God's mercy."

"After he drove our communicants out of the churches at Norwich and brought these pulpits to the brink of Popery? No, boy, it is impossible."

Wilkins suggested, "Suppose Bishop Wren admitted some of his errors?"

"Matthew Wren!" exclaimed Cromwell. "He is as obdurate as iron!"

"Now you should respect that, sir," said Christopher, "for it is reputed to be one of your outstanding virtues."

"There is a logic to that. But he will not submit."

"Suppose he does? Suppose he agrees to worship God privately?"

Wilkins said, "Oliver, that is an excellent idea."

Yet none of this mattered, Christopher reflected, Cromwell was not influenced by learning or the amenities, or even by the music the soldier treasured, but by his regard for strength and will. So, as powerfully as he could, he strode up to Cromwell, and while the General towered over him and seemed twice as wide with his broad, burly body, he said—with an amazing force for one so young and small, thought Cromwell—"He is my flesh and blood. And honest in his faith. Must I see him bleed?"

Cromwell wavered, then said abruptly before he could change his mind, "If your uncle acknowledges Parliament's authority he will be released."

"Thank you, General." Christopher felt a surge of hope.

"I will give you a safe conduct pass to visit him in the Tower and to ask his submission. If Wilkins will vouch for you."

Wilkins looked as if his own reputation depended on this mission, but Christopher's expression was so imploring, he said, "I'm sure our prodigious young scholar will present the situation in the best light."

"I hope so. Wren, report your uncle's reply to Wilkins and he will convey it to me. If the bishop refuses, we will not be so merciful again."

Cromwell's safe conduct took Christopher to Matthew's cell in the Bloody Tower the next morning without hindrance. But as the heavy prison door clanged shut behind him and the yeoman warder assumed his position outside and the chill of the cell penetrated him he shivered. Then, as his uncle embraced him, he was glad he had come, whatever the risk.

He felt his uncle shake with emotion and his uncle was so scrawny.

Matthew said sternly, "Nephew, you are thin! Have you been ill?"

"I was sick a few months ago. But I'm fine now."

"Have these Puritan dogs treated you badly?"

"No!" But he shivered, for the December cold dominated the cell in spite of the fire in the fireplace. "How are you, Uncle?"

"As well as can be expected. Considering the circumstances."

They moved apart to see each other better.

Matthew was very thin and looked much older. His features were sharper, his beard and hair were white, and Christopher was shaken by what time and imprisonment had done to him. Yet his voice was as severe as ever as he declared, "They will not break my spirit whatever they do."

Matthew thought sadly, Christopher has grown hardly at all, he will always be small and delicate, but his features had matured and were strongly cut and properly proportioned.

Christopher was pleasantly surprised that the cell was large and had two windows, a fireplace, and a pallet and rushes in the corner.

Matthew said, "As prison quarters go, I am not badly treated. They call the Bloody Tower the Ecclesiastical Tower these days. Laud, my dear friend and martyr, was confined here and since they consider me their greatest clerical enemy, now that he is gone, I occupy his quarters. Archbishop Cranmer and the Bishops Ridley and Latimer were also confined in this cell until they were burned at the stake at Oxford for heresy."

Christopher exclaimed, "It is to prevent this that I am here!"

"God knows I am not a heretic. I am not afraid. Even of fire. Besides, I hear that the Puritans, like Henry, prefer the axe. I have much company. Raleigh spent many years in these quarters and is reputed to have written his *History of the World* here. Ghosts walk with me often."

Did his uncle agree with Oughtred and the popular views about witchcraft, too?

"If I listen carefully I hear many voices. I met Raleigh."

"What was he like?"

"He was too free with his thoughts."

"I would have liked to have known him."

"I hope the New Learning hasn't corrupted you. Is it pious?"

"Uncle, many in The Invisible College are clergymen."

"That doesn't make them pious. Or aware of the true faith."

Matthew's tone was so critical his uncle reminded him of Cromwell and he changed the subject and asked, "Are you writing, too?"

"The warders are more merciful than I expected; perhaps they believe the King will rule again and want me to speak for them. They allow me a chair and desk of English oak, paper and ink, quills, but no penknife to sharpen the quills when the points become blunt, they are afraid I could use it to take my life. Fools, I wouldn't give them the satisfaction."

"What are you writing?"

"A defence of Laud. I am a hardy scholar. I am up at five and never in bed until eleven. They will not give me any bibles or religious tracts except their own, but I have Greek and Latin grammars to study. I wash myself daily, clip my fingernails and beard. What brings you here?"

"Cromwell has said . . ."

Matthew interrupted, " . . . that if I submit to him, I will be freed."

"How did you know?"

Matthew said scornfully, "Why else would he allow you to visit me?"

"Uncle, if . . ." Christopher halted; it was difficult to continue.

"Since I've been here I've walked around the world several times. It keeps me alive. I must not die in this cell, it would give them too much pleasure. They would say that we are weak. But I fear the chill. I do not want to die of a fever or the ague, or have these ills force me to tremble unwittingly in the presence of the Puritans. You must never tremble before anyone. Not even me. What did Cromwell say?"

"If you agree to Parliament's rule, you will be released."

"What about my fidelity to the King?"

"The King is a prisoner of the army. There is talk they will try him."

"They wouldn't dare!"

"They will dare anything. But I think Cromwell would keep his word."

"I would be a useful trophy. And if I don't submit, Christopher?"

"I don't know. But perhaps . . ."

Matthew cut in angrily, "You haven't succumbed, have you?"

"To what, Uncle?"

"To the Puritan heresies. It would be a betrayal of my whole life."

"I still follow your teachings and my father's."

"Then how can you expect me to betray them?"

Christopher didn't answer.

Matthew said, "This is aptly called the Bloody Tower, it reeks of blood. Almost no one who has been confined here has lived to talk about it. But surrender of my faith would be surrender of my soul."

Christopher thought of the heads spiked on London Bridge, withered by time and weather beyond recognition, and he longed to flee. He disliked fortresses and the Tower was that, too closed in, too cramped, and dedicated to death. Space should be used to spread out, not to shut out the sun and life with a pompous, hostile suspicion. Whatever anyone else honoured here, the Tower was a vast mausoleum and the work involved in expanding and strengthening it was not worth the effort. But who would listen? Who possessed the Tower, possessed London. Yet it was difficult to leave.

Matthew saw his sombre expression and said, "Christopher, you are not deserting me. It is better, even for me, for you to be free. I rejoice to see you grown up and your visit will lighten the dark days."

"Uncle, what should I tell Cromwell?"

"I *am* the Church of England, not the Church of Rome, but not the Church of Cromwell either. I am no more Catholic than Cromwell and I will not reject my God." Matthew strode to a window and pointed to a flower pot which contained a flower. "I've kept it alive by placing it where there is still sun and water. Look at its goodness and beauty. I cannot despair of God, however sinful we are, as long as it grows."

Wilkins listened solemnly to Christopher's report of his visit to his uncle and thought about it a long time before he answered. Then he said, "Despite the Bishop's refusal, I will ask Cromwell to be merciful."

"Do you think that is likely?"

"I don't know. But it is possible. If Cromwell succeeds in punishing the King, he may think that your uncle's death is not necessary."

"Is the King going to be tried?"

"It depends whether Cromwell and the army feel strong enough."

"If he decides to be merciful, can he enforce his decision?"

"Yes. He controls the army and the army controls the country now."

"Then perhaps he might pardon my uncle."

"Not as long as the Bishop supports Charles' Church."

Christopher sat silently in Wilkins' room at Gresham and thought, It is no use, my uncle's skull will join the others spiked on London Bridge.

Wilkins said, seeking to console him, "Do not despair, he may lessen his punishment to life imprisonment. I will suggest that to Oliver."

That was scant consolation but Christopher mumbled, "Thank you, sir."

"Be wise. Concentrate on your inventions. You have an ingenious, mechanical mind with excellent powers of invention. Your pasteboard model with which you demonstrate the motion of the moon has helped me. If you develop it further we could investigate some of Galileo's assumptions. Christopher, do you know Edward Bagshaw?"

"Yes. He was at Westminster when I was. He went off to Oxford."

"He requested admission to The Invisible College. He said he knew you."

"His scholarship was not notable."

"I know. I have rejected him."

"But he was a King's Scholar, with influential friends in Parliament."

"And not qualified." Wilkins added gently, "You must not speak for anyone else, not even your uncle, but only for yourself."

Yet who would speak for St. Paul's? It was a week later, a miserable December morning darkened by low grey clouds and rain mixed with sleet and snow, and as Christopher passed the cathedral on his way to Gresham with Sam, expecting to hear Cromwell's verdict, for Wilkins had promised to have it for him today, a troop of cavalry clattered up to the entrance. Instead of dismounting before the west portico, they rode directly into St. Paul's in an obvious profanation of the cathedral. They were so assertive, he was certain the King was going to be tried. He ran after the soldiers before Sam could halt him, not sure he could stop them, but he must do something. Someone had to speak for St. Paul's!

By the time he was inside the west portico the disorder was so prevalent he didn't know which way to turn. The soldiers were using the nave as a stable for their horses, smashing the panelling and choir stalls into wood for bonfires to keep them warm, and more soldiers were breaking up the pavement in search of hidden communion plate and other treasures. He protested to the officer in charge, who replied, "It is very cold and it is time Paul's was put to sensible use. I have orders to quarter my troops here, and here they stay." Captain Lind was young, determined, and vigorous.

"But you will destroy the fabric. And you're ruining the interior. Where are the beautiful candlesticks that were on the altar?"

"They were idolatry. We have removed them. No more preaching by bishops in Paul's," he gloated. "Paul's Walk is still permitted, but we have gotten rid of the whores and whoremongers as we have gotten rid of the bishops and deans. Why is it your concern?" he asked threateningly.

Sam, who had caught up with Christopher, explained apologetically, "He is interested in architecture. He admires the fabric."

"We'd pull it down if we knew how to remove the scaffolds."

"But why do you have to rob St. Paul's?" Christopher cried.

"You are a fool. The silver vessel in Paul's was sold for a train of artillery and the brass and iron are to be used for guns and pikes, and the silver and gold communion plate will pay the wages of my men. Now get out of my way, or I will jail you. The Deanery in the churchyard has become a camp for prisoners of war. Do you want to join them?"

Sam said, "Christopher, you were going to find out Cromwell's views?"

Lind's tone softened, "Are you a friend of the General?"

"No."

"An enemy?" The young captain's tone hardened.

"An acquaintance." God have mercy on their souls, he thought, several of the soldiers were using an axe—just like the executioners on Tower Hill—on the organ loft, pews, and the new woodwork, chopping them into more firewood. He was further shocked to see that the stained glass windows were shattered, the pillars chipped and blackened with smoke, monuments broken and being used for target practice, and the soldiers were using the west portico to play ninepins and were making a great clamour.

Unable to endure these desecrations, he hurried outside and came upon Captain Lind looking even more triumphant. He paused, finding it difficult to believe what was happening. The Puritan officer was pulling down the statues of James and Charles which the King had placed on the stately west portico as a lasting memorial to himself and to the Stuarts.

Captain Lind proclaimed, "On orders of the Commonwealth!"

Sam stood behind Christopher and watched in amazement, too, whispering, "He should have said on orders from Cromwell," but Christopher didn't reply, horrified. They were damaging Inigo Jones' work beyond repair.

A mob gathered and cheered the soldiers while ropes were tied around the two statues. James, and finally Charles, were toppled over accompanied by a mighty roar from the crowd. Christopher thought his heart would break. No wonder Jones had lost his desire to be a surveyor. The mob and the soldiers kicked the top of Charles' head down the marble steps. Then, they were not satisfied until they spitefully shattered it into many pieces, and Christopher was sure that the King's fate had been decided, that the trial was just a charade, however just they claimed it would be. And they were leaving only the bare bones of the cathedral. They were making a funeral pyre of St. Paul's, of his father's Church, the Church of England, and the Church of God. He was furious enough to shout them all down. But he didn't, turning away heart-sick, for he knew none of them would listen.

Scarburgh was also in a rage. He strode up and down his room at Gresham while Harvey sat in a corner disconsolately. Christopher and Sam had just arrived, still shaken from the ravaging of St. Paul's, and Scarburgh, hearing their news, grew even angrier and shouted, "Harvey is right! Man is no better than a baboon! Puritan soldiers sacked his London home and destroyed his papers and his anatomical collection!"

Christopher exclaimed, "But why? Cromwell did ask him to be his doctor."

Harvey said, "When I refused he withdrew his protection."

"He must have a more sensible reason."

"The soldiers claim they found arms in my house. My jewelled sword that the King gave me, my dagger, which I wear as a gentleman and as protection and as was the fashion in my youth. If I were only younger I would have used it, but with my gout I can hardly walk. And they said because I was educated in Italy I have Romanist sympathies. Which is nonsense."

"What about Wilkins? Couldn't he stop them?"

Scarburgh snapped, "He wrote me that he has been unavoidably detained at Oxford, but he isn't here so that he can avoid the issue."

"But Wilkins assured me that he would be here today so he could give me Cromwell's answer about my uncle."

"You have it," Scarburgh replied, "And so has Harvey."

Christopher felt ill as he asked, "You think my uncle will face the axe?"

"Wouldn't Wilkins be here if he had good news?"

"Perhaps he has been honestly delayed."

"Perhaps the King will be tried justly, but I wouldn't count on it. If the King is condemned, as it looks now, who knows who will be next?"

Harvey said sadly, "I could endure the seizure of my rooms, even the stealing of my furnishings, although I miss my stove, but to destroy my papers? No wonder the Puritans doubt that the blood circulates."

Christopher asked, desperately needing something affirmative to grasp, "Sir, do you recall any of your new work?"

"Some of it."

"If we could write that down not all of it would be lost."

Harvey hesitated, then said, "Get a pen, Christopher. We can try."

Christopher did and he dictated: "All animals, even those that produce their young alive, including man himself, are evolved out of an egg."

"*Omne animal ex ova,*" Christopher suggested.

"Yes, every animal comes from an egg. Christopher, you write a far better Latin than mine." Then he began to laugh.

"Have I done anything wrong?" Christopher asked apprehensively.

"You could still outwit those Puritan baboons."

"How, sir?"

"Outliving them. If I were younger, it would be my chief resolve."

Harvey decided to stay with Scarburgh at Gresham for the time being, but Christopher, although he sought to heed his advice, could not feel cheerful these days. Wilkins was still absent from The Invisible College and there was no word about his uncle, and Christopher was convinced more than ever that his uncle's fate depended on what happened to the King.

On January 9th, 1649, a sergeant-at-arms, attended by two troops of horse and six trumpeters, proclaimed before St. Paul's: *"Charles Stuart, King of England, is to be tried in Westminster Hall by a High Court of Justice that has been called into being by an Act of the House of Commons."*

Christopher heard this declaration with Sam.

Sam said, "Cromwell's House. Everybody else has been purged."

"So the conclusion is certain from the start."

"Probably. It is really the army against Charles, and Cromwell against Charles. Cromwell and his supporters feel a trial is essential, that everything must be done in a legal manner, but actually it will be an assertion of one authority over another authority."

Neither of them said anything more. Sam knew it was futile to object to the way things were going, while Christopher felt trapped by events.

Yet when he heard the trial was to start on January 20th, he rose early that morning, and not telling anyone, not even Sam, he hurried to Westminster Hall. It was a bitterly cold day, there was ice on the Thames and the air was so chilled he could hardly catch his breath in the grey gloom of the sunless sky, but outside the Hall there were many people waiting in line to witness the trial. Parliament had announced that it would be an open trial, to prove to the world, London, and the rest of England that it was going to be just, but Christopher remembered Sam's words and wondered. The weather was even worse here as strong winds from the river lashed those waiting and the sky was dark and dismal. It was too cold to stand in one spot, he thought. Nobody with intelligence lingered in the streets except from necessity, and most of the people waiting to view the trial were lean from the wars, and yet the line grew long. Soldiers were everywhere in the New Palace Yard which was the main entrance to Westminster Hall and Christopher saw that they were heavily armed. Suddenly he was possessed with grave doubts about the wisdom of attending the trial, for he had heard that Parliament had issued an order forbidding the presence of any Royalists in London. But when he saw that no one, not even the soldiers, were checking the identity of the spectators, except to allow a privileged few to enter first and to have the best seats—although soldiers were guarding every inch of Westminster Hall—he decided the order was not being enforced and was issued to scare Royalists away from public places, especially the trial, so that the supporters of the King would not cause a commotion or display their support of the King.

Money was being paid to many waiting in line for their seats and he saw that their places were being reserved for the rich. He found a hungry boy, not much younger than himself, in the front of the line and when he gave the boy two shillings, which was a fortune to the youngster, he got a choice seat. And as he entered the gallery of the Hall, which he knew from the trials of Strafford and his uncle, he was glad he had come. Now he felt he must; he owed it to the Stuarts, who had given his family preferment, and to his father and uncle, who were devoted to Charles.

But he was apprehensive until he realised he was anonymous in this very crowded Hall. He had never liked the design of this vast Gothic structure in spite of its size and space and this morning he liked it even less, for it was jammed to the last inch of room, denuding it of whatever grace and beauty it possessed. Everyone was solemn; the unbelievable was about to happen, a sacrilege of a text he had been taught from birth.

Then, as Charles entered, it was as if his childhood passed before him: The Prince of Wales, Sir Anthony, Hollar, the Earl of Newcastle, and Seth and the pony, Monk, and he hadn't thought about riding lately.

He was brought back to the present by the appearance of the King.

Charles wore the brilliant blue silk ribbon of the jewelled George around his neck, and on his cloak the great silver star of the Order of the Garter, and Christopher thought of his father and that this would please him. The King strode swiftly to his red velvet chair and sat in it and faced the judges without expression.

Many soldiers, armed with tall pikes, separated Charles from everyone else. Most of the spectators were too far away to hear the arguments. They could not cause a disturbance, and clearly, giving the King an open trial was just a gesture. But Charles wanted no pity or mercy. His manner expected obedience. He sat where Strafford had sat, and Christopher thought, If he had supported him, he might not be sitting here, and ghosts were beside Charles— Thomas More, Essex, Anne Boleyn, all of whom had been tried here—and he understood his uncle's view of the Tower better.

He was shocked by the change in Charles, the King was so much thinner, aged, and pale. He looked at Cromwell, sitting inconspicuously among the Commissioners. Like Charles, Cromwell was impassive, and he felt the two men should face each other; they were the true adversaries.

Cromwell's hair was still black, plainly combed, and fell to his neck. His moustache was small yet thick, his features round and fleshy. But while Charles' hair fell to his shoulders and was waved, it was grey, as were his carefully trimmed beard and long moustache. And although there was only a year's difference in age and it was Cromwell who was older, Charles had aged so much he looked like Cromwell's father. As if each pound of flesh that had fallen off the King had fallen on the General. Charles' features were gaunt and his eyes were sad and thoughtful in a way they never were in the years at Windsor. His long, thin hands rested quietly on his chair, while Cromwell's burly hands were clenched. And both of them were all in black except for the white trim at their necks and wrists.

Yet as the trial began Cromwell didn't say a word but sat even more inconspicuously among his followers while Charles' presence dominated. For the man who had stammered and spoken with a heavy Scottish accent and often had found words difficult replied now with remarkable eloquence.

Charged with *"high treason and high misdemeanours"*, of being *"a Tyrant, Traitor, and Murderer"*, Charles retorted without a trace of a stammer, *"I am your lawful King. I have a trust committed to me by God, by old and lawful descent; I will not betray it to answer a new unlawful authority."*

Charles, whom he had not liked, who, he felt, had brought many of his defeats upon himself with his intrigues, his changes of mind and policy, defended himself with dignity, bravery, and skill. Yet while Charles won most of the arguments, Christopher sensed he lost the trial. He refused to submit to the authority of the court, to admit its competence, to even plead. His refusal, his defiance were regarded as an admission of guilt and when the day ended Christopher was convinced that the King was doomed.

He didn't return until a week later and then it was to hear the verdict: *"that the said Charles Stuart, as a Tyrant, Traitor, Murderer, and public enemy shall be put to death by the severing of his head from his body."*

He was stunned. This was against everything he had been taught, yet Cromwell sat rigidly, not saying a word, as if this was an act of God. When Charles tried to speak, even more the King in his dignity, he was silenced abruptly, and Christopher thought sadly, Now only his behaviour on the scaffold would speak for him.

This occurred several days later, on January 30th. Christopher stood with Sam before the scaffold which had been erected outside of his beloved Banqueting House and he was appalled by its wounds. All of the grand, beautiful windows were broken and boarded up except for one.

"Which the King is to come through," Sam whispered.

"Do you think he will have enough voice to reach the crowd?"

"I think they will let him speak. They can't be that cruel."

"After the way they tried him? I doubt it."

"Fifty-nine members of the Commonwealth signed the death warrant."

"As if it were a mandate from heaven, a holy sacrament, a sign of divine revelation and retribution. They are so righteous and foolish."

"They have won. To them that is proof they are right."

"They haven't won. Not as long as the heir to the throne is alive."

"Are you thinking of joining his cause?" Sam looked at Christopher in amazement. "I never thought you would take up arms against anyone."

"I never thought I would be standing here."

"Are you sorry that you are?"

Christopher paused, then sighed. "I have no clever answer."

"This has gone on for thousands of years. And will go on for many more."

"That doesn't mean we approve. I came because of my father and uncle. They would want to be here if they could, to show their support of the King. If I cannot help, I can pray, I can speak in my soul for him."

"To whose God? Cromwell's?"

"Even Cromwell's. He had mercy when I first met him years ago."

"He wasn't so powerful then."

Charles stepped through the window of the Banqueting House that was enlarged for that purpose and on to the scaffold. The wood was draped in black and the scaffold was crowded with the presence of the executioner and his assistant, representatives of the Commonwealth, and soldiers to guard the King should he seek to resist or escape. But while Charles was momentarily bewildered by the bright sunlight, the intense cold of the afternoon, and the crowd watching, he stood straight as he saw the block and axe and was concerned only that he would be allowed to speak.

Christopher couldn't hear his words and doubted that anyone in the crowd could, for the Commonwealth deliberately had placed so many rows of soldiers around the scaffold they kept the crowd far away.

He recalled the first time he had seen Charles, arrogant, indifferent, ill at ease with others except his family, but now, while the King was only five feet four and his legs were bowed, Charles towered over everyone, even the burly executioner, as he spoke with a dignity that conveyed his courage with an eloquence greater than words. Finished, he took off his George, the insignia of the Garter, handed it to Bishop Juxon who attended him, and said loudly, determined to be heard, "Remember!" He discarded his doublet, told the executioner not to strike until he gave the sign by stretching out his hands, placed his head on the block and prayed. The executioner moved forward to make sure everything was in order and the King, believing he was about to strike, said commandingly, *"Stay for the sign."*

"I will, an' it please Your Majesty," said the executioner.

Christopher joined Charles in prayer and so did many in the crowd. The soldiers looked unhappy and Christopher saw several of them praying.

A few moments passed and as Charles stretched out his hands a terrible silence followed. Christopher was grateful that Sam, who stood before him at the instant the axe fell, was taller and shut out the sight. He knew it was over for an awful groan rose from the crowd.

He entered Westminster Abbey which was nearby to pray for the King and found Busby leading his students in public prayer for Charles. This was open defiance of Parliament, but he joined them, and listened to Busby conclude, "We must never forget this bleak and infamous day when the King was murdered and his sacred head was struck off."

So Busby was not a Puritan vessel, he thought with relief.

Busby saw him and asked, "Wren, why aren't you at the university?"

"I thought I could learn more at The Invisible College."

"Without a formal education? Nonsense! You should enter Oxford."

"I'm not sure they will admit me."

"They will. Wilkins has influence and you are one of his favourites."

"You may exaggerate, sir. I was supposed to hear from him recently, but there hasn't been a word."

"I never exaggerate!" For a moment he thought Busby was going to flog him, and then the Head Master regained his self control and said, "You have too much intelligence to waste it in London."

"In times like these?"

"Once Cromwell is gone there will be no one to succeed him. And now that Charles is a martyr, the English will want the Stuarts back. You must not think of stopping your schooling because of the Puritans."

But in spite of Busby's advice he couldn't think of anything except the execution of Charles and whether it would condemn his uncle by example. There was still no word from Wilkins, although he was at Gresham every day in the hope there would be; sometimes he was the only member of The Invisible College present. He sought to distract himself by pursuing his inventions, but his anxiety about his uncle made his study of perpetual motion and the investigation of submarine navigation seem pointless. And since the death of Charles, he was unable to approach Anne, although she indicated she was willing. He said he didn't feel well, and she accepted his excuse. Then he was upset because she didn't insist.

Two weeks after the execution Sam said someone wanted to see him alone at The Invisible College. He assumed it was Wilkins with news about his uncle. When Seth entered he was so disappointed he couldn't hide it, and Seth blurted out, "I didn't want the King killed! Remember, I knew him. He was a difficult man, but he liked a good horse and a well kept garden."

He was shocked to see that while Seth was only in his twenties the gardener was turning grey and was uncertain and apprehensive.

Seth said, "You look well. I am so glad to see you."

The Seth who smiled was the old Seth and Christopher said, "So am I."

"Did you get the registers of the Order of the Garter?"

"Yes. I thought you were the one who left them. Thank you very much."

"I couldn't tell anyone. It could have meant my life."

"That is why I was surprised to see you. My uncle is in the Tower and visiting me could be held against you. And won't your father mind?"

"We are Dissenters, not Puritans. I never thought they would go so far."

"Sit down, Seth. Would you like some wine?"

"Thank you, sir, but I can't stay long."

"My father was very pleased to receive the records of the Garter. They have helped his health, they have given him a reason to stay alive."

"It was the least I could do. You were kind to me and when the King's son comes back you can testify that I was a loyal subject."

Christopher noticed that Seth was hiding a package under his cloak with unusual care and he asked, "Is it something for me?"

Seth hesitated, not sure how to proceed. Then he whispered, "This could be dangerous for both of us, but I felt I had to do it."

"What is it?"

Seth unwrapped it and said softly, "The Garter of Gustavus Adolphus."

The diamonds shone in the sunlight and he realised that the gardener had taken a great risk. If Seth was caught, it would not be a simple beheading for him, but the hideous death stated by law for traitors: of being hung, then cut down while still alive and castrated, disembowelled, and quartered.

"I remembered this was important to your father because it was the first treasure given into his keeping when he became Register of the Garter."

"Won't this be found out? Won't they miss it at Windsor?"

"This Garter has been hidden ever since we buried it in the Treasury. The Puritans, to keep anyone from reading the Book of Common Prayer and the King's version of the Bible, locked the Treasury. They didn't have the courage to destroy these books, for in their own way they express the word of God, but they are determined to keep them from anyone's eyes. So the Treasury is boarded up as a place of sacrilege and no one goes there. No one will find what we hid there. No one is allowed to enter it. But I got in." He gave Christopher the Garter of Gustavus Adolphus. "Don't tell anyone, even your father, where you got it. Just in case it is discovered."

Christopher embraced Seth and the gardener declared, weeping with emotion, "Those Puritans are not proper people. They ruined my garden. Used it for their horses. Even the manure didn't help."

"It was such a beautiful garden." Christopher felt like weeping, too.

"And it will be again. But now Windsor is cursed. Although it may be redeemed some day. They buried Charles there a few days ago."

"I didn't know. I hadn't heard anything about it."

"They don't want people to know where the King is buried. They are afraid it will lead to demonstrations and become a place of pilgrimage."

"Seth, are you positive about the burial?"

"I witnessed it. I was still on the grounds of Windsor trying to save my garden from complete ruin. It was snowing heavily, even for February, and threatening to become a blizzard, when the funeral party arrived at the castle. The King's burial was being arranged by the Duke of Richmond, who was in charge, and the body was accompanied by two troops of horse to make sure that none of the rules Parliament had laid down would be violated. But I heard that the Commons said Charles could be placed in St. George's Chapel, so he wouldn't be totally humiliated. Charles' head was sewn back on his body, which was embalmed, placed in a coffin, and now the Duke was looking for the best spot to bury him. While the Duke and his friends decided, they placed the coffin on your father's table in the Deanery."

"The great oak table that I loved so much?"

"Yes. It hadn't been used for years, ever since your father was driven out. I was glad the table was long, sturdy, for while Charles was not a large or a tall man the coffin was heavy. I remembered all the good times you had on the table and how much you liked to write and draw on it."

"Charles used it, too, once."

"He lay on it now. They opened the coffin while it was on the table to be sure it was the King and that everything was in order. I was allowed in, for they wanted to talk to someone who knew the castle, and while I was known to be a Dissenter, the fact that I had worked for your father was in my favour and I was permitted to help them and to look at him."

"His face was as I recalled it, only thinner, sterner, and the insignia of the Garter, the George, was around his neck, which was his wish, it was his favourite decoration, and it gave me the idea to take this Garter."

"While I was wondering how, the Duke said, 'We must bury His Majesty as befits his rank. With another sovereign. Henry VIII is buried in the choir of St. George's Chapel. Isn't he, gardener?' "

"I nodded. But I didn't recall where and no one else knew. It looked as if we would never find the vault but I remembered how you had found the burial place for the treasures and I tapped on the floor of the choir until I heard a hollow echo and then I knew we had found it. They lifted the stone and found a large lead coffin with rotting shreds of a purple pall, which told the Duke it was Henry VIII, and a smaller coffin, with his third wife, Jane Seymour, and room for Charles' coffin."

"Were there any services?"

"None. They were forbidden. But like almost everybody else there, I bowed my head in silent prayer and some of the soldiers did, too."

"Seth, how can I hide this Garter until I see my father?"

"Pin it inside your doublet. No one will think of looking there."

Christopher did. Then he asked, "Seth, are you returning to Windsor?"

"No!" Seth's face was white. "They say that Charles' ghost will haunt the chapel until he receives a proper Christian service."

Christopher, with the Garter of Gustavus Adolphus pinned inside his brown doublet, wore it every day. So repeatedly Anne commented about that, but he was too nervous to hide the Garter anywhere else, and he replied, "It is cold these days and this is the warmest doublet I possess."

She didn't dispute that, and after weeks of waiting Wilkins returned to The Invisible College. When he approached Christopher he didn't apologise or explain the delay, but said, "Your uncle's case has been reviewed. Despite his being such a staunch supporter of Charles."

Wilkins was sombre and he was certain the verdict was death.

"I have obtained a reprieve. Your uncle's life will be spared."

"Thank you!" Christopher was so grateful he could hardly speak.

"Cromwell has agreed to be merciful. He has reduced your uncle's sentence to life imprisonment." But now Christopher's gratitude turned to despair and Wilkins added hurriedly, "You can do no more for Matthew Wren. Considering his history, his sentiments, and refusal to acknowledge the authority of Parliament, he is fortunate to be spared the axe."

"He may not think so."

"Perhaps, but many were of a mind to execute him, but I persuaded Cromwell, as much as anyone could persuade him, that it wasn't necessary."

"Why didn't he feel the same way about Charles?"

"'Cruel necessity,' he said, 'and the will of God.' But he may have spared your uncle because he respects your candour and logic. Christopher, won't you join me at Wadham? You will be admitted. I will see to that."

"To further preserve Puritan intolerance and rigidity?"

"To preserve learning. Now that the wars are over it is time we healed the wounds. I will be honoured to have you at Wadham where I hope to establish the same learning we possess at The Invisible College. It is the reason I took the post as Warden. Join me, please."

But foremost in his mind was to put the Garter of Gustavus Adolphus in his father's hands. It might compensate, at least in part, for Matthew's life imprisonment. He was packing for his return to Bletchington, when he couldn't find his brown doublet. He was afraid it had been stolen, yet Anne was the only one who came into his room in Fetter Lane. He didn't know how to ask her if she had seen the precious doublet. The day was dark and grey and the rain poured through the leafless branches of the trees in the garden, and he had put off telling her or Sam of his departure this afternoon until the last moment so they wouldn't have time to persuade him to change his mind.

Now however, he had to approach her. She was cooking the dinner in the kitchen and when he mentioned the brown doublet, she replied, "I have it."

"Why?" Was she really a supporter of the Puritans after all?

"I was going to sew it. You've worn it so much the cloth is torn."

"I need it now."

"At once?" Anne looked surprised.

"Yes. I'm leaving today. My father isn't well and I must see him."

"Is that the only reason you are leaving?"

"What other reason could there be?" He tried to sound innocent.

"Don't be angelic, it isn't becoming. You won't be back."

"Yes, I will."

"No, you won't. You haven't approached me for weeks. Ever since the King was executed. As if that was my fault."

"That is not the reason!" he blurted out.

"What is? That you are tired of me?"

"I've been distracted, upset. London is chaotic these days."

"So you will go to Oxford with Wilkins and forget us all here."

"I haven't decided yet."

"You will. Sam told me Wilkins asked you to join him and it is too great an honour to refuse. And you are a natural scholar and I am only a poor girl without a dowry, with no future, with nothing to share or help one."

"After I see my father, I will be back."

"No promises, Christopher. Do not promise what you cannot keep."

"May I have my doublet? It is cold and I will need it to keep warm."

Anne gave it to him and when he felt the Garter on the inside of the doublet he smiled with relief. But she thought this was pleasure at the thought of leaving and she said angrily, "I am good enough to be a nursemaid but not a wife." Before he could deny that, she was gone.

Sam said he understood why Christopher had to leave, but he was brusque. Then suddenly and abruptly he asked, "Does Anne know?"

"Yes. She thinks I'm deserting her."

"Aren't you?"

"I will be back, Sam."

"A year from now. It won't matter then. So Wilkins has won after all."

"I will make up my own mind."

"Of course. Wadham and Oxford are your focus now."

"I do hope if I should return to London, I will be welcome here."

"Certainly. I should have known that Anne was not for you."

"I intend to continue at The Invisible College."

"Naturally. Many of them will meet at Wadham now that Wilkins is one of the rulers of the university."

H*

Christopher adjusted his brown doublet so he could feel the Garter and said, "You've been my friend, but I have a choice to make and I must face it. And you were the one who warned me not to become involved."

Sam shrugged, and opened the door; the coach Christopher had ordered was outside and must not be kept waiting; he might not get another one for days.

But as the coach pulled away Christopher had to look back at Fetter Lane and he felt better as he saw Sam and Anne waving goodbye to him.

When Dean Wren received the Garter of Gustavus Adolphus from his son, he knew it had not been a waste to have Christopher educated with the royal family; his son had learned what was truly important in this world.

He was overcome with joy, but all he could say was, "I hear that the King died wonderfully religious, and well prepared for heaven. As Matthew will, if the occasion should arise. When are you entering Wadham?"

"I've not come to any decision. Why are you so sure I will enter?"

"You will want to show your gratitude to Wilkins and you are a scholar. And now that I have the Garter, we must preserve it for the return of Charles in the person of his son." After what Christopher had endured, he might survive his frailness and grow up.

1 6 5 6

See it There

See it there
Know its spaces
See it there
Feel its air
See it there
Its near distance
See it there
Its far nearness

Hear its wind's word
Make sure make sure
See its sight
Know its vertical reaches
　See its unknown source
Fit your mountain
into its hill
Breed its beginnings

See it there
　Whatever it is
　　　　Stymean Karlen

See it There

THE WINTER SUN WAS RISING AND CHRISTOPHER, AFTER A NIGHT spent at his telescope, stared out the oriel window of his favourite room in the Tower of Wadham and wished he could see all of Oxford with one viewing. The sky was clear and fine for seeing. But while this room was the largest in Wadham and was called the Astronomy Chamber because he had erected a telescope here, he was dissatisfied with how little he saw of Oxford. Yet this was a prized chamber. It belonged to the Warden and it was a special mark of Wilkins' favour that the Warden had given it to him.

On one side he saw the quadrangle and on the other side he looked out upon colleges that spread over the landscape. Even so, he could not see enough, for spires cluttered the skyline and hid most of the colleges from his view. He was constantly improving his telescope; he doubted the same could be said for the appearance of Oxford. He preferred the landscape to be more tidy. But no single style prevailed, he noted critically. The Oxford within his sight was a profusion of spires, arches, quadrangles, buttresses, towers, and roofs in patterns that were Saxon, Norman, Gothic, Renaissance and Tudor.

He shouldn't be surprised, he thought, the lack of order reflected the times. Seven years had passed since the execution of the King, yet there was no calm in England because of the deed, although Cromwell said it would bring peace to the land. Cromwell ruled now as Lord Protector and many expected him to become King. But the longer he governed, felt Christopher, the more the people yearned for the return of the Stuarts in the person of the King's son. Yet Oxford was academic again after the havoc of the civil wars. The Puritan conquest of the British Isles seemed complete with Cromwell's victories in Ireland and Scotland, and the King's son, proclaimed Charles II by his followers, had fled to the continent.

He told himself he must not be discontented. No one persecuted his father now, although the Dean's churches had not been restored to him; his uncle was still alive, while yet in the Tower; and he was the first Fellow to be elected to All Souls since the end of the civil wars, a great honour. But his discontent remained. He wondered if it was because of his weariness. He had been up all night studying the stars, but he had not found anything new. Yet, he thought, the year he was born Galileo was forbidden by the Inquisition to pursue his inquiries and the year that Parliament seized power in England the astronomer died. Such a conjunction of events must be coincidental and was no reason for him to become an astronomer. Tired by his doubts, he decided to nap, so he would be rested for the afternoon. Scarburgh was expected in Oxford then, to finish a medical experiment with other members of The Invisible College. They had transferred their activities to Oxford because of Wilkins' growing influence at the university; and he was Scarburgh's assistant due to his skill in anatomy and his ability to construct models.

Still undecided where his future was, he could not fall asleep as he wondered if the heavens were as mysterious as the human body. He was troubled by this, for he didn't love anatomy the way Scarburgh did, although he was curious about how the body worked. And inevitably, even as he nodded from fatigue, his eyes returned to the buildings of Oxford.

But his affection for architecture was an indulgence, he thought. There was no Chief Surveyor since the death of Inigo Jones a few years ago and long before that the architect had been discredited. Besides, he wasn't sure he approved of Oxford's preference for the Gothic.

Then, in a change of mood, as if it were not right for a Fellow of All Souls to feel otherwise, he assured himself that in his heart he loved the look of Oxford, the grace of the quadrangles and the courtyards, the tone of the buildings, often charming, dignified, even serene, suited to the student life. He had devoted six years of his life to study and Wadham and All Souls were a roof over his head— the best roof in England, scholars said—and he was weary of all the contemplation; he yearned to do, do, do. Abruptly now, as if that beat on his brain like a hammer, Christopher strode to the door where he measured himself. He hadn't grown at all, and he hadn't since he was sixteen, and he was going on twenty-four now. He must be content to be shorter than most men, although his hands had grown strong from riding and the constructing of models, and his shoulders had widened from his muscular activity. They were as firm as oak, he thought proudly, and these days he rode as skilfully as Cromwell, who possessed a superb seat in the saddle.

When he couldn't fall asleep, he thought of what had happened to Anne.

After he left London, he did not return to the city for a year, and then Sam told him, "Anne left. She decided there was no future here."

"But if I had become involved with her?"

Sam shrugged.

"Did you want that, Sam?"

"It would have been useful to Anne."

"Then you did desire it."

"I desired you to be happy. Have you married yet, Christopher?"

"Where did Anne go?"

"I think she got a position with a grand lord who likes pretty maids."

"In London?"

"I hear he travels abroad most of the time now that the Puritans are in control. Parliament passed an act in 1650 which makes adultery punishable by death and fornication liable to imprisonment. This lord feels it is safer to reside abroad, especially in France where they make a virtue of fornication. Have you met any attractive faces at Oxford? Are you ever going to marry?"

"I hope to be a Fellow of All Souls and they're not supposed to marry."

"I know. It is why I was expelled from Cambridge. But it is against nature, and they are treating you like a child."

Christopher's reverie ended as Robert Hooke ran up his steps, shouting, "You must hurry! Scarburgh has arrived from London and needs you to set up the model. Cromwell is arriving this afternoon to inspect your experiment. He is Chancellor now and Scarburgh is afraid he won't approve."

"But we are working in Boyle's rooms, which are not college property."

"The apparatus is. Cromwell is coming here, too. The telescope was put here with college money. I hope he has more sense than I think he has."

Christopher was startled by Hooke's excitement. He was used to his enthusiasms, but he had never seen Hooke so emotional. Highly charged, unable to sit still, Hooke paced up and down while he put on his old brown doublet. He treasured it as an omen of good luck and his worn clothes would give him the look of a scholar, and Cromwell preferred plain dress. But as he dressed carefully and slowly Hooke could hardly contain himself.

"We mustn't waste any time. All our work in Oxford could depend on this experiment."

He paused. Much as he liked his friend, he disliked being prodded.

"I hear two Puritan Visitors are with Cromwell, that they are critical of our work. If they have their way he will stop our experiments. They say in Oxford that our experiments are dangerous to the Puritans. We will have a full meeting. Everyone will want to see what happens."

Christopher fixed his white stockings so they fitted neatly—he abhorred black and untidiness in dress—and said, "At least, we are clean-shaven."

"I don't understand." Hooke was annoyed.

"Beards are forbidden. And ruffs and any finery."

"Sometimes I don't understand you. We are facing a crisis, you are the only one who can do the experiment and you waste time on clothes."

Christopher glanced reflectively at his friend. Hooke, who was at Christ Church and a member of The Invisible College despite his youth, was three years younger than himself, and even shorter, with a small, pale, crooked face. Yet while his body was ugly, he was hardly more than skin and bones, and deformed—his back had been bent from birth—he was imaginative, he was always inventing.

Now, with all his concern for haste, Hooke stated, "I've devised thirty ways of flying. Your Tower is a good place to try them."

And as Christopher took him by the arm and led him down the winding stairway and outside, where they had to walk carefully to avoid falling on the ice and snow as they hurried toward Boyle's rooms, Hooke never stopped talking. "We need a better lens for your telescope. I must put my mind to it. At Westminster I mastered six books of Euclid in a week. I can be a second Euclid, but I prefer mechanical pursuits. When my father died, I was sent to London to be an apprentice to the painter, Peter Lely, with a hundred pounds to pay for my instruction. I was only nine and I wasn't supposed to know my own mind. But I didn't like the properties of paint, you can't measure paint, so I kept my hundred pounds and went to Busby and he lodged me in his own rooms when he saw how clever I was. I learned to play twenty lessons on the organ. I could play for Cromwell. He likes music. It might soothe him. Did you hear that Wilkins is marrying despite the university rule against it?"

"No. Wilkins says he loves Oxford above everything else."

"Perhaps he does. He is marrying Cromwell's sister, Robina, the widow of Peter French. Perhaps he is doing it to preserve Oxford."

"If it will be allowed."

"It will be allowed. Do you think Wilkins will defend us if Oliver Protector is critical?"

"Not if you refer to his patron so disparagingly."

"He won't mind as long as our experiments enhance his reputation."

"Wilkins has more courage than you think."

"Possibly. At least he is marrying. You have known Mary Hart for years, she has a thousand pounds per annum, is pretty, well-formed, her father is an Oxfordshire landowner who has prospered because of his support of Oliver. You could have her the moment you proposed. With your Royalist connections, she would be protected whichever side survives."

"Hooke, you sound as if Mary is your preference."

"I don't intend to wed. I haven't time. But you are properly formed and have a good nature. I have a peevish temper, I am mistrustful, I have no prospects for wealth. But you have. Yet you let her dangle."

He sighed. Mary was attractive, well-proportioned, and just his height. Only he didn't love her. She was so proper. And he couldn't tell anyone about the women he had known sexually at Oxford. While neither was a lady, neither was a whore or a serving girl either. He paid five shillings each quarter to his bedmaker and laundress, but he hadn't touched them, although many students did. The Puritans set strict rules for the students on pain of dismissal: no more fighting in the streets, or velvet waistcoats or powdered wigs, or the study of poetry or plays—that was immoral. Swearing, drinking, and gambling were forbidden also, or any mention of Laud, who had dominated Oxford. But the worst sin of all to the Puritans was sex. That was punished harshly. Students caught in fornication were whipped and jailed. Eager to change the subject, he said, "Wilkins says that I can be a professor, once I decide between anatomy and astronomy. And it is preferred that scholars do not marry."

"He is. And you could if you wanted to. He would see to that. Boyle is lucky, he has three thousand pounds per annum from his father, the Earl of Cork. I wish I could afford his rooms. He has a whole house."

It was on High Street and it was the favourite meeting place for The Invisible College, even more than Wilkins' rooms in Wadham, for Boyle's laboratory was the best in Oxford because of his wealth and passion for chemistry. The instant Christopher reached it he felt urgency. Members of The Invisible College were there and while Cromwell and the Visitors had not arrived yet, Scarburgh anxiously awaited his coming. For a moment he felt as important as Cromwell. Then, dismissing that as vanity, and so, useless, he set up the apparatus with the single-minded concentration that had become characteristic of him. He made the laboratory more tidy, too, for Cromwell liked neatness, and the room resembled an apothecary shop—Boyle's love of chemistry caused him to hoard drugs and they were everywhere. Only when he was finished did he allow himself to observe who was there.

He was surprised to see Harvey sitting humbly in a corner. William Harvey looked very old—the physician must be almost eighty, thought Christopher—and was feeble, and could hardly walk from the gout.

But when Harvey got Christopher's attention, he murmured, "I was Warden of Merton until the surrender of Oxford to Parliament in 1646."

Scarburgh said, "This was where I met him. I studied at Merton."

Harvey said, "This experiment will show Cromwell the blood circulates."

Christopher wasn't so sure, but he was glad to see Harvey, who was joined by Oughtred, who was even older, but who possessed more energy.

Boyle examined the completed apparatus and he looked so severe that Christopher expected him to be critical, but Boyle was silent. The fourteenth child of the Earl of Cork was five years older than himself, and tall, over six feet, straight and thin, with a long, narrow nose, full, soft lips, and brown eyes.

By his side was John Locke, another former Westminster like Hooke, who had become a close friend of Boyle's, although he was Christopher's age.

Yet that was natural, reflected Christopher, for they resembled each other in many ways. Locke, too, was tall and thin, with long, lean features, a large nose, full lips, and heavy-lidded eyes that seemed bigger than they were and appeared to see everything. Boyle had introduced Locke, a King's Scholar at Christ Church, to The Invisible College. And they had other things in common. Both expressed disdain of women and they were interested in medicine but not in becoming doctors.

In a corner were two of the ablest physicians in Oxford, Jonathan Goddard and Thomas Sydenham. But their presence made Christopher uneasy, for Goddard, now Warden of Merton, had been Cromwell's body physician, while Sydenham, although he was younger than his colleague, in his thirties, and a good friend of Boyle and Locke, was an avowed Puritan.

His surprise grew when he saw his cousin, Matthew, and the poet, Abraham Cowley, in another corner. They were supposed to be studying medicine at Oxford, but he knew that everybody assumed this was a ruse, to give them protection while they spied for Charles Stuart.

Matthew had grown into a sturdy, muscular young man, clever at politics and intrigue, while Cowley—old to be studying medicine, Cowley was forty—possessed just a vestige of his once good looks.

They pretended to be as interested in the experiment as any one.

Matthew said, "Christopher, you must be at your best today."

Cowley said, "A good heart can work good medicine."

Scarburgh stepped forward and whispered to Christopher, "We must not allow anyone to stop us, whatever the risk. Hooke, fetch the dog."

Hooke was halted by a commotion outside. Armed guards appeared at the door followed by Cromwell, but when he saw who was in the room he dismissed them. Wilkins and Owens, the two Vice-Chancellors of Oxford, were behind Cromwell and Christopher realised they were the Visitors that Hooke feared.

Wilkins was their friend, he thought with relief. Then, as he saw the scowl on John Owens' face, he wondered if he was being optimistic.

Owens, Cromwell's chaplain during the civil wars, had been rewarded with the post of Dean of Christ Church, the most influential college in Oxford, and, as Vice-Chancellor, was the Puritan Visitor with Wilkins. The middle-aged Owens had the reputation of being athletic yet scholarly, musical yet pious, and much respected by Cromwell despite his arrogance and temper.

Owens preceded Wilkins and Christopher's apprehension grew as he saw Bagshaw with the Vice-Chancellor. Bagshaw, who had been Owens' protege as a King's Scholar at Christ Church, regarded the scene before him with contempt and Christopher felt there was mischief in Bagshaw and a need to destroy The Invisible College which had rejected him.

Yet neither Owens nor Wilkins dressed in the Puritan fashion. Both wore powdered wigs and velvet breeches. To outdo each other in importance, thought Christopher, but he noticed all eyes were on Cromwell, soberly wearing a plain black suit, grey worsted stockings, and simple, straight, unpowdered hair. The Lord Protector also had wound a heavy black scarf around his neck to protect himself from the cold and Christopher realised that Cromwell had aged. The Chancellor moved painfully, as if his leg ached; he kept his scarf on although there was good heat from the fireplace and he moved close to it. His face was stern as he stared at the apparatus, his features roughened by weather and lined by care, and when Wilkins suggested, "Oliver, would you like a chair?" he declined sharply, as if that were a libel on his person, and stated, "I have been informed that there are offences and disorders taking place here."

"And impieties," added Bagshaw, "Sire."

Owens said, "Many questions are being asked about the worth of these experiments. It is possible that they are tampering with God's work."

Christopher blurted out, "We are trying to improve God's work!"

"Altering the natural course of life?" questioned Bagshaw. "Sire, they intend to dissect a dog and destroy the life that God gave it."

Cromwell asked severely, "Wren, is that true?"

"No, sir. We are seeking to investigate the movement of the blood. And eventually, perhaps, to transfer it from one body to another."

Bagshaw exclaimed, "That is witchcraft!"

"Or, at least," added Owens, "a profanation of God's work, sire."

"Owens, be explicit. What is impious about this experiment?"

"Sire, they intend to divert the blood from its natural course."

"That is not so," Boyle said with passion. "Our methods do not lead to any conclusion inconsistent with the Bible. I am an authority on that."

"But learning is not enough," said Owens, "Faith is vital, too."

Bagshaw said, "Sire, Dean Owens is right. We must destroy this apparatus before it destroys us. We know the blood does not circulate."

He went to knock it off the table and Harvey, with a great effort of his will, lunged at him with drawn dagger. Christopher restrained Bagshaw with one hand and Harvey with the other. Bagshaw was surprised by Christopher's strength; he was knocked sprawling to the floor.

Owens shouted, "No swords or daggers are allowed in our Lord Protector's presence! We must arrest the two of them!"

Christopher thought Cromwell was going to summon his guards, for he agreed with Owens until Wilkins reminded him, "Oliver, it would be a blot on your good name to attack the person of our greatest doctor."

"Goddard is our best doctor."

"No, sire," said Goddard, "I bow before William Harvey."

"Sydenham, have you lost your Puritan sentiments, too?"

"No, sire. But while I don't agree with everything that is done here, in medicine Harvey is a master of observation."

"Owens, even our good Commonwealth physicians disagree with you."

"Chancellor, Harvey did draw his dagger."

"Steady, Owens, he is not going to cut off my head."

"He should die for his attack on you."

Harvey shrugged at Owens' anger and said, "We are all dying. Some sooner than others." He sat back, exhausted by his effort.

"Sire, he is implying . . ." Owens halted as Cromwell frowned and spoke.

"Wilkins, what do you think about this experiment?"

"Oliver, if it works it will increase your reputation."

"But Scarburgh is a Royalist and so is Christopher Wren."

"Here they are experimental philosophers."

"Wilkins, you have always favoured Wren. Why?"

"He is the best student I have. It would be criminal to allow his genius to be wasted."

"What is he doing now at Oxford?"

"He is taking his superior degree at All Souls."

"Oh, yes, I remember. You vetoed our first choice, Mr. Heron, in favour of Wren. It was the only time that the veto was used."

"Oliver, you approved."

"I hope I don't regret it. You know his cousin, Matthew, has no intention of pursuing medicine, and neither will Cowley. Every word I utter here will be reported back to their master, Charles Stuart."

"At least it will be reported accurately."

"I doubt it. However, let them stay. At least Charles Stuart will learn I am not afraid. That I do not wear a suit of armour underneath for fear of assassination. Wren, what is the purpose of this experiment?"

"Sir, it is Doctor Scarburgh's experiment. I am just his assistant."

"But the idea was yours. I have informants, too."

"Doctor Scarburgh is a skilful anatomist. I am a student."

Wilkins said, "We hope to prove that the blood does circulate, and to show that the blood can transport an object from one part of the body to another part. Which may explain how disease spreads. And help us understand whether it is possible to transfer blood from one animal to another. And perhaps, eventually, from one person to another."

Owens cried, "It is sacrilegious, against God's will! And impossible!"

Nothing is impossible, Christopher said to himself, if observation and experience lead us to it, but he said, "We cannot be sure until we try."

Bagshaw laughed scornfully and said, "Sire, all they will do is poison your realm. If not with their drugs, with their ideas."

Cromwell addressed Scarburgh, "You refused to serve me. Why should I permit you to use college property now?"

"It is for the common good. I may find a cure for the plague. Perhaps it is transmitted by the blood."

"Goddard, do you share his views?"

"Not completely."

Christopher waited for Scarburgh and himself to be dismissed.

Goddard added, "But he is a fine physician and whatever he learns will be of value to all of us. As Harvey's discoveries are already."

Owens said, "But sire, Harvey wears a sword even when you don't."

"I do not need a sword here. I am Chancellor here. Nothing else."

Wilkins said, "That is why I felt you would approve of our experiment."

"Will it cure the plague? Or any of the many ills that afflict us?"

Christopher said, "Sir, we cannot find out unless we try."

Cromwell deliberated, slow to convince, and yet, he thought, there was so much logic and sincerity in Wren it was difficult to resist him. And he didn't wish to be remembered only as a General. When he had become the Chancellor of Oxford he had been honoured and he had resolved to widen the learning in the university. Whatever his enemies said, he was not a barbarian. Sermons must not be neglected, but neither must learning. He saw that Owens was waiting intently and his disciple, Bagshaw, was smoothing his waistcoat which had been rumpled when Wren had knocked him down, and he smiled at the thought. He respected physical strength, especially in scholars; it was one of the things he liked about Owens. Perhaps Wilkins was right in favouring Wren. He declared solemnly, "*The mind is man. If that is kept pure, a man signifies something. If not, I would not see what difference there is between him and a beast.*"

Christopher asked, "Sir, may we start?"

"Yes." But when Hooke brought in the puppy they were to experiment on, Cromwell asked anxiously, "You will not butcher him? You will have mercy?"

Christopher said, "Sir, we do not seek this dog's death, but his help."

He gently caressed the terrier as Hooke placed him on the table and, on Scarburgh's instructions and because he had the steadiest hand, he performed the necessary incision on the hind leg. Then Boyle injected opium into the incision. The puppy struggled violently until the opium took effect; then the terrier lay upon the table motionless.

Cromwell shouted, "You are killing him. Owens is right. I must not favour such experiments. They are cruel, barbarous, against God."

Boyle said, "They *are* God's work. He transfers the blood from one body to another when we are born."

Locke said, "Sire, my connections with the Parliamentary Army are well known, but God would not forgive us if we failed to perform *His* work."

Cromwell snapped, "What do my doctors think? Goddard? Sydenham?"

Goddard spoke first, as befitted his age and position, "Sir, before we pass judgment, we must see if the dog lives."

"If it lives?" Cromwell said ominously. "Sydenham, your views?"

"Sire, I served with your army faithfully and I do not always agree with Scarburgh's views. And Wren, Boyle, and Locke are not even physicians, but they are observant men and we must not interfere with that."

Cromwell said, "They may continue. But only if the dog lives."

Bagshaw said, "Wren, I wager you ten shillings the dog dies."

Christopher was doubtful now, too, for the puppy lay as if dead, and he didn't reply, but Boyle said, "It is the opium. The blood has taken the narcotic to the brain. Yet the terrier is still alive. Sire, put your hand on his ribs and diaphragm and you will feel him breathing."

But Cromwell looked shaken, as if Boyle had suggested a perilous act, while Owens declared, "This is another form of witchcraft."

"Nonsense!" stated Oughtred. The aged mathematician sat with Harvey, to comfort his friend should the experiment fail, and he added, "I cannot endure such falsehoods in the name of scholarship. I am an experienced astrologer and very lucky in my judgment of nativities, and a great lover of chemistry, but anyone with sense and learning knows that witches do not appear in dogs, but in old women, chiefly widows."

This shook Christopher out of his doubts, for while many people believed in witches with Oughtred, including several of his friends, he did not. He put his hand on the diaphragm to confirm what Boyle said, and he was relieved, the dog was breathing. Suddenly, although he didn't like doing it, he slapped the dog. Cromwell was shocked and when the puppy didn't respond Owens and Bagshaw smiled triumphantly. Boyle massaged the dog, and yet, despite the breathing, it was motionless. They were working from rote, Christopher thought, and he tried to recall what was the most sensitive part of the puppy's body—observe, always observe, Harvey said—and abruptly, while it hurt him to do it, he hit the dog on the nose.

The puppy yelped, but it was the most welcome sound Christopher heard.

An excited Scarburgh put the dog on the floor while Boyle whipped him, saying, "This will improve his circulation. Dispel the narcotic from his brain." The puppy, although it whimpered pitifully, was able to stand.

Christopher sat down, disregarding everybody else, and lovingly took the puppy on his lap and patted it gently until it licked his hand.

Now Cromwell desired to see the telescope in the Tower of Wadham, so Christopher, leaving the dog in the care of Hooke—the puppy had become important—led the Lord Protector to his

telescope. Goddard, Wilkins, and Owens stood behind Cromwell—
the others stayed in the laboratory to observe the dog further—
and Cromwell asked him, "Are you an astrologer?"

"No. My chief pursuits are anatomy, astronomy, and
architecture."

"We do not need surveyors, but we could use scholars."

Goddard said, "Sire, Christopher could be an outstanding
physician."

"I believe it," said Cromwell. "But what does the young man
desire?"

"Medicine is so imprecise. There is so little we can cure."

"You pursued your experiment although it was dangerous and
unknown."

"Sir, did that ever stop you?"

"Wren, that was different. I saw an end in view. Could you
pump new blood into my old veins? Give me blood that is eager
for life?"

"Some day, perhaps, but not yet, although I think we could do
that with dogs. But we don't know enough about the anatomy of
the body. We know hardly anything. We cannot cure one single
case of the plague."

"So my doctors tell me. When I complain about the ague, Goddard
says God is merciful, prayers will be said for me and the pain grows
worse."

Goddard said, "That is why our experiments must be continued,
sire."

"Owens, are there many prayers in the university these days?"

"Yes, sire."

"For me, no doubt?"

"No doubt, sire."

"Do not flatter, Owens. I know there is gutter vituperation against
my character. Each church that is ravaged, every one who is slain
unfairly is blamed on me. But some men hate me honestly, no
doubt. Do you, Wren?"

"I do not hate you."

"Even though Matthew Wren is still in the Tower?"

"That is wrong, sir."

"I would free him, if he would accept our authority. But he prefers
to hate me. It gives him more pleasure and a sense of righteousness."

"I try not to hate anybody."

"You are rare. Our countrymen's greatest joy is to hate and they
do it passionately. On both sides. The Royalists should know how
often I have had to restrain my Puritan friends."

Goddard said, "You must relax, sire, you've just come out of a
sick bed."

Cromwell grimaced as if the physician revealed something he preferred hidden, but he said, "My health is not of my choosing. But Owens has been after me to stop the experiments and I had to see for myself."

"It is witchcraft. You saw how they brought that dog back to life."

"Owens, I wish they could put some young blood into my veins."

"Sire, you are going to live a long time."

"Do not exaggerate. I look in my glass. I am mortal."

Goddard said, "That is why I am interested in the nature of the blood. Perhaps, if I inject you, I could drive the vapors from your system."

"No!" Cromwell was emphatic. "That was a foul draught you put into the dog. It could have poisoned him. But it was an interesting experiment."

Wilkins asked, "Then you approve, Oliver?"

"I observe. Approve? That depends on whether it is God's work. Wren, do you think astronomy is God's work?"

"It is *His* universe, sir."

"Do you intend to pursue astronomy?"

Christopher hesitated, and thought, Cromwell believed he didn't have long to live whatever the doctors said, and he did appear to prefer outspokenness, as long as it wasn't political or theological.

"Come, young man, do not be afraid."

"After what happened to Galileo, I am not sure."

Cromwell's voice rose as he retorted, "We are not the Inquisition. That was why the Great Rebellion took place. I would not have become Lord Protector if it were not necessary."

A cruel necessity, reflected Christopher, as he saw Cromwell's hand shake from fatigue and strain.

Wilkins repeated insistently, "You do approve of what we do here?"

"You are Vice-Chancellor. You and John Owens."

Owens stated, "I do not approve. There is much impiety here. Many students like Wren do not support our views or attend our sermons."

"Yes," said Cromwell, "I hear the Puritan Visitors have forbidden oaths, whores, drinking, gambling, and other sports."

Owens said, "The students study and pray."

"What do they do for diversion?"

Wilkins said, "That is why experimental philosophy is vital."

"That is your view. But can you be sure that every man, inside of himself, John Wilkins, studies and prays as you wish?"

"I do not try, Oliver. I do not resent a difference of opinion. And I do not believe you do either, as long as you are allowed your own."

Christopher expected Cromwell to castigate Wilkins and for an instant the Lord Protector was stern, staring at his future brother-in-law with cold, unsmiling eyes. Then Cromwell, as if other thoughts penetrated his slow, deliberate brain, straightened with some of his military vigour, and said, "Owens, may God protect you if you persecute learning."

"I punish impiety, witchcraft, and disloyalty."

"In your eyes they are the same thing. Wilkins, may I have your hand? These winding steps are treacherous and my vision is not as good as it once was. England would be a silent, melancholy land without learning. I have been warned never to lose the friendship of scholars, or God will think less of me. Wren, I hope those who work here will be my friends, not my servants. Although your versatility could be a curse."

Only Goddard remained in the Tower of Wadham to help Christopher fix the telescope, and he sensed it was really to talk to him.

When the others were gone, Goddard said, "Christopher, you should become a physician. You have a rare talent for anatomy and observation."

"But I do not love medicine. Often I do not even respect it."

"Anatomy could lead to quick and great advancement."

"I could become Cromwell's body physician as you were?"

"In some ways you are as unforgiving as your uncle."

"Yet if I could cure Cromwell all experiments would be allowed?"

"No man can cure him. He has his old trouble, a stone in his kidney, aggravated from so much time in the saddle, yet he refuses to give up riding. It is his great passion. He claims he is the best judge of a horse in England, that when he cannot ride he doesn't want to live."

They were interrupted by Matthew, who was very excited.

Goddard bowed to him and said, "Excuse me, Christopher. I'm sure your cousin wishes to speak to you alone."

Goddard was gone before Christopher could answer and Matthew declared, "He will warn Oliver Protector against us, but one of these days it won't matter, the Usurper will be dead. He is clearly not well."

Matthew's tone was so gloating Christopher was disturbed. He did not hate the Lord Protector, although he knew, as a Wren, he was supposed to. He didn't know how he felt about Oliver Cromwell.

Matthew said triumphantly, "As soon as the Usurper is gone from Oxford, Cowley will inform our King of Oliver Protector's poor health."

Christopher was relieved that Hooke stood in the doorway, giving him an excuse not to answer. But Hooke was upset.

"Our puppy is gone, Christopher. I thought he might have followed you here, his trust of you was plain, but he must have been stolen."

"Are you sure?"

"It is likely. He is a famous dog now."

Matthew said irritably, angry that Christopher was more interested in Hooke's news, "The loss of the cur is a trifle compared to our knowledge of Cromwell's uncertain health. That could affect all of us."

That annoyed Hooke and he retorted, even sharper than Matthew, "This is the trouble with all you politicians, you are all biased. You think your affairs really matter. But we cannot observe the experiment truthfully until we see the after-effects on the subject."

Christopher said, "Perhaps we will find him."

"It is not likely. The puppy is very valuable now. Unless Bagshaw did away with him, to destroy our experiment." Hooke looked ready to weep as he added, "Christopher, God must be punishing me because I agreed to hear Wilkins preach at St. Paul's and I said I would try to persuade you to join me."

"How could you? With my father robbed and my uncle in the Tower?"

"Wilkins said, '*If I preach there, it will not be destroyed.*' And I wanted to thank him for supporting us. Do you have any idea where Circulate may be?"

"Who?"

"The puppy. I named him Circulate in honour of Harvey."

"No."

Then Hooke smiled. "We did prove Harvey is right. With Wilkins' help. Will you come with me to St. Paul's? Wilkins is preaching next week."

Matthew cut in. "Of course not. Christopher is not a fool."

Christopher was annoyed. His cousin didn't speak for him; no one did. He was curious what Wilkins would say. He said, "Let us try to find Circulate. I will decide about St. Paul's and Wilkins later."

Surely Surely And Then Unsurely

Surely surely and then unsurely
Unsurely unsurely and then surely
Unhampered unhampered and then hampered
Hampered hampered and then unhampered
Surely surely and then unsurely

Stymean Karlen

14

Surely Surely And Then Unsurely

CHRISTOPHER TOLD HIMSELF THAT HE WAS ATTENDING WILKINS'
sermon at St. Paul's only because he wanted to see what had
happened to the cathedral, but he was curious also to observe what
his friend would preach. He and Hooke sat down beside John
Evelyn, whom he was surprised to find here. Evelyn was an avowed
and passionate Royalist whom he had met at Oxford. And, he
reflected, a dilettante who was interested in all the arts and master
of none, except his own views, which were very opinionated.

Evelyn was as surprised to see them as they were him. He
apologised at once for his presence. "I do not approve of Wilkins'
text, but he is a worthy and most obliging person and he would be
offended if I declined his invitation. Wren, won't your father resent
your presence here? The Usurper has just prohibited all ministers of
the Church of England from preaching and St. Paul's is our most
important ministry."

"Perhaps. But that is not why I am here." He wondered how
this slight, dark, middle aged landowner with his private means,
who considered himself a great traveller, connoisseur, and critic of
architecture, could judge Wilkins' text when Evelyn hadn't heard it
yet.

Hooke was still lamenting the loss of Circulate, although that
had occurred several weeks ago. He told Evelyn, "Scarburgh was
disconsolate."

Evelyn replied, "He has noble Royalist sentiments. It might be
revenge on the part of the Puritans. Was Cromwell present when
the dog vanished?"

"No. Oughtred thinks it could have been witchcraft."

"Our esteemed mathematician visited me recently. He is a
renowned astrologer and he told me that his experiments incline
him to strong apprehensions of some extraordinary event to happen

255

soon, perhaps the death of Cromwell. Cowley tells me the Usurper looks ill. I saw the poet just before he left to inform our rightful Sovereign of the hopeful news. Hooke, you have medical experience, do you think the Usurper is ailing?"

"Yes. His hand shook as he greeted us and his movements were feeble."

Both sounded so pleased with the possibility that Cromwell might die soon that Christopher could not endure their conversation. He turned his attention to St. Paul's while he waited for Wilkins to speak.

He was appalled by the devastation about him. The Puritan soldiers were gone, some of the scaffolding that supported the roof had been removed, and there were about a hundred people waiting for the sermon to start, but it was plain that St. Paul's present masters were treating the cathedral without reverence or affection. None of the damage he had witnessed during the trial of Charles had been repaired, but only had grown worse. A large portion of the roof where the scaffolding had been removed had collapsed and had reduced the south transept to a melancholy ruin. Nothing was being cared for. Vandalism dominated. Tombs had been broken into and robbed, more windows were smashed, screens were ripped and demolished, glass was scattered across the floor. Wherever he looked there was dirt and disorder. Even paving had vanished. To be used elsewhere, he decided; everything had been done that would humiliate the cathedral. Most foreboding, he observed, was the attitude of the Puritans. Now that they had diminished the grandeur, importance, and beauty of St. Paul's, they were allowing the cathedral to perish of its own weight, as much by neglect as anything else. It was no wonder, he thought, that when Jones had returned to London in 1652 to observe what had happened to his beloved portico, the sight of the broken cathedral with the mean shops under his great columns had speeded his death. The fabric, left without care or consideration, was decaying at a frightening rate. He told himself sadly, One hard blow from fate or man and the venerable cathedral could collapse. St. Paul's was standing, but just barely. The old foundation needed a new foundation.

Evelyn wondered why Wren was so solemn. He was certain he had not misjudged him. After he met him two years ago at Oxford in the company of his dear and excellent friend, Dr. Wilkins, he wrote in his diary, his most precious possession, where he kept his private thoughts: "*I visited that miracle of youth, Christopher Wren, that prodigious scholar and nephew of the Bishop of Ely, now sadly confined to the Tower, who presented me with a piece of white marble, which he had stained with a lovely red, very deep, as beautiful as if it had been natural. And he has contrived many other inventions too numerous to mention.*"

It would be foolish for a young man of such talents to think of becoming a surveyor, Evelyn decided, yet Wren was regarding St. Paul's with such intensity the older man felt this was his innate desire.

He hurried to warn him, "To be a surveyor today you would be no better than a carpenter or a plasterer, or at the best, a master mason."

Christopher answered, "Wilkins would prefer that I pursue astronomy. To verify his speculations about the moon. He thinks it could be habitable."

"Interesting. Did you hear now the Jews are admitted?"

"No." Christopher wondered if that would bring Daniel back to London.

"Yes. It was the Usurper's doing. Next, he will sell them St. Paul's."

"I doubt that." He wished Evelyn would find a better way to spend his time. He was glad Wilkins was starting; now Evelyn would have to be quiet.

Wilkins observed, "Obedience is preferable to sacrifice."

Evelyn whispered, "A most obliging fellow. He has taken great pains to preserve our universities from the ignorant, sacrilegious soldiers who, if they had their way, would demolish all places that cultivate learning."

Wilkins added, "All men should be free, however, to worship as they please, as long as their faith doesn't lead them to disturb peace or order."

Christopher thought, He hadn't met anyone who contended earnestly for toleration of Dissenters who wasn't one himself. His mind drifted back to the cathedral as he speculated on what he would do if—even as he knew it was an impossible if—he was given the power to repair St. Paul's. He was deep in reconstruction, although he wondered whether that was sensible, whether it wouldn't be wiser to tear down the entire edifice and build a new cathedral, when Wilkins' tone became sombre. This was unusual and now he listened intently as his patron and teacher preached:

"If we do not heal our wounds we will come to the dire end John Donne predicted in his last sermon as Dean of St. Paul's. He said, *'If we do not mend our ways the whole world will be but an universal graveyard, our common grave, and the life and motion that the greatest persons have in it, but as the shaking of buried bodies in their grave, as by an earthquake.'*"

Christopher recalled these words as he stood by his father's side a few months later and saw that whatever the doctor did the patient grew worse. May had come, bringing spring to William Holder's

I

garden in Bletchington which his father loved, but Dean Wren was too feeble to stroll in it or to sit up and view it from his bed. He had just arrived from London by horse express, where he had been discussing the post of Professor of Astronomy at Gresham, for which he was being considered on the recommendation of Wilkins, and his father was even worse than he expected.

Dean Wren lay motionless, a shrunken shell of the man that Christopher knew, looking far older than his sixty-five. Dr. Horace Arne was saying, "Good! It is better that he sleeps. He needs the rest."

But Christopher thought that he was unconscious.

Then, as if his father knew Christopher was there, Dean Wren stirred, opened his eyes and recognised his son. Dean Wren stared at him for a moment and suddenly, by sheer force of will, he murmured, "I remember Donne preaching how lame and crippled we are without God. You are not going to pursue science, are you, son? John Donne predicted that science would destroy God if we did not put it to God's use."

"Answer him," Susan whispered. "It gives him a will to live."

Christopher remembered that Donne had, in a different mood, praised science, but he said, "Father, I always heed what you say."

"The skies are cloudy today, aren't they?"

There must be a mist before his father's eyes, he thought, for the sky was clear, but he answered, "Yes, father. As you say . . ."

"As God says!" retorted Dean Wren with some of his old vigour. "I fear your devotion to astronomy. Since Copernicus and Galileo it treats our earth, God's earth, as if it were a mere province of the world."

His father was quoting Donne again, but he didn't mention that, not wanting to upset him, and he changed the subject, asking, "How can we help you, father? I have some experience in anatomy . . ."

"Are you going to be a doctor instead of an astronomer?"

"Father, you must conserve your energy."

"I will have plenty of time for that in the hereafter. Are you?"

"I don't know. But first, we must help you."

"Sometimes, I think it is my old trouble, the stone, but when I have fainting fits, heats and chills, I wonder if it is the dropsy, only sometimes, too, my stomach swells and I think I'll die of the cramps."

"What does Dr. Arne say it is?" The small, spry, elderly physician was busy mixing a prescription to give his patient, now that his patient was conscious and able to absorb his drugs.

"He doesn't tell me." Dean Wren fell back exhausted while Dr. Arne hurried to his side to administer the prescription.

Dr. Arne forced his patient's jaws open to pour in his drugs and as they penetrated Dean Wren he lapsed into unconsciousness.

"What are you giving him?" Christopher cried. The smell was repulsive and made him sick.

Dr. Arne said, "I've stopped bleeding him. It hasn't helped. And the purgatives have weakened him. So I've prepared some drugs and herbs that cured Queen Elizabeth when she was very ill with the dropsy."

"But my father looks as if his kidney or liver have been affected."

"Yes, they could be diseased. One cannot be sure. But, at least," Dr. Arne said with satisfaction, "We know it is not the plague or smallpox. I will look in later. There is a woman in the village I must see. They say she has been touched by a witch and I must drive the vapours from her. If what I have given the Dean doesn't help, we will try the dried flesh of viper, it is a very useful cordial and it is said to cure a stone in the kidney."

When he departed Christopher said they should change doctors.

"But who?" replied Holder. "Scarburgh has gone to the continent to treat the royal family, Harvey is too old and feeble to even leave his chair, and Goddard and Sydenham are in Oxford, and your father would never allow them to treat him. For they are supporters of Cromwell, and he would say that it is sacrilegious. He abhors Cromwell . . ."

His father stirred, as if the word Cromwell was a bell in his brain, and he mumbled, "Christopher, did they force you to take the oath of submission at Oxford? The oath of allegiance to Cromwell?"

"No."

"I was told all students were supposed to."

"Yes, they were supposed to, but John Wilkins did not insist."

"Is that why you heard him preach at St. Paul's? I'm sure in the Presbyterian fashion. Christopher, have you given up my faith?"

Dean Wren tried to sit up again, but his persistent weakness returned and Christopher sat down on the edge of the bed beside him, took his hand, and assured him, "Father, I will always remain faithful to your Church."

"Promise?"

"I promise."

His father managed to smile as he said, "I can face my maker now."

Christopher almost shouted as he saw his father drifting off, "You will live a long time yet. Susan and William and I will see to that."

His father said weakly, "God may will otherwise."

"If we consulted another doctor, perhaps he could help you."

"Dr. Arne is my doctor. I have known his family all my life. His father attended Elizabeth, and he has the most wit in his family and other excellencies and he is a good Anglican, loyal to the Stuarts."

Then, as if that was settled, Dean Wren became unconscious again, although this time he twitched and squirmed and moaned.

By the time Dr. Arne returned that night Christopher was sure his father was near death. He and William sat by his side and Susan's gentle hand on her father's brow seemed to soothe him, for his moaning stopped and the patient lay quietly, but Christopher was horrified by his own feeling of futility. There was nothing to do but to wait. He was mystified by his father's illness and powerless to help him. Yet he was positive that Dr. Arne knew even less than himself. The physician kept saying they must guard against convulsions, but his father was inert. And Arne forced more drugs into him that had been given Elizabeth, each more repulsive than the previous one, until the patient's teeth grew black and his breath foul.

Yet when Christopher protested, mentioning Harvey's belief that nature was the great healer, Arne ignored his patient to denounce Harvey, "A quack! It is no wonder the Circulator hesitated for years to publish his conclusions about the blood. None of my contemporaries accepted them. Or his patients either. When his book, *The Circulation of the Blood*, was published finally, his practice fell mightily until no one would go to him, they knew he was crackbrained. Wren, I'm doing everything I can. I've memorised Aristotle and Galen and the aphorisms of Hippocrates. The classical texts must be true because they are classical. I am an authority on herbs. I will try medical waters. They come from Astrop. Astrop is unfashionably situated, to the north of Oxfordshire, but the mineral properties of the water has therapeutic value."

Dr. Arne ignored their protests and poured the water into the patient and Christopher felt a flicker of hope as his father revived.

Dean Wren sat up as if the medical waters had given him strength, although he held his stomach as if that hurt, eyed his son and said, "I wanted you admitted to Holy Orders."

"I know. But I couldn't, father. That is not my nature."

"But I did give you a sound religious education. When you bury me, you will use the Anglican ritual and prayer book. Or I will be damned."

Holder said, "Dean Wren, we will do whatever you desire."

"Even though it is forbidden?"

"Even though it is forbidden," Christopher repeated, and Susan nodded.

"Good. Doctor, will you leave me alone with my family, please?"

Arne was irritated, but when Dean Wren insisted he stepped into the parlour while Christopher, Susan, and Holder moved closer to the dying man.

"I didn't want him to hear me. He is a worthy doctor, but talkative. Christopher, when the Stuarts return, give the King whatever I have preserved of the Garter. It will please him and it will help you."

Christopher said, "You must live to do that yourself."

His father smiled wanly and said, "I would like to see the Stuarts return. But it is not likely. Have you decided on your future?"

"Not yet, father."

"God has given you many talents. But a mistake here will be like that of marriage and war, it admits of no repentance."

Dean Wren remained in a sitting position after he said that and when Christopher replied, "I hope you will approve of my choice," his father didn't answer him but seemed to be staring into space. Then, with a sudden gasp, he fell back on the bed and Christopher didn't have to call Dr. Arne to know that his father was dead.

After Dean Wren's funeral, which was conducted exactly as he had requested, Christopher resumed his studies at All Souls, but now much of it seemed irrelevant. Despite what he knew of anatomy it had not helped his father. He informed Wilkins that he had no wish to become a medical doctor, or even to take his degree as Cowley was—to protect himself as Cowley was while serving the Stuarts—or as Boyle and Locke were, to pursue medical research and chemistry as experimental philosophers. And when Wilkins asked him why he was so critical of medicine, he replied sadly, "So much of medicine is going from uncertainty to uncertainty."

The following year, when he was offered the post of Professor of Astronomy at Gresham on the recommendation of Wilkins, he accepted. He was not sure it was the best choice he could make, for he would be the youngest professor at Gresham, only twenty-four, when most of the professors were twice that age, and Rooke, whom he was succeeding, had a distinguished reputation, but he would be close to St. Paul's and other parts of London that he loved, and there was still much to learn about the heavens.

Wilkins was pleased with his decision. He said, "Astronomy is a place where you can settle down for good, feel secure in; and call home."

Christopher didn't answer. They were standing in his new rooms at Gresham and he had just learned that he had to be at Gresham only one day a week and that he could continue to live in Oxford, and he wasn't as sure as Wilkins that astronomy was his first love. If St. Paul's ever was rebuilt, as he was coming to believe was necessary, better materials and methods must be found than had been used for the present cathedral.

Wilkins said, "You can become a *virtuoso*. Another Galileo."

But he wanted to be only a Wren, a Christopher Wren. As he sat by his telescope at Gresham and stared at the stars, he kept thinking of the nature of building materials.

After the Last Shot on the Field of Battle

After the last shot on the field of battle
Each one politely asked: DID WE HURT YOU?

Stymean Karlen

¹5

After the Last Shot on the Field of Battle

"Christopher, do you really think the earth revolves around the sun?"

He thought, Elizabeth Cromwell Claypole asked this as if she expected the earth to come out of one ear and the sun out of the other, but he smiled as he answered, "As your father revolves around yourself."

"My estimable father only revolves around *himself*. In his role of Lord Protector, which he guards carefully, he regards all the people of England as his children. And he treats them like children, actually."

"But you do have a special place in his heart. Don't you?"

"As Copernicus and Galileo have in yours, Christopher?"

He didn't reply, not certain how to respond. The views of these two astronomers possessed many moments of truth, he reflected, but they were not peaceful teachers. Yet he didn't like them to be ridiculed. They had not studied for glory or gold or to limit God, but had been scholars of great strength and purpose who had pursued their investigations because of their faith and from a need to find Him everywhere. And one central fact about them comforted him: Copernicus and Galileo both had studied medicine before they had turned to astronomy.

He and Elizabeth were standing in the Claypole parlour waiting for the maid to serve dinner. It had become a weekly custom for him to have dinner with the Claypoles the day he was in London to teach at Gresham. But always, he knew, at *her* invitation. The Claypoles resided on Cheapside, near Gresham and Guildhall— Richard Claypole's favourite location in London, for this wealthy Northamptonshire squire considered them the centre of the city's intellectual and mercantile life—and their large house contained a fine garden, often interesting visitors, and a clear, direct view of St.

Paul's. But now she was so insistent that the earth was the centre of the universe that Christopher was uneasy. Usually he preferred to be alone with her, but this evening he was relieved when they were joined by her husband, Richard Claypole.

Claypole asked, "Am I permitted to comment?"

Her husband was sullen, thought Christopher, as if Claypole was jealous, but he said, "Of course. We were discussing astronomy."

"Does Elizabeth still think the sun revolves around the earth?"

She said tartly, "Whatever I think, it is my own view."

"But not Wilkins' view, who you admire. Or your father's. Or Wren's."

"I'm not sure what my father thinks of astronomy. Are you, Richard?"

Claypole was silent. He was not one to question the Lord Protector. Only she did, she didn't fear anyone, not even her formidable father.

They sat down at the table which was set for several extra places, Christopher observed, and which possessed an elegance that was remarkable compared to the bleakness of most Puritan homes. Yet was Elizabeth a Puritan, he wondered. He knew that Claypole wasn't, a Cavalier who had attracted her because he was so different from her father's friends. Nothing about her household suggested the austerity of Puritanism. He was delighted with the gold candle-sticks, the solid china, the slender forks and knives of silver, imported from Italy, and rarely seen in England. Elizabeth Claypole was reputed to keep one of the best tables in London and Christopher could believe that as the maid brought in white wine instead of beer and many courses of flesh and fowl. Before anything was touched, Elizabeth said grace. Christopher followed, it was in his father's fashion, but Claypole waited until he was sure no one else saw him.

Then Elizabeth offered a toast. "To Christopher's astronomy! To whatever you believe! Even that the world is flat! And stands still!"

Now he felt she was teasing. He grinned, although Claypole gritted his teeth. What a strange marriage, he thought. How could they sleep together? At twenty-nine Elizabeth was one of the more interesting and attractive friends he had, while Claypole was one of the dullest. She had been named after her father's mother, who had been the greatest influence on him, and after, also, the great Queen, the ruler that Cromwell admired the most, for Queen Elizabeth had been thrifty and prudent, qualities Cromwell respected in a sovereign.

She said, "If the world is round we would fall off."

He smiled as she wished. Elizabeth was slim, pretty, with vivacious brown eyes, red curls that were un-puritan; and tonight she wore a lovely green dress that was cut low and revealing like a court lady.

She said, "I don't need morals to show me how to dress."

Claypole frowned but he didn't interrupt his eating. He professes a passionate interest in astronomy, thought Christopher, and he cultivates me in the hope I will recommend that he be admitted to The Invisible College, but he is not qualified, he is a champion of the banal, he comprehends only the obvious. Yet Christopher sensed this was Claypole's way of striking a bargain. If he was allowed to enter The Invisible College, he would allow the professor to court his wife. Christopher knew that if not for Elizabeth's beauty and charm he wouldn't be sitting here.

Hoping he wasn't noticed, he gazed at the long-boned Cavalier, who was older than his wife, a tall, thin, nasal-speaking country-man who affected London manners, but whose features were without distinction.

Claypole blurted out, "Wren, haven't you ever thought of marrying?"

"I haven't time."

"You would be a good catch. Unless you are not interested in women."

Christopher saw Elizabeth pause in her eating as she waited for his answer and he replied carefully, "I have great admiration for attractive women, especially one as charming as your wife, but I hope to be a professor at Oxford some day and female attachments are frowned upon."

"The old prohibitions against marriage have been removed."

"Not in spirit. The monastical tradition is still favoured."

"Your mentor, Dr. John Wilkins, is married."

"He is a Vice-Chancellor. He can live outside the university walls. But no master, provost, head of a house, or fellow that I know is married."

Elizabeth said, "Wilkins' was a political marriage. My aunt, Robina, has some wit and learning, but Wilkins always leaves her in Oxford. But Christopher might change his mind if the right woman came along."

He wondered: Did she think he was pure water? Elizabeth possessed many of the qualities he craved in a wife: she was slender, straight, yet his own height, with a graceful walk, beautiful hands; she loved to ride fast and dance energetically; she was blessed with courage and a natural elegance of mind that led her to prefer the ritual of his father's Church to the drabness of Puritanism. She had adopted its tenets even though consideration for her father pointed in the opposite direction. He said, "You are right, Elizabeth, but so far the right woman hasn't appeared."

Claypole waited for his wife to respond, but she regarded

Christopher intently, thinking, She didn't desire to be flirtatious, but this youthful scholar, although he was slighter and shorter than her husband, almost diminutive, was not a fraud like Claypole, but suggested virility with his strong, wide face, his resolute jaw. His silence was more potent than anything Claypole said. His features were no mask but were the man himself. He rode beautifully, his hands were firm, and she liked that he was clean-skinned and wore no wig and kept his breath clean. But she must not crave. It would devastate her father. Of all his six children she was his favourite, she knew, although he was affectionate to each of them. Claypole had become an unripe fruit, but Christopher was a blossom just about to bloom. "Do not wait too long," she said to him emotionally, "yet perhaps," with sudden bitterness, "you are wise to wait."

They were starting the main course when Cromwell entered without any guard, as if he had been here many times and felt at home. He had aged cruelly since Christopher had seen him two years ago at Oxford, but when he saw Elizabeth his sombre features brightened and he looked much better as his daughter embraced him and kissed him warmly.

Wilkins followed, wearing so much powder in his hair, reflected Christopher, he could have discharged a battery of cannons, and his velvet jacket was as splendid as any King Charles had favoured.

Cromwell nodded curtly to Christopher and Claypole, while Wilkins shook Christopher's hand affectionately and greeted Claypole pleasantly.

Elizabeth wanted to know how her father felt and Claypole asked, too.

"Better, Betty, when I see you. You are the best cure for pain I possess. God knows, the weather is oppressing. The streets are so uncomfortable, even in a coach and six. Mud, mud, mud. It has rained all day and now it is grey and chilly. I'm glad you have a good fire." He stood by her fireplace, warming himself, and shed his black cloak.

He was a husk of the man he had been, thought Christopher, for Cromwell's drab grey garb added to his sallowness and as he joined them at the table, with Wilkins behind him, he moved stiffly and awkwardly like an old man.

Elizabeth asked with concern, "Father, where are your guards?"

"Outside, Betty dear, with a grand show of burning and lighting of torches. As if to announce my presence to any would-be assassin."

Claypole said piously, "Sire, no one would dare such an attempt."

Cromwell shrugged, not wanting to worry his daughter, and said, "With my own family I must simply be just their father."

Elizabeth insisted that he sit beside her, moving Claypole away.

Cromwell glowed with pleasure and for an instant Christopher saw their resemblance: her face was round like his and she had inherited his force and purpose—it was in their eyes—but then, as the candles flickered Cromwell looked very old and tired again and she seemed distracted.

What am I? She asked herself. A daughter of Cromwell or a daughter of God? He is no king even though he is surrounded by soldiers. She asked, "Christopher, do the sun and earth ever quarrel with each other?"

"If they did, I doubt we would be sitting here."

Cromwell said, "Wilkins tells me you are a professor of astronomy now."

"Yes. At Gresham College."

"I thought your genius lay in medicine. And inventions. Have you any new ones? Like the one you showed me at Oxford?"

"None of any importance, sir."

Wilkins said, "He is too modest. He has fifty, all of consequence."

Cromwell asked, "But nothing that will stop pain? Or death?"

"That is in God's hands." said Christopher.

"You sound like my doctors. They talk much and cure little."

"Father, do you believe that the earth revolves around the sun?"

"Betty, we must not denounce learning even if we do not always understand it. Does your astronomer friend believe it? Do you, Wren?"

"Sir, I believe we must not take anything for granted."

"In learning," added Wilkins.

Cromwell looked sceptical but he listened.

"Oliver, it is only fifty years ago the telescope was invented. Fifty years exactly. In 1608. By a Dutchman who didn't know how to use it. No one knew until Galileo learned to observe through it, the first man to see a heavenly body, the moon, as it really was. Think, Oliver, now we can see Mars, Venus, and Saturn in the sky apart from the moon. After thousands of years in darkness in a few years we have learned more about the universe than Aristotle or Ptolemy or any of the ancients discovered in centuries. We are on the edge of a great age and you could be famous as one of those who encouraged it."

"Even if I don't always understand it, Wilkins?"

"I don't always understand it. None of us do. Not even Galileo."

"Wren, do you comprehend the heavens?"

"Not completely. But that is not our concern."

"What is, professor?"

"To observe. To discover. To find the design of the universe. It is a grand tapestry and we are trying to find the threads."

Cromwell sighed heavily and said, "It is difficult. Sometimes, I fear, we will see everything in the heavens but God."

"We will see Him, too," said Christopher. "In its purpose and design."

"God willing," said Cromwell. "Professor, you are persuasive." He turned to Wilkins and added, "We will grant your request for a new telescope, as long as it doesn't lessen our faith in God."

"*And you will be remembered as a star whom the whole world honours.*"

"I would prefer to be a good father."

There was little conversation then, as if everyone was hungry now. But when the dessert was served, fruit and tarts which Elizabeth favoured, although her father ate only an apple, saying, "Too much food clouds the brain," she said with deep feeling, as if she had been pondering this ever since the Lord Protector had arrived, "Father, I hear you intend to arrest and try Dr. Hewer, my dear friend and confessor."

Cromwell, who had been cheerful the last few minutes, frowned and replied wearily, "You mustn't distress yourself with affairs of state."

"Then he is to be tried."

"It is said he has been communicating with Charles Stuart."

"But the sin you really hold against him is that he married me in a Church of England service in St. Gregory's, next to St. Paul's."

"Betty, I do not indulge in such behaviour." Tears filled Cromwell's eyes and he said with sudden tenderness, "I wish only your happiness."

"Spare him. He is a good man. He loves God as much as you do."

Elizabeth spoke eloquently about Dr. Hewer's virtues but the more she praised him, the more unhappy Cromwell became. When his silence didn't halt her, he said abruptly, "Wren, your uncle has been long in the Tower."

"He has, sir. Almost sixteen years. He bears his affliction with great patience and resignation."

Cromwell gazed at Elizabeth until he was certain she would hear him. When he saw that she was listening, he said, "He may come out if he will."

"Now? You offered that years ago and he refused."

"Age can mellow a man. I do not insist that he worship as I do, but only that he obeys the laws of the land."

"Father, what has this to do with Dr. Hewer?"

"*Betty, I am tender towards all even when they are of different judgments. If the poorest Christian, the most mistaken Christian, shall desire to live peaceably and quietly, to lead but a life of godliness and honesty, let him be protected.*"

Christopher stood up, determined not to waste any more time while the Lord Protector was in this benevolent mood, and asked him, "You will permit me to take my uncle this from your own mouth?"

"You may."

It was many years since Christopher had seen his uncle. Seven or eight, he didn't remember exactly, and he expected to find an infirm, tottering old man. Cromwell's safe conduct pass opened all the necessary doors the following morning, and Christopher was relieved there were no withered heads spiked on the entrance to the Tower, the Traitor's Gate, or on nearby London Bridge. This was a kind of peace and order, he felt, although he knew there was much discontent with the Lord Protector. But Matthew, although he was seventy-one and fourteen years older than Cromwell, was not infirm or tottering and had aged less. While his uncle was even thinner than before and his features had continued to sharpen with his imprisonment, he moved with surprising vigour as he embraced his nephew.

Christopher thought, His uncle was determined to outlive Cromwell.

Matthew had been moved to the larger Bell Tower and Christopher was pleased to see a good fireplace in his cell, three pointed windows with stone heads and deep stone window seats and space enough to pace. The Yeoman warder stood outside the great oaken door. Thanks to Cromwell's personal pass, reflected Christopher, they were being allowed the most blessed of privileges in the Tower—privacy.

"I have more comfort," growled his uncle, "but I am, as you see, still under lock and key. I am their most important prisoner now. Elizabeth was confined here before she was Queen, in the reign of her half-sister, Mary. By Mary. But why should I complain. I was born when Elizabeth was Queen, just a few years before the Armada. They were grave days, too."

"You look . . ." Christopher paused, not sure how to express himself.

"Better than you expected!" snapped Matthew, pacing agitatedly. "They permit me to walk on the leads, from the door of the Bell Tower to the Beauchamp Tower, but always with a guard behind me and one in front, but at least I am allowed light and air and some movement. But I don't see why they are nervous about me. The walls are eight feet thick. The Normans built these cells for eternity. Yet I should feel honoured to be here. Thomas More, the Lord Chancellor, was confined here, and so was John Fisher, Bishop of Rochester, and both were executed for refusing to accept Henry VIII as the supreme head of the Church. And were canonised. Can I behave any different to the Usurper?"

"Cromwell doesn't claim that he is the head of the Church."

"Is that why he forbids any sermons to be preached in our fashion? Did I ever tell you that at my Tower window I saw Laud pass on the way to the block? At least he was spared the pain and humiliation of hanging, drawing, and quartering. How many have they murdered lately?"

"None. That I know of. Now that all the fighting is over." Christopher's voice grew sad. "Uncle, my father is dead."

"I know. May he rest in peace. How did he die, nephew?"

"Wonderfully religious, and prepared for heaven."

"I will follow his example if I have to." But when he saw the sadness on Christopher's face he stopped pacing, his agitation lessened, and he took his nephew's hand and Christopher felt callouses as thick as warts, and yet there was a softness in his uncle's touch as he added, "But nephew, I see you have no taste for martyrdom. Why have you come?"

"Cromwell sent me to tell you that you can have your liberty."

"On what conditions?"

"None, except to obey the laws of the land."

Matthew was silent for a minute and then he said, "My son tells me that you are a professor of astronomy now."

"I thought he was in France on a mission for our Majesty."

"He is. But he communicates with me. The warders are friendly, should the King return when the Usurper dies. You will not allow the telescope to alter your faith? Are you sure the sun is the centre of the universe?"

"No."

His uncle looked relieved.

"But I do believe that the earth revolves around the sun."

Matthew was sombre as he said, "I hope your investigations do not shake your faith. Astronomy is hardly more trustworthy than astrology. We were better off when the world possessed an immutable stability."

"Uncle, Galileo was a great, a far-sighted man."

"That has not been proven. His Church did silence him."

"As the Puritans have tried to silence you."

"That is different. You must not commit sacrilege. I do not trust the new astronomy. It could shake our Church to its foundations."

The sun was obscured by a cloud and the cell was dark and although his uncle lit a candle and Christopher longed to shout, I am a devoted believer in Him, he disliked his uncle's scorn of astronomy. And Matthew had not answered the question. "Uncle, will you come out?"

"Did you know that I was not tried for life as your friend Wilkins said, but imprisoned until further orders?"

"No." Had Wilkins lied to him? That hurt almost as much as the sight of his uncle in the Tower. "Are you certain, Uncle?"

"Certain!" Matthew's thin lips tightened and the lines of his face showed that he knew he had suffered abuse and outrage. "And the Usurper was on the committee that impeached me."

Christopher reflected, His uncle was even less forgiving than Cromwell.

Matthew strode the length of the cell, denouncing the Puritans, but it was the stuff of the past, thought Christopher. His uncle was making a powerful speech, eloquent and moving, his voice beautiful once more, and it was helping no one. Except possibly, himself, by using his agitation to rid himself of emotion and to comfort his own self-righteousness. Then Christopher felt guilty; he knew he wasn't supposed to be critical of his uncle. As Matthew's tirade against the Puritans continued he stopped listening and stepped toward the door of the cell.

"But I haven't given you my answer, nephew!"

"I thought . . ."

"I wouldn't give in. But I want you to tell the Usurper my answer."

Christopher waited, wondering whether it was necessary to be angry.

"Tell him Matthew Wren declines to acknowledge his favour or authority."

"As you wish, Uncle."

"To do that would be to denounce my religion. My God. Allow me to worship privately? When I am a public man? Everybody would know!"

Christopher yearned to say goodbye affectionately, but his uncle stood in the centre of the cell still shouting scornfully.

"The Usurper will not outlive me now. All I need is patience. He has the stone, from too much riding, and each day grows increasingly feeble."

"How do you know?" He wished his uncle didn't sound so pleased.

"I have sources of information. I will come out soon. Without help."

"I hope so." He wasn't as sure.

"And the Usurper will have a longer imprisonment than mine. When he dies he will burn in hell for eternity."

His uncle was a tiger now, convinced of his own rhetoric, but when he saw the sadness on his nephew's face he softened.

"Christopher, I didn't mean to offend you, criticising astronomy. Do you think there are other worlds like ours?"

"We can only speculate." He was not certain he wanted there

to be, if they were like earth. Although now, his uncle kissed him goodbye and there were tears on Matthew's cheeks as the door closed behind him.

At the Claypoles the next week Cromwell and Wilkins were there for dinner, but the Lord Protector was distracted. Christopher sought to put in the best light the reason his uncle had rejected Cromwell's offer and he realised that her father was not really listening. The Lord Protector nodded absent-mindedly, as if Matthew Wren was of little importance now, and directed his attention to his daughter. Elizabeth had learned that Dr. Hewer was being charged with communicating with the Stuarts.

She said bitterly, "You will call it treason. He won't have a chance. But it is a lie that Dr. Hewer was a spy for the Stuarts."

Cromwell said, "Betty dear, we have proof."

"You want to punish him for marrying me in the Anglican faith."

"It is out of my hands."

"Nothing in the Commonwealth is out of your hands."

"There is *prima facie* proof that intelligence has passed between him and the Stuarts. The judges have no choice."

"If you murder him, you murder me. It will say I was wed illegally."

Stunned by Elizabeth's accusation, Cromwell sat in a stupor, able only to think of the child who had given him such pleasure with her love of life, while she retired to her room in tears. Claypole followed her to comfort her, although he hadn't said a word in defence of Dr. Hewer.

Wilkins asked Christopher, "Are you sure Matthew won't change his mind?"

"My uncle said he was not tried for life. As you told me, John."

"He is a passionate man. He feels deeply. As does our Lord Protector."

Cromwell looked up and asked, "What is it? Where has Betty gone?"

"She wanted to rest, Oliver. She doesn't feel well."

"It is not my fault. I brought her up to think for herself and now she will not listen to me. Professor, did your uncle say no?"

Christopher nodded.

"I thought that would be his answer."

Christopher couldn't tell whether Cromwell was pleased or sorry.

Elizabeth stood in the doorway, her face tear-stained, and cried out, "Father, if Dr. Hewer dies, his blood is on your head!"

"Betty, I bought you a new carpet. Imported directly from Turkey. You've wanted one for years. It is the best carpet I could obtain."

Claypole was with her, but she ignored his efforts to restrain her and shouted, "If Dr. Hewer is executed, I will never forgive you!"

"Betty, please!" He halted, feeling helpless; she wasn't listening.

She pulled away from Claypole's effort to calm her and screamed, "You are as wicked as the Papists, acting like you are infallible, too, but that doesn't justify murder!" She fled back into her room, sobbing loudly.

Cromwell mumbled, looking stricken, "She is resolved to make a martyr out of him. My hands are tied. We have proof Hewer conveyed intelligence to the Stuarts. Under the law that is treason. I cannot change that."

A few weeks later, June 8th, 1658, Dr. Hewer was executed on Tower Hill for *"having intelligence with Charles Stuart"*.

Evelyn witnessed this. "So I know the truth," he informed Christopher. "The minister went to his death like the excellent preacher he was, a resolute martyr, speaking with his last breath of his devotion to His Majesty, and he will be revenged. The week which preceded his cruel death was cursed with exceptional storms of hail and rain, with northerly winds as savage as winter, which foretells dire events for the Usurper."

Christopher didn't reply. He doubted the weather had anything to do with anyone's fate, the barometer he was developing showed the storms were due to atmospheric conditions and he had observed that English weather, even in summer, was unpredictable, but he knew Evelyn preferred his own beliefs.

A month later Elizabeth fell ill and Christopher realised it was grave when Wilkins asked him to visit her. He was surprised by the concern in his friend's voice.

"Did she request it?"

"No." Wilkins sighed. "She has been in a coma most of the time. Her father did. He said, 'She likes him and Wren is a skilful anatomist.'"

"But I am not a doctor, John."

"Do you hate Cromwell that much, too?"

Christopher knew he could reply, I don't hate anybody, but it was complex, Cromwell was a complex man. "Do you think I can help her?"

"I don't know. Goddard and Sydenham, our two best doctors attend her, and they haven't accomplished much. But it would help Oliver, it would give him the feeling he has tried everything. And Elizabeth likes you. You might comfort her. Oliver has taken her to Hampton Court, his favourite palace, in the hope that the fresh air will help her recover."

Christopher had never seen Hampton Court and his first sight of it disappointed him. The Tudor palace was large, its size was meant to impress, he reflected, yet it was too much like a fortress to suit his taste, too cold and foreboding to be ill in. He was surprised, too, by the ceremony surrounding the Lord Protector's favourite residence. There were a hundred scarlet-coated guards and many servants in a livery as bright as any he had seen around the King, and fifty gentlemen in splendid uniforms of black and grey with silver trimmings. Many of them were escorting the Lord Protector as he approached his visitors, but when he saw who was waiting for him, he dismissed everybody else.

He whispered mournfully to Wilkins, "Betty is worse. She is in a coma most of the time. Does the professor think he can help her?"

Christopher said, "If Goddard and Sydenham can't, I doubt that I can."

"When she is conscious, she won't even talk to me." Cromwell looked ravaged, as if she was draining all of his remaining strength from him. He led them into her bedroom. "Wren, if you could only correct her misapprehensions about me. She likes you very much."

Christopher had eyes only for Elizabeth. She lay on a great four-poster bed and he was shocked and deeply saddened by her appearance. She was gaunt, except for her swollen stomach, which was visible under the sheets. Cromwell motioned for him to examine her, and he did, softly tracing the size and contour of the swelling with his sensitive hands.

Meanwhile, Cromwell asked Goddard, "Could Harvey have cured her?"

Goddard reminded him, "Harvey is dead, sire. He died last year."

"Could Scarburgh?"

"He is not in London, sire."

But abroad, with the royal family, thought Christopher.

"And you can do nothing, Goddard?" Cromwell cried desperately.

"Nothing else, sire."

"Wren, what have you observed? Could she be pregnant?"

"No. She has the symptons of a malignancy." He felt stricken, too.

"Perhaps she suffers from a disorder of the liver."

Christopher thought, Cromwell was frantic to believe it was a medical illness and not a curse she had inherited from him. "I don't think so."

"Yet, like myself, she always has had a weak stomach and a tendency to suffer from constipation. I have pills that are painless and quickly soluble." He felt that Wren was staring at him strangely and he added, "Professor, I've never liked vandalism. Wilkins informs me you are distressed by the appearance of St. Paul's. I didn't want the cathedral desecrated. It was done against my wishes, but I am blamed for everything. My Puritan friends wanted to destroy it entirely, they said the cathedral was no longer necessary, that was why I had Wilkins preach there. If he hadn't, they might have had their way."

"Thank you, sir."

"Can you save Betty? God must not treat her like a hostage."

Christopher tenderly caressed her brow and his soft touch awakened a breath of life in her. Elizabeth's eyes opened and when she saw that it was Christopher she smiled wanly and whispered feebly, "I'm dying."

"You can't!" implored her father.

She turned her back on him, refusing to talk to him.

"Where does it hurt?" asked Christopher, not wanting to show his own fear.

"Everywhere. Those accusations against Dr. Hewer were false. The judges were bewitched. They have turned my blood into poison. I am cursed. It is my father's doing. No, I will not forgive him."

She was seized with a new attack of pain and she held her stomach as if something alive writhed within her. Then, mercifully, thought Christopher, she fell into a coma again, where at least she was free from anguish.

Several days later she died, never having recovered consciousness. At the funeral Cromwell, who was able to stand only with a great effort of his will, insisted on speaking to Christopher privately. "Professor, they say it was God's punishment for Dr. Hewer's death."

Christopher felt it was more likely because of a malignant growth, but it was forbidden to cut open the body and find out. He hesitated, not sure whether to console or to condemn the Lord Protector. He was filled with such a sorrow for Elizabeth it was impossible to feel anything else.

Yet as the coffin was laid into the grave and Cromwell looked ready to follow her, he whispered, "Goddard said it was a growth. I think so, too."

"She asked God to curse me. I've lost the dearest thing in life."

At Gresham a few days later Wilkins told Christopher, "The Lord Protector has fallen gravely ill. This time he may not recover."

"Do you think it is because of Elizabeth?"

"Partly. But he had a serious coach accident, just when she got sick, and he should have been in bed, too, instead of being at her side constantly. And the bad weather has made him feel worse."

Christopher's heart was heavy. Something vital and precious had gone out of his life, too. Death was an everyday occurrence and yet he couldn't accept Elizabeth's passing as inevitable. "I hope he gets better."

"Despite what happened to your father and uncle?"

Christopher was silent.

"I suspect it is out of our hands."

The next few weeks Cromwell lingered between life and death, and then he was taken to Whitehall, at his request—to be away from the scene of his daughter's death, and because he believed he could receive better medical treatment in the capital. And, as he fought to stay alive, on August 30th the fiercest storm that England had experienced in a hundred years swept over the country. Even Christopher, who didn't believe in such omens, was shaken by the torrential rains, the gales that threatened the stability of the land itself, knocking down trees and houses with a malevolent fury, while Evelyn, like most of the citizens of London, felt the terrible storms foretold Cromwell's death. When the Lord Protector died several days later, he told Christopher, "It was the will of God."

He was proud of his wisdom but Christopher thought, It was more likely that Cromwell had died of an ailing body and worse medicine.

Evelyn was jubilant as he added, "Now His Majesty will return."

Instead, a great quiet fell upon the land. Cromwell's son, Richard, was appointed his father's successor and everyone seemed to peacefully accept this situation. Cromwell's body lay in state for six weeks and then on October 22nd Christopher witnessed his funeral with Evelyn.

Evelyn invited Christopher; he wanted his friend to celebrate with him. But Christopher wasn't festive and wasn't sure how the great crowd felt.

Cromwell's cortege was borne from Somerset House and on to the Strand and toward Westminster Abbey, where he was to be buried. The Lord Protector lay on a black velvet bed of state drawn by six white horses—that Cromwell would have admired, reflected Christopher—and was dressed in royal robes and crowned with a crown, sceptre, and globe. As if that mattered, Christopher said to himself, staring critically at the imperial banners, the heralds in their scarlet coats, the excessive ornamentation.

Evelyn said as the cortege rumbled slowly past them, "*It is the most joyful funeral I have ever seen. There are none that cry but dogs which the soldiers hoot away with barbarous noises and their drinking.*"

Christopher said, "He was a great man, whatever his nature."

Evelyn regarded him as if he had uttered a sacrilege and added, "I was right. His death was the work of God. A golden age will follow now."

Christopher hadn't seen anything to justify such a view. He had been at his telescope often lately and he had not observed any change in the heavens. The moon had not altered its position and neither had the sun or any of the planets, and they were God's work, too.

Say Something

Say something
   you have never said before

Think something
   you never thought before

Know something
   you never knew before

Understand something
   none understood before

Be the source of origination
   solo conception

And you will be born
   as you have never been born before

Stymean Karlen

16

Say Something

SOON AFTER CROMWELL'S FUNERAL A TROOP OF SOLDIERS SEIZED Gresham.

Christopher's cousin Matthew, who returned to London with the death of the Lord Protector, wrote him this news and that it could be dangerous to try to assume his teaching post there and safer to remain in Oxford.

But Christopher had to find out for himself how serious was the situation at Gresham, and so he arranged to meet Matthew at the entrance a few days later. It was a Wednesday afternoon, the day he taught there, and he was determined to proceed with his class if he could. Matthew was waiting for him in front of the arched medieval gate, but they were halted by a guard with a musket who barred their way and asked their business.

Christopher said, "I am the professor of astronomy."

The corpulent, middle-aged, makeshift guard, who looked more like a butcher than a soldier, replied, "There is no admission on that account. The college has been reformed into a garrison."

Matthew asked, "Is anyone inside? Aside from the soldiers?"

"Dr. Goddard. He who was the Lord Protector's body physician."

Christopher asked, "May we see him?"

"Who should I say attends him?"

"Christopher and Matthew Wren."

The guard summoned other soldiers to watch them and after he bolted the door he disappeared inside while they waited on Bishopsgate Street.

Matthew was self-assured as he pulled his cousin out of the hearing of the guards to advise him. He thought, Christopher might be an able scholar but his cousin had some strange ideas and was not always practical.

He whispered, "I wouldn't concern yourself with Gresham.

When the Stuarts return, and that grows more likely each day, greater things than teaching are possible. I took many messages to the Stuarts and I will be rewarded. I have been told I will have a high post upon the resumption of their rule. And you could have one, too, if you cultivate the proper people. I wouldn't praise Goddard, he will be out of favour soon and so will Wilkins. And yet," Matthew added quickly, "I wouldn't tell them. I would wait a little while longer. Until we see how the wind blows."

Christopher shrugged, thinking, The entrance to Gresham was so filthy it needed a careful sweeping and yet the bricks in the ancient Roman wall nearby were still firm and they were very old. They were effective building materials. He decided that he must use bricks some day.

He was brought back to the present by the return of the guard who said, "Goddard says you can enter. But you will be escorted. Gresham is army property now." The makeshift soldier assigned two other middle-aged men as guards, who were uneasy as they pointed their muskets at Christopher and Matthew, but who scowled to show that they were resolute.

"Tradesmen from the City," Matthew whispered, "who want to show that they are going to rule London, now that the Usurper is dead."

The interior of Gresham smelled so vilely that Christopher felt he was in the infernal regions. The grand hall was strewn with manure where the horses were stabled and there was garbage everywhere.

Goddard, who was the physic professor, was in the laboratory of The Invisible College and was distressed. The room was so dirty and disorderly he explained hurriedly, "I almost arrived too late. The soldiers were about to destroy our experiments as impious. If not for my connection to Cromwell, I could not have stopped them."

Christopher asked sadly, "Are there no classes here at all?"

"None. Troops are quartered here while it is decided who is to rule. No one is sure. I think it will be major-general against major-general."

As if to confirm Goddard's view, a small, elderly, but spry officer marched in and announced himself as "Major-General Lukens".

His uniform fitted awkwardly, his posture was poor, and Christopher recalled what Elizabeth had said of her father's major-generals, *"They ought to be helping their wives with their dishes as they used to do."*

Yet a troop of soldiers stood behind Lukens, prepared to obey him as he declared, pointing to the instruments and drugs in the laboratory, "Now that the Lord Protector is dead, we have no need of such impieties."

Goddard said, "But we meet here because of the convenience of obtaining and inspecting drugs from the apothecaries. With Cromwell's permission."

"I have heard about you *vertuosi* for years," sneered Lukens. "Quacks, salvers, apothecary boys. Were you able to cure our Lord Protector?"

Christopher thought, If Lukens had his way Goddard will wish he had. This major-general, who looked more like an innkeeper than a soldier, acted as if he believed he could be another Cromwell and was itching to fight, as long as he outnumbered his foe, any foe. Christopher wondered if Lukens knew how to use the pistol he wore at his side, and suggested, hoping to distract him, "Sir, would you like to gaze through my telescope?"

Lukens glared at him and snapped, "I know what my eyes can see! Are you one of those who says the earth revolves around the sun?"

"Yes, sir."

Lukens was horrified and he exclaimed, "That is an impertinence. I see with my own eyes that it is the sun which moves, not the earth, and you deny that. As you would deny the word of the Lord." He ordered his soldiers to confiscate everything in the laboratory and he added, "I will decide later whether these are instruments of the devil and should be destroyed." He motioned for his soldiers to evict the intruders.

They stood on the street outside of Gresham a little later and Matthew said, "Doctor, I warned my cousin not to come here, but he wouldn't listen to me. He would have been better off if he had stayed in Oxford."

Goddard said, "Matthew is right, Christopher. Oxford is safer."

"Unless," said Matthew, "We raise a troop of soldiers and ride out with pistols and swords as some did at Oxford a few years ago."

Christopher said, "They were led by Owens, in support of Cromwell."

"But if they succeeded why shouldn't we follow their example."

Goddard said, "I was part of this troop, but now it will only incite men like Lukens to destroy our work. We must wait and see what happens. Now no one knows for certain what is going to occur."

Christopher resumed his work at Oxford while the country teetered on the brink of a new civil war. Owens raised another troop of horse soldiers to hold Oxford in the name of the Commonwealth, but while they patrolled the town and colleges vigilantly and were armed with pistols and swords they did not have to use them the next few months. Everyone was waiting to see in which direction the wind would blow.

Gresham remained closed and under military control and many of the members of The Invisible College stayed at Oxford and they met often.

Christopher was surprised when Richard Cromwell, the Lord Protector's oldest living son, was proclaimed the new Protector. He had met him at Elizabeth's house, and he thought him an amiable man but more suited to be a country gentleman than an omnipotent ruler like his father.

He was not surprised that Richard Cromwell was forced to call into being the Parliament his father had dissolved in 1653. He assumed that the new Lord Protector was doing this to protect himself from the army.

When the army forced Richard Cromwell to dismiss Parliament a few months later, it was what Christopher expected. The next step became inevitable. Nine months after Cromwell's death Richard abdicated.

Evelyn informed Christopher during a visit to Oxford to attend a meeting of The Invisible College: "*So perishes the House of Cromwell. The favourite penny ballad sung these days is: 'Richard the Fourth has deserted himself. Tumble down Dick has kissed his tail.'*" When Christopher didn't reply, he asked irritably, "Aren't you pleased?"

"It depends on what follows. The major-generals could be worse."

Evelyn sighed. "Our nation is in confusion. God have mercy on us!"

While a new Parliament, named the Rump, and the major-generals and the army struggled for control of the country, Christopher sensed that support for the return of the Stuarts was increasing and he was pleased.

Indian summer was beautiful at Oxford that year and although he spent much time at his telescope, he was most absorbed by observations of the human brain that he was working on with Hooke and Thomas Willis, a doctor who lived and practised in Oxford. Gresham was still closed but Oxford was open, and his father had left him enough to live on if he was frugal, and only the shape of the buildings filled him with a yearning for change. There were many moments when he saw the medieval contour of so much of the grey stone as too bleak for the warmth of his mind. Yet the weather was pleasingly variable, with light showery mornings, afternoons of prolonged sunlight, and nights when the fresh, persistent winds brought colour to his cheeks and he loved the briskness of the air.

But there were times during his studies of the structure of the brain and his astronomical observations that he wondered if he was taking the wrong turn. Sometimes he wanted to reshape Wadham.

Sometimes the design of the other colleges took a new form in his mind and he longed to alter them also, to fit them to this moment, not to a world long dead. Sometimes he yearned for a stark simplicity instead of a capricious ornamentation. Sometimes he wished his dialogue with the stone could be masculine and unaffected. So much of the fabric of the Oxford colleges was desultory where he preferred a meticulous order. He disliked over-emphasis; it embarrassed him. He kept these thoughts to himself.

He knew that Evelyn loved to record Evelyn's thoughts; his friend had told him so proudly. But he didn't believe that his ideas were that important.

Yet he did agree with Evelyn that some of the churches in Oxford and elsewhere were, as Evelyn wrote: *"Heavy, dark, melancholy, monkish piles, mountains of stone, ugly and depressing."*

There was too much leaning on the past, reflected Christopher. Most of the builders were still constructing as if they were in the middle ages, he decided, and for them there should be reserved a special place in a medieval hell. Then, feeling unfair, he was uneasy, and that drove him back to his study of the brain. But now even this was unsatisfactory. Dr. Willis expected to obtain a human specimen soon, but that seemed unlikely to Christopher, for such dissections were forbidden by the Puritans, who were still in power. Yet without a genuine specimen he could only speculate and not observe. It was almost as discouraging as astronomy where so much had to be taken on faith. He wondered if this year since the closing of Gresham had been wasted. He thought, It was not enough to say something, he must say something that had never been said before.

He sat by his telescope in Wadham later, tired of staring through it without finding anything new, while Hooke examined his drawings of the brain and declared, "They are too speculative. I doubt they are accurate."

Hooke was even more round-shouldered and misshapen than before, for he spent most of his time bending over his experiments and he hated exercise, as if that reminded him painfully of his infirmities. His impatience and irritation had increased, too; he knew he was a more sensitive machine than his colleagues acknowledged, and more skilful with his hands than any of them, even Christopher Wren. One of these days he was determined to fly out of the tower to prove his mechanical artifice. Only his assistant wasn't paying any attention to him. The astronomer was as preoccupied as he had seen him in a long time. "What's wrong?" he shouted loudly.

"The telescope is defective. The lenses are blurred."

"We need someone who can grind them properly. I would do it if I had the time. I am the best mechanic in The Invisible College."

And more suited to be a professor of astronomy than Wren, he thought angrily, if he only had the right apparatus. "I can do anything if I set my mind to it."

Christopher nodded, thinking, Hooke's mechanical skill was remarkable and he was always inventing devices to further this skill, but he rarely remained with one subject until he reached a conclusion.

Hooke saw a man in the doorway and snapped, "No visitors allowed!"

But it was Seth, Christopher realised, looking apprehensive and disconsolate. The gardener had aged sadly; now he resembled his father.

Seth's clothes were ragged, his shoes were worn through so that he was walking on his bare feet, yet he carried a large load of firewood. "From the royal forest of Windsor," said Seth. "Choice wood, sir. I came on foot, with my pony. Not Monk, but his son. I thought you could use wood, it is the best firewood in England and it is bitterly cold outside."

Hooke asked irately, "Christopher, who is this fellow?"

"Our gardener. Seth, what brings you here?"

Seth started to cry and Hooke turned away in disgust, but Christopher put his arm around him and consoled him until his tears stopped. Then Seth blurted out, "Times are very hard, sir. The harvests are bad, the civil wars have ruined the crops, most of the horses have been seized by the army, and Windsor is full of unemployed people and paupers."

"Why aren't you at the Castle? You were the best gardener."

"That ended after I saw you last." Seth regarded Hooke suspiciously, but when Christopher indicated that he could speak freely, although Hooke was crotchety, he added, "And our farm is gone. My father insisted on addressing our Lord in his own way. We are Dissenters, you know, not Puritans. When Cromwell became Lord Protector, ten armed men, several who were neighbours and most of whom we knew, seized our farm in the name of the Lord Protector. Didn't he have enough without our tiny bit of land?"

"They used Cromwell's name to justify their behaviour."

Hooke said, "Christopher, you are too merciful. The Stuarts, if they return, will not regard that lightly. This man is a Dissenter."

"But he is not a Puritan. Or a rebel."

"He is not to be trusted."

"I will judge that. Seth, what happened then?"

"The armed men forced us to sit in the village stocks. I was accused of being too friendly to the gentry, they meant you, and after we were released we returned to our farm to find that our house had been pulled down, our crops had been stripped. Soon after, my father died."

Even Hooke was silent, the gardener was so sad and hopeless.

Seth said, "Sir, I thought things would change with the Commonwealth, but it is the same as before for us ordinary folk, maybe worse. I have no place to go." His voice broke. There was so much fatigue in his legs he desperately wanted to sit, but he didn't dare in the presence of the gentry. Cromwell had said there would be a levelling, but there hadn't been any.

Christopher took the wood from Seth's aching arms and placed it on his fire and asked, "Where is your pony?"

"A horse soldier who was patrolling the street outside of Wadham, sir, confiscated him in return for allowing me to visit you."

Christopher started for the door to retrieve the pony, but Hooke halted him with the reminder that the thief must be miles away.

Christopher turned to Seth, asked, "Then you have lost everything?"

"Yes, sir. But I am still a good gardener, as you remember."

"A fine gardener. Sit down, Seth."

"Sir, it is not allowed!"

"Sit here. By the telescope."

"Sir, I don't know anything about it."

"You can keep it clean. And please, do not say sir all the time."

"Christopher!" Hooke was horrified. "This man is a Dissenter!"

"And aren't you, Robert?"

Hooke was indignant and he snapped, "Of course *I'm* not!"

"Yes, you are. You disagree with everyone in The Invisible College."

"This is different. This fellow cannot be trusted."

"I need someone to take care of these rooms. Especially when I am in London. Seth, there is a room off the corridor where you can sleep. I can't give you any wages as long as Gresham is closed, but I can give you food and lodging." The gardener knelt at his feet, and now it was Christopher who was embarrassed, who blurted out, with a lack of composure that surprised himself, "My father was happy about the Garter," and then he paused, realising that this admission could be dangerous.

When Seth noticed how often Christopher's gaze wandered from his telescope to the buildings within his view, he sensed that his master's heart was there, whatever Christopher professed. So he made sure that the windows were always clean, no matter how much it rained and snowed and both occurred constantly that winter. He was gratified that his master looked through them eagerly and repeatedly. He also kept the rooms spotless, although that was difficult, for Hooke, who worked in them often, was untidy. He didn't like the firewood that was available—it didn't compare with the wood from the royal forest of Windsor—but he was clever at building a fire and he performed this task with the utmost seriousness. But one thing saddened him. There was no garden for him to cultivate and he wasn't sure that Christopher desired one, although there was a fine one near Wadham, a physic garden which was reputed to possess six hundred herbs and medicinal plants. He was pleased at how relaxed his master was out of doors. He thought, Men of wisdom loved the sky while men of wit loved the earth and men of taste loved both, and to erect buildings was to embrace both sky and earth and that was his master's nature. It ruled his heart no matter how intently he pursued astronomy and anatomy. The life of Oxford was in its buildings, Seth decided, and he wished he could learn the height of each college, as if somehow, that would help Christopher. He spent much of his leisure watching the movement of the sun on them.

One day in January, 1660, Hooke came with a summons from Willis for Christopher to attend him at once. Hooke conveyed this irritably. He felt he was being used as a messenger again, but Christopher soothed him by saying it was an act of friendship, and that it was unusual for Willis to stress such urgency. Yet Christopher also resented Willis' impatience, even as he wondered about it and he hurried to obey.

Willis lived and practised on Merton Street in a dark, gloomy house across from Merton College and the room where Harvey had worked. He said the only doctor who had enriched him had been Harvey, that he treasured the latter's learning. His lodgings were also close to Christ Church, where Willis had studied theology in addition to anatomy.

The doctor greeted them excitedly. He was dressed all in black— he had sworn to wear black until the Stuarts returned, and he had done so since the death of the King. He was a slight, bony-featured man, whose skin was so tight the contour of his skull was taut, and he was very thin.

He whispered importantly, "I want you to attend me before the others arrive. I have finally obtained a human brain, a fine specimen, newly hanged, and there is no chance of this one coming back from the dead."

This reminded Christopher of the time, ten years ago, when Willis and Petty, another doctor, had revived Nan Greene, a serving maid who had been hanged for murdering her bastard child, and this had been regarded as a miracle and both men had become the best known doctors in the country.

Willis proudly showed them his specimen and Christopher tried to stifle his horror as he stared at it, while the doctor said, "I separated it at the neck, so we can concentrate on the brain. Wren, observe it closely, so you can illustrate it for me. It could lead to a valuable discovery."

Hooke asked irritably, "Why do you want me here?"

"To observe the specimen. You have the keenest eyes among us."

Hooke said disgustedly, "My eyes are not good enough."

"Perhaps you need a microscope. I have corresponded with Leyden, where they inform me, they have developed such an instrument, which detects objects too small for our eyes to see. Hooke, why don't you inquire about it?"

"You are the anatomist. My preference is for mechanical things."

Christopher suggested, "Possibly the brain performs that way, too."

Hooke was sceptical, but Willis said, "Wren, illustrate what you can."

Willis handed Christopher paper and pencil but before he could start there was a loud, impatient knock on the front door. He was annoyed, for his interest had grown stronger than his horror and now he was driven with a passionate desire to explore this unknown matter before him. He wondered: did it leave any record of its past life? Or had that eroded? This was as grand as any structure, this was the grand point of creation. Poetic Shakespeare. Fiery Marlowe. How could it be nothing? It was an architectural achievement and the cornerstone of the world.

Willis said, "It was too difficult finding this specimen to risk losing it. Even some of my Royalist friends do not approve of such experiments. They say we are destroying the soul. I must hide it." He did, locked his laboratory, and then opened the front door where stood Scarburgh, Evelyn, and Matthew, as if they were expected.

Christopher was surprised by Scarburgh's presence; he had heard that the doctor was attending the Stuarts, and Scarburgh was dressed more like a courtier than a physician. His hair was long, in the fashion of the late King, and his sharp features had become rounder.

He asked immediately, "Are you certain there are no Puritans here?"

"None," said Willis. "I made sure of that."

Now Christopher realised why neither Goddard nor Sydenham were present, although they were the best doctors in Oxford and were friendly with Willis and resided nearby. All those here were Royalists. Yet to verify his suspicions he asked, "Where is Wilkins, Boyle, and Locke?"

Willis said severely, "Wilkins supports the Commonwealth. And

K

Boyle refuses to declare himself and Locke doesn't know which side to be on."

"But they are members of The Invisible College."

"We have more vital matters to consider."

Matthew blurted out, "I have hopeful news. General Monk, who controls the army now, has left Scotland for London with his army, and I have reason to believe that he is sympathetic to our sacred cause."

Scarburgh said, "That is why I have returned to England and Oxford. To ascertain how much sentiment there is for our Majesty's return."

Hooke asked, "Isn't there danger if you are found out?"

"I'm not sure. Even the most ardent supporters of the rebellion are starting to temporise. In the event that Monk should support the King. No one knows for certain what this major-general will do. Willis, did we disturb you in the middle of an experiment?"

"No, Scarburgh. We were discussing the political situation."

"With Wren here?" he asked sceptically.

"You forget that I am a professor of natural philosophy."

"I forget nothing. Especially your interest in experimentation. Willis, don't you consider me worthy of your experiments?"

"Scarburgh, what is the news from His Majesty?"

"He is prepared to return."

"With an army? Is he thinking of mounting an invasion?"

"Goodness, No! He has had enough of that! His Majesty is interested in learning how much support he will find in Oxford. He hears so many tales of Puritan depravity and misrule he expects to be invited back."

Matthew said, "That depends on Monk. He is becoming the most powerful man in the country. He could take London without a shot being fired."

Evelyn said, "If he would only declare for the King it could solve everything, but I fear that he will try to be another Lord Protector."

Christopher noticed that Willis subtly but firmly led them into his parlour and away from his laboratory. He wondered why Willis complained about his situation. The doctor owned enough chairs for all of them to sit in, where usually, one had to sit on a hard, backless bench. There was also a fine long table in the centre of the parlour around which he seated them, a thick carpet, and a miniature on the wall of the dead King.

Willis ordered his serving maid to bring his guests coffee, and she gave each of them the beverage in a carved jug. No one wanted to show that they distrusted this drink, yet all of them hesitated except Willis, who said as he drank, "I acquired this taste from

Harvey. He assured me that coffee has medicinal properties and is a useful stimulant."

Christopher wasn't sure that he liked coffee, although he had tasted it before, but this drink was a hotter and stronger mixture.

Matthew didn't touch his coffee until Scarburgh took a sip, while Evelyn was torn between curiosity and apprehension. He hated to be left out of anything, but the taste was strange, almost bitter, an odd brew.

Finally however, all of them followed their host's example, who said, "A coffee house has just opened in Oxford, but I have hesitated to visit it. I am not sure whether the proprietor is a Royalist."

This brought Matthew back to the reason for his visit. He said, "I have evidence Monk could be. When he was imprisoned in the Tower for having supported Charles, he cultivated my father. They conversed with the connivance of the Tower authorities, who were not sure which side was going to win. Then, at the time Monk was in danger of losing his head because he had fought for the King, he asked the Bishop to conduct Episcopal services for him. He told my father that he didn't want to die an unbeliever. This convinced the Bishop that Monk, in his heart, would always be loyal to the Stuarts. When he discovered that the soldier was popular with the army, that the rebels were eager for Monk's sword and that the King's cause was lost, my father persuaded him to yield to Cromwell's request and to accept a commission in his Irish army, where he would not have to fight against Charles. But before Monk was freed he asked the Bishop for his blessing and as he knelt before him, he swore, *'never to be an enemy to our King . . . I will do our Majesty the best duty I can against the rebels in Ireland, and I hope I shall one day do him further duty in England.'* My father is convinced Monk meant that."

Evelyn said, "He has never given us any hint of his intentions."

Scarburgh pointed out, "The King has written Monk, but he has refused to even receive his letters. How can we trust the Bishop's views?"

Willis said, "Question the Bishop of Ely? We must have faith in him!"

Willis assumed this was settled and he guided them authoritatively into a small hall which was arranged like an Episcopal chapel. Christopher was startled by this direct violation of a strict Puritan ordinance, as was Hooke, but the others knew about it as Willis boasted, "I have been holding Episcopal services here ever since the start of the rebellion."

Christopher said, "You never told me."

Willis replied, "I wasn't sure that you could be trusted."

"Despite my father and my uncle?"

"You are close to Wilkins. And Hooke didn't seem interested."

"Then why do you include us now?"

"The Bishop wrote me that you could be relied on even though you were friendly with supporters of Cromwell, even with Cromwell himself, that your heart would be in the right place even if your head strayed."

Angry, Christopher thought of withdrawing; then he realised it would be misunderstood; they would assume he was turning his back on his faith, and that wasn't his intention, that would be a rejection of his father. But, as he stayed, he reflected Wilkins, who knew about almost everything that happened in Oxford, probably knew of these services, yet Wilkins would never think of interfering, that was against his nature.

Hooke said, "Willis, I have no influential relatives to vouch for me."

"You are too valuable a student to be lost to the Puritans."

"I can still be saved?" Hooke asked mockingly.

"Busby thinks so. And none of your thinking is contrary to our faith."

Hooke, however, stood undecided until Christopher reminded him, "You told me that your father was the minister of his parish. And a devout Anglican. You said it was one of the reasons you entered Westminster."

Hooke remained, but he sat close only to Christopher.

The makeshift chapel had a small organ, prayer books, and surplices. Willis donned one while the others knelt as he prayed for the return of the Stuarts and for divine aid to guide Monk to support such a step.

Then he intoned, *"Dear God, we must rebuke the followers of that great beast, Cromwell, for the blasphemy they have committed against Your name. We must smite them down. In Your name. And for our martyred King."*

Willis was finishing his sermon when a dozen horse soldiers carrying muskets and pikes burst into the makeshift Episcopal chapel, led by Bagshaw, who wore the uniform of a Puritan cavalry officer, and as he saw who was there he said gloatingly, "I have a fine catch!"

"What are we charged with?" asked Willis, discarding his surplice.

"Blasphemy. You are violating the ordinance that no one is allowed to observe the superstitions of the Stuart Church." He ordered his aide to write down their names, although he knew all of them, and he shouted, "You will be committed to prison! Now without question!"

Bagshaw commanded his soldiers to search the prisoners for arms and incriminating papers, and while he found nothing, he was forcing them to leave under armed guard when Owens strode in, dressed as a major.

Bagshaw said, "They offend grievously. Their prayers are nothing more than a mass in English and they were praying for Charles Stuart."

Christopher addressed Owens, "Sir, as you are no longer Vice-Chancellor, you no longer have authority over any part of the University."

"This chapel is not part of the university," said Owens, "but it is a part of the Commonwealth."

Bagshaw declared, "And it is to suppress heresy that we are fighting. We have caught them in an open profanation of our faith. We will never have a better chance or more cause to punish them."

Owens was silent for a moment, almost sombre. Then he said abruptly, "Bagshaw, you push too hard. Times have changed. Cromwell is dead."

"What about the ordinances against Episcopal services? Dr. Hewer was beheaded for such acts. Even though he wed Cromwell's daughter."

"He was executed for conveying intelligence to the Stuarts. This is not charged here."

Bagshaw drew his loaded pistol and pointed it at Christopher and said accusingly, "Wren abandoned the Lord Protector when he was dying. Wren was ordered to attend him and he deliberately refused."

Owens hesitated, not certain whether to believe him or not."

Bagshaw said, "I heard that from those present at the deathbed."

"I was present," interrupted Goddard. "And Wren was not asked to attend the Lord Protector. He is not a doctor, although he is a skilful anatomist." Goddard stood in the doorway, having heard about this raid. He glared at Bagshaw as he exclaimed, "Bagshaw, you want to destroy the best brains in the country! Owens, you cannot consent to such a sacrilege!"

"I haven't. It is Bagshaw whose piety has flooded his brain."

"Then stop it! Before he brings shame upon all of us!"

Owens looked unhappy, but he ordered Bagshaw to release the prisoners.

Bagshaw cried, "Sir, I thought you wanted to destroy heresy?"

Owens said, "You think this is the only Episcopal chapel in the land?"

"No. Of course not. Yet . . ."

"We must become used to them. There will probably be more of them in the next few years rather than less. It is the mood of the land." But when Bagshaw continued to confront Christopher with his loaded pistol, Goddard looked scandalised, Willis smiled contemptuously, and this was more than Owens could bear. He strode in front of Bagshaw, a remarkably muscular man, reminding everyone, but especially his subordinate, that he was still very athletic—it was one of the reasons he had been chosen to be Cromwell's chaplain—and he said, "Bagshaw, give me your pistol!"

Bagshaw put his pistol back into his holster and before Owens could do anything, he hurried to the door at the rear of the chapel and when Willis tried to block his way, he said gleefully, "Sir, as I thought, they are hiding something treasonable. Communications with the Stuarts or something worse. May I force open the door?" Owens saw Willis' apprehension and he ordered Willis to stand aside. Willis didn't want to, but Goddard motioned to him that he should obey, and he did, although reluctantly. Bagshaw forced open the door with the pikes of his troopers and burst into the laboratory. At first he was disappointed, this wasn't what he expected; then he found the specimen in the glass jar and his eyes lit up. He cried out, "They are performing a dissection! And on the brain. Sir, you cannot excuse that! This is impious. Where the soul is lodged."

Christopher stepped between Bagshaw and the specimen, to stop him from destroying it, and said, "The brain is not the seat of the soul. And it is not impious to observe it. How else can we learn how it functions?"

Scarburgh exclaimed, "Willis, you were experimenting without me!"

Willis apologised, "I know that you are a fine anatomist but lately . . ." He didn't finish, realising that this could incriminate Scarburgh.

Owens asked, "Wren, do you believe the soul is not lodged in the brain?"

Everyone had followed Bagshaw and Christopher into the laboratory, and Bagshaw interrupted, "Of course he believes that. Heretic. Sir, if he dissects this brain, he will destroy its soul."

Owens said, "I asked Wren, not you. I know your opinions."

Christopher said, "I believe the brain is the seat of our intelligence, the sum of our knowledge, the centre of our nervous system, but not our soul. That is elsewhere, perhaps in the air we breathe, perhaps in the spirit with which we live, and the devotion with which we worship God."

"Just so," Goddard said approvingly.

Hooke said abruptly, "I must write to Leyden and ask them to send me a microscope. Then perhaps, we can know for certain where the soul is."

Christopher said, "The brain is the centre of sensation."

Owens said, "But the heart has always been regarded as that."

Bagshaw said, "As Aristotle said . . ."

"I know what Aristotle said," Owens interrupted him testily. "Now I want to know Wren's reasons."

"The activity of the brain is sensation, for while it neither sees nor hears nor smells nor tastes nor touches it does all these things."

Even Scarburgh looked sceptical of Christopher's views and Matthew wanted to change the subject, afraid his cousin would commit blasphemy, but Willis said, "Wren could be right. That is why we must pursue our inquiries."

"Dissections," Owens reminded him.

Goddard said, "Dr. Willis practises with distinction. You admitted that yourself, Owens, for you asked him to attend you when you were ill, and he cured you. You told me so yourself. Remember?"

Owens remembered when he was a student at Queens College he had been told he had a brilliant future as a scholar; if he continued to delve into every kind of learning, that he could become another Francis Bacon. But he had been more ambitious, he had become a theologian and Cromwell's right hand, only to find as Vice-Chancellor that there was too vast a distance between himself and the scholars. It was a mistake to oppose the experiment with Circulate; he must not make such a mistake again or he would lose whatever scholarly reputation he still possessed. He thought of what Cromwell had said when the Lord Protector had become Chancellor: "*The mind is man, if that be kept pure, a man signifies something; if not I hardly see what difference there is between him and a beast.*" He braced his strong body and declared, "I would not destroy the work of a colleague"—he bowed in the direction of Willis and Wren—"as I would not have them destroy mine." He ordered Bagshaw and the troop to leave and he followed them to be sure that they obeyed him.

Willis asked Goddard, "Could Owens truly want our good opinion?"

"It is possible. He knows now he was mistaken about Circulate, and that with Monk's growing strength the Royalist enthusiasm is increasing."

Matthew asked, "Aren't you afraid of what could happen to you?"

"Did I hurt you?"

"My father is still in the Tower."

Goddard was silent.

Christopher said quickly, "That was not Goddard's doing."

Goddard smiled wryly. "I doubt others will be so merciful. But I joined this troop, as I think Owens did, also, to prevent excesses. Now that it is possible the Stuarts may return, Owens is more like his true self. At heart he is a tolerant man, but when he thought he might succeed Cromwell as Chancellor, his ambition got the better of his judgment. However, Willis, I would close this chapel for a while. Not everyone will be so understanding. The Puritans cause is still quite strong."

Christopher asked, "Is that why Bagshaw is so vindictive?"

"He was appointed second master at Westminster a few years ago, on the recommendation of Owens, who as Dean of Christ Church and Vice-Chancellor, was a man to please. Then Bagshaw tried to replace Busby as Head Master, expecting Owens and other powerful Puritans to support him. Instead, while Owens and some politicians did help him, Busby won by the simple and direct expedient of having the students bodily evict Bagshaw from the school, which showed the true sentiments of Westminster. And since you, Christopher, are considered a protege of Busby, Bagshaw is seeking to get revenge by attacking you. He has become a scavenger."

"Whatever he is," said Christopher, "he is wrong about the brain."

"I agree." Goddard added wistfully, "We must not allow the bitterness of factions to erase our sense of comradeship."

After Goddard left, Evelyn whispered, "I still don't trust him. He was too close to the Usurper. Christopher, do you really believe the soul is not in the brain?"

Matthew said, "He was joking. He professed that to confound the Puritans. And to confuse them. We know where the soul is. In the brain. And we must be very careful, we must not damage the soul."

Willis said, "I'm not sure where it is, but I will be careful."

"For God's sake!" exclaimed Hooke, "None of us really knows where it is!"

"Anyway," Scarburgh said, "where the soul is doesn't matter now. Willis, you should have included me in your experiments, even though they are not important. I must tell His Majesty that the Puritans allowed your chapel to stand. It is a favourable omen."

Christopher was sad. The light was gone and now it was too dark to examine the specimen. Yet it was foolish to argue with them; their words were echoes from the past. They were still bewitched by the old rituals and superstitions, even Willis, but he must find out for himself.

Scarburgh asked Willis, "Are you going to close the chapel?"

"No."

Matthew said, "And if Willis is watched, we can meet in Christopher's rooms. No one will suspect him, he is so friendly with Goddard."

"His serving man is a Dissenter," said Hooke. "He might betray us."

"He will not," said Christopher, but no one was listening.

They agreed with Hooke and decided that if it should be necessary to have more meetings, they should be held in Hooke's rooms at Christ Church.

"But I doubt I can take part in them," added Evelyn, "for I have an appointment to meet with Colonel Morley, now Lieutenant of the Tower. He is an old schoolfellow of mine and I am trying to persuade him to hand over the Tower to forces that are friendly to His Majesty."

Christopher suggested, "If you could introduce me to him, perhaps I could convince him to release my uncle."

"I will mention it," said Evelyn, "and let you and Matthew know."

"A splendid idea," said Matthew. "I would be delighted to help you, but I have to see His Majesty, also, to report the good news."

Matthew and Scarburgh prepared to depart for the continent, although Christopher wondered why both had to go, unless it was to make sure that neither acquired more influence with Charles Stuart than the other.

As he took a last look at the specimen, so he could remember it as a work of architecture, Scarburgh took him aside where no one else could hear him and said, "I don't understand what you see in Hooke. He is so untidy, poorly dressed, a dirty, unfortunate looking fellow, without any prospects. He will not be of any value to you when the Stuarts return."

"He has one of the best minds I know," answered Christopher.

Hooke was discussing his theories of flying with Willis, who regarded that as verging on blasphemy. Only God could fly, thought the doctor, and his angels—and we cannot presume too far, he said to himself—and he changed the subject and he uttered a silent prayer to be forgiven for listening to such dangerous ideas.

Christopher was relieved that Scarburgh had stopped talking and was departing with Matthew, each determined that the other would not reach Charles Stuart first with the good news. Whatever Evelyn said, he must visit London and his uncle. He yearned to see the city again. Perhaps when Monk reached London, Gresham would be cleansed and St. Paul's repaired. If he could restore the cathedral to its normal self, he would feel he was speaking for his father. He told no one of this, for there was no profession of architecture as such, and his dreams would be regarded as foolish. He did make an appointment to meet Evelyn outside the Tower in a week, to give Evelyn time to speak to Colonel Morley.

He journeyed into London the next day, eager to see what was happening there, and he left his rooms at Wadham in the care of Seth.

He was saddened to find St. Paul's closed and that Gresham

K*

was still occupied by soldiers who were treating the college as if it were a bawdy house and that he could not enter either building. He sought to distract himself by observing what was happening in London while the city waited for the arrival of Monk and his army, but that was equally depressing.

The streets were muddier, dirtier, noisier, fouler smelling than before, and very uncomfortable. They were crowded with cattle, pigs, drays, carts, coaches, and rolling barrels in a profuse and profane confusion, and it was difficult to walk on them without being run down. Frequently a troop of soldiers or citizens converted into soldiers, marched through the streets and shouldered everybody else aside. Most of the city converged on St. Paul's, as if the cathedral, even closed, even in its neglect and decrepitude, was still the heart of London.

Wild rumours dominated. Christopher didn't know what to believe.

Londoners stood in front of the unfinished portico of the west front and declared that the cathedral had been bought by the Jews, who had been allowed back in England by Cromwell a few years ago, although not officially, that they were going to convert St. Paul's into a synagogue. Others said the cathedral had been closed by Puritan edict. Yet when Christopher said this was more likely he was shouted down. There were also rumours that the apprentice boys intended to fortify the city, even the Tower and St. Paul's, against anyone who planned to return the government to the Stuarts, that Monk was going to pronounce himself Lord Protector, that Charles was seen in the city with a French guard, or more frightening, with Spanish soldiers and a Papal legatee, who was going to return the country to popery. This caused fierce agitation. At the mention of the Roman religion the women wept while their men cursed and shouted that this would bring massacres and ruin upon England and this was why the winter was so terrible, God's blessing was gone from England.

But Christopher's attention returned to St. Paul's, whose presence struck him as vital to London amid all these threats and distractions. However, as he viewed the broken steeple, the crumbling walls, the shaky fabric, the unfinished portico, the cracked stone, the grotesque scaffolding, he was stricken with pain and a deep discontent. He reflected unhappily, One strong blow from the weather or man and much of it could fall down and no one seemed to care. Yet he felt beholden to St. Paul's, it was London's past honour and future hope, it bore witness to a faith that had survived centuries of travail and changes of rule. It bore witness to the country's endurance. It was sufficient unto itself. With its death, many ages would vanish, a vital aspect of England would die.

Unable to bear the melancholy that assailed him, he decided to visit Sam, perhaps rent a room and re-live the excitement he had felt there.

The fat, ageing, sad man who opened the door was a ghost. Sam's face was etched with bitter lines and he moved painfully, and Christopher thought, Time was a thief, it took so much without even a thank you.

Sam was stunned when he saw who it was. He forced a smile, but when Christopher asked him, "How are you?" he grumbled, "I am all alone. My father is dead, Katherine and Lucy left me when Gresham closed and my income was reduced to nothing." But as he saw the pity in Christopher's eyes, he added quickly, "I manage. I take in roomers."

"Would you have a place for me?"

Sam hesitated, then said slowly, "I'm not sure."

"You don't want me?" Christopher was surprised.

"It isn't that. Professor, why are you in London?"

"I am going to try to get my uncle out of the Tower."

"I hope that you are willing to pay for his freedom."

"I hadn't thought that was necessary."

"It is more necessary than ever, now that no one is sure who is going to rule. Money is a language that everybody understands."

"Do you ever hear from Anne?"

"I have been told she is back in London, but I haven't seen her. I am a poor relative now, to be ignored rather than acknowledged."

"Sam, why do you hesitate to rent me a room?"

"Fetter Lane is full of Puritans and your family are well known."

"Suppose Charles returns. Lodging me would be a useful recommendation."

"I was never a Puritan, as you know. I will give you my father's room, so you don't have too many memories. How long do you intend to stay?"

"As long as is necessary. It depends on what happens."

Christopher met Evelyn at the appointed time, who said, "I have treated privately with Colonel Morley concerning the deliverance of the Tower to the King. I begged him to declare for His Majesty. I pointed out it would bring him renown and position, but he refused. He doesn't believe that Monk is coming to London to do the King any service. There is no chance of your uncle being released now. Are you returning to Oxford?"

"Not until I see what happens here."

"London could be dangerous for supporters of His Majesty."

"Are you leaving the city?"

Evelyn regarded Christopher with amazement. "Of course not!

Someone has to observe for His Majesty in his capital. They will not touch me. Wilkins and Goddard and other prominent Puritans are my friends."

Christopher watched Monk's progress closely. When the General pulled down the gates of London and entered the city triumphantly, he felt that hope of a Royalist victory was gone and that Monk was going to declare himself Lord Protector. But when Monk dissolved the Rump Parliament and ordered the churches reopened, this was announced with a great ringing of the bells and Christopher felt that the Commonwealth was done. Yet no one knew whether Monk was doing this for Charles Stuart or himself. Then he heard encouraging news from Evelyn.

"Wren, Morley has asked me how much money would be needed for his pardon, should he turn over the Tower to the supporters of the King."

"What did you tell him, Evelyn?"

"I said that first he would have to declare, and then the price would be decided. But he still hesitated, so I took my leave of him."

Weeks passed while Christopher, like all of the country, waited for Monk to indicate what was to follow. But although the General controlled the land with an iron grip he gave no sign of his final intentions.

Christopher kept his room on Fetter Lane. It was not a happy place, there were too many memories of Anne, and Sam had lost his cheerfulness. He spent most of this time studying the structure of St. Paul's and he began to believe a new cathedral might be wise, the old one was in such a poor condition. He wondered whether Willis had pursued his inquiries on the brain with him absent, and he hoped not.

Just as he was sure his uncle would not be released, Evelyn told him, "Morley has received the following order: '*Dr. Wren, Bishop of Ely, is to be discharged from the Tower.*' Tomorrow. Do you wish to attend?"

"Yes." He was afraid to be joyful, he wasn't sure the Bishop would accept freedom unless it was on his own terms and that wasn't likely.

Yet as he stood at the entrance to his uncle's cell in the Bell Tower with Evelyn and Colonel Morley, a sturdy, middle-aged soldier, who looked stricken with the fear that it was too late to join the victorious side, he gathered hope as his uncle greeted them without a reproach.

The first thing the Bishop asked, "Where is my son, Matthew?"

Evelyn replied "With the King, on the continent. On his business."

"Good. Morley, what are the conditions of my release?"

"None."

"I will not accept it if it comes in the name of the Commonwealth."

"It comes in the name of General Monk."

The Bishop was relieved and as he stepped outside and saw his nephew. He said, "I told you I would outlive the Usurper. God has shown Himself to us today." But he refused to leave the Tower until he paid his respects "to my great colleague, the Archbishop of Canterbury, William Laud".

Colonel Morley did not protest as the Bishop entered the Chapel of St. Peter-within-the-Tower and prayed for the soul of Laud. Now Christopher was almost sure the Stuarts were going to return, for his uncle performed an Episcopal service. Then he was not so sure as the Bishop paused in the graveyard and whispered, "Here lie many who were beheaded. Thomas More, Anne Boleyn, Catherine Howard, Thomas Cromwell, the Earl of Essex."

Tears came into the Bishop's eyes as he thought of how close he had come to lying here, and he said, "It was fitting that I pray for Laud. When he died, I was confined to my cell and they gave him a Puritan service."

There were still no withered heads spiked over the Traitor's Gate, which was a relief to Christopher, while his uncle smiled with pleasure at the sight of the barge waiting for him in the river.

He cried out, "What shall I do with my freedom? I must build a memorial to our Lord as thanks for my deliverance. Possibly a chapel."

When Christopher heard that the barge was taking his uncle to Monk, he was positive the General was going to support the return of the Stuarts.

He was not surprised that the day after his uncle was freed, Monk gave a secret interview to an emissary from Charles. He thought, the only real business that remained was for Monk to arrange for Charles' return to England as King in such a way as to bring them both the most glory and power. The official announcement came six weeks later.

As Charles Stuart was proclaimed King Charles II, on the orders of Monk, Monk wrote the new King: "*I beg your Majesty to forgive all that is past, since whatever the appearances, I was ever faithful in my heart, but was never in a condition to do you service until this present time.*"

His uncle had spent eighteen years in the Tower and had become an old man of seventy-five during this confinement. He hoped that the Bishop's faith in the Stuarts was worth the imprisonment. He was not sure.

What A Risk Life Is

What a risk life is
You are handed a perfectionist
And given a vulgarian
Both on one cracked plate

The perfectionist stands
on the crack
The vulgarian idyll-like ballets
on the perfect part

But suddenly you see that the
perfectionist
has mended the plate

Stymean Karlen

17

What A Risk Life Is

CHRISTOPHER STARED AT THE KING APPROACHING ON THE STRAND
and he thought, Charles II was a very different kind of a man from
Charles I. It was his first sight of him in many years and now the
differences were marked. It was Tuesday, May 29th, the King's
thirtieth birthday, and he was celebrating it by returning to his
capital in triumph. He was accompanied by a great guard of honour,
twenty thousand horse and foot soldiers were welcoming him and
escorting him from London Bridge to the palace at Whitehall.

May 29th was also the day Christopher's father had died and the
memory saddened him. Dean Wren had longed to live for this day.
How happy he would have been to see *his* King restored! The
memory hurt Christopher too much and he returned to the present.
He stood on the Strand with Evelyn, who stated triumphantly,
"This is a historic occasion indeed!"

Indeed, reflected Christopher, not so long ago the same crowd
that was acclaiming Charles II was driving Charles I out of London
with scorn. But then, his mind ran on, that was another time and
this was another man.

The King riding on the Strand to his restoration to the throne
looked fit to sit upon it. Even astride his horse he was tall, with
long legs and a long body. He rode with an easy, elegant grace
that resembled his father. But he was much taller and darker, and
his curled black hair was combed in ringlets. He looked more like
a Bourbon or a Medici—whose blood was in his veins—than a
Stuart. He was so dark it was obvious why he was called "The
Black Boy". Not at all like the child he had played with, decided
Christopher, except in the authority of his manner.

Evelyn exclaimed, "The air is so clear I can distinguish the
colour upon His Majesty's cheeks! His eyes are sparkling, he knows
great work is to be done. Look, Wren, the common joy is everywhere

305

to be seen. It is past imagining, the greatness of it. Now I no longer have to secretly toast the health of my sovereign. God has blessed us this glorious day."

Evelyn was ecstatic. He had waited for this moment for eighteen years. The sunny sky was a favourable omen and as the procession neared, hours after the appointed time of noon, no one cared about the delay or were troubled by the weary waiting, their joy was so great. He noticed the houses on the Strand were adorned with their richest tapestry, and the balconies were hung with banners.

The bells rang constantly. Evelyn heard St. Paul's, the first time he had heard these bells in years. Trumpets sounded for the King and as he passed the roar that rose drowned out even the trumpets and the bells.

Charles waved to the multitude lining the Strand and he smiled as he bowed to the ladies on the balconies and in the windows.

The exultation was almost more than Evelyn could endure. As the crowd threw their hats into the air and cried adoringly, *"God Bless our good King Charles!"* it was the grandest sight he had ever seen. Proudly he watched the parade led by the Lord Mayor, aldermen, and the companies in their liveries and chains of gold. Colonel Browne's carefully chosen regiment trotted by in their silver doublets and black scarves. The King's brothers, the Dukes of York and Gloucester, rode on each side of Charles. The Duke of Buckingham, bare-headed like his monarch, galloped directly behind the King to show that he had returned to favour. Many nobles and gentry followed, clad in their richest cloth of silver and gold and this train of courtiers stretched for miles. Evelyn thought gleefully, All this was being done without one drop of blood being shed, by the very army that had rebelled against the King's father. He was sure it was the Lord's doing; the procession was so vast it took hours to pass.

Christopher was bored until he thought he saw Anne. But it couldn't be her, this beautiful young woman sat in a coach behind Buckingham. Yet George Villiers was notorious for his amorous life. The coach was escorted by a private troop of soldiers and there were other women in it and Evelyn said, "The Duchess and her attendants. The Duke married Fairfax's daughter to protect himself in the event of a Puritan victory."

He observed his cousin riding with Edward Hyde, the King's chief adviser, and further back in the procession, Scarburgh. After they passed, Evelyn said, "There is no one else worth seeing," and he didn't protest as Evelyn pulled him out of the crowd so they could talk privately.

"Wren, will you be at the Banqueting House this Sunday?"

"I hadn't planned to attend. Why do you ask?"

"Charles is having a reception at the Banqueting House. After services are held and he performs the ceremony of the *touch for the evil.*"

"So soon?"

"Yes. It is fitting that Episcopal services and the Office of Healing are done in conjunction. To show our Majesty's support of our English Church and to remind the public that the King's Touch, that his hands, *His Sacred Hands*, possesses, as God's anointed sovereign, a *Miraculous Gift of Healing*. So his subjects will be doubly impressed."

Christopher doubted the value of the Office of Healing. More often, he thought, those who believed their ills were healed by the King's Touch were suffering from a hallucination. But he kept his doubts to himself.

"Wren, you should be there. Many places of advantage will be decided."

"Already? Charles will have been home just a few days."

"Many places have been given out—already. They were decided when Charles was acknowledged as King. My services to the throne are being rewarded. And there could be a place for you, too. I hear that your uncle is to perform the first Protestant service as a reward for his devotion to the King and to demonstrate His Majesty's firm support of our blessed Episcopal Church. Haven't you been invited?"

"No. I haven't involved myself with political matters."

"You were too friendly with Wilkins and Goddard."

"I am supposed to be in Oxford. Perhaps my invitation miscarried."

"I doubt that. I received mine. But come with me and I will speak for you to His Majesty. I am to be one of his special guests."

Sunday was dry and hot and Christopher met Evelyn outside of the Banqueting House, where there was an enormous throng, who were being held outside by many armed soldiers. But Evelyn possessed permission to enter and they were admitted at once.

Evelyn was absorbed in seeing who had been invited, but Christopher had eyes only for his beloved Banqueting House. He thought, It was fortunate that Cromwell had used it, so that it had survived the Puritan neglect of royal buildings. The boards were gone from the windows and there was new glass in them and the stone was freshly cleaned. There was no trace of the scaffold where Charles I had been beheaded. And plate, hangings, and pictures which had been pillaged from the building had been restored.

He was surprised by the way the great hall was arranged and he realised that only its extraordinary length made this possible. There was an improvised chapel at the far end and the King sat in his Chair of State, which was elevated on a dais above all the other seats, while ecclesiastics and high officers and others in favour stood around him. There were galleries in the rest of the Banqueting House and they were divided in the centre by a railed-in passage, which was lined with Yeomen of the Guard and the royal chirurgeons. He had heard much about the ceremony to *touch for the evil*, but he had never seen it performed, for Cromwell had banned it as a Royalist ritual and superstition.

Evelyn said, "Many will be cured by the King's *Sacred Touch*. If only my son had lived to this day, but he died while the Usurper was in power."

There were so many people inside the Banqueting House that Christopher could not view the dimensions he liked so much. Yet as he saw the jubilant faces, the fashionable clothes, the sparkling jewels which appeared suddenly from hiding, it was extraordinary, he thought, it was as if nothing unpleasant had happened here, not Cromwell's use of the Hall for his own audiences and receptions, not even the death of His Majesty's father on the scaffold outside the spotless, newly shined windows.

Christopher was gratified that his uncle was conducting the services. The Bishop of Ely was preaching before the King in lawn sleeves because of the heat, but he wore a surplice and he led the prayers in front of an altar, performing the rituals the Puritans had hated and banned.

Charles looked detached to Christopher, but the Bishop was fervent as he stated that for purity of doctrine, substance, and decency, the Church of England was the most perfect under heaven. Then his tone grew stern.

He declared, "To avert God's heavy judgment on this land, we must not neglect to exact justice against the offenders of our Holy Church."

Christopher saw the King struggle to suppress a yawn.

His uncle added, "But God has been merciful to this dear land, restoring our beloved and blessed Sovereign to us."

Now the King was interested and he smiled beneficently.

"Today there must be no surrender to false doctrine. God must have our assurance that we will worship Him only in our true Episcopal fashion."

Christopher thought, This was more like a warning than a prayer and he saw the King frown. Suddenly the Bishop assumed his most eloquent and sonorous tone of voice and gave Charles his blessing pontifically.

Charles indicated the *touch for the evil* should start, as if the two ceremonies were part of each other. Christopher watched fascinated while Evelyn was full of wonder. The King sat in his Chair of State as the diseased stood in the railed-in passage in the centre of the Hall.

Evelyn, who was on the aisle, shrank from those waiting for the King's *Sacred Touch,* many of them looked shocking and depressing and they were so close, and he whispered, "The King is mighty indeed to cure these."

Christopher wished he could be closer to them so he could have a fair chance to diagnose their ailments. The most common appeared to be scrofula, but he saw sores that could be syphilitic and signs of scurvy, starvation, and simple cases of ague and the gout—he could tell these ills by the way they shivered or limped—and ailments he couldn't detect.

At the King's sign a chaplain moved to the side of the throne and quoted Jesus: "*He that Believeth and is baptised, shall be saved; but he that believeth not, shall be damned.*" Christopher's attention wandered to his uncle, who was nodding approvingly. Then he heard the chaplain conclude: "*They shall lay their hands on the sick, and they shall recover.*"

As this was pronounced the patients were arranged between a passage formed by the Yeomen of the Guard. The royal chirurgeons examined their petitions, a certificate signed by their minister or churchwarden.

Evelyn said, "In the past the sick had to have written certification that they had not been touched by the King, but since he was absent for many years, it is not necessary now. But those whose certificates are signed by anyone who is not of our Episcopal Church are barred. Rightly."

Those approved were brought one by one to the throne by the chief chirurgeon while the King, as the sick knelt before him, gently stroked their faces with both his bare hands, at which moment the chaplain in attendance declared, "*He put his hands upon them and he healed them.*"

The King did this naturally and tears came into the eyes of many of those Charles touched, Christopher noticed, and he understood the people's faith even as he wished he knew more about their illnesses.

When all the patients were touched by the *Sacred Hands,* they returned to the throne in the same order and another chaplain delivered them to the King, who, to mark the occasion, placed the Angel of Gold around the patient's neck. This gold coin with the stamp of St. Michael was on a white ribbon. And each time Charles put the Angel of Gold around the neck of a patient, a chaplain said, "*This light is the true light, which lights the way of every man that comes into the world,*" and he blessed the one who had been touched.

Christopher asked Evelyn, "How long do they wear the Angel of Gold?"

"Until they are cured. Many are. As soon as Charles was declared King, he touched for the evil. Even before he left for England he cured at Breda, Bruges, and Brussels. Over two hundred and sixty. Very successfully, for he drew a great number of the diseased from the most remote provinces of Germany."

After the last patients were led away there was another prayer. Christopher saw his uncle praying and he joined him. The sun was shining through the windows, forming a kind of halo around Charles' long, black hair and he didn't know what to believe. The ill were gone now and some of those who had limped in had walked out energetically. When the Benediction was finished, the Lord Chamberlain and the Comptroller of the Household brought a basin, ewer, and towel for His Majesty to wash.

As soon as Charles' hands were clean his audience began. There was so much kneeling and kissing of his hand Christopher thought he would be exhausted quickly. Instead, he loved this adulation. Word circulated through the crowd that the King had ordered, "None should be kept out," and Christopher was amazed by the passion of the mob converging toward him, kept from overwhelming him with their emotion only by the heroic effort of the Yeomen of the Guard. The simple thing was to turn away and wait for a more appropriate time to approach Charles, but Evelyn was adamant that they must act now. Evelyn brought Christopher forward, with help from an officer of the Guard whom he knew, so they would not waste their appearance here, but it was still impossible to reach the King at this moment, there were so many people around him. Then Christopher's attention was attracted by a sudden stir. At the King's command the crowd dissolved to permit a small party to approach him. Christopher saw that it was Monk and Hyde and their entourages.

Evelyn said, "They should approach together. They are the men most responsible for his restoration." He added reflectively, "Monk, the man of the hour, victor yesterday, the Duke of Albemarle today."

Christopher said, "I see he is wearing the Order of the Garter."

"Charles wasted no time. As soon as he landed in England and he was sure he was safe he invested Monk with the Garter. At Canterbury."

Evelyn was full of gossip but Christopher stopped listening, his interest caught by the commotion Monk and Hyde were causing. Monk's short, stocky figure, his cold grey eyes, his tight lips, inconspicuous in themselves, held everybody's gaze because of his power. But no one among the onlookers paid much attention to the man who had negotiated with him, whose patience and persistence had made this occasion possible. Hyde was small, with red cheeks and bucolic features and an awkward gait. Yet this unremarkable man, Christopher thought, this typical Englishman, who looked like an obscure country gentleman, held great power now also.

He observed his cousin trailing Hyde step by step. At first Matthew ignored him, although he saw Christopher, as if nothing was more vital than being with Hyde, but then they came within the view of the Bishop, who motioned to his son to acknowledge Christopher. Matthew did, and at his father's insistence, he invited Christopher and Evelyn to join him.

Everyone was still as Monk knelt before Charles and kissed his hand as if this was the final public acknowledgement of Charles' regal authority.

Charles looked amused and sniffed the air; Christopher saw flowers strewn at the King's feet and noticed that the atmosphere about the King was heavily perfumed. Then Charles embraced Monk and the spectators shouted, *"God Bless good King Charles the Second!"* Hyde was next to bow and kiss the King's hand, but this ceremony was perfunctory.

Matthew, seeing Hyde speaking to Charles who listened attentively as a mark of his favour, paused in his march forward and asked, "What do you want, cousin? This is the time to ask. Before all the posts are given out."

"I am content to be a professor of astronomy."

"When there is so much to be gained?" Matthew regarded him critically.

"I am a scholar, not a politician. Besides, I have Puritan friends."

"That might be overlooked. But your lack of ambition won't be."

"Matthew, it isn't lack of ambition, I'm not indifferent to the world."

"You give the impression you are. At Gresham and Oxford it is said you have the best brains in England, yet you allow others to take the credit. You are careless about your reputation, as if it doesn't matter."

This was not true, thought Christopher. Behind his apparent disregard for position was a very strong desire to assume responsibility and to become a figure in the world, to find in his work a confirmation of his judgments. But he didn't want to pay the price that was being asked.

Evelyn said, "Matthew, he is not interested. Come, I must talk to His Majesty before it is too late. I have plans to repair St. Paul's."

"Just a moment." Christopher put out his hands and halted them.

Matthew was astonished by his cousin's strength. Christopher was such a short man but his shoulders were wide and his hands unusually muscular. And now his grey eyes gleamed and his firm chin looked even firmer.

"I would be interested in being the King's Surveyor." Then he, too, could repair St. Paul's, for surely that would be a royal building again.

"Is that what you want?" Matthew was disappointed.

Christopher nodded.

"It is impossible. It has been promised to Sir John Denham."

"But he is a poet, not an architect!"

"He will have John Webb to assist him, Inigo Jones' man."

Evelyn said cynically, "Denham was His Majesty's eyes and ears in England during the Usurpation and conveyed much intelligence to him. As did your cousin. And now they are being rewarded."

Christopher shrugged, hid his disappointment, and said, "Congratulations, Cousin, I am sure you deserve whatever post you receive."

Matthew said proudly, "Secretary to Sir Edward Hyde, first Earl of Clarendon and Lord Chancellor. It is all settled."

"That is why I am in a hurry," said Evelyn. "Before everything is settled." He pushed forward until he was before the King.

Matthew followed instantly so Evelyn would not precede him, while Christopher remained where he was, finding this struggle for place and preferment distasteful. Hyde officially introduced Matthew to Charles, who graciously received him and acknowledged the services he had performed for the crown. Evelyn was next and Christopher observed that the King treated him with precisely the same degree of cordiality and charm, as if that was measured carefully. Neither Evelyn nor Matthew paid any attention to Christopher as they stood side by side in front of the King.

Christopher thought, Court attendance could be infinitely tedious.

Willis appeared unexpectedly, behind Scarburgh, but the latter, after he knelt to the King and kissed his hand, didn't introduce his colleague.

Matthew did, for Willis was not competing with him for position.

After Charles accepted Willis' devotion, Willis announced, "Sir, I still wear mourning. I have worn black ever since your dear father was opposed."

Charles said, "Doctor, you can take it off now. You have paid your proper respects to the dead. And black reminds me of the Puritans."

Evelyn added, "Begging your pardon, but I wore black, too, Your Majesty. Ever since you were forced into exile I have worn mourning."

"How boring and uncomfortable! Willis, what is your pleasure?"

"Whatever is your pleasure, sir."

"You desire to be a royal physician?"

"How did you know, sir?" Willis was astonished. "You are prescient!"

"Why else would a distinguished doctor journey from Oxford?"

"Sir, I have kept our services for eighteen years despite the risk."

"Now that I am back, no one seems to have done anything but support me."

"Exactly, Your Majesty. But I was always constant."

Scarburgh interrupted, "Sir, I was greatly moved by your touch. I am sure your *Sacred Hands* cured more patients than any doctor will."

"Now I must knight you, Scarburgh."

Christopher felt Charles was sarcastic but Scarburgh beamed and stated, "Today, more souls were healed by Your Majesty's *Sacred Hands* than have been cured by all the physicians in your three kingdoms this year."

"A pretty speech," replied Charles. "Willis, you see Scarburgh is quite suitable to be my body physician." But when he saw Willis' disappointment, he added, "I am sure you will do worthy things at Oxford."

Charles' tone was mocking still, thought Christopher, yet it was evident that the King was susceptible to flattery, for he smiled graciously upon Scarburgh and ordered him to stand nearby. Evelyn motioned to Christopher to approach the King, but he hesitated. Many courting Charles were so fulsome they were nauseating. He saw Monk returning with Morley and a lady and his curiosity got the better of his desire to depart. Monk introduced both of them to Charles and Christopher was surprised by the warmth the King bestowed on Morley.

Evelyn noticed Christopher staring incredulously and amused by his bewilderment, he whispered, "Just common sense. Since Morley didn't actually harm the person of our martyred King, a thousand pounds has secured him a pardon. The lady is Monk's wife, the Duchess of Albemarle."

She was fat, dowdy, plain, but Monk wore the Order of the Garter now, and while she looked ridiculous as she knelt, Monk stood as if this was the conclusive proof that he had been right to support the Stuarts.

A moment later Buckingham presented his wife to the King. He was slim and handsome, almost as attractive as his father who had been reputed the most beautiful and graceful courtier in Europe, but Christopher was startled by his wife's appearance. She was extremely plain and swarthy, short-legged and wide-hipped, a little, round, crumpled woman and she wore such finery it framed her plainness by its prominence.

This became insignificant as Christopher saw Anne. Now he was sure it was her. She was one of the Ladies in Waiting kneeling behind the Duchess. This young woman's features were the same delicate ones that had given him so much pleasure. But her garments were of the finest quality, inferior only to the Duchess. In the years that had intervened Anne had matured beautifully; she was miraculously alluring and lovely. His heart palpitated; he was so attracted by the sight of her. She was even more appealing than before, still slim, still with the same soft skin and clear, rosy-cheeked complexion he had adored, and her thick red hair, skilfully combed, was vividly enticing. But the suddenness of her beauty, of her appearance, the excitement, the uncertainty, the thought of her being possessed by someone else, possibly Buckingham, was too much to bear.

He turned away, determined to depart, telling himself that he could not beg, even of the King—it was remarkable how many were gazing at Anne, her appearance was so pleasing, she must be one of Buckingham's mistresses—when his uncle saw his gesture and halted him.

The Bishop said, "Nephew, you can't leave now, you have not had your audience." Buckingham's retinue had retired, but the Duke stood next to the King, closer than anyone else, and before Christopher could protest, his uncle pushed him forward until he was directly in front of Charles.

"Sir, I would like to introduce my nephew, Christopher Wren, who has performed valuable services for the crown."

Christopher knelt and kissed Charles' outstretched hand, but as he stood up at the King's signal he saw that Charles was eyeing him intently. Charles said suddenly, "We knew each other as children. At Windsor."

The Bishop smiled triumphantly as Christopher replied, "Yes, sir. My father was Dean of Windsor and Register of the Order of the Garter."

"You shared my tutor for a short while. You were clever for one so young."

"Sir, he still is. He can do anything he sets his mind on."

"Your son mentioned that to me. Wren, you are a professor of physic."

"Astronomy, sir. At Gresham."

"A modest post. Physic seems to please more people, there is so much sickness in the world. Did you ever learn to ride?"

"Yes, sir. A little later. Comfortably, now."

"You have good posture." Charles stood up and moved down

from the dais until he was face to face with Christopher.

This made him appear even more impressive, thought Christopher, for now the King accentuated his tallness at the expense of his subject's shortness. Charles towered over him, several inches above six feet in height, and it gave the King an extra touch of royalty. And his clothes were drab by comparison with Charles. But, of course, that was supposed to be fitting. This Charles bore little resemblance to his former playmate. The King's lips were thick, sensuous, his cheeks sagged, his complexion was swarthy, his thin moustache stressed the strength of his large nose, but his manners were easy and his voice was charming.

Charles was puzzled. This short, almost diminutive scholar didn't appear to want anything. That was so rare that it was intriguing. A useful person, perhaps, as long as he didn't create any difficulties. Difficult courtiers were such a bore. "You drew me." he said suddenly. "It was a good likeness, although my father tore it up. Do you still draw, Wren?"

"Sometimes. Sir, I have ideas for repairing St. Paul's. I . . ."

Charles halted him irritably, "St. Paul's is falling down upon our ears. I fear to hold services there, it is in such a lamentable condition."

"Sir, that is why I brought it to your attention. The cathedral is in a disreputable state, yet it is the most important structure in the kingdom."

Even the Bishop was startled by Christopher's passion, he was usually such a quiet person who never made a noise that disturbed anyone, but now his nephew stood as if he were viewing St. Paul's at this very moment. He didn't want the King to think his nephew pushing or presumptuous and he hurried to say, "Your Majesty, he intends no offence."

"It doesn't matter," Charles said curtly. "St. Paul's is Denham's duty. Besides, you are not an architect, Wren."

"Neither is Denham, sir."

For an instant the Bishop thought Charles was going to dismiss his nephew, but he said, "Why do you think repairs are essential?"

"No time must be wasted, sir. It is miserably dilapidated. You enter the nave, the choir, and the ruins and desolation are everywhere. If it is not repaired soon, as you said, it will indeed fall upon our heads. That would be a great tragedy, for St. Paul's is the best hope of bringing together our divided country. It should be the soul of London."

Charles frowned as he said, "But you are a physic professor, Wren."

"Astronomy, sir."

"The difference doesn't matter. You have no experience in

building."

"Neither has Denham, sir. But I respect his poetry."

As Charles seemed to hesitate, the Bishop said, "Sir, he will have experience soon. I vowed that if God saw fit to spare me from my confinement in the Tower, I would express my thanks to the Almighty by the erection of a chapel at Pembroke, for the ornament of the university and in grateful remembrance of my education, which was received there. My nephew is going to help me design it."

Christopher didn't know what to say, he wasn't sure he wanted such an assignment, and yet if it helped with St. Paul's it might be sensible.

His uncle continued, "Sir, my nephew is right. St. Paul's is the heart of our Episcopal faith. If you recommend that it be repaired it will show your blessed support of our English Church."

"Bishop, you are persistent."

"Your Majesty, I spent eighteen years in the Tower because of my support of your cause and your Church."

"I am not unmindful of your sacrifices. I, too, spent the same eighteen years in a kind of prison."

"Sir, that is why I must purge my diocese of disaffected ministers."

"Softly, Bishop, softly. That may not be necessary."

"Sir, we must have no Dissenters in any pulpit in England."

"Please, give me no further disturbances. I have had enough of the subject." Charles' voice grew stern. "You grow presumptuous."

"Your Majesty, I know my way to the Tower."

For an instance, Christopher thought the King was going to take his uncle at his word and order him there. Then, as if he remembered his father's rigidity and what a mistake that had been, Charles smiled and said, "Bishop, you are fortunate that I am magnanimous or your impatience could be a considerable embarrassment to yourself."

"Sir, I only want to cleanse our country. We will have no peace unless we rid ourselves of Presbyterians and Papists and possess a united Church. Quickly, before they sow their seeds again and poison the ground."

"Bishop, you weary me." Charles started to dismiss him angrily, then forced another smile and turned to Christopher, "I hear you conduct many interesting experiments. Could you perform one for me?"

"Sir, would you prefer to view experiments with the pendulum, or a lunar globe as I have observed the moon from my telescope, or a weather wheel to measure the expansion of the air, or . . ."

Charles cut in abruptly, "A lunar globe. Your findings on the moon."

"There is one other matter, sir."

"Yes?" Charles paused, looking prepared to be displeased.

"My father saved many of the treasures of the Garter from the Puritans, and he asked me to restore them into Your Majesty's hands."

"Give them to the new Dean of Windsor, when he is appointed."

"But sir, the Garter of Gustavus Adolphus contains hundreds of diamonds."

"They belong at Windsor. In St. George's Chapel. But I will consider your feelings about St. Paul's. Your cousin has mentioned them to me."

The King turned to those waiting nearby and when Evelyn said, "Sir, we have waited long and devotedly for your return," he replied, "That is obvious. Everybody has told me how much they wanted me back that if I had known of their devotion, I would not have waited so long. I have been foolish indeed, not to have come home before, since every man in England is protesting that he has always longed for my return."

Evelyn left the Banqueting House soon after with Christopher and informed him that, in fact, this was a most successful audience, "Now that it is settled that our Sacred Majesty is peacefully and by the grace of God, restored to his martyred father's throne."

"What place did he give you?"

"He suggested a number of posts, but I am not sure which one to accept. Why did your uncle put himself at such a disadvantage?"

"He feels very deeply."

"I am as strong a supporter of our Church as any man, but I wish he had been more cautious. The King leans to toleration, but surely, the Bishops will triumph, yet your uncle has offended the King. I doubt he will be given any advancement."

"I doubt he expects any. He is an old man. Seventy-five."

"Yet vigorous. But they will say his health is failing, that is the excuse they will give to pass him over. And you could be ignored, too, if you are not more careful. I share your views about St. Paul's, and privately, I have made several surveys of the damage already, but the suggestion should come from the King, it is more fitting. Wasn't it a wonderful audience! Everyone of importance was there."

Christopher had hoped to return all the possessions of the Garter into the hands of the King himself—it had been his father's dying wish—but he knew he must hide this disappointment. They walked down King Street quite a distance without another word.

Then Evelyn, as if silence was unbearable, cried out, "You are upset, aren't you, by the King's apparent indifference to St. Paul's?"

"We must take into account the character of Charles. He has

endured much pain and suffering and it has made him prudent. But I would like St. Paul's repaired, if that is possible, before it is injured further."

"Of course, it is possible to repair the cathedral."

Christopher didn't share Evelyn's certainty, but he kept that to himself.

Many Have One Heart

Many have one heart
and hundreds of daggers
You have
hundreds of hearts
and no dagger
This quality happy-s
me
     Who made you

Stymean Karlen

18

Many Have One Heart

GRESHAM OPENED THAT SEPTEMBER AND CHRISTOPHER RESUMED HIS lectures on astronomy. He was pleased to be teaching again, but he was disappointed that nothing was being done about St. Paul's. The cathedral was used for Episcopal services while the extensive damage remained untouched. He stayed away from Court, although Whitehall was near and Evelyn and his cousin chided him for being absent. They warned him that this behaviour would never attract the attention of the King. But the Court bored him and he did not want to risk seeing Anne, the sight of her aroused such a desire in him. He hated feeling thwarted and he believed that she was the mistress of Buckingham, for the Duke was a notorious libertine.

In October he was visited at Gresham by Evelyn and his cousin. They were excited by their news as Evelyn told him, "The King has expressed an interest in The Invisible College. He has a taste for experiments. He has a physic garden where he cultivates herbs for his laboratory, and a chemist, Le Febvre, whom he brought from France, who says cordials can be composed that dropped into the wine of guests, will cause them to babble secrets. Charles finds this amusing and asked if we can do this."

"What did you tell him, Evelyn?"

"I told him that we could do many wonderful and strange things."

"I am not interested in performing tricks."

"What about the lunar globe he requested? Haven't you started it?"

"Charles was just being polite." The King's indifference to his father's efforts to preserve the treasures of the Garter was irritating. He had gone to Windsor in August and delivered these precious items to the new Dean of Windsor and received a written receipt for them, and he was angry at this perfunctory appreciation of his father's devoted services.

L

Matthew sighed. "Christopher, when will you cease being a recluse?"

"When I will cease to have to be a beggar."

"Would you command the King?"

Christopher didn't reply.

Evelyn said, "Christopher prefers to be a natural philosopher. But now he can be and still advance himself. If we organise The Invisible College into a Philosophical College or Society, in the name of the King, and present it to him properly, we might obtain his support, royal support." Evelyn was very excited. "Don't you think it is a wonderful idea?"

Christopher said, "It depends on the circumstances."

"What do you mean?" Evelyn frowned; Wren was being difficult.

"We must be allowed to perform our experiments without interference."

"Of course we will be able to!" Evelyn was impatient, irritated.

"With our gracious Majesty as our benefactor? I doubt that."

Matthew said, "He is an amateur philosopher and he is sympathetic. As long as our discoveries are done in his name and he is acknowledged as our patron, it is likely our findings will be accepted."

Evelyn said, "We must include Sir Robert Moray and Lord Brouncker. Moray is close to the King and Brouncker has wealth and position."

Matthew added, "And Buckingham. He has some knowledge of chemistry."

Christopher said, "The manufacture of love potions, probably. I do not think he is worthy. Brouncker, at least, is a skilful mathematician."

Evelyn said, "Buckingham has great influence with the King and he can be intelligent and inquisitive when he sets his mind to it."

"Next you will tell me that he is a Raleigh and that we should dedicate our work to him. As Raleigh deserved. But not Buckingham."

"Shakespeare dedicated his work to Southampton. For worse reasons."

Matthew said, "Evelyn, we cannot be certain."

"I am sure. The other day I saw *Hamlet Prince of Denmark* played but these old plays disgust our refined age. And his father was a butcher."

Christopher said, "I find it a moving tragedy, full of compassion."

"It makes me uneasy. So afflicted with a mad discourse. It is clear that Shakespeare was not a gentleman's son, not a man of quality."

"A man of spirit. As is Hamlet. If your father had died strangely . . ."

Matthew interrupted, "Christopher, we have more vital matters to discuss. I have compiled a list of those suitable for admission to our proposed new society." He pulled out a scroll with many names on it. "Clarendon approves this and if he approves the King will."

"But Hyde has not yet been appointed Earl of Clarendon."

"He will be. Charles is delighted with the way he has been received."

Evelyn said, "Matthew, read the list. It will do us all honour."

"So you have had a hand in it, too!" exclaimed Christopher.

"Who knows better about the worthy philosophers of our realm than a well travelled gentleman like myself. Don't reproach me as if we are indulging in a conspiracy. We have included experimental philosophers."

"Like Lord Brouncker, with his wealth and position?"

Matthew read proudly, "Like Lord Brouncker, the Duke of Buckingham, Robert Boyle, the son of the Earl of Cork, Sir John Denham, Knight of the Bath, John Evelyn, Esquire, William Holder, Doctor of Divinity, Sir Robert Moray, Knight, Charles Scarburgh, physician to the King, Matthew Wren, Esquire and secretary to Clarendon, and Christopher Wren."

"Are you going to be Clarendon's secretary?" This was interesting news!

"I am already, but the announcement will not be made until His Majesty officially declares that Clarendon is his Lord Chancellor."

Matthew had not wasted any time. He wondered whether his cousin was worthy. Matthew was shrewd, patient, but not truly curious or thoughtful, more disposed to intrigue and calculation than wit, and always discreet.

"Aren't you proud, Christopher? It is a great honour for our family."

"I'm pleased." At least Matthew would be no worse than most and perhaps, if influenced, also disposed to the restoration of St. Paul's.

Evelyn said, "It is a noble honour. And a voice in the King's ear."

Matthew said, "A privilege which must not be abused. The others yet to be proposed for our society must be carefully chosen."

Evelyn said, "Such as Abraham Cowley, the poet, who performed many distinguished services for the crown, and Samuel Pepys and John Aubrey."

"I know Cowley and Aubrey," said Christopher, "But Pepys . . .?"

"Pepys will do us credit," said Evelyn. "While his father was a tailor, he comes from a good family and he is a cousin to Sir

Edward Montagu, who commanded the fleet that welcomed the King back to these shores."

"He comes from an *old* family," Matthew reminded Evelyn, "And he is well educated, a graduate of Magdalene. Montagu is his patron and Montagu is close to the Duke of York. Pepys has become Clerk of the Acts. Secretary to the Navy Board. A useful post. Of some influence."

Evelyn said, "Pepys is an inquiring fellow with a very curious mind, Aubrey is a gentleman and learned, and Cowley has a clever wit."

Christopher walked to his window and looked out. He was surrounded by many things he loved, in the last few weeks he had restored the laboratory to a working condition, but some of the best brains in the land were absent from this list. He asked, "Why haven't you included Wilkins and Goddard?"

Matthew replied, "They supported the Protectorate. And Wilkins was Cromwell's brother-in-law and Goddard his body physician."

"Quite so, and one of the best doctors in the land. And it was Wilkins who kept The Invisible College alive through the difficult days of the Protectorate. Evelyn, you are the one who always refers to Wilkins as '*My dear and excellent friend, who took great pains to preserve the universities from the ignorant, sacrilegious Commanders and soldiers who would have demolished all places and persons that pretended to learning.*'"

Evelyn was uncomfortable as he admitted, "That is correct. But he did preach in the Presbyterian fashion and many in power desire revenge."

"Like my father," said Matthew. "He wants all dissent rooted out."

"So Wilkins and Goddard are to be punished," said Christopher.

"They have been already. Wilkins left Wadham last year for Trinity College in Cambridge, but he has been removed from the mastership despite a petition from the fellows of the college in his favour, and Goddard has been deprived of his post as Warden of Merton. And worse could follow."

"Will they be jailed?"

"That hasn't been decided. Charles is inclined to mercy, as is Clarendon. They feel that everyone should be exempt from death except the Regicides who signed the warrant for the execution of the King. But it is unlikely that Wilkins and Goddard can avoid some degradation."

Christopher stated positively, "I will not agree to any proposed Philosophical Society that does not include Wilkins and Goddard."

"You are risking the King's displeasure."

"Wilkins, as much as anyone, created The Invisible College, and

Goddard protected us despite our different views. I cannot betray them now."

"You will offend the King."

"He may be proud to count a mind like Wilkins among his subjects and he surely could use Goddard's medical skill which is rare. I would also like to suggest we include Hooke and Sydenham."

"Sydenham says he is not interested. But we have Scarburgh."

"Sydenham is the better doctor."

"I doubt that. Scarburgh has more influence. Sydenham has none."

"What about Oughtred, since we should have mathematicians?"

"He died a few months ago. It is said from an excess of joy upon hearing of the return of the King."

Evelyn cut in, unhappy at being left out, "Christopher, I think you will like Samuel Pepys. I will bring him along next week when we have our first full meeting of The Invisible College to discuss our proposals."

Christopher added, "And I am inviting Wilkins and Goddard. If our society is not strong enough to contain them it is not worth continuing."

Evelyn kept his word about Pepys and brought him the following week, but Christopher wasn't sure he liked him. Pepys was uncomfortable as he was introduced to the members of The Invisible College he did not know, and Christopher was surprised by his boyishness, although Pepys was almost the same age as himself. Pepys had a smile for everyone around the table, even Goddard and Wilkins, and Christopher was intrigued by his appearance and obvious curiosity. His features were round and soft and suggested sensuality, with a large mouth, thick lips, a long, fleshy nose, and a dark complexion and olive skin. His wide, deep brown eyes were never still, and as he acknowledged Christopher's greeting the latter saw that Pepys' eyes were everywhere, and that he was vain about his clothes, which were fashionable and yet not of a taste equal to their pretension. They made him look stocky rather than sturdy, although his five foot six inch body was strong. He sat next to Evelyn and a safe distance away from Wilkins and Goddard, and he seemed intimidated by Christopher's learning.

Aubrey, who arrived alone, was more to Christopher's preference. While he dressed like a courtier he was pleasant looking with his large, fair features and light brown hair, and Christopher felt his good nature and a surprising naivete. He liked that Aubrey placed himself beside Wilkins, whom Aubrey knew and regarded with a respect that verged on awe.

When Pepys spoke about the trial of the Regicides, saying, "There will be no trouble. No one will riot to save them. I looked in on Old Bailey, nearby, where the twenty-eight of them—as many as could be arrested—are being tried, and the spectators were shouting for their blood and they will be condemned without question," Aubrey added, "We must look beyond. The public wants the Regicides to dance like monkeys on the gibbet and scaffold, but the country needs moderation."

Christopher asked, "Aubrey, do you think they should be executed?"

"That is for His Majesty to decide. But we must not make a God of the rope and the axe. William Harvey told me, in private, that the blood comes around full circle and that it is against nature to disturb it."

Christopher was preparing the laboratory some days later for the next meeting of The Invisible College, grateful that so far Wilkins and Goddard had not been punished further, when Pepys rushed in with exciting news.

"Wren, today, I had a great treat. I, who saw Charles executed" —he didn't add that at this time he had supported the Commonwealth and the execution of the King—"saw the first blood shed in revenge."

Christopher had come to Gresham by a different route to avoid witnessing the execution at Charing Cross, but now there was no avoiding it.

Pepys continued, "I went to Charing Cross to see Major-General Harrison hanged, drawn, and quartered, which was done there, he looking as cheerful as any man could look in that condition. He was presently cut down, and his head and heart shown to the people, at which there were great shouts of joy. It is said that all the rest will be hanged and quartered, too."

He wished Pepys didn't sound so pleased and triumphant, even though Harrison had supervised the death of Charles.

"It was one of the finest sights I have ever seen. Before Harrison was executed, he was drawn on a hurdle to the gibbet at Charing Cross and there hanged with his face towards the window of the Banqueting House from which his own victim stepped out twelve years ago."

A few days after this Evelyn arrived at Gresham with more news. He told Christopher, "Unfortunately, I was too late when Scott, Scroope, Cook, and Jones suffered for their iniquities at Charing Cross, in sight of the place where they put to death their natural Prince, and in the presence of the King, his son, whom they also sought to kill. I did not see their execution, but I met their quarters mangled and cut and reeking as they were brought from the gallows in baskets on the hurdle. Oh, the miraculous providence of God! We should not have any more difficulties! The hand of God is powerfully against these cruel murderers! No one pities them!''

Christopher was grateful that after ten of the Regicides were hung, disembowelled and quartered, the King scribbled across the table to Hyde, *''I confess I am weary of hanging—let it sleep.''*

Matthew told him this. Aware of Christopher's distaste for the killings, he wanted to assure him that the executions were over. He had come to Gresham to talk to his cousin privately on a matter of urgency.

When he saw that his words eased Christopher, he asked, ''What has happened to the lunar globe we discussed? The King has mentioned it to me again. The moon has aroused his curiosity. If you could construct it now, it might persuade Charles to grant us a royal charter.''

''I will do it if Wilkins is appointed to the chair.''

''Of what?'' Matthew was puzzled.

''Cousin, of the council we must organise to design a College for the Promotion of Physico-Mathematical Experimental Learning.''

''A good title. Then you have been considering my proposal?''

''Yours and the King's. If Wilkins is your nominee, too.''

''After what happened at Charing Cross that could be risky.''

''It will demonstrate our support of our members without respect to their politics or theology. It will do credit to us all.''

Matthew wished Christopher wasn't vital to his plans, but Charles liked experiments that amused him and had set his heart on a lunar globe and no one in The Invisible College could construct it as cleverly as his cousin. And if he brought the best minds in the land together and with a royal charter expressed their support of the King, it could solidify his position at court. He was proud that he was the only one who realised this was an admirable approach to Charles' good will. Other courtiers offered the King money, piety, adoration, and women, but this would give Charles great prestige without any cost or difficulty. And Christopher would be too involved in his work and in Wilkins to compete for credit.

Christopher repeated, ''You support my nomination of Wilkins to the chair, it will assure his selection, and you will have the lunar globe.''

''Haste is needed. It would be best to present our globe before the coronation next year. As a gift from The Invisible College.''

''As soon as Wilkins is in the chair, I will work on it. That is, if there are no further distractions or disturbances.''

Matthew thought disgustedly, Now what? but he asked, ''What do you mean?''

"This senseless blood-letting. Isn't it ever going to end?"

"I told you the killings are over. The thirst for revenge is satis-fied."

"I hope so. They serve no useful purpose. Is it agreed about Wilkins?"

Matthew hesitated—if he showed doubt Christopher would be more appreciative—although his mind was made up already, and then he nodded.

Two months later Christopher showed his lunar globe to The Invisible College in his room at Gresham. He had worked intensely. He had shut out the world to complete the lunar globe, for Matthew had arranged an audience with the King and regarded an immediate presentation as vital. The last week he had not seen anyone; he had arranged with Sam to leave food at the door for him, and he had postponed his astronomy lectures. Yet as he fixed the lunar globe on its pedestal, he thought, It was odd, but this had been one of the most exciting times of his life and he had not minded the solitude. Although there were moments he had felt exhausted, now that he was finished and the moon looked as he wished, he felt full of energy and he had a great desire to continue constructing.

But while the other members assembled Christopher sat quietly beside the lunar globe and gazed outside. A fine misty rain fell and became fog and the winter light faded. Sam, who was working at Gresham again because of his recommendation, lit the candles and put more wood on the fireplace.

Wilkins was in the chair, considering everyone's opinion as always, moderate and gentle, and Goddard was the first to examine the globe and to admire its exactness. Christopher was pleased that many members of The Invisible College were present: Matthew, Evelyn, Scarburgh, Hooke, Boyle, Pepys, Aubrey, and Willis. The first motion, passed without any dissent, was to invite to the next meeting Lord Brouncker, Sir Robert Moray, the Duke of Bucking-ham, Sir John Denham, and other important courtiers.

Christopher didn't protest, for Matthew said, "To aid us to design a College for the Promotion of Physico-Mathematical Experimental Learning."

Matthew stood at his full height of five foot eight as he added proudly, "It is a clever title. I am glad I thought of it."

Christopher didn't correct Matthew's claim, as the members con-gratulated him on his wit. It didn't matter, he thought; vanity made men into children and Matthew was quite pleased with himself.

Then, instead of there being discussion of the lunar globe, as

Christopher expected, Matthew said in a pious voice, "Lord, forgive us our former iniquities. Yesterday and the day before, Your justice was done."

Wilkins shook his head in angry disagreement, which was rare for him, and Goddard was quite upset, and several others looked uneasy, but most of the members nodded approvingly and encouraged Matthew to continue.

"I propose we express a formal statement of gratitude for the events of the past two days."

"What events?" asked Christopher. The more triumphant Matthew became, the more ill at ease Wilkins and Goddard were.

Matthew said, "I forgot, you have been confined to your laboratory."

"For almost a week. What are you talking about?"

"Ask Evelyn. Pepys. They saw God's work. His glorious revenge."

Evelyn said, "Only some of it. Sadly, I missed the most vital part."

Wilkins and Goddard looked as if they wanted to sink through the floor, but there was no escaping the revenge of the Royalists, Christopher thought, and while he counted himself one, too—the son of a Royalist churchman, the nephew of an influential bishop—he felt outside their need for revenge. Whose head, he wondered, had been struck off now?

Evelyn said, "By the grace of God and the mercy of good King Charles, the Lords and the Commons concurred in an order to dig up the carcasses of the arch-usurper, Cromwell, Bradshaw, the judge who condemned His Majesty, and Ireton, son-in-law to the usurper, from out of their fine tombs in Westminster Abbey among the Kings. So, on the anniversary of His Majesty's execution, this command was carried out with a stupendous roll of drums, while this day was declared a solemn day of fasting and prayer."

Christopher was shocked by the way almost everyone except Wilkins and Goddard sat listening placidly while Evelyn spoke. And now Pepys followed.

Pepys said gleefully, "I saw most of what occurred afterwards. The three carcasses, in their open coffins, were drawn on a sledge to Tyburn, then taken out of their coffins, and in their shrouds, hung by the neck."

Christopher wanted to shout, Until they were dead! but who would understand? Everyone, even Goddard and Wilkins, sat as if petrified.

He shivered as Pepys continued, "They were left hanging until the going down of the sun while thousands of spectators, who had seen them in their pride and infamy, cheered as they were forced to eat dirt. For at six that night, when the light was gone, they

L*

were taken down, beheaded, and their bodies were buried in a deep pit beneath the gallows, that fatal and ignominious monument, without their coffins."

Christopher prayed that this was the end, this was too much to endure, and no one was paying any attention to his lunar globe.

Pepys added, "This was not the end of their punishment or their public humiliation. The coffin in which the body of Cromwell had lain was a very rich thing, full of gilded hinges and timber of the best quality and some of the soldiers began to fight over possession of it. It was quite amusing. But when they began to play with the heads, their officer halted them, for there was one more ceremony to perform."

It was frightening, thought Christopher, the pleasure and gratification he saw in some eyes, and he asked, "Wasn't everybody satisfied?"

"No," said Pepys. "Yesterday, their heads were placed on spikes over the entrance to Westminster Hall as a lesson to everyone. I saw them myself." Pepys trembled despite his enthusiasm. "It was my washing day. I took this precaution so I would not catch the contagion, but the heads were green and grinning and then, even as I stood there, only a few feet away from the spiked heads, a gust of wind came up and the head in the centre, that of Cromwell, was blown to the ground. A Yeoman guarding it picked up the skull and said to me, 'I served under him. He was a good soldier.' I saw that the usurper's head was carefully embalmed and looked lifelike. Yet the brain had been extracted by dividing the scalp and the skin resembled parchment, and the beheading was done badly, hacked by a hand not used to the work, for there were cuts at the vertebrae."

"I saw it, too," said Matthew, "but spiked as was fitting."

Pepys, not to be outdone, said, "The officer in charge hurriedly took the head from the guard and in his haste so clumsily impaled it on the ashen pole, pointed with iron, that the spike emerged from the crown of the head. Then I went home."

Aubrey said, "It is rumoured that Cromwell was not buried in Westminster Abbey, that his body was secretly and privately interred next to his favourite daughter, Elizabeth Claypole. But now no one can be sure."

Christopher rubbed his eyes. The lunar globe looked like a skull. The spots were eyes, the whiteness of the surface Cromwell's complexion in the last days of his life, the eminences and cavities of the moon his features. He closed his eyes and remembered the meetings with Cromwell, Elizabeth. Was the face a mask for the soul after all? The globe was winking at him and smiling and appeared about to speak to him.

"Speaking of God . . ."

He opened his eyes. It was Matthew, sounding like the Bishop.

"We must give thanks to our blessed Lord that His will has been done."

Not my God, thought Christopher, in a sudden spirit of rebellion. He could not believe that, whatever his uncle preached. Yet he saw that Matthew was determined to use his prayer to extract loyalty to the King and to evoke a final renunciation of Cromwell. His eyes were playing him false. The globe did possess the shape of Cromwell's head. For a mad instant he wanted to smash the globe, it was a grinning skull green and grey and stinking of death and Wilkins was its brother-in-law and Goddard its physician extraordinary, and then he looked at the others to regain his self control. Matthew was still praying and everybody bowed their heads as if to give thanks for God's punishment of the Regicides. But Christopher, who was praying, too, that God would have mercy on Cromwell's soul, saw tears trickling down Wilkins' cheeks and Goddard suddenly had to go to the water closet and the physician did not return for many minutes.

When Matthew proposed, "At the time we present the lunar globe, I suggest we ask His Majesty for permission to establish a permanent Philosophical Society with a royal charter to signify his approval," this motion passed without a dissenting voice.

But Christopher kept hearing Pepys' parting words, "Wren, you should see the skull of Cromwell, it is quite a sight."

Take Your Own Firm Hand

Take your own firm hand
when no other is there
It will take you
to where
your own soul plans

Stymean Karlen

19

Take Your Own Firm Hand

THE NEXT NIGHT MATTHEW TOOK CHRISTOPHER TO WHITEHALL
Palace to present the lunar globe to the King, and with it the
petition for the creation of a Philosophical Society which would
have His Majesty's approval. He guided Christopher into Charles'
audience chamber, past stern-faced Yeomen of the Guard who knew
the Lord Chancellor's secretary and admitted him without question.
Yet he paused after they entered the doorway, for Charles, sitting
behind a handsome marble table, was engaged in an animated
discussion with Hyde and Monk, each of them standing at his elbow
in their efforts to win his attention over the other.

Christopher realised this was not the moment to interrupt them,
even before Matthew held up his hand to be silent and patient.
He did not mind. It gave him an opportunity to observe his surroundings. He was more interested in the fabric of the palace than
in the intrigue which permeated its functions. He liked that the old
Tudor palace of Whitehall was being restored to its former
splendour, but he disliked the way it sprawled without order from
Charing Cross to Westminster and from the Thames to St. James'
Park. Whitehall Palace and its grounds were immense, yet except
for the Banqueting House, there was no plan, as if the bits and
pieces had been added helter-skelter, lacking dignity or nobility,
beauty or symmetry, comfort or sense, and it was vulnerable to fire.

But the audience chamber, which was part of the King's apartments, was spacious, attractive, and in a choice location. It faced
the river, fifty feet long and twenty-five feet wide, with the kind
of mathematical proportions he preferred. Typical of Stuart taste,
he thought, as he noticed the mixture of elegance and sumptuous-
ness.

Walnut had replaced oak as furniture, a taste acquired from the
court of France, he realised, and the chairs were higher-backed

than he recalled from Windsor and more extravagant in their carving and gilt. Thick Persian carpets covered the marble floor and muffled the sound of their footsteps. Charles, involved in his ministers' arguments, had not heard their entrance. Christopher recognised the full length portrait above the fireplace as that of the King's father. Not by Sir Anthony, he was surprised to see, but by Daniel Mytens, who had portrayed the short, thin, austere Charles I as a handsome, elegant figure. Huge tapestries were on the wall, imported from France, and they depicted the fountains of Rome. Their architectural beauty aroused his interest, and he was intrigued by the paintings by Holbein of Henry VII and Henry VIII. But in the most conspicuous place was a representation of the King's birth, which declared his right to his dominions, and spoke of his miraculous preservation. He could not make out the artist.

This brought him to the heart of the chamber: Charles. While the King's chair was just a few inches above the other chairs, he sat with a presence that dominated. Christopher saw that Charles' long black wig was combed to the last hair, that he was perfectly groomed. It made him aware that his own shoulder length brown hair, without a wig, looked unruly by comparison. The plain brown knee-long breeches and doublet he favoured because they matched his colouring were nondescript next to the King's brilliant blue breeches and doublet, scarlet robes, silver stockings, and diamond garter and ear-rings which glittered brightly.

Christopher had entered through an anteroom crowded with courtiers in feathered hats, fancy thigh-length cloaks, lace ruffles on their sleeves, ribbons on their shoulders, and swords on their hips to indicate their nobility, but none of them matched Charles' magnificence in dress.

Christopher wondered what the King wanted with a simple lunar globe.

But suddenly Charles looked from side to side as if to be free of Hyde and Monk pressing in upon him and saw Christopher and Matthew. He motioned for them to approach, as if welcoming this diversion.

Christopher placed the lunar globe on the top of the marble table and began to kneel and was halted by the King. "Enough of that. Wren, you are certain this is a faithful representation of the moon?"

"As certain as we can be from our telescopes, sir. We know something of the moon's anatomy, but no more than we know of our own. If we possessed better telescopes we could learn much about nature and God."

Charles frowned. "Your words smell of money. It is the universal need. My Lord Chancellor tells me there will not be enough shillings to feed even my own family unless I pursue economy, while Albemarle warns me that if I do not pay the army we will be left defenceless. Wren, has your society found any way to create gold? I could use a good alchemist. I would be tempted to make him my chief minister."

This time it was Hyde who was upset, but before he could reply or any one could, Buckingham entered without pause or announcement, dressed as magnificently as the King, and approached Charles as a familiar. Christopher was surprised that Charles was not offended, but regarded him indulgently as the Duke said, "Sir, I have a piece which I am sure will please you, that I have taken from Beaumont and Fletcher."

Charles brightened as he asked, "Is it a cheerful enterprise?"

"Very much, sir. It will not displease you, I assure you."

Charles turned to Hyde and Monk and said, "Buckingham is wise. He realises that even a King needs relaxation from the cares of state."

"Thank you, sir," said the Duke. "But it will be costly to make this piece sufficiently entertaining for one of your discerning taste."

Charles bit his lips, as if for a moment he regretted what he had just said, then he added, "Buckingham, we must do our best. Hyde, you will see to it that the Duke is given what he needs for this entertainment."

Hyde exclaimed, "But Your Majesty, it will be said that Whitehall is ruled as much by singers and players as the Escurial is ruled by dwarfs and priests. And even Providence will be hard pressed to find the money."

"I am confident that your affection and wit will suffice. You will obey my instructions or go elsewhere to seek your dinner."

Hyde bowed, his mouth trembling, while the Duke gloated and Monk was impassive. Wood was added to the fireplace, yet Charles, with disdain, ordered the windows opened. While the air was frosty and the strong wind blew the tapestries about, he declared, "I like fresh air even if there is ice on the Thames. I have survived foul weather before."

Charles returned to the lunar globe and he examined it carefully as everyone, Buckingham, too, was silent as they waited his judgment.

Christopher was amused by a similar design in Buckingham, Hyde, and Monk despite their rivalry for the King's favour. All three had grown heavier, even in the brief time that had elapsed since the restoration of Charles. Hyde and Monk had acquired a second chin and the younger man was on the verge of one. Hyde had a new moustache and beard in the fashion of Charles I and his cheeks were fuller, but he still had the florid complexion. It was Monk in his brown dress uniform and gold sash who had become appallingly fat, as if power brought weight and he was standing behind himself. But his expression, as usual, revealed nothing.

Charles said, "Wren, you make the moon attractive. Acceptable."

"It is, sir," Matthew said. "And it is suitably inscribed." He read the inscription which he had dictated to Christopher.

> *"TO CHARLES II*
> *King of Great Britain, France, and Scotland*
> *For the Expansion of whose Dominions since no*
> *One Globe can suffice,*
> *Christopher Wren dedicates another in this*
> *Lunar Sphere."*

Charles said, "Thank you. I am glad that is established."

"As we hope, sir, you will establish a Royal Philosophical Society."

"How much will that cost, Matthew?"

Christopher said, "Only patience, sir, and your approval."

"I wish I could trust that."

"Sir, we do not need funds."

Charles stared at Christopher as if he would have liked to have believed him, but was afraid to; no one wanted something which cost nothing.

Matthew said, "Sir, you can trust my cousin."

Charles said sharply, "I have known him since childhood. Before you did. And you presented him last year. I have heard much about him." He returned to Christopher. "Wren, I am told you are an authority on mathematics and anatomy and have some interest in building."

"Sir, if you would consider my views on St. Paul's?"

"Not now! You must have other interests beside that cathedral."

Christopher was silent. He thought, None greater than St. Paul's, but that was not something to define.

"Wren, I may be marrying the Portuguese Princess, Catherine of Braganza. Part of her dowry would be the town of Tangier. It is an important seaport. With Tangier in our possession, our navy will be able to put down the Moorish pirates who have been harassing our sailors. But the mole, harbour, and fortifications of the citadel are in such a ruinous condition they should be repaired immediately."

"Sir, I am sure you have many competent to perform that service."

"You have been recommended."

Christopher was surprised and he blurted out, "Sir, who recommended me?"

"That doesn't matter. I am told you are one of the best mathematicians in Europe. And your lunar globe is cleverly done."

"Your Majesty, what do you want me to do?"

"Go to Tangier as my Surveyor, report on the repairs that are needed and rebuild them or do whatever is necessary to strengthen them properly."

"Your Majesty does me much honour."

Charles regarded him suspiciously. "You do not want it?"

"It is, as I said, sir, a great honour, but . . ."

"Wren, I am not amused. You are an engineer, aren't you?"

If he denied that, he would never have a chance at St. Paul's. Yet he had little interest in Tangier and less in fortifications. He said, "Yes, Your Majesty, in some ways, but I am in a dilemma. I have given my word to my uncle, the Bishop of Ely, to help him with the chapel he is planning at Pembroke and I do not think my health is suited to Tangier."

"After English weather?" Charles exclaimed sceptically.

Matthew said, "Your Majesty, my cousin was a very frail child."

"I know about his childhood. Wren, did you know you are also being considered for the Savillian Professorship of Astronomy at Oxford?"

"No." This was exciting. This was the best chair of astronomy in the country. "I am honoured."

Hyde handed Charles a paper and he read: "*'It is required that the holder of this chair should explain the Ptolemaic and Copernican and other modern astronomical systems.'* Do you qualify, Wren?"

"I believe so, sir. So far." He knew there were other conditions.

"*'He is to be of any nation in Christendom, provided he has a good reputation, a knowledge of Greek, and is twenty-six years of age '*"

He thought of Daniel, but he said, "I am twenty-eight. Old enough."

"Furthermore," Charles read on, "*'The choice of the professor is to lie with the Archbishop of Canterbury, the Lord Chancellor, the Chancellor of the University . . .'*" Charles paused and then added, "And myself. Wren, your refusal is hardly likely to put me in an approving temper."

"I am sorry, sir, I would like to be Savillian Professor but . . ."

"Your health forbids?" Charles said cynically.

"Partly. And I have no taste or talent for military fortifications."

Charles turned to Hyde, asked, "Are you going to approve of Wren's appointment to Savillian Professor? Clarendon, you are free in this."

Hyde hesitated, then said, "Sir, I haven't decided yet."

"Albemarle, what would you do?"

"Your Majesty, the fortifications must be repaired."

Buckingham said, "Sir, I have several other prospects."

Matthew added, "Your Majesty, perhaps my cousin will reconsider."

"I doubt that. Am I right, Wren?"

"Yes, Your Majesty."

"I have been told that you knew the Usurper quite well."

"I wonder if anyone knew him that much."

"You supped with him, you were friendly with his daughter, his physician and brother-in-law. I hear you don't want them punished."

"Wilkins is a distinguished scholar and Goddard is a fine physician."

"Does that excuse their crimes?"

"Sir, they didn't harm anybody."

Even Monk, who had served Cromwell, was disturbed by this reply, but Charles said, "Now that the Usurper is safely dead and in the winding sheets of posterity, was he really so able? Wren, did he really impress you?"

There was a force in Charles that had to know and Christopher thought, However they sought to obliterate Cromwell, he would not melt away, but it was not that simple, nothing about Cromwell was. He said, "Cromwell respected the arts and the sciences in the universities."

"So do I!" Charles said hurriedly. "I have great respect for them. But that was not why the Usurper won. Why do you think he did?" Wren, at least, would give him an honest answer, if anyone would.

"Perhaps he knew how to finish what he started."

"Is that why you insist on having his brother-in-law and physician included in your Philosophical Society?"

"Please, sir," said Matthew, "not everyone agrees with that."

"I asked your cousin, not you."

"Sir, they are the best in their field and we want the best, don't we?"

Matthew apologised for Christopher's behaviour, Hyde was annoyed, Monk was uneasy, Buckingham laughed, but Charles asked, "You believe that the Usurper must not outdo me in support of the arts and sciences?"

"Precisely, sir."

"Matthew, I will give you my view of your Society at a suitable time. Buckingham, is the entertainment ready?"

"Sir, the maids of honour wait outside for your pleasure."

"Bring them in."

The Duke motioned to the Yeomen at the door and a moment

later a half dozen attractive young women entered and curtseyed before the King. What caught Christopher's attention was that Anne was among them. When he saw Charles' eyes wander to her, as the Duke said to Charles, "Sir, whoever is in my service, is at your service, I am aware that you need beauty about you to relieve you of the cares of the day," he wondered if Anne, too, was at the King's disposal. She wore a lovely red satin gown with a veil of black lace over her stunning red hair and her bodice was cut so low it revealed much of her full, white, voluptuous bosom.

If Anne noticed him, she didn't show it. She stood in the rear, but there was no question where the King's interest was now. Charles stared at her intently and he seemed finished with everything else.

Yet when Charles detected what he thought was a censorious look in Christopher's eyes, he felt compelled to say, "Wren, you mustn't be like Hyde who thinks beauty and pleasure are vulgar and unworthy."

Christopher didn't reply and turned to go, only to be halted by Charles.

"Wren, what do *you* really desire?"

He felt that Charles was taunting him, particularly in front of Anne, and then he told himself this was ridiculous. Thinking he might as well ask for the moon while he was about it, he said, "Sir, I would like to be Surveyor General of the Kings Works so I can restore St. Paul's."

"Denham is Surveyor General. You know that. We discussed it."

"Sir, you asked me. May I go now, Your Majesty?"

"Just a moment." Charles gazed at Christopher and thought, *This young astronomy professor is a strange one. He has no self praise when everyone is full of it. And no one has to tell me about St. Paul's. I know it has become as barren as a barn and its bones are brittle but that is not the end of the question.* Despite his cynicism, he had a sudden need to justify himself to Christopher Wren—after all, he rationalised, they had played together as children—and he said, "I am aware that St. Paul's in in a lamentable condition. But there is no money for it. Whatever is in the treasury has to go for our army and navy."

"And Tangier, sir," suggested Christopher.

"Yes. Wren, if you want to repair St. Paul's, fix Tangier, and once that is put in order, your wish might be granted. If you accept this post, you will be given an ample salary, a leave of absence from your Professorship, and possibly, succeed to Denham's office when he passes on."

It was tempting and yet as Christopher appeared to consider it, he knew he could not accept. He said, "Your Majesty, you are very kind and I am deeply honoured but I have no talent for fortifications. I would not know how to prevent an invasion."

Charles was freshly shaved and his dark skin was smooth and it glistened with a healthy glow but now he flushed angrily. For an instant he was inclined to dismiss this recalcitrant professor without another word, and then he remembered there might yet be a time when he could use Wren. And when he saw him looking anxiously yet eagerly at the maids of honour, he said abruptly, "Buckingham has good taste, don't you think?"

"Yes, sir." Christopher stood like stone, determined not to betray himself.

"My maids of honour are one of my most pleasant charges. I am responsible for their welfare. It is one of my obligations that I enjoy very much."

If he could only say good night, thought Christopher, but no one left the King's presence before he was dismissed.

Charles said mockingly, "If you do become Savillian professor, it is understood that you do not marry. Celibacy is the custom. Although some of those chosen have strayed. But you wouldn't, would you, Wren?"

"I haven't the post, sir." Out of the corner of his eye he saw that Anne was watching him. "So that is not my concern."

"I wonder how much self control you would have then."

What was the point of telling him this? What cynicism. But Christopher stood motionless, without change of expression, saying nothing.

"But you do listen well. Very few do. Wren, you are dismissed."

A Seed Will Not Grow

A seed will not grow
in sawdust
But plant it if you must
A planter's instinct
grew The Creation
And he who can does

Stymean Karlen

20

A Seed Will Not Grow

DANIEL STOOD IN FRONT OF THE ENTRANCE TO GRESHAM AND PAUSED to catch his breath after his climb up the hill from the Thames and Paul's Wharf.

So this was where Christopher and his Society met, he thought, and he recognised that the college had been a grand Elizabethan town house and he was glad that Gresham, with its medieval gate and spacious quadrangle, was allowed to remain as it was in the heart of a growing city.

From nearby St. Paul's, he heard the bells boom the hour. It was the middle of the afternoon, when he had planned to arrive, but now that he was here he was not sure he should enter. It was many years since he had seen Christopher and his school friend must have changed greatly. Yet he had come so far, it seemed foolish to turn back. But he hesitated.

It was cold for the end of April and the coal smoke caused Daniel to cough and he noticed that many of the stones of Gresham were black. He had refused a hackney coach at the river, so he could renew his knowledge of London first hand, but now he was sorry he had. The trudge through the narrow, winding streets was tiring, the noise was appalling, and the stench was disagreeable. He paced along Warwick Lane, where his father had lived, and instead of feeling pleasure it reminded him of the gulf that had developed between him and his father. St. Paul's still stood as he remembered it but the ruined tower and the eroded stone was more like a skeleton than a living fabric and it was blackened by coal smoke, too.

He felt betrayed by his nostalgia. Perhaps, he reflected unhappily, he should not have left Amsterdam. It was one of the great cities of Europe, with one hundred and fifty thousand inhabitants, but London was even more jammed than it was years ago. There were more houses than he recalled, more houses crowded together, more carts, coaches and commotion, more cold winds and only a little sun and fresh air. Worst of all was the dirt that was everywhere and which made London ripe for plague and fire.

He was a fool to have come here, he decided, despite his discontent with Amsterdam. He felt for the letter close to his heart and that gave him some confidence. His doublet was tailored to fit, his grey breeches and dark stockings, while not brilliant, were of good quality, and he wore a fine cloak that indicated fortune had treated him well.

But what would Christopher do? Now that he was important?

Daniel wavered again before the entrance and a voice within him said, *If Daniel Van Doorn was asked by Fate what old friend it would please him most to meet again, it would be Christopher Wren.* Push open the door. Go inside. He might just still care. Daniel stepped on to the cobblestones of the quadrangle, his heart pounding, his pulses racing, thinking, Will I be able to say *My Friend* without feigning?

The quadrangle was quiet after the noise outside but as he entered he was accosted by a fat-faced, squinty-eyed, small-mouthed, officious man.

Sam asked him, "What do you want?"

"Are these the quarters of the Royal Society? I was told . . ."

Sam interrupted suspiciously, "You are a foreigner, aren't you?"

"I'm Dutch, if that is what you mean."

"I thought so from your accent and dress. Who are you looking for?"

"Christopher Wren."

"What do you want with Doctor Wren?"

"Is he an anatomist, too? I heard that he was an astronomer now and an experimental philosopher, but I didn't know he was a doctor, too."

Sam said proudly, "Doctor Wren is a learned man. Two years ago, in 1661 he was appointed Savillian Professor of Astronomy at Oxford and was given his degree as Doctor of Civil Laws at Oxford and he received a similar honour from Cambridge. And he persuaded the King to grant The Invisible College a royal charter which has His Majesty's approval and support."

"Thank you. May I see Doctor Wren?"

"What do you want with him?"

"We were friends at school."

"Friends?" Sam made no effort to hide his scepticism.

"Yes. I have a letter from Henry Oldenburg, who is secretary to the Royal Society, to a friend of mine in Amsterdam, Baruch Spinoza. Mr. Oldenburg wrote Mr. Spinoza, who experiments on lenses, that Christopher Wren is also interested in such experiments.

Mr. Spinoza gave me the letter and said he would like to communicate his ideas on lenses to your master. Doctor Wren will be upset if I am turned away." Daniel halted angrily. What right had this servant to stand here like an inquisitor?

"I don't know whether he is available. He is conducting an important meeting this afternoon for the Royal Society and he doesn't like to be interrupted." But when Daniel moved toward him threateningly, his hand on the sword he wore, Sam retreated, deciding that this Dutchman did wear clothes of a quality that indicated some worth, and asked, "Who should I tell him wants to see him? If Doctor Wren is in?"

"Daniel Van Doorn. From Westminster."

Daniel waited nervously, thinking, This servant was too possessive, he wouldn't even inform Christopher of his presence, or if he did it would be so unflattering his old friend wouldn't want to see him. And why should Christopher? Seventeen years was a very long time. He couldn't blame him. He could hardly endure this waiting. He hated to wait; Christopher always had been more patient.

Suddenly Sam was back and he led Daniel down the length of one of the longest halls the latter had seen. "Built by Sir Thomas Gresham, Elizabeth's greatest merchant," Sam said. "Now the entry to the apartments of the Society. The next room is used only for special occasions, as today's meeting. The Society has two other rooms and a fine gallery."

At the end of the hall Sam turned into a chamber almost as large. Christopher sat at a huge table, adjusting the model of a building upon it. There were dry rushes on the floor at the entrance, to wipe muddy feet on, and their feet crackled on them. Christopher looked up, but he was silent, formal. Daniel thought, with a shudder of apprehension, Flee, Flee! But he had a need to see his old friend, however difficult the encounter, and so, in spite of his fear and pride, he approached Christopher, who stood up slowly. For a moment they were both motionless.

Daniel saw that Christopher was working hard, for he was sweating despite the chill that pervaded the meeting room, and was preoccupied, groping to straighten out the threads of a tangled web, turning inward for his feelings and thoughts. Daniel was startled that Christopher had grown so little. But he liked that his shoulders had widened and that his hands were beautiful in their maturity, slim, long, and smooth. And his features had become stronger. Christopher's high cheekbones were more pronounced, his chin was firmer, and his grey eyes were bright and clear. Daniel was relieved that there was nothing ostentatious about Christopher; he wore a plain brown doublet and breeches, and no periwig or powder on his hair which fell in long waves below his shoulders.

Christopher reflected, Daniel stood as if to plead his case—yet he was also erect and defiant in his effort to be composed. Yet this was not his nature, he thought. Daniel had grown into a tall, slender man, but his hair and complexion were still fair and he was dressed fashionably, although not like a dandy or a gallant, and Christopher was surprised to see that he was wearing a sword.

Then Daniel smiled and Christopher thought, How true it all was! I, for one, never forgot our happy days! With a feeling he hadn't realised he possessed Christopher offered his hand and as Daniel took it, he was surprised at the depth of his emotion. He exclaimed, "Daniel, when did you arrive? You look fine. Are you back for good?"

"I'm not sure. Christopher, you look well, too."

"I'm to present a model for a building I'm designing for Oxford." He pointed to the edifice on the table. "To show the others when they arrive."

"It looks like a Roman theatre."

"It is based on one. But most of the design is my own."

"Do the other members of the Royal Society have to approve?"

"No. But I am interested in their reactions."

Christopher sounded so humble Sam blurted out, "Doctor Wren is famous for his inventions, a weather clock he calls a barometer, new ways of engraving, experiments in perpetual motion, the grinding of glasses, the . . ."

Christopher cut him off sharply, showing impatience un-expectedly. "Enough!"

"Doctor, you should feel proud of your achievements."

"My work is not something to talk about. It is better to do than to talk about it. Daniel, what has brought you back to London?"

"It is a private matter."

Christopher asked Sam to watch at the entrance for any early arrivals and to delay them a few minutes if any came now. Sam showed disapproval but Christopher didn't reprimand him. After Sam was gone, he told Daniel, "You think I'm indulgent, but I've known Sam a long time and he acts like my steward. Can you tell me why you are here?"

Daniel gave him the letter from Oldenburg to Spinoza and after he read it and said he would enjoy meeting Spinoza to exchange their views on lenses, Daniel said, "This letter is just my excuse, my calling card."

"Did you study with Rembrandt van Rijn?"

"So you remembered!" Daniel was pleased. "Have you seen his work?"

"No. Is he like Rubens?"

"Not at all. He is not like anyone. That was my trouble." When

Daniel saw that Christopher was genuinely interested, he continued, "I found myself imitating him, which was impossible. I was too literal. Rembrandt suggests rather than states." Aware that while Christopher was listening attentively he might not be comprehending what he was saying, Daniel hurriedly unwrapped the bundle he was carrying with love and care and held out the contents for Christopher to examine.

They were two portraits of elderly men and Christopher didn't know what to make of them. The background that framed the faces was so dark and gloomy. The paintings had no finish, not like Sir Anthony who suggested Italian sunshine. Yet, as he stared intently at the portraits he felt that the painter was blessing the soul—whatever the mortifications of the flesh, the more he gazed at these old men the more he felt linked to them.

"Who are they?" he asked.

"The man with the beard is my father. What do you think of it?"

"The background is so dark, so full of shadows."

"It is the way Rembrandt views life."

Christopher was surprised that the portrait of Daniel's father showed a countenance and dress more like a courtier than a merchant. The small, pointed chin beard, the matching moustache, the starched white collar, the wide-brimmed hat seemed to have nothing in common with trade.

Daniel asked, "Don't you like it?"

"It isn't that. I thought your father was a learned man, but . . ."

"He looks like a courtier?"

"Yes, he does. At least in this portrait."

"While he rose in the world by trade, he wanted me to be a gentleman. That was why he sent me to Westminster and taught me to be skilful with a sword. But he also has a great reverence for learning, he speaks many languages, he reads widely, so he had me study with Spinoza, whom he esteemed as a scholar. And when I refused to be a merchant like himself, he allowed me to work with Rembrandt, whose painting he respected. He says a man who can draw accurately can always make a living."

"Is he still alive?"

"Yes. But we differ about Spinoza and Rembrandt now. He thinks the difficulties that have befallen them are their own fault."

"What difficulties?"

"Rembrandt van Rijn was declared a bankrupt and Baruch Spinoza was excommunicated by his synagogue for his so-called heretical beliefs."

"Daniel, you don't agree with these judgments?"

"No, I don't. It is one of the reasons I left the Republic. Any country that can allow such injustices to occur is not worth living in."

"Do you think England will be any better?"

Daniel was startled by Christopher's reply. He didn't expect it from him; Christopher was doing what Christopher wanted to do and appeared sure of himself. But perhaps there were more contrasts in him than he knew.

"We have gone through a terrible civil war. Death was everywhere and the preoccupation with its throes, to the very decomposition of the corpses, was horribly depressing. Why do you think I work so hard?"

"Because it is your need, desire, purpose."

"I am also a mathematician who observes. Who is the other portrait?"

"He is supposed to be St. Paul."

Christopher couldn't hide his surprise. This man looked like a Dutchman. He stared at the portrait again, but still he was incredulous.

"Knowing your interest in the cathedral, I thought you would like it."

But that was not why he was infatuated with that church. And Paul had been a Hebrew, not a Dutchman. His scepticism grew.

Daniel said, "Rembrandt was given a commission to paint St. Paul two years ago, in 1661. But when he came to do it he painted himself."

"It is an interesting portrait but the English will never accept an ageing Dutchman as St. Paul. At least if he looked a little English."

"I warned him of that but he merely shrugged and said, '*Who knows what Paul really looked like? Every painter depicts the figures of the Bible as natives of their own land. The Italians, the Spaniards, the Germans, so why not the Dutch?*' To reiterate that, he painted a second portrait of himself, named it St. Paul, too, and gave it to me as a farewell present and refused to take anything for it, although he had no money. What do you think of it as a painting? He couldn't afford a model."

"Rembrandt looks so old, tired, lonely, suffering."

"He was only fifty-five when he painted this, but he aged prematurely."

"Did he sell the original?"

"No. It was rejected on the grounds that it was not faithful to the Bible. He laughed and said that when I felt blind I should look at it, that it might teach me to see. Christopher, look at it carefully, without any preconceptions. Concentrate on the eyes."

Who had said the eyes were the windows of the soul? It didn't matter, Christopher told himself, it was a familiar saying but this portrait wasn't. He couldn't move, transfixed by the eyes. He thought, Most observers would say Rembrandt van Rijn was a fat old man infected with compassion and a need to express it. *But not if you truly looked. You might kill a man like you killed a chicken or a pig and ignore the noises he made and yet here was a man whose eyes came out of his soul.* Christopher yearned to touch the paint, to make sure it was dry, to feel the eyes, they were so alive. But Daniel was waiting for him to speak. He said, "I have been engaged in many discussions about where is the soul and now I know. It is in this painting."

"And not in God?" asked Daniel, almost mockingly.

"God is in this painting, too. His eyes draw you toward Him. They outstrip everything else in this work."

Daniel hesitated, as if pondering a vital decision, and then he said quickly, before he could change his mind, "Take the painting. It is yours."

There was so much anguish in Daniel's eyes, Christopher replied, "I can't. It means too much to you. I will appreciate it but you love it."

Daniel breathed deeply, to gather energy, and said curtly, "If that is what you wish. I trust I haven't interfered with your meeting too much." He took the two portraits and turned to go.

Christopher halted him and asked, "Do you have a place to stay?"

"No. After Cromwell's death my father sold his house on Warwick Lane."

"Would you like to stay on Fetter Lane? I have a room there, in Sam's house, the Steward's, which I am not using at present. There is no obligation. As soon as you find better quarters you can move out."

"I don't think your Steward likes me."

"He is jealous. But that far I do not indulge him. Please stay."

Christopher sounded sincere and Daniel paused in his departure.

"And you can meet the members of the Royal Society."

Daniel reminded him, "I am Jewish."

"Does that matter?"

"It could cause difficulties."

"Then we won't discuss it. With your Dutch accent you will have enough difficulties. We are on the verge of war with Holland and the people are eager to fight. As long as it doesn't take place on their soil." When Daniel still hesitated, he took him by the arm and sat him by his side and added, "Your accent has one advantage, they won't assume you are a Spaniard and a Papist. Holland is a Calvinist country, isn't it?"

"Very."

"Good. While we may be at war with Holland soon, it is the Spanish and the Papists who are feared and hated. But I wouldn't refer to Holland as the Republic. In England that is considered an obscene thought."

A minute later Sam entered with Hooke, who as the curator of the Royal Society, arrived ahead of the others to see that everything was in order. While Sam built up the fire and arranged the room as Hooke commanded, Daniel resolved to be courteous and cheerful, but he felt vulnerable.

Hooke, whose slight, misshapen body gave him the look of a half-grown child, recognised Daniel. As Christopher started to introduce Daniel, he interrupted sharply, "I entered Westminster before you left. You were in an upper form. Why didn't you study to be a King's Scholar?"

"I was going to Amsterdam to study painting."

"You were the Dutch boy who drew all the time. Did you pursue it?"

"Yes. I worked with Rembrandt."

"Who?"

"Rembrandt van Rijn. The Dutch painter."

"I was a King's Scholar. I went to Christ Church. Did Busby flog you?"

"A few times."

"He never flogged Wren." Hooke was envious. Moving about briskly, his long dark brown hair uncombed and loose, he examined what Sam had done. Then he dismissed Sam curtly and turned to Christopher and stated, "I don't trust him. Have you seen our apothecary bills? Six pounds! And the hangings for this chamber are costly. He must be pocketing some of the money. Van Doorn, did you give Busby any Christmas presents?"

"No. Was that necessary?"

"You know it was practically compulsory. If you wanted to be a King's Scholar. Wren, what are you going to do about Sam Taunton?"

"There is nothing to be done. He has not committed any offence."

"My suspicions are usually right." He saw the model and the table and Hooke asked, "Is this the building that Sheldon is giving to Oxford as a parting gift to celebrate his elevation to Archbishop of Canterbury?"

When Christopher nodded, he took a closer look at it and said, "It will never work. Your roof is not supported by any pillars. You are a clever mathematician, but that won't solve this problem. But you won't allow me to help you with the design, even though you have no practical experience in building. How large is the span of the roof?"

"I haven't decided yet. It depends on what size will work."

Hooke repeated urgently, "You must use columns to hold the roof."

"I want it to resemble a Roman theatre. Since Latin is the

fabric of learning and this structure is for a university, it should be in the fashion of Rome. If I use columns to carry the interior load I will destroy the resemblance to an ancient theatre that will be suitable for an academic audience. But don't worry, I will solve this problem.''

Before Hooke could correct him, other members of the Society arrived.

Christopher introduced Daniel to them as: "My old friend, Daniel Van Doorn, who attended Westminster with me. He is a fine artist."

Daniel bowed respectfully to the members who returned his greeting.

Viscount Brouncker, President of the Society, sat at the head of the long table, and next to him Sir Robert Moray and Henry Oldenburg, the Secretary. Daniel sought to remember all the members: Robert Boyle, Dr. Jonathan Goddard, Bishop John Wilkins, Samuel Pepys, William Holder, John Aubrey, Sir Charles Scarburgh, John Evelyn, Abraham Cowley, John Dryden, whom he recalled from Westminster, and Sir John Denham.

The middle-aged Brouncker, strongly built but softly spoken, began the preceedings with a prayer to God and to the King, then said, "This meeting of the Royal Society for the pursuit of Natural Experimental Philosophy is hereby declared open." Hooke, as curator, carried in the royal mace that had been presented to the Society by the King as a sign of his support. The silver mace, which bore the royal arms and emblems, was very heavy and the frail, stooped Hooke staggered under its weight. But he placed it proudly on the table in front of the President, although its weight caused him to drop it awkwardly and he almost knocked over the model. After the business of the past meetings was reviewed by Oldenburg, a stout, dark man with a strong German accent, the members who were present were asked to propose new business, if they had any. Boyle spoke about the vegetation of plants; Hooke discussed his experiments on the vibrations in the air and that they corresponded to musical notes and after further investigation he hoped to tell how many strokes a fly could make with its wings; Evelyn said that prices were increasing so rapidly they must bear in mind the possibility of changing the currency from fifteen shillings for every pound weight of gold to ten shillings; Pepys talked about the history of saltpetre and gunpowder and how both were essential to the Royal Navy.

There was a brief pause when Sam returned to serve wine and everyone sipped it and seemed to relax as Wilkins said, "I want to bring to the attention of our Society, a newly invented musical instrument, a harpsichord with gut strings," and it was agreed, although Hooke questioned its value and Evelyn was sceptical, that

M

Wilkins should submit it to the next meeting for their inspection and possible approval. Then Scarburgh announced there would be an anniversary oration in praise of Dr. Harvey in the Anatomy Theatre of the College of Physicians on Warwick Lane and that all members of the Society would be welcome.

Finally however, the members turned their attention to the model on the table. Christopher said it was to be a theatre to provide Oxford with a meeting place and a structure where the public ceremonies of the University could be performed with suitable space, dignity, and comfort.

Brouncker and Moray excused themselves, saying they had royal business to attend to, and Denham followed them with the same excuse.

Hooke said to Daniel, "Denham, as chief surveyor, wants to avoid committing himself. Too bad, with his presence, we would possess the most illustrious living poets in the realm, Cowley, Dryden, and Denham. But one has to be a true man of science to understand building, like myself."

Daniel didn't reply, for Evelyn was holding forth. He wore the ribbon of St. Andrew's Cross—"our patron Saint," said Hooke— but Evelyn's long face, nose, and chin reminded him of the snout of a dog as he said, "I bow to no one in my admiration for Doctor Wren's many talents, but I do not comprehend how such a building can be successful." Evelyn didn't say why, but added, "Charles has appointed me to the commission for reforming the buildings and streets of London and His Majesty consults me on many architectural matters. I doubt he would approve of it any more than I do."

Wilkins reminded him, "Christopher isn't building the theatre for the King. Sheldon, the Archbishop of Canterbury, is supplying all the funds."

Pepys asked, "Wren, are you going to call it after Sheldon?"

Christopher said, "I'm not interested in the name but how it works."

"Hear! Hear! Hear!" cried Pepys, but he didn't commit himself.

Daniel noticed that Pepys was running to fat, although still a young man, and wore a fine cloak with gold buttons and a silk suit which must have cost much money and he wondered how Pepys could pay for it, since this member was just a Clerk of the Acts. But Pepys kept talking about how often he saw the Duke of York, the King's brother, as if York was an intimate acquaintance, and each time Pepys mentioned York, Evelyn spoke of how frequently the King consulted him. Daniel doubted that many of the members were honestly looking at the D-shaped model of a

Roman Theatre, but those who didn't disagree with it nodded sagely as Christopher said it was still in an experimental stage and there might be many changes before the final design was decided. "After all," he pointed out, "the corner stone hasn't been laid yet and won't be for another year."

Evelyn said, "Even so, you must broaden your architectural vocabulary. I am having translated the *Parallel between Ancient and Modern Architecture* from the French of de Chambrary, which proves we must return to classical architecture. As soon as it is ready, I will give it to you to read. It will make you more expert."

"Thank you," said Christopher. "It may be helpful."

The conversation became general and Oldenburg approached Daniel. Christopher had told Daniel that the German-born philosopher possessed valuable ties with able men of science on the continent, like Spinoza, and the moment Oldenburg heard that Spinoza was Daniel's friend, he was friendly, too. But before they could talk Pepys cut in.

Pepys asked, "Mr. Van Doorn, have you seen the sights of London?"

"No. I just arrived."

"Too bad. You have come just a little too late for one of the great sights of the capital. The skull of Cromwell, spiked over Westminster Hall, vanished recently. It was quite a sight. It established who truly won the civil war. Its disappearance is a great scandal, some even say the King possesses it and argues with it secretly, but others think it may be witches who took it, to resist extermination. Is Holland as afflicted with witchcraft as we are?"

"No." Daniel didn't believe in witches but Evelyn supported Pepys' views and Oldenburg looked interested. But before anyone could pursue witchcraft any further Matthew Wren rushed into the chamber and cried out, "Christopher, the King wants to see you. Now. It is important."

"After I see Daniel settled." Despite his cousin's urgency, he told Sam to give him room and board and stated it so insistently that Sam didn't argue but nodded. Then Christopher addressed Daniel, "I will see you here tomorrow afternoon. If you are willing?"

Matthew asked, "What about the King? Suppose he needs you then?"

"He will be able to spare me."

That was unthinkable to Matthew, but he knew it was futile to argue with his cousin. Once Christopher made up his mind, he was stubborn.

"Daniel, should I expect you here tomorrow afternoon?"

"Christopher, I will be honoured."

"So will I."

Daniel picked up his pictures and followed Sam to the door, but paused there, quite curious about this urgency in Matthew Wren as Christopher asked, "Cousin, do you know what His Majesty wants of me?"

Before Matthew could reply, Evelyn said, "It may have to do with the new Queen. Charles wants a chapel built for her. Wren, you have so many friends about the King, like myself, it will be your own fault if you fail to get what you desire. Considering how incessantly Charles is beset with suitors for place and advantage, you must use your own industry."

Sam pushed Daniel through the door, but then Daniel halted, still within hearing distance, for Matthew was answering Christopher.

"Cousin, I'm not certain why the King wants to see you, but you must not keep him waiting. His Majesty has a just esteem for your parts. Charles has kept your lunar globe in his cabinet."

I Will Be Connected

I will be connected
with all the silences there

I will be connected
with all the sounds there

I will be connected
with all the peaceableness there

I will be connected
with all the bones of the corpse there

I will be connected
with all the mortal breath there

I will be connected
with all the immortality there

Not to be connected
is to be twice abandoned, here and there

I will be twice connected at one time
through all of time

All my instincts told me and tell me this
Commanding me

Stymean Karlen

21

I Will Be Connected

"Sir, are you offering me the post of Assistant Surveyor of Your Majesty's Works?"

"Yes, Doctor Wren. Are you surprised?"

"I am. And honoured, sir."

"Deeply honoured, Your Majesty," Matthew added fervently.

Christopher stood in the audience chamber of Charles' apartments in the Palace of Whitehall and faced the waiting King, with only Matthew in attendance, and he longed to shout Yes. Building was his temptation and St. Paul's the prize, but he didn't want pride to lead him to fail. Yet as he looked into himself, he knew that it was not only the building but the planting, especially the planting, and the thought of someone else restoring or rebuilding St. Paul's made him heartsick. Even so, he temporised and asked, "Sir, are you sure I am qualified?"

"Lord Clarendon thinks so. And so does your cousin."

"That is kind of them, sir, but . . ." Christopher paused uncertainly.

"Doctor Wren, what is troubling you now?"

"Sir, are there any conditions?"

Matthew was horror-stricken at Christopher's temerity and he expected Charles to dismiss his cousin. But the King, who was dressed informally as a sign of royal favour, smiled indulgently and said, "You are a stubborn man. But, at least, I know your views. I am surrounded with so many who flatter me it is difficult to know whom to trust."

How like Charles, thought Matthew, to make a virtue out of necessity.

Charles continued, "The main duties of the office of the works are in the hands of Denham, the Surveyor General, and his deputy, Webb, who was Jones' assistant, but I have a special task for you."

"Thank you, sir. As I said . . ."

"You are honoured," interrupted Charles, "But not sufficiently, even if it means restoring St. Paul's to its ancient glory?"

Christopher flushed. Charles knew where he was vulnerable. He said, "Sir, it would be a noble task, but I'm not sure I'm fitted for it."

"You are designing a building for the Archbishop of Canterbury."

"And a chapel for my father, the Bishop of Ely, sir," said Matthew.

Christopher said more happily, "Sir, I have the designs for the Oxford building with me. I deposited a set of plans in the archives of the Royal Society, but I thought you might like to look at them, too."

"Later, later. I'm sure they are competent."

Matthew, afraid that Charles was displeased, said soothingly, "Sir, the Royal Society is deeply honoured by your support. The venison, the iron chest, and the hundred pounds you presented us have been put to good use."

"I am interested in the sciences and St. Paul's. As you are, Doctor."

"Indeed, Your Majesty. But there is little I can do if others override my plans." Then Christopher wished he had held his tongue and he waited anxiously and unhappily for the King to make the next move.

Charles didn't reply but addressed himself to his own thoughts. Ever since he had wed Catherine of Braganza and allowed her to worship in her Catholic faith, and pressed for freedom of worship, the Anglicans, who dominated the country now, regarded his support of the Established Church with suspicion. Even when he had accepted the English Bible as the Authorised Version of the Bible from a deputation of Anglican clergy as he had entered London and he had thanked them for it and told them, *"the greatest part of this day's solemnity I must ascribe to God's Providence and I will make this book the rule of my life and government,"* he felt that many of the bishops didn't trust him. And still didn't. Such as Matthew Wren, Bishop of Ely, and Gilbert Sheldon, the Archbishop of Canterbury, churchmen of great influence and close to Doctor Wren. But if he made the proper gesture toward St. Paul's, the most important Episcopal church in the land, it would dispel the rumours that he favoured Popery. There was no reason why the Office of the Works should not be put to political use, everything else in the country was, especially piety. And Wren had nothing better to do. He congratulated himself that this professor of astronomy was a clever choice. Clarendon and his secretary might think they were responsible, but Wren, as the son of a Dean of Windsor and the nephew of the Bishop of

Ely, possessed irreproachable connections. What Wren proposed didn't have to be accepted. There were always the problems of materials, money, design, but if Wren's proposed repairs would silence his clerical critics it would be worth much. He was determined that St. Paul's condition must not have a deleterious effect on his fortunes or those of his family. He was not half-witted, even if many about him were. He asked, sounding kinder than he felt, "Doctor, what troubles you about St. Paul's?"

"Sir, my plans will be subject to Denham and Webb's approval."

"Not with St. Paul's. You will be in full charge." When Christopher still hesitated, he said, "I didn't think you were a coward."

"A coward!" exclaimed Christopher. "Sir, I . . ." He halted; he was on the verge of snapping back and that could be fatal.

"Your globe is well made. Do you think there are angels on the moon?"

"I doubt it, sir. We have no evidence to support such a view."

"They must be somewhere. I think about that often. Doctor Wren, your cousin will discuss your duties. And as soon as that is done Denham and Webb will be shown in. They are waiting in an adjoining chamber."

Christopher thought angrily, So Charles assumed he would accept even before he had decided and Denham and Webb could resent his appointment.

"Of course, you know Denham from the Royal Society."

No wonder Denham had left today's meeting early, reflected Christopher.

"And Webb is a good architect, if touchy like his master, Jones."

"Thank you, sir."

"It would be useful if you appeared at court tonight. We are having an entertainment provided by Buckingham and many ladies will attend. Now that you are a surveyor you don't have to remain chaste. Or aloof."

Was Charles taunting him? Or testing him? Or compelled in other ways? But Christopher asked, "Sir, do I have to give up my post at Oxford?"

"No. And whatever Denham says, you will submit your reports on St. Paul's just to me. I will be the only one who will have final approval."

After the King left Matthew said, "You wish to restore St. Paul's and yet, when I get the chance for you, your stubbornness almost ruins it."

"I do not like being pushed into it."

"You are not being pushed. You are being invited."

"And if I had refused?"

M*

Matthew shrugged. "You would not have been invited again."

"What are the other difficulties I will face?"

"Privileges, not difficulties, cousin," Matthew said grandly. "Denham lives in Scotland Yard, next to Whitehall Palace, so he can be close to the King, and you will have a house there, too. It won't be as fine as Denham's, he has sixteen rooms, but it will be pleasant. And the King implied that when Denham dies his residence and office will revert to you."

"That is a ghoulish thing to say."

"Why?" Matthew was distressed. "Everyone knows that Denham has aged prematurely with his gambling and other dissipations. Reversion of the office to you is an important consideration. You should feel honoured."

"It sounds to me like another bribe."

"Don't be righteous. Webb has a house in Scotland Yard, too, as Jones had when he was Chief Surveyor. It is one of the privileges of the office."

"What are the other privileges?"

"Denham gets eight shillings a day and two shillings for travelling expenses, and eighty pounds per annum for his basic recompense, and his assistants get six shillings a day or four, depending on what they do."

"How much will I receive per annum?"

"That is not stated for Assistant Surveyors of the Works, but if you are clever it could amount to many pounds a year. It is said Denham has earned thousands of pounds in the three years he has been Chief Surveyor, and Webb has bought a fine house in the country. If you are clever, you can engage yourself in many lucrative enterprises."

"What do you mean, Matthew, if I am clever?"

Matthew sighed as he said, "This should be one of the happiest days of your life and you make it sound melancholy and without purpose."

It came into Christopher's mind that Matthew's feelings were typical and had no place for the simplicity and severity of the best of building. Matthew was not interested in his sensibility, or even his model for the structure at Oxford, but in advancement.

"Don't be a fool. It is understood that the Chief Surveyor and his assistants avail themselves of any worldly rewards within their reach."

Before Christopher could dispute this or declare that he would perform his duties differently, Matthew ordered Denham and Webb to be ushered in.

Although Christopher knew both men, when Matthew introduced him as the new Assistant Surveyor, he felt young and inexperienced.

Denham and Webb were about fifty, and while they politely acknowledged his cousin's announcement, he felt immediate criticism. Neither by expression or word did either of them appear to desire his help or opinion. Webb frowned and Denham looked uneasy and he sought to relieve his own discomfort by saying, "Sir John, I am honoured to be at your service."

"I am the one who is honoured. Doctor Wren, you have met Mr. Webb."

"Yes. I have respected his work ever since I learned he was Inigo Jones' assistant. The Banqueting House is a beautiful building."

Webb said sharply, "I was his first assistant. I drew many of the preliminary sketches myself. Even though I was a very young man."

Denham said, "Mr. Webb has a capacity for invention."

"It will be needed," said Matthew, "All of you will be needed, for London is continuing to grow with amazing speed and changes daily."

But there was no ease here, thought Christopher; the conversation, whatever its purpose, was self-conscious and makeshift.

Matthew said, "This could be a great time for construction. And His Majesty desires that Doctor Wren examine St. Paul's."

Webb said, "But sir, I was the one who helped build the portico."

Matthew said, "His Majesty desires several opinions. Yours, too, Sir John. As he does with Greenwich and Windsor, also."

Denham and Webb were surprised and so was Christopher. He had heard that Denham's work at Greenwich was going badly and that Windsor was in even worse condition than when he had lived there but Charles had not mentioned either. He knew the King could be devious, evasive, selfish, but he had no wish to be a pawn in Charles' intricate manoeuvres. Yet he couldn't act as the injured party. It would betray Matthew. Even if he was being used. And Webb looked so censorious and Denham aggrieved.

It was a good moment to observe them more closely and Christopher, apparently waiting for the Chief Surveyor to command him, saw Denham as a tall, lanky man, who, approaching fifty, looked much older. His thin, yellow hair, long as befitted a gentleman, with his fair complexion and painted skin, polished except for traces of smallpox, must have been attractive, thought Christopher, especially for a romantic poet. But now Denham was round-shouldered, almost misshapen like Hooke, and as he walked, or rather stalked, his lean legs had an awkward, unnatural gait. Then Denham appeared querulous one moment and ready to cry the next, nervous and impatient, and he had a habit of staring and guiltily turning away when caught. Yet it was impossible to read the Chief Surveyor's thoughts.

Webb's face, square and blunt, was even more of a mask, but behind it Christopher sensed a permanently worried expression. No smile escaped his features and none would if Webb had his way, Christopher reflected, or acknowledgement of any other surveyor's worth, except Jones, who was safely dead. Webb wore a wig to show that he was as much a part of the restoration as any of them and a hand pistol, of the finest Dutch design, to prove that he was also one of the gentry.

Matthew said, "Gentlemen, I am delighted that each of you will be serving His Majesty with your fullest devotion."

Denham nodded grudgingly but Webb said, still far from content, "Sir John, you assigned Greenwich to me after you started it."

"I am very busy with Windsor," Denham explained apologetically.

"Of course," said Matthew. "That is why His Majesty has suggested that Doctor Wren should survey St. Paul's. He desires all your views."

That evening Christopher sat between Pepys and Evelyn at the rear of the Great Hall of Whitehall Palace, which was arranged as a theatre, with a stage, boxes for the royal family, and stalls and a gallery. The Court was in attendance to Charles and his new Queen and while she understood very little English—a slight, sallow, unattractive young woman who was remote from everyone but the attendants she had brought from Portugal—Buckingham's entertainment was *Twelfth Night*.

Pepys said, "It is acted well, but it is a silly play and not at all relating to the name or the day," while Evelyn declared, "It is typical of a butcher's son, with foolish poetic fancies, careless of fact, teeming with bogus romantic sufferings, and it is unfashionable," but Christopher liked the poetry, beauty, and satire. Evelyn added, "It is criminal to waste such a fine audience on such a stupid story," but Christopher stopped listening when he saw that Anne was sitting just ahead of him.

Jugglers and acrobats followed *Twelfth Night*, but now he had eyes only for her. He told himself he was not indulging in nostalgia, that she was just the most attractive woman here and he was simply curious to learn how she had attained her present position. Yet when he tried to speak to her after the entertainment ended, she avoided him. He wondered why; he did not intend to reveal her origin. Finally however, he caught her by the arm as she tried to avoid him on the river terrace. She didn't challenge his grasp, but she was frightened. There were lines around her neck, but her red satin gown displayed her full breasts and she was still beautiful.

Yet she could scarcely speak.

"Anne, I intend no harm. And I am glad to see you again."

She was not sure. So much could be at stake.

"After I saw you, I couldn't look at anyone else."

She noticed that although Christopher must be in his thirties now he hadn't grown much, but his expression was mature while his body was still youthful. She thought approvingly, He had remained slender and trim, with a slim waist, broad shoulders, well-turned legs, dressed like a courtier yet not over-dressed, with a clean brown wig which matched his colouring. And as she saw that he had developed into a handsome, if rather short gentleman, the light came back into her eyes.

After a moment of doubt, she agreed to remain on the terrace with him.

He stared downstream and said suddenly, "There is St. Paul's, still without a covering. I remember when I spoke of putting a dome on it and you said that was in the style of Rome. No one else noticed that."

She replied abruptly, "I don't want to discuss my connection with the King or Buckingham. They have enough mistresses without me."

"I agree," he said very quietly.

She spoke less fast now. "Have you ever been threatened with starving?"

"No, fortunately."

"I have been. Do you see Sam?"

"He is my Steward at Gresham and I have a room on Fetter Lane."

"Have you discussed me with him?"

"Why should I, Anne?"

"I would have thought . . ." She halted, feeling incoherent.

"I asked him about you only when I returned to London to teach. I was concerned. But since then I felt it was none of his business."

"Did he know—that is, about us?"

"Anne, we will achieve nothing looking back. Will I see you again?"

"You are a professor of astronomy at Oxford. I doubt I will be visiting Oxford soon. This Court is not university minded."

"I will be at Court more often now that I am an Assistant Surveyor."

"Is that what you want?"

"It is what the King wants."

"But you accepted."

"Anne, does one refuse the King?"

"I did!" But when he did not answer, she couldn't endure what she felt he was thinking. She added passionately, "It is not what you believe. I know Buckingham acts only for his own amusement and loves whoever suits him at the moment and has no principles, and Charles is no better, but, I assure you, it is my presence that pleases them and not my person. I couldn't see Sam. It would ruin everything. I am the daughter of an English nobleman who was in France during the civil wars. I know Spanish and French now and since the English are bad with these languages and usually too lazy or disdainful to learn them, it gives me a great advantage at Court. I wait on the Duchess of Buckingham and Charles likes pretty women around him and I am helpful with the Queen. Because I speak a good Spanish and French the Queen, who dislikes to use what little English she knows, prefers me to many others. Christopher, you do believe me, don't you?"

There was such entreaty in her voice he nodded. He didn't know what to believe, but when she was close to him everything else was unimportant. He didn't expect any guarantees, that was not the nature of the Court. He was silent so he wouldn't say the wrong thing.

She thought his silence indicated disapproval and that she couldn't endure. Yet how could she tell him of the fright deep inside her of not belonging to anyone? She must belong to *someone, somewhere,* as a flower needed a garden to grow in. She had been obsessed with this feeling all of her life. As if she were searching for an explanation of herself. Anne recalled that when she combed her hair or dressed, or dressed the Duchess of Buckingham, part of her feelings and thoughts were on this quest of hers. She wondered: Did the Duchess or the Queen ever feel this way? Years ago it had been one of the reasons she had given herself to Christopher. Almost gratefully, she reflected, for then, at least, she had belonged to *someone, somewhere.* But she could not tell him this. He would not believe her. And how else could a poor girl, without family connections, advance herself in the world?

He asked, "Anne, may I see you again?"

"I can look after myself."

"I am sure you can. But it is good to see you once more."

"Softly. Someone is coming." She pulled him behind the high plants on the terrace and they hid there while the approaching voices grew louder.

Webb declared, "Sir John, I'm shocked you accepted Wren's appointment without question. He has no formal training and he has built nothing."

"I have no choice. His cousin is close to the King through the connection to Lord Clarendon and his family were friendly with the Stuarts."

Webb said savagely and contemptuously, "This brood of Wrens, a real Wren's nest. All of the Bishop's four sons have achieved prominence with the Restoration, although none of them have any special merit."

"You must realise that is the way Charles rules."

"I realise. But Wren has no gift for architecture. He has a few inventions, but they have nothing to do with building. He is an amateur."

"Webb, you are still my Deputy Surveyor."

"But he is to survey St. Paul's, that noble and pious work."

"That doesn't mean it will be restored. Charles won't find the money. He is doing just enough to please Parliament and the clergy."

"Perhaps, but I worked on it, Wren didn't. I helped the most gifted builder our realm has known, Jones. Did you know that Inigo Jones' original ambition was to be another Michelangelo?"

"No, but you must not take any action that will offend the King."

"I only accepted the post of Deputy Surveyor because I was promised that I would succeed you when you retired."

"You must not retaliate. Time will take care of Wren. You must be flexible. He will fail. The most he has ever built is a lunar globe."

They walked on and a minute later they were out of sight and hearing.

Christopher was unusually quiet and Anne whispered, "You mustn't take them seriously. Denham's only experience as an architect was running royal errands and now he has personal difficulties. He wants to wed the twenty-three-year-old Margaret Brooke, who is half his age and looks less. Denham has children older than she is. And that is not all."

Christopher said, "We mustn't be malicious even if they were."

"But everyone knows that she is the mistress of the Duke of York."

"Have they any proof?"

"She is quite beautiful and whenever she is at Court the Duke has eyes only for her and she is very responsive. York is even more free with his affections than his brother, the King. And Denham knows this, yet he seems determined to marry her, as if to prove that he is still young."

"At Court it always seems to come down to that."

"Women are the food upon which the royal brothers feed. I must return to the Great Hall before the gossip starts about me. Everyone here is judged by their appetites. It is the only taste that is totally approved."

Christopher walked her to the entrance, wishing that they could be alone, and as she paused, waiting for him to say goodbye, he said with an assurance he didn't feel, "As I told you, I will be at Court often now. As Assistant Surveyor of the King's Works, I have been given a house in Scotland Yard, next to the Palace."

"Did you know that I was living there, too?"

"Anne, there are almost two thousand rooms in Whitehall and the buildings attached to the Palace."

"I must be independent."

He sighed. "If you insist."

"It is a problem. Christopher, are you married?"

"No. Professors at Oxford are not supposed to marry."

"Would that prohibition stop you?"

"I don't know. I haven't considered it so I haven't thought about it."

Anne leaned close, kissed him lightly on the forehead—more like a sister than a woman he desired, he thought irritably—and just before she went through the door and back to the Court, she said, "I wouldn't worry about Webb. Everyone knows that he is still talking like Inigo Jones."

When The Creative Being

When the creative being
enters
from your soul
Do not instruct it
It wants the freedom
to be whole
on its own
    As you do

Stymean Karlen

22

When The Creative Being

CHRISTOPHER WAS STILL THINKING ABOUT ANNE WHEN HE MET Daniel at Gresham the next day. He wondered why she had to assure him that she was not the mistress of Charles or Buckingham. Was it because of her need to protect herself? Or her desire to please him? Or a reason he could not fathom? He decided it was beyond the realm of reason to comprehend her motives, a futile pursuit, and he tried to halt his speculations. Yet a strange discontent remained in him. After their meeting he took a room in an inn at Charing Cross so that Daniel would not be disturbed, but when he was unable to fall asleep, the usual ways of overcoming insomnia did not suffice. Instead of thinking of his designs for St. Paul's, Oxford, and Pembroke, Anne kept intruding. Vivid in his mind were her wistful eyes, her lovely complexion, and her sensuous walk as she had left him.

However, he didn't mention her to Daniel when the latter asked him if yesterday had progressed as he wished, but said, "The King offered me the post of Assistant Surveyor. And I accepted."

"Congratulations, Christopher."

"I'm not sure I deserve them. Neither Denham, the Chief Surveyor, nor Webb, his deputy, are enthusiastic about my appointment and there may be many difficulties. Did Sam make you comfortable?"

"He still regards me with suspicion, but the room was clean and the tavern he recommended at Charing Cross served an excellent meal."

"Do you have any of your own work with you?"

Daniel hesitated, then nodded and said apologetically, "I have some drawings. I thought you just might be interested in them."

But Christopher was silent as Daniel placed a dozen drawings of buildings on the table in front of him. They could put their friendship on trial, but as he looked at them he sighed with relief;

this was quite safe; Daniel's drawings were precise, accurate, and skilfully executed.

"What do you think?" Daniel asked anxiously. "Rembrandt stressed that the artist must see exactly, whatever the spirit of the subject."

Christopher stared at the drawings again and said, "I prefer the work you have done with pen and ink on white paper. They are the most exact."

"Rembrandt said I was a better draughtsman than a painter. He taught me to use chalk, too, black rather than red, but he favoured working with a quill pen, then later, a reed pen. He said less gifted artists needed chalk or a pencil, especially for preparation, but that I should work directly with a pen, boldly. Although you can't erase it or wipe it out."

"Don't worry about that. They can always be done over if necessary."

"I don't like to go back. It irritates me."

"When one designs buildings, one is always doing them over. But you must not be embarrassed, your drawings are effective." He waited a moment before he asked, "Have you planned what you are going to do here?"

"Draw, paint. I hear that your King fancies Dutch craftsmen like his father did. I'm no Van Dyck or Rubens but I can do a good likeness."

"Would you consider working with me? I can't pay much, but . . ."

Daniel cut him angrily, "I don't want charity. I don't need the money."

"That is not why I asked you. With my teaching at Oxford I need help. My duties are more than I expected. They have grown already, in less than twenty-four hours. My cousin left a list of new instructions here with Sam. I think Matthew was afraid to face me with them."

"What are they?"

"Remember, not a word to anyone. Promise?"

"I promise."

Christopher read: "*Dear Cousin, I am sorry I could not inform you of the following, but before I left Whitehall the King gave me instructions for your eyes alone. He wants you to examine Greenwich. Heavy rains have flooded the grounds, the river has risen, the work there is in danger and he desires your views. The same heavy rains have afflicted Windsor and leaks have developed in the fabric of St. George's Chapel and in the royal apartments. After you look at Windsor, survey St. Paul's and recommend what should be done. Webb and Denham should be at Greenwich when you arrive there tomorrow, and perhaps the King himself, who is sailing on one of his yachts, but all that has passed between us must remain private. Please destroy this paper after you absorb it.*"

"Are you going to obey?"

"Yes. The instructions are easy to remember."

"Why did you tell me?"

"Because I believe I can trust you. That is another reason why I asked you to work with me. Faced with Webb and Denham's hostility, I need a friend by my side. Who is also skilful. Will you consider it?"

Daniel wavered. When he had decided to return to London he had thought of working with Christopher. But not as a beggar. "I will consider it."

"Good. Then come along with me to Scotland Yard where my quarters will be. My cousin also enclosed my new address there and a set of keys. And it would be helpful if you could view Greenwich with me. It will give you a better idea of the difficulties we might have to face."

"Won't the others resent me? Especially since I am a Dutchman."

"They already resent me. One more resentment won't make a substantial difference. And you are right, Charles does like Dutch craftsmen."

"Even though he may be at war with Holland soon?"

"Charles never allows such things to interfere with his pleasures."

Scotland Yard, so named because it had been the residence of the Kings of Scotland when they had come to London to pay their respects to the Crown of England, was a large rectangular courtyard enclosed with wooden and brick houses. Daniel remembered it from his days at Westminster. Scotland Yard was on the way to Charing Cross, just below Whitehall Palace and the Banqueting House, and he had passed it often.

Christopher saw that it was next to the Privy Stairs, the main access from the Palace to the Thames, but only for the private use of the royal family and their guests, and a quick, convenient way to reach Scotland Yard without being seen. Most of the buildings were a nondescript jumble of many styles, some picturesque, some of one storey, some of two and three, and a few that were orderly and of great size and magnificence.

Denham's residence possessed such distinction, with a fine entrance, many rooms, attached stables, and was a short walk from the Privy Stairs. Christopher knew it, for it had been Jones' residence, and while at school he had slipped out to see it and he had been disappointed that it lacked the strength of the Banqueting House. In those days he had expected that anything associated with Jones would be in the Chief Surveyor's taste.

He stood in front of his new residence, a much smaller Tudor house of two storeys, set amid a hodgepodge of gabled roofs and twisted chimneys.

Then, across the courtyard, on the river side of Scotland Yard and close to the Privy Stairs, he saw Anne leaving a neat brick house for the private entrance to the Palace. She didn't notice him and before she could, he pulled Daniel back into the doorway of his new residence.

But Daniel thought her so attractive he wanted to take a closer look at her. After she departed by way of the Privy Stairs, which led also to the King's apartments, he asked, "Christopher, do you know her?"

"She is just an acquaintance. In the service of the King."

Christopher looked so secretive Daniel didn't pursue the subject. Yet he knew he would remember her if he saw her again, she was so beautiful.

The new residence was clean with a parlour, dining room, kitchen, two bedrooms on the second floor, a cellar, and a housekeeper in attendance.

Mrs. Mary Mallory was a slight, thin-faced, middle-aged Londoner, alert and emphatic in manner, and she expected Doctor Wren. She greeted him warmly and quickly informed him, "Sir, you do not have to worry. My wages are paid by the Crown and so, too, is the cost of rent and food. It is an honour to serve the nephew of Bishop Wren, a true martyr and hero. Not like Grace Burrows next door," she added contemptuously. "She had to wait on John Milton, who lived there when he served Cromwell, as the Usurper's Latin Secretary. Milton called on me when his infant son fell ill but I wouldn't help him—he advocated the death of our lawful sovereign. And his child died soon after. Some said it was bewitched but I am sure it was God's will. Doctor Wren, is this gentleman your guest?"

"Yes, Mrs. Mallory. Would you have any cool water?"

"There is a small well nearby. I will have it fetched."

After she left Christopher said, "I knew Cromwell and I find it distasteful to regard him as a devil. Sometimes his behaviour was cruel, but he was a remarkable person and he had a high regard for learning."

"What happened to Milton when the Stuarts returned?"

"Fortunately, nothing serious considering his services for Cromwell. Charles can be merciful when he is in a good humour and perhaps he didn't think Milton was important enough to execute. I hear that Milton now lives on Bunhill Row with his third wife and his two daughters and while he has gone blind, he has returned to poetry, that he is writing about the conflict between

God and Satan. Wilkins proposed his admission to the Royal Society, but Milton declined before this could be voted on."

"Would he have been admitted?"

"I don't know. I would have voted for him, but there is still much animosity against him. Daniel, you are welcome to stay here with me."

"Can you really afford to use me? From what I have heard . . ."

"From Sam," interrupted Christopher.

"That doesn't matter. I heard Charles will not pay for my services to you and that it will come out of your private purse."

Already reproached by Matthew for employing Sam and Seth, Christopher was in no mood for further criticism. He said, "I inherited money from my father with the Restoration and that, and my earnings, are ample, for my needs are modest. Besides," he added curtly, "that is my business. Do you want to work with me? I won't ask you again?"

There was a severity in him that frightened Daniel. What he feared most was that Christopher would reject his outstretched hand. He said, "I think it would be better if I stayed on Fetter Lane. But I will be happy to accompany you to Greenwich, if I can be of any service."

"Good. I will pick you up at Paul's Wharf at noon."

The voyage down the Thames was easy, but the grounds of the old Tudor palace at Greenwich were in a shocking condition. Christopher stood with Daniel on the banks of the river and he wondered how Denham could have made such a dreadful mistake, putting his piles for the new palace at the brink of the river. The Thames overflowed the shore and the newly laid piles and he saw that they were not strong enough or secure enough or sufficiently well placed to carry the weight of a great palace. The foundations were absolutely wrong, he thought, both in their location and design. But how could he tell Denham, or penetrate Webb's arrogance?

While he tried to decide what to do and Daniel was silent, Webb approached, followed by Denham, and to his surprise, Matthew and Evelyn.

As he introduced Daniel as his assistant the others barely hid their disapproval. No one said, An excellent idea, or paid any compliments. Webb regarded Daniel as a foreigner, Denham was indifferent, Evelyn ignored him, and Matthew said, "The King will pay only your salary."

"I know," said Christopher. "Daniel is an old friend of mine."

"Cousin, you never mentioned him."

"He was away in Holland for a number of years."

"Cousin, I came here to see that everything goes properly."

And to keep an eye on me, thought Christopher, but he nodded.

Evelyn said, "I sailed this morning with His Majesty on one of his yachts from Greenwich to Gravesend and back. He entertained me with his intention of building a palace here, once the old one is demolished, and he wanted me to declare my thoughts on the virtue of placing it here."

Webb replied defiantly, "My designs will please the King. I am Jones' nephew and deputy and I am carrying out his plans for Greenwich."

Denham added, "Which His Majesty agreed to. Just the other day."

"Of course," Evelyn said soothingly, "Charles merely wanted my opinion."

Webb asked irritably, "Does he want us to consult with you?"

Evelyn answered, "His Majesty does."

"That suits him," Webb declared, "but I'm not sure it suits me."

Denham said appeasingly, "We must not be offended. Our good friend, Evelyn, intends no harm. Is that the King's yacht lying in the river?"

"Yes," said Evelyn. "He may bless us with a visit later to observe how the work is going. Unless he decides to race the Duke of York again. At the moment the wind is contrary. His Majesty wonders whether the pilings should have been placed so close to the river."

Denham explained, "I wanted to make it possible for Charles to sail into the new palace, since he loves boats so much. And the patch by the Thames is unsightly, so I thought it should be covered."

"In any event," Webb added hurriedly, "the piles can be changed. Since the Queen's House, which Jones built and Charles likes, is too small for a palace—the new one, once the old one is demolished, will possess the same symmetry and distinction in the classical style."

Christopher said approvingly, "The Queen's House is a marvellous example of classical authority and form. I admire it greatly."

"Anyway," Webb said, "We have to demolish the antiquated Tudor palace before we can do anything else and it is an exhausting task, requiring resolution and strength, although already, I've knocked down much of it."

Christopher stared at the ruins of the old favourite palace of Henry and Elizabeth and he was appalled by the devastation and chaos in front of him. Webb was proud of what he had accomplished; Denham was unsure; Matthew had no opinion; Evelyn was critical; Daniel was still silent and Christopher didn't know what to say. Some of the ancient palace still stood amid the parts that had been demolished. He saw two Gothic towers and turrets where the royal flag had flown, foundations, massive pillars of a forecourt, solid blocks of masonry, and a number of heavy stone walls.

Great lives had treasured this palace, Christopher recalled, Greenwich was Henry's pride and Elizabeth's joy and where Raleigh had made his reputation, and now its *very being*, its brick, wood, granite, limestone, glass, sand, and mortar lay in an aimless mess. The lack of order offended Christopher most of all. Daniel looked melancholy, overcome by the sight of the terrible ruins. Then Christopher saw that Denham and Webb were concentrating on a part of the palace that was still standing.

They were surveying timbers that shored up walls of what had been a royal apartment, deciding how to demolish them, and Evelyn took Christopher aside and whispered so no one else could hear him, "I would put the new palace between the Queen's House and the river, with a large square cut into the Thames like a bay, but Sir John was all for setting it on the brink of the river, which I cannot assent to. Be wise, keep away from this project, as I am, it will be safer. Sir John is a better poet than he is an architect, even if he has Jones' man to assist him."

"How could he make such a mistake!" Christopher muttered.

"Denham will make more," Evelyn said. "But he is in a strong position. He carried letters for Charles during his exile, helped convey the Duke of York out of England to Holland, attended Charles' mother in Paris, and collected money for the royal family in Scotland. It is useless to oppose Sir John. His connections are irreproachable."

Christopher turned to Webb and Denham who were quarrelling about the best way to demolish the portions of the palace that were still standing. Denham wanted to employ a battering ram; he said it was safer. But Webb proposed using gunpowder; he insisted that it was more efficient, that it was the only way to knock down everything with one blow.

Christopher wished there was something he could do or say.

Webb said, "Denham, we can't wait any longer. As it is, we will be criticised for building so late in the year. We must demolish the old palace now, before we are exposed to winter and we will have to cease all work. Masons, bricklayers, and carpenters won't work in the bad weather."

"I was just wondering," Christopher started to suggest then stopped.

"What were you wondering?" asked Webb, glaring at him.

"If the ground under and around these walls and foundations were investigated it could be determined whether they could stand gunpowder."

Webb said, "I thought of that. I have built a tunnel behind and under the walls, but no one will enter it. They are afraid."

"Where is it?"

"Here." Webb showed him the tunnel whose opening was just large enough for one man to enter. "I would go in but I'm too big to navigate it."

Christopher could believe that. Webb's stomach bulged like a barrel of beer and his feet made a deep, heavy impression on the soft earth.

"I wouldn't risk it, Christopher," Daniel said suddenly, sensing what his friend was thinking, then he wished he had bit his lips, he had not been diplomatic, for it only spurred Christopher into further action.

Christopher examined the entrance to the tunnel. This earth was firm. Then he studied the pillars overhead. They were an ominous sight, and yet . . .? Suddenly, Christopher, who was proud of his reasonableness, who could usually see the other person's point of view, felt that the others were watching him critically, except for Daniel.

He shook his head as if arguing with himself and crawled into the tunnel before anyone could halt him. He was the smallest one here, he reasoned, and so the best one to investigate. Besides, he would understand what he found. But he knew that none of these reasons really mattered. He must show that he could face risk as much as anyone. He was in a dark, foreign space now where nothing was familiar. In the tunnel there was no space but to squirm forward, squeezing himself into the smallest possible shape and size. The walls seemed solid but sand trickled into his eyes and he had a moment of panic, then he was tired, the air was difficult to breathe, and he knew he must get out. Sand was in his eyes and he couldn't see properly. He was no coward, he told himself, but there was water in the tunnel and a shortage of air. Yet when he went to back out he couldn't manage until he recalled how a worm moved. Wriggling slowly, grateful for once that he was small, but wishing his shoulders were not so broad, he reached the opening. He was wringing wet with sweat and the hot, fetid air made him look pale, exhausted. He gasped, "I could hardly breathe. But the ground seems safe. It should hold during the demolishing."

Matthew was white-faced; Evelyn was stunned, Daniel was relieved; he couldn't tell what Webb or Denham thought. "I knew what I was doing."

No one replied, and as he looked up he realised why. The King stood nearby, watching him with a curious smile. "Doctor, what did you find?"

"That a builder needs a good pair of hands and a strong heart, sir."

Daniel said abruptly, "It was not worth the risk."

Christopher said, "Your Majesty, my assistant, Daniel Van Doorn."

Daniel bowed and Charles asked, "A Dutch artist?"

"Yes, Your Majesty."

"They are good craftsmen. Do you favour gunpowder or a battering ram?"

"Sir, I don't favour either method at the moment."

The Court had caught up with the King and Christopher noticed that the courtiers stayed behind Charles, stepping gingerly on the ground, not venturing close to the rubble, it was too dirty for their dainty clothes. He saw Buckingham, growing fatter despite still being a young man, the Duke of York, tall and fair and imperious, the Lord Chancellor, looking seasick, Pepys, self-important, and trailing the Duke as if every word York uttered was gospel, although the Duke was a dull conversationalist.

Charles asked, "Doctor, why do you differ with Denham and Webb?"

"Sir, demolishing may cause more flooding. There is water in the tunnel."

"There can't be!" Webb exclaimed. "This ground is dry!"

Christopher pointed to his doublet and breeches which were wet and he said, "I am soaked. And not from perspiration, sir."

Charles didn't seem to be listening. The King stared at what remained of the old palace and his expression was sorrowful. He appeared to be in another time and he declared, solemnly for him, "Sometimes, I think we are tempting God's mercy, demolishing this palace. Henry was born here, wed Catherine here, courted Anne Boleyn here and became suspicious of her here. His daughters, Mary and Elizabeth, also were born here. No wonder the palace was named the Placentia. Henry spared no expense to make it magnificent. He was partial to it because he was born here. Many sumptuous entertainments and splendid receptions took place in this palace. Some say the attack on the Armada was planned in it, and now, with a few blows of the battering ram or the explosion of gunpowder, all gone."

Denham said, "Sir, I'm sorry, but you've already given instructions."

"I know," Charles said curtly. "But even a King can have second thoughts. Do you think Henry had any second thoughts about Anne Boleyn?" He didn't wait for anyone to answer, but added, "If I cut off the heads of all my mistresses who knew another man, I might not have any. Well," he sighed, "that was a bloody business. And a snare and a delusion. You can't buy trust with an axe." He turned to Christopher, who looked very young. "Doctor Wren, would you preserve the old palace?"

"Sir, that depends on whether it could be preserved."

"I doubt it. Although the Usurper used it, it was greatly decayed. The necessary repairs could cost more than a new palace. So I ordered it taken down and a new palace erected in its place."

Denham said, "Sir, would you like to inspect what we have done?"

Charles nodded, as if to shake himself loose from the past, and followed Denham across the grounds, the Court behind him.

The moment Denham's back was turned and Webb was alone with Christopher, he drew him out of the hearing of the others and said, "Thanks for investigating the ground. I could have been damaged by the flooding."

"I'm glad I was helpful."

Webb said, "You know that Denham hasn't the slightest idea of what he is doing. But we could work together. And when I succeed Denham, you could become my deputy and we could purify English architecture. In addition to talent and experience, I have just as good credentials as Denham. During the civil wars, I fortified Oxford for the King's father, and performed even greater services. I carried his father's jewellery through the enemy lines, and when that was discovered, I was imprisoned for a month. If you support me with Greenwich, I will help you with St. Paul's, although I have already carried out repairs on the cathedral." Christopher showed his surprise and he commented, "In 1662. Didn't you know?"

"No, Mr. Webb. I'm sure you will improve Greenwich."

"I'm getting two hundred pounds, as much as Denham, and it could be your fee in a few years, when I'm Chief Surveyor and you are my deputy."

Matthew had said Webb was getting eighty, yet he must have known that wasn't true. The Lord Chancellor controlled the Office of the Works.

"Will you support me about the placing of the new Greenwich palace?"

"If you are right."

"I'm right about the pilings and the gunpowder."

"I'm not sure about the gunpowder. I would investigate further."

As Webb saw Charles returning with the Court, his voice rose so the King could hear him, "Wren, I'm honoured that you support my views!"

Before Christopher could correct him, Charles said, "Doctor, your assistant, Van Doorn, informed me that he attended Westminster. I am glad those in my service have such a good classical education.

Busby was a good loyalist. Although sometimes contrary. When I visited the school recently, he didn't excel in humility. Unlike my other subjects, he didn't take off his hat in my presence." Charles laughed. "So I took off mine. It was most amusing. Are you happy with Webb's proposal?"

Matthew was motioning for him to say, Yes, but he couldn't. Webb was a better architect than Denham, but he couldn't say yes on demand. Instead, he replied, "That is for Your Majesty to decide. It is dangerous for any design to have more than one master. Three surveyors are apt to build in three different styles. And that could be dangerous, too."

Charles asked, "As dangerous as burrowing through a twenty-foot tunnel?"

"It was necessary, sir."

"Doctor Wren, I didn't think you would be that impulsive."

"Sir, neither did I."

If I Were Two Gods and Not One

If I were two Gods and not one
as I am
I would be a true God
And not compete with Him

He would be a lesser God
Since He would wish to win against me
And He would
In my mercy I would not lift a hand

Thenceforth my people
would be His people
under His reign
But I will not forsake them

I will remain one God as I am
Even though I be only half a God
The other half
being Him

Stymean Karlen

23

If I Were Two Gods and Not One

WINDSOR WAS A RETURN TO THE PAST. CHRISTOPHER STOOD IN ST.
George's Chapel for the first time in years, a week after his
visit to Greenwich, and memories flooded him. He recalled the
quarrel between his uncle and Jones over the need for
repairs and the installation of Charles as a Knight of the Garter
when the King had been the heir-apparent. He wished his father
could be by his side and he had a yearning to see Susan; he
had not seen his sister since she had visited Oxford two years ago
when the university had given William Holder the degree of Doctor
of Divinity.

Yet he shouldn't be nostalgic, he thought, the past few days had
been busy ones. The Royal Society had discussed the prevalence
of pheasants in South America and the possibility that salt water
could be sweetened by freezing. Daniel had offered to get a
microscope from Holland for Hooke, and while he had accepted
this proposal grudgingly, Hooke was pleased. Matthew had said that
Webb had exaggerated the amount of his wages and had assured
him that Charles would meet with him after he looked at Windsor
and St. Paul's. And gunpowder had been used at Greenwich, and,
as he had feared, two workmen had been killed by the falling
debris and four badly hurt, but what Webb had wanted demolished
had gone down.

Christopher sought to return to his survey of St. George's Chapel.
He had come without telling anyone in authority of his mission so
he could see what he wished. There was new gold plate on the
altar, watched by an attendant so that it would not be stolen, the
great sword of Edward hung on the wall of the chapel and he felt
he had contributed to this, and the building had been cleaned. But
he saw that the fabric was in even worse condition than it had been
in his father's time, there were many leaks and stained glass windows

were broken. The royal apartments showed dire neglect and made him homesick for the Deanery.

It was closed. The Dean was away and two workmen were moving furniture into the Deanery. He wondered if the great table was still in the study. But when he tried to enter the Deanery the Steward barred his way at the gate and said, "You can't go in. The Dean doesn't permit visitors."

"I used to live here. My father was the Dean at one time."

"When?" The Steward was sceptical. This man was dressed plainly.

"Until the Commonwealth drove him out."

"Where is he now?"

"He is dead. Is there a great table in the study?"

"On which the dead King was laid out?"

"Yes."

"No. The Dean moved it. He said to use it to sew the head back on the King's body was sacrilegious." The Steward shut the gate in his face.

Christopher was tired, discouraged. He wanted to assess the damage carefully, but he felt that whatever he recommended, it would be ignored. And his heart was not in the repair of Windsor; it was in St. Paul's.

"Daniel, could you make drawings of St. Paul's?" he asked the next day when they approached the cathedral. After Daniel assented and asked him what he had found at Windsor, he said, "Much decay, yet I doubt anything will be done there, but St. Paul's is different. It is the most vital and conspicuous structure upon the landscape of London. It can be seen for miles, long before one is in the city itself, and from whatever side one approaches London, silver-grey if the sun is shining and black if there is no sun. If anything is the soul of London, St. Paul's is. Even Denham knows this. Long before he could have thought of becoming chief surveyor, he wrote about it in his best known poem, *Cooper's Hill*." He quoted:

> *"that sacred pile, so vast, so high*
> *That whether 'tis a part of earth or sky*
> *Uncertain seems, and may be thought a proud*
> *Aspiring mountain or descending cloud . . ."*

He added, "When I learned it was about St. Paul's I memorised it."

"It is appropriate," said Daniel. They were close enough to St. Paul's to touch it, standing in front of the damaged west portico, and he sketched the cathedral as he listened. He agreed with Christopher that it was the best known church in England, a vast structure whose length and brooding immensity gave it an air of grandeur and importance. But St. Paul's was also an odd mixture of Norman, Gothic, and Jones' classicism. And the decay was everywhere. Daniel wondered why anyone hesitated about repairing it the need was so obvious.

Christopher asked, "Did you study with Hollar, the engraver?"

"No. But I know his work."

"He is a remarkable engraver. I hear he is back in England. This is an excellent drawing. Everyone but a blind man should be able to see from it what has to be done. Your exactness is just what I need. Now I must itemise what has gone wrong. And if I miss anything tell me."

Daniel followed Christopher into St. Paul's and they itemised: the steps and pavement of the west portico smashed to pieces, the Corinthian columns mutilated, the foundations of the stone towers shifting and no longer properly supporting the building, deep cracks in the vaulting, and the upper walls of the nave bent outwards.

Christopher said, "This ought to convince the King if anything will."

"You don't sound hopeful."

"The repairs should be done at once but that doesn't mean they will be."

There were shouts outside, the clamour of a bell, and Daniel was surprised that Christopher wasn't alarmed until black rats scampered in front of them and across the floor of St. Paul's. Now however, Christopher flinched and said, "It is a fire. Our wooden houses with their overhanging roofs are so crowded on our narrow streets that fires are frequent. One of these days we will have a fire we can't put out. And the rats are fleeing from it."

Daniel shivered. "They are so black, ugly, large, and so many of them."

"I've noticed that when these black rats appear we have the plague. But no one knows why or makes any attempt to clean up the filth which breeds these rats, but prefer to blame the plague on Popery or witchcraft."

"Christopher, believing that old women are witches is nonsense!"

"I agree, but Charles' grandfather, King James, believed in witchcraft so fervently he wrote a book to support his views. I doubt that Charles feels that way, but many Englishmen do. Much of the damage to St. Paul's is blamed on witches, although I saw the Commonwealth deface it with my own eyes. And what they don't blame on witches, they blame on Papists. That is easier than rebuilding London and reforming our building laws. But

388 *Myself, Christopher Wren*

one of these days plague and fire may leave us no choice."

Several days later Christopher was granted a new audience with Charles. He carefully prepared his recommendations for repairing St. Paul's and he gave the King the reasons why, with Daniel's drawings. Charles liked the drawings, but he preferred to discuss Windsor, and when Christopher returned to the subject of St. Paul's, he said irritably, "These demands you are making are very tiring. We do not have money for everything."

Clarendon and Matthew, in his post as secretary to the Lord Chancellor, were in attendance, and Christopher sensed this was an official occasion.

Charles added, "A Royal Commission has been appointed to supervise all matters concerning St. Paul's, particularly the raising of money, and to determine the true state of the church. When that is decided, they will order the necessary repairs and supervise their execution."

Clarendon said, "His Majesty has graciously appointed me one of the commissioners. It is a great honour and I am deeply grateful."

Matthew said, "Buckingham is another member of this noble commission and a hundred of the most illustrious subjects of His Majesty."

Christopher winced. Nothing would be done now, he thought sadly, with so many involved; there would be only more confusion. Yet perhaps this was what Charles wanted; possessed with the Stuart capacity for self-delusion.

Clarendon continued, "The commissioners have consulted Denham and his deputy, Webb, about the state of the cathedral, and to make certain that His Majesty is properly served, they have called in three other surveyors for consultation. Hugh May, Roger Pratt, and yourself."

He wasn't flattered. He thought, Charles doesn't really trust anybody. He knew May and Pratt, who were older than himself, and who were active at Court. Hugh May was the cousin of a prominent Court official—like himself, he realised suddenly, and he wondered if it was his connection with Matthew that had pushed him into the service of the King as Webb had said, and that possibility caused him to feel self-conscious and guilty.

May was also a protege of Buckingham, inclined to vacillate, easily influenced, always heeding other people's judgments. But Roger Pratt was very sure of himself and he had built houses for the nobility, all alike, as if he had one idea and he was determined to practise it assiduously.

Christopher couldn't resign himself to submitting to these evasions and delays, which he felt they were waiting for him to accept. He said, "Sir, I appreciate your wish to obtain the best opinions on the subject, but I doubt that St. Paul's will endure much longer in its present state."

"Denham assures me that it could last a long time."

"Denham, I'm sorry to say, sir, was wrong at Greenwich."

"Webb insists that if Jones' portico is restored to its original state the remainder of the cathedral can be repaired gradually."

"Sir, the portico is artful but St. Paul's is crumbling. It was so badly handled during the civil wars some of it is actually ruinous."

"That is not Pratt's view. He supports Denham and Webb."

"Sir, the fabric is extremely insecure. I beg of you, advise its repair before it is utterly destroyed. It should be done for the safety of your realm. The people will take it as a bad omen if it collapses."

Charles was astonished by the Professor's passion. He had not thought him capable of such feeling. Or that he would risk his future for an old, decayed church, which was more of a symbol than a practicality. Then Charles felt pushed and that he couldn't endure. He said curtly, "May, as paymaster, says repairs will cost thousands of pounds and this money is needed to outfit our fleet for protection against the Dutch."

Matthew said, "Cousin, war may begin at any moment."

"And I doubt we have enough money to pursue that properly," said Clarendon, "begging your pardon, Your Majesty, if I may speak candidly."

"You always do, Hyde," Charles said wearily. "Professor, Pratt who has visited Italy, France, Holland, and Flanders, points out that you have never been abroad, that you have never seen a building outside of England. And he assures me that he can patch up St. Paul's without much cost."

"Your Majesty, there is also the danger of plague and fire."

"Are you sure?" Charles grew pale.

"I saw black rats the other day in the city and there was a large fire near St. Paul's which drove them into the cathedral in search of safety."

"Hyde, why didn't you inform me of these signs?"

"Sir, Doctor Wren is easily alarmed. There have been no reports of plague and the few fires that have occurred have been put out quickly."

Matthew added, "Your Majesty, it is my cousin's concern for your welfare that has caused him to be so apprehensive."

"I know," Charles said even more wearily. "My subjects love me so much I wonder how any harm can come to me. Hyde, have the Bills of Mortality checked. They will tell us if there have been any cases of plague recently. We will find out if the Doctor is as clever a prophet as he thinks he is."

"Sir, I investigated the weekly Bills of Mortality and only four years in the last sixty has London been free of the plague. I think the infection still exists in the city, there have been many suspicious deaths lately, and so does the danger of fire, with the overcrowding and the dirt."

"What do you propose?" The plague was an old, terrifying enemy.

"Sir, order health precautions to be observed in the city, and change the building regulations so that houses can't be crowded together."

"And have the City accuse me of taking away their living? It could start another civil war."

"Sir, it is better than taking away their life. If the citizens see the Crown doing something about St. Paul's, it will encourage them to obey the health regulations. It could collapse, if we don't protect it now."

"If?" Charles shook his head sceptically and added, "St. Paul's is the work of more than twenty surveyors and you dispute their results."

"Your Majesty, is anything going to be done? By anyone?"

Charles frowned angrily, but before he could reply Hyde said, "Sir, forgive me for having to bring such matters to your attention, but the Office of the Works has already contracted a great debt at Greenwich and Windsor and our exchequer is empty. There is no money to spare."

"Professor, I cannot go against the advice of my most trusted advisor." Who, he thought, always keeps my interest close to his heart, since it is also his own. "At this moment, with war on the horizon, the repair of St. Paul's would only be an unnecessary expense. As King of England I am also ruler of the sea and if I am to take to the sword to protect our realm, I must not allow anything to distract me."

Charles sounded as if the war with the Dutch would be more like an entertainment than a bloody battle, thought Christopher, but he kept that to himself. The King held out his hand to be kissed and he did so, although he doubted that anything would be done about St. Paul's, despite the commissioners and the assigning of five surveyors to report on it.

He took Daniel with him to Cambridge where he intended to review his plans for the chapel at Pembroke with his uncle. He had decided on the final design, a plain, rectangular structure resembling the shape of the Banqueting House, but without its grandeur and spaciousness.

Daniel was disappointed by the planned simplicity of the interior, which resembled a long box, but he liked the classic shape of the exterior. He didn't express his views, although Christopher encouraged him to speak. He thought Cambridge beautiful and the location of Pembroke felicitous.

Christopher introduced him to his uncle, who stood by the foundations which had been laid the previous year, and Daniel was surprised by the old man's vigour. His friend had told him that his uncle was almost eighty, but Bishop Wren, while his body was bent and narrowed by age, was alert and determined to show his competence. The Bishop still wore an ancient Elizabethan ruff, although that was long out of style, and his beard was pointed in the fashion of Charles I, and he was easily irritated.

When the Bishop heard Daniel's name and accent, he asked, as sharply and suspiciously as Sam had, "Nephew, is he a foreigner?"

"Daniel was born in Holland but we met at Westminster."

"Then he is an Anglican?"

"Does that matter?"

"Yes, it does. Do you expect me to accept the aid of a non-believer?" When his nephew didn't reply, he blurted out irritably, "Is he a Papist?"

"No, he is not a Papist."

"Is he a Dissenter? They exist in Holland, too."

"He is a fine draughtsman." Christopher handed his uncle several of Daniel's drawings of St. Paul's. "They are clear and precise."

"Where was your friend during the Usurpation?"

"In Holland, sir," said Daniel. "With my family."

"So was the King," Christopher reminded his uncle, "part of the time."

"That is why we must be careful. We have curious goings on at Court. Our Episcopal King weds a Portuguese Papist, which is very disturbing. That is why our chapel must be Anglican. Why it is appropriate that I am building it to give thanks to God for my liberation from the Dissenters."

"Uncle, he is not a Dissenter."

"Oh, a Calvinist. Well, it could be worse. Van Doorn, it is our need to worship God correctly that impelled me to will the five thousand pounds I received on my release from the Tower to the construction of this chapel. Since the first stone was laid last year, I have been a hardy scholar. I am up at five and seldom in bed until eleven. I supervise the workmen. I drink no wine, eat off only a wooden trencher, I practise fasting and abstinence with great strictness. I learned in the Tower that it was possible to live austerely if I worshipped faithfully and accurately."

Christopher thought, No wonder his cousin was political, the Bishop had not spent any of the revenue from his livings on his children, but had made the chapel his heir, bestowing upon it his estate at Hardwick.

"Van Doorn, our people are terrified of the Papists, rightly, and you were wise in Holland to get rid of them. The King is too lenient to the Catholics. Christopher, did Charles approve your plans for St. Paul's?"

"Not so far."

"I didn't expect him to. He will do as little as he can for our Church. When I insisted on purging my diocese of the disaffected ministers who supported the Usurper, he resisted me. But he didn't stop me. I rid my diocese of them and when Charles begged me, '*to give no further disturbance,*' I told him bluntly, '*Sir, I know my way to the Tower.*'"

Daniel asked, "And he didn't punish you, sir?"

"He didn't dare, for he knew that God was on my side."

But that was what Cromwell believed, reflected Christopher, and it was probably his uncle's resistance to the King that had kept him from further advancement, although the official excuse was old age.

His uncle surveyed the foundations proudly and declared, "I will die wonderfully religious and well prepared for heaven. We must not allow any religion to be practised in England but my dear Episcopal one."

He sounded so violent Christopher tried to change the subject.

Yet when he spoke of his designs, his uncle ignored them and said as if he were addressing a large congregation, "Of all the failings of man, the basest is when he shall shift his religion with the time and the tide. As long as I live, I will face my task of imposing the right religious practices on our land, as the King should. The Anglican Church is the soul of the state. Without it the body politic is lifeless."

Christopher motioned to Daniel to depart and only then, as they started to walk away, did the Bishop heed his nephew.

He asked curtly, "Nephew, are your final designs ready?"

Christopher paused, nodded, and handed them to his uncle.

He studied them and said, "It is a plain box. How big will it be?"

"Seventy-five feet by twenty-five feet. As you requested."

"I wish the design wasn't so simple, so severe."

"I'm using red brick because you said you can't afford anything else."

"The limits of my private purse oblige me to put a stop to the bolder strokes of your pen. But the chapel should have more ornamentation."

"I won't design it in the Gothic fashion. That is not fitting, that is barbarous. But you should like the windows. They will be large and light."

"I don't like the way they look on your plans."

"They are Venetian, in the classical style. As will be the chapel."

"But not Roman," his uncle warned. "I want no Popery in my chapel."

"Uncle, we are in a new time and our buildings must fit that time." When the Bishop differed, Christopher refused to submit. He had to stand up to him and in his need he grew unusually forceful. He declared, "Just as I wouldn't interfere with your sermons, you mustn't interfere with my designs. I don't like the endless elaborating of the Gothic forms and details. My proportions must be mathematically correct, or I will quit."

Bishop Wren looked very old as he asked, "Even if I don't like it?"

"I will teach you to like it. As I must teach myself how to build."

"Normally, I would have built this chapel myself, as I built one at Peterhouse across the street when I was young. But I've been ill of the ague, an old enemy, and can no longer do what I used to do easily."

Daniel said, "Sir, you can trust your nephew."

"Van Doorn, do you approve of his plans?"

"On the whole, yes. They should work."

"I want the chapel to be useful," said Matthew. And a monument to his generosity and fame, he hoped. "But most of all to be an Episcopal chapel. I will not barter any portion of Church truth or discipline for the doubtful advantages of comprehension or toleration. If I'm to be buried here, it must be an Established church. Nephew, what is happening at St. Paul's? My oldest son says he arranged for you to survey it."

"Uncle, he has been helpful, but the King only has money for ships and not for St. Paul's. Charles says repairs will cost too much."

"I'm not surprised. I think Charles would have St. Paul's destroyed, except that it would cost too much, also. Did you know Laud left eight hundred pounds to the repair of the cathedral and I'm the overseer to his will?"

"I knew you were his executor but not that he left the money."

Matthew walked them to their coach and said, "Van Doorn, most people who come to Cambridge think of it as a green oasis in a world of strife, but here, too, we must address God in the right way."

Daniel wondered if the Bishop truly understood the nature of architecture, but he said, "Sir, I trust that you will live a long time."

"At seventy-nine? Not likely! And they use that as the excuse for passing me over. Nephew, I hope your Royal Society doesn't concern itself with God and the soul. That is better left in trained hands." But when he saw that Christopher and Daniel looked uncomfortable, he added, "I don't expect young men to agree with me, but as long as you are not a Catholic, Van Doorn, I do not mind if you work on my chapel."

Christopher said, "Uncle, he is not a Catholic."

"Good. Then he can assist you on this work in hand."

The foundation stone for the theatre at Oxford was about to be laid and as Christopher discussed it with the donor, Gilbert Sheldon, the Archbishop of Canterbury and a former Warden of All Souls, he realised he might have to alter his plans a few times before this building was finally completed. Sheldon was an attractive, strongly built prelate, with a fresh, ruddy complexion and penetrating grey eyes, who was admired for his vision, courage, firmness of opinion, and practical turn of mind.

His opening words resembled his uncle's admonitions. "Doctor Wren, I respect your illustrations, but my purse is limited. I'm very much aware of your abilities but we must be reasonable in our ambitions. This is not to be a place for preaching, but since it is to be used for secular needs, it must be practical as well as attractive."

Not as magnificent as I want, Christopher thought, or as large, and there isn't as much space as I would like, which means compressing, and thus, compromising, but it is challenging, with a circular back and a flat front, and I do respect the Archbishop's taste and temperament.

Sheldon rarely got cross as his uncle did and was inclined to listen rather than to lecture. The Archbishop was intrigued by Christopher's determination to design the seventy-foot roof without any load-bearing columns, so the interior would resemble an ancient Roman theatre. He gave him permission to try this daring experiment, but repeated, "Watch the cost." He was paying Christopher a flat fee and time was not supposed to be a problem. Sheldon said the Professor could take as long as was needed, but so much had to be done with so little! There was not enough money, not enough material, the timber was shoddy and the stone inferior, the workmen felt underpaid, and the masons and carpenters —who regarded themselves as authorities on building—were doubtful about his design.

Sheldon, after he examined his present design, said, "It could be fine, but I suggest it remain fluid, so you can make changes after the building starts. Often the masons and carpenters are very good at that."

It was a relief to do the illustrations of the brain for Doctor Willis. There was no arguing over the design, or about the materials to be used, or masons and carpenters to be pleased, patrons to be satisfied, or any money crisis. Not even Willis interfered. And no one halted the doctor's dissection of the brain, whose one request was that Christopher give the most significance to the arrangement of the blood vessels. Much of the time he worked alone. He saw no trace of a soul and he also returned to astronomy. But this didn't absorb him as it had in the past. No matter how often and intensely he gazed at the heavens, his mind turned to St. Paul's, Pembroke, and Oxford. One night he stared through his telescope at Saturn and scribbled his findings on a scrap of paper and afterwards, when he went to examine his astronomical research he discovered that he had sketched a new, classical St. Paul's cathedral, with a dome on top.

The Moth

The moth
clings to the window's
glass
Is it breathing or not
Still it clings
through the hours
I cannot stir it
It may be between
breathing and not
Which would it mind more
Being awakened
Or finding itself dying
I won't make it find out
I have mourned for moths
before
I cling to the window
with it
Both of us unresolved

Stymean Karlen

24

The Moth

THE BALL WAS HELD IN WHITEHALL PALACE TO CELEBRATE THE anticipated victory over the Dutch. It was also to honour the Duke of York, who was to lead the fleet. Everyone seemed to assume the coming war would be a triumph to equal the one over the Spanish Armada, and Christopher felt if he expressed his pessimism about this he would be greeted with derision.

He stood at the entrance to the Great Hall of the palace with Daniel, who had come with him reluctantly and he saw many people he knew: Charles, the Duke of York, Buckingham, Clarendon, his cousin, Scarburgh, Evelyn, Pepys, and the four surveyors, Denham, Webb, Pratt and May. Their presence reminded him of what Daniel had said when he had invited him.

"Christopher, my Dutch accent could be resented."

"Daniel, you are an artist. That will be forgiven."

"My religion won't be if it is discovered by your fellow surveyors."

"Cromwell allowed your people to return to England even though it was not agreed to officially and Charles feels as Cromwell did. When the Jewish immigration into England is questioned he ignores it. He shares Cromwell's view, that since Jewish brains and blood helped Holland become great this should do the same for England. As long as you don't cross yourself and mutter Roman oaths you should be safe. If you are going to be my assistant, you must become accustomed to the Court and its ways."

"I'm not sure I'm capable of that. Especially with my background."

"I will decide that. If you are willing?"

Daniel assented, but now this decision was made Christopher wasn't as sure about it as he sounded. Daniel was attractive and capable enough, he reflected, but his background could cause difficulties. Yet Court was the place to find out if there were any and what they might be.

He led Daniel into the crowded ballroom. They had come from his new quarters in Scotland Yard, which he had found pleasant and comfortable, while Daniel was still using his room on Fetter Lane.

Then ladies entered behind the Queen and her maids of honour, many of them the most important and ambitious at Court. There was Lady Castlemaine, the King's mistress, the Duchess of York, the Duchess of Buckingham, and other ladies that he knew. They were elegantly dressed and some of them were considered the most beautiful in the realm, but when he saw Anne in attendance to the Queen, she was the one he longed to approach.

He was glad he had taken special pains with his dress. His grey doublet matched his eyes and his simple brown wig set off the natural colour of his hair. And while most of the courtiers wore finer lace and powdered wigs, he felt he fitted this occasion. Daniel looked appropriate, too, he thought, with his blue doublet and his well turned legs, a personal adornment that was admired by the ladies at Court.

After the King and Queen and the Duke and Duchess of York were seated, Charles started the ball by taking out the Duchess of York and the Duke took the Queen, and many of the lords and ladies followed. Then Charles ordered a country dance and led it with the comment, *"Cuckolds attend."*

Christopher watched for Anne, but she wasn't dancing, while Daniel observed everything intently, but he couldn't tell what his friend was thinking. Charles danced very well, far better than the Duke of York, and of the ladies Castlemaine was the best and ended in Charles' arms.

When the dancing ended Charles motioned for Doctor Wren to join him.

Christopher wished he could avoid the royal command, for the King had summoned the other surveyors, too. But he knew that if he ignored this, the King, despite his laxity, might never use him again. So, leaving Daniel in the company of Evelyn and Pepys, who were still curious about his Dutch friend, he responded to Charles' command, but slowly.

Charles smiled slyly as he saw Christopher's reluctance. He had invited the five surveyors to the ball in the hope that they would disagree. If they did, their disagreement could become his excuse for not pursuing any of the building or repairing, and as King he was above rebuke.

He said, "I trust you gentlemen are acquainted with each other."

Christopher bowed to Pratt and May, who returned his greeting;

Webb and Denham nodded, pretending they were delighted to see the others, but Christopher felt they were annoyed by his presence and Charles' cunning.

Charles said, "I want to hear your views on the rebuilding of my realm."

Denham said, "I'm sensible of my obligations, sir, I won't fail them."

"We mustn't fail, Your Majesty," said May, "Since you've honoured us."

"We won't fail, sir," Pratt assured him. "I never have."

Webb shrugged and Christopher was silent.

What kind of a game was Charles playing? Christopher wondered. He knew that five heads would never agree. Was this the comfort Charles needed?

Webb said suddenly, "Your Majesty, the situation at Greenwich is difficult but not serious. There have been no more casualties and the ground will now hold the greatest of foundations. As they did for Henry."

Christopher added, "Sir, I wonder if it wasn't premature to demolish the old Tudor palace. I've had second thoughts on the subject."

"Professor, why didn't you raise these objections at Greenwich?"

"Sir, I found illustrations of the palace. While some of it resembled a fortress, most of it was a pleasant mixture of Renaissance roofs and Tudor towers. Henry liked it so much he made constant additions to it and Elizabeth favoured it, too, particularly in summer and because it gave her the feeling England was a great maritime power, for it is close to the sea. And you also expressed second thoughts about demolishing it."

Webb said hurriedly, "Your Majesty, it is too late. The errors at Greenwich have been rectified and now are in hand. I've stopped the flooding and virtually all of the old palace has been demolished."

"But two workmen were killed. You may have trouble getting more."

"Sir, that is part of the cost. It frightened a few faint-hearted workmen, but work is scarce, so I have had no trouble replacing them or the dead men. I am devoted to Your Majesty, as I was to your martyred father."

"I hear so many tributes to him, I cannot conceive how he lost."

"I served him faithfully, sir," said Webb, and Denham joined in, and so did Pratt and May, but Christopher was silent, unable to cheapen himself.

Charles said, "Professor Wren, why are you so quiet?"

"Sir, I thought the subject in hand was architecture, not loyalty."

"You are not deficient in wit. It's never too late for such avowals."

"Sir, about Greenwich and the restoration of the old palace. If . . ."

"No!" Charles halted him regally. "You had your chance when we met there. We cannot keep changing our minds. Pratt, what are your views?"

The stout, heavy-featured Pratt replied, "Your Majesty, I bow to no one in my admiration for Professor Wren as a lecturer on astronomy, but he has designed nothing and has never been abroad. As I have been. Frequently."

The short, slight May added, "Sir, Wren's repairs for St. Paul's could cost thousands of pounds, enough to outfit several fine men-of-war."

Webb said, "Sir, I hear that his chapel at Pembroke is no more than a box and he expects at Oxford to support a seventy-foot roof span without pillars, which is obviously impossible. Inexperience shows, clearly."

Christopher said, "I'm lucky to be among such good friends," but no one seemed to hear him except Charles, who replied, "You are over-ruled."

Yet, he thought, if they think I'm giving up they are fools.

"Thank goodness, Your Majesty," said Webb. "I do have experience."

But Charles was tired now; Webb's persistence exhausted him and he had achieved his purpose. The surveyors were governed by self-interest, he reflected, everybody was. That would stop them from ever agreeing, which was what he wanted, for to repair St. Paul's and Windsor was to commit himself to projects his treasury was incapable of supporting; it would be difficult enough to support the war against the Dutch. He stretched out his hands to welcome the approaching Castlemaine. He felt grateful to her; she was less demanding than these surveyors and he had a sudden desire for her. She was his one continuing satisfaction and sustenance. As he felt her touch, he dismissed the others with a weary, regal wave of his hand.

Daniel was still talking to Evelyn and Christopher compared Castlemaine to Anne. Her height was impressive and she carried herself gracefully and yet voluptuously. But while he knew she was supposed to have the most exciting figure at Court, with swelling breasts and a small waist, he preferred Anne's charm and simplicity. Their hair was the same red colour, but Castlemaine's was darker, and her features were vivid and bold where Anne's were touching. The King's mistress possessed a striking complexion, lively eyes, and an expression that indicated she would omit nothing to catch a lover and that suggested she would do anything to hold on to him, while Anne's manner implied that would never happen, even if it did.

Before he could approach Anne, Denham insisted on introducing him to his bride-to-be, Margaret Brooke. The gossip had not exaggerated, he thought, Denham looked like an old man beside his youthful fiancée. She was very pretty, but slightly built, fair and pale, with a delicate complexion and a languid affectedness she assumed was inviting and tender.

Yet Denham, who had hardly spoken at all in the company of the other surveyors, was proud and animated now, as if Margaret was his greatest possession and he must guard this acquisition with his life.

Denham was trying to appear young and manly, talking about how cleverly he danced, although Margaret said, "I rarely indulge," when the Duke of York abruptly took her off to dance. She didn't protest but looked pleased, while the tall, blond, athletic Duke strutted as he led her about the floor.

Denham was aware of James' interest in his fiancée, for he flushed angrily as the Duke's hand caressed Margaret's lovely, exposed shoulders.

Bored with this intrigue, Christopher searched for Anne until he found her in a corner, alone, and near the river terrace where he had accosted her several weeks ago. This time she didn't seem to want to avoid him, but appeared glad to see him, as if she half expected him to look for her.

Suddenly he felt, What had been a search had become something else.

She moved closer to him and asked, "Christopher, do you dance?"

"Not if I can avoid it, Anne. But if you would like to, I will try."

"It is not necessary."

There was a brief pause and then he said, "We are neighbours."

"I didn't know." Anne was honestly surprised.

"As Assistant Surveyor to the Office of the Works I have been given a house in Scotland Yard. Across from yours. Are you ever free?"

"Forgive me for being a bit cynical, but is that an invitation?"

"Anne, I would like to be friends again."

"Is that all you desire, Christopher?"

"I recognise that I care for you. It is not something to ignore."

"Even though I may have known the King or Buckingham or others? Don't deny that it is thought. Half the Court assumes that and the other half thinks that if I haven't, I should have. Isn't that your understanding?"

"I'm not interested in gossip. Anne, I do want to see you again."

And then I would belong *to someone, somewhere*, she thought proudly yet desperately, and it might not be too late. No man she had met had been as genuine as Christopher. She could almost trust him. She hesitated, and then, even as she feared the consequences, she longed to agree with him. She whispered, "I will be home later tonight." Her hand touched his and he felt something metallic and she added, "It's my key. Tell no one. Promise?"

"I promise. I will be discreet."

A moment later Anne was with the Queen, fluently translating her Spanish, and the usually ill-at-ease Queen became relaxed, which was rare.

Matthew said accusingly, "You never told me you knew Lady Beaufort."

Christopher replied, "Were you aware that when you extended Charles' invitation the other surveyors would be here, too?"

"Yes. When did you meet Beaufort? Through Buckingham or the King?"

"No. Is she . . . ?" He paused, not wanting to reveal his emotions.

"I don't know. No one seems to know. But they have favoured her."

"I doubt Charles will support any surveyor. It saves him from assuming any responsibility if anything goes wrong, even with St. Paul's."

"Christopher, you mustn't regard St. Paul's so pessimistically. There are reports the Dutch may invade us up the Thames and that must be our first concern. But after we win the war, if you don't antagonise Charles, you could become Chief Surveyor. Do you know Lady Beaufort well?"

To avoid answering he joined Daniel, who was annoyed by all the questions Pepys and Evelyn had asked him. They wanted to know how the theatre and the chapel were progressing and when he referred them to Christopher, they inquired about his own background. The expression that came into Daniel's eyes was even more undecipherable and he changed the subject. He asked them whether he would be badly treated because of the impending war.

Evelyn said that if the English won he would be tolerated but if they lost he could suffer for it, while Pepys, who was supposed to have inside information, for Pepys worked for the Admiralty, didn't reply.

Pepys saw an attractive young woman whom he fancied and he excused himself to pursue her. And to Daniel's relief the King motioned for Evelyn to attend him. Evelyn's haste to accept this invitation was so frantic he tripped over a lady's long train which brought a hearty chuckle from Charles, who appreciated an embarrassment, when it was on someone else.

Christopher wanted to depart, to prepare himself for his meeting with Anne, but Charles summoned him, also. He excused himself to Daniel, after making an appointment to see him at Gresham the following afternoon, and approached the King even more reluctantly than before. Scarburgh stood beside Charles, very much the royal physician and courtier and he bowed stiffly to Christopher although they had known each other intimately.

Charles asked mockingly, "Professor, do the learned gentlemen of the Royal Society ever concern themselves with the phenomenon of chastity?"

Christopher didn't reply for a moment. He gazed at the brilliantly lit candles and torches, the musicians still playing, although no one was dancing and hardly anyone was listening, and everywhere there were the signs of great wealth and extravagance. He knew that virtually all preferment depended on the sovereign, that to rise in the world attendance at Court was considered essential and to kiss the hand of the King and to heed his instructions a sacred duty not to be neglected. But when he replied he couldn't resist being just as mocking, "Sir, we do not have enough evidence to make any judgments. But perhaps, at Court, I will learn."

"Who would you choose to observe?"

"Sir, that would be for you to decide."

"Wouldn't it be wiser to examine your fellow scholars at Oxford? Where marriage is frowned upon and chastity is virtually obligatory."

"Sir, I wouldn't assume such precepts are always obeyed."

"Professor, I never assume anything. But you do have the reputation of being a fine scholar, a prodigy of a scholar. Your cousin and others assure me that is so. How could you have time for other inclinations?"

Christopher felt Charles was taunting him and it irritated him. "However, as a surveyor, celibacy is not essential."

Christopher, containing himself, bowed and said, "Thank you, sir."

Was the Professor being sarcastic? That far, Charles thought angrily, no one presumed, not even Buckingham or Clarendon. "Unless, like so many scholars, you bury yourself in scholarship because you're afraid of women."

Charles sounded like a rival and Christopher was glad he had kept his private life secret. He said, "Sir, if you have no more need of me may I depart?" He saw Evelyn nearby, waiting for the King to return to him, while Scarburgh looked triumphant as Charles asked his opinion.

Then Charles said, "My eminent physician informs me that many years ago Dr. Harvey prescribed the same remedy for an illness of yours."

"Sir, he was a great man."

For an instant Charles didn't know how to regard this remark, but Wren's face was expressionless and suddenly, tired of this game, he snapped, "I never demand of my subjects what they cannot fulfil. Good night!"

Christopher's meeting with Anne loomed larger now, even as he felt that Charles might not regard it favourably. He was glad he had stood up to him. The key fitted in her door and inside he felt less cold. There was a fire in her front room and he saw Anne waiting for him. She pressed her face against his and he was surprised, her eyes were wet. Then he realised that she was crying.

Quite a long time later, after they had been joined together, he felt that at last his sword had found its proper scabbard. Within the walls of her body he felt alive and blossoming. And when she said, "I have not known Charles or Buckingham," he replied, "Anne, you do not have to justify your conduct to me." It was enough that she was extremely skilful now and this was the best love-making he had known.

Then she was crying again and when he asked her why, she didn't say what she was feeling, that she was struggling for self-respect and a sense of identity, of belonging to *someone, somewhere*. She was afraid he wouldn't understand, but she allowed him to dry her eyes and she sighed gratefully and she agreed to see him a week from this joyful night.

In love, she thought, Christopher didn't have to be a conqueror like so many men, but was content to share. He didn't demand subjection but asked for affection, and thus, was the best man she had known.

He fell asleep, but she had to awaken him, so he could leave before it grew light and he could be seen.

He tiptoed across Scotland Yard, delighted that he was so close to her.

You Can Only Be

You can only be
as wise as you are
Later you can only be
wiser than you were

Stymean Karlen

25

You Can Only Be

Now, as Christopher predicted, nothing was done about Windsor or St. Paul's and activity was stopped even at Greenwich. The preparations for the war with the Dutch became the country's passion and for the remainder of 1664 all work on buildings under the royal jurisdiction was halted.

But Charles, while he was pleased with the support this feeling evoked, hoped to avoid the actual conflict. He wrote his sister: *"I am the only man in all my dominions who does not desire war,"* and he tried to persuade the Dutch to pay him not to fight. However, they refused to buy him off and when Parliament voted him two and a half million pounds for the conduct of the war—a sum far greater than he had received for any other purpose—he decided it would be more profitable to declare war.

Christopher resumed his lectures on astronomy at Oxford and returned to London each week to visit Anne, although the reason he gave others was that he was attending the Royal Society meetings at Gresham. He told no one about her, except Daniel, and then, only that she was his friend.

The work on the theatre at Oxford stopped because of a lack of wood—the good timber was confiscated by the Navy—and he needed the best wood for the roof. He sensed that Daniel was restless and to keep him by his side, he asked him to supervise the completion of the chapel and offered him half of his surveyor's salary. Daniel protested that the twenty pounds was more than he deserved, and that he didn't need the wages, that he had independent means of his own, but Christopher insisted so strongly Daniel gave in, not wanting to risk a break with him.

The war finally began in 1665, after much hesitation on both sides, and was indecisive. When it appeared the struggle could become interminable Christopher grew impatient. Now that his desire for Anne was satisfied he was not sure she was essential to his happiness. He still enjoyed their love-making, but her skill aroused his suspicions. While he told himself it was none of his business whom she had known, that troubled him. Yet she had much to offer and she gave willingly and he was grateful.

By the spring of 1665 he realised he was more interested in architecture than anything else. But there was no work in England, for energies focussed on the war which seemed likely to continue for years. He remembered the accusation that he had never seen any architecture outside of England and this nagged him. When he heard that the King of France, Louis XIV, had embarked on a vast building programme and had invited Bernini, the great Italian sculptor and architect—who was considered the foremost authority on architecture in the world—to remodel Paris and the palace of the Louvre, he decided to visit France. In his imagination that country became a school of architecture.

The chapel at Pembroke was a few months from completion, but he was not satisfied with it. He felt it might fulfil his uncle's needs, but not his own. It was more immature than he liked, revealing a narrowness of view and his own inexperience. He wanted his next design to turn out more uniquely, to be more aware of the present than the past.

It was easy to obtain a leave of absence from his professorial duties at Oxford, for there was hardly any interest in astronomy at the moment. Most of the students preferred to achieve a reputation at arms.

Yet to leave Anne was difficult and he reflected many days before he decided to break the news. But when his cousin gave him a letter of introduction to the English Ambassador in France, Henry Jermyn, the Earl of Albans, and a man of influence in Paris, he felt he couldn't procrastinate any longer. While the French were supporting the Dutch, they were still at peace with the English. He thought, Anne must sense by now that he didn't intend to marry her. He must tell her how much he loved architecture. But would she comprehend? He wondered and was doubtful.

He didn't tell her about his visit to Paris until just a few days before he was to depart, so she couldn't change his mind. Then, after a sensual night together, as he was about to leave, he said abruptly, "Anne, I won't be able to see you next week. I have to go to Paris."

Her eyes grew misty and she asked, "Will you be there a long time?"

"Not very long. A month, perhaps. But no longer, I think."

She was lying in bed while he dressed, but now she jumped to her feet and cried, "I've lived for our weekly meetings, Christopher!"

"They matter greatly to me, too. And they will when I return."

"You won't return. Not for months. Can't your journey wait?"

"No. This is the moment to go. If I wait it will be too late."

"Is it a mission for the King?"

"It is to learn how to be an architect." She was puzzled by this and he added, "It is an opportunity I can't afford to miss. There is a great surge of building taking place in Paris and I must view it and study it now."

"And I'm forsaken because you love buildings more than you love me."

He thought, *Anne, I owe much to you, but I cannot throw away my present needs and future hopes, for they are the things I value most. If I am to live in this age, I must make it my age. I must do what I believe. Or part of me dies, the best part of me dies. I must go, and without any regrets. While it is still possible. Or I will never forgive myself.*

"Christopher, if you truly loved me, you wouldn't go."

"Anne, I have no choice, and it has nothing to do with you."

"That is the trouble," she said sadly. "I am never considered."

"Do you need any money?"

"Christopher, must you insult me, too?"

"I don't want you to suffer in my absence."

"The Court takes care of my needs as long as I serve the Queen."

"Anne, I have to go. I do."

"I know my place," she mumbled. "I've always known it with you."

He didn't know what else to say or do. It would be easier to leave quickly, but he felt badly about her tears and he said, "The time will pass soon and then I will be back, standing at your door."

"And I won't be here," she said sharply. "Who knows where I will be?"

As he said goodbye she stared at him as if he were a ghost already. It only made him feel more stubborn in his resolve to visit Paris. Building rejuvenated him. Everything else, he thought, was just an escape. Yet at her door, unable to endure her sorrow, he turned back suddenly, kissed her passionately, and then was gone.

She uttered a silent prayer: *Dear God, bring him back soon. Before I die of wretchedness. Or forfeit my future and be as melancholy as the grave. I am so tired of waiting.* Long after her candle flickered out she gazed in the frosty moonlight at his house across Scotland Yard.

Daniel understood his reasons for going to Paris and assured him that he would take care of his affairs. He said, "Your uncle doesn't always listen to me, but he does seem to respect my views, and I believe he will follow your design. I will write you how the work progresses and about the state of St. Paul's, although the decay there grows worse."

"I expect to be back in time for the completion of the chapel, but if I'm delayed, would you keep an eye on Lady Beaufort?"

"Write you who she sees?" Daniel was surprised; he didn't expect Christopher to be jealous—his friend must be intimately involved.

"I didn't mean it in that sense." Christopher didn't want to sound like her lover. "I just don't want anything unfortunate to happen to her while I'm away and it could, for she is in a vulnerable position at Court."

Daniel didn't ask for any further explanations but told him, "I will protect Lady Beaufort to the best of my ability."

Then it came time to say farewell and neither knew what to say.

By now Daniel realised that Christopher's journey to Paris was of the utmost importance and could test his cleverness and tact.

And a search for sanity and survival, reflected Christopher, who almost said that to Daniel, but was silent, unable to strip himself totally. Instead, he cried out, "Don't be too trusting! Evelyn could be right. If the war turns against my countrymen, they could turn on you."

"You must be careful, too," Daniel answered. "You will be a foreigner in Paris, and while France is not at war Louis favours Holland."

They embraced silently and parted.

Christopher arrived in Paris a few days later and went directly to the residence of the ambassador which was near the Palais Royal. Jermyn expected him, for Matthew had written Jermyn in advance about his visit, over Clarendon's signature. The ambassador had a footman show him into his drawing room and greeted him graciously, for this youthful astronomer came highly recommended. He was surprised when Doctor Wren asked to meet Bernini and the other architects remodelling the Louvre.

While Jermyn pondered his reply—he had learned a long time ago never to give a quick answer even if he had one—Christopher surveyed his surroundings. The drawing room was one of the most lavish he had ever seen and the heart of what was a small château within Paris, and which contained a magnificent courtyard and beautiful fountains and gardens.

Jermyn thought, With Wren's connections he would be a fool to deny him.

Christopher was disappointed by the Earl's appearance. He recalled him vaguely from his childhood as a tall, handsome, stately man, but now, at sixty, Jermyn had become ponderous and fat, possessed of an insatiable appetite for food and drink and the other luxurious amenities. His once strong, regular features had become jowly and soft and his gigantic wig sat on his head like an uncertain crown and accentuated his bulk.

But Jermyn was amiable, reflected Christopher, although he moved painfully because of his gout as he rose to assure him, "I had no idea you were interested in architecture or in meeting Bernini, but I will do what I can. Louis is giving a fête at Versailles, to celebrate the completion of part of the renovation. He is turning this old hunting lodge into a grand palace to prove his greatness as a King. Now that he is absolute ruler of France he is determined to rebuild the country."

Christopher was envious. How different Louis was from Charles! Then he stifled these feelings, resolved to be just an eye.

The day of the fête Jermyn took him in his coach to Versailles, which was about twenty miles outside of Paris. The Earl's coach was comfortable, well sprung, two footmen rode on each side to serve them, and the driver was skilful. The May afternoon was sunny and the fields near Versailles a brilliant green. Almost as green as the fields about Oxford, thought Christopher, and that made him homesick. It was an effort to focus on the architecture. And the château at Versailles was not as interesting or exciting as he had expected and Jermyn saw his disappointment.

He said, "It is unfinished. Building here will go on for years."

What a marvellous opportunity for an architect, Christopher reflected.

"Most of Louis' courtiers differ with his enthusiasm for Versailles. They say his plans will cost a vast sum. That it is sand and marsh, that the drainage is poor, there is no water, no woods, no view, and worst of all, no town, that it is a barren and melancholy place, but Louis thinks the location is marvellous. He is a country person, he spends hours in the saddle. He is miserable when he is confined to a town, even one as worldly as Paris, and he is determined to remake Versailles in his own image. He has grandiose plans to erect a great palace here, although many think he will fail. But you will judge for yourself, Doctor Wren."

Indeed I will, Christopher said to himself, and looked about intently.

They stepped out of the coach and Jermyn skinned his shins on a stone a workman had failed to remove and he cursed. Yet, as he led Christopher toward the King, he was affable and smiling. Great porticos had been erected in front of the entrance to the château and between them was a dais on which sat Louis XIV. There was a great crowd of courtiers in attendance to the King, but Jermyn, to show his influence, spoke to one of the royal footmen, who brought them immediately to the King.

There was still sun in the clear May sky and it beat down upon the King and Christopher wondered why Louis XIV was considered handsome. While he was just twenty-seven, his features—like Charles'—were becoming fleshy and sensual. His nose was large and curved and although his lips, mouth, and cheeks suggested power and strength, they were also softening into roundness and sensuality. His small moustache resembled Charles', but was dark brown where the English King's was black. Christopher liked his well-shaped head and that he was broad-shouldered and muscular.

Louis acknowledged the English Ambassador as he introduced Doctor Wren to him and Jermyn was gratified. But Christopher felt his name meant nothing to the King, for when a handsome young woman approached Louis a moment later, he curtly dismissed them to address her.

Jermyn whispered apologetically, "Montespan. Many say she is going to be the King's next mistress. I'm sorry, Doctor, but he is susceptible."

Montespan was dark, voluptuous, with excellent features and a fine complexion, but Christopher thought her over-dressed and her expression sanctimonious. He was more interested in surveying Versailles, but Jermyn said impatiently, "Later. The fête is about to start."

The setting, in a small theatre which had been built for the occasion in the vestibule of the château, was ostentatious and lavish. Christopher sat in the rear of the audience with Jermyn, while the King and Montespan were in the royal box next to the improvised stage.

Music began the programme. "By Lully," Jermyn told Christopher. "He is leading the fête with his musicians. He is the King's first musician."

Lully's music was too loud and repetitive for Christopher, but the comedy that followed enchanted him. He had refreshed his French before leaving England, and while he distrusted his accent his ear seemed satisfactory, for he could understand most of what was happening, and he found the pantomime charming yet quite satirical.

Jermyn, who was determined to prove he was a wit in addition to being a diplomat, told Christopher, "It is by Louis' favourite dramatist."

"His views of the folly of much of our medical practices are amusing yet accurate. I would like to meet such a clever, witty man. Who is he?"

"Jean Baptiste Poquelin. But now, as the King's servant, he is called Molière. You don't want to meet him. He is just a paid entertainer."

But when *The Doctor In Spite of Himself* ended, Christopher applauded so loudly that Jermyn was embarrassed and hushed him. He repeated his wish to meet Molière and the ambassador ignored his request.

Jermyn said, "I will introduce you to the three men who have the most influence with Louis in architecture." He led him across the hall to Colbert, the King's chief adviser and supervisor of his purse, Charles Perrault, a poet whose ideas on building were fancied by Louis, and Louis Le Vau, who Jermyn introduced as, "the King's First Architect."

Christopher thought, Jermyn was proud of his French and the help he was giving him, and Le Vau was plainly committed to his own importance. Le Vau was dark, stout, round-faced, with a moustache in the fashion of the King, a long black wig, and wore extravagant lace and several medals.

Charles Perrault was closer to his own age, Christopher noted— Le Vau was of the previous generation, as was Colbert—and was slim, vivacious.

On first sight, Christopher liked Colbert best. Although all three Frenchmen were dark, the minister's wavy hair had an attractive reddish tinge, he was still lean and strongly built, and he seemed a good listener.

Yet when Jermyn mentioned that Wren was an astronomer who had come to France because of his interest in architecture, the three Frenchmen looked sceptical and Colbert said, "This could be considered a trespass."

"Sir, I came to observe and learn. From yourself, Monsieur Le Vau."

Le Vau bowed graciously and said, "I can teach you much."

"I also hope to meet Signor Bernini," Christopher added.

"He isn't present. He considers us beneath him," Le Vau said sharply.

"I thought he was designing additions to the Louvre."

"He is incapable of understanding our art."

Perrault nodded and Colbert added, "Bernini's ideas are extravagant. He bites off more than we can digest. Monsieur Wren, I would avoid him."

"But I heard he has come to Paris on the direct invitation of the King."

"That is true," said Le Vau. "Only he doesn't understand our ways."

Colbert said, "I doubt that we can afford his extravagant designs."

Christopher felt trapped. If anything, the Frenchmen's hostility to Bernini increased his desire to see him, yet he realised that if he did it could end whatever chance he had to be friends with them.

However, the thought of not seeing him made Christopher feel as if he were in a jail and he said, "I heard Bernini is the first artist in the world."

"He is, Monsieur, as a sculptor." The young lady who stated this knew the others who bowed to her respectfully, while Jermyn introduced her to Christopher. The Countess de Chambeau acknowledged his presence as if she knew about him and continued impulsively, "Doctor Wren, Bernini is greatly honoured where he is not feared. But not loved, is he, gentlemen?"

"No doubt about that, Countess," said Colbert. "No doubt whatever."

The King motioned for Colbert to attend him, and as Colbert obeyed, Le Vau, Perrault, and Jermyn followed the chief adviser, determined not to allow anyone else to excel them in Louis' favour. Christopher expected the Countess de Chambeau to join them, but instead, she said in perfect English, "Dr. Wren, you must not mind their dislike of Bernini. They are jealous of his reputation. Are you interested in architecture?"

He nodded, glad she had stayed. She was very pretty and well spoken.

"Jermyn informed me that I should converse with you, that you were a learned astronomer, but he didn't mention your regard for architecture."

Her interest was so genuine he told her why he had come to France and he was surprised and pleased by how much she knew about building. He had felt attacked by the men, but not by her. She didn't regard his passion for architecture as just a diversion, for when he expressed his feeling for it, she replied, "Then you must remain firm in your views."

"I will, Countess. Where did you learn such perfect English?"

"My father was an admirer of Queen Elizabeth. He met her as a young man and was able to converse with her in French, English, and Latin. He was much taken with her wit and intelligence, and he swore that if he ever had a son he would teach him such graces. But I was his only child and so he made the best of it, perhaps reluctantly, and had me tutored by the best teachers in the realm. Using Elizabeth as an example, I was taught English and Latin and Greek, astronomy and building. When he rebuilt our château, I became his assistant. I learned much."

He remembered that she was a Countess and suddenly he felt at a disadvantage and he blushed, for he did want to see her again.

"Do you consider such learning in a lady sacrilegious as so many do?"

"No." Now he knew why she attracted him. It wasn't that she was pretty, although she was. He was aware of her slender figure,

the same height as his own, which he preferred. He noticed that
the beauty of her complexion was accentuated by her bright black
hair and vivid brown eyes. He was fascinated by her perfect teeth,
extraordinary for one raised on rich French cooking. But what
appealed to him the most was that her manner was as pleasing as
her voice. If he could only see her again.

"Dr. Wren, are you staying over at Versailles as some guests
are?"

"Jermyn suggested it. So I could become better acquainted with
France."

"He meant, to know who is influential and useful. Would you
like me to show you the grounds tomorrow? I know Versailles.
I live nearby."

"I would be delighted. If it is not too much of an imposition."

"It is not. And perhaps you could examine the Louvre with me.
Le Vau desires to remodel my château and he is sure I will be
suitably impressed and employ him. Has anyone offered to introduce
you to Bernini?"

"No."

"Perhaps I can. He is difficult to see, but I will try if you
like."

"Countess, it would be . . . ." He caught hold of himself. He felt
so much exhilaration with her it was dangerous. He must be careful.
He added, "You are very kind, but I don't want to cause you any
difficulties."

"I never endure difficulties when I don't want to. I think it will
be a good idea if we use my coach and four. It is well sprung
and spacious."

After they arranged the time and place to meet and parted, he
hoped, that with all of her pleasing ways, she was not using him
as a diversion. Yet why else would a lady of her quality, so intelligent
and attractive, desire his company? He almost asked Jermyn later,
as they prepared for bed in quarters arranged for the King's favoured
guests, then decided, as was his nature, to keep his private affairs
to himself.

Jermyn asked, "Did you enjoy the Countess?" and he replied,
"She is quite learned." Jermyn smiled and added, "She is one of
the best educated ladies in France. It troubles many courtiers. They
feel ignorant in her company, and thus embarrassed by her, which
they consider unforgiveable in a lady. But this shouldn't concern
you. You can match her learning."

Christopher pretended that he wasn't interested, although he was,
while Jermyn continued, "She prefers men of learning and you
might amuse her. She is a rare creature at Louis' Court. Although
she is probably in her middle twenties, she is unwed and no one

o

has been able to discover any scandal about her. This is most unusual. And you are well informed."

And he was stimulated by her presence and the thought of seeing her again, but he merely shrugged and didn't answer Jermyn who was curious.

The King and his guests were gone the next afternoon when the Countess met Christopher to show him about the works at Versailles. Jermyn had left for Paris early, after Christopher assured him that he would have transportation back to the city. She took him through the various rooms which had been built, rebuilt, and refurnished with many luxuries, curiosities, and ornaments. She noticed that while he observed everything carefully, he became most interested when they met Colbert and Le Vau beside a marsh where Louis had insisted a lagoon should be created.

Both men were disturbed. While they acknowledged Christopher's presence and bowed graciously to the Countess, obviously determined not to offend her, they were preoccupied with their construction problem.

Colbert said apprehensively, "Drainage of these marshes will cost an immense sum of money. Our resources should be concentrated on the Louvre which is built already, but when I venture such an opinion Louis is very angry and insists I rearrange our finances to include both works."

Le Vau shrugged as if to say that was not his concern.

Colbert added bitterly, "Yet if you fail, I will be blamed."

"I never fail," declared Le Vau. "But these marshes present many difficulties. There is more water here than soil. It is a poor place to build a great palace, particularly the size the King desires."

Christopher wondered why other possibilities couldn't be considered, but they ignored his attempt to suggest something else, while the Countess was silent as Colbert said irritably, "One of the workmen drowned the other day and his mother accused Louis of indifference to his subjects' lives. When she publicly called him '*A whoremonger, a stupid tyrant,*' he was furious. Louis is proud of his learning. He ordered her whipped and silenced, but he was upset. He told me that if there are any more deaths on his works, they must be kept from the public, that the lives of the workmen are the responsibility of the architect, that he, on pain of death, must not be bothered by such irksome matters."

"I've done my best," Le Vau replied. "But if Louis wants building to continue at Versailles, risks must be taken and some lives lost."

Christopher saw a dozen workmen sinking into the mud of the marsh up to their hips while they laboured, yet Colbert and Le Vau, fastidious and perfectly groomed, stood a safe distance away, disdainful of the workmen and repelled by the mud. He had an impulse to investigate the condition of the marsh itself to determine its solidity, as a sensible surveyor should before he risked anyone's life, but as he moved toward the marsh where several workmen were struggling desperately to keep from drowning, the Countess caught him by the arm and whispered, "Leave them alone. Colbert and Le Vau will argue about Versailles interminably and then if it is not built as Louis wishes, they will blame each other."

He felt sad. More workmen would die before this palace was finished. And while he had gained some information he had not learned enough facts.

She took him to the Louvre the next day to observe what was being done to complete it. Most of a very large palace was built already and it needed only an east front and a main entrance to finish it. But while a vast amount of work was going on, Christopher couldn't tell whose designs were being followed. He saw no sign of Bernini or Le Vau or any other architect and he was startled by the attention that was given to the rubble being carefully carted away.

The Countess explained, "The wood and stone is the property of the architect and there is much money in it. The wood is used for gallows, they are in constant demand, and the stone can be used elsewhere, for other patrons are not fussy or as powerful as the King."

"Who is responsible for the work itself?"

"Le Vau. But Colbert has also consulted our greatest architect, François Mansart. He is in his sixties and has retired, but his opinion carries great weight. Yet the final designs are Le Vau's, unless Louis changes to Bernini's. That hasn't been decided so far."

There was beauty and symmetry in the Louvre, he thought— what he could see of it behind the confusion and the dirt, and the workmen seemed industrious and skilful—but he wondered why the architect wasn't present. At this moment in the reconstruction it seemed vital.

Christopher was so interested in the work on the Louvre he returned to it often until the Countess reminded him there were many other fine works to be viewed in France. He agreed to be guided by her, grateful for her assistance and enchanted by her company. She introduced him to many examples of French architecture by showing him churches, country houses, and châteaux. Then, just as he had given up all hope of meeting Bernini, she arranged for him to meet the sculptor-architect. But she warned him, "Bernini says he can give you just a few minutes. He is sculpting a head of Louis and he will see you after a sitting. Briefly."

But Christopher was determined not to be intimidated by Bernini who had a reputation for arrogance. He arrived at the designated time and he was ushered into Bernini's audience chamber in Louis' palace at St. Germain and was informed that he would be seen as soon as possible. Then he waited. After two hours he decided this delay was a disaster; if he waited any longer he would only be humiliated further. He rose to go, tired of surveying the palace which was designed as a castle, when a footman in the King's livery halted him and ordered him to attend Signor Bernini.

He was led into a large studio where an elderly man stood by a large, unfinished marble bust. It was Bernini, he realised, and he was disappointed—Bernini looked so old. The sculptor-architect was deep in thought, but then he heard him and turned angrily. Now nothing mattered to Christopher but Bernini. It was *his head* that should be sculpted, he thought, not the King's. Bernini's long, powerful features were a daring and extraordinary composition of nature. He noted the strong jaw, the fine nose, the sensuous lips, the piercing eyes, the spacious forehead, the wavy, ample white hair, the arched carriage of the head, the passionate expression. If he could only sculpt, what a superb bust this could be!

Bernini said in Latin, "The Countess de Chambeau tells me that you are interested in my designs of the Louvre. Why? You are an astronomer."

"Sir, some of my activities include building," he replied in Latin.

"Some? Either it is everything or it is nothing!"

"But you sculpt, sir."

"In stone. As I do in architecture. God had given me this gift and I cannot refuse Him. What did you want to view? I have much on my mind. Louis was restless today and I don't trust his expression."

Christopher gazed at the head, which was partially done, and thought, It flatters Louis, for it looks more like an idyllic Greek god than a man fattening into sensuality, but he said, "Sir, it looks satisfactory to me."

"Satisfactory!" exploded Bernini. "That is for mediocrities and the French! As Michelangelo Buonarotti used to say, God wants more from us. What is your reason for being here? The Countess has taste, which is rare in France, but I have no time to spare. Be quick."

"Sir, if I could see your designs for the Louvre, I would be honoured."

"So you will copy my invention?"

"No, sir. It is to learn. I am learning to be an architect."

Bernini stated contemptuously, "One does not learn. Either one is inspired by God or he is a Frenchman. I only have some early designs."

"Sir, whatever I see of yours should teach me something."

"If you have eyes. And know where you are going. As Michelangelo Buonarotti used to say, all work should be measured by his and Raphael's. What do you think of my designs for the Louvre?"

Christopher hesitated. The five dusty designs on the paper he held were unfinished and he couldn't tell whether the soil of the Louvre could maintain such colossal columns. Everything appeared so heavy. Yet they possessed grandeur, although he doubted they fitted what stood already.

Bernini sensed his doubts, for he took them away from Christopher abruptly and said, "I have received many thousand of pistoles for them."

"May I copy them, sir? I'm sure they will be most instructive."

"No! God must furnish you with your inspiration. If you have any." He returned to the bust of Louis as if Christopher didn't exist. Yet when the latter reached the door, he swung around with a quickness that Christopher didn't think him capable of and declared in Italian, "However, if you are serious you may build something that will support life. Your Latin is better than I expected. especially from an Englishman. Although your accent could be better. More Italian, preferably."

Christopher was grateful that his Italian was better than his French as he answered in that language, "Sir, may I see you again?"

"And show me your own designs?"

"Perhaps."

"And I will say, how well done!"

"If they deserve it."

"How horrible." But when he saw Christopher shrink from him, he added hurriedly, "I'm not malicious, Signor, Signor . . ."

"Wren, Christopher Wren."

"Signor Wren, I'm not malicious at all. But God has taught me that one cannot afford to be charitable in matters of art. I have toiled years, with His inspiration, to achieve my greatness. I cannot indulge others. It is childish and wearies me. No one is as hideous as an amateur. I am the direct descendant of Michelangelo Buonarotti. Although he was very aged and ailing he waited until I was born to die. It was no accident."

"Thank you, sir."

"For what?" Bernini stared at him fiercely—was he mocking him?

"For giving me this time. I trust your bust will turn out as you wish."

"It always does. My invention is still fertile."

Now he had a need to tell Daniel about his experiences. He wrote:

"I have been busy surveying the most esteemed fabrics of Paris and the country. The Louvre for a while was my daily object where no less than a thousand hands are constantly employed in the works, some in laying mighty foundations, some in raising storeys and columns with vast stones, by great and useful engines, others in carving, in laying of marbles, plastering, painting, gilding, which together makes this a school of architecture, the best probably at this time in Europe.

"The College of the Four Nations is generally admired, but the artist has purposely set it in an ill-favoured manner so that he might show his wit by purposely struggling with an inconvenient situation.

"An Academy of painters, sculptors, architects and the chief artificers of the Louvre meet every first and last Saturday of the month. Colbert comes to the works of the Louvre every Wednesday, and if business doesn't hinder him, on Thursday, and the workmen are paid every Sunday.

"I was introduced to Bernini, who showed me his designs of the Louvre and the King's statue. This was at the antique mass of the Castle of St. Germain, whose hanging gardens are delightful.

"I have tried not to miss the King's houses. Fontainebleau has a stately wildness and vastness suitable to the desert it stands on. I have viewed the palace of Versailles twice. The mixture of brick, stone, blue tile and gold makes it look as if it has a rich livery, and every inch within is crowded with little curiosities and ornaments; many of the women are attractive and several are acquainted with architecture and philosophy. But building certainly ought to have the attribute of the Eternal and therefore is the only thing incapable of new fashions, but so much at Versailles is concerned with only what is fashionable.

"After visiting the incomparable châteaux of Vaus and Maisons, I have seen Ruel, Constances, Chilly, Essuane, St. Maur, St. Maude, Issy, Mendon, Rincy, Chantilly, Verneuil, Liancour, all of which, and many others, I have surveyed. And that I might not lose the impression of them, I shall bring you all France on paper.

"Bernini's designs of the Louvre I would have given my skin for, but the old Italian gave me but a few minutes' view; it was five designs on paper, for which he received many thousand pistoles. I had only time to copy it in my fancy and memory, and shall be able, by discourse and crayon, to give you a tolerable account of it. I hope I shall have an accurate report on all the best artists in France. My business now is to investigate their trades and arts. I put myself into all shapes to humour them, it is a comedy to me, and though sometimes expensive, I am reluctant to leave it.

"I have been asked to remain until Christmas so that I will have enough time to perfect what I have on the anvil—observations on the present state of architecture, arts and manufacturers in France."

After he posted this letter to Daniel, he wrote in the same vein to several other friends.

The next day there was a letter from Daniel, who wrote:

"I trust you will not be cross with me, but I have bad tidings. The plague has afflicted London, and uninvited, has brought many deaths to the city and all those who can afford the expense have fled London. I would like to, but Lady Beaufort is living now on Fetter Lane despite the danger. I think she has come here because she believes it will keep her in touch with you. Sam Taunton refused to take her in until she gave him ten pounds, which is excessive, and they are barely civil to each other, but she seems determined to stay here until you return. I do not think she needs any money, since she still has some jewels, but when I asked her why she left her house in Scotland Yard she didn't answer. But I have made inquiries through Evelyn, Pepys, and others at Court, and I am led to believe it has something to do with Buckingham or the King.

"You are fortunate not to be in London at this time for the plague grows worse and if you value my advice, you will remain away. There is so much imperfection here it reminds me of Amsterdam. The war drags on, still without signs of victory for either side, and I will keep an eye on Lady Beaufort. She does talk to me, for she knows I am your friend, although her manner is full of suspicion and I doubt she trusts any man.

"Nothing has been done on your theatre at Oxford and St. Paul's only grows worse, even more neglected with the spread of the plague, but your chapel at Pembroke is almost finished, for Cambridge is free of the affliction and your presence there is not required.

"Many die in London now and our whole mode of life has changed.

"You will be wise to stay in Paris."

Christopher considered returning to London at once, but when he told this to Jermyn, the ambassador replied, "I don't think that you will be able to obtain passage. There are no boats visiting England now because of the plague. And the channel is full of Dutch men-of-war, who would imprison you if you managed to survive their attack."

Then there was his feeling for the Countess. By now she insisted that he call her by her name, Françoise, and she invited him to her château to suggest repairs and possible improvements.

They sat in her beautiful gardens, bathed with a soothing summer sun, and he was enchanted with the setting and the design, and her presence and charm; and pleased that she was turning to him for advice when she knew Bernini, Le Vau, and Mansart. He noticed she wore a new, fragrant perfume and that her dress was the most

424 *Myself, Christopher Wren*

voluptuous he had seen. And suddenly she declared, "I will stay unwed before I marry a man I do not love. I have always loved what is beautiful. Too many architects I have consulted, know nothing except to make a hall on one side, a room on the other, and a staircase in the middle. I expect more from you, Christopher."

He did, too, but he wasn't certain how to proceed. Her château had a refined and delicate feeling, with a classical simplicity he liked, and which was characteristic of her temperament, and it was difficult to suggest any improvements. He said, "I would like to help you, but I'm not sure you need any here. Did you consult Bernini?"

"Yes. He informed me, '*Art is a continuous activity between God and man.*' and he added, '*and I have agreed to listen only to Him. I must create only masterpieces in the time left to me.*' And Christopher, I prefer you to Le Vau."

"But your château is almost perfect."

"That was my father's doing. I was fortunate."

Twilight spread quietly over the gardens and the fragrance of the flowers was like a part of her and as she leaned close to him, he yearned to take her in his arms. They had shared so much the past few weeks, but did she care? Perhaps, with all of her apparent innocence, she had been pursuing. Yet he hesitated.

Françoise was glad Christopher had begun to wear lace on his sleeves and collar and to groom his hair carefully. It was a good sign, and that he liked to ride, a pursuit she enjoyed. And he had the best mind she had met. But she couldn't be his servant, or, on the other hand, exact any promises from him. He must give willingly or not at all. She asked, "Is it true that everyone at the Court of Charles has a mistress?"

"I don't know, Françoise. I am not a courtier."

"Nevertheless, that is generally true, isn't it, Christopher?"

"It is difficult to say what is true at the Court of Charles, just as it is at the Court of Louis. Besides, I dislike gossip."

"That wouldn't halt any of Louis' courtiers."

He reached for her hand and to his surprise, she withdrew it, although not far. Yet he was in no mood to flirt, to cajole, to implore. He returned to their discussion of architecture, for once, reluctantly. She sat motionless now, neither coming closer nor pulling away, and he wondered unhappily whether their shared interest in building, fascinating as it could be at other times, was doing him more harm than good.

The next day he wrote to Daniel again, asking him if he should return to London in spite of his friend's advice that this was unnecessary.

"Unless," he added, "you can assure me that Lady Beaufort is safe."

He composed this letter at Françoise's château, where he had remained overnight, although, to his regret, everything had been circumspect.

Now That I Went Mad

Now that I went mad
      none will I tell
   I will seal
the fact
      well
   not to threaten
their prejudice

They think they know how
      to deal with
   their insane
      so what would
they do
   if they lost
      their only forte

Since they do not know
      what to do
   with their sane
and their
      sane don't
         know what
to do
   with them
      like I do.

Stymean Karlen

26

Now That I Went Mad

"Unless you can assure me that Lady Beaufort is safe."

Daniel reread those words in the hope they would help him formulate a sensible reply to his friend and thought bitterly, no one living in London these July days was safe. Instead of the warmth of summer bringing relief to the stricken city, it brought desolation. The Bills of Mortality were increasing at a terrifying rate. Hundreds were dying of the plague each week and no sane person returned to London willingly. But if he wrote this to Christopher, his friend might be impelled to rush back from a sense of duty, despite the difficulties, and that was idiocy. He must reassure him, whatever the truth was, and keep him in Paris.

He sat in Christopher's old room which overlooked the court and garden and lit a candle, for the daylight was finally leaving the July sky. He reflected mournfully, That was another terrifying thing, the better the weather the worse the plague. No rain had fallen for weeks, which was unusual, and the heat was intense, and this added to the apprehension and gloom, for it aggravated the savagery of the pestilence. The blue sky, seldom cloudy, had become hateful. The lack of wind was like the hand of death upon London and nothing seemed to stir but the plague.

In June he had heard the guns of a battle at sea between the English and the Dutch, and later he had learned that the English had won. But he felt neither glad nor sorry, only numb, for the fighting dragged on while the war on the streets of London became far harsher.

Death was everywhere and coming closer each day. Already several houses on Fetter Lane were shuttered and shut up, their doors padlocked so none of the inmates of these infected buildings could leave and infect anyone else. And to be sure everyone knew of the presence of the plague in these houses, the watchmen scrawled on their front doors the dreaded red cross and the words "*God have mercy upon their souls.*"

Then, with the coming of nightfall, Daniel heard the worst sounds of all: the ringing of the church bells announcing the deaths in their parishes and rarely quiet now, the rattle of the death carts on the cobblestones, the shouts of the drivers, "*Bring out your dead!*" the creak of the death carts stopping, the clamour of the searchers breaking into the silent houses to dispose of the dead, but always, rising even above the echo of the church bells, the cry, "*Bring out your dead!*"

He shuddered and his horror grew as he noticed the smell of brimstone coming from the house next door. The Rowleys—husband, wife, and four children—must be desperate if they were using brimstone. This was the favourite treatment to get rid of the plague, to fumigate the infected quarters with the strongest smelling disinfectant possible, but it also revealed the presence of the pestilence and could bring the feared locking up of the house and its occupants for forty days. The poor man's portion, he reflected sadly, by then it was almost impossible to survive. He also smelled saltpetre, amber, tobacco, other favoured disinfectants.

His alarm increased as he saw the Rowley house being shut up. Now they were prisoners of the plague for forty days, if they survived, and that was unlikely. As he saw the watchman stationed outside the Rowley dwelling to prevent anyone escaping from the infected house, heard the padlock snap on the front door, observed the red cross drawn across it, with the inevitable, "*Lord have mercy upon their souls*," he shivered and knew that he, Anne, and Sam must flee London before it was too late.

His need was spurred as he noticed black rats scurrying from the Rowley house. There was still light enough for him to see they were black—he was familiar with their appearance, for with the spread of the plague he had seen them often—with their bluish-black coats, their long snouts, their large ears, their preference for human habitation.

But no one else seemed to share his view that these black rats had anything to do with the plague, he thought wryly. All dogs and cats had been killed but the rats had been ignored. Yet wherever these vermin appeared, he noticed, there was the pestilence.

Daniel hurried downstairs to warn Anne and Sam and found her in the front room staring anxiously at the Rowley house. She was so intent she didn't notice his entrance and he paused a moment to observe her.

He wondered whether she was a lady. Sam refused to call her anything but Anne and then with contempt, and she was at home in these plain quarters. But she spoke well, she carried herself with dignity, she wore expensive perfumes and painted her face and reddened her lips like a lady, and she was beautiful, although traces of age and wear showed.

He asked, "Can you hear their groans and cries?"

She turned abruptly, "They are horrible! Their pain must be awful!"

"We must leave. As soon as possible. Before we are infected, too. I have enough money to hire a coach and to reside in Cambridge, where I am working on Christopher's chapel, and I can take you and Sam with me."

"What will be your excuse?"

"That you are my sister and brother."

"No one will believe it with your Dutch accent."

"Then you are my cousins. Hurry, get your things and warn Sam."

She replied desperately, "I can't."

"What's wrong? What are you afraid of?"

She said agitatedly, "I think Sam has the plague."

Daniel gasped, "Are you positive?"

"He collapsed in the parlour. Come, look for yourself."

She led Daniel into the parlour where Sam lay on the floor and Daniel felt a chill of apprehension. Sam was unconscious, his colour a shocking grey, and as Anne motioned that they should lift him and put him in bed Daniel imagined his own body infected with the plague and he hesitated.

Anne said, "I'm not strong enough to do it by myself," and Daniel, ashamed of his fear and the scorn he saw in her eyes, helped her carry Sam to his bed. Sam was sweating profusely and as Anne undressed him to bathe him there were the dreaded plague spots, and she exclaimed, "The tokens!"

As Daniel saw the spots he felt faint and sick and he said, "It is too late to help him. There is nothing we can do for him now. We must leave before the searchers discover the pestilence is in this house and lock us up like the Rowleys for forty days and the plague destroys all of us."

"I can't leave him!"

"But he hasn't even been civil to you. I think he hates you."

"I don't blame him for being bitter. All his women deserted him."

"Were you one of his women?"

"Sam helped me when I was a child. When no one else did."

But Daniel felt the main reason Anne wanted to stay at Fetter Lane was that it was *the* link to Christopher, whatever the danger. Anything else, for her, was limbo. He had to object, pointing out, "You are risking your own life. Once the spots appear there isn't much chance of recovering."

"Would you leave Christopher in such circumstances?"

Probably not, he thought, but that was no comfort. Annoyed that she was involving him when he wanted to flee, he snapped irritably, "You are not really Lady Beaufort, are you?"

She replied coldly, "Buckingham thought so and the King did, too. I must nurse Sam until we get a doctor. Could you fetch one?"

"Where? I hear that most of them have left the city."

"Try St. Paul's. The booksellers there should know, or Archbishop Sheldon, who is conducting services. He knows Christopher."

Compelled beyond common sense, he reflected unhappily, he dressed for the street. Then he recalled some of the other dangers and he cautioned her, "Don't burn any disinfectants. I doubt they will do any good and they will tell the searchers that the plague is in this house and cause them to lock us up for forty days. We will never survive that."

"Don't worry," she assured him. "I have other remedies. Some quite remarkable. Marigold and purslane for his fever, cordials and pills for his nausea, which have been prepared under the proper astrological charts, an amulet to keep away evil spirits and poultices to apply to his sores."

Daniel had grave doubts about these remedies, but he had nothing better to suggest and so he didn't criticise her. He must find a doctor, he decided, if any were available, although he didn't have much faith in them either; he wished he knew as much about anatomy as Christopher did. But then he got a new idea and asked excitedly, "What about the Royal Society? Its members may know a cure for the plague."

She said, "Sam told me the plague forced them to discontinue their meetings, that the members have left for the safety of the country, where Wilkins and Hooke are pursuing problems of chemistry and mechanics. Sam is proud they are true scientists and philosophers. He admires them for not allowing anything like the plague to distract them."

Was Anne being sarcastic? He couldn't tell from her expression.

"But you might try the College of Physicians first. It is on Amen Corner, near the cathedral, and Christopher knows some of the doctors."

He nodded and as he started out Anne whispered, "Be careful. Anyone with a Dutch accent will be regarded suspiciously. And the streets are ridden with the plague. Fortify your stomach with bitters and your breath with tobacco, the smell keeps off the pestilence. And here is a dried toad. An eminent physician at Court gave it to me. He assured me that it will stave off any malignant humours such as the pestilence."

He didn't share this view, but he took the dried toad to please her.

Fleet Street was darker than Daniel had ever seen it and as he turned toward Ludgate and St. Paul's he was chilled, although it was a hot night. Could he have caught the contagion already? he wondered, and then he decided it was fear, for there was much to fear. Many houses were shut up and shuttered with the red cross scrawled across the front door and the inevitable *"God have mercy upon their souls,"* and he felt in an inferno.

The silence on this once busy thoroughfare was unearthly. Where there used to be many hackney coaches there were none. The many pedestrians he was accustomed to seeing were absent and the few he passed were silent. The only sound he heard was the church bells tolling for the dead, the sound of the death carts, and the repeated, *"Bring out your dead!"*

As he neared Ludgate he heard shrieks from a padlocked dwelling and the imploring words, "Dear God, save me! I'm shut up with six dead!"

He moved toward this cry and he was blocked by a burly watchman, who warned him, "No person can be conveyed out of an infected house." When Daniel didn't stop, he added, "On pain of being locked up with them."

The next instant garbage was flung out of the window, but it missed the watchman and almost hit Daniel. He shrank against the wall, for it was assumed that all things from an infected house were also infected.

The desolation grew as he neared St. Paul's. The shops he passed were empty; no garbage had been taken away; there was the smell of brimstone and the stench of death was so nauseating he had to hold his nose to pass through it and he prayed for the strength to go on. He felt better for a moment when he saw a vehicle approaching that was not a death cart, for no one was shouting, *"Bring out your dead!"* Then he had a new feeling of horror for it was piled high with freshly constructed coffins.

People he passed recoiled from him, muffled in their cloaks, and he realised they were hiding their sores so they would not be shut up.

There was a loud commotion in a large house on Ludgate, at the foot of the hill leading to the cathedral, and several people paused, curious to see what was happening. Daniel was shocked when two elderly women dragged out the body of a child with their death hooks while the mother clutched the body, screaming, "You can't put her in the death cart! She is still alive!"

"The old hags are searchers," a middle-aged bystander whispered to Daniel. "Drunks and harridans who can't get any other work. They are paid by the body. If you try to halt them, you'll end on the death cart."

One of the searchers, a filthy, ragged, blowsy woman, said to a man watching the house, who looked equally disreputable, "If she is still alive, we must hustle her out of the parish so the cost of the burial won't fall on our parish and we can pocket the money. It is worth a shilling. Hurry, be sensible!"

But as the watchman grabbed the body from the searcher it came alive and the little girl whimpered, "My name is Rosemary."

The mother, who was restrained by another searcher, cried out, "She is my eldest child," and turned to the spectators and shouted, "Pray for me!"

Before anyone could move, two watchmen were propelling the little girl, who looked about ten, into the next parish while the searchers pushed the sobbing mother back into the infected dwelling and padlocked the door.

The bystander said to Daniel, "There is no remedy. We can't allow those who are infected on the street or they will infect everybody else. You mustn't fall ill on the street, even if it isn't the plague or you are just drunk, for they will throw you into the death cart."

Everything had happened so fast Daniel had been unable to do anything.

"Besides," said the middle-aged man, "this is the best way."

"Then, even as Daniel still stood there, the bystander shook violently and collapsed on the cobblestones crying, "I have the contagion!"

"There is no doubt about it," said a searcher, and with her hook and the help of a watchman, lifted the bystander on to the death cart.

The others watching faded into the shadows and it was very quiet.

The College of Physicians on Amen Corner was deserted. A porter next door informed Daniel that its members had gone into the country to take care of their wealthy patients. But before he was able to shut the door in his face, Daniel was able to inquire about the whereabouts of Dr. Sydenham, a friend of Christopher's, and was told, "He left for the country, too, so he could pursue his medical observations."

At St. Paul's a large, bright moon had risen and it shone down on the cathedral and Daniel saw the west front clearly. It was the least damaged portion of the church and almost worth preserving, he thought, except the remainder of it was such a patchwork, and then he noticed a number of people standing in front of the portico.

A royal proclamation was being read: "*Since the sickness continues to spread and infect our realm, it is hereby declared that a day of solemn fast and humiliation must be observed before God to prevent the disaster that threatens our entire country.''*

Daniel wondered who had hatched this great cuckoo. There wasn't a word about preventive measures or aid. The instant the liveried servant of the Crown posted a new Bill of Mortality on a column he hurried away.

It was twice as large as the previous week. Over a thousand had died in the past seven days. The figures shocked Daniel. It was as if death was greedy beyond satisfying.

A man with a blotched, plague-cured face began to argue with an older man, whose visage was grave. The first was William and the second John, and William said, "No wonder the booksellers have fled. When Paul's Walk is deserted, as now, we must expect all of us to be swept away."

John replied, "It is God's will. We are cursed because of the King's unnatural practices. Even now, while we suffer, he enjoys himself at Hampton Court with his harem. That is why London is a vast pest house."

"But what is being done?" Daniel asked.

"Why do you want to know? You're Dutch," John said suspiciously.

Daniel mumbled, "Of course not. I attended Westminster School."

"You don't sound like an Englishman," John declared ominously.

"What do you want?" William asked.

"A doctor. I was told I could find one here."

"Do you have the contagion?" William shrank away from Daniel. "No."

But now they regarded him even more suspiciously and John said, "Most of the doctors have fled and your accent isn't to be trusted."

There was a disturbance at the other side of the portico and Daniel saw a man being beaten and he asked, "What is happening?"

"It is not our affair," said William. "He is just a Frenchman."

"How do you know he is guilty of anything?"

"He is a Papist," said John. "I don't believe you. Many say the Dutch are to blame for the plague. They have written, '*The English nation is now brought so low with the plague that one man with his finger may run them down.*' I read that in L'Estrange's news-sheet." Suddenly he called over to the crowd who were beating the Frenchman, "We have a Dutchman!"

The mob ran toward Daniel as if he had committed sacrilege and he recoiled, not knowing where to go, and a third man stepped out of the shadows and pulled him into St. Paul's and whispered, "Follow me. Before they thrust you into a pest house or Newgate. I've hidden many in here."

His rescuer knew St. Paul's very well and he led Daniel silently until he was sure they had escaped the mob. Then, in a small chamber behind the north transept, he said, "I am a Friend. George Whitehead. When the people have no one else to blame, when they run out of Papists, Jews, and Frenchmen, they turn on us. I've used this passage often. What are your needs?"

"I need a doctor quickly. Is Archbishop Sheldon here? He knows a friend of mine. Perhaps he can recommend a physician."

"He did preach here recently. He is the only important High Churchman who has remained in London, but he has gone back to his palace at Lambeth. I can recommend a doctor to you if you don't mind that he is a Friend."

"I will be grateful." But as Whitehead took him out of St. Paul's by a secret passage, he asked, "Why are you helping me? I'm not a Quaker."

"It is God's way. And our Friends have found liberty in Holland."

Whitehead was disappointed that Elisha Biddle's wife told him that her husband was out and the parish he was visiting was so plague-ridden she didn't know how soon he would return. But she promised to inform the doctor of Daniel Van Doorn's need.

Daniel also wrote down Whitehead's address, which was nearby, and as he said goodbye to this Friend, who assured him, "I will return to Dr. Biddle's later to remind the physician of the urgency of your need," he was deeply touched that this Quaker risked so much, especially for a stranger. The Friend was of modest stature, with pleasant but unassuming features, a man who might have been a tradesman or a yeoman farmer. In his gratitude he offered to pay him, but Whitehead would have none of that and for a moment the Friend was offended. Yet as he realised that Daniel was trying to thank him, he said, "It is a common report that today over a hundred houses were shut up. We must do God's work wherever we can."

Sam was worse. Anne was agitated; she hadn't expected Daniel to come back as several hours passed. In her relief and anxiety she almost wept.

There were new swellings on Sam's groin and fresh running sores and the room stank, for all the windows were shut as was the custom, and after Daniel assured Anne that the doctor would come as soon as possible, he rushed upstairs, driven with an irresistible need to cleanse himself.

He discarded all his clothes and he scoured his skin until he thought it would crack and he yearned for the night to end, and he heard voices in the distance. At first he thought it was the doctor, then he realised it was Sam speaking to Anne. He dressed hurriedly and as he entered Sam's room he heard him cry out to Anne, who stood next to him, "Is it a man or a woman? I can't make it out! Please, don't bury me in a plague pit!"

Anne tried to caress him gently to soothe him, but Sam recoiled and shouted in his delirium, "Anne was always in such a hurry. She had to hold herself like a flame at the end of the candle but that scorches the skin. Will somebody please stop the pain? In God's name!"

Daniel felt helpless yet guilty as she suggested, "They say if you take a pigeon and put its feathers against the sores it draws out the poison," for he didn't believe in that, yet he had nothing better to recommend.

"Do not let them bury me in a common grave! I am a man! Promise?"

Daniel said, "Sam, you have a long time to live."

"With this pain?" For the moment Sam seemed fully conscious. Daniel stood numbly.

"I have a will. I left the house to Christopher. He was the one person who didn't desert me. Promise me you will bury me in a churchyard. In a coffin where the rats can't get at me. Please, I'd do the same for you!"

Anne wanted to refuse point-blank, that could be dangerous, but before she could say anything, Daniel nodded, and Sam, who had sat up suddenly, fell back into unconsciousness, his eyes half open as if he was dead already.

They were still sitting by the inert Sam the next morning when there was a knock on the door. Anne didn't want to answer it, afraid it was the searchers to shut up the house, but Daniel reminded her that they came only at night, and as he expected, it was Dr. Biddle.

He was the same age as Whitehead, plainly dressed in grey cotton stockings, simple knee breeches, a long coat of black cloth, and he held a flat-headed cane, without any ornamentation, which was a sign of his calling. He felt Sam's burning head and he said, "You must keep him warm, sweating. Wrap him in your heaviest blankets." Dr. Biddle dressed the sores which had increased during the night, and added, "What the patient needs now is endurance. And you must protect yourselves. Drink a glass of sack three times a day to prevent the infection from lodging in your stomach and rest if you feel hot." But even as he spoke Sam turned his head like a knob from side to side, gasped for breath, and lay like a broken doll, his mouth wide open, his eyes staring starkly and as Dr. Biddle closed them slowly and sadly Daniel realised that Sam was dead.

Daniel couldn't turn his back on his promise. After he burned all of Sam's things in the hope that would prevent the contagion from spreading, he retraced his steps to Whitehead's house. If only Sam wasn't so cold!

Whitehead read the request in his eyes and said, "You can bury him in our cemetery. We make no distinctions of faith, but you must be careful. If you are caught, you will be put into Newgate. You must bury him when it is dark and late. If the watchmen see a coffin coming out of your dwelling they will assume it is a plague victim and shut up your house."

Shortly before dawn a coffin was delivered to the house on Fetter Lane. The box was barely six feet long but Sam had shrunk and as Daniel and Anne placed him into it, while the Quaker cart waited, she reminded him, "Sam didn't like Quakers. He could hate us for this."

Daniel thought there wasn't time to argue. But when he saw how unhappy she looked, he asked, "What should we write on the record?"

"That he was a scholar. That was what he wanted to be. It was why he admired Doctor Wren so much."

As Daniel helped the Quaker driver load the coffin on to the cart, he told Anne there was no need for her to come with them. He was glad she didn't insist and that the streets of the city were empty. The Quaker cemetery was clean despite the ruins around it. Whitehead supervised the burial while the driver said, "He is one of the lucky ones. Most are laid in the pest pits like faggots, one on top of the other, until even the earth is crowded out, but here he should find peace. God willing."

Anne hadn't done what Daniel had told her. Instead of being prepared to leave when he returned to the house, she was lying down. "I don't feel well," she complained. "I'm so dizzy I can't stand straight and my muscles are so heavy. I can hardly lift my arms and my head burns."

"Do you think you are sick?"

"You don't have to stay. You don't owe me anything. I can take care of myself. As I always have. Don't worry about me."

Daniel touched her forehead. It was feverish and he replied, "I will fetch the doctor for you. Right away. Before you get worse."

Ignoring her protests, he hurried to Dr. Biddle's house and was told the physician had fallen ill, probably of the contagion, and wasn't seeing any patients. He went to Whitehead's residence nearby and heard that the Friend had been arrested and imprisoned in Newgate, charged with ministering to the afflicted in the blasphemous Quaker fashion.

At Fetter Lane Anne was worse. She was alive but that was all there was to console him. In her delirium she babbled, "Buckingham learned about Christopher and had me dismissed from the King's service, but the Duke hadn't been my protector for years, he used me only to serve his own purposes and to please Charles. If Christopher was here, if he had stayed in London, he wouldn't have permitted this dismissal."

Daniel applied poultices to the sores which had spread to her face while he wondered if they would destroy her beauty and he tried to decide what to do. He was afraid to return to St. Paul's after what had happened with the mob, yet he felt that without a doctor Anne was lost.

It was the middle of the day and Daniel, judging there were enough hours of daylight to find a doctor and that she should survive until he returned, decided to leave her alone while he searched for a doctor.

But he had serious doubts. He wrapped her in blankets so she would perspire profusely; he lit a candle and put it in the window so it would look as if the dwelling was occupied without illness; he gave her sack as Dr. Biddle had advised, which he was able to force down her throat without causing her to vomit. And he wrote a note, explaining where he was going and that he expected to return soon, and left it for her to read should she recover consciousness. At the moment she lay in a stupor and he could only tell that she was alive by her faint breathing. More spots had appeared on her body, but what worried him most were the plague sores on her face, as ugly and deforming as the pox. A blow, he thought, from which she might not recover. He sighed and closed the door carefully.

He was appalled by the gloom that hung over Whitehall and Westminster. The Palace was deserted, the Abbey was empty except for a few plague victims, heavily shrouded to conceal their sores, praying for deliverance, and he felt in a grim, ghostly world without life or purpose. His next stop was at Westminster School to consult Busby. While there were things about the Head Master he disliked, he respected his intelligence and courage. Busby should know a good doctor, he thought. The porter told him that Dr. Busby had removed the boys to Chiswick for safety. Scotland Yard was near and he knocked on Denham's door, but there was no reply, no sign of anyone living here at the moment.

He saw a row boat at the Privy stairs and Lambeth Palace across the Thames, and although he didn't trust what he was doing, he decided to visit the Archbishop even as he thought it would be fruitless. Yet he felt better rowing, less thwarted, but at Lambeth Palace, while Sheldon's presence was admitted, he was not allowed to see him until he said he was Doctor's Wren's assistant. Then he was ushered in quickly.

Daniel had met the Archbishop briefly, but the prelate didn't remember him. Yet Sheldon listened carefully to his story and replied, "Mr. Van Doorn, the difficulty is, the doctors I know, I regret to say, have fled London. It is a scandal. Have you approached the Duke of Albemarle, who has remained to rule in the King's name? Monk is a brave man and if anyone should know a worthy doctor, he should. He is residing at the Cockpit in St. James' Park and I will give you a letter of introduction."

Sheldon's note brought Daniel into the Duke's presence, but Albermarle stated, "There is nothing I would like better than to recommend a doctor, but when I refer one he is gone. Are you acquainted with Samuel Pepys?"

"We have met, sir. At the Royal Society and through Doctor Wren."

"Pepys knows everybody." Albemarle gave him Pepys' address but by now he was desperate with frustration. He had been gone from Anne far longer than he had planned and he felt panic at the possibility that even if he found a doctor, it would take so long she would be dead. And he didn't expect to find Pepys in, for his Admiralty Office was on Seething Lane, in the middle of one of the worst plague-afflicted districts of London.

But even as he felt hopeless, he couldn't turn back. He crossed the city with uncertain steps and while it was a warm, sunny day the streets were barren again. On the entire journey he met just two vehicles and both of them were death carts, although it was usual to bury the dead only at night, and a rare pedestrian. Most of the day was gone and he felt mad, as if he had left his wits on Fetter Lane, and even if Pepys was in, the Clerk of the Acts would regard him as a fool. To Daniel's surprise, Pepys was at his desk in the Admiralty Office, working on a column of figures, and Pepys was curious why Van Doorn was here.

Pepys had gained weight which made him look shorter, Daniel noticed, and he sipped sack as he worked and he said, "To help me pass water freely. And it keeps me from being melancholy when I am alone. We must not allow the plague to interfere with the conduct of the war. I trust you are not suffering too much these dire days. What can I do for you?"

"I need a doctor at once. A friend of mine and Wren's is very ill."

"Is it the plague?"

"Probably. Archbishop Sheldon referred me to Albemarle who sent me to you, saying you would be acquainted with a competent physician."

"The Duke flatters me, but my good friend and neighbour, Dr. Burnet, who treated the infected bravely, discovered the plague in his own house and has locked his door to everyone to prevent it from spreading. Now, I hear, he is infected. Does Wren know of his friend's illness?"

"No. I wrote him about the plague but that is all."

"It doesn't matter. He couldn't return from Paris now even if he wanted to. Our ports are closed and Dutch privateers hover about them."

"I doubt he would have left London if he had known about the plague. But it was a secret until it was impossible to hide it any longer."

"The deaths were kept quiet so the country could go on with the war."

Pepys was quite willing to talk, reflected Daniel, but at the idea of Anne lying helplessly, probably dying, he cried out frantically, "Don't you know any doctors at all? I have tramped all over London and . . ."

Pepys interrupted, "It must be a woman, you are so agitated. Yours or Wren's? I've wondered whether he had a mistress. What is her name?"

"She is just a friend. Of both of us. Don't you know any doctors?"

There was contempt in Daniel's voice and this Pepys couldn't endure. He said, "I will take you to Lord Brouncker, the President of the Royal Society, who has remained in London. He is virtually the only nobleman who has. He will know a doctor. Have you heard from Wren?"

"Yes. He has met Bernini and examined the rebuilding of the Louvre and a new palace Louis XIV is building at a place outside of Paris called Versailles. He has doubts about it, but he says the châteaux are splendid."

Pepys' interest in Daniel grew and he took him to Brouncker's mansion in the Piazza at Covent Garden. Brouncker greeted Pepys warmly and said, "I'm happy to see you looking well these awful days." He nodded curtly to Daniel, but when Pepys told him that Van Doorn had heard from Wren and what his needs were he was friendlier. He added, "Van Doorn, I know a doctor who might be available, but I doubt you will want him. He is a Jew."

Daniel stiffened but he asked, "Lord Brouncker, is he a good doctor?"

"I presume so. No more of his patients die than anyone else's."

"May I have his address?"

Pepys asked critically, "You will use a Jew?"

"Should I allow my friend to die? Wren would never forgive us."

"Maybe. I'll go with you. I've never seen a doctor who is a Jew."

A little later, at the address Brouncker gave him, Daniel hesitantly knocked on the door of Dr. Joseph Mendez Bravo. Until now he hadn't thought much about his Jewishness, except when it was thrust on him, but now he was troubled at the idea of hiding it. Yet if Pepys or his friends discovered his Jewishness, it could cause the Crown to force Christopher to dismiss him from any project which was part of the Royal works.

An attractive, dark-haired young woman answered the door and wasn't surprised by his mission. She called her father, who appeared quickly.

Dr. Bravo didn't ask them in, for they could be bearers of the plague, but stood in the doorway of his small timber house and inquired about their business. He wore a beard in the fashion of Charles I, and his black moustache and hair and swarthy complexion reminded Daniel of the King, for the doctor was about the same age and quite tall and slim.

He refused to visit the patient until he heard Daniel's name and Dutch accent. Then Dr. Bravo asked excitedly, "Mr. Van Doorn, were you born in the United Provinces?"

"In Amsterdam. I studied with Rembrandt. I am an artist." While he seldom mentioned his calling, he wanted this Jewish doctor to know.

"I was born there, too. But my parents came from Spain. Perhaps we know some people in common. My father knew Rembrandt, too. When the painter had better times. Where did you live in Amsterdam?"

"Dr. Bravo, my friend may be dying. Every moment is precious."

"I'm sorry to hear that. But truly, this is not unusual these days."

"I will give you five pounds."

"That is not necessary. I'll attend your friend."

While they waited for Dr. Bravo to leave, Pepys said approvingly, "Van Doorn, you used your birth cleverly, but I wouldn't give him so much money."

"I'll give him whatever he wants. I'll keep my word."

The patient must be his mistress, thought Pepys, or Wren's. No one else would be worth so much. He asked, "Do I know your friend?"

"No. Are you coming with us? That will satisfy your curiosity."

"I can't. I have Admiralty business to finish at my office."

Pepys' curiosity didn't extend to visiting a plague victim, but after he left, assuring Daniel of his interest, Daniel almost believed him. He liked Pepys better now; Pepys in his own way, had tried to be helpful.

Daniel and Bravo turned on to Fetter Lane an hour later and the doctor looked weary from the long walk but he didn't complain. Twilight had come and it was growing dark rapidly and Daniel had a sudden feeling of apprehension. A death cart stood before the Rowley House and he heard the inevitable and melancholy, *"Bring out your dead!"* He saw one of the Rowley children carried out and dumped, half-naked, only in her shift, on a stacked pile of unclothed corpses, and as the parents fought to stop this, they were blocked by two watchmen and pushed back into the house.

He halted, to hide the presence of the doctor from the searchers, for that would reveal the existence of the plague in Sam's house, and the death cart, already overloaded, moved a few feet, then paused in front of Sam's house. Two elderly women searchers, ugly, evil-smelling creatures, with huge, floppy breasts and soiled, blood-stained dresses, entered the house and emerged a minute later carrying a limp Anne in their hooks.

But she couldn't be dead, he thought, he hadn't been gone that long!

He caught the searchers as they were about to throw her on top of the dead bodies and shouted, "Doctor, examine her! She can't be dead!"

"She's dead!" snarled a searcher. "Look at the sores on her face!"

Daniel wrestled Anne free and held her in his arms for Bravo to examine.

The doctor did so carefully. He felt her pulse and he put a small hand mirror to her mouth and then he said, "She is still alive, although I'm not sure she will want to be when she sees her appearance."

Daniel, however, satisfied that there was still breath in Anne, carried her back into the house.

A watchman said, "Your house will be shut up for forty days."

"But she should have fresh air."

"And you with it. Unless you leave now."

Daniel wavered. Anne was right; he owed her nothing. But he couldn't cease feeling. He cried out, "Can't the doctor prescribe for her?"

"Not unless he wants to be locked up with you."

Daniel thought, Others needed Bravo, too. But as two watchmen pushed him inside and padlocked the door, he shouted after the helpless Bravo, "Doctor, what should I do for her?"

Bravo shouted back, "Keep her as clean as you can. And charms won't work. Fresh air may help and untainted food, and don't bleed her, it will only weaken her. Give her a light diet of eggs, broth, and wine, and if carbuncles appear, make poultices for them, of vinegar and honey."

"What about your fee?"

"May God be with you!"

Daniel lost track of the days. Most of the time Anne was unconscious and there was always a watchman outside the door.

The night one, a squat, middle-aged butcher, was more affable than the day one. On a lonely evening Daniel, eager to talk to someone, asked him, "How did you know there was plague in this house?" and he answered, "Mr. Rowley told us he saw a coffin coming out of your house." And when the watchman saw his shock, he added, "Don't worry, you will be revenged. I don't think any of the Rowleys will survive the plague." That wasn't what Daniel wanted, but he didn't reply. He knew he must not offend the night watchman; as long as he paid him generously there was enough food.

While Daniel was tempted to use Anne's jewels, which he found, he spent freely from his own money so she would have the proper diet of eggs, broth, and wine, all of which were expensive. Yet even when she was conscious, which was seldom, she seemed unaware of what she was eating. He washed her daily, and himself, too, and he sought to keep the house as clean as he could. He was grateful that Sam could read and had books in the house, but after reading Raleigh's *History of the World*, Erasmus' *Praise of Folly*, and Foxe's *A Book of Martyrs* he became more depressed rather than less.

By the middle of August he knew the plague was worse, for the church bells rang continually now and the cry, "*Bring out your dead!*" was frequent. The only activity on Fetter Lane was the movement of the searchers looking for new corpses, and their voices, hoarse and rough. They stopped regularly at the Rowleys and he counted the bodies removed, two, three, four, five, and then there was only one left, the father, and he wondered how this could be endured, and then, in September, the last call was made at the Rowleys. By now it didn't matter what the father had done; Daniel felt as if he was losing a companion, that he was all alone. He began to believe he would be the last survivor. The night watchman told him the Bills of Mortality were still increasing. He saw the smoke from many fires and he thought London was burning but the watchman informed him that the fires were being lit to destroy the infection.

The watchman added, frightened and amazed, "Over eight thousand died last week, just in one week, from the plague. No one knows where it will end. It is thought that since the pestilence began in the spring over a quarter of the population of London had died, over a hundred thousand. No one, nothing is on the streets any more. There are no more coffins. Everyone, even the few well-born who perish, are thrown into the plague pits. You are fortunate, Van Doorn, that you are locked up."

The next few days Daniel heard only the tolling of the church bells and the shout, *"Bring out your dead!"* There was no sign of life anywhere, except those concerned with death.

Then gradually, several weeks later, the sound of the church bells began to diminish and he saw and heard the death carts less frequently.

At the beginning of October the night watchman smiled for the first time in many weeks and said, "Finally, the Bills of Mortality are less. The worst may be over, Van Doorn."

Indeed, thought Daniel, for he was starting to think that Anne might live after all. None of the dreaded carbuncles had appeared; she was no longer feverish and sweat-soaked and the spots had vanished, even from her face, although her skin and complexion still showed she had been ill.

Yet he thought he was dreaming one morning when he heard her voice, "Oh, God! I must smell like a fishwife! How long have I been sick?"

He hurried to her side and said, "Many days."

"It feels like a lifetime." She felt her face and asked suddenly, frantically, "May I have a mirror?"

"Not yet, Anne. You're not fully recovered. You'll look ill."

She reached under her pillow where she had hidden a small mirror and stared into it before he could halt her. For a moment she looked puzzled, as if she didn't recognise the person she saw, and then she screamed, "You shouldn't have lied to me!"

"I haven't lied to you. You have been very sick. Near death."

"You should have left me to die," she wept, "I've become so old!"

"You should be grateful that you are alive."

"And you took care of me for this?" She smashed the mirror and lay face downwards and refused to be consoled.

However, she was out of bed the next morning to test her strength and while she didn't thank him, she asked, "What happened to the Rowleys?"

"They all perished. One after another. Six of them."

She walked into the strong sunlight and he noticed that she had put on powder and paint and was wearing a scent that reminded him of rosewater, but in the bright light her complexion was faded. And he was angry at himself, for he realised his look of sadness revealed this change.

She flinched and turned away from him abruptly and with her back to him, she asked, "Have you heard from Christopher?"

"Not a word. I was unable to write him. No letters were handled these past few weeks because of the fear of infection."

"It doesn't matter. He won't come back to me. Not now."

"Anne, you look fine."

"I've been picked apart by the pestilence. What is that I hear?"

"The church bells. They toll for the dead."

"They toll for me," she said to herself softly.

She didn't want to be comforted, but several days later, when she recovered more of her strength, she asked him, "When are you supposed to be in Cambridge for the completion of Christopher's chapel?"

"Later this month. If I survive and can get out of London."

"You will survive," she said confidently, "if you survived Sam and myself. I would get out if I really wished to. The night watchman will look the other way if you pay him enough."

"Anne, what are you going to do now?"

"The house belongs to Christopher. I'm a trespasser now. Are you going to stay?"

"I have two paintings here I value. Otherwise, it depends."

"On me?"

She turned so that he could see her clearly and she looked much better, although traces of the plague remained on her skin and he had a feeling these marks would stay. But that was not really the issue, he thought. He did care for her, he knew now, perhaps loved her in a way. He had put so much of himself into her these past months and he admired her spirit, independence, and intelligence, and she still possessed her stunning red hair, fine figure, and attractive features, if too tart a tongue. But she must have known Christopher intimately—by now he was convinced about that, although he would never ask—and that made her inviolable. He couldn't explain, least of all to her, that Christopher's presence, however shadowy, would stand between them, whatever he felt toward her.

He said, "I respect you, but you are waiting for Christopher."

"And he can promise nothing."

"He did ask me to care for you."

"You have. Your duty is done. You can go now."

"Why don't you come with me to Cambridge? It will be safer there."

She turned her back on him and the rest of the day she didn't talk to him. And when he awoke the next morning she was gone.

There was a note for him: "*I have risked your life enough, I cannot risk it any more. When you read this, I will be far away. But do not worry, I have some jewels and wits. And my outer skin. And a memory of ninety-two days.*"

Had it been that long? Suddenly, without thinking, his eyes filled with tears. Yet she was absolutely right. But he missed her so. A part of him had died. And the more he thought about her, the more he cried.

That night when the watchman approached to find out if he wanted any food, he said, "My patient is gone." As he expected the friendly watchman didn't seem surprised, but shrugged, and Daniel asked, "How much was it worth to you?"

"I'm a poor man. And this is not the time to be cruel and rigorous. I cannot watch the door to the garden and the front, too. If someone wants to break out, they should be able to spare a few shillings."

Daniel reached into his pocket but the watchman halted him. "Later. Leave ten shillings on the window sill and the back door will be open. But make sure no one is on the street. The death cart will be calling a few doors above. Wait until it departs, then put the money out."

Daniel followed these instructions and at midnight he found himself on the streets of London, holding the two paintings by Rembrandt close to his side. He saw no one and he walked many miles before he found a hackney coach outside of the city—none were allowed in London. And that evening he arrived in Cambridge. He went to Bishop Wren's residence at Peterhouse, which was across from Pembroke, and Christopher's uncle didn't seem surprised to see him, but said reproachfully, "Mr. Van Doorn, I expected you sooner. The chapel is to be consecrated in a few days."

"I was delayed by the plague. Have you heard from your nephew, sir?"

"He wrote me a week ago. He said he wanted to return but that there were no ships available because of the pestilence and the Dutch privateers. I hear that London has suffered terribly."

"Yes. Almost beyond belief."

"It is a visitation from God," Bishop Wren said sternly. "The city has been wasted as a punishment for our people's sins and the King's. He is in Salisbury now and I hear that he prays often at the great cathedral. But God doesn't forgive transgressions so easily. If you wish to write my nephew, your letter will be delivered."

Daniel was in no mood to do so, but he felt he must, and thus, with mixed feelings he wrote Christopher: "*You were wise not to return to London. The city was desolate these past months and you would have accomplished nothing. Sam died from the plague and Lady Beaufort was dangerously ill but she has recovered and she has gone elsewhere, I don't know where, but I suspect to a different kind of life. I am in good health and your chapel at Pembroke is finished and much as you designed it. Your uncle says it is God's truth. I hope so.*"

As You Pray

As you pray to God
God must pray
to you
I cannot conceive
anything
being human
  one way

Stymean Karlen

27

As You Pray

DANIEL'S LETTER SHOCKED CHRISTOPHER. HE HAD BEEN TOLD THAT the plague had ravaged London and that it was impossible for him to return to the city until it ended, but when he hadn't heard from Daniel he had assumed that his friend had taken Anne and Sam safely out of London. The news of Sam's death and Anne's illness was a sickening blow. And there was a sharpness of tone in the letter that was not like Daniel.

This darkened his mood as he prepared for the farewell party Françoise was giving Bernini, who was leaving for Rome. As he arrived at her Paris mansion on the Rue François Miron, he told himself he would have gone back to London if it had been possible, but in his heart he wasn't sure. His stay in France had been fruitful, he rationalised, he had learned so much about building it had become one of the best periods of his life. Yet Daniel was cryptic about Anne, as if there was more to be said, which his friend didn't trust to a letter. Christopher was pleased about the news of Pembroke, but this was the only news he relished.

Françoise detected his disturbed feeling as her footman ushered him into her drawing room and that worried her. She had asked him to come before the other guests, so she could show him their designs for the Louvre without them knowing it, but when he seemed distracted she wondered whether her efforts on his behalf were worth the risk. If Le Vau or Bernini found out what she had done, they might never speak to her again. Yet while her party was supposed to be for Bernini, actually she was giving it for Christopher. She wanted him to see her native land in the most favourable light, in the hope it would influence him to remain in France. So she had obtained the designs he was interested in, and had invited those she thought he would find most intriguing and influential, Bernini, Le Vau, Colbert, and Perrault. This should please him, if anything did.

She was still unsure about his feelings toward her, for while he had spent more time in her company than any other man, he had been proper, not once had he tried to make love to her. His reserve was not an attitude she treasured, she reflected ruefully. She dressed with extreme care this evening in October, wearing her most elegant and enticing blue gown, cut low to display her lovely white shoulders and perfect breasts to the best advantage. And as Christopher approached her and kissed her hand, she hoped that his heart beat faster as hers did. Instead, his distraction appeared to increase.

Despite her pride in her poise, she blurted out, "What is wrong?"

"The news from London is bad. An old friend of mine died."

"In the plague?"

"Yes. I should have been there."

"But you were told that you could do nothing. That no one could. And you said that a friend was taking care of your interests."

"It might have been too difficult for him."

"I'm sorry. Perhaps this is the wrong time for a party."

"Oh, no!" he answered quickly. In some strange way she was suffering, too. "It is gracious of you and you look enchanting."

"Do you like the way I have arranged the salon?"

"The design is beautiful. It expresses your nature, gentle, intelligent, fanciful, and in the best of taste."

She glowed and felt much better as she said, "I hoped you would like it. The salon has been designed and decorated with great care."

"I love your dome. Whose idea was it to cover your salon that way?"

"My father's. He was enchanted with this possibility when he saw St. Peter's in Rome. So I followed his wishes."

"Did you design this mansion?"

She shrugged and said, "I'm more interested in what you think of it."

"I've always admired your salon, that it is a double cube, symmetrical and beautifully balanced, lyrical yet restrained, possessing warmth and intimacy despite its palatial proportions, a lesson in good taste."

He was passionate now and she wondered if this was all he truly cared about and if she had been wrong to stress her interest in architecture, but she said, "The house is Italian outside, French inside."

"A useful marriage. I enjoy the design of the entire building. It has a classical and controlled feeling, combining convenience with comfort and spaciousness, yet always, in each detail, pleasing to the eye."

This reminded her why she had invited him early and she showed him Bernini and Le Vau's new designs for the Louvre. He studied them carefully. Bernini's were more detailed than those the Italian had allowed him to look at months ago, but little changed. His east front curved like his approach to St. Peter's, creating a concavity utterly different from the French style of straight, strict decorum. On the other hand, Le Vau's designs were a repetition of what was done already, a rigid imitation without imagination or initiative. He preferred Bernini's plans, although they didn't totally satisfy him.

Françoise saw his doubts and said, "Neither architect has been heeded. Louis is so much in love with Versailles he has no interest in the Louvre and he has left that to Colbert and his chief minister doesn't care for any of their designs. So he has turned to the Perraults."

"But you told me that the one I met, Charles, is a lawyer, and that his younger brother, Claude, is a physician."

"You are known here as a professor of astronomy. Has that halted you?"

"I'm also a mathematician, with engineering experience."

"Charles Perrault is a courtier. Which is most important. As it is in England. You said that is why Denham is the Chief Surveyor."

"Then what advantage would it be to me if I migrated here?"

"There are opportunities. Private houses, châteaux, and work for the King. Charles Perrault has been appointed Inspector-General of the King's Works. That is why I invited him tonight. For your sake."

The footman announced the first arrivals and she hurriedly hid the designs in her cabinet. He thought, the important men he was going to meet—Bernini, Colbert, Le Vau, Perrault—had only one thing in common, their own ambition. He couldn't share this kind of devotion. He wasn't a courtier and he had no intention of becoming one. Not even for the sake of St. Paul's. And certainly not to shout the praises of Louis XIV.

Yet he stood by her side as she greeted her guests.

Colbert, Le Vau, and Perrault arrived together, so no one would gain an advantage, thought Christopher. As soon as they assured Françoise how honoured they were to be her guest, and politely but briefly acknowledged Christopher's presence, they plunged into a discussion of Bernini as if drawn to it by an inevitability stronger than themselves.

Colbert told Françoise, "The Italian had a touch of colic this morning, but he assured me that he would come. He blames it on French food, but I have been anxious. His absence could cause an international scandal."

"We have had enough trouble with him as it is," added Le Vau.

"His plans for the Louvre don't possess enough conveniences and comforts."

Perrault continued, "Bernini ignores our nature, our climate, our affection for our own past. And the Louvre is not a Papal palace like St. Peter's, but a royal palace. Isn't that so, Françoise?"

"His plans have a power that could suit the King's temperament."

A power the French designs lacked, reflected Christopher, the French were merely extending the Louvre into a larger royal mansion while Bernini desired to express grandeur rather than cleverness. But since no one asked his opinion he didn't volunteer any, but listened.

Colbert said, "Worst of all, Bernini considers himself infallible, but in France not even the Pope is, only Louis."

Le Vau nodded in agreement and pointed out, "We are the richest, most populous and powerful nation in the world. *Le grand monarque.*"

Perrault stated contemptuously, "His designs have nothing to do with French feeling, they are pure Italian. Exaggerated, wild, so bombastic, that all they would accomplish is to declare the genius of Bernini. We have had enough of the extravagances of the Italian style. We must demonstrate that we are the greatest nation on earth. This is what Louis desires. And to prove that we are a country of gentlemen."

Colbert and Le Vau agreed while Françoise was embarrassed and glanced at Christopher to see what he was thinking. He was impassive and she sighed with relief; surely he would forgive a little patriotism.

Bernini entered and the Frenchmen assured him that they were honoured by his visit and spoke to him in Italian to prove their respect.

Dinner was served and Bernini ate heartily, explaining, "I took a physic and a noon nap. They cure the colic, even the French kind."

Colbert smiled as if that were a witticism but no one replied. The meal passed in silence, broken only by Bernini's approval of the food.

Finished, he said, "It is gracious of you to come here to bid me farewell. I appreciate the courtesy you have shown me, but I have to return to Rome for the winter. I cannot endure this abominable climate."

Colbert nodded to express his condolences and said, "But we trust, Maestro, that you will come back and grace our country again."

Bernini shrugged and now Perrault and Le Vau implored him to stay, *He must lead them and they would follow and obey*, and Françoise joined them.

Only Christopher was silent and Bernini turned on him suddenly —he had not spoken to him at all—and asked, "Wren, do you share their views?"

"I think French architecture will be less if you leave."

"But you are an astronomer," said Le Vau, "not an architect."

Françoise cut in, "Doctor Wren is an Assistant Surveyor of the English King's Works and has designed a number of successful buildings."

He loved her effort to defend him even as he wanted to correct her exaggeration of his work, but before he could say anything Bernini asked him, "Do you believe the earth moves? No one has proven that."

"It will be proved. If we continue to study and investigate. We are only on the threshold of learning about the universe."

"Then you agree with Galileo?"

"Yes."

Colbert said, "His theories are banned here. Do you understand them?"

"I think so." Christopher didn't want to discuss astronomy, but architecture. And he could see by the emotion on their faces that astronomy had become a matter of theology rather than reason.

Bernini said, "The Church was right to punish him. He was too stubborn."

Christopher was silent, aware he couldn't change anyone's views.

Françoise, sensing his dismay, changed the subject and said, "Maestro, you did tell me that you liked Mansart's work."

"Some of it. If he had gone to Rome he could have become a great artist, like Poussin, who has lived and worked there for forty years."

Le Vau said, "I'm glad you found a French artist at last you admire."

"Like. Not admire."

Christopher was wondering whether architecture was too noble a profession to be left to the architects, when Colbert asked him, "Wren, what buildings have you designed?"

"A chapel and a theatre for Oxford University."

"Is that all?" asked Perrault.

Françoise said, "They are buildings of great importance."

None of the others thought so, Christopher observed, for they were ignoring him as Bernini rose to go. He stood in the centre of the salon, a short man actually, unimposing in stature, bald except for his long white hair at the back of his head, in many ways an old sixty-six, and yet his eyes and expression had a vitality greater than any of those about him. He stated, "The execution of a work may be the labour of many hands but it must be the design of only one mind. You err when you seek more than one view."

Colbert, feeling attacked, replied, "Two minds can be better than one."

"Michelangelo Buonarotti didn't think so when he painted the Sistine Chapel. And do you think God consulted anyone when He created the world?"

Colbert shrugged but Perrault said, "Granted, Maestro, but we mere mortals have to depend on many hands."

"Precisely. That is why your work is never heavenly. But when it is a gift from heaven, as with Michelangelo Buonarotti and me, we must carry our work to a triumphant conclusion without interference."

"Such individuality becomes disorder."

"As you will it. But *I will* otherwise. As God does."

"I am as devout as anyone," Perrault retorted indignantly.

"No doubt. But that is not a point of view."

A heavy silence fell upon the salon and Françoise said hurriedly, "Maestro, I am privileged that you could come. It is a great honour."

He bowed in response and said, "Countess, I'm honoured, too. Your taste and hospitality transcends whatever ill treatment I have received." Before any of the Frenchmen could protest that this wasn't so, he asked Christopher, "The Countess said you have designed a chapel. Do you intend to devote yourself to church architecture?"

"When it interests me. Why do you ask?"

"In religious architecture the art must always bow before the function. It is good to be pleasing but first we must serve God."

"Signor Bernini, why do you advise me?"

"Wren, you have a good mouth, you do not abuse it or over use it. Remember, you cannot satisfy people who cannot understand you."

Bernini was gone before anyone could answer him, so Colbert addressed the others. "The Italian wants to smash our traditions, but he is naive. Louis is clever, he is friendly to Bernini and the Italian likes him, but I have to hear the King's objections to his plans for the Louvre. Where will Louis' mistresses sleep? Will there be rooms for his servants? What about the water closets? The kitchens? Bernini is full of grandiose designs and ignores the necessities. I had to reject them. For all his talk, they would leave the King cramped and uncomfortable."

"Indeed, indeed," said Le Vau. "You understand architecture."

"Anyway," added Perrault, "The Italian will be in Rome where it will be impossible for him to execute his designs. Monsieur Colbert, it was clever of you to suggest that he complete them there."

Christopher thought, They were all critics, except of their own work. He prepared to depart with the others when Françoise restrained him. As he paused Le Vau spoke to him for the first time.

"Wren, did you know the Countess designed this house herself?"

"I thought so, but she has not mentioned it."

"She is modest. But she is a good architect. If she didn't regard building as a diversion, she could do fine work."

Colbert added, "And her lovely complexion is much admired by Louis. He likes beautiful complexions. We all adore her amiable countenance."

Françoise blushed but said quietly, "I am fortunate that my reputation is in such gallant hands. Gentlemen, thank you for coming."

Christopher couldn't tell whether the others were aware of the sarcasm underlying her words, but they did comprehend her hint to go, for a moment later they left.

As they stood face to face, exactly the same height, he enveloped her suddenly in his arms. He kissed her again and again and she didn't push him away as he had feared, but whispered, "I wondered when you would."

He followed her to her bedroom. Then she faltered as they stood by the huge canopied bed. Not from a lack of desire, he sensed, but from something she must find out first. Yet he felt excited when he saw her bedspread thrown back, and a pink nightgown on her pillow. He told himself there must be no hesitancy, there was nothing here to disturb them, but as he went to lift her up and carry her to the bed, she pulled away and said, "I must marry in my faith."

This crashed on his ears like breaking glass. Was their world coming to an end? He could feel her body responding intensely, with only the final intimacy to come, and yet, she was speaking again, "I am a Roman Catholic, you know."

Her words made him feel impotent. He asked impatiently, "Françoise, does it have to be discussed now?"

"Now," she replied, "For there will be no turning back once we start."

He released her abruptly, asked, "What are you trying to say?"

"Christopher, I cannot marry outside of my faith."

He tried to be rational as he said, "But I am not a Roman Catholic."

"I promised my father I would be faithful to his teachings."

Confused, he took her hands and said, "They are so cold. But lovely."

"Then you agree with me? See my point of view?"

"I see your point of view." He relinquished his grasp.

"Christopher, I have to warn you."

"Yes, you have warned me."

P*

She had never seen him so stern. She asked imploringly, "Why are you so upset? We do love each other."

"But you love your God more."

"Our God."

"Then in different ways. If I changed I would betray my father."

She wavered, then said, "As I would mine."

He hadn't decided when to leave France, but suddenly he sensed that his idyllic months were coming to an end. He was shocked to see how rigid she had become. He couldn't change, he thought sadly, and she wouldn't. He stepped back and his hands dropped to his side.

"Don't be angry with me," she pleaded.

"I'm not."

She couldn't tell. His jaw had tightened but he was quite still. She thought of how much she wanted Christopher to love her, but in her life, where so much was uncertain, where courtiers had courted her without conviction, where little could be trusted, her faith was the unshakeable foundation, the changeless thing, the one dependable thing. She said, "You wouldn't be the first Englishman to become a Catholic."

He felt drained. "No," he said. "But I'm not the one, Françoise, that is not my nature."

"Be sensible. You have great opportunities here. And I could make many more for you."

He paused a moment as if considering her proposal, even as he knew that this had become impossible, then said, "I have put off my return to England too long. I left my best friend in London to take care of my responsibilities during the plague and he could have lost his life. I'm not sure he will forgive me. If I had been present, I might have saved Sam's life. I do know something about anatomy."

"One can always speculate on such matters but that is futile."

For an instant he longed to blurt out, *It isn't even enough to put my trust and faith in architecture and God is such a muddle*. But that was no consolation either and whatever it cost he must not savage her. He said, "It's not your fault. It's no one's fault."

"That's the awful thing about it," she said, almost regretfully. "It would be easier if we could blame someone."

His tone grew more composed as he changed the subject. "If we could only see Paris from above. Fly over it and record what we see, the circular roofs, the domes, the total perspective."

"You must build so high that this becomes possible."

"No such works are available."

She looked at his high cheekbones, his clear grey eyes, the mouth he used so intelligently, his clean, smooth skin. Courtiers were always flattering her complexion, but his was easy to love. Yet she had failed.

He was adamant. He was as devoted to his father's faith as she was to her father's.

He said, "Françoise, you have made my visit to France memorable and I will always be grateful for the kindness you have shown me. I will never forget it." He bowed and departed before she could stop him.

Why did she have to fall in love with the son of a Dean? she thought bitterly. Tears streamed down her face and she felt blasphemous.

The People Who Go Away

The people who go away
by changing

The people who go away
by dying

The people who go away
by remaining

Stymean Karlen

28

The People Who Go Away

JERMYN UNDERSTOOD CHRISTOPHER'S WISH TO LEAVE FRANCE. HE
sat in his drawing room, so stricken with the gout that every
movement hurt, and said, "I don't blame you, Louis is thinking of
declaring war on us and this could be an awkward country for an
Englishman. Would you do a favour for me?"

Christopher hesitated. The ambassador was devoted to intrigue
and he didn't want to become involved in such matters. Yet Jermyn
was insistent, which was unusual, and he answered, "If I can, sir."

"I would appreciate if you could convey dispatches to Charles."

"Why me, sir?" He was surprised by the request.

"If the Dutch capture you, they will never suspect that a professor
of astronomy is a courier." When he saw Christopher's apprehension
he added, "You have nothing to fear. Charles is sending a man of
war to Calais to convey these dispatches. He expects me to bring
them, but I have decided to remain in Paris to conduct further
negotiations with Louis. I may be able to persuade him not to fight,
he needs money for Versailles and he dislikes the Dutch, they are
too bourgeois. And even if he does declare war on us, he would
never harm me. We are noblemen and gentlemen."

"Are the dispatches important?"

"Very. It is essential that Charles comprehend Louis' intentions.
And the possibility that money could avert Louis' hostility."

"I heard that our King's purse is empty."

"Yes. It is distressing. I must say Cromwell never allowed money
to interfere with his policies. But I doubt that England itself has
much to fear. The French, if they fight, will do so at sea. Like the
Dutch."

"How has the war progressed with the United Provinces?"

"Not as smoothly as we expected. Fortune has favoured them.
The plague has hindered our efforts and lost us valuable taxes."

"I've often wondered why we are fighting the Dutch. Religion cannot be the excuse, for we are both Protestant countries and there is much about the Dutch we admire. We have imported many of their ways and arts."

"The Dutch threaten our supremacy of the seas, our trade. But for a country so small, they are remarkably resourceful. Charles is at Oxford because of the plague and you will be conveyed to our docks at Chatham."

Christopher paused, unable to admit his distaste for this mission.

"You will not take the dispatches?" Jermyn was astonished.

"My Lord, you are quite sure I will."

"Sir, you are an Englishman and a gentleman!"

"And you are a diplomat," Christopher said, almost disparagingly.

"Every man serves his country the best way he can. The risk won't be great. Charles is sending a man of war as an escort and in November the channel is foggy and it is easy to evade the Dutch guns. I thought you would be honoured to serve the King in this way. As Denham, your superior, did during the late troubles. But perhaps I misjudged you."

"No!" Christopher replied rapidly, even as he disliked himself for allowing his pride to overcome his judgment. "I will do what you wish." Although, he thought, he didn't believe in this Dutch war and never had.

"As our sovereign wishes." Jermyn ordered his footman to fetch the dispatches and then, as they waited, he half-asked, half-suggested, in a sudden change of mood, "You saw the Countess often?"

"She was gracious."

"She is a great lady." Jermyn's expression asked: What else happened?

"I learned much about French architecture from her."

"That is why I introduced you to her."

But Françoise had introduced herself. He didn't correct Jermyn and when the footman brought the dispatches he took them and turned to go.

"Doctor, I heard she left Paris. Do you know where she has gone?"

"No. Is there anything else you want to tell the King?"

"If the Dutch capture you, although it shouldn't occur, destroy the dispatches. They mustn't be intercepted. But if you are able to hand them to the King, he will be pleased. You might even rise in his favour."

A week later Christopher boarded a huge man of war that docked at Calais. He was startled by its size. *The Sovereign of the Seas* was the largest man of war in the English fleet. It carried one hundred and two guns and was under the command of Vice-Admiral Sir William Berkeley.

This, he was told, was because the ambassador was expected and must be shown the proper honour. But he knew Berkeley, too, who regarded him favourably as he was escorted aboard. Christopher recalled that while this tall, lean, dark, middle-aged gallant danced cleverly and pursued the ladies of the Court avidly and fancied himself a successor to Drake, he also considered himself a philosopher, for he dabbled in astrology and was interested in becoming a fellow of the Royal Society. Christopher wasn't surprised when Berkeley invited him to his cabin for dinner and wanted to discourse on the stars, not as a guide to navigation which Christopher preferred, but for their influence on the course of the war.

The Vice-Admiral asked him whether he thought the stars favoured their cause and he replied, "Sir, I haven't looked at the heavens lately."

"But you are an astronomer. A learned one. Savillian Professor."

"Sir, I'm also an architect, Assistant Surveyor of the King's Works."

"You still understand the heavens. Doctor, there is a new comet in the sky, which could be a good omen. On a clear night it shines like a liquid flame, but tonight there is too much mist and rain to see it. What do you make of the comet? Does it favour our cause?"

"I prefer that this ship is heavily armed and properly manned."

"It is. We carry more guns than any ship afloat and our hull is built of the best timber, it is no easy matter to drive anything into her, even a nail. Charles, to impress the French, sent his greatest man of war to escort his envoy. If we meet any Dutch ships, I will defeat them."

"I heard there is a fleet of ten Dutch sail in the channel."

"This foul weather will disperse them. We have nothing to fear."

Yet while Berkeley ordered his ship to set sail for the naval base of Chatham on the river Medway, he didn't do anything else. Christopher wondered about this and the Vice-Admiral said, "The master, Hatton, is responsible for the navigation of the ship. I tell him where to take her and I command her when we fight. Hatton is a supple and cunning fellow. He knows these waters like the palm of his hand."

As they sailed into the open waters of the Channel and pointed for Chatham, Berkeley stood defiantly on the high poop deck and invited his guest to join him. Christopher did so reluctantly; he felt no need to prove his bravery. And it was hard to tell what was the worst danger, the Dutch or the foul weather. The wind was so strong, the waves so rough he could hardly stand and as the mist became fog there wasn't anything to see. He thought, This was carrying courage to ridiculous extremes. Yet as the weather grew worse Berkeley acted as if the elements were delicious.

The man of war lurched in the darkness, then righted itself slowly, but the violent rocking continued. The sea washed over the bow and waves smashed across the deck and Christopher couldn't tell what was soaking him more, the blinding rain or the heavy wash, and he expected to be totally submerged at any moment. He was dizzy, sick, he would have given much to stand on dry, stationary land. But Berkeley refused to move from the exposed poop deck and shouted, so he would be heard above the shrieking wind, "If we are engaged in a fight, although I was ordered to avoid one if possible because of the dispatches you are carrying, follow my dog, he always seeks out the safest place in the vessel, but keep away from the powder room, there are many barrels of explosives there." As he saw Christopher reach for the rail to vomit over it, he cried urgently, "Go below! You will be told when we land. What a splendid storm!"

Berkeley's dog cowered in his cabin, whimpering piteously, and never stopped. Christopher tried to sleep, but that was impossible, the dog was so noisy and there was such a creaking of timbers and flapping of sails and shuddering and shivering of the ship itself that he was sure it was coming apart from the force of the storm. Even when he chained himself to the bunk he fell out of it from the roll and pitch of the ship. Many foul hours passed and it was daylight before the weather improved and they reached the calm of the Medway estuary. He came out on deck and saw the shores of England with tremendous relief. Enough of ships, he thought, he had no wish to work or fight this vessel or to be a mariner.

The Vice-Admiral was friendly but patronising, for he had managed to remain on deck most of the night, proving his courage and resolution.

He invited Christopher to accompany him to Oxford in his coach and six, and said, "You are on the King's business and a hackney coach is dangerous these days, for the plague is still about." When Berkeley's luxurious coach arrived at the dock there was such a gathering of beggars and begging that Christopher was embarrassed. Berkeley ignored them, assuring him, "My Intelligence tells me the storm scattered the Dutch. But if they had attacked, I would have made their ships swim with blood."

Christopher thought, Berkeley was full of rhetoric and had fine legs and bright feathers on his hat, but the beggars looked ill and starving.

A shrunken, withered child thrust his trembling hand inside the coach and cried, "Mercy, sirs, I'm hungry. A shilling, please, great sirs?"

Berkeley recoiled in horror and slammed the door so quickly it bruised the child's hand and ordered the coachman to drive away at once. "I might have known we would be bothered. The plague has reached here, too."

"I could have spared a shilling. He may be sick but he is not dead."

"No! We must not suffer them to approach us once they are ill. Even the air they breathe is infected. Doctor, you must not encourage them."

Christopher saw many seamen on the street, some obviously wounded, others in rags, and several brandished pistols and swords at their coach. He said, "I thought we were winning."

"We are. They are the lice and vermin of our navy."

And no longer recognised, Christopher reflected sadly, now that they were no longer usable. If this was victory, defeat didn't matter.

They rode by houses with a red cross on the front door and written below it, "*The Lord have mercy upon us*," and Berkeley ordered the coachman to hurry, to go faster, much faster, and mistaking Christopher's concern for fear, he stated, "If I could help, I would, but nothing can be done. You must smoke tobacco, it will take away the smell and the apprehension."

Berkeley smoked furiously, but Christopher didn't follow his advice.

They passed a coach with its curtains drawn and all in black and Berkeley said, "A pest coach. Its occupants will die soon. You are fortunate that you were in France and missed much of the contagion."

"I was told that the plague decreases."

"So it is reported. The Bills of Mortality have diminished since the beginning of October and last week, for the first time in months, they were under a thousand dead in London. Perhaps it is because the days are shorter, colder. But no one is sure. Except that it is God's will."

Berkeley didn't stop smoking until they reached the next town and got out of the coach to stretch their legs while the coachman gave the horses water, and suddenly, even as Berkeley and Christopher stood nearby, the coachman was struck sick, blind. He couldn't see the horses and he felt his groin and cried out in horror, "I have a bubo!"

Berkeley said, "He must have caught it from that child." Christopher wanted to examine the sick coachman, who had fallen upon the ground, to see if he could be saved, but Berkeley dragged him away, crying, "We must take sensible precautions. I'm as brave as any man and you are learned, but the coachman is infected and we are in the service of the King."

He hurriedly hired another coach, after making sure that the horses were fresh, the coach clean, and the driver without any trace of the plague, and commanded the new driver to leave this rancid town at once.

They arrived at Oxford late that afternoon and while Berkeley reported to Albemarle, who had been appointed Commander of the Navy, Christopher went immediately to the King's audience chamber. It was not as large or lavish as the one at Whitehall, but it was finely furnished in gilt and gold, which he didn't expect— he had heard so many dire reports about Charles' empty purse. Matthew was there, for Clarendon was in attendance on the King, and after embracing him affectionately, he said, "Cousin, you look healthy but tired and thinner."

"I've travelled without any sleep since I left Calais. I have dispatches for the King. Jermyn said they were important."

"Yes. Charles will be pleased to get them. But you will have to wait, for he is at Lady Castlemaine's lodgings where he is having supper."

"The ambassador said they were also urgent."

"I know. But he dislikes being disturbed when he is with her. I will inform him of your presence as soon as he arrives here. He is expected later. If you are restless Pepys will keep you company."

Christopher turned to greet Pepys, who approached while his cousin retired to watch for the King. He noticed a new air of assurance about Pepys, who wore a new black silk suit with gold lace on its sleeves, and who had gained weight, more round-faced and fatter than before.

When Pepys saw Christopher observing his appearance, he said proudly, "It is quite handsome and expensive, it cost me above twenty-four pounds. The first gold lace I have ever worn, my wife tells me that the close knees become me most nobly. I was wondering if you would ever return from France. You must have had important business to keep you there."

"I saw many new buildings. You look quite well, despite the plague."

"We have suffered much, but God has seen fit to preserve me. You were wise to miss the contagion."

"It isn't all gone, is it? I saw a number of plague victims today."

"You are safe here. There is no fear of the plague in Oxford. No houses have been shut up. You were sensible to stay away until it abated."

Christopher said angrily, "That isn't why I remained in France."

"A lady? Are the French women as flirtatious and easy in their ways as is reported?" When Christopher didn't reply, he said, "No ill feeling. Most people envied you. Did you know that Van Doorn approached me on behalf of a friend of his and yours who he said had the plague?"

"No."

Christopher's surprise showed and Pepys added, "I thought he was using your name as an excuse to obtain help but I aided him."

"It was a friend of mine. And they had the plague."

"I thought it was his mistress, Van Doorn was so urgent and anxious."

"Was the patient helped?"

"I didn't hear from Van Doorn again. Was it a close friend of yours?"

"Close enough. Was Denham able to do any architectural work?"

"No, but he did write a poem celebrating our victory over the Dutch."

"Were you frightened by the plague?"

"One got used to it. What else could I do? Someone had to supervise the accounts of the Navy with the Dutch at our door."

They were interrupted by Evelyn, who also looked better than Christopher expected for one who had been in the midst of the plague, too. While Evelyn was pleased to see his dear friend, Doctor Wren, he was unhappy that he had to wait, for he had important business with the King. After Evelyn greeted Christopher and observed that Wren hadn't changed much, fortunately, and Pepys told him why Charles was delayed, he blurted out, "No wonder every boy in the street cries openly, '*The King cannot move until Lady Castlemaine is finished with him.*' Meanwhile, the sick and wounded Dutch prisoners die from want of care and provisions."

Pepys informed Christopher, "Our honourable friend has been appointed one of the Commissioners for the care of the sick and wounded prisoners."

"*The Commissioner*," Evelyn said curtly. "No one else cares at all. And with two thousand sick it is not employment even for a slave."

Christopher asked, "Is their condition that bad?"

"Worse. They die like flies. Like from the plague."

"You look well."

"Last month I was forty-five. But I feel wonderfully preserved and for that I bless God's infinite goodness. I knew His faith would protect me. I wear a leather amulet on my arm containing the right devotional words. It is a charm against the devil and his instruments, even the plague."

Pepys thought, Evelyn's natural countenance inclined to severity and yet he was capable of mirth, when he didn't regard himself with too much self-importance. Unfortunately however, while an estimable fellow, Pepys' mind ran on, Evelyn was inclined to conceit, believing himself very good at many things, poetry, books, plays, painting, plants, and the design of great buildings, so positive of his excellence he was certain of his being above all others, except perhaps a Doctor Wren or a Doctor Wilkins, and thus, inclined to be tedious in his knowledge.

Bored, Pepys recalled with savour a dream he had enjoyed last night.

The best dream he had ever dreamt. The more he reflected upon it the more he enjoyed it. Lady Castlemaine was in his arms and not the King's. She was allowing, nay imploring, that he use whatever dalliance he desired of her, with a passion that was lustful, the most obliging mistress he had ever known, encouraging the many variations of his amorous fancy.

It was such a pleasurable dream he didn't want it to end. What a fine thing it would be, he thought, if he could dream such dreams in the grave, as Shakespeare suggested. Then he would not be so afraid of death. As everyone was in plague time. That too, might be God's way.

Evelyn said sharply, "Samuel, you are not listening!"

Why should he? he reflected, he had heard Evelyn's complaints before, but he said, "Of course I am." He remembered the corpses he had seen.

"It concerns you. This war is governed like children play. The King is wretchedly abused, the only man who honestly serves his interests is Albemarle. The Court is more interested in their pleasures than in the war. The plain fact is that Charles borrows money from his Lords but has none for the navy. If matters do not improve we will lose the war."

Pepys reminded him, "We captured their chief settlement in the New World." He added proudly, "New Amsterdam has been renamed New York, in honour of the Duke of York. They say that while it is a savage place it may have possibilities as a port. It might amount to something one day."

"I doubt it," replied Evelyn. "The colonists are a rude, rough breed and it will take great diligence to make true Englishmen of them. Many are willing to follow Charles but all are afraid to disagree with him."

Evelyn was silent suddenly and pale as the King appeared, trailed by Albemarle, Clarendon, Matthew, and Scarburgh. Charles nodded briefly to Christopher, and when he saw Evelyn, with a gesture of cordiality, he walked toward him impulsively with out-stretched hands. Evelyn flushed with joy and bowed and kissed his hand, and Pepys, not to be outdone, did the same. Christopher followed their example and said, "Your Majesty, I have dispatches from the Earl of St. Albans."

"I know," said Charles. "Berkeley has informed Albemarle." He took the dispatches from Christopher, but he didn't look at them. "Evelyn, I'm heartily glad to see that you are safe. I hear that you have been much among the sick and plague-ridden these difficult days."

"I'm honoured to serve you, sir. I'm but a plain country gentleman."

Christopher thought, Evelyn doesn't mean a word of that, he is deeply flattered by the attention of Charles and regards it as quite appropriate.

Pepys said hurriedly, "Sir, I'm devoted to your interests, too."

"I give thanks for your good services all this year, Pepys. I assure you that I am sensible of it. My brother says you know so much about the administration of the Navy that you have become indispensable."

"The Duke of York is very kind, sir, but there are difficulties."

"Speak up, Pepys," Albemarle said suddenly, "Have your say."

"Your Majesty, our Navy is in desperate need of money. Now our ships are little more than scarecrows, for we have neither credit, stores, or provisions, and the pressed men are more of a liability than a help."

Clarendon added, "And, Your Majesty, there are other grave needs."

Evelyn took this hint and said, "Sir, if there is not money to buy clean straw and give our prisoners that and wood for fire they will all die."

"Gentlemen, I appreciate your problems and concern." Charles sighed.

"Thank you, sir," said Pepys. "I'm glad you understand our plight. For the ropemakers have discharged themselves for want of money and have gone into the country to make hay, and the joiners, sawyers, and blockmakers all refuse to work any more without money. Their pay is much in arrears."

"Deplorable, absolutely deplorable," declared Charles. "The condition of my country and my people troubles me greatly. It has made me ill. I haven't been able to sleep, I'm out of humour, tired of everything. Scarburgh says it is from the damp of Salisbury, it is one of the reasons I returned to Oxford, and he attends me daily, watches my bowels and makes sure that I'm free from the contagion."

Scarburgh, who stood silently behind the King, was far different to Christopher from the young, inquiring physician who had introduced him to William Harvey. He was dressed like a courtier and he nodded acquiescently as Charles spoke, no longer asking questions but expressing Charles' text.

"And now Berkeley informs me that France is about to declare war on us. Wren, is that true?"

"Your Majesty, I believe that the exact view is in the dispatches."

"More bad news, no doubt." He put them in his pocket still without reading them. "I would be better off if I devoted myself to natural philosophy."

Albemarle said urgently, "Sir, we cannot ignore the French threat."

"*You* cannot ignore it. You are in command of the Navy now. Wren, you are an observant scholar. Do you think the French will fight?"

"Their King needs money for Versailles. It might distract him."

Charles looked at Clarendon who said, "Sir, with the plague our taxes from London are gone and our trade has diminished by more than half."

"Money is the eternal problem. Clarendon, you must find ways to raise revenue. Is all the money gone from the sale of Dunkirk to the French?"

"All, sir," said Clarendon. "The only remedy is to make peace."

"No." For once, Charles was positive. "We cannot risk moving the country out of its desires. England is as avid for this war as a cuckold is for his conscience. Clarendon, Albemarle, I'm sure that in the company of such devoted subjects of mine you will find a solution."

Everyone bowed as Charles strode out, languid and distant.

Clarendon and Albemarle didn't want to hear anything from the others. They knew what was wrong; they had heard the complaints before, many times. They dismissed the others as soon as the King was out of sight.

Seth had kept Christopher's rooms in Wadham in meticulous order. And at the sight of him, he cried out, "There were times I thought I would never see you again. But we have been free of the contagion in Oxford and you look fine. I heard you were returning but I wasn't sure when."

His eyes filled with tears and Christopher instinctively felt that Seth's emotion could be trusted. He wasn't sure about anybody else's, except possibly, Daniel's. Caring was caring, there was no substitute for that, he thought, and Seth, who had aged, seemed all that was left of his childhood. And with Sam gone, Seth's presence was more precious.

A few days later he was in his Oxford routine—he was available to students once more and using his telescope, although his mind continued to wander to architecture—when Daniel appeared. As his friend stood in the doorway he wanted to shout for joy. And there was such a multitude of questions he yearned to ask him, but there was something in Daniel's manner that discouraged this. Daniel held a bag and two paintings, apparently prepared to stay if invited, but he couldn't tell whether his friend was glad to see him, Daniel was so reserved. Maybe they had learned a different view of reality, he reflected, or of responsibility.

He asked Daniel to come in, to have dinner, and Daniel accepted.

It was a fine, clear, frosty evening and Seth cooked them a plain but substantial dinner, served with wine, and then disappeared so they could talk freely. They had eaten silently which was not natural for them.

And now Christopher asked the expected. "How did you know I was back?"

"Your uncle told me. He heard the news from his son."

"Is he satisfied with the chapel at Pembroke?"

"Enough. As much as anything he didn't design himself."

"Will I like it? I know you wrote that I would, but . . ."

Daniel interrupted, almost impatiently, "As I said, it is much as you designed it. It is functional. It does what it is supposed to do."

Suddenly Christopher asked, "Daniel, what did really happen to her?"

"She vanished. I wrote you."

"You don't know where?"

"She didn't say."

"Did Anne, at least, say why?"

"She left a note."

"Do you have it?"

"Yes."

"May I see it?"

Daniel's lips tightened as he handed it to Christopher.

Christopher was surprised by how carefully the note had been kept. He read it silently, re-read with great care, "*I have risked your life enough, I cannot risk it any more . . . But do not worry, I have some jewels and wits. And my outer skin. And a memory of ninety-two days.*"

Ninety-two days?

Christopher didn't know what to say. There was a tension, a tightness in Daniel he had never seen before, and something in this tone of Anne's that he had not known. He realised that Daniel didn't want to discuss her and yet he had to ask, "Did she ever tell you why she was dismissed?"

"Dismissed?"

"From the palace as a maid of honour."

"Oh!" Daniel paused, then said, "Once, in her delirium, she

babbled that it was Buckingham's doing, but that if you had . . ."
He halted.

"If I had *what*, Daniel?"

"It is not important."

"It is to me. What did Anne say?"

"*If you had been here you wouldn't have allowed her dismissal.* But I shouldn't have repeated that. I'm sure you couldn't have stopped it."

Christopher wasn't sure, or that Daniel was, yet he said, "I know you don't want to discuss her, but I must thank you for what you did."

"No thanks are necessary. You would have done the same."

"I hope so. Did Sam suffer much?"

"Anyone who had the plague did."

"Yet you escaped unharmed." Christopher marvelled at that.

"I was fortunate."

"And not spared by God's providence like Pepys and Evelyn?"

"They will believe what they want to. I see no reason why God would single me out for special favours. Did you find what you wanted in France?"

Christopher paused, then said, "For the most part. Daniel, stay with me? Please?" As Daniel wavered this time, he added urgently, "Once the plague and war are over much building will be done and I will need you."

"Did France convince you to be an architect?"

"Possibly. Daniel, why do so many have to die unnecessarily?"

"If I knew, perhaps I would be God."

Then Christopher had to say what troubled him most of all, "I'm sorry I didn't return sooner and help you. I didn't realise how bad things were."

"You made a good start at Pembroke. There was no sense spoiling it."

"That was thoughtful of you."

"May I have Anne's letter?"

Christopher handed it to Daniel and he put her note inside his doublet with loving care.

How Up is Up

How up is up
How down is down

When down is up
To the worm in the ground

And up is down
To the kite on the moon

How up-down is down-up
How down-up is up-down

To all of us

Stymean Karlen

29

How Up is Up

JANUARY, 1666, FRANCE DECLARED WAR ON ENGLAND AND WHILE there was no fighting at this time, Christopher felt that was rubbing salt on a wound that was festering already. Charles and his Court returned to Whitehall in February and the next month the Royal Society resumed its meetings at Gresham. Now Christopher believed that the plague was over but he didn't consider visiting London until the Archbishop of Canterbury asked him to report upon the repairs required for a suitable renovation of St. Paul's.

They met at Gilbert Sheldon's private quarters in Oxford and the ruddy, vigorous, outspoken Archbishop was surprised by Doctor Wren's reluctance and he said, "I didn't expect you to question my proposal."

"I'm honoured, Your Grace, but when I offered recommendations before they were ignored. The other surveyors were jealous of my plans and the king made it plain that he has no money to spare for the cathedral."

"Charles may be more sympathetic these days. His interest in St. Paul's will demonstrate that he supports our faith and is not a Papist as is rumoured. And he needs a worthy project to distract the country from its present troubles. If you give me a detailed report for the next meeting of the Royal Commission it will be considered seriously." When he saw Christopher's continued pessimism, he asked, "What is wrong now?"

"How can I get wood for St. Paul's when I can't get it for the theatre? Only the outer shell is done because of the war. All the good timber has gone to build or repair men of war and the carpenters have been pressed into the Navy. Sir, nothing is being constructed except for the war."

"Work on the theatre will be resumed when the war is over."

"If it will ever end, Your Grace."

"It will end. Be patient, you are still a young man."

Not that young, but he didn't pursue the subject.

"Then you will have recommendations for the repair of St. Paul's?"

"If you desire, Your Grace."

"If you desire, Doctor."

"Sir, what about the other surveyors, Denham, Pratt, Webb?"

"Denham has been ill and Pratt's ideas are rigid."

"Webb is a competent surveyor, sir."

"But not liked. The King finds him too pushing, an awkward fellow. He doesn't like bad manners, he says vulgarity upsets his digestion."

Before Christopher left for London, he visited his uncle and his chapel at Pembroke. The Bishop greeted him critically. "I was beginning to wonder if you would ever leave that God-forsaken France. Papist bigots."

"I saw many examples of worthy architecture."

"Very pretty, too, I'm sure, but not godly."

Christopher stood in front of the chapel with his uncle and he was dissatisfied with it. The variety he had seen in France gave him the feeling that this building was hardly more than a rectangular box, without distinction. But he did like the three Venetian windows on each side and the neat belfry perched at the top of the chapel. Then he frowned.

Matthew saw that and said apologetically, "I was forced to use red brick for most of the outer walls because I couldn't afford anything else."

"That isn't what is wrong. But it is such a simple structure."

The bishop asked suspiciously, "What fine plans have you now?"

"The Archbishop wants St. Paul's returned to its former greatness."

"As it was under John Donne," Matthew said contemptuously. "I knew him. I didn't like his face. It was more Italian than English, with his dark hair and eyes, his long nose, thick lips, lewd and lascivious. No wonder he had such amorous proclivities in spite of his preachings."

"I heard that Donne had a lovely voice."

"It was too sensual, there was too much of the world in it." As his nephew turned to leave, he added, "I hope you are not going to war."

"No."

"Sometimes I think the Dutch war was declared for the purpose of destroying our most worthy young men. Nephew, you are not angry with me?"

Christopher smiled and said, "I know you mean well."

"The road to hell is paved with good intentions. And I am an old man."

"Uncle, you have many more years ahead of you."

"At eighty? You must not exaggerate!" But when his nephew started off without another word, he said hurriedly, "Pembroke is quite good, considering that it is your first effort at design."

Finally there was the need to persuade Daniel to come to London with him. But at this suggestion Daniel said, "My presence will antagonise the other surveyors, especially now, with the Dutch war going so badly."

"I need your drawings of St. Paul's."

"That doesn't require my presence."

"I require someone whose views I can trust."

Daniel was silent, then he said, "I can't go back to Fetter Lane."

"You can stay in Scotland Yard." Christopher handed him the key.

Daniel thought, It was a faint hope but it was possible Anne might come back to Scotland Yard. He was sure she wouldn't return to Fetter Lane.

Christopher saw that Daniel was wavering and he said, "I can use all the help I can get. The Royal Commission wants my views on how St. Paul's can be returned to its former beauty, glory, and strength."

"You will be opposed by Webb, Pratt, and May. And possibly, Denham."

Christopher was melancholy until he packed his luggage with his designs of the best of French architecture and added to them the drawings of St. Paul's that both of them had done and said, "I'm going to suggest a dome to replace the ruined steeple."

"I doubt that they will approve. There are no domes in England."

"Then it is time we had one."

"You may merely be amusing yourself."

"*I know. But even if my proposals and designs are not accepted, I shall not repent the great satisfaction and pleasure I have taken in the contrivance, which equals that of poetry and composition in music.*"

Christopher was so earnest Daniel was persuaded. He took the key to the house in Scotland Yard and said, "I will help you any way I can."

Daniel did visit Fetter Lane with Christopher to help him get settled. Christopher was touched that Sam had left the house to him, and he felt, to keep Sam's memory alive, the house should be occupied. He was startled by what they found. The heavily scrawled red cross remained on the front door and was still the most prominent thing to be seen, and underneath it was written, *"God have mercy on their souls."* No wonder Daniel looked so pained, he thought, the past was too recent, too dreadful here. The Rowley house was empty and the blank, dirty windows stared at them with sightless eyes. The home above them on the street was vacant, also, as were most of the buildings on Fetter Lane, although there was no more plague on it.

Daniel told himself, He must not expect others to feel the way he did. He saw pedestrians on Fetter Lane and the nearby Fleet, and many of them were dressed in soft, expensive cloths and fine, high-heeled shoes stepping discreetly above the mud and on to the egg-shaped cobblestones. There were sounds of laughter and the cries of street hawkers which echoed loudly in his ears and he felt they profaned what London had endured.

The house had a stale, unused odour, but after Christopher scrubbed off the red cross and the words underneath and Daniel cleaned and rearranged the interior the house appeared fit to live in again.

Damn it, Daniel told himself, it was no longer his concern. It was Christopher's house now. He came on a pair of Anne's shoes and when his friend wasn't looking he put them into his luggage quickly and secretly.

Christopher kept staring at the garden and as he saw Daniel regarding the Rowley house with a terrible sadness, he asked, "Did they all die?"

"Yes. But Sam was lucky. He was buried in a grave, not a pest-pit."

"Did you see any rats during the plague?"

"Many. Particularly just before the contagion infected Fetter Lane. I took special notice because of what you had said. Big, black rats. But no one paid any attention to them. And now it is assumed the plague has abated because of the hard frost and the freezing weather this winter."

"I still think the rats caused the plague, but no one shares my views. And with all these old wooden houses on the narrow, filthy alleys it will recur, if fire doesn't strike first. Trust London to do everything in excess. I love the city but sometimes its ways are very strange."

"If you are really so afraid of fire why don't you do something?"

"No one listens to those views either. Whenever there is a calamity they say it is God's will or blame it on the stars. They have more faith in astrology than in cleanliness, efficiency, and proper building."

Daniel shrugged and said, "It was wise of you not to be here during the plague. It wouldn't have helped and people's disregard of each other was obscene. I'll never forget it. London was a vast graveyard."

Christopher knelt and prayed for the soul of Sam. He didn't mind that Daniel didn't join him, but still was staring at the Rowley house. This way his friend couldn't tell that he was praying for Anne, too.

Daniel felt better living in the house at Scotland Yard. Gallants strode the streets around Whitehall and he liked the hope it gave him of seeing Anne once more. Her brick house was empty and he didn't want to talk about her to anyone. And the housekeeper only wanted to discuss Denham and his young wife, Margaret. She told him, "What's going on there is scandalous. Sir John has lost his senses and when he isn't in his house the Duke of York is. Yet no matter how the husband loses his wits, his wife doesn't care, her only concern is to please the King's brother."

"It could be a problem for Doctor Wren. He has to work with Denham."

"He won't be able to. Denham has aged prematurely. He never should have wed a young woman. Mr. Van Doorn, when will Doctor Wren stay here?"

"When His Majesty requires his presence."

"Denham is so ill he can hardly walk. Any old man who weds a young woman deserves to be miserable. Don't they know what is wrong with him?"

We all have our secrets, Christopher reflected. He sat on the edge of the bed he had occupied with Anne and as his bare feet felt the wooden floor, the thinness of the surface, the scrape of the splinters on his flesh, he hoped he had both feet planted firmly on the floor. But he wasn't sure. A misery filled his eyes. He wasn't clear what gave him such sadness, Françoise or Anne or his distaste for the meeting with the Royal Commissioners and the other surveyors, but he hated idleness. Why couldn't he be getting up instead of going to sleep? Idleness was boring and gave him too much opportunity to recall. He jumped up and ran across the floor and opened the shutters on the windows and he saw the immense space of the sky and the stars. Nothing was asleep in the sky, he told himself, and he must not have any doubts tomorrow. Once he plunged ahead with the repairs on St. Paul's, astronomy must become secondary. When he designed a structure his body time was different than anyone else's. Time must wait then, as the Archbishop had suggested, time was celestial, time had brought him here, time must bring a better St. Paul's. He clapped his hands together to applaud that idea. He must be heard, whatever the opposition. He must make sure they knew the facts despite the risk. The cathedral was not just paste and stone or a toy with which to play.

The Royal Commission for the repair and renovation of St. Paul's met at Whitehall the next night with Archbishop Sheldon, William Sancroft, the new Dean of St. Paul's, Lord Clarendon, the Duke of Buckingham, and the Duke of Albemarle in attendance, and they were joined by Matthew, as secretary to Clarendon, and Webb, Pratt, and May. But there was no sign of Denham. And six commissioners were needed for a quorum.

Matthew, eager to prepare his cousin properly, told him privately, "The King will be the sixth and deciding voice if anything has to be decided. He is watching an entertainment in an adjoining chamber. He prefers to avoid meetings such as these, he says they are tedious. And some say that Denham is ill, but I hear he has gone to the island of Portland to survey the stone quarries there, at the request of the King, to see how much of the stone is available. And to earn a bit of profit for himself."

The audience chamber was converted into a conference room and on the large walnut table in the centre were two models of St. Paul's, one of the present church and one of the cathedral when it had been without damage. Sheldon sat at the head of the table to direct the inquiry and had placed beside him the new Dean of St. Paul's, William Sancroft, a small, grave, middle-aged man, who was taking notes and acting as the Archbishop's assistant. Christopher was most interested in Buckingham's appearance. The once handsome young man had become, although still in his late thirties, fat and flabby, his face loose and self-indulgent.

Sheldon called the inquiry to order and said, "My Lords, since we know the other opinions, I would like to start with Doctor Wren's proposals."

No one objected, although Buckingham looked bored and Webb and Pratt irritable, and Christopher got to the point at once. "I believe the whole central tower should come down. As Sir John and Mr. Webb recommended."

Webb said, "I recommended that Jones' great portico be preserved. Wren, if St. Paul's is repaired, it must be done in an orderly way."

"Mr. Webb, that is why I believe the central tower should be done away with altogether. Or the same problems will arise again."

Webb retorted, "Doctor Wren grossly overstates."

Buckingham asked suddenly, "May, what are your views?"

"Sir, quite apart from anything else, it will cost too much."

Albemarle turned to Pratt, asked, "Do you share his view?"

"I don't approve. I can patch up St. Paul's without much cost."

Sheldon said, "Nonetheless, we must hear Doctor Wren's remedy."

"If we don't tear down the tower now a worst disaster could occur."

Pratt said mockingly, "Any day the whole church could be destroyed?"

"Any day," Christopher replied deliberately.

"Problems, problems," said Clarendon. "And they cost so much."

"Sir, if something isn't done about St. Paul's it will cost much more."

"Doctor Wren, what do you propose?"

"Lord Clarendon, to open up the entire central space of the cathedral and instead of another Gothic steeple, to erect a noble classical dome."

Even Sheldon, his supporter, was surprised, while Clarendon gasped and exclaimed, "It will cost a fortune! We cannot afford it!"

Pratt was outraged, Webb disgusted, Albemarle, May, and Matthew were puzzled, and Buckingham said, "Our astronomer is very self-indulgent."

"Sir, we have neglected St. Paul's too long. But a dome would enrich London's sky and restore the cathedral to a full life again."

"And cost hundreds of thousands of pounds," Pratt said indignantly. "To give us a Roman church that doesn't represent our views in the least."

"A dome will be an appropriate match for Jones' noble portico."

"But you are not *a* Jones," said Webb. "I was his deputy. I knew his mind. I was working with him when you were just a student at Westminster."

Pratt said, "Doctor Wren must remember he is only an adviser. The cathedral is not in such grave danger. In Paul's churchyard they are selling books again and he has never been to Italy. He has never seen a building by Bramante, Bernini, or any of the masters. As I have."

Dean Sancroft said quietly, "I've observed the great buildings of Rome. Doctor Wren has learned their principles correctly and his designs for a dome are accurate in the classical tradition."

Christopher added, "What is most important is that the restored church be all of a piece, all to be contained within a dome."

Sheldon said strongly, "Go on, Doctor."

Christopher felt in an unique situation, this was a chance for a clear thinking effort to exert a direct influence on the shape and structure of his country. His previous study was like a prelude to this moment; his thoughts were ordered, purposeful; his mind keyed to a high pitch. He had laboured long on his preparations; he had re-examined his drawings of St. Paul's and Daniel's; he recalled what he had seen in France. He spoke with fluency as he described the inadequacies of the present St. Paul's. Everyone, even Buckingham, Pratt, and Webb were listening intently, if not agreeably, when Charles entered followed by a frantic Denham.

Even the usually poised King looked distracted and upset.

Denham shouted, "Sir, you should know me better! My life wasted, my future gone, and now you deny that I am the Holy Ghost!"

Charles said, "Sir John, you know I deny you nothing. But you must not pursue me into my private chambers. Don't you know who I am?"

"His brother." Denham was too weak to stand without his crutch as he cried out, "I'm a fine soldier, too. I've joined the army of Jesus, I'm His Ghost. His Holy Ghost. I'm dead to this foul world as if I am already in the grave, but I will be resurrected. Oh!" He glanced around. "Where is my bride? How long has she been absent?"

Christopher asked Matthew, "How long has this madness gone on?"

"Since he discovered that his wife prefers the Duke of York."

Denham looked eighty, Christopher thought sadly, he had become so old.

"No man may insult me now! I am Him who no one dares offend!"

Sheldon said, "Sir John, you are blasphemous."

"He is ill," said Charles. "We must not hurt him. He took my brothers to safety during the troubles. He has served my family well."

Denham asked, "Is the sun shining?"

"It is night, Sir John," Christopher said. "We are discussing the repair of St. Paul's. See the models on the table."

Denham limped around the models on his crutch and declared, "They are the Tower, but they will not put me into it. I'm the Holy Ghost and I'm free from prosecution. Has anyone seen my virtuous bride? She must be paid for her services. Do not put her into the grave."

Two guards entered, aroused by the commotion, and Charles motioned for them to take Denham back to his house. "But gently," he said.

As Denham felt the hands of the guards he announced, "Friends, I'm not yet dead, but distracted. Do you understand?"

The King said kindly, "Yes, Sir John. Trust me."

"I trust no one. But Jesus. My clothes are in rags and my heart is in tears but Jesus will save me. I'm His Ghost, His Holy Ghost."

Charles said to the guards, "Make sure no harm comes to Sir John."

He cried out, "Do not fear, Your Majesty, I cannot be harmed. I'm the blessed Jesus Christ, and you will have a good place in heaven. But before you come to enjoy it, Your Majesty, you must live a better life, as my own wife must, if she desires a good place there also. My poetry has led me astray. I should have been Milton, a scourge, a prophet. I should have beaten my wife as Milton did. What fools men are!"

As the guards carried off Denham, Clarendon said, "Your Majesty, you must take official cognizance of his madness."

"His incapacitation. What do you suggest?"

"I suggest our friend here, Hugh May, paymaster of the Works, executes the office of Surveyor of the Works until Denham comes to his senses."

"Granted," Charles said curtly. "What other business have you here?"

Sheldon stated, "Doctor Wren has proposed plans for the repair of St. Paul's, featuring a dome to replace the ruined steeple."

"A Roman dome," Buckingham sneered.

"Like St. Peter's?" asked Charles. "Is that what you intend, Doctor?"

"In a way. Sir, it would add lustre to your reign."

"How much would it cost?"

May said, "More than we can afford, Your Majesty."

Sheldon said, "There is no harm in having Doctor Wren submit his final plans. They could be helpful. Don't you agree, sir?"

Charles thought, He needed the support of the Church, matters were going so disastrously elsewhere. He nodded.

Sheldon addressed the others on the Royal Commission and Clarendon, Albemarle, and Sancroft added their approval to his recommendation that Doctor Wren submit his final designs for the renovation of St. Paul's for their further consideration. The Archbishop declared that this motion was carried by a vote of five to one and turned to tell the King. But Charles had left with Buckingham to inspect the latter's newest novelty, a gold toothpick set, of a nature no one had seen before. Buckingham was a great man with a toothpick and he was glad to see that noblemen were using them now, for they were good for the teeth and a mark of distinction.

Christopher told Daniel about Denham's insanity and Daniel replied, "He may not be as mad as they think. I've seen York coming out of his house. His doubts about his wife's infidelity may not be an illusion."

"Nonetheless, it is sad. Denham is ill, a ruin of a man."

"Will it affect your designs for the cathedral?"

"I doubt it. He won't be one of the judges, but even if he was . . ." Christopher paused and sighed, "I don't think he would approve."

"It seems to me that it depends on whether the King does."

"I don't expect him to approve either. Unless the war ends suddenly, and that is not likely. I'm told it grows more ruinous each day."

Early in June the battle between the English and Dutch fleets began off the coast of Holland, then moved down the Channel. On the fourth day of bloody conflict, while Christopher and Daniel were surveying St. Paul's, they could hear the sound of the guns. When news reached London that the English fleet was shattered and citizens were talking of repelling the expected Dutch invasion, Christopher thought of taking up arms himself. He was shaken by the news that Berkeley had been killed after refusing to surrender to superior forces and now was regarded as a hero. But the Dutch, while they had won the four day battle without any help from the French, were so exhausted they could not follow up their victory.

At the Royal Society a few days later Christopher heard from Pepys, who had come to obtain a table on naval matters from Wilkins and Hooke, that there were still enough English ships afloat to repel an invasion. Pepys was more interested in discussing Denham's madness.

Pepys told Christopher, "You could become Chief Surveyor soon. Some say he has the fits, others that he has the pox, and there are those who believe he has syphilis and is suffering from too much venery."

Hooke and Wilkins had moved into another room to continue their work on the latter's book on a universal language, and Christopher wanted to join them, but Pepys was determined to tell him all the news. "I hear that York, despite his being ruler of the Navy, is wholly given up to his new mistress, Lady Denham. He visits her every day in Scotland Yard."

"How can you be certain, Pepys?"

"Everyone knows. Lady Denham said, '*I will not be his mistress, as Mrs. Price, to go up and down the privy stairs, but I will be owned publicly.*' And so she is. And very proud of it. Lady Denham has become lady of the bedchamber to the Duchess of York, so he doesn't have to reach far to take her in his arms."

Pepys' envy upset Christopher. He realised he mustn't confide in him or his private life would be public mischief, but he had to say, "Don't you think you should hear Denham's views before gossiping about him?"

Pepys was indignant. "What I told you is common knowledge!"

Christopher was pleased when Denham asked to see him a few weeks later. The fear of invasion was gone, the summer had become hot and dry, as the previous year, but there was no recurrence of the plague. There was to be a meeting of the Royal Commission to review his final plans for the repair of St. Paul's and Christopher assumed this was what Denham wanted to discuss. Instead, while the Chief Surveyor greeted him naturally, which pleased him, when he said, "The surveyors are meeting in a month to discuss St. Paul's," Denham dismissed this with an indifferent shrug.

It was a sunny afternoon and Denham sat by the window, although all the blinds in his house were drawn, and said, "To keep the prying eyes of my neighbours out of my affairs. I've been ill, but I'm fine now. Just tired, troubled with the ague in my legs. Have you seen my wife lately?"

"No. I'm rarely at Court, Sir John."

"She is always there. It is my misfortune and has made me melancholy."

"What did you want to see me about?"

"I am simply trying to defend my family name and honour."

"How can I help?"

"By being here. Accepting my invitation. Not everyone does. Even though I'm still a member of Parliament and I was knighted by the King."

"I'm suggesting a dome for St. Paul's. What do you think, Sir John?"

"As long as it is decent and honourable. I tell you, Wren, whatever they accuse me of, I'm innocent."

"I believe you," said Christopher, trying to be consoling.

"I've sought many cures for the melancholy, prayer, diet, herbs, fresh air, physic, merry company, purges, wine, sleep, blood letting, hot baths, but I'm bewitched. No matter what I do I'm sick at heart. My wife is the open and acknowledged mistress of the Duke of York, the second most important person in the Kingdom, and I can do nothing."

"Sir John, why do you tell me this?"

"I can trust you, Wren. Thanks for coming." He motioned for Christopher to leave and put his head into his hands and started to cry.

Daniel was in the house on Scotland Yard and he was surprised by the vehemence with which Christopher urged him to move into Fetter Lane. His friend stressed again how much he needed him, but Daniel felt there were other reasons. But to be wanted was a good feeling, and so he joined Christopher at Fetter Lane, although he still disliked living there.

Now Christopher hoped that his voice carried the conviction he felt. He had waited for this day a long time and as he stood in front of the west portico of St. Paul's with the designs he and Daniel had prepared, he had to struggle to conceal his nervousness. It was the 27th of August, another hot, dry afternoon, and St. Paul's was etched vividly against the clear blue sky. He expected to see Pratt, May, and Dean Sancroft, and even the Bishop of London, Dr. Humphrey Henchman—who held the post his uncle had coveted—but he hadn't thought he would meet with John Evelyn, Thomas Chichely, and Henry Slingsby.

He didn't worry about Henchman's views; this old, benign cleric was the most handsome bishop in England and one of the most ineffectual, and would support Sancroft in anything the Dean proposed. But Chichely, wealthy, self-important, vain about his knowledge of building, might be difficult to convince, while Slingsby, the Master of the Mint in the Tower, and a good mathematician with a working knowledge of mechanics, preferred to support the popular view, and Evelyn, although his friend, had strong opinions and was eager and ambitious to be a surveyor.

Sancroft took him aside and told him, "Doctor, it was decided by the Commission to obtain a technical opinion of your proposals. So they appointed a committee of three architectural authorities to act as judges of your designs, Evelyn, Chichely, Slingsby. They will rule on them."

Christopher, with a sinking heart, moved back to the others, clutching his designs for the dome he had carefully done with Daniel's help. The concepts were his but some of the drawings were by Daniel, who had a precise hand. They expressed what he believed, but would the judges believe? He doubted that, his proposals were so new. And as Daniel had said, "*There are no domes in England, domes are regarded as Papist.*"

He said, "We will keep the portico, as you can see in my designs."

Everyone nodded and Sancroft said, "Continue, please, Doctor Wren."

"However, we must remedy the infirmities of the present design."

Evelyn looked startled while Chichely was shocked and Slingsby said, "It can't be that infirm. St. Paul's has stood for centuries."

"Nonetheless, sir, it is dying."

"I don't agree!" Pratt exclaimed and regarded him as if he were insane.

"The cathedral is dying in time. It has been neglected so long that only a drastic rebuilding will preserve it. We must rebuild most of it."

Pratt cried out dramatically, "What transformations does our doctor of astronomy desire now? What pillars and blessed arches to be pulled down? What new ones to be erected? The smallest alteration he proposes, to lessen in one part and to add in another, how difficult, tedious, and changeable this will be! He will weaken the cathedral on one hand and deform it on the other! Even if this is done with the best thrift and prudence in the world we cannot support such wild proposals and expense!"

As Pratt's attack gathered vehemence, Christopher noticed that it annoyed Evelyn with its anger and upset Slingsby with its violence, as if it was not gentlemanly, which, to Slingsby, was a sin.

Christopher replied simply and directly by kicking at a pillar and dislodging a piece of stone which came loose and fell with a jolt.

Sancroft said apologetically, "Since the war there hasn't been any revenue available for the maintenance of the fabric."

Christopher said, "That is why we must have a new dome."

Chichely said, "The faithful will bewail the loss of a steeple and feel blasphemous if they don't see a hopeful successor rise in its place."

Pratt said, "Doctor Wren wants to make St. Paul's *his* St. Paul's."

"I want to restore it before it falls down completely."

"You are obsessed with that, sir. The cathedral has stayed up for centuries, nothing will knock it down now, for it has survived plague, civil war, all kinds of torments, natural and man made."

"And has become faceless, an object of derision, when it should reach up and up with love, with a feeling it doesn't possess any more."

"That is too vague," Pratt declared. "As are your proposals."

Evelyn asked suddenly, "Doctor Wren, what are your proposals?"

"Beyond the dome," added Sancroft.

Slingsby remarked, "All of them," and May, who had been silent up to now, said, "So we will truly know how much it will cost."

Christopher pushed caution aside and led them to the base of the tower and said, feeling as if he were uttering a funeral oration over the old cathedral, "*Concerning the repair of St. Paul's, some may desire too great a magnificence, which the disposition of the age will not accept. Others may think of piecing up the old fabric, here with stone, there with brick, and cover all faults with a coat of plaster, leaving it to posterity as an object of charity.*" He paused, for in his passion he had become breathless. He saw Sancroft regarding him approvingly; Evelyn

Q*

was listening intently; the others, at least, weren't trying to halt him.

He plunged on, for what he felt he knew by heart. He had thought about it for years and had memorised it to himself many times. "*But none of this solves the problem, for the cathedral is a pile for ornament and for use. It could be repaired at less expense, but it would want grandeur. It must be a monument to our country and to our faith. As it was when London had not a fifth part of the wealth it now possesses.*"

Pratt said abruptly, "What has this to do with your proposals?"

"*I will proceed now to the defects of the building. It is evident from the ruin of the roof that the work was both ill-designed and ill-built from the beginning. Ill-designed because the architect didn't give butment enough to counterpoise and to resist the weight of the roof from spreading the walls. The eye alone will discover this. That the pillars, as vast as they are, even those eleven feet in diameter, are bent outwards at least six inches from their original position. Thus, it follows, that the whole roof must fall open with large and wide cracks along the walls and windows, and eventually, infect the pillars until they yield to the stress. This bending of the pillars was facilitated by their ill-building. They are cased outside only with little stones, no larger than a man's hand, and within there is nothing but a core of small rubbish, stone and more mortar, which crushes easily and yields to the weight. This outward coat of stone is so torn with age and neglect that it is a rare piece of stone that is not mouldered and flawed away with the saltpetre that is in them. This is an incurable disease, which perpetually throws off whatever coat of plaster is laid on it, and therefore not to be cured.*"

Pratt cried out, "It is easy to be critical, but what is your remedy?"

Christopher's passion grew—they must believe, or whatever was left would collapse about their heads. "*My remedy is to open up the central space by cutting off the four inner corners of the cross and to raise above the crossing a noble dome.*"

Pratt shouted, "That won't accomplish anything!"

"*By these means the deformities of the cathedral will be removed. St. Paul's, which is much too narrow for its height, will be made spacious in the middle. The outward appearance of the church will swell in the middle from a large base, rising with a rotunda bearing a cupola, and ending in a lantern. And this with incomparably more grace than it is possible for the lean shaft of a steeple to afford.*"

Slingsby asked, "Doctor Wren, what material would you use?"

"*Either we build a timber roof, which under certain circumstances will soon decay, or a thinner and lighter shell of stone. Perhaps a light brick vault covered with stucco like those in the French renaissance churches.*"

Pratt sneered critically, "French Papist stucco in an English church?"

Christopher replied, "*The stucco I would use is firm in many ancient*

Roman buildings to this day. If we are to build, it must be for eternity."

Sancroft said, "I've seen such buildings in Rome."

"So have I," said Evelyn. "Worthy structures, classical and grand. And, as Doctor Wren says, the building does recede outwards."

Pratt declared, "It was built this way, to give the proper perspective in regard to its height."

Chichely agreed with him, but Evelyn said, "I'm of another judgment."

Pratt retorted, with Chichely's approval, "It is not enough to repair St. Paul's on its present foundations," and Evelyn examined the foundations, especially the pillars, and said, "They are in a very mean condition."

Sancroft summoned everyone about him and asked, "How do you vote?"

Pratt stated, "The foundations of the tower are sound, to remove them is impracticable, for they conform to the rest of the cathedral. Wren's scheme is too costly, too difficult, and I'm firmly against it."

Henchman waited for Sancroft's opinion; May hesitated; Slingsby looked uncertain, but when Chichely supported Pratt, Evelyn said abruptly, "I reject Mr. Pratt's views."

"Then you approve of Doctor Wren's proposals?" asked Sancroft.

"I approve of giving our cathedral a sense of His ultimate purpose and design."

Slingsby said suddenly, "I've listened carefully to all that has been offered and John Evelyn is right."

Gathering courage, May said, "I agree. I'm persuaded, if not totally convinced. This soil is barren now, but perhaps Doctor Wren can seed it."

Sancroft said, "Doctor Wren's proposals are accepted. Even without my vote and Bishop Henchman's"—who was nodding his approval of what Sancroft was saying—"they are carried by a vote of three to two."

Christopher sighed with relief. He yearned so much to rebuild St. Paul's he felt he was part of it, yet only now did it appear possible.

Pratt said harshly, "So you are going to put a Papist dome in a Protestant city! It will give aid and comfort to our Papist enemies!"

Sancroft said, "We are going to recommend that a committee of able, qualified workmen be appointed to examine the present foundations. To verify Doctor Wren's views."

And there his plans might end, Christopher thought apprehensively, buried behind the façade of still another committee. Yet Evelyn had supported him and that pleased him, and now Evelyn was saying, "Doctor Wren, a dome might look impressive. You should be overjoyed that so much attention has been given to your opinions. This could be a vastly important commission. You are still a young man.''

Christopher felt, however, that his work was just starting. No one had asked to see his designs for the dome. He glanced about him. An unusual calm hung over London. He was relieved that there had been no recurrence of the plague, that the Dutch war, although undecided, was still free of invasion. With plans for a dome in hand this should be an autumn he could enjoy. He prayed that nothing would disturb the quiet that prevailed in London these waning days of August. He wondered, staring at the remains of the ruined steeple, visualising a great circular dome in its place, how far up was up.

This Paralysed Hour

This paralysed hour
Its limbs stiffened beyond anticipation

Knowledge failed to re-alive them
Philosophy tried but ended in travail

Its sight was the last sense remaining
Until it too came to be out of use

Denial stamped its visage
Claiming nothing moved all was stricken

But the time-piece
Magically gifted to a point of genius

Lured this paralysed hour
Making it rise

And walk outside of distance
So relieving the ever waiting heart
                                    waiting

Stymean Karlen

30

This Paralysed Hour

THE SMELL OF SMOKE SPREAD OVER LONDON AND INFECTED THE CITY with a strong stench. It awoke Daniel early Sunday morning and as the acrid air irritated his throat, he sat up with a start. He thought he detected the odious odour of brimstone and he was appalled; he was afraid that the plague had returned. Apprehensive, he hurriedly aroused Christopher who was sleeping soundly in the next room.

Christopher was dreaming of the dome he was designing for St. Paul's—it was six days after he had presented his plans, and in the interval he had thought of little else. He was startled by Daniel's fear. He wished he could go back to sleep and his happy dream of a perfectly proportioned cathedral. But Daniel was determined to find out where the smoke was coming from, so he said, trying to be reassuring, "Smoke isn't unusual in London, there are so many fires in the city, mostly at night. While there is no need for heat this second day of September, wood and coal are burnt for so many purposes that a fire can start at any moment."

"This is different. The smoke smell is very strong. There is something evil about it. It could be brimstone. I'm going to look."

"You've become nervous since the plague. Next you will tell me that you believe Mother Shipton's prophecy: '*London in sixty-six will be burnt to ashes as punishment for her sins.*' That is a stupid superstition."

"Whatever you do, I'm going to take a closer look. Now, if London is going to be afflicted, I want to know in time to get out."

Reluctantly, but prompted by Daniel's urgency, Christopher followed him to the highest part of the house, the attic, threw open the window, sniffed the air and said positively, "It is not brimstone. Scarburgh used that on me years ago and I've never forgotten it. That was such a foul odour. This smell is more like burning wood."

Dawn was near and there was a red haze in the east and Daniel said, "It is close to London Bridge. I can't tell if it is the sunrise or a fire."

"It could be a fire. The wind is strong and we have had one hot, dry day after another. Much of the city is a tinder box."

"The weather is the same as when the plague occurred. Do you notice how the glow is spreading? It is not the right shape for a sunrise."

"But the city is very quiet. There are no sounds of trouble."

"Perhaps, because it is a Sunday morning. Everybody is asleep."

"An excellent idea. If it is a fire it should be put out quickly, for it is by the river, where the means of quenching it are best."

Daniel couldn't close his eyes after Christopher went back to bed. He sat by the attic window and even when the sun rose and assumed its natural shape, the glow in the east grew, faster as the minutes passed. The sky was clear and sunny, a blue and white sky except for the spreading red haze. It was quite far away, he thought, but the width and height of the glow was increasing. He was sure now that it was a fire and he decided that it could be a serious one—it could be seen at such a distance.

He wondered if it had reached London Bridge. He eagerly welcomed Christopher who joined him at nine o'clock that morning; he was anxious to discuss this fire with his friend. It wasn't like Christopher to sleep that late, and he didn't want to press him, but the rapid growth of the glow was worrying. In the last hour it had spread across a considerable portion of the eastern London sky and the acrid smell of the smoke had become much stronger and he couldn't see the sun.

Christopher still didn't share his apprehension, but he admitted that if it were a fire, it could be a big one, and he added, "There is much wood but very little stone about the bridge. It is the most inflammable part of the city. Let us go to St. Paul's, where we can see better."

At St. Paul's there were the usual worshippers and Dean Sancroft was conducting the services. Christopher didn't ask Daniel to join him inside, aware he would be uncomfortable in a pew, but suggested, "Why don't you visit Pepys? He will know what is happening. He knows almost everything that occurs in London. You can ascertain how dangerous this fire is."

"Then you agree that I'm right to be apprehensive?"

"I agree we must observe carefully before we jump to any conclusions."

"The glow is the largest I've ever seen and the smoke is heavy."

"I'll see what measures have been taken to protect St. Paul's, although I doubt it will spread this far. We've had many serious fires in London, but none have threatened the cathedral."

"Here I can see the flames and they are many feet high."

"I'll meet you back at Fetter Lane. And be careful. Since our Navy burned a Dutch town recently, this will be blamed on the Dutch."

"Don't worry, I'll assume my best Westminster School accent."

"When you become angry, you lose it."

"I'll stay calm. Are you going to attend the services?"

"Of course. Sancroft isn't a Donne, but he is a sincere preacher."

The Dean was occupied with a different text than Christopher expected. He thought Sancroft would give thanks for the planned rebirth of St. Paul's. Instead, as Christopher sat down, shivering at the decay about him, the Dean's voice took on an unexpected severity, almost contempt.

"*Some hours ago a fierce fire started in the neighbourhood of London Bridge and it is reported, so swiftly does it burn, that it was set by Papists, Fanatics, Nonconformists, the French or the Dutch. But this is a devious way of avoiding our responsibility to God. We must repudiate all charges of incendiarism. Dream no more of grenades or fire-balls, or the rest of these mischiefs. Search no more for scapegoats, for incendiaries, Dutch or French. The Dutch pride and the French vanity and the rest of their sins, which we are so fond of, are infinitely more dangerous to us, than the enmity of either nation, for we have made God our enemy, too. If you would find the incendiary, turn your eyes inward. There lurks the devil, the fire-maker. If this conflagration is as fearful as reputed, it is the afflicting hand of God in judgment upon us for our sins.*"

Christopher wondered why fire was regarded as the instrument of the devil, it warmed a man, cooked his food, lit the world, was a form of life. But he listened intently to Sancroft as the Dean resumed his sermon.

"When Donne, one of my recent predecessors, was accused of profaning his office of Dean with poetry, he replied, '*As we consider with a religious seriousness the manifold weaknesses of the strongest devotions in time of prayers, it is a sad consideration. I throw myself down in my chamber and I invite God and His angels there, and yet when they are there I neglect Him and His angels for the noise of a fly, for the rattling of a coach, for the whining of a door. I talk on, in the same posture of prayer; eyes lifted up, knees bowed down, as though I prayed to God. And if God or His angels should ask me when I thought last of God in that prayer, I cannot tell. Sometimes I find that I had forgot what I was about, but when I began to forget it, I cannot tell. A memory of yesterday's pleasures, a fear of tomorrow's dangers, a straw under my knees, a noise in my ear, a light in my eye, an anything, a nothing, a fancy, troubles me in my prayer. There is nothing, nothing in spiritual things perfect in this world.'"*

Sancroft paused, then said, "Prayer is not just a refuge, not just a bowed knee, but what is in our hearts. Otherwise, we are composed only of straw and will burn on earth as in hell, and perhaps more fiercely here."

Yet how can I avoid looking at the walls of the cathedral? thought Christopher, they are in such grievous need.

He told Sancroft, "We should remove the scaffolds. One stray spark could ignite them and bring St. Paul's down on our ears."

The Dean listened intently, but he replied, "To remove the scaffolds I have to obtain permission from the Archbishop and he is in Oxford now, and there are no workmen available, they have been pressed into the Navy. Doctor, would it help if we soaked the wood with water?"

"It wouldn't help enough. The sun and fire will dry the wood quickly."

Christopher stepped outside. Only an hour had passed since Daniel had left, but the sky had darkened in the east. He rubbed his eyes. They smarted from the smoke. He was irritated. He remembered Sancroft and Donne's words, but once again, his mind ran on bitterly, nothing will be done, nothing at all. Until it was too late.

Daniel was determined to find the truth about the extent and severity of the fire. As he hurried downhill to Thames Street, which ran along the river, he found the path blocked by the inhabitants from the burnt part of the city. They were fleeing from the flames, the fortunate moving their possessions in heavily loaded carts, the less fortunate carrying their belongings on their backs, the most fortunate able to hire boats. No one was helping anyone else; the struggle was to be first. He pushed his way through the mass flight and then he could not go any further on Thames Street. The smoke was thick, choking, blotting out the sun and much of the daylight; many houses were burning in front of him, not one by one as in an ordinary fire, but unnervingly, in groups of four, five, and sometimes ten; the fire coming directly at him, driven by a fierce east wind. He saw that part of London Bridge was burning, too, where there were houses on the northern end, but it still stood, although it was impassable, while many boats were on the river carrying people and their possessions away from their burning homes. Yet as Christopher had said, the fire was still a safe distance from St. Paul's, possibly half a mile away, but it was spreading in size and intensity and to go on to Pepys' house he had to circle around the flames by way of Cannon Street.

Pepys was irritated, frightened, and bursting with news. The instant he saw Daniel, he exclaimed, "Van Doorn, I wish you had brought Doctor Wren with you. As a surveyor he might have convinced Our Lord Mayor to pull down houses in the path of the blaze. That worthy will not listen to me."

"Is the fire that bad?"

"Worse. It burns everything in its path. Yet when I first warned him about the fire early this morning, he said contemptuously, '*It is nothing to fear. An old woman could put it out by pissing on it.*'"

"Did his Honour try?"

"He went back to bed. But later, when I was able to convince him of the seriousness of the fire and begged him to pull down houses between those on fire and those still untouched, so the blaze could be isolated, he cried out, '*Who will pay for the charge of rebuilding the houses we tear down? I dare not do it without the consent of the owners.*' Fool! I went to Whitehall and told the King and the Duke of York that unless His Majesty orders houses to be pulled down nothing will stop the fire. They agreed, but so far little has been done. Did Wren send you here?"

"Yes. He is concerned about St. Paul's."

"I passed it on my way back from Whitehall. It looks safe to me."

"Have you seen the Lord Mayor since?"

"Indeed. I gave him the King's message, but he cried, like a fainting woman, '*Lord! What can I do? I'm spent; people will not obey me. I've been pulling down houses, but the fire overtakes us faster than we can do it. And I'm exhausted, I must go home and sleep, or I will collapse.*'

"So he left me and I came home, everywhere seeing people distracted and no manner of means used to quench the fire. If it gets worse, I will have to convey all my possessions from here. Tell Wren, he is clever, that the wind is so strong it carries showers of sparks for long distances, dropping them on many buildings far from the fire. If something drastic isn't done soon, much of London could burn. The rush of people fleeing prevents the use of what appliances are available and the water supply at the river has been cut off by the fire at the foot of the bridge."

"And it is in the poorest part of London. Nothing will really be done until the rich mansions are threatened. How and where did it begin?"

"I believe near Fish Street, by London Bridge. The city is so tightly built there two people can hardly pass through it, you stretch your arms and you can touch each side, and the tops of the houses are just a foot away from each other." He halted, interrupted by shouting outside.

Daniel followed Pepys on to Seething Lane and they saw a mob beating a slight, elderly man with a bloodthirsty relish. He grabbed a burly young fellow who was hitting the prone victim and he asked, "What has he done?"

"He's a Dutchman."

"Is that why you are trying to kill him?"

"Someone heard his accent. They say two hundred Dutchmen and Frenchmen set fire to the city. So they can cause chaos and invade us."

"How can you be sure of this? There is no sign of an invasion."

"Everyone knows," said the dark, heavy-faced young man. "I hear there are four thousand Dutchmen and Frenchmen outside of London, waiting to seize it when the entire city is aflame. Every foreigner is dangerous."

"Where is your proof?" continued Daniel.

"The foreigner said this Sunday is the hottest day he has ever seen."

"It is very hot. But it could be, it is still early September."

"And someone saw him carrying fireballs. Even now, he hides them."

Daniel forced his way into the mob about the victim—they had paused to regain energy—and uncovered what he was carrying, some tennis balls.

The man whimpered in heavily accented English, "They are for the King. His Majesty will never order them again if I don't deliver them."

Daniel threw several balls into the air. They didn't explode and he said, "See, they are not fireballs! No one need be afraid."

In the diversion caused by Daniel's intervention the victim was able to escape. This enraged the mob and desperate to vent their rage on someone they turned on Daniel, who would have been beaten up next if Pepys hadn't pulled him into his house. Daniel was cut on the hand where the victim had scratched him in his effort to hold on to his precious tennis balls, but otherwise he was unscathed. Pepys advised him, "Wait until the crowd disperses. The worse the fire becomes the more terrified the citizens will become and the more they will blame the blaze on foreigners. Watch your step and don't try to protect any Dutchmen. With your accent you could be mistaken for one."

"Why is the mob so overwrought? The fire is a natural disaster."

Pepys said piously, "Their wrath is the will of God."

At Fetter Lane that night Daniel told Christopher what he had learned and his friend replied, "The real reason why the Lord Mayor doesn't want to tear down any buildings is the City law that says: '*Any one destroying another man's property must pay the cost of rebuilding it.*'"

Christopher decided the best spot to judge the size and severity of the fire was at the Bankside on the south side of the Thames. He and Daniel hired a boat, although the waterman demanded an excessive fee to row them across the river. This neighbourhood along the south bank of the Thames was filled with thieves and prostitutes, but also, Christopher recalled, where Shakespeare's theatre, the Globe, had stood until it had been destroyed by fire about fifty years ago. Then, as he stood directly opposite St. Paul's and its silhouette was illuminated by the flames, although they were still quite a distance away from the cathedral, Christopher thought, Very lovely, My Lord, I can see Your temple precisely, I must make it worthy of You, a treasure beyond price.

The fire had grown so much since Daniel had observed it this afternoon he felt it had become a living presence, an animate being.

He said this to Christopher who replied, "Yes, and a natural force."

They were silent, amazed by the speed with which the fire had spread.

But, Christopher told himself, he could not hide his head before such an impending disaster and he said, "I've never seen a fire as fierce as this one, and still the blaze moves west, fanned by the wind."

Daniel noted, "And the wind is especially strong by the river. That is why it took hold here and is spreading so rapidly."

Christopher said angrily, "Another reason is that Fish Hill Street and Pudding Lane are so densely constructed, most of the buildings are of timber, coated with pitch and plaster, which catches fire quickly and burns with a devouring flame. Even at this distance you can see that no barriers are being built to halt the fire, no houses are being blown up or torn down to isolate it, as if everyone is waiting for it to burn itself out, or for the wind to slacken or end. But the wind grows stronger, particularly from the east and if it becomes northerly most of London could ignite, it is such a wooden city." Then he paused in wonder, for despite his forebodings and the savage fury of the fire, it possessed a natural force that he had to respect, and even, in a way, admire.

Daniel said, "It has grandeur with all its terror. Doesn't it?"

Christopher felt guilty that his friend had sensed his awe and he said, "It is a fearful spectacle. London feeds the fire rather than foils it. If it ever reaches Cheapside the cathedral could be doomed."

Neither of them slept that night. Daniel heard Christopher tossing in the next room, which was not like him—his friend was usually a sound sleeper, while he couldn't fall asleep. Finally, compelled as a moth hovering about a flame, Daniel got out of bed and sat by the attic window and stared at the widening glow in the east. It was impossible to tell when the sun rose this Monday morning, for while the sky lightened eventually, the brightness of the flames and the dense yellow smoke was nightmarish and obscured the sun. Yet Daniel, looking toward Whitehall, where there was no fire, saw that there were no clouds in the sky, and that, apart from the conflagration, it was a warm, sunny, beautiful day.

Christopher joined him at the window and said, "It is a fire like we have never seen before. We must go to St. Paul's and warn them, and do what we can to prevent the cathedral from burning."

"I don't think you can prevent that if the fire continues to grow."

"Perhaps. But we must do what we can. There is real danger now."

They hurried down the Fleet and on to Ludgate Street and mounted the hill leading to St. Paul's and Christopher was upset that the exodus of people had turned upon the cathedral. The King had ordered that no carts could enter London, so the streets of the city would be free for his soldiers to fight the fire. Thus, the people who had been driven from their homes by the fire and who had been unable to flee the city with their goods, were storing them in St. Paul's, assuming that such a sacred, long-standing, powerfully-built cathedral would be secure from any fire.

Christopher didn't share their faith, and he shouted, "St. Paul's is a frail refuge and not to be trusted in its present condition!"

No one heeded him in their need to preserve themselves and he looked for Sancroft. He found the Dean in the nave of St. Paul's arguing with a group of excited, middle-aged men. Before he could suggest that those putting their goods into St. Paul's should be stopped—it would add to the danger to the cathedral—the Dean said, "The booksellers who keep their books on Paternoster Row want to store them in St. Paul's, but I'm not sure it is safe. Doctor, what do you think?"

"I'm not sure anything is safe here. The wind is turning north."

One of the booksellers, a stout, swarthy man, stated, "We have no choice. Our stock is too large to be conveyed elsewhere, it contains the richness of centuries, and no carts are available. If we put our books into St. Faith's, which is under St. Paul's, they will be safe."

St. Faith's was not the ideal refuge, thought Christopher, but it was better than the exposed Paternoster Row. This old, small church under the choir of the cathedral might shield the books if the fire reached here, although its Gothic vaulting was in a state of poor repair.

None of the booksellers were waiting for him to decide, for when the Dean said, "I sympathise with your problem," they assumed Sancroft agreed and began to store their books in this church under St. Paul's.

Daniel knew of the existence of St. Faith's, but he had not seen it before. He found it a curiosity, more like a crypt and cellar of St. Paul's than a church in its own right. He was oppressed that the roof above his head was the floor of the cathedral, and he was amazed by the vast number of books the booksellers were storing here. The Dean said, "This is the safest place in London," but he didn't agree. The Gothic vaulting was worn and decayed in many places and he saw cracks in parts of the roof. And Christopher was surveying St. Faith's to make sure that this ancient church was free of inflammable material, although it was evident that these books, most of them old, were very inflammable.

After they returned to the outside of St. Paul's, Daniel said this to Christopher, who nodded and added, "But the booksellers are convinced that the fire cannot reach below ground and I can't change them. They believe, like those storing their goods here, that this church is invulnerable."

"Do you think so?"

"It is very vulnerable." He turned to Sancroft, who was relieved that the problem of the booksellers had been settled, and asked him, "Dean, has there been anything new on my recommendations for repairs?"

"Be patient. Rome wasn't built quickly. Would you investigate the direction of the fire? It appears to be changing, moving north-easterly, invading the City. I will remain here as long as the danger lasts."

When Christopher saw that the Royal Exchange had caught fire he felt that the blaze was out of control, for this was one of the vital buildings in London and the heart of the City. He realised, with a sickening sense of impending disaster, this was no longer a riverside fire but was moving swiftly across the entire city. Threadneedle, Cornhill, and Lombard Streets were burning fiercely, and most frighteningly, the wind had swung toward the north with renewed vigour, and the flames were spreading with an insidious yet insatiable inevitability. He didn't like what this portended. He felt better when he came upon the King's own regiment and the Duke of York at a fire post around the Exchange that the King had established, and saw Charles himself and York order a squad of soldiers to pull down the buildings about the Royal Exchange.

Charles led them personally as his soldiers fixed their long thirty-foot fire hooks to the ridge beams of the burning buildings and pulled down the fragile timber. But even as this was done successfully and the wood fell with a shattering crash, the fire leaped over the cleared space and caught hold of the structure they were seeking to protect. Charles, still determined to bring order out of the confusion dominating the Exchange, dismounted and commanded water to be thrown on the burning building. And as the line formed to handle the buckets of water from hand to hand, the King strode up and down the length of it, exhorting, demanding, encouraging, and sometimes carrying a bucket of water himself to lead by example. York remained on his horse, saying he could see better from this position; Christopher noticed it was Charles who was taking the risks, not his brother. The King's lace sleeves caught fire from flying sparks and he put that out impatiently; his face grew black with dirt and soot; then he noticed Christopher and Daniel and called them over.

Charles stood before the burning Exchange—the water being thrown on it was not halting the expanding flames at all—and he asked urgently, "Doctor, you are a surveyor, is there anything else we can still do?"

York rode up and advised, "Charles, blow up the buildings around it."

"Wren, what do you think of this proposal? Will it help?"

"Sir, it is too late to save the Exchange, there is too much wood in it and the fire is too advanced. But if you build fire breaks on Cheapside, you might save the rest of London, particularly St. Paul's."

"Nonsense!" exclaimed the Duke. "I can still save the Exchange!"

Christopher said, "Begging your pardon, Your Majesty, but it will be futile, it will waste time and energy that could be used elsewhere better."

Daniel agreed, but Charles ordered York to blow up all the buildings around the Exchange. Gunpowder was laid down but before it could be lit properly a spark fell on it and the gunpowder exploded with a wild, uncontrolled fury, barely missing Charles, York, and the others.

Charles shrugged and he didn't move, although more sparks carried by the high wind fell on him, York, Christopher, and Daniel.

One grazed Daniel's hand and he felt terror at the possibility of losing his ability to draw and he was relieved that it left only a slight burn. Christopher brushed his off; York rode out of danger; Charles continued to disregard the sparks and he strode closer to the Exchange.

Christopher thought, It was as if Charles' rule over his kingdom depended on halting the fire, the King must force the fire to halt if he was to retain his sovereignty over the people—there was no alternative.

Christopher followed Charles in his effort to halt the blaze, then York joined them, not to be outdone by a commoner. But suddenly, all of them, even the King, had to retreat hurriedly, the air and the heat became so stifling. The entire Royal Exchange had caught fire and Christopher paused, still closer to the approaching flames than the others. Despite the murky, suffocating air he had to watch what was happening. He told himself, It will aid in the defence of St. Paul's, but he knew he was rationalising, It was his need to observe, to learn, to do.

The flames mounted to the highest part of the Exchange with a quick ferocity, as if seeking out the bell tower and the steeple with a calculated malice. Then the fire descended down to the bottom of the lowest vaults and cellars, marched along the galleries and walls with such a roaring noise that Christopher was deafened. It invaded every inch and corner of the long, four-storeyed Elizabethan building. Sheets of flame even leaped across the spacious quadrangle, Christopher noticed with awe, wondering if this fire could be halted anywhere, and now the entire Exchange, even its brick and stone, was covered with flame.

The fire threatened to singe the King as he stood transfixed in front of it and his brother had to pull him back to safety. The King looked wounded, as if the fire was a personal insult and challenge, but York said, "Charles, you mustn't worry unduly. Much of London still stands."

But as York spoke the statues that stood in their niches in the façade of the Exchange in glorious splendour fell down on their faces. All those of the Kings of England shattered into many pieces with a dreadful clatter. Even Charles was shaken, for the only statue that survived unbroken was that of the founder of the Exchange, Sir Thomas Gresham.

York cried, "An omen! That the Exchange will survive even this fire!"

Charles thought, No one could foretell now what would happen. Then, as if to regain control of himself and his Kingdom, he said, "We must stop the fire elsewhere. Jamie, where is the most peril now?"

York said, "Along the river. There it still spreads west with awful speed. Couriers tell me that Billingsgate is threatened and Baynard's Castle, in spite of all the stone in its structure. If the flames move any further west, Whitehall itself could be threatened."

As Charles ordered the soldiers to follow York, Christopher said, "Your Majesty, begging your pardon, but what about St. Paul's?"

"What about it, Doctor?" The King was annoyed.

"The Poultry has caught fire and Cheapside could be next. Cheapside is in a direct line with the cathedral."

Charles, once more the King despite his blackened face and singed clothes, marched to where he saw St. Paul's up the length of Cheapside. He stood so that his height dominated everyone about him, especially the short Christopher Wren, and he stated, "The incline on Cheapside will halt the flames. They will not burn up hill."

"Sir, that hasn't halted the fire so far. And the incline is slight."

"Wren, you mustn't allow your enthusiasm for St. Paul's to bias your judgment. Jamie, we must prevent the fire from reaching Whitehall."

Soon after Charles and York started for Baynard's Castle, where they were determined to halt the fire along the river, the flames began to creep up The Poultry toward Cheapside. Christopher reported this to the waiting Sancroft and added, "The flames are coming in our direction now. Dean, if Cheapside catches fire, St. Paul's will be next."

"You're too pessimistic. The fire is much stronger along the Thames."

"That is what the King and York say, but it has made a circular sweep in the past twenty-four hours. It moves freely through the city now."

"It will stop on Cheapside," Sancroft said confidently. "Most of the houses on Cheapside are owned by rich merchants and are built of stone. You know, as a surveyor, they will not burn like the poor wood structures along the river. They will be a formidable obstacle to the flames."

"But not insurmountable. This fire will no longer stop of itself."

"Perhaps the wind will change. That would do the trick. Doctor, I must take care of the people who have come here for divine guidance."

Christopher and Daniel climbed up the scaffold on the southeastern side of St. Paul's to see how far and fast the fire was moving through London. Night had come but much of the city to the south and east of St. Paul's was brightly lit. They were stunned to see that London was burning in a vast curving arc from Baynard's Castle to The Poultry. Christopher was alarmed that Paul's Wharf and Blackfriars, below St. Paul's on the south, were starting to burn. He thought sadly, The fire was reaching out to devour the cathedral on two, perhaps three sides, and there were flames everywhere in front of him.

"Good heavens!" Daniel said, "It will take more than gunpowder and a pair of hands to halt this blaze, it burns with such fury, like hell."

Christopher asked suddenly, "Daniel, do you believe in hell?"

What the devil could he say to a friend who believed in God, thought Daniel, but he shrugged and said, "If there is a hell, it must look like this fire." The moon, which he had seen last night, was no longer visible in the yellow glare and the thick smoke. Yet where London burned and much of it was burning this Monday night, he reflected unhappily, it was as light as day. "Christopher, do you think God caused this fire?"

"Do you really mean that?" The usually calm Christopher was upset.

"Why not? Many are blaming the fire on God. And in some ways it does have grandeur. As if a new kind of sunset is being painted."

"Grandeur? When it destroys everything in its path?"

"Yet even as it does, even as I fear it, even as I know it can end all of us, even London, I find myself admiring its beauty and magnificence."

"I find it hard to believe anything is beautiful that destroys."

"However I worry about its consequences it fascinates me."

"Don't tell anyone how you feel. They will blame the fire on you."

"I won't." But now Christopher wasn't listening to him and he asked anxiously, "Did I offend you? Did I say something wrong?"

"I've been thinking how I should rebuild the burnt out part of London. A new city has been in my mind. I've thought about this a long time."

"Then you've expected St. Paul's to be destroyed?"

"No. The last thing I want is to see the old church burned. It needs such effort to obtain permission to have a dome on St. Paul's, can you imagine what effort it would take to construct a whole new cathedral!" Christopher laughed ruefully. "That would require a lifetime. More years than I can spare." His tone grew more serious. "But with the burning of the city, much of London will have to be rebuilt. It will be a severe but a great challenge to a surveyor. If we survive this fire." His face became sombre as the sky above Cheapside lit up with a bright orange flare of flame, then turned red and yellow, and fiery.

As the fire continued to spread Christopher couldn't sleep, he couldn't even try, and Daniel insisted on staying with him when Daniel saw how worried he was. Daniel thought, His friend must not be left alone, his friend was so determined to protect St. Paul's he was prepared to fight the blaze single-handed. Every hour Christopher surveyed the books in St. Faith's, still growing in number; the goods stored in St. Paul's, piled high and indiscriminately; the structure of the cathedral, the nave, choir, tower, vaults and scaffolds; the fire-fighting equipment, the axes, ladders, fire hooks, casks of water, leather buckets, portable cisterns mounted on wheels; and always, a long and careful survey of the burning city. Daniel went with him, helping him wherever he could. Yet nothing changed, Daniel thought, except to get worse. The fire was burning more fiercely each hour and London was becoming a vast charnel house.

Sancroft retired to the Deanery for the evening, exhausted from his labours, but Christopher awakened him at daybreak, for Cheapside had caught fire and a wall of flame was creeping slowly but inevitably toward them.

The Dean was surprised, and angry and disappointed, as if the fire was betraying him, but as he realised that Christopher's fears were justified, he agreed to help him in any way he could.

Christopher said, "We must blow up the buildings between the fire and St. Paul's. Create a fire break that not even sparks can be blown over."

"We can't," said the Dean. "Only the King has that authority."

Daniel said, "The King and York are concentrating their efforts at Blackfriars below us." He had looked from a scaffold on his own, sensing that Christopher could use such information. "Nothing is being done on Cheapside. It is obvious the King is afraid Whitehall will burn next."

"Dean, could you use the cathedral equipment to make a fire break?"

"Doctor, you mustn't be so persistent. It is unseemly."

Christopher shook his head in despair.

"You've done your best. We must trust the will of God. Maybe He will alter the course of the fire, or the wind will die down, or the stone houses will not burn. Why don't you rest, things will be easier then?"

Christopher tried to nap in the Deanery and Daniel joined him, but after several hours he was aroused by a messenger from Sancroft. He was almost grateful, for he had been unable to sleep. But the news was dire.

The messenger said, "St. Mary-le-Bow is on fire."

Christopher told Daniel, "It is the most vital parish church in London, second in importance only to St. Paul's. Built in the reign of William the Conqueror, shortly after 1066, its Caen stone is considered safe from fire. Its bells are the sound of London itself. It is said, '*To be born within the sound of Bow Bells is to be the true*

Londoner.' My worst fears are being realised. It is halfway up Cheapside."

Christopher hurried to the eastern end of St. Paul's and saw that the news was grave indeed. The steeple of St. Mary-le-Bow—one of the landmarks of London—was aflame. He felt the heat of the approaching fire, although it was still some distance away. But it was moving relentlessly, and now it was near Bread Street, where, he recalled, John Milton lived. He wondered whether the poet was staying there now.

Daniel had him by the arm. "Sancroft wants to see you. Pratt, May, and Webb are here, and he wants you to hear their suggestions."

"Are there any new ones to make? The fire comes closer as we talk."

Hour by hour that was evident. It was the only thing on which all the surveyors agreed. Pratt stated, "St. Paul's should be abandoned." Christopher opposed that and said, "We must fight the fire with any means that are available;" and this caused May to cry out, "How much will it cost?" While Webb declared, "None of these methods will work. We must make a fire break by separating the east end of the cathedral from the centre, and then, afterwards, I will build a portico on it like Jones' masterpiece on the west front. It will give St. Paul's a better face."

And again, Daniel observed, nothing was being done. The Dean grew confused; Pratt became more vehement; Webb turned surly when he was ignored; May threw up his hands in horror at the destruction the fire was doing to the King's precious revenues; and Christopher, unable to listen to this bickering while London burned, to this utter waste of time, hours had passed in a kind of paralysis, left all of them, even Daniel.

He hurried to where Paul's Cross had stood for centuries in the north-east corner of the cathedral grounds until the Puritans had torn it down during the Commonwealth. He told himself that he had come here to view the fire which was approaching from the north now, in addition to from the east and south, but somehow, he hoped to find consolation here. Paul's Cross had been the pulpit of St. Paul's and London. He wondered why the Puritans had razed it; then he realised that to the Dissenters it was a cross, and a cross was clearly, unmistakably, Popish.

Several preachers were exhorting their listeners where the cross had been, but Christopher's attention was attracted by the tremendous spread of the fire. He knew that it was night again, for the sky had darkened behind him, but the fire burned so brightly that now everything in front of him was as light as day. Seconds, minutes, hours, and days had lost their shape and significance and all that mattered was the conflagration. Tuesday had passed in a maddening blur of smoke, flame, and ruin and he had lost track of the time and all he was able to count was the destruction. The fire was far vaster and fiercer than on Monday, many times worse, he thought with horror, it had increased tenfold. Not only was the Royal Exchange gone, but many churches, hospitals, public buildings, monuments, and thousands of houses, so much of London reduced to ashes and the sky a flaming red, as if heaven were on fire, and if it didn't abate there might not be anything left. He felt that hell was at hand.

The blaze had swung around to the north and was on three sides now, but the immediate peril was from the east and Cheapside. Bread Street and St. Mary-le-Bow's had vanished in a wall of flame and most of Cheapside had been consumed and now the fire was scarcely a hundred yards away.

Christopher thought, The only saviour was rain, such a downpour like the flood, that would make St. Paul's his Noah's Ark, rain that not even wet England had ever experienced; but it hadn't rained for a long time; this Tuesday was hot and dry as had been all the days lately, another deadly dry day. He wondered if any of London would be left after this fire finished. He told himself, This blaze was a seething holocaust such as no one had ever seen, not even a Nero had witnessed such a fire. *His* London was much larger and greater than Nero's Rome. So much of the blood, history, and character of London was perishing before his eyes. He felt his eyes fill with tears. But he couldn't retreat; he was on duty; St. Paul's was his responsibility, even if he never put a stone here.

His reverie was interrupted by Daniel, who was worried about him. Daniel looked so glad to find him unhurt, he didn't have the heart to reproach his friend for intruding on his privacy. He was grateful for Daniel's help and support; Daniel hadn't questioned his judgment, even when his friend didn't agree with him. But before they could speak to each other a loud, dominating voice caught their attention.

A gaunt, hollow-eyed, haunted-looking preacher declared, "Such unnatural practices have afflicted our country with the return of the Stuarts, it is inevitable that God would see fit to punish us for our sins. He has brought war and plague upon us, and now fire, for we have become another Sodom and Gomorrah, and only if we return to Him, to our true Presbyterian faith, free from idolatry, will we be redeemed. If we do not heed Him, all of our world will be laid waste and destroyed."

A commotion erupted in his audience as a man shouted, "The fire is not the will of God, but a Popish plot, aided by the Dutch and French. They, not the hand of God, set London ablaze with their powder and fire balls."

Another listener yelled, "False! The fire has come because you have ignored His teachings, and so the Archangel Gabriel has brought the flames to smite you until you love God in the true Roman faith."

Daniel said to Christopher, "They are mad."

"And accomplish nothing. It is absurd. Yet many share their views."

A squad of the King's guard approached and the preacher and his audience vanished. A moment later Charles and York arrived, and Charles said, "Doctor Wren, Dean Sancroft says you have judged the course of the fire correctly. Where do you think it will strike next?"

"Here, sir. At St. Paul's."

"Then your views haven't changed," Charles said sharply.

The King had, thought Christopher, the lines in his face were deeper, the colour of his skin was more sallow, his thick lips were tighter. But he was still surprisingly relaxed in his elaborate satin doublet, lace, and plumed hat, and Christopher wondered what Charles was truly feeling. Although Charles was one man, he was also many, and a consummate actor.

York said, "Brother, we can do nothing here. Our soldiers are overworked and are needed elsewhere. It is too late to save St. Paul's."

Charles was not persuaded and he said, "Doctor, do what you can."

"Your Majesty, I need many men."

"Use these." Charles pointed to the soldiers protecting him.

"Sir, I need carpenters, too."

Charles shrugged, as if to say, What do I know about carpenters? What comfort could they be? But when he saw Christopher's persistence he said, "Doctor, we need God's help and love. And blessing. Especially now."

"Your Majesty, I also need trained men to pull down the scaffolds."

Daniel said, "Christopher, I investigated whether any carpenters are available, as you requested, and I am told they are all in the service of the Royal Navy at Greenwich, Chatham, and Woolwich."

Charles turned to York and asked, "Can they be obtained quickly?"

"No, brother. They can't be spared. Whatever carpenters we have, are repairing our wounded ships to prepare for a Dutch invasion."

At that moment John Dolbein led a group of Westminster boys to the King. The vital, middle-aged Bishop of Rochester and Dean of Westminster, who had fought bravely during the civil war on the side of the King, had formed his pupils into regular ranks and they marched after him more skilfully than Charles' own guard. Dolbein kissed Charles' hand and said proudly, "Your Majesty, these boys, all King's Scholars, as I was, have saved the church of St. Dunstan in the East by fetching water and putting out the fire. Sir, they are prepared to do the same for St. Paul's."

"Very good," said Charles, "If they have Busby's permission."

"Of course, sir. I wouldn't dream of employing them if the Head Master had not approved. He would have come himself, but he has the ague."

Christopher looked at the dozen eager boys, and he found it hard to believe that he had been that young. Then he recalled how he had been part of the band who had defended Westminster Abbey from the Apprentice Boys and he wanted to warn them that rocks could fly here, too.

Charles cried out, "Hurry, Doctor! This dismal fire threatens us even as we stand here! It burns like no other in man's experience!"

Christopher saw that the entire horizon around St. Paul's except to the west had become a wall of flame. He felt like a general surrounded on all sides but at his back. Blackfriars, on fire all day, was spreading the flames from the south up what York had said was impregnable Ludgate Hill, and was threatening the high ground on which St. Paul's stood. To the north the fire was curving around St. Paul's in a direct line from Newgate to Old Bailey. And in front of them, where the peril was deadliest, Cheapside was being devoured by a mass of flame searing upwards and forwards into the sky and he heard it crackling mercilessly.

"Sir, may I blow up the houses still standing between us and the fire?"

York said, "Charles, we have no more gunpowder with us."

"Your Majesty, then we must tear them down with our fire hooks. To create a fire break. It is our only hope. Our last hope."

Charles motioned for Christopher to proceed and he ordered the King's Scholars and the soldiers to fetch the fire-fighting equipment. Daniel led them to it and they returned quickly with fire hooks, leather buckets, and cisterns of water. But before Christopher could use the equipment the remaining houses between the conflagration and St. Paul's were on fire in a rising crescendo of flame. He realised, The only thing he could do now to save St. Paul's was to bring down the scaffolds, although he had scant hope that would suffice. And even then he had to beg the King's permission, but it was granted. The King's Scholars were too short and frail to handle the fire hooks, so while he had them bring up the portable cisterns of water, he directed the soldiers to yank down the scaffold on the south-eastern side of St. Paul's, where the peril appeared most immediate. The scaffold shook a moment and seemed about to fall, and just as he sighed with relief, thinking, There might still be a chance to save St. Paul's, the fire hooks broke, rotted from age and disuse.

Daniel ordered the boys to throw water on the wood, but the cisterns were empty. Christopher felt weary, impotent, helpless. He hated such feelings and he longed to cry out in his anger.

One of the Westminster boys shouted—Christopher couldn't tell whether it was from excitement or anguish—"St. Paul's on fire!"

He stared upwards and saw that a board on the roof was burning, ignited by a spark blown by the fierce wind. But there should be no boards there, he thought angrily, it was contrary to sensible building precautions. Then he remembered that dry timber had been put above the stone vault of the roof where the lead had broken away while the Royal Commission had disagreed about what should be done to repair the damaged cathedral.

The fire was very small at the moment, just along the ridge of the board. He had an urge to climb the scaffold and stamp it out— he could still do it with his bare hands, although the climb would be difficult and dangerous. But as he placed a ladder against the scaffold to extinguish this fire Daniel halted him. Daniel ignored his anger and pointed upwards. Other wooden boards on the roof of St. Paul's were aflame and even as they looked the fire spread rapidly to the scaffold.

Ashamed of his lack of self-control, Christopher regained his composure and suggested, "Daniel, will you survey the condition of St. Faith's? The books are so inflammable. Perhaps they should be removed before it is too late. And the goods stored inside St. Paul's, too."

When Daniel did as he asked, he caressed the wood of the scaffold, thinking, Wood could be such a marvellous material for design, but now it was becoming an instrument of death. And then all the scaffolds caught fire and the entire cathedral was wrapped in flames.

Christopher and the others retreated to the west portico where Sancroft watched sadly, holding a Bible, praying, and muttering, "I am so troubled, and yet the fire burns so brightly I can read every line clearly."

"Sir, what about the books in St. Faith's?"

"The cathedral roof has collapsed and broken through the floor of St. Paul's and into St. Faith's, and with it many fiery embers. I've been told that all the books are burning. It is most melancholy."

But what of Daniel? Christopher thought anxiously.

Daniel reached the entrance to St. Faith's and came upon an

R

avalanche of molten lead running into the old church. Its roof was smashed by the falling debris from St. Paul's, and he backed out of both churches as they went up in flames.

Christopher cried out when he saw him, "Lord God, are you hurt?"

"A few scratches. No matter. Everything is ruined inside."

Wherever Christopher looked there was fire. He saw pigeons hovering about the windows of St. Paul's, as if they could not leave it, in spite of the danger. While he watched them the poor pigeons fell down, wings burnt, dying at his feet. He felt his skin blistering from the intense heat. It was becoming impossible to breathe. Molten lead swept toward him in a monstrous stream and forced him from the west portico.

Fire reached it and that saddened him. Jones' work was the part of St. Paul's he wanted most to preserve. But nothing could be saved now, he realised. Parts of the cathedral fell as he had predicted and its stones split off and flew about like grenadoes. He saw the King, York, Sancroft, and Daniel nearby; Bishop Dolbein had withdrawn the Westminster boys to safety and the King's guard had followed them.

Charles said, with a mixture of shock and awe, "This fire will reduce us to nothing if we don't halt it soon. Jamie, our only hope to save the rest of London is to blow up Fleet Street to Fetter Lane. If the blaze burns beyond there, Whitehall and all of the city will be gone."

The others followed him down Ludgate. It was the only escape left to them and they reached the bottom of the hill just in time, for a few moments later fire swept through Ludgate and closed the exit from St. Paul's.

Christopher heard the preacher who had predicted God's wrath snarl at the King, "Charles Stuart, when you are an honest man, God will halt His wrath. Let St. Paul's burn. Let her waste. The whore's cap is off!"

The preacher disappeared into the crowd before he could be caught.

Christopher remembered the pigeons who had died because they had refused to leave St. Paul's, and for an instant he thought that it was raining. Then he realised that his eyes were full of tears and grief. He paused when he was out of the reach of the fire and turned to take a last look at the old cathedral. Proud, imperfect St. Paul's had lived for centuries, it was a history of London, he reflected, and now it was dying. He stared where the cathedral was and saw a tower of flame.

You Can See Through Fire

You can see through fire
You can see through wood
You can see through
   whatever
is before you
when you can see through
the unimagined
   and still see

Stymean Karlen

31

You Can See Through Fire

IT WAS IMPOSSIBLE TO SLEEP THAT NIGHT. CHRISTOPHER AND DANIEL stood on the roof of the house at Fetter Lane and watched London burn. It was a fine evening, crisp and clear, perfect for visibility, except for the heavy clouds of smoke swirling over the city, and much of London was in their view. Christopher saw that the fire had spread from Bridewell on the south to Holborn Bridge on the north and as far east as the Tower, although he couldn't tell whether this fortress-prison was burning.

Daniel, more concerned with the immediate danger, warned, "The flames are nearing Fetter Lane. The dry, timber-framed buildings on the crowded, narrow Fleet are burning like tinder and the fire is still spreading fast."

"I wonder if the King knows this?"

"Let us see. In another hour the flames could reach here."

Christopher felt better as daylight arrived as they descended to the street, and he noticed that Charles had ordered York to establish a fire post and a fire break at Shoe Lane, some distance from Fetter Lane.

Daniel said, "That won't help. The wind is too strong and it will carry the sparks over the fire break, as it has done often these last few days."

"The wind is slackening a little and veering to the south."

"Not enough to make any difference."

"Not yet. But it is a hopeful sign."

Daniel shrugged and thought, The King didn't think so. Charles had just ridden up to Shoe Lane, escorted by a few soldiers, and for once he wasn't autocratic and composed, but nervous and irresolute.

Charles asked York, who sat on a great white horse while he ordered soldiers to blow up the buildings on the Fleet from Shoe Lane to Fetter Lane. "Jamie, do you think this will help?" His voice was doubtful

"Eventually. We have to explore all the means at our disposal."

"We must halt the fire here. There isn't much of the city left to burn."

Christopher thought, Charles was very clever but now he looked baffled by forces he couldn't control or manoeuvre. Then, as if action was essential, he dismounted and handed gold guineas to the soldiers to keep them from wavering in their efforts to stop the fire. He ordered more water to be used and he passed the leather buckets as he had done at the Exchange. While he was spattered with soot, mud, and ashes, at this moment he was everything he had promised to be. But the flames leapt over the fire break and even Charles had to back away to avoid the falling timbers.

At Fetter Lane the blaze swung up the street and Daniel was frightened. His blessed paintings were threatened. He told this to Christopher, who was helping York establish a new fire break, and his friend said, "Take them to Scotland Yard. They should be safe there."

"You won't mind, Christopher? I don't want to desert you."

"You won't. I know what these paintings mean to you."

"What about your own possessions?"

"I've nothing I value there, except my designs for St. Paul's, and I'm not sure they are worth anything, now that the old cathedral is gone. And the clothes can be replaced. Go. Before it is too late. Before the King wants your services and you cannot refuse him."

"I'll take your designs, Christopher."

"Thank you." He put his arm around Daniel and then pushed him away.

Although Charles was absorbed in fighting the fire, he noticed Daniel's departure and asked Christopher, "Doctor, where is Van Doorn going?"

"To store some paintings he owns at Scotland Yard. That he values."

"Dutch ones, Doctor? By Rubens? Van Dyck?" Charles grew interested.

"No, sir. By Rembrandt."

"Oh, I see!" Charles' lips tightened.

Christopher couldn't tell from the King's enigmatic expression whether Charles knew Rembrandt's work or cared. He said, "Sir, begging your pardon, but shouldn't we be guiding the troops fighting the fire?"

"I've set the example. Enough is enough. And I've done what I can. Now it depends on the wind. Doctor, Van Doorn is a good servant, isn't he?"

"Sir, Mr. Van Doorn isn't a servant."

"Are you republicans?" Charles was surprised. "With your family?"

"Sir, we are friends."

"You are fortunate. I wish I had someone I could trust."

"Your Majesty, there is your brother."

"That is a comfort." Charles' tone was sarcastic.

"Daniel Van Doorn was at Westminster School with me."

"And many joined me in exile. I don't know whether it was to save my skin or theirs. When this dreadful calamity is over, you must submit your designs for a new London to me."

"I will be honoured, sir. I have thought much about a new London, even before this fire, and such plans are in my mind."

"An audience will be arranged when your designs are ready."

"Next week, Your Majesty?"

"So soon? The fire hasn't stopped burning yet, Doctor!"

"Sir, the truth of a new city is evident."

Charles nodded, thinking, His subjects must be diverted as quickly as possible, and the best way was a London rising renewed and rebuilt. He turned back to the flames moving up Fetter Lane and said more hopefully, "While the blaze still pushes forward, it burns more slowly." He was relieved that it was no longer spreading in the direction of Whitehall.

"Yes, sir. The wind is abating and changing to the south."

"Yet the vagaries of the wind are a frail thing to rely on, Doctor."

"Your Majesty, it may be all that is left."

Daniel wrapped the two paintings by Rembrandt into a neat bundle so they would seem like a simple package of clothing. He put Christopher's designs inside his doublet and tied them to his skin so he could not lose them. He did this hurriedly, for the empty Rowley house next door was burning, and as he left he told his friend what he had done. Christopher was advising soldiers to blow up the Rowley house, at the command of Charles, and he whispered, "Hurry, Daniel, while the way is still clear to Whitehall."

"What about yourself?"

"I'll get out if I have to. But I think we can halt the fire here. The houses beyond Sam's are of stone and Sam's will make a good fire break."

"Are you going to blow it up?" Daniel was stunned at the idea.

"If it will stop the fire. It doesn't really belong to me and Sam is gone and so is Anne. And with the wind altering and slackening, a fire break here might be effective. I will see you at Scotland Yard later."

York rode up and stated, pointing to Sam's house, "Doctor Wren,

His Majesty informed me that you need assistance, that you want to demolish this house and require soldiers and gunpowder."

"Yes, sir. If you are agreeable."

"My brother is King. Of course I agree. Is Van Doorn assisting?"

"No, sir. He is on the King's business." Christopher turned to Daniel and added, "Remember, Mr. Van Doorn, since you are in His Majesty's service, you must be careful." He pushed him away again, this time strongly and urgently, and set about to demolish the house that Sam had left him.

The Fleet at Fetter Lane was blocked by fire, so Daniel hurried north until he came to High Holborn. Then he turned west, circled Lincoln's Inn, and only when he reached Drury Lane, where there was no trace of the fire, did he feel more at ease. But the horror of the flames didn't decrease as he arrived at the Strand, the main route to the west, but grew worse.

A vast exodus from burning London was occurring on this highway. Much of the city was on the move here, Daniel observed, mostly on foot, many without anything, others carrying tremendous loads, some pulling carts, a few being conveyed in carts, and occasionally, but rather rarely, a lord riding in a coach. No one could travel quickly or easily in the press of the bodies and many appeared to Daniel to be more impelled by a fear of God than by a horror of the fire. He decided, for the sake of the paintings, that he had to endure the pushing and shoving, although he hated it. By now he was exhausted. He hadn't slept at all the past few days and he wondered how Christopher could continue working, yet when he had left him there had been animation in Christopher's eyes as his friend explained to the soldiers what had to be done on Fetter Lane.

He felt less sorry for himself as he saw mothers carrying babies in their arms, others with a sucking infant at their breast, a number who were pregnant and frantically seeking to protect their exposed bellies. There were the ill who were borne on a servant's back and those who couldn't afford such a service and who limped along, some so sick they could barely crawl. No one helped anyone else. Preservation was all that mattered. And to save their possessions. Many of those fleeing the fire could hardly be seen beneath the huge, heavy loads they bore on their backs. Yet in the next instant he saw burly porters, carrying small bundles as they forced their way through the crowd with loud curses, while the prosperous merchants who had hired them followed humbly, for the porters were the masters, bearing the merchants' prized possessions to safety.

At Charing Cross, just as Daniel felt better, for he was near Whitehall, two men moved to each side of him. He sensed it was deliberate; they knew each other. The one on his right was tall, about twenty-five, with narrow blue eyes and a quick step, while the other man was forty, short, stocky, and slower-gaited. Both of them wore old clothes, their shoes were worn and thin, and he wondered if they were vagabonds or thieves.

The younger one said to his companion, "Henry, our friend is in a hurry."

Henry replied, "Ralph, he must be on the King's business."

"I am," Daniel said curtly, and he sought to elude them by walking faster, only to find his path blocked by a commotion in front of him.

Ralph said, "It is nothing. They are only beating a Dutchman."

Henry said, "He must be one of those who started the fire."

Daniel asked indignantly, "Do you have any proof?"

Ralph said, "He is a foreigner. Where do you come from?"

A squad of the King's guards dispersed the mob and rescued the bleeding Dutchman, and Daniel thought of joining them. But they were marching into the city to fight the fire and he couldn't go with them because of the paintings, and with the arrival of the soldiers the two men had vanished.

He was relieved and he turned toward Whitehall with renewed energy. He was at the entrance to the forecourt of Scotland Yard when he heard footsteps behind him. He swung around and saw the two men close to him. The crowd was gone, having split off at Charing Cross, and he felt alone, for there were no other pedestrians on King Street.

Ralph said, "My, you are a nervous gentleman! What are you afraid of?"

"You are a gentleman, aren't you?" asked Henry.

"Yes," Daniel said sharply. "Why?"

Ralph said, "You're not very worthy. You have no servants."

"What do you want?" Daniel demanded angrily.

"What are you carrying?" Henry asked. "Is it that precious?"

"It is of no value except to me."

Ralph asked, "Are you really on the King's business?"

"Of course. Can't you see that I am going to Whitehall."

"You stopped at Scotland Yard. You carry that bundle close to you."

"It contains clothes."

"You don't look like you care that much for clothes. You are dressed like a gentleman, but indifferently."

"I got dirty fighting the fire. For the King, at Fetter Lane."

"It hasn't gone that far yet, has it, Henry?" Henry nodded, and Ralph continued, "We know the ways of Court. A gentleman or a lord would never allow his clothes to get soiled. I served a Duke as a groom and Henry was a scrivener for one of the King's mistresses.

R*

He wrote all her letters. Until the King's favour was enticed elsewhere. What do you really have in that bundle? Gold, silver plate,
jewels? A gentleman would never carry his own clothes and you
hold it as if it is mighty precious."

"I told you. It is clothes. And two pictures." Daniel grew irate
despite Christopher's warnings and his voice lost his careful English
accent and he added furiously, "You will suffer if you touch me!"

"Without a sword?" Ralph said sceptically. "What gentlemen
there are on the streets today carry swords for their own protection
or employ armed companions, but you are unarmed, alone. Are
you Dutch?"

"What would I be doing here if I were Dutch?"

"Your accent isn't English. Henry, see what he is hiding."

Evelyn approached with another squad of the King's guards.
When he saw Daniel disputing with the two men—obviously
rogues from their dress, he decided—he approached them, and with
the soldiers at his back, he asked, "Mr. Van Doorn, have you
seen Doctor Wren recently?"

"I'm performing a service for him."

"On His Majesty's business?"

"Yes. Doctor Wren is aiding the King at Fetter Lane."

"That is my destination, too. I have vital matters to discuss with
His Majesty. Do you want these scoundrels arrested?"

Ralph and Henry were abject now and the former said, "My
Lord, we were simply trying to aid this gentleman to find his way."

Evelyn said sharply, "I'm certain Mr. Van Doorn knows his
way here."

"I do, Mr. Evelyn. I'm going to Doctor Wren's residence here."

"Say the word and I will have them imprisoned in Newgate."

"Newgate, begging your pardon, sir," said Ralph, "has burned
down."

"We can find another jail. What do you say, Mr. Van Doorn?"

Daniel hesitated. Both men regarded him imploringly and after
all, he thought, although they had been threatening they had not
attacked him. And once they were jailed they could sicken or starve
or suffer an even worse fate, and now that he was at Scotland Yard
in broad daylight he was safe, and Christopher made a virtue of
being reasonable. He said, "Let them go, Mr. Evelyn, as long as
they keep away from me."

Evelyn looked dubious about this display of mercy, but Ralph
exclaimed, "We will, Great sir!" and Henry cried, "It will be a
noble act!" and when Daniel nodded and added, "Doctor Wren
would prefer that we be kind," Evelyn said strongly to the cringing
men, "I wouldn't be so forgiving and easy, but if this is Doctor
Wren and Mr. Van Doorn's wish, so be it." He waved an im-

perious hand and declared, "Be gone. Before I change my mind."
He pointed to Charing Cross and Ralph and Henry hurried away.

"Wicked men," Evelyn said to Daniel. "I must represent to His
Majesty the case of the French and Dutch prisoners of war, they
are in such a pitiable state. And aid him in his efforts to subdue
the flames."

"He is at Fetter Lane off the Fleet. With York and Doctor Wren."

"I will help them quench the fire there. I am particularly concerned with the hospital of St. Bartholomew, near Smithfield,
where there are many sick and wounded in my care. The impetuous
fire hasn't reached it yet, and it would be grievous if it does. They
cannot flee as the others can. Did you see the burning of St. Paul's?
Doctor Wren is so devoted to it."

"Yes. He tried to halt it. But that was impossible."

"I know," Evelyn said passionately. "I saw the burning of St.
Paul's, too. I thought Guy Fawkes had returned, the fire exploded
with such fury, stones splitting off and flying about like grenadoes,
the roof falling, walls collapsing, timber crashing. It was a sight
such as the world has not seen since its foundation. Ten thousand
houses all in one flame. It was like Sodom, Troy. As I viewed
it last night I thought the final hour of the world had come, nothing
seemed to satisfy the appetite of the fire. The flames could be seen
for fifty miles. It was as if the hand of God was purging London
of its sins. We can not expect the help of men to halt it, only
the Almighty power of God can save us. And perhaps that is so,
for today it has pleased God to abate the wind, and to give us a
King whose bravery and industry have lessened the spread of the
fire."

"Thank you for your aid, Mr. Evelyn. It was gracious of you."

"Are you sure you are safe? That these rogues won't return?"

"I'm just a few feet from the house. The key is already in my
hand."

"Good. I must go to the King and Doctor Wren. Charles consults
me on many matters, I have a superior knowledge of architecture,
and I am a member of the Commission to reform London. My
services are much in demand."

Daniel put the key in the lock, but it stuck instead of opening
the door easily as he expected. He knocked, but there was no
response. He thought, The housekeeper must have fled, afraid of the
fire. He was still struggling with the key and the lock when he
heard someone call him.

"Van Doorn?"

"Yes." He instinctively answered and turned around to see who
it was.

Ralph and Henry stood behind him, with ten men. A few minutes had passed since Evelyn had left him and he realised they had planned slyly, there was no one else in Scotland Yard except the mob with them.

"See!" Ralph shouted, "I told you he was Dutch! His name *is* Van Doorn!"

The mob surged toward Daniel and he shouted back, "As I told you, I am in the King's service and this bundle contains only paintings."

Ralph pulled the package away from him and tore off the wrapping. When he saw it was two paintings in his disappointment and rage he went to smash them while the several members of the crowd pinned Daniel's arms.

But Henry, who knew about paintings, said, "Let me see them first!"

Daniel said, "They're by Rembrandt van Rijn."

Ralph repeated, "See, he is a Dutchman, as I told you."

The mob closed in on Daniel, who pleaded, "Don't harm the pictures!"

"Quiet!" yelled Ralph. "Why are they valuable, as you claim?"

"Rembrandt is a friend of mine."

This angered the mob more, while Henry, who examined the paintings, said, "They're worthless. They're dirty, dark, of a couple of old men."

"One of them is of St. Paul," Daniel declared frantically.

"He is mad," said Henry. "Both subjects are Dutchmen. I can tell from their appearance. I met several Dutchmen when I was at Court."

"May I have the pictures back? Since, as you say, they are worthless."

"Why do you want them then?" Henry asked.

Daniel knew that if he said why it could be an admission that he was Dutch, but it seemed the only way to regain the paintings. He explained, "The other man is my father. It is all of him that I possess."

For a minute the crowd appeared moved by his feeling, then Ralph said, "This proves that he is Dutch. One of those who started the fire."

The mob attacked Daniel and as he sought to protect himself and to retrieve the paintings he was hammered to the ground. He screamed for help and he heard a furious clatter on the cobblestones like people running. He couldn't tell how much time passed as he lay on the ground. He put his hand to his head and it was covered with blood and he realised he was bleeding profusely where he had been hit on the forehead.

He looked up and he saw Denham standing over him, supported by four footmen armed with swords. All of the mob were gone and so were the paintings. He wanted to die, the paintings were himself, the best part of his person, without them he felt only half a human.

Denham said, "Van Doorn, you are fortunate I heard your screams. I thought it was my wife. She is afraid someone wants to kill her. I tell her that is foolish, but she will not heed me. Did you lose something?"

"I was robbed of two paintings."

"Is that all? These days you are fortunate you didn't lose your life."

"They are irreplaceable. By Rembrandt."

Denham shrugged and said, "That is not likely."

"Do you know his work?"

"Vaguely. But only a poem is worth preserving. However, if it is any comfort, these scoundrels don't know anything about paintings."

"Then they could be destroyed. If they are not already."

"So they will not profit from their knavery. That should please you."

"I would rather they have the paintings, if it will keep them alive."

Denham looked at Daniel as if he were mad, but said, "You are in an awful state. You should clean the blood off your face. It is unclean."

After Daniel was within the safety and privacy of the house, his key finally opening the recalcitrant lock, he held his head in his hands and wept. Not knowing what had happened to the paintings was, in a way, the worst blow of all. Not knowing what to do next, what to trust, who was to blame, was too much to endure. And suddenly he had a new guilt. He felt Christopher's designs against his skin and he realised that he had forgotten about them. But while he was grateful that they were secure, it didn't console him. He loved the paintings more than anything else. Without them, there was nothing else he yearned to possess.

When Evelyn reached the fire at Fetter Lane he found that for the first time since the blaze had begun it was checked and under control.

Charles said, "Our good fortune is due to the houses Doctor Wren blew up on Fetter Lane, wisely choosing to create a fire break where there were stone houses beyond. But Evelyn, I'm grateful for your services, too."

Evelyn said, "Thank you, sir. I'm honoured."

Christopher said, "It is gracious of Your Majesty to appreciate my efforts, but it was your example, sir, that spurred us on."

"And the frequent use of gunpowder and the quieting of the wind."

Evelyn said, "Sir, you jest. If I may say so, Doctor Wren is right."

"No. It is the wind. It has fallen almost to a dead calm and now no sparks fly about." Messengers from other fire posts brought the King news that the fire had slackened elsewhere and he managed a smile.

Christopher begged to be excused. He had not slept for days and he felt so tired it was as if he had been beaten into insensibility.

Charles nodded, and said, "Doctor, it would be useful if you could accompany me tomorrow on my survey of the devastated parts of London."

"Sir, I will be honoured."

"You can determine what has to be done. As we discussed earlier."

Evelyn said hurriedly, "Sir, I've plans for rebuilding London, too."

"They will be considered," Charles said wearily, exhausted by Evelyn's insistent eagerness and ambition. "All reputable plans will be."

After Daniel told Christopher what had happened, all his friend could say was, "Somehow, we must find the paintings." Daniel was so stricken that it worried him deeply. "I will help you whatever way I can."

"We will never find them. There is nothing you can do. I must return to Amsterdam, to Rembrandt. I must find there what I have lost."

"The King has asked me to survey the city with him and suggested that I design a new London. Come with me. I can use your keen eyes and perhaps we will find a clue to where the paintings are."

"Among the hundreds of thousands of impoverished people who are homeless? No! It is an impossible quest. And the King will not be grateful for my presence. He will regard me as an outsider. Which I am."

Christopher was silent, thinking, Daniel wasn't the only one who had lost something. Now that the excitement of fighting the fire was over and the wind no longer blew and the flames had abated, he was sad, too, about the memories Sam's house had possessed. He felt almost as disconsolate as Daniel, for he had demolished a vital part of his growing up, a part he recalled with fondness. He had made the destruction of the house appear unimportant to Daniel so it would be easier and lessen Daniel's objections. But now that it was done he felt, in a sense, that he had buried Anne and Sam, irrevocably, and he could better comprehend Daniel's pain. And part of himself was gone with the loss of the house. Yet he couldn't force Daniel to do something that was against his nature. But as Daniel continued to talk about returning to Amsterdam and Rembrandt, he had to say finally, "At least, wait until the war is over, when you can go back in safety," and he was relieved that Daniel apparently agreed with him.

Charles was decisive as he rode around London on horseback. By Thursday the wind was calm everywhere and what remained of the fire was completely under control. Christopher followed him, coming to his side only when it was requested. He liked the feeling of being in the saddle, it was one of his favourite pastimes, and he enjoyed the King's interest in his views, although he didn't altogether trust it. And Daniel seemed less distraught, although still quite depressed.

Christopher observed that on the west the fire had been halted at Fetter Lane, on the east it had reached the walls of the Tower but had been blocked by the moat, on the south much of the bank of the Thames had been burnt but none of the flames had touched the other side of the river and to the north some of Smithfields had escaped the conflagration.

Charles sighed as he saw that most of the city was gone, while Christopher was grateful that the flames had stopped at the walls of Gresham College. He was shocked that he could stand on Cheapside and see the Thames. Every building between there and the river had burned down. Only the stone and brick fabric stood and he called the King's attention to this fact.

The King, surrounded by gentlemen and soldiers, asked, "Doctor, is that important?" The more he saw, the more he was depressed, for the destruction was even vaster than he expected.

"I believe so, sir." Christopher replied. "London must never again be a wooden city. Stone and brick is all that has escaped the flames."

However, the real tragedy to Charles was that in all of the City, the mercantile heart of his country, where so much of his revenue came from, there were only two main streets of houses left untouched, on Leadenhall and Bishopsgate. But he said, "Doctor, I don't underestimate the difficulties facing us, yet first, I must take care of the homeless."

They were camped mostly at Moorfields and while the courtiers were nervous, afraid that the anger and despair of the citizens would turn on the King, he was resolute in his determination to comfort them.

Christopher stayed close to him, eager to observe how the people would behave. Charles rode up to the multitude sitting on the ground by whatever they had been able to save from the calamity, and with his face streaked with ashes, close enough to be touched, he addressed them:

"We must not change our character. Just as we have repelled enemies in the past, we must repel them now. But do not be misled, this fire was no plot by Dutchmen or Frenchmen or Papists—we have examined many and have no evidence of such a design—everything convinces me it was due to the hand of God upon us, a great wind, and that the season has been so very dry. I assure you, now that this lamentable calamity is over, I will, as your King, do everything in my power to help you. There will be food for everybody, and shelter. Wooden huts will be erected immediately and we will start rebuilding London at once."

By the time Charles finished speaking everyone was cheering him and Christopher thought, He couldn't blame them, Charles had been steady-voiced and had expressed a genuine interest and affection for his people.

Christopher's eyes turned to St. Paul's which stood like a gaunt skeleton, a burnt-out shell of a cathedral. Yet, to his surprise, while flames had attacked all of St. Paul's, much of the fabric still stood, for most of it was constructed of stone. But no pigeons fluttered about its charred windows. The ruins were still smouldering and it was impossible for him to tell to what extent the cathedral had been stricken, although he could see from even casual observation that the roof was gone, a pillar had collapsed, the walls were sagging precariously, and the inside of St. Paul's was a desolate waste. He thought, It was so weakened and defaced that it was beyond restoring. But he mentioned none of this to the King. At the moment Charles seemed interested only in the rebuilding of London.

He listened intently to Charles' views and said, when the latter ended as they reached Whitehall—the King had asked him to ride by his side—"I will have a design for the whole of the burnt-out part of the city, sir. Next week, if I may have an audience."

"You inform me when it is ready and I will see you."

Daniel was gone. He had left a note for his friend at Scotland Yard.

"Dearest Christopher, I appreciate everything you have done for me, but I must return to Amsterdam. There, perhaps, I may find what I have lost here.

And please, do not worry about my safety. My father has many friends among the sailors of England, and there are still ships sailing between both countries. You are a clever man and you do not really need me, much as you have said so. May fortune favour you and if fate is kind, possibly when the war is over and the present calamities cease, we will meet again. I write this in affection and gratitude for the friendship you have given me. It is a comfort that I shall always treasure. May God bless you and keep you safe."

Stunned, Christopher was grateful that he had something to preoccupy him such as the designs for a rebuilt London. But how could Daniel have made such a choice? Why? Even as these questions tormented him, he heard hammering and his heart leapt for joy, thinking it was Daniel returning and knocking on the door. Then his heart sank as he realised that it was a soldier banging his musket against the cobblestones, ordered to protect them because of the attack on Daniel.

If You Look Too Intently

If you look too intently
You may not see freely
It would suggest an objective
And what is to be seen there
may be outside such
                    boundaries

Stymean Karlen

32

If You Look Too Intently

CHRISTOPHER SUBMITTED HIS PLAN TO REBUILD LONDON SIX DAYS later. He missed Daniel's precise hand, but he drew his design clearly and strongly.

Charles was amazed by the speed with which Doctor Wren had carried out his command. As he sat in his audience chamber at Whitehall Palace, he studied the plan carefully. No one else was present; he was determined to give this matter his complete attention. Then Charles saw that Doctor Wren was waiting patiently for him to comment. He had to comment, he thought wryly, he was the King. And London was in dire need. But there was one thing about the plan he wasn't sure he agreed with, and he asked critically, "You have made St. Paul's the heart of the rebuilt city?"

"Sir, not only St. Paul's, but the Royal Exchange, also. They should be the two most important buildings in a new London. The Exchange is the centre of our worldly life, St. Paul's is the heart of our spiritual being."

"Do you believe that a new cathedral is that vital?"

"Yes, sir. It must be the spirit behind what we do. We must erect a cathedral that will make London different from every other city on earth. That will express the glory of your reign for hundreds of years."

"Doctor Wren, you flatter me."

"A new St. Paul's must also show that we love God as He loves us. It must express His message to us. It must be our resurrection."

"Enough, you must not be so extravagant! We are also creatures of the earth as well as of the spirit. And there are practical problems. But I like the way you designed wide, straight streets to run through the city and to converge on St. Paul's, and the handsome *piazza* you have placed around it. This gives the cathedral grace yet grandeur."

"Sir, St. Paul's must have space around it to set it off properly. No more should we allow houses to be pushed against it or buildings to be erected all about it, destroying our view of it and marring its contour."

"What about the rest of the city?"

"Sir, we must do away with timber structures and spread out the city and rebuild on wide streets so there will be no danger from plague or fire."

"It sounds sensible."

"It is essential if London is to be a clean, beautiful, orderly city, sir. Spacious, not crowded, greatly planned. A city we can treasure."

Charles was intrigued by this prospect and he took another look at the plan. He liked the way the streets radiated from *piazzas* at a new Royal Exchange and at St. Paul's. Surely the wide, straight streets would develop a safer, more comfortable city to live in; this would be a vast improvement on the winding, narrow roads and lanes of the medieval town. Attractive long vistas would be everywhere and important buildings would be easily accessible. It could be marvellous. As if a magician was at work. But a magic wand might be essential to put this design into reality, Charles couldn't help thinking, for was it possible? Or practical? Or even feasible? Despite the aspects of the plan that impressed him, he wondered if it wasn't too imaginative, too extraordinary, and too different for his subjects to comprehend, however much of it was worth realising.

He could hear their objections: "*We cannot sacrifice our land to a wide roadway. It is impossible to wait for such building when we don't have a roof over our heads. And it will destroy our past. Our heritage.*"

Charles, unable to give a direct reply when it might be unpleasant and uncomfortable, distracted himself by observing Christopher's presence. He recalled how they had met as children, that they were almost the same age, although he looked much older and different. He was very much aware that Christopher was short where he was proud of his height, fair while he was dark, broad-featured where his face was lean and long, direct where he was devious, and single-minded when he had to heed many views. What puzzled him was that Wren seemed to lack self-interest. No one at Court was like that, he reflected. At the first sign that the fire might threaten Whitehall many of the courtiers had fled and most of the others had not done anything to fight it, except in the rare instances where their person, property, or possessions were in danger, yet Wren had blown up his own house to halt the fire. Wren had not told him: he had learned this from Evelyn, who was bewildered by such quixotic behaviour. This was a man he might almost trust. He was pleased they both possessed philosophical curiosity. But Charles was concerned that Wren didn't appear to be interested in women, when they were his chief interest. He was about to ask the surveyor whether there were any women in his life, then he caught hold of himself. He stood up, aware that he had allowed himself to come closer to Wren than he preferred. He disliked that. Even his mistresses were kept at a distance; even in the most intimate moments a part of himself was detached. It was his way of protecting himself.

He moved to the door as a gesture of dismissal, but when he saw the look of dismay on Wren's face, he said, "I will review your plan."

"Your Majesty, although I have given it to you quickly, it has been in my mind a long time and it is carefully planned."

"Knowing you, I'm certain it is." Yet when he saw the look of pleasure on the surveyor's face, he hurried to add, "As I said, I will consider your design carefully. I'm favourably impressed with it. It shows ingenuity and thoroughness. But acceptance will depend on many circumstances."

Evelyn submitted his plan for a rebuilt London several days later. Hooke followed with one of his own soon after.

Christopher found out, for they told him quite proudly.

They were so self-assured they sounded as if they were certain *their* plan would be the one accepted. Yet Matthew informed him that the King had submitted all three designs, and a number of others, to the Privy Council for its consideration, but that he favoured Christopher's.

While Christopher waited for a decision to be reached he surveyed the present condition of the burned part of London. He estimated that five-sixths of the city was razed to the ground and all that stood untouched was east of the Tower, north at High Holborn, and west from the Temple and Fetter Lane. Nothing had burned on the Strand or at Charing Cross or around the curve of the river to Whitehall and Westminster, where most of the nobility resided, the fashionable neighbourhood had escaped the fire.

Some of the time he rode about London, but most of the time he walked, for much of the old city was impassable, many of the streets were blocked by fallen buildings and other debris. He trod gingerly over heaps of smoking rubbish, for the ground under his feet was often so hot it burned the soles of his feet, the fire smouldering in many places. It gave Christopher the feeling that the scorched part of London had become a vast volcano with lava continuing to sputter up from the earth where occasional fires burned in cellars and beneath the rubble. Yet on this enormous crater where not a roof was visible against the blackened horizon and scarcely a wall stood above one storey, he saw many chimneys and stone walls, and the skeletons of many parish churches, the heart and soul of London, their burnt-out towers and steeples still penetrating the sky. And dominating everything else was the charred fabric of St. Paul's. The roof was gone now in addition to the tower and the steeple, but the walls remained and it lay like a long, broken bulk across the face of London, and was still the most vivid sight within view for miles. Even in ruins it could be seen from Greenwich and Whitehall and Southwark and the hills to the north. It gave him an even fiercer determination to restore it whatever the obstacles and he sensed there would be many.

His moment of pleasure vanished as he passed people searching through the cinders and charred remains for a blanket, a bed, poking in cellars for one thing saved, a cup, a spoon, anything that was familiar, and so, friendly. He saw an old man uncover a sword, so twisted it was useless, but the owner fondled it as if it were the Order of the Garter, for it was his. Another found his dead dog and wept. But most of those he saw walked about looking like ghosts moving across a desolate landscape.

He knew many had moved into hovels and cellars and the rooms of relatives in the tiny portion of London that had not burned, but there was a huge multitude that was not housed. Then, just as he was afflicted with despair and wondering where the hundreds of thousands of homeless people were living, he saw a sight that excited him. A middle-aged man, his wife, and their ten-year-old son were erecting a flimsy shack by placing wood across the one-storey walls that remained of their house.

He inquired of the father where the wood had come from and Guy Jobe regarded him suspiciously and growled, "I'm not surrendering it."

"I just wondered where you obtained the wood. I'm a surveyor."

"The King has put Albemarle in command. A good thing. He will do something. Already, he has sent in tents from the army, timber from the Navy, but no carpenters can be spared, they are still repairing the ships damaged by the Dutch, but bread and corn has been rushed into London, too, from the naval stores. Do you have any nails to hold this together?"

"I'm sorry, but . . ."

Jobe cut him sharply, "Everybody is sorry, but does nothing. But I will reside on my own land before I permit them to lodge me in a hovel or a cellar. I've always had my own house and nothing will take it away from me. Not even the fire. What do you really want?"

"I'm surveying the city so that it can be rebuilt properly."

"Amid all these ashes? It will be the old face with a new coat of paint. Do you think I'm the only one building on an old site? Look!"

Christopher did while Jobe urged his son and wife to work harder as they put straw over the cinders. Wooden huts were going up around them, mostly sheds and lean-to shacks, and he asked, "What is the straw for?"

"Fool!" snapped Jobe. "To sleep on, of course! We are not vagrants to rely on someone else's charity. Not that there is any!"

His son found a stone flower pot that had survived the blaze and jumped with joy while his parents congratulated him and helped him clean it.

The next day Christopher returned to St. Paul's at the request of the Dean to survey the present condition of the cathedral. Sancroft had built a small wooden shed on Warwick Lane, which was close to St. Paul's, and to demonstrate that he wasn't daunted by the disaster, he called it "*Saint Paul's House*". When the Dean's servant told Christopher that his master was busy with visitors, he took his first close look at the cathedral since the fire had ended. The ruins were cruel and sad; before, at least, with all the imperfections there was life but now there was none. Irreparable injury had been done to the portico, the ancient walls sagged even more precariously, the roof was gone, the inside was a picture of devastation and chaos, rubble and debris was everywhere, with fallen masonry, smashed tombs, charred timber, ironwork and bells melted by the heat, ornaments burned, the altar cracked. And worst of all, he felt, and almost unbearable, every book stored in St. Faith's—a storehouse that had contained the treasures of centuries of learning—had become cinders when the vault of the roof of St. Paul's had fallen into St. Faith's, for fire and molten lead had followed.

"Yet God is merciful," he heard Sancroft saying in the nave. He turned and saw the Dean speaking to an elderly blind man and a young woman. "Mr. Milton, there is still warmth to be found in the house of God."

"No doubt," Milton replied. "But I never thought I would see such a disaster in my life. St. Paul's in ruins, London burned to the ground."

"Not all of it." Sancroft saw Christopher approaching and he introduced him to John Milton and the latter's wife, Elizabeth, who was pale and thin.

"Christopher Wren," Milton repeated. "Son of the Bishop?"

"Nephew, sir," said Christopher. "My father was Dean of

Windsor. We met many years ago, when I was a child, but I doubt
that you remember it."

"Oh, yes," Milton said, but Christopher doubted that he was
listening.

"Mr. Milton has come to discuss his property on Bread Street."

"Dean, what are you talking about? Bread Street is the only
property I own, but I can bear its loss if I must. It is my work
that brings me here. Work is vital, little else. Pray God you will
realise, what I scratch with my pen on paper is all that is left to
me and if I appeal to you for a licence to publish it, it is because
circumstances force me to do this."

"Mr. Milton, this is a service I cannot offer you."

"Why not? You are a power in the High Church. Dean of St.
Paul's."

"The power to license is in the office of the Archbishop of
Canterbury."

"Gilbert Sheldon?"

"Yes. His office has the power to approve or disapprove."

"Will he read the work himself?"

"It depends. Doctor Wren, what do you think?"

Christopher said, "The Archbishop is a learned man. Well read."

"And he is fond of you, Doctor Wren," said Sancroft.

Milton said, "My life has not been easy. I have many afflictions,
but God must take pity on me and allow this work to be published."

Sancroft said, "I hope for your sake it is not a political tract."

"I've written only poetry since 1660. It is a godly work, although
I've put it in the form of an epic. *It is in English heroic verse without
rhyme, as that of Homer in Greek, and of Virgil in Latin.* I call it *Paradise
Lost.* But I will be unable to find a publisher unless and until I
obtain a licence from the official censor, which is assigned now to
your Church, Dean Sancroft. Will you speak to the Archbishop for
me?"

"Doctor Wren might be better. The Archbishop fancies his
views."

"You are very kind, but I'm not qualified. I'm a surveyor."

"And one of the most learned men in England. With a good
clerical background and a rare devotion to the public interest."

Milton said, "Wren is right. He is not qualified. He is not a poet."

"You are better off with him. Another poet will be envious."

Milton was perplexed and he paused and Christopher stared at
him, startled by how much he had altered and that he was much
older than his wife, who looked like his daughter. The poet was in
the sober black garb of the Puritan, but his long hair was still
attractive and carefully combed, his one vanity, and his eyes were
so large and his manner so positive it was hard to realise he was

blind. But suddenly he complained that his gout stool had been destroyed in the burning of his house on Bread Street.

Sancroft asked, "What is the significance of the title, Mr. Milton?"

"Dean, it must be read to be understood."

"Does it pertain to our world?"

"To my world. And to the world of my imagination."

Christopher said, "Could it have anything to do with the fire?"

"It was finished before then. My learning goes beyond that."

His wife blurted out, "We were affected by the flames. We were in our house on Bunhill Row, scarce a quarter of a mile from the blaze, and even Mr. Milton was troubled by the flames. He was as frightened as I was. He kept asking me whether it was approaching, whether it was very close."

"Naturally," Milton said angrily. "I was afraid for my work. Doctor Wren, did you ever have anything you loved destroyed by fire?"

Sancroft said solemnly, "He just did, Mr. Milton. St. Paul's."

"Doctor, then I don't have to tell you what *Paradise Lost* means to me."

Sancroft added, "And Doctor Wren was friendly with the Usurper despite his Royalist connections and was Doctor Wilkins' favourite protege."

Milton asked, "Doctor, do you still see the estimable John Wilkins?"

"Indeed! He is secretary to the Royal Society."

"Did you know that the conflagration destroyed his vicarage house, his papers, and his library, one of the best and most valuable in England?"

"No!" Christopher was shocked. "I haven't seen him recently."

"If you speak to the Archbishop it will be appreciated."

"Even if I haven't read the work."

"The only copy is in the hands of the ministry. Assure the Archbishop that he has nothing to fear. *Paradise Lost* is beyond the trials and tribulations of the moment. And my previous work should suffice to convince you of the worth of my latest enterprise." Milton strode away.

Sancroft said, "Poor old blind schoolmaster. Too bad he still lives in the past. His great days are over. Considering the spite with which he attacked our late King and his fanatical support of the Usurper, he is lucky he is alive. Charles was merciful to spare him. Men who sinned less were beheaded, rightly so. Do you think St. Paul's can be used?"

"It is unlikely. What is left standing is in danger of falling."

"We must take that chance. It is important that I conduct services there. Or our Episcopal faith will suffer greatly. For the time being, we must patch it up. As soon as the debris is cleared away, I will use the west end for temporary cathedral worship."

"But sir, that is where the most danger of collapse exists."

"We will improvise, Doctor. We will manage. We must."

Christopher didn't argue. For once, something else was more vital in his mind than St. Paul's. He wanted to help Milton, but could he?

Long after Milton and his wife were gone Christopher recalled how the poet had walked out of devastated St. Paul's from memory, needing his wife only to avoid the debris. He was distressed about the news of Wilkins' calamity. But when he visited him to console him, Wilkins said, "It was God's will. All I regret is I lost original manuscripts I can't replace now, for I'm too old to do them over. If one could only have two sets. I hope you can help Milton. He is a thorny man, but anything he writes should be read. And he may have omitted all political references."

When nothing was done the next few days about the rebuilding of London, Christopher returned to Oxford as Savillian Professor of Astronomy.

Sheldon, who spent much time in Oxford, was glad to see him. He said, "Once the war ends, and I'm hopeful it will be soon, you should be able to finish building the theatre. Then materials should be available."

"Your Grace, there is another matter I would like to discuss."

"Sancroft tells me that you don't approve of services in St. Paul's."

"Sir, I don't like risking people's lives when the remains of the cathedral are in danger of collapse."

"An immediate start on a new building is impracticable. Perhaps impossible."

"Sir, that isn't what I wanted to talk about. It is Milton."

"The Usurper's Latin Secretary? He was one of our worst enemies."

"He can do no harm now. Your Grace, he is writing poetry."

"He may interject seditious ideas."

"That is what I wanted to talk to you about, Your Grace. He has written a new work which he has to submit to your office for licence to publish."

"What is it called?"

"*Paradise Lost.*"

"It is not a title I favour. It sounds as if it could be blasphemous."

"Your Grace, if you could read it, then you could decide for yourself."

"I haven't time. I'm too busy. But Milton will receive justice, more justice than he and the Usurper meted out when they ruled England. If his work is godly it will be licensed. My domestic chaplain, the Reverend Tomkyns, will consider the matter. He is a learned man and he has distinguished himself with publications he has written in a zealous High Church and Royalist spirit. What is Milton's work called?"

"*Paradise Lost*, Your Grace."

"Tomkyns will examine it with the utmost vigilance. His stricture, *The Inconveniencies of Toleration*, expresses many views that I share. If there are any passages in the work that are dangerous to Church and State he will find them." But when he saw that Christopher was distressed, he offered one concession. "Doctor Wren, I will inform you when John Milton's work is submitted officially to my office for licensing. Then you can present your views to the Reverend Tomkyns. I will advise him to hear you."

"Sir, it should be read by anyone who expresses views on it."

"Tomkyns knows my mind. It is the character of John Milton that concerns us. I'm interested in whether he is properly repentant. You must not be too merciful. It is often mistaken as a sign of weakness."

"Thank you, sir." He respected the Archbishop for his courage and vigour, as he respected his uncle, but he wondered if they had to be so devoted to their own certitude. "I will look at Milton's work if it is allowed."

"As you wish." The Archbishop stood up in the same commanding manner as the King and reminded him, "But don't make it too important. After all, it is just a poem. Remember, Doctor, as a child of our Church your first duty is to restore St. Paul's to a state of worship."

New Day New Day

New day New Day if you want of me
what I want of you
I would have to be a new me New Me
for you

Do make me Make Me new to please you
Since that is all All I want of you
That you be a new kind New Kind of day
for me

Stymean Karlen

33

New Day New Day

NOTHING HAPPENED AT ST. PAUL'S THE REST OF THE YEAR WHILE the King appointed a Commission of six surveyors to advise him on the rebuilding of London. Christopher thought apprehensively, Whenever Charles wanted to evade making a decision he appointed a Commission. It was no consolation to be told that he was one of them, for Pratt and May were, too, and he doubted they would agree with anything he recommended; the other surveyors were from the City, men without imagination or initiative.

Charles met the Commission at Whitehall, submitted Christopher's plan for a rebuilt London to them for their consideration, and asked for their opinion. It was the beginning of 1667 and Christopher waited uneasily; Charles was as formal as he had been friendly at their previous meeting.

Pratt was the first to respond. He examined the plan hastily, as if he knew what he thought about it without having to study it, and stated, "Your Majesty, this design destroys Elizabethan London, the London of our greatest glory, that has caused our city to rival Rome and Athens."

Christopher replied, "And will make it unique among cities. Spacious, grand, and comfortable, and most of all, considerate of its residents."

Pratt said even more insistently, "Your design is only a replica of Rome, with such wide streets you obliterate many houses and properties."

"We must start now to make London orderly and comfortable."

"You have too many open spaces, more *piazzas* than buildings."

"We must give easy access to every part of London."

"And in the process you wipe out Cheapside, you tear down Guildhall, make the Fleet unrecognisable, and destroy London as we know it."

"It is time to stop living in the past, to think of those here today."

"Your plan is just a rectangle. At Shoe Lane, an unimportant site, you put an enormous *piazza*, as if you expect the city to grow far beyond there. But that is poor planning. That will never happen."

Evelyn, who had just entered to support his own plan, interrupted, "Mr. Pratt, I think Doctor Wren's design is a great achievement. I am honoured that mine coincides with his in many important details."

Wren's was an admirable design, thought Charles, but was it wise? He had suggested it to his advisers and they had found many objections.

Hooke followed Evelyn into the audience chamber to advocate his own plan and he said, "Your Majesty, I respect Doctor Wren's philosophical views, and he may know what he is doing with this design but I'm not sure."

Charles grew uncomfortable. Now that he had learned what he wanted to know, this argument tired him. He said, "All the plans will be reviewed and circumstances will determine which one is chosen. If any are."

"None will be," Evelyn told Christopher as they left Whitehall. He was eager to talk and he accompanied his friend to Christopher's residence at Scotland Yard. There, outside the house, Evelyn paused and added, "Did you notice that His Majesty affects the French fashion in dress again? It may reflect his views on building. I've been told no one wants to give up what they possessed before the fire. Improvements will be made, but it has been decided to keep the design of the medieval city and the buildings are going to be re-erected where they were originally."

"Then why did he want to meet us if a decision has been reached?"

"You know how he is. He doesn't like to say No, that wearies him. But I don't blame you for being upset. Your plan is splendid in many ways, but too visionary for our age. Yet now, at least, all buildings will have to be of brick and stone, and the streets, lanes, and alleys will be wider, although not with the grandeur and spaciousness you and I proposed."

"No wonder May and the City surveyors never said a word. They know that was useless. And Denham and Webb weren't even there."

"Webb is out of favour. His need for self praise has lost him friends."

"He is a competent surveyor. More competent than Pratt or

May. And Denham is still Chief Surveyor and he is in a healthy mind again."

Evelyn asked increduously, "Haven't you heard?"

"Heard what?" Evelyn was bursting with news.

"Denham's wife was exceedingly ill, although she was very young. It was the talk of the town, particularly of the Court."

"I haven't been to Court lately except to see the King."

"She has just died. It is the great scandal of the season."

"Because she was reputed to be the mistress of the Duke of York?"

"That is only part of it. Everyone knows that York was wholly given up to this bitch of Denham's. He was seeing her three times a week."

"Poor Denham." Christopher sighed. "No wonder he went mad."

"Many at Court believe he still is. Most of the Court thinks she was poisoned, by Denham himself, because of her behaviour with York."

"I don't believe it. It is not Denham's nature. He is a gentle man."

"I doubt many agree with you. Pepys, in particular, is sure Denham has murdered his wife. But that may be because Pepys wanted to defend York."

"Pepys is a gossip. And sometimes malicious."

"Perhaps. But her illness was common knowledge, as was her affair with York. She made sure of that, even flaunting it in Denham's face."

"She could have offended others, too. She was very ambitious."

"That is what Aubrey thinks. He says that Anne Hyde, York's wife and Clarendon's daughter, had reason to hate Lady Denham. The bitch intrigued against the Duchess' father, and some suspect Anne Hyde of the poisoning."

"Has an autopsy been taken? That could dispel the gossip about poison."

"Her body is being opened by the doctors, but their reports will not be accepted. The Court enjoys the scandal too much to relinquish it."

"I must talk to Sir John," Christopher said suddenly. "Console him."

"It could be dangerous. Yesterday, when he went out he was stoned and his neighbours threatened to tear him to pieces if they caught him."

Christopher stared across Scotland Yard at Denham's fine, spacious house. There was no one in front of it and he walked over to it and asked Evelyn, "Do you want to join me? Your presence would please him."

Evelyn said uneasily, "I would love to, but I have an appointment, to discuss my new rebuilding scheme. You must express my regrets to Sir John." He walked away so quickly his feet hardly seemed to touch the ground.

Christopher knocked on Denham's door. But no one answered until he saw a face peering through the hangings on the window. Then a footman admitted him into a dark, shrouded reception room, lit only by candles.

Denham sat at a large oak table and as Christopher was ushered in, he said, "Doctor Wren, forgive me for not rising, but I have the gout, it makes me quite lame. Do they still gloat and threaten me outside?"

"Sir John, no one is there."

"They will return. No matter what I say, it only makes matters worse. They are determined I play the jealous husband, like themselves. But it is good of you to come. You don't believe I poisoned her, do you?"

"No. I came to express my regrets over your wife's death."

Denham said woefully, "It is so sad. She was so young, lovely, full of life. She adored the world of the Court, the dancing, which I could not indulge in, I am troubled with lameness. But she ate carelessly and she could have poisoned herself with overeating. She had an avid taste for sweets. While my preference is for poetry. It is all that keeps me from ending my miserable existence. I'm trying to compose an ode now."

"Sir John, do you know Milton's work?"

"Very well." Denham's aged, sombre features lit up for the first time. "A recently published poem, *The Second Advice to a Painter*, which satirises the conduct of York during the war, has been attributed to me and Milton. I am greatly flattered, although I did not compose the poem and I doubt that Milton did either. It is not worthy of him."

"I have been asked to read his newest work, *Paradise Lost*."

"An appropriate title for our time. It sounds as if his genius is searching for the truth. I must read it. Anything Milton writes, I must read. I disagree with his politics, but his poetry has a moving effect on me. A new work from him could be a great occasion."

"It is kind of you, as a fellow poet, to say so."

"Not at all. Never believe gossip. I am accused of impotence, York of carnal knowledge of my wife, but none who accuse have actually witnessed any of this. Doctor Wren, the Holy Ghost came for her. That stopped her blood running. But no one understands this."

"I do. I think."

Denham was reflective, then he asked, "Have you ever been in love? You are a private man, but it is helpful to talk to one who is a friend."

Christopher replied carefully, "I have admired beauty and loved the way a woman spoke and smiled and walked. And found that in individuals."

"Then you know that with the best intentions love is not always pure?"

Christopher nodded.

They were interrupted by the harsh impact of stones on the house. Denham limped wearily to the window, looked out, and said, more in sadness than in anger, "It is the mob again. They are resolved to hate me, even if they don't know me. Hate makes them righteous, which they enjoy."

Christopher saw a crowd outside throwing rocks at the door and the windows. In another moment, he realised, the windows would be shattered.

Denham threw open his front door and faced the mob. They yelled, "Murderer! Poisoner!" Stones followed, just missing him, yet Denham faced the menacing mob with composure and ordered his footmen to bring wine.

The crowd was so surprised by this good deed they stopped to see if the Chief Surveyor would carry out this gift. A minute later his footmen were distributing large portions of burnt wine to the mob.

"To mourn my dear departed wife's funeral," he announced. "Four times as much wine as has ever been drunk at any funeral in England."

The mob adored the wine, wanted more and more, and soon most of them had fallen into a drunken stupor in the courtyard or had staggered away, singing boisterously or shouting the praises of Sir John Denham's generosity, proclaiming that he was truly a benefactor of humanity.

Then he said, "Now it is safe to depart. I didn't want them to see you, for when they are sober again they could vent their spite on you."

"What will you do when they become sober again?"

"Give them more wine. Especially at the funeral. Such an amount as has never been given on a public occasion. I must read Milton's *Paradise Lost*. It is the most godly thing I can do. Whatever our Church says."

A week later Christopher was summoned to Whitehall to hear the royal decision on the rebuilding of London. This was announced by his cousin, who was curt. Matthew said he was distracted because his father was ill and he told Christopher in his most official tone, "Every design has been rejected, including yours. London is going to be rebuilt on the old lines of the medieval city. I'm sorry. Now you must excuse me. Clarendon wants my presence at once." Matthew left him abruptly.

Christopher had heard that Clarendon was blamed for the failure of the Navy to defeat the Dutch—the French had not done any fighting, standing by to pick up the spoils—and that Clarendon had been warned that if there were more defeats he could fall from power. But Christopher, while he was distressed about his uncle's illness, thought of the rejection of his plan and told himself, Once again expediency had won over imagination.

At the door of the Presence Chamber he was halted by Pepys, coming from a meeting with York. Many were in dire need in London, it was the most severe winter in years, but Pepys wanted to talk about Denham.

Pepys said, "Denham was shrewd. He gave his wife such a sumptuous burial at St. Margaret's in Westminster and such a liberal bestowing of wine it appeased the mob, although there were still some shouts against him."

"But I heard that the autopsy found no evidence of poison."

"That doesn't prove anything. But I heard something more intriguing. *The doctors found a vessel about her matrix which had never been broken. This shows she wasn't carnal and that York didn't lie with her. But it makes Denham more of a cuckold, even more likely that he poisoned her.*"

"I felt he was broken-hearted over her death."

"Or relieved. No one likes to be a cuckold or to be suspected of being one. You mustn't worry about London. It will be rebuilt in its own way."

"Do you know Milton's work?"

"A scandalous man! I wouldn't read what he wrote. It is dangerous!"

Christopher visited his uncle, who was at High Holborn, but the Bishop lay in a coma. When he died a month later his nephew was deeply shaken.

But the Bishop would have been pleased with the funeral, Christopher reflected. A huge procession bore the Bishop's body across the Essex countryside to Cambridge, where it was met by the Vice-Chancellor. It lay in state for two weeks and in May, before most of the important officials of Cambridge and his family and friends, his uncle was buried in the tomb at Pembroke which he had had Christopher build for this occasion.

His sister and brother-in-law were there. He had not seen them recently and as he sat beside them in the Bishop's rooms after the funeral, he was eager to talk to them. William Holder had contributed so much to his early schooling and Susan had been a vital part of his growing up.

Susan looked in good health, although she had lost her girlish slimness, while Holder had grown portly.

Susan informed her brother, "William has become an authority on deafness and is eminent in music. He has composed several anthems and he is a great disciplinarian. He has many gifts. Like yourself, Christopher."

Holder nodded and added, "I am happy that I was helpful to you when you were young. Bishop Wren often commended me on that score."

Christopher was uncomfortable. He felt there should be a mood of sadness here—one of the most alive persons he had known had died—and yet everyone was concerned only with their own pursuits. His cousin joined them and said, "Clarendon is in dire difficulty, he is blamed for the Dutch disaster, but never fear, if he falls I have been promised the post of secretary to the Duke of York," and when Christopher pointed out, "But if York commands the Navy, isn't he responsible for the Navy's defeats, and not Clarendon?" his cousin regarded him as if he had uttered treason and hushed him with the remark, "York could be our next King. It is unlikely that the Queen will ever give Charles any children."

Susan said. "What a pity! For the monarchy must always be asserted."

Christopher stopped listening. A young woman approached Susan to express her condolences and she was pretty, slim, fair-skinned, and light-haired, and her grace and manner appealed to him. Susan introduced them.

"Miss Faith Coghill, my brother, Doctor Wren. Miss Coghill's father was Sir John Coghill and she is a neighbour of mine at Bletchington."

Christopher drew her aside on the excuse he wanted to show her the design of Pembroke Chapel, but as they walked on to the quadrangle he didn't expect her to be interested. To his surprise, she had some knowledge of building and the questions she asked were intelligent. Yet, as he saw her framed by the bright green grass it was her presence that pleased him the most. Then, remembering his uncle lying nearby, he felt guilty, and to hide that, smiled.

This flustered her and she asked, "Doctor Wren, have I offended you? My father taught me some of the principles of building, for he improved our own residence several times, but there is much I don't know."

"Perhaps I could teach you."

"You are kind. But you are a learned man."

"Miss Coghill, when may I see you again?"

"Doctor Wren, I live at Bletchington."

"Susan told me. Have you known my sister long?"

"Since she moved there with the Reverend Holder. I reside near them."

"Do you ride?"

"Often."

"I love the motion of the horse, the wind in my face." Then he frowned.

"What is wrong, Doctor Wren?"

"I am imposing on you."

"Not in the least," she said with unexpected forcefulness. "No one does that. We do not have a Court at Bletchington where one must cater."

"May I call on you this Sunday? Escort you to church? And then, perhaps, we could go riding?"

"Your sister didn't mention that you were visiting her."

"I haven't heard my brother-in-law preach for a long time. And my uncle would like that. William was a protege of his."

"Were you close to the Bishop?"

"I respected his courage and vigour, although he could be too insistent in the pursuit of his own views. I don't think he was ever satisfied with the way man behaved. But he seemed pleased with this chapel."

"Are you, Doctor Wren?"

"Pembroke is an early work, Miss Coghill. My first. An introduction to surveying. But I like its simplicity. And I was fortunate to have the practice. Will I see you this Sunday? I would feel privileged."

"I think your sister will be happy to have your company. She tells me often how much she misses you and how seldom she sees you these days."

"If you tell Susan when it is proper to call on you, I will be there at the exact minute." He escorted Faith Coghill to the coach which was waiting for her. Then he realised that he knew very little about Faith.

Every Other Has Another

Every other has another
definition of poetry
But every poem
has its own

Stymean Karlen

34

Every Other Has Another

THE NEXT MONTH CHRISTOPHER SAW FAITH AT CHURCH EACH
Sunday. He came to know Holder's sermons by heart and they
bored him, they were so righteous, but he endured them so he could
be with her. After the services they rode through the country and
he was happy when he was beside Faith. Her father was dead and
she was mistress of her estate and she ignored the custom that
an unwed lady must be chaperoned. Faith knew the fabric of the
country and she enjoyed showing its beauty to Christopher. She
rode as gracefully as she walked; she loved to jump, to gallop, to
race, and so did he. Yet while formality ripened into friendship he
didn't express what he felt.

When Susan asked him, "Are you courting Faith?" he said,
"We're just friends." Susan was sceptical and William announced,
"She is eligible. Faith has had many proposals of marriage, she is
rich, but she has declined all proposals so far, yet she is highly
esteemed in the parish for her virtue and her grace. Christopher,
are you in love with her?"

"Are you going to present your views on deafness to the Royal
Society?"

"Yes. I have a paper prepared. Will you be there?"

"If I can. I want to hear what you say."

"I intend to publish on the subject. The Archbishop has given
me a licence already, without reading it, and he assures me of his
support."

Susan interrupted, "Christopher, why are you hesitant about
Faith?"

He didn't reply, for he wasn't ready to move any faster. His
future was uncertain; his only secure post was at Oxford, and as
a professor he was not paid much and it was understood—although
no longer stated—that he was not supposed to marry. The preference

for celibacy was a residue of monastic days, and it was not always enforced, but it was still preferred. But each time he saw Faith, he longed to see her again, and he disliked living between bursts of happiness and denial.

"I'm your sister. You don't have to hide anything from me."

"I'm still unsettled. I'm almost a surveyor, yet not quite."

Early in June he was summoned to St. Paul's by the Dean. Sancroft had adapted the west front for temporary services and he wanted Christopher to view what he had done. Then he asked, "Will it be safe?"

"Not permanently. The sensible solution is to erect a new cathedral." Some of the debris had been removed but the burnt-out fabric looked even more precarious than before. "Or worse could happen, sir."

"Nothing worse could happen after plague and fire." Sancroft gazed sternly at Christopher and asked, "What do you hear now?"

"It sounds like guns."

"If you listen hard enough, you can hear anything."

"No, sir, it is the thunder of guns."

They were joined by an aged canon who said, his voice trembling, "The Dutch are sailing up the Thames. They are attacking our ships on the Medway and London will be next. The King has called his militia to Tower Hill to defend the city, to make a stand there, and all is in peril. London lies exposed and helpless, without any fortifications since the fire. Nothing will be left now. Everything is lost. This hour is our epitaph."

Christopher waited with the rest of London for the Dutch to invade the city, for it didn't possess the strength to resist despite the King's militia. He wondered why the Dutch wanted London, the city was still a ruin. In the nine months that had passed since the fire little had been done. There had been royal proclamations but only a few buildings had arisen, there was such a shocking shortage of materials and labour. He thought ruefully, The Dutch will conquer an already conquered city.

The thunder of the guns was heard in London for days, but the Dutch didn't attack the city. Perhaps it wasn't worth much, Christopher decided. The Dutch burned and sank many of the King's ships on the Medway and the English Navy suffered a humiliating defeat. Charles took personal command of the army; he moved about London to reassure the citizens of his presence and protection; he smiled often and informed everyone that he would repel any danger. Gradually some of the fear lessened. The Dutch withdrew from the Medway and now many wrote: "*A lamentable and*

deplorable shame has befallen this poor Kingdom . . . The fire was but a flea
bite to this disaster . . . We have been betrayed, let the blame light where it
will . . . Things were better ordered in Cromwell's time . . . Oliver made all
the neighbour princes fear him . . . But the Court is as frivolous as ever and
the King, amid all these tribulations, continues to be attracted to Lady
Castlemaine as a moth hovers about a flame."

Six weeks after the Dutch victory on the Medway the war ended
with a treaty of peace between the two countries. But instead of this
bringing happiness, Christopher sensed that the prevailing mood
was of despondency.

He met Evelyn at Whitehall where he had gone to see his cousin
and his friend said, "Doctor, the times are evil. Wise men prepare
to remove abroad what they have, for we must be ruined, the
Kingdom is in so much debt, and the King minds nothing but
his lust and Lady Castlemaine."

Evelyn hurried away to arrange his affairs properly, in the event
that his dire predictions came true, and Christopher felt guilty.
He hadn't seen Faith since the Dutch assault on the Medway, and
he felt he should have. He had written her explaining that he had
been held in London, and he had received a polite acknowledgment,
but that didn't please him. And now Matthew looked more stricken
than he had ever seen his cousin.

When they were alone in the Presence Chamber, Matthew
whispered, "Clarendon has fallen. It is not official yet, but it will
be soon."

"What about yourself?"

"I hope to become York's secretary. I know more about the
affairs of state than anyone, Clarendon confided in me, but it hasn't
been decided yet. Don't be too friendly with Denham. York could
resent that."

"Matthew, what will happen to Clarendon?"

"It is impossible to foretell. The great mansion Pratt designed for
him on Piccadilly has been stoned and the trees in front of it have
been cut down and a gibbet has been set up, but I don't think
Charles will allow Clarendon to be hanged. He said, *'If everyone who
has made a mistake in my Kingdom was hanged, we would have no more trees
in London.'* But he will not defend him more than that, for it would
risk his own neck. Clarendon will be a useful scapegoat. It will divert
the nation's rage and criticism from him. So Clarendon is sacrificed.
He will be exiled. Nothing else will satisfy the jackals. But you could
profit from it."

Christopher was startled and he exclaimed, "I don't understand!"

Matthew regarded him indulgently as if he were distressingly
naive and explained, "Pratt built the mansion with material taken

from St. Paul's. There is even a poem about it. I remember some of it."

Matthew quoted:

> "*God will revenge, too, for the stones he took*
> *From aged Paul's . . .*"

His cousin added, "Pratt is in disgrace, too. He will not get any more royal patronage. You will have less opposition. You should be pleased."

"I have no affection for him, but he has some sense of the classical style. Is there any talk at Court about Milton's application to publish?"

"None. Be wise. Don't involve yourself. The Archbishop will have anything Oliver's secretary wrote examined with his usual vigilance."

When Christopher stood in front of Clarendon's house, he realised why the public resented it. Clarendon House was one of the most lavish private residences he had seen. He respected the classical style that Pratt had used, with the wings jutting out from the main pile. But he felt it was ostentatious, seeking to be a palace yet not quite daring this final audacity, handsome but too grand to be comfortable, pompous and solemn, designed to impress and overwhelm. There was also a large park around Clarendon House, a wall of trees and a fine Roman gate.

Then he shuddered. Matthew hadn't exaggerated. There was a gibbet, newly erected, just outside the gate. What a dreadful thing to look out upon, he thought, and he wondered if Clarendon was in residence.

There were lights within the mansion and soldiers formed an armed guard around it while a mob circulated about the gibbet. He noticed that some of the trees before Clarendon House had been cut down to build this gibbet and now he was angry, there was such a sickening lack of good timber to build any kind of a shelter in the still devastated city, and this was such a waste. He heard people in the mob declare vehemently:

"*Clarendon is a Papist at heart . . . We must have a Pope-burning . . .*"

"*We can creep around the rear and break the windows . . .*"

"*It is a bawdy house . . . The King brings his whores here . . .*"

"*Pratt robbed St. Paul's to erect this mansion. I saw many wagons conveying materials from the cathedral to build this pile. It cost fifty thousand pounds. No wonder it is called Dunkirk house. Clarendon stole the money from the sale of Dunkirk to the French to build it. Hang him!*"

Christopher questioned this and an elderly woman retorted,

"This is better than bull-baiting. More godly. Those who sin must be punished."

The soldiers forced the mob to retreat, but they didn't back away far, knowing that the troops would not carry out their threat to shoot.

He was glad there was still light in the sky this long summer day; he felt a little safer. After dark no one was on the streets of London or its outskirts without an armed guard, especially since the disorder caused by the fire. He was just a short distance from Scotland Yard. As he started homeward he wished that Clarendon House was simpler, more honest.

A few days later the Archbishop of Canterbury ordered him to appear at Lambeth Palace. Christopher was relieved that the mob before Clarendon House had been dispersed, and he assumed that Gilbert Sheldon wanted to see him to discuss the theatre at Oxford, where work had resumed.

He entered the ecclesiastical palace and it reminded him of Laud and his uncle; it had been Laud's palace, too, and his uncle's favourite. He was ushered into the Archbishop's audience chamber and while he waited amid the oak walls and under a large wooden lantern, he thought, This palace was vulnerable to fire, also, yet he doubted that Sheldon would like to hear this. He looked out a small Gothic window and wished he could be riding across the open fields of Southwark with Faith. He hadn't seen her recently, still unsure of his future, yet the wide green stretch of turf bordered by stately trees reinforced his yearning for her. Then he turned to acknowledge the entrance of the Archbishop.

Sheldon was in white robes, like an angel of God, and he said, "Doctor, you asked me to inform you when Milton's poem, *Paradise Lost*, is submitted to my office for licensing. That has been done."

"Thank you, Your Grace."

"Didn't you want to read it?"

Christopher blushed. He had forgotten about that request. He said, "Unfortunately, I haven't had the time. I've been busy."

"I know, Doctor. Glance at it now. Before my chaplain and Milton arrive. The manuscript is on the table."

He stared at the huge pile of papers and said, "It is so long, sir."

"Very long. Over four hundred pages. I'm told."

"I can't read it now, sir. There isn't time enough to form a judgment."

"You will not have to read much to judge the work."

"Have you read any of it, Your Grace?"

"A little. The work's tone is established at once."

Sheldon looked so insistent he started to read. The script was distinct, written by a painstaking hand, and he recalled that the blind poet dictated his work. He realised quickly that *Paradise Lost* was not a quarrel with Sheldon's Church, or *his* Church, or any Church, but if it were an argument, it was between God and Satan, good and evil, and an expression of the poet's views. And Milton was wrong about the universe. The earth was not the fixed and immovable centre, as the poem declared, and yet, fascinated by the music of the poetry, he re-read the opening.

> *"Of Man's first disobedience and the fruit*
> *Of that forbidden tree whose mortal taste*
> *Brought death into the World, and all our woe"*

He thought, Milton's words were severe, but they were fitting. He didn't feel them as he felt Shakespeare's; Milton didn't look inward as the dramatist did, and his words often verged on bombast, but his views possessed substance and there was much in them to respect and esteem.

"What do you think of the work?" asked the Archbishop.

"Sir, it is an immense work of the imagination and quite moral."

"Perhaps. But Milton likes Satan too much to please me."

"Your Grace, I thought you hadn't read it."

"I said that I glanced at some of the poem."

"Sir, it does possess religious reverence."

"I will see what my domestic chaplain thinks. He has read most of it." He summoned the Reverend Thomas Tomkyns, dark, short, not yet thirty, and asked him, "Have you determined Milton's intention?"

"I believe so, Your Grace. It is a Puritan view of the universe."

Christopher said, "I didn't find any political references."

Tomkyns said, "It is in the theology."

Sheldon asked, "Have you found anything dangerous?"

"Sir, there is a passage that might be considered offensive."

Christopher asked, "Reverend, have you discussed this with the poet?"

"No. He is waiting in the porter's lodge with a friend and a printer."

Sheldon exclaimed, "We've not given him licence to publish!"

Christopher said, "Sir, perhaps that is his hope, and anticipation."

Sheldon ordered, "Have him brought in!"

Milton was ushered in, accompanied by the young friend who had guided him here, Thomas Ellwood, and a printer, Samuel Symmons. Next to the vigorous, ruddy-faced Sheldon, the pale, slight, cadaverous poet looked frail and grey. Ellwood was the same age as Tomkyns, Christopher observed, while he couldn't judge the printer's age, Symmons was so uneasy. Milton was dressed in a simple black serge but his hair was still long and attractively combed, and in spite of his blindness he gave Christopher the feeling that he was staring into the Archbishop's soul.

Sheldon said, "Milton, I've been informed by my domestic chaplain that your work is full of Puritan sentiments."

"Protestant sentiments, Your Grace, to convey my piety in my work."

"As you did in the time of the civil wars?"

"I did my duty, sir, as you did yours."

"And wrote against the King. You are fortunate you were not hung."

"Sir, the greater the King will be for having shown mercy."

"Yet you have natural gifts."

"Thank you, Your Grace, I esteem even your censure."

"But I find the title revolting and the poetry doesn't engage me."

Milton flushed angrily but he didn't answer this time.

Christopher said, "Your Grace, the poem does concern the redemption of mankind. The ideas arouse reverence or horror, but not political views."

Tomkyns said, "Your Grace, there is a reference to revolution." He read:

> "As when the sun, new risen
> Looks through the horizontal misty air
> Shorn of his beams, or from behind the moon,
> In dim eclipse, disastrous twilight sheds
> On half the nations, and with fear of change
> Perplexes monarchs."

Tomkyns added, "That is unworthy and could be misunderstood, sir."

Milton said, "Many things could be misunderstood, Your Grace, but kings are human, too, and are often perplexed. Aren't they, sir?"

Christopher nodded but Sheldon replied, "Milton, do not instruct me!"

"It is not my intention, sir, but to justify the ways of God to man."

"Is that why you have arranged already with a printer to publish your work even before you have received the permission of our Holy Office?"

"Sir, in view of the dismal situation which afflicted our country with plague and fire it seemed an appropriate time to publish."

Sheldon asked the printer, "Symmons, do you share this opinion?"

"Your Grace, it is a poor time commercially to print. Almost all the books in London were burned in the Great Fire because they were stored in St. Faith's under St. Paul's. Indeed, it is a monstrous bad time, sir."

"Then why do you want to publish now?"

"Your Grace, Mr. Milton has some reputation as a poet."

"What are your terms?"

The printer seemed to shrink within his small body and his grey, worn face looked even more pained and he said, "Sir, I cannot afford the risk, but because I'm merciful and generous I will pay him five pounds for the first impression of thirteen hundred copies, and if the work shows unexpected strength, I will give him another five pounds for a further impression of the same number of copies. And if there is a third impression he will receive five pounds more, and the same for a fourth."

"After that," Christopher blurted out. "After a fourth impression?"

"Nothing," whispered Milton. "But it will not sell beyond that."

Sheldon said critically, "Milton, you do not drive a good bargain."

"Sir, that depends."

Ellwood spoke for the first time. "There is nothing to fear in *Paradise Lost*. I have read most of it and it is an excellent poem."

Sheldon said, "And you are a Quaker. I can tell, young man, with your grey garb and obstinate and pernicious disrespect for manners and position."

Christopher said, "Sir, a Quaker saved the life of a dear friend of mine. And they have endured much for their faith. It is the poet's view of the universe that troubles me. It is astronomically incorrect."

"It is the Bible's!" Milton declared indignantly. "The story of Adam and Eve as expressed in the Holy Writ!"

"The Ptolemaic cosmology is wrong. Galileo proved that."

"I met Galileo when I was in Italy. In 1638 or 1639, I no longer recall precisely. He was old, blind, a prisoner of the Inquisition for thinking in astronomy otherwise than the Franciscan and Dominican licensers thought, for his stubborn support of the Copernican heresy. But I write of heaven and hell and chaos as the Bible says. My poem is a virtuous work."

"It is, Your Grace. Whatever his astronomical views there is much to admire in *Paradise Lost*. Even my brief reading makes that evident."

"Archbishop, I wrote the poem because of my faith in God. And, I hear, you respect Doctor Wren's opinions."

Sheldon looked vexed and waited for Milton to be abject, but the poet stood as much a prince as the Archbishop. Yet Wren, whose regard he enjoyed, hung on his decision as if he were the Angel Gabriel. And whether or not he assented to the publication he must be firm. He declared, "Milton, the supporters of the Usurper mutilated our churches and it is difficult to forgive such barbarous destruction. But as Doctor Wren has said, I am a merciful man. You will hear our decision soon."

Milton shivered as if the ground was hollow beneath his feet. Then he regained his composure and said, "I see that you are merciful, for you have heard me out. Sir, if God has given me a gift, I must use it, as you use yours. *Paradise Lost* is not a quarrel with our time, but a hymn of praise to our Creator, in the manner of the Iliad and the Aeneid."

His blind eyes seemed to glow and Ellwood took his hand lovingly and said, "Archbishop, I'm but a humble Quaker, but God will bless you if a licence is granted." Ellwood forced himself to bow, although it was against his principles, and led Milton out, with the printer behind them.

Sheldon sighed with relief and said, "Praise God, that is done."

"Sir, you will grant Milton a licence to publish?" Christopher asked. "I prefer Shakespeare but there is an eloquence here that should be heard."

"It is not my inclination. The work is not pleasing but full of woe and melancholy. And to give away all of his rights for twenty pounds is an act of foolishness, and yet, in some ways, he is quite vain. He regards himself as the equal of Homer and Virgil. Tomkyns, is there anything else in the work beside what you read us that is offensive?"

"I've found none, Your Grace." As Sheldon still hesitated, Tomkyns added, "Let it be printed, sir. Although it is, as I pointed out, full of Puritan gospel, you needn't concern yourself with it. Very few, if any, will read it. The work has no liveliness or wit, but is so wordy and grandiloquent it will not suit the popular taste. Moreover, it will not engage. We are concerned with re-demption and curious about heaven and hell, but he tells us what we knew before. It could be salutary, Your Grace, to show how ponderous is a Puritan poet's view of the universe and how peculiar is his mind."

Sheldon said curtly, "Let it be printed. With our imprimatur."

When the first issue of *Paradise Lost* was printed Christopher bought a copy of the book for three shillings. He liked the strong yellow paper, he thought it would wear well, and the good legible type, which was easy to read. He judged it was between three hundred and four hundred pages in length. The book was thick, but the pages were not numbered. He started to read it while he waited at Gresham for the Royal Society to meet—the college had escaped the fire—but before he could get into the work and form his own opinion he was interrupted by Pepys and Evelyn.

Pepys insisted on knowing what Doctor Wren was reading and when he saw what it was, he laughed and said, "The poet Waller just informed me the old, blind schoolmaster has published a tedious poem on the Fall of Man. Waller told me, 'Its length may have merit, it has no other.'"

Evelyn said, "Denham likes it."

"Sir John is charitable, since his recent troubles. But Milton is an old Commonwealth's man, whatever his fancy and invention. And he wrote in defence of the murder of the King. Very few will dare to read him now."

Christopher asked, "Evelyn, what did Denham say?"

"He declared it is a book for both wise men and fools. Sir John rose in the House of Commons with a sheet, wet from the press, and in his most lucid manner, stated, '*I have part of the noblest poem that was ever written in any language, in any age. It is called Paradise Lost.*'"

"Granted that he said that, his view is not important," Pepys replied. "Everyone knows that Denham is mad. He dotes on controversy and is in a state of fatal decay. I hear that Clarendon is exiled. Doctor Wren, is there anything new about St. Paul's?"

"Nothing," Christopher said sadly. "Each time I recommend that a new cathedral must be built or the ruins of the old will topple on our heads, it is ignored. There is much ignorance about."

It is Only in the Instant

It is only in the instant
after pain
that heaven is revealed
And the greatest peace
is yours
Were the instant to last
heaven would be lost

Stymean Karlen

35

It is Only in the Instant

CHRISTOPHER WAS IMPROVING HIS TELESCOPE AT OXFORD BY designing apertures that could let in more or less light, as the viewer desired, by opening and closing them like the pupil of his eye, when there was a new summons from Sheldon. The Archbishop was concerned about the final stages of the construction of the theatre. Everything was in place but the roof, yet the master mason, Thomas Strong, doubted that the unsupported span would work and Sheldon was inclined to agree with him. The three men stood in front of the almost finished structure and Christopher inspected what was completed and as he saw that his instructions had been followed, except for the roof, he asked, "Mr. Strong, what is the difficulty now?"

"Doctor, it is . . . ?" He hesitated, not wanting to offend the professor, for Wren's cousin was secretary to the Duke of York, even if this gentleman philosopher was not actually a surveyor but an astronomer.

Christopher hoped it wasn't a vital objection. He couldn't ignore Strong's views. Without a reliable master mason nothing could be built; in many ways he was more essential than the design. And this blunt man, a little younger than himself, was a mason to respect. He was one of five brothers who had inherited stone quarries in Taynton in Oxfordshire; he was a craftsman and clever at choosing the right materials; his father had worked for Inigo Jones' master mason. "Are you worried about the roof?"

"It is seventy feet wide. No single beam of wood is that long."

"I have designed a truss that will support the roof."

"It can't hold. This kind of a roof has never been built before."

"That is no reason why it can't be built now. I have devised this truss with short beams that are dovetailed together. It will be fitted in between the ceiling and the upper roof and it will support both."

"No timber will sustain that. It puts too severe a strain on the wood."

"My design will work. I have examined all the possibilities."

"In your imagination, Doctor?" Strong asked scornfully.

"In my mind," Christopher answered quietly but firmly.

"There is no precedent for such a roof."

"Then I will establish one. With planks of sufficient strength."

Sheldon said suddenly, "We must pray for heavenly guidance."

"Meaning no disrespect, sir," said Strong. "I love the Bible, but I seldom read it. I prefer Roman history, it teaches more about building. Doctor, would you place the boards under the roof like pies in an oven?"

"Piece by piece. Four across and three to hold up the truss."

"Impossible. No one can cover such a vast space with timbers none of which are equal to the span. No wood will hold. It is too hard to do."

"I will do it. We have the best oak in the world in England."

Sheldon interrupted, "It is the property of the Navy."

"Your Grace, with the war over that shouldn't be a problem."

"It is always a problem, Doctor Wren."

"Sir, everyone admits that the theatre is necessary, that we can no longer hold the public ceremonies of the university in St. Mary's. And the King and the Duke of York are great supporters of learning. I think they can be persuaded to spare Oxford some of their noble oak."

Sheldon thought, He might have to perform magic to get the wood Wren wanted, but he nodded, disliking—above all else—to display weakness.

"Your Grace, it must be timber that will not require renewal, oak that will be secure and yet not stretch the walls. Wood that can stand the vicissitudes of heat and cold, drought and moisture. Without decaying."

Strong asked, "How can you be certain that such timber exists?"

"It does. Otherwise, Venice and Amsterdam would fall."

"I still don't see why you avoid columns to support your roof?"

"Because this structure is designed like the Theatre of Marcellus in Rome, and the shape is suited to the needs of this building."

Strong said, proud of his knowledge of Rome, "Roman theatres were open or covered with an awning to protect against the sun."

"Can you imagine leaving a building in England unroofed?"

"Granted, but I'm surprised that the interior of your theatre is wooden when such good stone is available."

Sheldon said, "He has given it a marble effect."

"Sir, it is not the same thing. Yet the stone from my quarries made Oxford possible. They are close and the stone is of the finest quality."

Christopher said, "The wood in the auditorium is better acoustically."

Sheldon added, "Doctor Wren knows these things better than we do."

Christopher said, "In this structure the sound is vital. We will see marble, but we will hear resonantly. And since this is where our students will graduate, it is essential that they hear the speakers."

Strong said, "Perhaps, but the style doesn't fit Oxford.

"The university has placed too much reliance on the Gothic."

Sheldon said crossly, "Our spires reflect the glory of Oxford. Truly."

"And, begging your pardon, are of the past. Sir, we must look forward. We have no choice if we are to be a civilized nation."
Christopher handed Strong his new design for the roof. "You can trust it, I assure you."

The master mason studied it, then said grudgingly, "It might work."

"It must work. Every beam of wood is in the right place."

After Strong left to see if any reliable oak was available, Sheldon asked Christopher, "What are your plans for the exterior of the theatre?"

"Thirteen heads of Roman Emperors, sir. It will be fitting."

"Your master mason fancies himself a sculptor. Commission him to do the heads and you could win his complete co-operation."

"Your Grace, I must give it to the men best suited."

"A master mason requires as much consideration as the design. Have you planned for gutters on the roof to carry off the rain?"

"Of course, Your Grace. Who raised the question of drainage?"

"Strong. He wants to find out how much you know about surveying."

"Sir, he regards me as a philosopher, not a surveyor."

"It is not a profession for gentlemen, but you have some skill at it. Although not always the manners. Sancroft is insistent that a choir and auditory be rebuilt at St. Paul's, but you keep telling him that this cannot be trusted. He is unhappy about your indifference to his proposals."

"Sir, it is not indifference but concern. To try to restore St. Paul's in its present shape is to try to resurrect a corpse. Moreover, I'm only an adviser, not the surveyor, and even my advice hasn't been accepted."

"I trust your enthusiasm for an unsupported roof doesn't alter your gift for natural philosophy. Your feeling for St. Paul's may have distorted your view of it. As Sancroft says."

A week later Christopher stopped at St. Paul's on his way to a meeting of the Royal Society at Gresham and told the Dean what Sheldon had said.

"But it is His Grace who feels that way!" exclaimed Sancroft. "He is the one who is determined to patch up the cathedral. With Clarendon in exile, he has fallen out of favour at Court, for he was close to Clarendon. Now he is using his great energy for Church affairs. He has decided to devote himself to repairing the damage done to our churches during the civil wars and our other troubles. Look, it goes at a fine pace."

Scaffolds were being built around the ruined shell of the cathedral and work was starting on the shattered roof and the west end where the Dean believed St. Paul's could be used for worship. But Christopher could not smile with a sense of achievement, as Sancroft did. He saw that the pillars on the south side of the west end of the cathedral were still off their perpendicular and possessed other defects, even more dangerous than before. They could collapse at any moment with the extra weight and strain imposed upon them by the new scaffolds being erected about them. Yet no one shared his apprehension. Many wagons were bringing timber up Ludgate Hill for more scaffolds. What a waste, he thought sadly, here was oak he could use at Oxford. He saw other wagons carrying off the best stone and wood.

He asked Sancroft, "Where are these materials going?"

"Buckingham is using the stone and wood for a house he is building."

"But there is a terrible shortage of materials."

"Charles has given his permission. He can't deny Buckingham anything. But don't worry, we have enough for our needs. Once we secure the west end we will hold services. For the sake of our faith. The Archbishop has ordered this done at once, vigorously, without fail."

"Who is in charge?" The more he saw the pillars the worse they were.

"Joshua Marshall. Son of the King's Master Mason and a master mason himself. He says a surveyor isn't necessary, that he has more practical experience. While he is not much older than yourself, he has worked with Denham, Webb, and Inigo Jones as a boy apprentice for his father."

"He may be right. At least, about the experience."

"Doctor, many buildings have been constructed without a surveyor."

"You are very fortunate, Dean Sancroft."

"Then you don't object to what Joshua Marshall is doing?"

"I've objected and objected. Has it done any good?"

"Your advice is appreciated. Your services will be considered."

"Thank you, sir." Sancroft was so excited about repairing St. Paul's he couldn't discourage him. *Perhaps*, he thought, *in the hands of a good man the work might prosper beyond his expectations.* Yet knowing, even as he assured the Dean of his support, that the fabric of St. Paul's was no stronger than an eggshell. Miles of wagons loaded with the best oak, the finest stone could not repair the unrepairable. The only conclusion he could see for this ancient Gothic cathedral was English dust.

"Doctor Wren, you are a man of considerable philosophical attainments, but you have had no professional training as a surveyor."

"Are you finished, sir?"

"What do you mean?"

"I have an appointment at Gresham with the Royal Society."

"Most fitting. Your scientific ingenuity is much admired."

"Yes, sir. I hope that you will be able to hold services soon."

Yet, as he walked toward Gresham, he felt guilty. More than ever, he believed, if the burnt fabric of St. Paul's held, it would just be for a short time. He was unhappy. Only surveying pushed him to the limits of his being, but no one seemed to like the direction he was going. But he couldn't be a sheep, single-minded and stupid and like a thousand other sheep. Be content, a voice said within him, you are a professor of astronomy, well considered, in good health, without any torments.

But so much of London was still an ugly thing. He stood on Cheapside and while almost two years had passed since the fire— it was spring, 1668—little of the city was rebuilt. St. Mary-le-Bow was a skeleton, Bread Street was without a house and reminded him of Milton and he wondered if anyone was reading *Paradise Lost;* it was obtainable now, and possibly, a Godly work, whatever the Archbishop said. A few public buildings were being erected and some private houses, mostly by rich merchants. A thousand structures existed out of the many thousands needed and the perspective was appalling. No wonder his plan for a new London had been rejected, he thought, every man claimed his own house and plot of ground, every heap of rubble was the site of a home, every residence, even if it was just a few boards and straw, had its owner or tenant. There were still ashes and rubbish wherever he looked and signs declaring, *"Mine! Mine!"* For the first time in hundreds of years London could be a city of straight streets and confusion reigned. London was becoming as it was before the fire, with the same narrow lanes, crooked alleys, and crowded courts. Then he noticed that most of the buildings already erected were inns and he sighed: perhaps he was foolish to want to be a surveyor.

Hooke had no such doubts. Hooke, who was Curator of Experiments to the Royal Society and Professor of Geometry at Gresham, was excited when he saw Christopher and he cried out, "I have great news! I have been appointed a surveyor by the City. Because of my plan to rebuild London. It wasn't accepted by the King but it was approved by the City authorities. They have two other surveyors, but I will be the one who matters."

"Congratulations, Robert. I'm sure you deserve it."

"Of course I do. You're an amateur in architecture but I'm an expert."

Christopher ignored that—Hooke was often cantankerous because of his poor health—but his mind was one of the most active and curious he knew. No one else had arrived for this afternoon meeting of the Society and this was a good time to show him how he had improved the telescope; Hooke fancied himself as an astronomer, too. But Hooke wasn't listening, and finally, growing impatient at his lack of interest, Christopher exclaimed, "Robert, I'm still an astronomer, a professor of astronomy. Do you like this experiment? I'm thinking of submitting it to the Society."

"You are wise to confine yourself to such matters. I've contrived a rigging for ships, and a model for a chariot with four springs, easy for both the rider and the horse, a new kind of a coach. Evelyn says of me, '*No such person is to be found elsewhere in Europe for clever parts and ingenuity.*' Certainly I have a rare curiosity and imagination."

Christopher nodded, although he felt despondent.

The next moment his heart leaped with joy. Holder stood in the doorway accompanied by Faith and he said, "My lady has business in the City and expressed an interest in the proceedings of the Society, and I thought she would be pleased by some of your experiments and inventions, and so, I brought her here. I trust no one will object."

Christopher said happily, "We will be honoured."

Hooke grumbled, "Besides, it is done."

Christopher showed Faith the model of his new telescope and she was fascinated with it. Holder drew Hooke aside, who went unwillingly until the former asked him if it was true he had been appointed City Surveyor. Then Hooke was eager to show Holder his plans to rebuild the City.

Faith examined Christopher's *Instrument for Perspective*, his *Nocturnal Astronomical Device for Finding the Time at Night*, his *Perpetual Motion Machine*, and his *Ways of Embroidery for Beds and Hangings*.

She was surprised by his interest in embroidery and asked why.

"I want to improve our country's trade in domestic and foreign markets, and I must be an economist as well as a philosopher."

"And a surveyor!" she exclaimed.

"Not necessarily."

"But that is your natural interest and sympathy."

He didn't answer.

Faith felt this was too important to be ignored. "Are you giving up your desire to be a surveyor? Is that why I haven't seen you recently?"

"I wanted to call on you again but I have been distracted by building matters. What is your business in London?"

"I'm going to Drury Lane with the Reverend Holder and your sister. I need a vacation from the country. Would you like to join us?"

He hesitated. He enjoyed the theatre but he had gone rarely.

"The King's Company are giving a late performance. At five today. To suit the King's pleasure. So he can hunt earlier in the afternoon."

"What is the play?"

"I'm not sure but I believe it is by Dryden."

"He was at Westminster when I was. In a lower form. And he is a member of the Royal Society, although he seldom comes to our meetings."

Holder, who had returned, said, "He may honour us today and attend his play. It is a revival of his success, *Secret Love*, but the great interest in it is because the King's newest mistress, Nell Gwynn, displays her charms in the leading role. She is supposed to be very pretty and quite amusing. Charles is so pleased with this play he has graced it with the title of *his* play and has commanded this performance. It could be an exciting occasion. Our monarch is indeed profligate."

"What about the play? Is it interesting?"

"It is a success. As you know, I'm eminent in music and an authority on deafness and there is much I will learn about speech at the theatre."

And enjoy yourself while being a matchmaker, thought Christopher, but possibly that wasn't a bad idea. He hadn't seen any of Dryden's plays, although the latter fancied himself the successor to Shakespeare. He was curious about Nell Gwynn, but it was Faith that mattered. Her grey taffeta cloak was thrown open and revealed her beauty to the best advantage. Faith's blue velvet gown, which matched her eyes, was cut low on her shoulder and was finished with red muslin and a white lace collar which heightened her rose and lily complexion. He liked her long blue gauntlet gloves which reminded him of her love of riding. Her

charms were natural; she disdained the black face patches which
he felt were one of the vices of the age. He had missed her oval
features, her small, graceful mouth, her vivid blue eyes, and her
slender waist and full hips. He wondered why he hadn't seen these
qualities before.

Holder asked impatiently, "Christopher, are you distracted
again?"

Faith said, aware of his scrutiny, "Perhaps he doesn't want to
go."

"I do," said Christopher. "After our meeting. If you don't mind
sitting next to me, I will be happy to explain our proceedings if it
should be necessary."

"I just want to observe," she said hurriedly, "and learn." She
congratulated herself that this step, at least, had been taken.

None of the members commented on her presence although
Pepys' eyes widened at the sight of her, for he never could take
his eyes off a pretty woman, and she was very pretty. Evelyn had
known her father and he stated he was flattered by their friendship
and honoured by her presence.

Boyle viewed her critically; she felt disapprovingly, although he
bowed when Christopher introduced her. Matthew came in late,
making it obvious he had been detained by vital matters at Court.
Aubrey was pleased that she was present; she gave the meeting a
liveliness that was usually lacking.

Wilkins, now Bishop of Chester because of Buckingham's influence, presided and she thought, This broad-shouldered, strong-
featured divine was without gall, which was rare. He was gracious
to everyone, while Hooke, who exhibited his plans for the rebuilding of the City, regarded everybody suspiciously. Hooke, by the
side of the well-built Wilkins, looked even more crooked and stooped.
Of all the members there he was the most lean and pale, and except
for Christopher, the only one without a periwig, wearing his own
hair, which hung, a dark brown, very long, uncut and uncombed,
to his shoulders. She didn't comprehend all that he said, while
Pepys told her, "His ideas are fine but too clever," and Christopher
said nothing.

Evelyn was the next to speak. He stated there must be sex in
trees and plants, for they had such a difference in hardness and
softness, and everyone knew that men's bodies were hard while
women's were soft.

Not all of the members listened until Boyle spoke of his experiments in alchemy. He was convinced he could convert quicksilver
and mercury into gold and this interested the members. Only
Christopher was sceptical of this ardent alchemist's confident asser-

tion that it was just a matter of time before he coined gold out of the baser metals.

The meeting was about to end when Wilkins mentioned Doctor Wren's new telescope and asked, "Christopher, don't you want to exhibit it?"

"Not yet. I've not perfected it. Bishop, what about your investigations into the possibility of creating a universal language?"

Wilkins said passionately, "With all our new ideas, experiments, and discoveries, the only surety against ignorance is the development of a language, learned in nature, that will make all philosophical knowledge available to men everywhere. The true philosopher is not concerned with religious or national distinctions but in universal information." Some of the members were uneasy, as if what Wilkins said was heresy, but Christopher nodded and Wilkins added, "I have an example now where a universal language would be beneficial. Doctor Wren has devised a *Way Wiser*. He is too modest to present it himself, and so I take the liberty of doing it." He rushed on before Christopher could halt him. "Wren's *Way Wiser*, fitted into a space cut into the axle tree, has five indexes and measures distances"—Christopher interrupted, "I prefer to call it a *milemeter*"—"As the Doctor says, in miles, tens of miles, and hundreds of miles."

Before Wilkins could explain this invention further, for most of the members were puzzled, which made Faith grateful that she wasn't the only one, Hooke stated irritably, "This experiment is not new."

"Vitruvius talks about it," Evelyn added knowingly.

"I never maintained it was wholly original," said Christopher. "Very few inventions come from one mind. Almost everything grows out of what someone else has learned. Most knowledge is a step, a growth, not a beginning or an end. We must understand, as astronomy tells us, that there is still so much to learn and we stand only on the threshold."

Susan met Holder, Christopher, and Faith in her coach, which had brought Faith and the Holders from Bletchington. Two footmen rode on each side of the coachman, which assured their safety, and as the coach rolled toward Drury Lane and His Majesty's Theatre, Holder sat next to his wife so that Christopher could be by the side of Faith, and remarked, "Miss Coghill has just purchased this new livery. It is in the latest fashion and is one of the finest I have ever ridden in."

Faith said modestly, "It is necessary if I want to travel."

Susan added, "Faith can't risk the common hackney coaches, for every fop and licentious courtier would approach her with indecent advances."

Christopher said, "The coach rides easily despite the mud and cobbles that afflict our travel. Too often riding in London is a hazard, but this coach is well sprung. Each year there are more vehicles on the road, more than the city can endure comfortably. One day, with the increase of vehicles, there will be no space in London for anything else to move."

Faith said, "That is why I bought a small coach."

With two beautiful black horses, he noticed, their manes and tails tied with blue ribbons and the footmen and coachman dressed smartly.

Soon after they turned off the Strand and into Drury Lane and arrived at the theatre. It was Christopher's first visit to this playhouse which was under royal patronage and while the afternoon was no longer pleasing, having grown rainy, windy, and cold, he was eager to observe what had been built here. Heavy, lumbering carriages crowded the street and he thought them clumsy and he disliked the neighbourhood, which had escaped the fire, for the buildings were old, often rotting, and most of them stood with a kind of sunken, depraved hopelessness. Drury Lane was a maze of medieval courts, dark brothels, narrow alleys, and dismal poverty. He imagined the fine, clean, spacious *piazza* he would have constructed about the theatre if he had been asked; instead he saw wooden buildings pressed tightly against the playhouse and decaying timbers overhung the facade and again he was aware of the danger of fire. But if he mentioned this he would be regarded as a scold and so he was quiet. Yet this was not a Queen of a theatre as he desired but a drab. There were just two entrances, narrow passages only ten feet wide, and as he followed the Holders and escorted Faith, whores and orange girls solicited around them. Holder assured them that they would have a fine box, for he had paid a boy a shilling to hold their seats. Susan said this was extravagant, but Faith said nothing, observing everything that was visible with curiosity and eagerness.

Christopher noticed that their box was within sight of the other boxes but had a poor view of the stage. Faith discussed the audience with Susan while the pit filled with whores and orange girls, too. In the gallery there were women who were not selling their services and Christopher was amazed by the commotion. People strolled in and out and shouted to friends all over the theatre. But no one seemed to mind the din but himself.

Holder admiringly pointed out that the boxes were handsome with their green baize linings and bands of gilt leather, but Christopher saw the orange peel that littered the aisles and the green cloth-covered benches in the pit that were filthy from the feet of the men standing on them. As he observed the crowded seats, the poor sight lines, he found himself redesigning this Drury Lane theatre so it would be more comfortable, more for drama and less for spectacle, with the benches in the pit elevated and curved in the shape of an amphitheatre, each row higher than the one in front, and the boxes arranged so one could see rather than be seen.

Then the fiddlers in the music room above the stage struck up an air to announce the arrival of the King. There was a scraping of feet and a hum through the audience as they rose and faced the King's box over the stage, and draped with scarlet velvet and the royal coat-of-arms.

Charles entered accompanied by York and he smiled to the audience, pleased with their homage, and raised his hand in acknowledgement.

Faith had never seen Charles in person; she hadn't expected him to be so tall and swarthy. She thought, While he was almost the same age as Christopher, he looked much older, and dissolute. His jowls sagged, his eyes had heavy pouches, and his complexion was sallow despite his love of hunting and riding, but she liked his easy, graceful posture. She felt that Christopher's appearance was more individual, with his mobile mouth, his sharply defined features, his wide grey eyes, high cheekbones and vivid chin, and skin that was unblemished by age or dissipation. And while he was short, he was compact, a man interested in everything and everybody, not just himself. What she preferred most about him was that unlike most of the courtiers, he didn't strive to imitate women in his apparel, with a long periwig, a patched and painted face, breeches like petticoats, but dressed simply but sensibly as befitted his masculinity.

She mentioned her dislike of periwigs, particularly those down to the waist, and he replied, "They must be the scalps of hanged men, they are worn so proudly. Most courtiers seem ashamed of their own hair."

She nodded, although she knew little about the Court except what she had heard, and then she was distracted by the entrance of Dryden into the box on their left, for some of the audience applauded him.

Pepys arrived in the box on their right and as soon as he saw Doctor Wren, he said, "I didn't think you were addicted to pleasure."

Christopher smiled as he answered, "It is easy, if it is genuine."

"I'm much addicted to the theatre. It has its own wisdom. But sometimes I think it is folly to attend so much, like wine-drinking."

"Do you know this afternoon's play?"

"Very well. I've seen Nell Gwynn in *Secret Love* six times." His voice grew lively and cheerful. "I've never seen a better performance

T

in a comical role. If I may say so, without vanity, my views of the theatre are well thought of." In his enthusiasm he didn't notice someone had thrown a burning ember out of the gallery and that it had fallen on his wig and set it afire. Christopher became aware of this when the burning wig sputtered with a strange noise and lost its perfect curl and he grinned. Pepys tore the wig off his head and smacked it angrily on the floor until he put out the fire. Christopher realised that Pepys' once black hair was turning grey like the King's, but Pepys ignored that and said, "I paid three guineas for the wig. I hope it isn't ruined."

"The curl is gone and it is shorter."

"I think three guineas was a fair price. And I can afford the best serge now and I will be buying my own coach this year. Do you want to meet Nell Gwynn? I know her well. She may wield much influence soon."

Christopher hesitated, but Faith, who heard this invitation, said, "Yes, Mr. Pepys," while Susan added, "It isn't fitting for my husband to be seen with her, so we will wait for you outside in the coach."

Pepys said, "Nell Gwynn is a fine actress. I much admire her."

It was difficult for Christopher to get a clear picture of her. He could only see part of the stage from the box, and while it was only five in the afternoon the grey, rainy sky had darkened the glass above, there was an opening on top of the theatre, and he was upset by the spectators in the pit shifting to avoid the dripping water. This offended him; he thought it irresponsible to allow this leak. The many bright burning wax candles in the chandelier above the stage were all lit but they brought smoke, haze, and mist. He lost interest in the play, which he found insipid, written to exhibit her charms. He wasn't sure he cared for her acting but she was pretty and the lines suited her. Dancing and skipping about the stage, Nell Gwynn swayed with a voluptuous desire to please.

She sang a bawdy song, which he doubted was in the text—it was not typical of Dryden—but her voice gave it a sensual and insinuating quality. The audience liked her best when she appeared in tight breeches and a thin white blouse in which she could display her chief charms. She held her ribs high to show off her full breasts and small waist and as she ran the length of the stage, ending near the King's box where he watched her closely, she raised her skirt above her knees so that her legs could be seen.

Christopher felt Charles was appraising her as carefully as if he were buying a horse, but now she looked beautiful, although he still wasn't sure she could act. He noticed that only when she was playing did the audience quiet down; there was some laughter and talking, but no one left or entered the playhouse, as they did when she wasn't on stage.

Pepys led them backstage as if he had gone there often. Nell Gwynn greeted him familiarly and curtsied to Christopher and Faith. She knew that Doctor Wren was a professor of astronomy, a renowned philosopher, and a gentleman surveyor, and she was gracious to Faith, who, for once, was not self-possessed, as if Faith didn't know how to treat an actress.

After all, reflected Faith, it was just a few years that women had been allowed to play women's parts and she wasn't certain she approved.

Christopher realised that Nell Gwynn was even prettier in person, with a clear skin, hazel eyes, full lips, a generous mouth, dimples, and the voluptuous breasts which were prominent by contrast with her small face and slender waist. Her voice had a touch of cockney but was appealing.

Pepys declared, "Madame Gwynn, I've never seen you act better," then paused, for the King entered. Charles was alone and he frowned when he saw Pepys, but as he noticed Faith he grew affable. He bowed as she curtsied to him and he asked to be introduced. Christopher did so, reluctantly, not liking the approval that appeared in Charles' eyes.

Charles asked, "Miss Coghill, are you a friend of Doctor Wren?" He sounded surprised.

"Yes, Your Majesty. He has shown me much of his work."

"He is a fine inventor but I'm not certain about his surveying."

Christopher asked, "Sir, you think ruined St. Paul's should be used?"

"Why not, if the Dean thinks so. It will surely cost less. And there is doubt about the roof you propose for the theatre at Oxford."

Nell Gwynn said suddenly, "Your Majesty, I grew up in the shadow of St. Paul's. No one loves it better than I do, but now it is a ruin."

Charles laughed. "Madame Nell, what do you know of surveying?"

"I know what is fitting. Especially in a church, sir."

"Next you will want to design a building yourself."

"Your Majesty, I couldn't do worse than some of those who serve you."

Charles was silent. He knew that most of the fulsome expressions of devotion he received were false but it was not always wise to admit it.

Christopher said, "Your Majesty, may we be excused?"

Charles ignored that, curious to find out whether Doctor Wren really was interested in this very pretty lady. "Miss Coghill, why haven't I seen you at Court? Your presence would add beauty and grace to it."

"Thank you, Your Majesty, but I have had no occasion to come."

"You should persuade Doctor Wren to bring you. And to be more attentive."

"Sir, he is attentive enough." She halted, embarrassed.

Christopher said, "Sir, I'm honoured by Miss Coghill's presence. Madame Gwynn, it was nice to meet you. I hope I shall have the pleasure again."

Charles said sharply, "I trust you are going in the same direction as Mr. Pepys. He has more experience in the ways of the Court than you do."

Pepys was elated as he left the theatre with Christopher and Faith. Now, after the King's praise, he was positive he could afford a new coach.

Christopher said nothing, not even to Faith, who was critical of Nell Gwynn, which he felt was jealousy. The Holders wanted to know what had happened backstage, but Pepys had to go in the opposite direction and Faith was uncommunicative and Christopher refused to tell them.

At an inn nearby where they spent the night—Susan and Faith shared one room while Holder and Christopher slept in the other—they went to bed early. Holder couldn't sleep; he had to tell Christopher of Faith's many virtues. *"She has a thousand pounds a year, she knows Latin and Greek, she likes music in addition to the theatre, and she would grace any man's home."* Christopher remained silent in the hope that Holder would take the hint, but the last thing he remembered as he fell asleep was Holder saying, *"She has a fine estate, her income would be dependable . . ."*

He dreamed all night and in his dreams he was ringed by Sheldon, Strong, Sancroft, Pepys, and the King, who were seeking to trap him. Their words were in a language strange to him and he couldn't escape them. His doublet was falling down about his legs, his hose and shoes were gone, his collar torn, his hair shorn, his heart exposed, and they were treating him as a puppet, jerking him to the ground and then into the air where he hung helplessly, feet dangling, while they shouted at him, *"Look again, your roof is faulty . . . you do not love St. Paul's, your concern is for yourself . . . Jones is dead and your designs are not safe . . ."* When he awoke he felt much older. The dreams were so real they had a life of their own.

Faith asked to see his new telescope and the next week he showed it to her. She stood in his observatory at Wadham and saw that he wore a new brown doublet and a fine lace collar to set off his long flowing hair. She had never seen him so carefully and attractively dressed and she was pleased. He seemed in a good humour, but when she asked to look at the theatre, he said, "It is pointless. It is unfinished and it may remain so."

"But you have made your final designs."

"My master mason hasn't approved. While he agreed to put timber in as I ordered not a plank is in place or looks as if it ever will be. I'm not yet equal to a master mason and I doubt I ever will be."

"I felt you would like to redesign Drury Lane."

"How did you know?"

"It was in your eyes."

"I thought you were absorbed by the performance."

"The stage fascinates me, but it is no place for a lady."

"The same could be said for surveying. It fascinates me, but I'm told it is no work for a gentleman. Only I'm a philosopher, not a gentleman."

"I thought you had your heart set on being a surveyor."

"I did. But what they have never seen before they say is incredible, and thus, impossible. When I was a child Windsor needed repairs. It still hasn't been done. Things are always being put off. Now the excuse is that Denham is ill, Pratt is in disgrace, May—who is in charge of Windsor—has no opinions, Hooke is too difficult, and Webb is ignored."

"And Christopher Wren?"

"He is regarded as a dreamer, a visionary, which is even worse." It was odd, he thought, her questions were as if she searched for an explanation of herself. He added, deeply interested in what she felt, "Faith, why is it important to you?"

She couldn't tell him of her ambitions; it wasn't fitting in a lady. The only way she could realise them was through a husband and he had the most ability of any men she had met. "Because it is important to you."

In this moment he felt as close to her as he had felt to anyone and he was tired of holding in his emotions. "Surveying depends on many things apart from the design, on carpenters, bricklayers, and most of all, on master masons. Since they do the actual building, they often think they know more than anybody else, especially the surveyor."

"Do they, Christopher?"

"It depends on the designer. A Bernini, a Jones must be heeded." She listened so intently, he was able to say to her what he hadn't said to anyone:

"In their hands, architecture aims at eternity. Yet it also has other uses. Public buildings can be the ornament of a country, establish a nation, make the people love their arts which passion is the original of great actions in a country. The design of the cities of Greece was the true cause of their greatness. The obstinate valour of the Jewish people was occasioned by their love of their Temple, and was the cement that held them together through many ages and changes."

"Go on."

"Even when my work is taken seriously there is interference."

"You must still do what comes from deep inside of you."

He was so grateful for her encouragement he reached forward to embrace her. Then he halted; he heard someone approaching. "I appreciate your support but I should give up surveying. Before it breaks my heart."

She was furious at this interruption; she had worked so hard to evoke a display of emotion. But she said quietly and firmly, "It doesn't have to. You mustn't let it. You mustn't let anything or anybody stop you."

"They are not interested in my style but prefer the Gothic. I'm going to stop being a surveyor and concentrate on being a natural philosopher."

He had such an air of resignation she believed him. As she approached him to console him, treasuring this moment, they were interrupted by Seth. His servant ignored her irritation and ran up to Christopher and cried, "Master, I've a message from London for you. It came by special messenger, who is waiting downstairs for your reply. There is an express coach now which travels from London to Oxford in one day."

Christopher took it and said, "Faith, it is from Dean Sancroft."

She asked, "What does he write?"

He read:

"What you whispered in my ear at your last coming here has come to pass. Our work at the west end of St. Paul's is fallen about our ears. Your quick eye discerned the walls and pillars gone off from their perpendiculars, and other defects too, which are now exposed to every common observer. A week ago, while we were working at the third pillar from the west end on the south side, it threatened a sudden ruin so visibly the workmen removed themselves and the next night the whole pillar fell and carried scaffolds and all to the ground. The second pillar stands alone now with an enormous weight on top of it; we cannot hope it will stand long and yet we dare not venture to take it down.

"This breach is due to defects in Inigo Jones' work. It is the opinion of all men that we can proceed no farther at the west end.

"What we are to do next is the present deliberation, in which you are so absolutely and indispensably necessary to us, that we can do nothing, resolve

on nothing, without you.

"*You will think fit, I know, to bring with you those excellent designs you formerly favoured us with, and in the meantime, until we enjoy your presence here, consider what to advise that may be for the satisfaction of His Majesty and the whole nation. An obligation so great and so public that it must be acknowledged by better hands than those of—*

Your very affectionate friend and servant,

W. Sancroft."

Faith asked, "What are you going to do?"

"I have to respond. I have no choice."

Seth cut in, "Master, the messenger is waiting below for your reply."

"I will answer in person."

Faith said, "That is a mistake, Christopher. The Dean didn't ask for your immediate presence, but for your opinion and help. Do not be too available. Now that they need you it will be better if you are delayed. Write and say that you are so busy in Oxford that you cannot come to London at once, but you will arrive as soon as you can. Possibly, next week. That will make them want you more."

Seth agreed and Christopher thought, Faith was more practical than he was. He wanted to embrace her to express his gratitude but he had a letter to write. Phrases were developing in his mind. He must not gloat, yet in his heart he was almost glad that the pillar had fallen down.

With her help he composed the end of the letter he was writing. "*Sir, I shall only put my business in order so that it may not stand still during my absence and I shall wait upon you and His Grace about the middle of next week, bringing the old designs with me . . .*"

He turned to Faith and asked, "Do you like it?"

"It should be suitable and useful."

He thought about this a moment, then said, "Seth, tell the messenger I will have a written reply for Dean Sancroft shortly."

After Seth left, she asked, "Were you serious about giving up surveying?"

"Quite serious. I'm still not sure I should pursue it. I will see what happens in London next week. Now I must complete this letter. I will take you to your coach." He took her hand to help her down the stairs and when he felt her tremble, he had to assure her of his feelings. He embraced her and she responded as fervently as he did.

Then she wondered if he had the same doubts about her that he had about surveying, and she withdrew as if her virginity had been threatened and exclaimed, "I will never see you again!"

"You must!" he cried. "You've been so helpful! I will visit you in Bletchington as soon as a decision is reached about St. Paul's.''

Faith didn't reply but stepped into her coach and waved goodbye.

He hurried back to his desk to finish his reply to the Dean.

I will not Discard the Inch of Thread

I will not discard the inch of thread
It is red
And will make a bright stitch

I will not leave this left-over brick
It is jagged and stunted
But will be the holder of my stubborn door

I will not abandon the lost button
It is simple and without distinction but
It will be a fine model for a quaint design

These bits of fame tendered by me will not
be taken from you
But if you need a bit of fame too

I would surely give it to you

Stymean Karlen

T*

36

I will not Discard the Inch of Thread

CHRISTOPHER FOLLOWED FAITH'S ADVICE. HE WAITED A WEEK BEFORE
he replied to Sancroft's request in person. And, as she predicted,
when he arrived at St. Paul's, the Dean greeted him even more
eagerly than he expected.

Sancroft exclaimed, "How good of you to come!" and led him
to where the pillar had collapsed and asked, "What do you think
should be done?"

"I must examine everything before I know."

"As you will, Doctor. You will be heeded now."

Despite his desire to build a new cathedral, Christopher was
stricken with horror. The pillar lay shattered into many pieces.
The stone was in fragments, crushed by the impact on the cathedral
floor. He thought, It had been shaped with pride and honour and
now all life was gone from it. He wanted to repair it, but that
was useless, the pillar was beyond saving. Everything about the old
St. Paul's was. Wherever he looked there was rubble and the
devastation had increased. A heavy misty rain fell on the burnt-out
fabric and the dark afternoon sky was sombre and added to his
sense of desolation. He thought, This was no longer a church but a
death. They were mourning the end of the ancient Gothic cathedral.
It had died many times, he told himself, but this was the final
funeral. Without any doubt now, whatever life had been left in old
St. Paul's, was gone. Gross rot had set in, the last vestige of hope
of repair had vanished, although many walls still stood and a vast
amount of stone, lead, and other materials would have to be
demolished and removed. It was a task almost as difficult as constructing a new cathedral. But all patching had ended. No wagons
brought materials, the scaffolds that remained were half-finished.
He shivered and reflected, He had nothing to celebrate yet.

Sancroft, surprised and worried that Wren had not replied and he had not arrived as soon as anticipated, perhaps he was offended by their previous attitude, asked anxiously, "Won't you consider helping us?"

"Not if I'm held on a string to be pulled one way and then another."

"I assure you that will not happen. The Commissioners have met and decided old St. Paul's must be demolished and that we need a surveyor."

"And not a Master Mason? He could remove the debris."

"We need a design. Did you bring your designs with you?"

"Yes, but they may need revising and how do I know you will use them?"

"Doctor, don't be difficult. The Commissioners have decided to allow the surveyor to handle the problems of demolishing and design."

Christopher picked up a fragment of the crushed pillar and said, "Even Inigo Jones could make a mistake. And I thought he was a giant."

"Don't mock us, sir. You can be the surveyor. If you desire."

"If I desire?" Christopher exclaimed. "Dean, now you are mocking me."

"It has been decided privately that you are the most suitable."

"You are flattering me to find out what to do."

"We have appraised you. The Archbishop and I agree that you are the best choice, and the other Commissioners will agree with us."

"What about Webb? He is qualified, too."

"After the way Jones' work collapsed? He would be impossible."

"And Denham is ill, Pratt disgraced, May incompetent, and Hooke . . ."

"He is not a gentleman and you are much better qualified. You are the only one who foretold what was going to happen. Don't you want the post?"

He coveted it so much he felt the new fabric in his bones but he didn't want to remove a dunghill and then be cast aside. He said, "Charles will not approve. He appointed me Deputy Surveyor, but he has not allowed me to complete anything. Whatever I propose he finds an excuse to put off."

"He will not put off work on St. Paul's. It has become a matter of national honour and now that the rebuilding of London takes shape, there is enthusiasm for a new cathedral. As long as Charles doesn't have to dig deeply into his own pocket, he will support us. And we have spoken already to him about you and he has agreed to your appointment. In this, you are not the King's servant but ours. As your uncle and father were before you."

Christopher stared at the naked, wretched, mangled cathedral and yearned to say yes, and yet? He blurted out, "What about my theatre at Oxford?"

Sancroft was startled and retorted, "How does that concern St. Paul's?"

"The Archbishop questioned the roof I proposed. If my design is not followed there, how do I know it will be accepted here?"

"Doctor, we must reserve the right to criticise."

"And I," he said proudly, although it came hard and he felt he was choking off his own breath. "Must reserve the right to refuse."

Decline if you must, Sancroft longed to shout back, but solve our present problem. Only Wren looked so adamant his tone was softer than he felt as he said, "I will speak to Sheldon about your roof. If that is the surety you wish. I'm sure now that your invention will be carried out."

Soon after work started on the roof of the theatre as Christopher intended. He wrote a letter of thanks to Sancroft and said he would do anything in his power to help him and a few weeks later he was notified by the Dean: "*The Royal Commission appointed by His Majesty, Charles the Second, for the repair, rebuilding, and maintenance of the Cathedral Church of St. Paul's, have appointed you the surveyor. God save the King.*"

Christopher had to tell Faith the good news. He hired a coach and left Oxford early in the morning to make sure he would find her in, but when he arrived at her home in Bletchington she was out. Her steward said she was in London and he didn't know when she was returning. He stopped at the rectory in the hope Susan would know when Faith would be back, but she didn't, and said, "Why didn't you write her that you were coming?"

"I wanted to surprise her."

"You've surprised me. May I give her a message?"

"I'll write her."

He turned to go and she asked unhappily, "Aren't you staying for dinner? William will be disappointed to miss you."

"I've much work to do. I've been appointed surveyor of St. Paul's."

She looked at him in amazement—he had not said a word to her about this possibility, although she knew he loved the cathedral. She threw her arms about him and cried, "Christopher, I'm sure you deserve it!"

"I will find out." He was pleased with Susan's excitement but he didn't want her to overdo it. Don't tell Faith. I would like to tell her myself."

"So you do care for her! Christopher, have you ever thought of . . ."

He halted her. "Susan, my future is still uncertain. Work on St. Paul's may go on for many years and a professor's pay is not large."

"Faith has enough for both of you."

"I will never marry anyone I can't support."

"But you should settle down and have a place you can call home. Not a passion for an old, ruined cathedral. That is not fitting."

"Susan, you sound like William now."

"I should. He is my husband. I should follow him in all things. As Faith would. As any dutiful wife would."

He kissed her lightly on the cheek to quiet her and smiled as he said, "Remember, you promised not to tell Faith about the surveyorship. I prefer to do that myself." He returned to the coach he had hired, driven with a new urgency to work on St. Paul's as soon as possible.

These plans distracted him as he wrote to Faith the next day. He wanted to tell her how much he missed her, how much he cared for her, and his designs for a classical cathedral intruded and blotted out the endearing phrases he intended to write. Instead of revealing his feelings about her, he asked if he might see her again soon because he had important news to convey to her. He had Seth deliver this letter in person.

Seth returned without an answer.

He asked, "Did you give my note to Miss Coghill?"

"Yes, Master. Personally. She had just come back from London."

"And there was no answer?"

"None. I thought she swallowed whatever she intended to say."

He was startled when Faith appeared at Wadham the following week. It was a warm afternoon at the end of June and he wore an old brown doublet and a grey shirt that was open at the collar. He was working on a tentative design for a new St. Paul's, with a dome and pillars that would endure. His room was untidy, drawings were scattered over his table—he missed Daniel, Daniel drew better than he did—and, as he heard the approaching footsteps, because his friend was on his mind, he hoped it was Daniel. He didn't expect Faith. He wished she was more formal, as was the custom. He respected her independent ways, but her sudden visits were disconcerting. His shock showed and as abruptly as she had entered she started to leave.

He stopped her at the door and said, "I'm delighted to see you. It is just that I'm not dressed appropriately, not prepared for company."

She liked the way he looked when he was not formal. His appearance was the quintessence of what he was. His open collar gave him an elemental yet romantic manner and displayed his fine, long, brown hair and strong neck to splendid advantage; altogether, he was a most attractive man. But perhaps her forwardness was a mistake; it was not the fashion.

He said, "I was afraid you meant it, Faith, when you said you would never see me again."

"Is that why you visited me? To mock me to my face?"

"I never want to mock you. Or to hurt you in any way."

"You left word that you had important news for me."

"Yes, I think you will be pleased."

"That is why I came and broke my resolve not to see you any more."

"I'm happy you did. It is why I visited you when I found out about my good news. I was disappointed that you were not at home."

"What news?" Her voice was quiet but full of anticipation.

"I have been appointed surveyor of St. Paul's. And you helped."

"Oh!"

Instead of appearing pleased, she sounded upset. "Faith, didn't you want me to obtain this appointment? You encouraged me to seek it."

"I wanted you to obtain the post. But I knew that you had."

"Who told you? Susan? She promised . . ." It was his turn to be upset.

"It wasn't your sister. But Holder was so proud of you, he had to tell me. I thought your important news was . . ." She bit her lips, blushed, and was silent. She had assumed too much, she thought bitterly, like a country lass fresh from her father's nursery. She mustn't make that mistake again.

He realised she had translated his good news into a proposal of marriage. He said, "I treasure your friendship, but I'm in no position to offer anything permanent. St. Paul's may take years to rebuild and my prospects at Oxford are modest."

"Holder says you will be the King's Chief Surveyor when Denham dies."

"That is macabre."

"But his failing health is a fact, isn't it? And you like facts."

"Denham's poor health is a fact. But the rest . . .?" He shrugged.

"And you have good connections."

He frowned.

"No offence meant. But your cousin, Matthew Wren, told me."

"He considers himself one of those connections. But it is a frail reed."

"Your background is fitting. Susan told me that your father and uncle designed several buildings and that you have always loved to draw."

"Susan exaggerates."

"So does her brother." As she started to leave, she added, "This time, I will not see you again."

"Faith, don't go! Please! I would never forgive myself if you left now!"

"But sit here and watch you work, only to be dismissed summarily when your desire to design overwhelms everything else in you. No thank you."

"What if I stop work this instant?"

"You would never do that, not for anybody, not even for the King."

He sensed he faced one of the vital decisions of his life. Faith was not like other women he had known, although she had Anne's independence and Françoise's learning. She was intricate, demanding, imperfect, but he had waited so long for love since Françoise and Anne, and he had such a need for affection, understanding, companionship, and a family before it was too late. He had gone slowly in this but where would he find two persons better suited? Faith's education was excellent, she was thirty-two, mature, yet close enough in age, four years younger, which was thought ideal. Their station was the same which could make living easier, and for a beautiful woman she was not vain. And she possessed the whitest skin he had seen since Anne's, and while her flaxen fairness was no longer the fashion it suited him. But he would have to wait, whatever he felt.

"Do you prefer me to be dull spirited, always succumbing to your work?"

"Would you like to see our garden? It is a favourite place of mine."

"Even more than your telescope, your drawing board?"

"It has so much of life and sweetness and beauty I think you will love it, too." He took her by the hand and led her down the stairs and into a secluded glade. It was deserted and she liked the quiet and peace of the grounds and she felt happy as she saw the relaxed, fulfilled expression on his face. The country part of her nature prevailed and she enjoyed the noble paths, carefully tended, the agreeable air, the birds warbling, the sweet turf of the meadow, the roses and violets which were lovingly cultivated. He added, "I have spent much of my free time here."

"It is beautifully kept."

"Seth does that. This makes him content, although there is little that has to be done. Oxford has many gardens. The meadow at

Christ Church is much larger and New College is reputed to be the prettiest, with an unusual open and spacious view, but I prefer this. It is more private."

"I understand why you enjoy it. But what is that statue? She pointed at a stone figure set upon a mound and holding up a gilded world.

"It is the creation of Wilkins, as is this garden. When he became Warden of Wadham during the civil wars, Wadham had no garden, and he declared that no true place of learning could flourish without one. So he built this one and with his universal curiosity he called the statue Atlas. I remember the time he showed Evelyn this, and the two transparent apiaries he made like castles and palaces, so as to take the honey without destroying the bees. Evelyn took one back to his garden at Sayes Court. He was proud of it and he showed it to the King. As if he had designed it himself."

"Evelyn told me. And how he met you years ago and you presented him with a piece of white marble. He informed me, '*It was stained with a lively red, as beautiful as if it had been natural, by Christopher Wren, that prodigious young scholar, that miracle of nature.*'"

"Evelyn flatters himself by flattering me. Here is what I like best in this garden." He showed her a magnificent copper beech, "It is said this tree was here when Oxford was established centuries ago, when Wadham was started in 1610. It is regarded as our foundation stone."

"Yet you said you need good timber for your theatre."

"Oak, Faith, not beech. And not a single tree. Sometimes I wish I lived when Wadham was built. Imagine, then oaks were felled at sixpence and eightpence apiece and brought here without stint."

"Some day you will have all the materials you need."

He saw her hand caressing the beech and he took it and she didn't move but smiled at him, half-expectant, yet a little fearful, and he lifted it to his lips and kissed it and said, "What a delicate hand—so lovely!"

"To match yours," she said.

He pressed her hand against his heart and suddenly she was eloquent.

"My father, unlike the King's grandfather, James Stuart, didn't believe my nature, being female, had to be devoted to spinning, sewing, and cookery. Since I was his only child and due to inherit his estate, he wanted me to know how to govern a house, how to dress and speak, and to be educated. He said it didn't harm Elizabeth and that it would have benefitted James Stuart. When he resolved to have no more children, he decided I should possess the same advantages as a son. My mother, whom he loved, died bearing me and he was determined not to wed again. He had me tutored from the age of five. And he wanted to prove that his blood could learn, despite being female. He was proud of his common sense; he said learning would protect me and make me less vulnerable to hasty emotional decisions."

"I'm grateful for his foresight. Will you wait for me?"

"Wait for what, Christopher?"

"Within a year I may know what my future will be."

"Will you be sad to leave Oxford?" His hands had clenched suddenly.

"I love Oxford but London fascinates me."

"London fascinates me, too." At this moment she felt that whatever the difficulties, now that he had loved her for one whole hour, they spoke the same language. She said, "I will wait. If it isn't too long."

"I'll do my best." He showed her a small pond that Seth had built. "He is unhappy because it hasn't attracted any life, but I assure him, Be patient, birds will come. Faith, do you have a keepsake I might have?"

She took off the watch she was wearing but in her eagerness to give it to him, she dropped it into the water. By the time he rescued the watch it was drenched and tears came into her eyes until he told her that he could repair it. He wasn't as sure as he sounded, but she seemed to think he could do anything mechanical, yet she added, "Do not promise miracles."

"It is a miracle that we met."

And because, she reflected, she had asked Holder to arrange it.

"Soon I will know when I can see you again."

"In between your various assignments?"

"No, Faith. Whenever it is suitable for you."

"I will wait, Christopher, as I said, but not forever."

A few days later the King issued a royal warrant: "*Whereas upon strict examination of the ruins of the Cathedral Church of St. Paul, by knowing and experienced artists, it is found that the walls now standing are in all parts so decayed by the late fire, they are judged altogether insufficient for bearing another roof, or any new work. It is therefore our express will and pleasure that immediate care be had for taking down the walls, and clearing the foundations to the east end, the old choir, and the tower, in such a manner as shall be judged sufficient to make room for a new choir of a fair and decent fabric, near or upon the old foundations, and also that care be taken to preserve the cornishes, ashlers, and such other parts of the former towards the west as shall be deemed useful for the new fabric; lest they be spoiled by the fall of more of the walls, which seems to threaten immediate ruin. And for so doing this shall be your Warrant. Given at our Court of Whitehall the 28th Day of July, 1668. Charles R.*"

The instant Christopher received this news from Sancroft he hurried into London to supervise the demolishing of the east end. He was not completely happy with the warrant, for it was still a compromise, but he decided to make the best of it, although that was against his nature. But it seemed enough for Sancroft. The Dean assured him that once work started on a new St. Paul's nothing could halt them. It was not a view which Christopher shared, but there was no questioning the Dean's purpose.

Sancroft had hired Joshua Marshall to organise the demolition and work had begun by the time Christopher arrived. Wood was coming in large quantities, some of which he wished could be spared for the theatre at Oxford, but Marshall was using it to erect scaffolding around the walls at the east end.

Sancroft led Christopher to where workmen were labouring and introduced him to Marshall, who was supervising them. Christopher felt this stocky, dark, middle-aged master mason, with his black hair, brown eyes, and weather-beaten skin, regarded him suspiciously. He recalled how the Dean had described him: "A man who thinks he could have built the Pyramids and the Temple of Diana, and he is a believer in the nobility of our Church. Vigorous, ambitious, fearless, although more inclined to be civil to those who acknowledge they know less about building than he does."

The master mason was prepared to dismantle the east end without any interference; he didn't need help; he knew the proportions of St. Paul's as accurately as any man. Yet he mustn't offend this surveyor, for this philosopher possessed the support of the Dean and the Archbishop.

Christopher recalled that Marshall had made a mistake with a fallen pillar; he could make a mistake here. Before these scaffolds were put up, a determination should be made concerning the strength of the walls. They towered eighty feet high, and while they were five feet thick, they could collapse, too, unless the proper precautions were taken.

He mentioned this and Marshall replied, "Professor, this is a great and troublesome work, but I've probed the masonry and it is secure."

"Did you examine it yourself?"

"No. But a trusted helper did."

In such matters, Christopher thought, it was wise to trust no one but yourself. Yet he didn't want to irritate an already antagonistic mason and he said, "You're probably right, but I'd like to look at it, too."

While Marshall watched disapprovingly and even the Dean was puzzled by so much care, Christopher examined the walls that were about to be demolished. Then he said, "The walls seem solid."

Marshall grumbled, "Too solid. They will be hard to knock down."

Sancroft said, "Doctor, you mustn't worry, he knows what he is doing."

"Yes, I do. Once the scaffolds are firm we will pull down the walls," Marshall assured them.

The first scaffold was ready and workmen climbed to the top of it and hacked away at the masonry of the cathedral wall with their pickaxes.

Christopher said, "That is dangerous. They should work more slowly."

"Why, Professor?" The master mason was aggrieved, sceptical.

"If they go too fast they could become careless and lose their footing and fall to their death."

Sancroft said solemnly, "Such an accident would be unfortunate. The church would have to pay the cost of the funeral. And should the victim be married, we would have to take care of his widow and family. We cannot afford that. We have very little money in the Repair Fund."

As the Dean spoke a large stone broke off the wall and almost took the workman wielding the pickaxe with it. He clung precariously to the scaffold poles until a fellow workman rescued him and pulled him back to safety.

Marshall shouted up to be more careful, to go slower, and as he was obeyed with haste and relief by the workmen, he asked the Dean, "I trust the Repair Fund will last through the demolition and rebuilding?"

"We cannot be certain. The Repair Fund has to rely on voluntary contributions and you know how unreliable they can be."

"Dean Sancroft, I thought the King was contributing, too."

"Charles said £40,000 should be spent on the work, but if he can't find money for the Navy I doubt he will obtain it for a new St. Paul's."

Christopher asked, "Then how will we manage?"

"That is why we have sold stone to the City. Don't worry, it is not the best, which we will use for rebuilding, but the rubbish, called Kentish rag. Come, tell me whether the remaining pillars at the west end will hold while the work goes on here. You can trust Master Marshall."

Christopher followed Sancroft to the other end of the vast ruin and examined what stood. It hadn't changed since he had viewed it last and it still shocked him. "It may hold a little while, but not permanently."

"Good. That will be enough for our present situation."

None of the debris had been cleared away and Christopher picked up a jagged fragment of the Inigo Jones' pillar and held it lovingly.

Sancroft asked, "Would you like some of the original stones from the old Gothic cathedral? They have been stored in St. Faith's."

Christopher nodded and Sancroft took him into the bowels of the earth. The ashes and fragments of the burned books still lay about indiscriminately, but workmen had piled up large amounts of broken stone and other rubble.

Sancroft said, "This stone comes from the Norman cathedral that was erected here after the old Saxon church was burnt in the great fire of 1087 which destroyed the City from the east gate to the west gate. It took centuries to finish the Gothic cathedral. I hope you will be quicker."

"It depends. The news about the Repair Fund is not cheerful."

"*We must have faith. The Commission is resolved to frame a design for a cathedral that is handsome, noble, and suitable, and which will serve all its purposes, and the reputation of the City and the nation.*"

"What about the money needed? Where will it come from?"

"*They have taken it for granted money will be had to accomplish it.*"

Christopher studied the fragment of stone he was holding and said, "These are very old. Yet very strong. They may go back to Roman times."

"It is possible. It is believed there was a Roman temple on this site."

"I will know better when I investigate the earth under the foundations."

That night Christopher put the three stones against the doors of his house in Scotland Yard to hold them in place. He was proud of them. They had survived war, plague and fire, and he was determined that they must live as long as he did. He gave his housekeeper strict orders not to remove them and the next day he went to visit Denham who was ill.

Denham was pleased to see him. He lay in bed and talked about Milton. "This past week I obtained a new binding of *Paradise Lost*. I'm re-reading it and it reinforces my faith in the work. Have you read it?"

"Just the beginning. I've been very busy."

"They are worrying you about St. Paul's. It is a nuisance. But I find peace in reading and writing poetry. But very few possess such taste. Only thirteen hundred copies of *Paradise Lost* were published a year ago, yet less than half of them have been sold. It is dismal. The new binding I have, I had my steward buy it for three shillings, doesn't contain the author's name, but merely his initials, *J.M.* So it will appeal to respectable persons. But I'm too close to death to care about that."

Christopher thought, Denham looked terrifyingly feeble but he had to say consolingly, "Sir John, you have many years ahead of you."

"I doubt it. They say it is my heart but I'm just wearing out. My heart was broken years ago. But my wits are sane. I'm working on an Elegy about old age and I've added to *Cooper's Hill*. If I'm remembered at all, it will be for that poem. Yet my critics invest me with madness."

Christopher reiterated, "Sir John, it is they who are mad."

"I pray that you are right. As Milton writes: '*The Mind is its own place and in itself can make a heaven of hell, a hell of heaven.*'"

"I agree. The concept is true and the expression worthy."

"Yet when I asked Waller, whose poetry has none of Milton's mighty line, if he had read *Paradise Lost*, he replied, '*The old blind schoolmaster has published a tedious work on the Fall of Man. If its length is not considered as merit, it has no other. He is an old Commonwealth's man.*'"

"There is much malice about. You mustn't allow it to trouble you."

"It ruined my life. But I will ask Dryden to read *Paradise Lost*. While he has changed his coat several times, like Waller, he is a better poet and has taste, and more influence. He may realise, with his admiration for Virgil, that Milton has redeemed himself with a grand godly work."

"Is there anything I can do for you?"

"It was gracious of you to visit me. Not everyone does. But I'm a good scholar. I translated Corneille's *Horace* which was played at the Theatre Royal, and the King attended, although there was no role in it for Nell Gwynn. Do not give your love lightly. It can bring anguish."

Marshall continued to supervise the demolition with a haste Christopher felt was risky, but Sancroft asked him not to interfere. He had confidence in the master mason and he reminded him that there was so much else to do.

Quarters were needed for the Dean, so he could oversee everything, and he ordered Christopher to design a suitable place next to the cathedral.

Christopher hadn't made any designs for a new St. Paul's, or shown his old ones, for no decision had been reached on the kind of church it was to be.

He was unable to visit Faith as he desired, but nights he worked on the repair of her watch. When he was puzzled what to do he consulted Hooke.

Hooke had done many experiments on watches, it was a speciality of his. He had invented a machine for cutting the teeth of watch wheels; he had used a spiral spring to regulate the balance of watches; he had built watches new in shape and strength. He was glad to show he could do things Wren could not do. He knew his mechanical skill surpassed all others and while he didn't hide his scorn of Wren's failure, he fixed the watch.

As Christopher thanked him, he said acidly, "Don't try to find out any more whether it has a water level. Watches are not designed to swim."

Christopher was so pleased that the watch worked—he had doubted that even Hooke could fix it—that when he was called to Oxford to face a new crisis, he decided to return it to Faith as a proof of his devotion. And to be sure she didn't misunderstand him, write her a letter to go with the watch. Strong, afraid the truss could still be a mistake, insisted he survey the roof of the theatre before it was put in. The master mason still didn't trust Doctor Wren's boldness, despite the Archbishop's orders.

The truss fitted precisely as Christopher visualised and he felt as if he had created a lofty tower, although the roof wasn't high. It gave him the courage and impetus to write what he was feeling. The roof of the theatre no longer usurped his thoughts, but shaped what he was writing and gave him a glimpse of joy. Then he ordered Seth to deliver the watch and letter in person and not to leave until he placed both in Faith's hands.

Seth was surprised by his tone—Christopher was more inclined to suggest—but he nodded and asked, "Should I expect an answer?"

"That depends on Miss Coghill. But I will be interested in the way she receives the watch and letter."

Faith was sewing when Seth's presence was announced. She had a girl to do such chores, but she had to do this work, for this was the dress she had worn when Christopher had wooed her for the first time. Moreover, it was the only way she could be patient, to prepare herself for waiting. The red thread made bright stitches and when she lost a button she could not abandon it but searched the floor until she found it. Now his servant stood in *his place*, handed her a box, and mumbled, "It is the watch."

She was furious and distraught. Christopher had asked for it as a keepsake and now he was returning it. This must be his way of rejecting her, she decided angrily, and she dismissed his servant, determined never to see Christopher again, whatever the circumstances.

Seth mumbled, "Madam, I can't go until I give you this letter, too."

She took it but she didn't open it or the box.

He asked, "Madam, aren't you going to read the letter?"

"Later. I'm busy now." But the servant didn't move.

"Doctor Wren said you should read the letter. He wrote it with care."

Seth's expression halted her move to have him dismissed. He looked so ready to sacrifice himself for Christopher, her sympathy was engaged. So, while she doubted it was wise, she opened the letter and read to herself:

> "*Madam—the artificer having never met before with a drowned watch, like an ignorant physician has been so long about the cure that he has made me very unquiet that your commands should be so long deferred. However, I have repaired the watch at last, and envy the felicity of it, that it be so near your side, and so often enjoy your eye, and be consulted by you how your time shall pass while you employ your hand in your excellent works. But have a care of it, for I have put such a spell into it that every beating of the balance will tell you it is the pulse of my heart which labours as much to serve you and more truly than the watch. For the watch, I believe, will sometimes perhaps be idle, and unwilling to go, having received so much injury by being drenched in that briny bath, that I despair it should ever be a true servant to you more. But as for me— unless you drown me too in my tears—you may be confident I shall never cease to be,*
> *Your most affectionate humble servant,*
> *C. Wren.*
> "*I have put the watch in a box that it might take no harm, and wrapped it about with a little leather, and that it might not jog, I filled up the corners with a few shavings and waste paper.*"

Faith saw the setting sun on this summer day and thought, No matter how high, mighty, and sovereign were the towers that Christopher built, she would treasure this letter above all of them. And while there was only an inch left of the red thread she couldn't discard it. Soon the moon would be out beautiful and full, but it was this little piece of red thread that made the bright stitch for her.

Seth asked, "Madam, is there any message?"

"Did Doctor Wren ask for one?"

"Madam, he said that depends on you. But I think he wants one."

"Tell your master that I will wait as long as it is necessary."

"Thank you, Madam. May I go now?"

"Yes. And thank you. Thank you very much."

"What for, Miss Coghill?" Seth was surprised.

"For bringing the watch." And a proposal, she thought, however it was worded. She was his love after all. Of that now, she was almost certain.

A Man of Rock

A man of rock
with a hand
Great and capable
A heart that leads
A mind that plans
takes me
From where I was
To where I must be
and makes me feel
That I took him

Stymean Karlen

37

A Man of Rock

A FEW DAYS LATER TWO WORKMEN FELL TO THEIR DEATH AT ST. Paul's when a hastily built scaffold collapsed. Christopher heard the news with horror and he rushed back to London from Oxford in the hope he could avert more accidents. Sancroft was holding an inquest and he was hollow-eyed and tired as he listened to the workmen telling him what had happened. He greeted Christopher as if he expected him and motioned for him to sit down. But the surveyor had to examine the broken scaffold before he heard the workmen's testimony, and he excused himself, although the Dean was annoyed that he didn't take his word but had to see for himself.

All work had stopped and Christopher walked to the east end, assuming that the men had fallen there. He was surprised to find that the accident had occurred at the middle tower which had borne the steeple. Someone had ordered the tower dismantled in spite of its height. It was nearly two hundred feet high, twice the height of any other part of the ruined fabric, it required a scaffold of the stoutest timber. He surveyed the poles that still stood and the splintered platform which lay on the ground. He picked up the cracked wood and saw that it was inferior maple, when the sturdiest oak should have been used, that the scaffold was not properly braced, the framework of the poles was insecure, the platform was thin when it should have been given the extra protection of a double planking with sound wood. Around him were the remains of the dead St. Paul's, the lead, rubble, and the sorted stones, those to be sold and those to be used.

A crowd gaped at the shattered scaffold where the accident had taken place and he heard: "*No wonder the Papists set the fire. Nostradamus, the expert astrologer, foretold the fire a hundred years ago, and pointed out the very year it would be burnt. It is the judgment of God.*"

"*To tax us for this ruin is a denial of our just liberties.*"

"Cromwell was right, it is ungodly and has come to a true end."
"The broken cathedral is not worth reviving after this calamity."
"St. Paul's is for wise men to avoid and fools to go into."
"This is God's will. Now the whore's cap is off for good."

Christopher felt he was the only one here who wanted to weep. The jeering was more than he could endure and he returned to the inquest.

He wondered why Marshall wasn't present. His foreman, Roger Quint, a spry, young, red-haired man, testified, "They were cutting the remainder of the unmelted lead from the roof when they fell. They were negligent."

Sancroft agreed but Christopher interrupted, "Sir, if there was negligence, it was in the scaffold itself. The excessive height and weight of the scaffold and the weakness of the wood put an unwarranted and unforeseen strain on it and caused the collapse."

Quint said, "The men were careless. They were working too fast."

"Were they ordered to?"

"They knew the dangers. All the workmen were warned."

"But not that the scaffold itself might not support them."

Sancroft said, "Doctor, does this give you any satisfaction?"

"It indicates where the blame lies."

"What good will that do? The men are dead and work is halted. There is a great outcry in the City and the Court against the building of a new St. Paul's, and now many are saying that it is not worth the cost."

"We must prevent further calamities. Guard the men's safety better."

"Are you implying it was the fault of the cathedral authorities?"

"Dean, it was someone's fault. It was not an act of God."

Sancroft looked wrathful and said sarcastically, "Whose fault? Mine?"

"Whoever ordered a scaffold to be built there and in such a poor way."

Quint mumbled, "It was Marshall. But he is a master mason."

"Did he examine the scaffold himself? Test it first?"

"How could he? He has so much else to do!"

"Where is he now?"

The foreman glanced questioningly at Sancroft, who indicated that he go on, and he replied, "His services are needed elsewhere. He is supervising the work on the Customs House and a new Royal Exchange."

Sancroft added, "It is the view of the Crown and the City that these buildings are vital, that they must be done first as an encouragement to the nation." He dismissed Quint, the workmen waiting to testify, then said, "You pursue some matters too avidly. The Church is merciful but there is only so much we can afford. We will pay for the funerals of the workmen, but the Repair Fund is so low we have to discontinue all work."

Christopher's heart was heavy and he didn't answer.

"There is talk of a new war with the Dutch and the rebuilding of London is still perplexing, but most of the streets have been measured and staked out and much of the rubbish has been cleared away. There is a want of money, materials, and labour for anything else. We can just afford to give the workmen one shilling and two pence a day, while the City pays them one shilling and four pence a day, and so the workmen don't want to work for us."

Christopher said, "Another reason, I hear, is that they were forced to labour while the scaffolds were slippery or they would be fired. It was raining heavily when the men fell."

"That is another problem. Winter is approaching and the bad weather has curtailed our work, so we have decided to wait until next year."

"It is only September, too soon to stop work because of the weather."

"We must give this reason or we will discourage contributions."

"It is sad that we have to halt. It will be hard to revive enthusiasm."

"Do not despair. While we are in desperate straits because of a want of money, all is not lost. You must bear yourself with courage, as I am. I was offered a bishopric this summer, of more consequence than St. Paul's, but to show I have faith there will be a new cathedral I declined it. We must find the money. And the labour and the materials. Somehow."

Christopher didn't know what to believe. St. Paul's became barren as its open spaces were used by Hooke and the City for their rebuilding, as a standing ground for their carts, as a storage place for their stones, and as dumps for their rubbish. He tried to accept this painful situation, and consoled himself that this gave him more opportunity to see Faith.

Her reply that she would wait as long as it was necessary was the one flame that lit the gloom that surrounded him. He wrote her asking permission to visit her and when it was granted immediately, he hurried to Bletchington, where she greeted him radiantly, as if she expected him to woo her. He wasn't certain he was ready for that yet, but he was happy in her presence. She thanked him warmly for the repair of her watch and she complimented him on his skill, and he was too pleased with her praise and joy to risk telling her that Hooke had done most of the work.

As they walked through her gardens, however, he felt uneasy. No matter how much he cared for her, he didn't want to reside in the country.

Faith sensed what he was feeling and said, "It is lovely here, especially in the autumn, but it can also be a small, confining world. Your place is in the world of London and Whitehall and the City."

"You have more faith in my future than I do."

"Christopher, you must persevere."

"You don't think I'm a fool to dream of designing a new St. Paul's?"

"If you could fix my watch, you could fix anything."

He was silent. He thought of the expedition he was contemplating and he wondered if she would be a suitable companion.

"Is there anything wrong?" He was sombre suddenly and she was alarmed. Now that they were this close, she didn't want to drive him away.

"I've been thinking of examining some of our more venerable cathedrals."

"And you were deciding whether to invite me to accompany you? I would be honoured to view them through your eyes."

"I thought you might be offended by such a proposal. People could talk."

"You don't mind what people say. Why should I? Besides, I will be happy to put my reputation in your hands." He looked agreeable, so she suggested, "May I take my coach and footmen? If you don't mind?" He scowled suddenly. "I don't wish to impose upon you, but it will be more comfortable than the hackney coaches you would have to hire, and safer."

So it was decided. Then, for many days, time was measured by the curve of an arch, the point of a spire, the style of a tower, the strength of a wall, the spaciousness of a crossing. Their first visit was to Windsor where he showed Faith the chapel of St. George and told her: "*I have lived with architecture all my life, even before I knew what it was or what it was called. I was born next door to it, for the chapel of St. George was my first memory, and my father and uncle were concerned with its repair, which still hasn't been done thirty years later. By the time I was eight I saw London, which meant for me, most of all, St. Paul's, and lived within sight of Westminster Abbey, Parliament Hall, and the palaces of Whitehall and Lambeth. Yet my interest directs me to the classical style.*"

"To your sense of order, to the mathematician and engineer in you."

"You are wise!" he exclaimed delightedly.

And learned my lessons well, she smiled to herself, from Susan. She knew her greatest gift was her ability to listen and to remember.

He was gratified by how easy it was to talk to Faith. Her interest, her animation, her recalling whatever he told her, spurred him to talk as he hadn't talked to anyone. She was a treasure; her faith and enthusiasm persuaded him that this venture was sensible. He had not expected so much wit in her; in some ways she was as clever as Françoise.

At Ely cathedral, where his uncle had been bishop, he said: *"Ely has its own logic, the language of the middle ages, standing dark and dramatic and dominating the entire landscape, as my uncle liked to do. But its superb octagon tower is original and poetic and the great lantern in it covers the crossing with authority and skill."*

He was critical of Canterbury cathedral which surprised her.

"It is reputed the masterpiece of the Gothic in cathedrals, but I find it too heavy, determined to be aware of its own strength and magnificence."

And he didn't completely approve of Westminster Abbey, as she did.

"In many ways, here is the triumph of the Perpendicular, which may be the greatest virtue of the Gothic. Not for its height or order. It is not unusually high and it is a mixture of several styles. But when it soars, it expresses the best of the Perpendicular, as close to heaven and immortality as we have so far come."

But it was the approach to Salisbury that took her breath away. They saw it from the plain and she loved this view so much she stared avidly. It rose into the sky with a beauty she found wonderful, while he said:

"The approach to Salisbury cathedral is the art. The view of it from the distance is what enchants the onlooker. The various parts unite to direct the eye to the spire, which is the loftiest in England, four hundred and four feet. But the inside of it is cold and the pile, while magnificent, contains some errors. The architect built on a low and marshy soil, and so the foundation is unsubstantial, a second fault was not raising the floor of the church, for at its present level it is too easily drenched with floods; besides, it is unhandsome to descend into a church."

Yet he was fascinated by this fabric, she thought, for he spent much time surveying it. Winchester, which was only eighteen miles away, was their last stop, and he was caustic about this structure. By now her head was crammed with information about cathedrals and much of it confused her, and she wished she could talk about what she knew, Viola, Ophelia, Portia, Cordelia, Kate, and Desdemona. She identified herself with these women, although she had no desire to live as they had. But she realised that she must be very attentive now, for his criticism of Winchester summed up what he disliked most about the Gothic style in cathedrals.

U

"Salisbury, at least, is all of a piece. It is pure Early English, one style, and the builders of it were fortunate, they were able to erect it within a space of forty years. Thus, it is outstanding for its harmony, uniformity, and freedom from foreign influences. But Winchester, which was begun before Salisbury, took much longer to complete, hundreds of years, which was a mistake, for it resulted in a mixture of styles ranging from Norman to Perpendicular. The transepts are Norman, the nave Perpendicular, the east end Early English, and the church was built as if many had to be pleased, which was a mistake. Consequently, it is badly designed."

His voice was contemptuous and as they entered her coach to return to Bletchington, she asked, "What about your design for St. Paul's?"

"How can I design it when I don't even know what space it is going to occupy? The exact site hasn't been determined yet."

"But you do have a design, don't you, Christopher?"

"Yes, foolish though that may be. Different from any other cathedral in England, a classic design away from the Gothic fashion, but of modest size to suit the Repair Fund. I have so little hope for it I have not shown it to anyone. Not even to Dean Sancroft or to Archbishop Sheldon."

"Maybe they will favour it. They know how your taste inclines."

"It is useless. They say there will be no work on St. Paul's until next year, and I'm not sure it will resume. They use lack of money as the reason for the cessation of work, but I think it is only an excuse. The King and the Commons have to be convinced and that may be impossible."

"Why don't you try to convince them?"

"I'm not a courtier."

"Perhaps you should be."

He regarded her irritably and for the next hour he didn't speak. But then, as he saw her unhappiness, he relented and talked about the parish churches in London that had to be rebuilt and that he was being considered for this task. She brightened and managed a smile of encouragement.

Faith was troubled he would use the postponement of the work on St. Paul's to put off proposing to her. She recalled what he had written with the watch—she memorised every word—but Christopher had observed all the proprieties and had not even implied that he was in love with her.

At her home in Bletchington, he said, "I will miss you."

"That is nice."

"Is that all, Faith?" He looked offended.

"Should I feel anything else? Do you feel anything else?"

He thought, Couldn't she tell by the way he had behaved? They stood in her drawing room while his hired coach waited to take him back to Oxford and he didn't want to leave her. Yet he must, for his prospects were no more favourable than before. She shivered as he started out and he turned, grasped her hands, and he was shocked by how chilled they were. He realised he had offered much to her, but not himself. She didn't wish to be admired; she yearned to be loved. And he didn't desire a companion; he craved a wife. He kissed her on the lips and she returned his touch emotionally. Then he drew back and she felt bitter again, afraid she would die a virgin.

He sensed her apprehension and he said, "I care for you very much. It was a wonderful expedition and it was your presence that made it so."

"I'm glad you found out what you wanted to know about the cathedrals."

"I've seen them before. But not with your eyes and emotion."

"What could I contribute to your understanding?"

"Your interest and appreciation brought a freshness I needed."

"But you took me. You explained. You showed me."

"Only physically, as was fitting. But, with your feeling, it was you who took me. You gave what I had seen before a new dimension."

"Whatever you described to me, I more than saw it, I also felt it."

He sighed.

"Christopher, does that disturb you?"

"I wish I could spend as much time with you as I would like to. But I have to return to Oxford, and to be available to go to London, also, if my presence should be required. May I see you next week?"

"If you wish to."

"I do. Very much."

This time as he kissed her, he embraced her passionately. His hands were strong, like the rock he loved, but his touch was gentle.

The next six months he saw Faith regularly while he waited, without much hope, for work to resume on St. Paul's. His cousin reminded him that he was still Assistant Surveyor for the King, but the Crown's Works were at a standstill. The only surveying that was occurring was the rebuilding of the City, and that was in the hands of Hooke, who hadn't consulted him.

Then, on a windy, rainy day in March, 1669, while he was at his house at Scotland Yard to see the King, who had requested his presence, he received an urgent plea from Denham to visit him. He wondered if the two summons had anything in common, and he hurried to attend Denham.

The Surveyor General looked ghastly and he had just enough strength to turn his head so he could see who had entered. He said laboriously, "It was good of you to come. I was never robust but now I am near death."

"Nonsense," said Dr. Scarburgh, who was examining him, sounding much more the diplomat than the physician. "You have many years to live. This is just a passing attack, the ague or the dropsy."

"Sir Charles has a great gift for putting a cheerful face on ill health. It is why he is in such favour with the King."

"Sir John addresses me wrongly. I've not been knighted yet."

"You will be. The King considers you indispensable to his humours."

"It is why I attend you. Charles has a high regard for you, and so he ordered me to examine you and to cure you. He admires your poetry."

"It is a taste some share. But his regard, more likely, is because, during the civil war, I conveyed his two brothers from St. James into France. The Queen Mother still owes me money for that. Ten pounds."

Christopher remarked, "She owes me the same."

"I didn't know that you served her."

"Briefly. Sir John, what is your business? I don't want to tax you."

"When Scarburgh finishes. Sir, do you intend to bleed me?"

"It is not necessary. A purgative will do." The physician ordered the nurse in the adjoining room to administer it in an hour and left.

Denham said, "Scarburgh has become a constant courtier, but that is necessary with Charles. You have a gift for medical matters."

"It is exaggerated. But I believe in using common sense."

"That is why I wanted to see you. I am making my will."

"How does that concern me?"

"I used to have a fine complexion, except for the smallpox. Did you know I had the pox? I survived that, the loss of the land my father left me, the civil wars, a young, beautiful wife, but I will not survive this."

Christopher didn't reply; he sensed that Denham probably was right.

"You also have a gift for seeing things as they are, not as people wish. If I am remembered, it may be because you were my assistant."

"Sir, you are in a state, you don't feel well."

"I'm dying, but my wit is sound. That is why I'm putting in my will that you must be appointed my sole deputy in the surveyor's office."

"I thought John Webb was."

"No longer." Denham feebly picked up the paper lying by his side, but read resolutely, "*By my patent I have the power to make a deputy, during my life. I have appointed Doctor Christopher Wren my sole deputy. If Mr. May or anyone else pretends thereto, it is without my knowledge or consent.* Which means when I die, you should be appointed Surveyor General."

"I am touched and honoured, but I trust your passing is far away."

"No, it is just a little way off. And you are the suitable choice."

"The King has the final approval. He has been distant lately."

"I have reason to believe he will approve. I was wise not to write any love poems. Did you ever hear my tale about George Withers?"

Christopher had, but Denham was so eager to tell it again, he said, "No."

"During the civil wars, Withers, the poet, who was also a captain in the Parliamentary Army, sought my estate. Then he was taken prisoner by the royalists and I begged the King not to hang him, on the grounds, '*That while George Withers lived I should not be the worst poet in England.*'"

"So you were responsible for his life being spared! You were merciful."

"I pray to God that He will be so merciful. I have tried to be faithful to my nature. If I have not been the best Surveyor General to hold that office, I may have been the best poet, although I do not measure myself with Milton or Dryden. But I have had a sound ear and a natural lyric."

"Sir John, your health could improve."

"It is not likely, I wanted you to attend me so that you would know from my mouth that I have recommended your succession to my office. Would you call the nurse, please? My powers are failing."

But Christopher felt that Denham wanted to avoid any expressions of gratitude, any emotional farewells, and as he called the nurse, who came at once, he said, "I'm honoured by our acquaintance."

"I'm the one who is honoured. I've been aware of your abilities for a long time. You could be a splendid Surveyor General, if they permit you."

The next day Matthew met Christopher in the audience chamber of Whitehall and informed him, "*The King has issued a grant for you to hold the office of Deputy Surveyor of his Works, at the request of Sir John Denham, on account of his weakness.*"

Christopher replied, "I still doubt I will become Surveyor General. The King hasn't told me, so he can always deny what someone else said."

"He is too busy to see you. And he dislikes details. But you should succeed to the office when Denham dies, which can't be far off now."

"Why shouldn't it be Webb, who was appointed Deputy before me?"

"Because your reputation is higher. And I have helped. Christopher, you have great natural gifts, but no talent for advancement."

Denham died a few days later and on the King's command was buried in the Poets' Corner of Westminster Abbey, near Spenser's tomb and Chaucer's monument. Otherwise, Christopher noted, it was a simple ceremony, without the pomp or eulogies that had attended the funeral of another celebrated poet, Abraham Cowley, two years earlier. Cowley had been given a state funeral and Denham himself had written the poetic tribute. But perhaps the simplicity was more fitting for the harassed, overburdened Denham, reflected Christopher, possibly his work would be his monument.

Christopher remained in London to learn what his duties were in his new office and when, after a week of waiting, he was told that the King wished to see him, he arrived at this audience sceptically. Work hadn't resumed on St. Paul's and it was a ghostly pile, although the weather improved daily. Since his promotion to Deputy Surveyor no one had consulted him about anything. And as he entered Charles' Presence Chamber, and he saw Webb and May there, in addition to Matthew, he was pessimistic. No one said a word but stood silently, as was the custom, for the King to arrive.

Charles strolled in many minutes later, viewed those waiting with a sly smile, sat down in his throne-like chair, and said, "As you know, the Surveyor General has the right to name his successor."

May said, "Begging your pardon, Your Majesty, with one exception."

"I have the authority to alter it. I know that very well."

Webb said, "Your Majesty, when I was appointed Deputy Surveyor I was assured of the reversion of the surveyorship after the death of Denham."

"Assured, Webb, but not promised."

Webb flushed angrily, but he didn't reply.

Charles turned to Christopher, "Doctor Wren, what is your claim?"

"Sir, I have no claim but I'm honoured by Sir John's wish and his will."

"Do you think this is enough?"

Matthew said hurriedly, "Your Majesty, I'm sure he understands that Sir John wouldn't have dreamed of recommending him without your approval."

Charles asked, "Wren, do you desire to be Surveyor General?"

"Very much, Your Majesty!"

"Even though it may interfere with your work on St. Paul's?"

Christopher hesitated, then didn't answer.

"You mustn't be peevish. Not everything can be done at once."

"Your Majesty, I realise that. But it would be unworthy of us if we allowed St. Paul's to perish. Don't you think so, sir?"

Charles was surprised by the emotion in Christopher's voice. He was accustomed to his courtiers showing this when they discovered infidelity or indifference in a female, or became infected with the French disease through folly or lechery, but a building, whatever shadows it made in the sunlight, was still just a pile, easily altered and easily forgotten. Yet Wren was so determined to mend it, his views must be taken seriously.

Webb said abruptly, *"Your Majesty, if Wren is appointed I cannot act under him, for he is far my inferior."*

May added tentatively, "Neither can I, sir, I think."

Christopher said, "If I should be appointed, I hope Mr. Webb will change his mind. I respect what he has done at Greenwich and for Inigo Jones."

"No," said Webb, "I will retire first. If he hadn't stripped St. Paul's of the scaffoldings, the pillar that fell would not have given way."

That was a lie, Christopher thought angrily, but he didn't reply.

Charles said, "Sancroft told me the fallen pillar was Jones' fault. And I would like to see St. Paul's rising on its ashes, but I doubt, whatever the effort, I will live to see a new cathedral completed."

Christopher said urgently, "Sir, Salisbury was erected in a man's lifetime, within forty years, and it is one of our chief glories."

Charles sat reflectively, while everyone stood and waited for him to resume. He didn't wish to commit himself, although many had recommended Wren for the post of Surveyor General, despite his inexperience, and had told him that the Professor possessed great gifts as a mathematician and engineer. He was the only one to foresee the collapse of the pillar at St. Paul's, and his theatre at Oxford was nearly finished and appeared sound, and his chapel at Pembroke was a suitable work, if not unusual. Yet a large part of Charles longed to avoid a decision and preferred to race at Newmarket, to hunt and sup with friends, but this matter had to be settled now. There was too much work pending for this affair to be deferred any longer. But this cold, distant Professor—Wren must be cold, Charles felt, for he didn't seem inclined to women, and distant, for he refused to flatter him—could be out of place in the world of Whitehall. As Surveyor General, he would have to work within the realm of the Court. Charles glanced down his long nose at the men standing before him like statues, and he was pleased that Wren, while he was the shortest, stood most erectly. He was the only one who was slim and straight, which he liked. Charles respected physical prowess, good looks and a fine carriage. May's stomach bulged; Webb was portly, too, and peevish; neither looked capable of agility, and as Surveyor General there could be much scrambling and climbing over the Works. Possibly Wren could save St. Paul's; he must see his new design when he had time. Now, Nelly was giving him a candle-lit supper party, and he yearned for her voluptuous body. Let his brother's secretary worry about the revenues for the Surveyor General's Office; Nelly was more immediate and appealing. Webb was a prying, pressing fellow, and May, while he knew his place, was without wit or inventiveness; but Wren had a sensible clerical heritage and an original mind. And if Wren failed, an excuse could always be found to dismiss him. He said abruptly, "Doctor, it is my wish that Denham's will be carried out. Matthew will inform you of the details." He dismissed Webb and May, and after a curt nod to Christopher, he strode out.

Matthew informed Christopher, "I was told you were his only choice, but he likes to keep people guessing, so he will possess the advantage."

"It seems to me that he is still making up his mind."

"With Charles, the appearance is not always the reality. The warrant for your succession to Denham's post has been issued already. Denham wished to put that into his will, too, but Charles forbade it. He wanted to take the credit for the appointment, in the event it turns out well."

"So I am to be the Surveyor General?" Christopher said reflectively.

"You are," Matthew said positively. "The King's warrant says so."

"Then why did he call us together and indulge in this farce?"

"He likes comedy. And so he could change his mind, if he had wanted to." Matthew sighed with relief. "But he didn't, and now, what we have worked so hard for has come true. Your unofficial six year novitiate is ended."

"I'm not sure. When I was appointed Assistant Surveyor, Charles told me that much would be done. Instead, very little was accomplished."

"Aren't you ever satisfied? I've worked hard to make this come true?"

"I want to be grateful, but in the years I've worked for the King, whatever you say, I've done nothing of importance for him. I've no wish to be a figurehead now. Like Denham was, whatever his virtues as a poet."

"You won't be. There is much work in hand. A new Customs House is being built and you will be in charge, and you will be consulted on the Royal Exchange that is being constructed by the City."

"Hooke is not a good or a willing listener."

"He will obey. You are above him. And you have other advantages. The office is for life, you inherit Denham's residence at Scotland Yard, and his salary. It comes to about £200 a year, but both Denham and Jones became rich in the office. You could, too, if you are wise."

"And if I accept money only for what I do?"

"Even Denham, with his madness, was not that foolish. He died wealthy."

Christopher disliked raising objections, but a plan was forming in his mind. But he wanted to be sure he could carry it out. "When I was appointed Assistant Surveyor, you assured me that I would receive eighty pounds per annum. Instead, I got a small fee for my survey of Greenwich, ten pounds for a report I did on Salisbury cathedral, but nothing for what I did on St. Paul's or for my plans for rebuilding London. How do I know I will be paid now? That I can afford to give up my post as professor?"

"Charles has been in hard circumstances, but matters are improving."

"The way he lives I think he will always be in such circumstances."

"You're not being moral, are you?" Matthew regarded him with horror.

"I'm being sensible. There are several decisions I wish to make, but until I know I'm certain of an income I cannot do that."

"I've forty pounds for you. As an expression of good faith."

This was the most money Christopher had received for his ability to design and he took it with a feeling of wonder. He had designed Pembroke for nothing, Sheldon had not paid him yet, often he had felt he would never be paid for his own designs. The forty pounds was a treasure.

"Is there anything wrong?" Christopher looked startled.

"I have to leave London briefly. I hope my presence can be spared."

"Are you going to resign at Oxford?"

"Matthew, I appreciate all that you have done on my behalf."

"You can rely on me. But don't be absent long. If you've suffered from a lack of employment in the past, you will not suffer from that now. You have a vast amount of work ahead of you even without St. Paul's."

"Has a decision been reached against its renewal?" His heart sank.

"The Commons refuses to give money for it and Charles has none."

U*

Christopher hired an express coach to take him to Bletchington.

"Faith, will you marry me?" It was the following afternoon, and he still felt breathless from the way he had hurried to see her.

She was wearing a plain dress, for she had not expected him; he had not even given her time to compose herself. All her life she had imagined this moment with the panoply of romance and gallantry, and frequently she had thought he would never propose, and she had never expected it to happen this way, yet she knew she must not appear surprised. She said, "Christopher, when you do express yourself, you are direct."

If he hadn't said it quickly, he thought, he might not have said it at all. "I must say directly what I feel. May I have your hand?"

She hesitated; she mustn't seem eager, however urgently it came from her heart. She regarded him intently and said, "What do you want with it?"

"To possess it. With your permission and love."

"You have never said you love me." Now this was out she was glad.

"Isn't it evident, Faith?"

"It is never evident until it is expressed. Are you afraid to say it?"

"I've told no one else about my good fortune."

"You haven't told me. Is work on St. Paul's begun?"

"I'm Surveyor General." He took her by the hands and danced her around the room. Her touch pleased him; she did have the finest hands of any woman in the world. "Will you marry me?"

"If you love me."

There was a long pause and he felt trapped. Yet the idea of living without her was too painful to endure and he said, "I do. Deeply."

"Will it require more years of waiting?"

"As soon as it is propitious. Don't refuse me, I implore you."

"When will we marry?"

"As soon as I can resign from Oxford. Professors are not supposed to marry, and I want to be free of such obligations. But that should be accomplished by the end of the year, and then we can set the date."

Faith had expected, when he proposed, to sigh and languish, and appear reluctant, but she couldn't resist the entreaty in his eyes. She said, "I am willing. If it is this year."

"But you said that you would wait."

"Not forever."

"I will ask Holder to arrange it by the end of the year."

"I would prefer a London wedding. We will live there, won't we?"

"Wherever you prefer." He thought, They complemented each other in many ways and possessed some traits the other lacked. Then, feeling he was too calm for such an occasion, he embraced her with an ardour he had not expressed before and she responded so passionately he realised there were depths of emotion in her, too, like himself, yet to be used.

After he promised to arrange their wedding in London by the end of the year, he returned to the city to resume his duties as Surveyor General.

He asked for a leave of absence from his post at Oxford and this was granted; he didn't tell Faith that he hadn't resigned; but he didn't want to be impulsive; he still wasn't certain about his new position.

Yet, as Matthew said, there was much work in hand. Matthew escorted him to the most important and immediate rebuilding occurring in London, the erection of a new Customs House, determined to help Christopher avoid any mistakes. It was being built on the site of the edifice that had been constructed by Elizabeth and which had been destroyed by the fire.

Christopher liked the location—it faced the Thames between the Tower and Billingsgate—but as they arrived in a Crown coach and he saw the work going on, he had doubts about the design. The ground plan had been staked out but he wasn't sure it had been done on merit.

He questioned this and Matthew replied strongly, "The space around the building will suffice. At least, for our time."

"But if the amount of our imports and exports continue to grow, as you say they will, we should make provision for future expansion."

"No. As it is, it was very difficult to obtain the £10,000 allotted to the rebuilding of the Customs House. No more money will be forthcoming."

"Nonetheless, as I showed in my design for the city, there should be a *piazza* here to give easy access to vehicles. Who supervises this work?"

"Joshua Marshall and his foreman, Roger Quint."

Christopher winced but he asked, "May I see them?"

"You are their superior now." He led him to the riverbank where Quint and Marshall were excitedly discussing Roman pottery that had been unearthed.

Marshall nodded politely to Matthew and curtly to Christopher.

Christopher asked, "Whose design is being used for the Customs House?"

Marshall replied, "With the death of Denham no one will take the responsibility, but some say it is by Webb or May."

Christopher studied the design and then said, "I believe it is by May. The Dutch influence is pronounced and he prefers that style."

"What is the difference? I know what has to be done. The King wants a large building with a fine courtyard, so it will impress. Nothing will fall here, it is a low structure. Or collapse, for I am using the most massive of the Roman orders, the Tuscan. It will be a robust building."

"I'm glad to see that no timber is being used. But it is being crowded in by old buildings that are being rebuilt as if they are new."

"This is the work of the City Surveyors. They do not consult me."

"The streets that are being rebuilt should be wider. Instead, they are just as narrow, crooked, and difficult to travel on as before the fire."

"Professor Wren, you are a critical man."

"Yes," said Quint. "He blamed us for what happened at St. Paul's."

"I'm interested in avoiding any more such tragedies."

Marshall held up bits of Roman pottery and stated, "Caesar thought he built for eternity and this is all that is left. I will construct a Customs House that will not harm anybody's reputation, not even yours."

Matthew said, "Mr. Marshall, I'm sure you can be trusted." Matthew pulled Christopher away but he didn't resist, for he wanted to clarify several matters and he preferred that this be done privately.

As they rode toward the Royal Exchange, he said, "The Customs House is being built too quickly and cheaply. Another fire will destroy it and it is too small for the growing commerce of London."

"Marshall knows what he is doing. He is one of the best known masons in London, and he has just been appointed His Majesty's Master Mason."

"To keep a watch on me, no doubt."

"To make sure there will be enough money for a new St. Paul's."

"You exaggerate."

"Not at all. In many ways this Customs House is the most vital work in the realm. The average income from imports and exports before the civil wars was over £300,000 a year, and Charles is determined to increase that. This is why the Customs House is being built first. The revenue it brings in is essential for Charles' survival. It could save his purse."

"What has this to do with St. Paul's?"

"The money to rebuild it will have to come from the Customs House. From a tax on imports that are in demand."

"So the sooner it is finished, the sooner work on St. Paul's starts?"

"It is the prevalent view. Even the King's, and your precious Sancroft."

The foundations of the new Royal Exchange had been laid two years ago, and Christopher realised this building couldn't be his, no matter how often he was consulted. The business was too far advanced. The design was by Edward Jerman, who was reputed to be the best carpenter in London. He thought, The most he could say for it was that it was symmetrical, but in style mannered and coarse. But there was not much wood in it, which was a step away from medievalism, and the brick and stone looked substantial.

Not all of the Guildhall had burned down during the fire and the walls that were framed with solid oak still stood. And what remained had been used. Instead of a new design, Christopher saw, what had been injured in the fire had been repaired at once. This actually, he told himself, was work for a carpenter, but when he asked who had done the renovations, no one was sure. Some said it was the work of Peter Mills, the bricklayer who had been appointed City Surveyor with Hooke and Jerman, but he felt it was the doing of Jerman—the timber work was a carpenter's dream. Yet Matthew insisted that Hooke must be responsible, for Hooke had talked much about the Guildhall at the last few meetings of the Royal Society.

When Christopher came before Charles to report on what he had seen, the King stood on the highest pavement of the stairs that looked out on the Thames, and it was not as if they were in Whitehall Palace but before the Royal Exchange. He remembered how Charles had ignored the flames on his sleeve. He wondered why the King couldn't show such courage now. The rebuilding of London was as vital, yet fire had succeeded where he couldn't. Charles waved aside his doubts about the three buildings.

The King gazed down the Thames where the ruined hulk of St. Paul's was silhouetted in the sharp spring sunlight and said, "Doctor, I realise that the cathedral is your mistress and the sight of a new, beautiful St. Paul's would please me mightily, too, but other business must come first. The City merchants cannot run their trade without a Guildhall and cannot support themselves without a Royal Exchange, which is a futile exercise without a Customs House." Charles wore a black velvet suit, his gloves were scented with jasmine; he gave Christopher ten pounds and said, "Since you serve me directly now, dress more fashionably, it will earn you more respect and obedience." Before Christopher could protest that, as

Chief Surveyor, this was not essential, the King halted him and added, "You mustn't struggle against the inevitable. While your *grand design* for the city was declined, not all of it was wasted. The new building regulations which forbid the use of wood will give London a new texture, and you are in a large measure responsible. Now it will become a stone and brick city, and when you consider how many churches have to be rebuilt, you will not lack employment. Perhaps, after we accumulate the small places of piety, we can concentrate on the crown of them all, St. Paul's."

"Thank you, Your Majesty. It will be a great step forward."

"But we must realise that building is performed by human beings, always fallible, and usually sinful. My people are more interested in seeing a fair woman naked than a cathedral clothed."

"Your Majesty, St. Paul's could still be a fine sight."

"It will be interesting to see how your theatre at Oxford is received. If it is favourable, possibly I can consider your new design for St. Paul's." He handed Christopher ten more pounds, pleased with the way this Surveyor General had listened, and retired to meet Nelly in his private chambers.

July 9th, 1669, Evelyn proudly noted in his diary: "*In the morning was celebrated the opening of the new Theatre, so magnificently built by the munificence of the Archbishop of Canterbury, in which he spent £25,000, and yet my Lord Archbishop told me that he has not seen it or never would see it. It is a fabric comparable to any of this kind of former ages, and exceeding any of the present, as this University does for all the Universities in the world. It is a noble pile and there was much said in praise of the Archbishop and the ingenious architect.*"

There was no doubt in Christopher that the theatre would suffice. A few morose scholars declared his design a corruption of the Roman style, but the roof was solidly in place, and most of those in attendance, including the Vice-Chancellor of Oxford, who dedicated the theatre in the name of Gilbert Sheldon, called it a worthy work. Christopher liked that it was called the *Sheldonian Theatre*, for that was appropriate. But he was disappointed to hear that the Archbishop was not in attendance. He wondered if this was a censorious act, yet afterwards he realised that his work was in favour, for Charles asked to see his new model of St. Paul's.

It was against his inclination to have so much depend on what was just a first model, but Sancroft was sure this would exhibit his work to good advantage. The design was smaller than he desired, but sensible, he felt, since so little money was available for the grandeur he preferred. He presented the wooden model to Charles and said, "*Sir, I have contrived a fabric of moderate bulk but good proportions, a choir with a vestibule and porticos, and a dome conspicuous above the house, and it is beautiful and fit for our way of worship, being possessed also of a convenient auditory.''*

"I like your wit," replied Charles, "but this, as designed, would be an insignificant cathedral, lacking the majesty of our great Kingdom. We desire a St. Paul's that will be a magnificent tribute to our greatness."

Most of his advisers disliked this design and their objections were many: the model varied too much from traditional cathedral form, it was not grand enough, and it would not serve the best interests of the nation.

When Charles said nothing about another design, Christopher decided that all plans for a new St. Paul's had been rejected and resolved to concentrate on his duties as Surveyor General.

But he had to assert himself more affirmatively. The large house he was given at Scotland Yard and the adequate income of his new office gave him the courage to arrange to marry Faith at Temple Church in London on December 7th, 1669.

He selected this church because it was one of the rare round churches left in England, and it had escaped the fire. Temple Church was the closest the Gothic came to the structure of a dome, yet as he stood by the side of Faith, who looked solemn, almost sad, he wondered if she had any regrets. He had hesitated to take this step, but in another moment or two he would swear eternal love, yet some doubts remained.

Faith knew she looked beautiful in her wedding clothes, but Susan and Holder and Matthew must be puzzled why she didn't appear happy, only even now, he hadn't said he loved her. She felt jealous of his designs. But it was madness to withdraw; she would never meet another Christopher.

Then he realised that if she didn't have all of his love, she had the best of it. As they were wed, he whispered, "Faith, I do love you."

"And I love you, Christopher."

Her eyes sparkled now, she looked elegant and beautiful, and now he was sure of how he felt. He thought, Faith was part of the fabric of his being. And he told her so.

Any New Beginning

Any new beginning has more religion than faith has
Faith suggests faithlessness

Any new beginning is without cunning doubt or bribe
It will be a total of giving and receiving

But especially of getting is the feeling
And where the feeling comes from

None will ever know
                    Except that desperate longing

Stymean Karlen

38

Any New Beginning

THE DAY CHRISTOPHER WAITED FOR THE VISIT FROM THE KING WAS an anxious one. It was supposed to be a great honour but so much depended on it that his concern grew. Four years had passed since Charles had rejected his first model for St. Paul's, yet it was just a few months ago that he had requested a new design. Then Christopher had worked passionately to complete what had been in his thoughts for many years. He was determined that this model contain all the mechanical and mathematical skills he possessed, his powers of observation and invention, and his abilities of hand, eye, touch, and mind. It must be the best expression of his art. But he didn't tell anyone of his dreams of a great church under a dome. Not even Faith or Daniel, who had returned to his service a few years ago.

Now the wooden model awaited the King's pleasure and he examined it to reassure himself that the joiners who had put it together from his designs had not taken liberties but had reproduced it accurately.

He stood in the studio of his official residence in Scotland Yard, and while it was not the kind of a house he would have designed, it suited his needs, and he liked its spaciousness and location. It was across from where he had lived before, and next door to where Jones had resided. Despite the defects of the pillars, he still remembered the surveyor's work with respect. This Tudor house had many rooms and a fine garden that Faith loved. The walls were a sturdy stone and the courtyard reminded him pleasantly of Oxford and the rooms were comfortable.

But nothing mattered now except the fate of his new model. He recalled Charles' words: "*We command you to prepare for a new structure, in form and fashion, a design which will equal if not exceed, the splendour and magnificence of the old cathedral, when it was in its best estate. His*

Majesty, to approve of it, desires a Model to be made thereof, in so large and exact manner, that it may remain in perpetual and unchangeable rule and direction for the conduct of the whole work." He didn't want to swell with pride but he loved this new model and it should please the King. It could become the finest cathedral in the world. He felt he had achieved a genuine majesty with this model. Then his anxiety grew. No such design had been seen in England. It was shaped like a Greek cross, when the essence of the English cathedral was the traditional Latin cross. He feared that Charles, and the clergy, who had to approve, would not accept such originality, although he felt it was an appropriate combination of grandeur and simplicity, beauty and suitability.

If he had made any mistakes with this new model, he thought, it was because he had been so busy. He had designed ten churches in 1670, ten more since then, and more were planned. He was creating a monument to commemorate the fire; a new prison at Newgate; another theatre at Drury Lane, which had burnt down as he had feared; he was rebuilding Temple Bar, the traditional entrance into the City of London. He had to approve the finished Guildhall, Royal Exchange, and Customs House, although they were not designed to his taste. Charles had commanded him to accept them; they were essential to the welfare of his realm and to his purse.

Most unwillingly and yet most necessarily, he had to administer the Office of the Surveyor of the Works. He was responsible for the upkeep of all Crown property, from the royal palaces to the royal stables, from the lodgings of the King's servants to the hunting lodges. He had to be sure the King's drinking water was free of pollution and that all of the royal drainage was satisfactory. He supervised the Comptroller, Clerk, Paymaster, Master Mason, Master Carpenter, Master Bricklayer, Sergeant Plumber, masons, joiners, carpenters, bricklayers, carvers, and many others. He directed the use of the royal stone quarries on the island of Portland. He had to understand how to make brick and tile, to know the price of lime and sand, what iron was available, and the different kinds of stone that were available. There was the carrying out of all royal proclamations that had to do with building regulations.

Christopher, reviewing this as he wondered uneasily if Charles would arrive, knew he should feel achieved but he didn't. The rebuilding of the churches faced many problems. The lay projects had other difficulties. Despite his feeling for the new model, he couldn't tell whether work on St. Paul's would resume, and if it did, which appeared unlikely, how long it would take. And now he faced a new difficulty. He could tell by the rage in Hooke's voice as the philosopher rushed in with Daniel.

It reminded him of how his friend had returned.

Daniel had come back to London the year after he had become Surveyor General and had refused to discuss what had happened to him. All he would say was: "Rembrandt died. Last year. In 1669." As if that was the only reason he would remember that year. "And Spinoza no longer lives there and hasn't for years. Amsterdam is a blind, ignorant city."

"Are you back for good?"

Daniel shrugged.

"Do you intend to stay in London?"

"Can I be of any use to you?"

"I need someone I can trust. I have so much to do."

"You will do it." Daniel paused. "Are you sure you can use me?"

"You can still draw, can't you?"

"Yes."

"And you are not a stranger."

Daniel smiled and looked more like the friend that Christopher had trusted. But Daniel felt that he had to say, "I may not be qualified to help you design churches and they are a large part of your work."

"You will learn. The materials are the same as any other building and you have a good eye and hand. One of the best I know."

Daniel was unhappy about Hooke's hand, but the philosopher drowned out his words by shouting, "I do not lack for praise, but this Dutchman does not comprehend my intentions. When I agreed to aid you with St. Mary-at-Hill, little did I dream I would be treated with so little veneration and honour."

Daniel said, "Sir, I do not wish to offend you. But your drawings are insensitive and unreadable. We cannot judge what materials are needed."

"If you refuse my design, the loss will be great." Hooke was outraged.

Christopher asked, "May I see your drawings?"

Hooke gave them to him rudely, as if to question his work was absurd, but Christopher, as he studied his drawings, understood what Daniel meant. He had planned St. Mary-at-Hill in the shape of a Greek cross, to see whether it could work with St. Paul's, but Hooke had altered that. Yet his friend was so easily hurt he must be careful what he said.

"Wren, it is appropriate," Hooke said positively.

"Perhaps, but not quite in harmony with my intention."

"It is a Dutch plan and I'm an expert on the Dutch style. Van Doorn isn't qualified to judge. He's a draughtsman, not a surveyor."

Daniel replied, "I can judge an accurate drawing when I see one.

The design for St. Mary-at-Hill is not as Doctor Wren intended the church."

They were interrupted by Faith but when she saw that her husband was busy, she hesitated, and Christopher asked her what she wanted. He was worried about her pale, wan expression. Since their son, Gilbert, whom they had named after the Archbishop, had died in infancy last year, she had languished. She paused to choose her words carefully, and he reflected sadly, Last year had been a bad one, Matthew and Wilkins had died, too.

In this moment of reflection he realised he was not satisfied with such medical judgments as: "Your son died of a congestion." Congestion of what? "Your cousin's symptoms could have been the dropsy." But Matthew had been only forty-two and dropsy was an elderly person's illness.

Wilkins had persuaded Sydenham to attend him because of their old friendship as supporters of Cromwell, and Sydenham, at least, knew what was wrong with Wilkins, even if he couldn't cure him. "Suppression of the urine," he told Christopher when the surveyor visited Wilkins near the end. "But the Bishop takes the pain well and remains cheerful and optimistic."

Wilkins' robust voice had become a whisper but he wanted to talk to Christopher while he could. "I've left my estate to Wadham and the Royal Society. Were you able to visit Milton? I heard that he has aged terribly and is ailing. And he respects your modesty."

"I haven't been able to see him. I've been very busy."

"I've heard. It is very kind of you to visit me. You, at least, didn't vote against Milton's entry into the Society as the majority did."

"I believe it was because of his association with Cromwell."

"That is likely. But Dryden supported the Lord Protector and I'm sure that Pepys did, too, although he doesn't admit it, and others did, also."

Christopher sighed with regret over Milton's rejection.

But Wilkins brightened as he reassured Christopher, "Soon, I will be free of this troublesome body of mine. Don't worry about my passing, I've introduced a new member to the Royal Society who will more than fill my place. He will far outdo me in learning and invention. I resign my place to him cheerfully and will seek my redemption in the everlasting."

"You mustn't talk that way."

"I can't dance any more but I can still judge a philosophical nature."

"Who is this new member you propose for the Society?"

"A young mathematics professor at Cambridge, Isaac Newton. He fancies himself a theologian but he is a better mathematician. In some ways he reminds me of Hooke, he is suspicious and easily wounded, but his mind is capable of nobility. He could improve the quality of the Society."

Christopher recalled these words when he met Newton after the mathematician was admitted to the Society on Wilkins' instructions. The professor, who was ten years younger than Christopher— having been born the year that Galileo died—was small, thin, sprightly, with a long, narrow face, a large, dominant nose, a sharp, determined chin, and a sober demeanour.

Hooke quarrelled with him immediately. Christopher wasn't sure which philosopher he agreed with; their views on the nature of light were both possible. But he liked the reflecting telescope Newton presented to the Society, and he differed with Hooke's criticism of it.

Hooke stated, "I possess a better instrument, and an infallible method of perfecting all kinds of optical machines," which Christopher doubted, and added, "Much better than Newton's," which Christopher doubted also, while Newton shrugged and retorted, "Not all things are as they seem."

Faith's voice brought Christopher back to the present. "I wanted to see if everything was in order for His Majesty's arrival. Wouldn't it be better to receive him in our drawing room? It might be more fitting."

"I don't want to move the model. That could damage it."

She hid her disappointment and said, "What about your drawings? They will be better received if they are neat and orderly."

"I was rearranging them when Hooke wanted to see me. I know you have put much into making this residence habitable and your taste is evident."

Faith hoped the King felt that way, too, but it was not pride only that caused her to spend much time, effort, and money on these quarters. It was duty also, which demanded that the Surveyor General's house be worthy. Christopher had chosen the room with the best light for his studio; he loved light; he designed everything with light in mind. But she felt, as his wife, that it was necessary to improve the comfort, beauty, and dignity of this official residence. She had hearths placed in all the rooms. She hung tapestries where they were fitting, and chintz in her audience chamber, and purple hangings in his studio to show that he was in the royal service. This was the precious place to Christopher, a fine, long room with numerous shelves built into the walls for books, papers, and drawings, all catalogued, and his most cherished possessions. The space between the bookshelves was wainscotted in oak, but all of it, she thought, served to frame the table and desk where he worked. The candles lit the room fully, twice the number actually that were needed, but he wanted the brightest light. He had allowed her to furnish everything, except his working materials, and he seemed pleased and proud of her taste. But now, she sensed, he was preoccupied, for he didn't even notice the time, that the King was very late.

She cried out in her anxiety, "Perhaps His Majesty isn't coming!"

Christopher assured her, "Charles is almost always late."

Faith looked at her watch. "Unless this timepiece is incorrect."

It was the watch that had fallen into the water and Hooke said proudly, "Madam, it is not incorrect. No watch I repair fails to work properly."

"But Christopher said . . ."

"He helped me, Madam. But I repaired it. I am the one who regulated the balance. This is a truth too important to be ignored. And my new Dutch microscope verifies my conclusions about watches."

Which I brought him from Amsterdam, Daniel smiled to himself, but he was silent. Madam Wren looked upset, as if Christopher had deceived her, and Daniel wasn't sure she fancied him. There were moments he felt she was jealous of him because he possessed memories which she couldn't share.

Christopher looked harassed and overburdened, but he said, "Faith, I fixed it in spirit. I asked Hooke's aid so it would work perfectly."

"His Majesty is very late!" she exclaimed.

"But not too late, I trust, Madam."

Charles stood in the doorway and she curtsied and said, "Your Majesty, we are honoured by your presence."

"Madam, I'm delighted that Doctor Wren has such a keen eye for beauty. I didn't expect that in him. It is my pleasure to attend you."

Faith was happy that she wore white with trimmings of blue and gold lace which heightened her fairness. It was the least she could do for Christopher. And as she blushed, her complexion was rosy and good again.

Christopher said, "Your Majesty, would you like to see the new model?"

Charles nodded languidly, motioned for York and Buckingham, who were behind him, to accompany him, and strolled leisurely over to the model on the oak table. The sight pleased him, for his dark eyes widened and he grew animated and he asked, "Doctor, is this your final model?"

"No, sir. This is my working model."

"How long will it take to construct it into a great model?"

"A few months, sir."

"That should be built as was done with St. Peter's. Have you seen it?"

"Only in a drawing, sir."

"Strange, for it reminds me of St. Peter's."

"Your Majesty, perhaps it is the dome."

Charles glanced at his companions and asked, "What do you think?"

Buckingham said, "Sir, much of it is borrowed and laborious."

York added, "And he neglects the altar." He preferred the cathedral to be rebuilt in such a way it could be suited to Roman Catholic services, if necessary, but this was not the time to say that.

Christopher explained, "Sir, the design is more concerned with the human act of worship than the physical object, the altar."

York said, "It is more regular than our existing cathedrals."

"Sir, I want nothing superfluous, yet everything fit for human needs."

Charles, whose natural curiosity was engaged now, said suddenly, "It is far grander than your first model for St. Paul's."

"And I believe, sir, more soundly constructed."

"Hooke, what do you think of this design? You are a surveyor."

Hooke appeared to be looking elsewhere, distracted because he wasn't involved, but when he saw that the King truly desired his opinion, he said, *"Sir, I have differed with Wren on occasion, but I must affirm that since the time of Archimedes there scarce ever met in one man so great a perfection and so mechanical a hand in so philosophical a mind."*

Christopher was startled by Hooke's praise; Faith wanted to embrace him; Daniel found it hard to believe, yet Hooke's expression was serious; while Charles asked, "So what do you recommend, Surveyor?"

Hooke said, "In matters such as St. Paul's, sir, he should be heeded."

Daniel suggested, "Your Majesty, you spoke of the need to construct a great model that will display this design to the best advantage."

"It will be done. I will call it the *Great Design*. It will be an ornament to our nation and evoke reverence with its grandeur. Doctor Wren, we will have the *Great Design* constructed into an eighteen foot high model to display to the Commission for St. Paul's. It will show why we must resume work on the cathedral. As soon as this is possible."

Christopher wasn't certain Charles meant what he said, "Your Majesty, what about the cost? It forced us to halt four years ago."

"Things have changed. The Commons have taken a thousand pounds from the tax on coal and allotted it to St. Paul's." Charles surveyed the studio and said, "You have a vast amount of work ahead of you, don't you?"

"Yes, Your Majesty. But it won't interfere with St. Paul's."

"I hope not. The city churches are essential and we need the Monument to honour our rebuilding efforts, and a new theatre at Drury Lane so we will not get bored. You will need a comprehensive mind for all these matters."

"Sir, Mr. Hooke is generously assisting on the Monument and Mr. Van Doorn is helping me in the same way with Drury Lane."

"But both must have your personal supervision."

"They will, Your Majesty."

"The *Great Design* could be a great occasion. I feared you were planning an insignificant St. Paul's, but I should have known, that with your wit, you would have better judgment. Isn't that so, Jamie? Buckingham?"

York agreed, but Buckingham said, "I prefer more passion in our Surveyor. He should be pleasing and entertaining to suit all humours."

Charles said, "You have too much sympathy for Pratt and May, who have better manners perhaps, but lack Wren's taste and originality."

Daniel asked, "Your Majesty, should we go ahead with the larger model?"

"Yes. That is official."

Christopher added, "Sir, what about the demolishing and the debris?"

Charles was annoyed and he snapped curtly, "What about it, Doctor?"

"Sir, until the entire ruin is cleared away, no design, however grand and pleasing, can be final. The dimensions of a new St. Paul's cannot be determined until we know what space is available."

"I said, work will resume on St. Paul's. When the weather is better. I will command a royal warrant to that purpose. To take effect no later than the spring of next year. As I expressed, Doctor, when I ordered you to prepare this new design. And it is not suitable for my Surveyor to be a professor of astronomy. It is advisable that you resign."

Christopher looked stricken by this but Faith said, "Your Majesty, you are wise. My husband cannot long survive in good health with all the activities he attempts now. One day a week he is at Oxford for his lectures, one day at Gresham for the Society, one day at Windsor . . ."

Charles halted her. "Madam, I've not commanded him to go to Windsor."

"Nonetheless, he goes, Your Majesty."

Christopher mumbled, "It was my home." He couldn't tell anybody, least of all Faith, whom he wanted to surprise, that he was designing a new country house for her at Windsor on the banks of the river.

"Your Majesty, he is so occupied with other matters, I don't know how he can carry out the projects of his Office. Yet when I implore him to resign from Oxford he refuses."

"Madam, he cannot refuse me. Wren, this is a command."

"But, sir . . ."

"Unless you regard it as too high a price to pay for being knighted."

Christopher stammered, amazed, "But I wasn't aware, sir, that . . ."

"Would you consider resigning from Oxford now?"

"Whatever you wish, Your Majesty," Christopher murmured, still stunned.

"This will give you authority for the tasks ahead of you. People will hesitate to oppose you, for they will be opposing their sovereign, too. And I desire you to stand, with my support, as a candidate for the University in the Parliamentary by-election which is about to occur."

"But, Your Majesty, what reason could I have for such an act?"

"Commons has to be influenced, too, and your voice in it could help pass some of our more ponderous acts, especially on behalf of St. Paul's."

"Sir, will my new model be accepted?"

"It is a work of art. I will recommend that to the Commission."

The King was as good as his word. Another Royal Commission for the Rebuilding of the Cathedral Church of St. Paul was appointed, and Charles informed them that he favoured the Surveyor General's new model. And that as soon as this *Great Design* was constructed to a scale fitting its scope and grandeur, it would be shown to them for their consideration and approval. He assured Christopher that his recommendations would be followed, and shortly after Christopher resigned as Savillian Professor of Astronomy at Oxford he summoned him to Whitehall and knighted him.

Then reluctantly, but to express his gratitude, Sir Christopher Wren became the King's candidate for Parliament from Oxford University.

He wished Matthew was alive. His cousin would know what to do. Nothing perplexed him more than University politics. On one hand he was accused of being an academic, and so, unworldly and unfit for office as a member of Parliament, on the other he was sneered at as a court favourite and not to be trusted intellectually. He couldn't devote much time to seeking the office; he was busier than ever with his work as surveyor. He never heard the name of his opponent mentioned; the chief subject of his effort to be elected was Cromwell. Although he was the King's candidate, the opposition said he was Cromwell's. His acquaintance with the Lord Protector was used as if he had served him rather than Charles, which was a lie. But once that was uttered, he noticed it was believed. He was not surprised when he lost.

Now, at least, he could return fully to his true vocation. With the coming of spring and better weather the Royal Commission ordered the demolishing of the old cathedral to resume and to continue until all of it was cleared away. The eighteen foot high model of the *Great Design* was almost finished now and he was told by Sancroft, "It is a virtuous plan, *handsome and noble and suitable*, and with the King's approval it is likely that all the Commissioners will approve, it is the custom."

That prospect brought such joy to Christopher he was relieved by the defeat at Oxford, now he could concentrate on what truly mattered.

Faith was hurt by it. She felt that as a member of Parliament, everyone would listen to Sir Christopher Wren, but he disagreed with her. He said, "Not everyone even listens to the King. He is not always obeyed."

She retorted, "It is a pity. I still think you should have won."

"I couldn't, Faith dear. I was running against Cromwell."

The Blind Wall Looked At Me

The blind wall looked at me
But I knew the wall well
It saw through me
As I saw through it

I understood and walked away
Knowing
It misunderstood me
As blind walls do

In a world whole
    With blind walls

Stymean Karlen

39

The Blind Wall Looked At Me

AT LAST IT WAS BEING DONE. THE RUINS OF ST. PAUL'S WERE COMING down.

It was the first of May, an appropriate time to start. The day was fair, mild, and fine for working, for clearing the ground for the new foundations. Christopher braced himself for the task ahead and surveyed the area in front of him once more. He had done this many times in the last few weeks, waiting for the weather to improve enough to allow him to begin. He knew he couldn't be too careful. Yet everything was prepared.

Edward Woodruff, whom Sancroft had appointed to aid him, had collected workmen, pickaxes, and material for scaffolds. As surveyor for Westminster Abbey, he was considered competent to arrange the technical details.

The profusion of other projects in work, Christopher's other concern, seemed properly arranged. Daniel was supervising the rebuilding of Drury Lane; Hooke was continuing the work on the Monument; Thomas Strong was directing the work on St. Stephen Walbrook; and Joshua Marshall was in charge of St. Mary-le-Bow. They were his favourite churches, although many more were being projected, designed, and built. His eighteen foot high model for the *Great Design* was finished and it had been submitted to the newly formed Royal Commission for Rebuilding St. Paul's. All his aides, even Hooke, assured him that it would be approved but he wasn't as sure. He had refused to make any concessions to the old forms of worship and he had no feeling of certainty that his innovations would be accepted.

Now he focused on the work in front of him. He began at the east end, where demolishing had gone on until the two workmen had died. He had not forgotten this; he was resolved that this must not happen again. The beginning was vital. If the work began safely it would encourage the workmen to toil hard; otherwise it would be difficult to get capable labour. The Crown might have to press men into a work gang, which he hated.

These walls were not the highest he would have to knock down, but they were high enough to be risky. Eighty feet high, their masonry was five foot thick and solid enough to have been built for eternity.

He chose the best wood and supervised the erection of the scaffolds.

Woodruff was horrified that the Surveyor General was soiling his hands. "Sir, this isn't necessary. I will see to it that all is done correctly."

"I must do this myself. We must not have any deaths this time."

"Sir, on work of this kind casualities are unavoidable. Inevitable."

"That doesn't have to be. The workmen's lives are my responsibility."

"Everything is as you wish, sir. And you have so much else to do. I can take care of the details. This is a great and troublesome task."

"Woodruff, I know you wish to spare me difficulties. But some I must face. It is my duty to see that these scaffolds are completely reliable."

He insisted on testing them himself, although he wasn't sure that was foolproof, for he was smaller and lighter than most of the workmen who had to climb them. So he carried up a twenty pound rock to verify that they would hold the men's weight. He was pleased he was strong enough to carry the rock without strain, although he was almost forty-two. He wondered what his father would have thought of his delicate son if the Dean had seen him now. Then, in this moment of distraction, he almost lost his balance. He looked down at the ground many feet below and the sudden change of perspective made him feel dizzy. The faces beneath him became a blur. He clutched a scaffold pole, dropped the rock where he stood; he was relieved that the planking held. Yet, he thought, if this happened to him at eighty feet and he had experience at heights, how would the workmen be affected at two hundred, where the remains of the broken tower stood?

On the ground he didn't tell anyone of his dizziness or apprehensions, although Woodruff asked him if he were feeling well, he looked so pale.

"I'm fine," he replied. "It is the first time I've climbed a scaffold this year." He must find a better way to demolish this towering ruin; the scaffolds were dangerous at such a height.

Woodruff thought, Sir Christopher Wren was insane, no Surveyor General in his right mind would climb scaffolds to test them, and now that he was knighted he had no need to assert his authority.

Christopher sensed his criticism and he wanted to retort, Walls can be stubborn even under the most extreme pressure. Instead, he ordered work to start on the eighty foot scaffolds. He stayed close to this work until he was certain everything was progressing efficiently and safely.

So he proceeded, gaining every day more space and confidence, until he came to the middle tower which had borne the steeple. The remains of the tower were over two hundred feet high and the workmen who toiled on the eighty foot walls, which were almost down, with pickaxes, told Woodruff it was dangerous to work so high. Woodruff replied that this was nonsense and brought the rebellious workmen before Christopher to have them punished, but the surveyor agreed with them and refused to chastise them.

Woodruff exclaimed, "Sir how else will we get the tower down?"

"I will find another way."

Woodruff was dubious and said, "Sir, if I have them whipped and their leaders put in Newgate, the others will go up. Men have been hung for less."

"I will not punish workmen for being afraid of an unnecessary risk."

"Sir, some risks may be necessary."

"I will determine that."

"Sir, I'm sure, with your wit, you will solve the situation."

But Christopher was troubled. When he found no solution the next few days, he feared that scaffolds might have to be used. He re-read his warrant to give him reassurance: "*Sir Christopher Wren, Surveyor General, who draws all the designs of the building, has the universal care thereof, gives all directions to workmen and other officers, examines all accounts, agrees for the price of workmanship and materials. His salary is £200 per annum.*"

Yet that didn't tell him how to bring the tower down. He wanted to build a house for God to enter, but perhaps God had gone away.

One night, unable to sleep, he drove to the ruins with only his driver in attendance. It was a beautiful moonlit evening and he gazed at the moon above him, and thought, This was an undiscovered country, too, in spite of Copernicus and Galileo, and astronomy could become an enterprise of great moment and substance. Then he visualised a cathedral that was heroic and monumental, not reduced to ashes, and he recalled that Van Dyck and Donne had been buried here. He wondered where their bodies were. Corpses had been unearthed by the fire, but most of them were unrecognisable. He felt he was burying a ghost. Yet, he asked himself, how could he bury what was without flesh or material matter? But he must have this ruin down soon if he was to proceed with his *Grand*

Design. He walked over to the tower, whose steeple—before it had been wrecked by lightning—had been the sign of old St. Paul's splendour and London's permanence, and heard a stirring.

At first he thought it was a rat and he drew back in alarm. Then he remembered that the rats had been burnt out by the fire, and so far, neither the rats nor the plague had returned. He approached again and now his curiosity was aroused, for he saw a pile of rubble that was built to serve as a shelter. It was shaped like a tent and he poked his head into it, followed by his coachman, Walt Bray, a youthful, alert Londoner, who knew the city intimately, and accidentally awoke a sleeping beggar.

The grizzled, elderly man was indignant. He had bedded down for the night by clearing a space on the ground to sleep on; he had wrapped a rag around the stone he used for a pillow. He snarled, "What do you want?"

The coachman said, "You're trespassing. We'll have you whipped."

"Can't you let a body sleep?"

"Sir, I'll call the watch and have him put into Newgate."

"Wait!" Christopher asked, "Aren't you afraid to sleep here?"

"No one will harm me. I've nothing they can steal."

"Don't you think about the people who have been buried here?"

"If I don't disturb them, they won't disturb me."

Christopher inadvertently dislodged a loose stone and the tent collapsed with a loud crash. No one was hurt but it brought the beggar to his feet, moaning that there was no peace anywhere, even in hell.

It also brought the watch, two husky men armed with swords and staves. In the flickering glow of their lantern—Christopher hadn't taken any light, he knew the way by heart—they peered suspiciously at the three men.

The leader said, "I'll have to arrest you. No one is allowed here at night. There have been too many thefts of stone, timber, and lead."

Bray said hurriedly, "It is the Surveyor."

The watch looked more closely and when they saw Christopher's fine clothes they recognised him and the leader's tone grew obsequious. "Sir, is this villain bothering you? We can dispose of him easily."

"We're bothering him. Let him sleep." Christopher walked over to him and added, "I'm sorry about the tent. I didn't intend to knock it down."

The beggar grumbled, "I've been knocked down before. In the Dutch war, where I served in the King's navy. By a charge of gunpowder. It blew me the length of the deck. I'm lucky I'm alive.

It knocked down the main mast and it was only a small charge, for loading a few cannon. But now, I'm not even fit to be a grave digger. I survived the plague, the fire, Dutch shot and English gunpowder, but this weather, it will kill us all."

It was starting to rain, a heavy, chill downpour, which meant there would be no work tomorrow, the scaffolds would be too wet and slippery, and yet Christopher felt exultant. Gunpowder could knock down the tower, properly applied. He must reckon a way of doing it safely. He gave the beggar two shillings and ordered the watch to allow him to stay.

The leader of the watch nodded, but added, "Sir, next time you venture out at night, you should be better protected. London isn't safe then."

After exploring the foundations of the tower, Christopher measured the effects produced by gunpowder. He used small amounts on a thick, low wall where there was no danger of flying debris. When this worked as he had estimated he felt fine.

Woodruff and Sancroft said gunpowder was too dangerous to use, that many would be mangled and killed by the explosion, but he didn't listen to their warnings. His assistant shrugged but the Dean was offended; he felt the Surveyor didn't trust him; he wondered if he was wise to support him.

Christopher consulted with the Tower of London's chief gunner on the effects of gunpowder. When Phillip Brilock's conclusions agreed with his own, he decided to proceed with the plan he had evolved.

Early one warm, dry morning, he prepared to demolish the huge central tower with a charge of gunpowder, although the universal belief on the site was that it wouldn't work. Even the chief gunner, who was setting the charge, was sceptical. But the Surveyor General also supervised the care of the Tower of London, so he had to obey his orders, even as he feared the blast that followed would fill the breach with English dead.

Christopher knew exactly what he wanted to do. He cleared away the area about the northwest pillar of the central tower. There were four pillars here, each fourteen feet in diameter, and the gunner said this small charge—his deal-box contained only eighteen pounds—would never demolish walls so thick and fixed. "That is not my intention," the Surveyor answered, "Just follow my instructions, or someone else will."

Sancroft, who stood within view but far enough away to feel safe, had never seen the Surveyor so determined. Christopher thought, Only Daniel, whom he had invited to attend, believed he would succeed. He hadn't told Faith, afraid she would worry about the danger to him; he had told Hooke, who had shrugged critically and said, "You should have asked my advice, but you always have to do it your own way. I'll repair the damage."

For a moment Christopher hesitated. The price in arms and legs and shattered bodies could be large. But everything he knew, he remembered, convinced him that his plan would work, whatever anyone else feared.

Workmen dug a hole four feet wide by the side of the northwest pillar. Next, with tools that Christopher had constructed for this purpose, they cut a hole, two feet square into the centre of the pillar. The gunner placed a little deal-box containing the eighteen pounds of gunpowder into this pillar. "No more," Christopher told the perplexed gunner, whose leatherly face showed his doubts. He ordered the gunner to fix a cane to the box of powder and a quick match within the cane, which reached from the box to the ground below. Next the gunner laid a trail of powder along the ground. But before he lit it, Christopher made sure the mine was carefully closed up in the pillar with mortar and stone. Then he commanded everyone to stand back while the gunner set fire to the fuse.

Even Daniel, with all of his faith in Christopher's inventiveness and skill, shivered and recoiled apprehensively.

The blast occurred exactly as Christopher planned. There was a muffled roar, but now, instead of the pillar exploding outward in a thousand pieces as everyone expected, the gigantic block of masonry rose a few inches in the air, and almost leisurely, lifted up part of the roof and tower and it crumbled into an enormous heap of rubble.

Sancroft was the first to congratulate Christopher on his cleverness, and Woodruff exclaimed, "Sir, you have performed a miracle! With only eighteen pounds of powder, you have lifted up three thousand tons of cathedral and you have saved the work of a thousand labourers."

And no one was hurt, he thought, but he was unhappy that the fall of so much weight from a height of two hundred feet caused such a concussion that many people ran from their houses in terror, believing an earthquake had hit London. He must take more care next time to avoid such a shock. If he only had time to study the forces of gravity closer! He must discuss this with Hooke and Newton, who seemed to have a flair for such matters.

He excused himself from the crowd praising his ingenuity as if he were a magician, which displeased him. If this explosion was a triumph, it was of reason. He asked Daniel, "Has Hooke returned St. Mary-at-Hill to my original design?" He was alone with Daniel now.

"I don't know. He refuses to allow me to look at them now. Christopher, knocking down this pillar was quite a trick."

"It is not a trick. Do you think that Hooke will listen to me?"

"I doubt it. He is convinced he knows more than anybody else."

"I will take care of St. Mary-at-Hill later." In his desire to have privacy with Daniel, he had backed away from the ruins so that his perspective had improved, and as he viewed what he had done he sighed.

"What's wrong now? Aren't you ever satisfied?" Daniel was pleased he didn't have to call Christopher sir, except when others were around, but his friend looked doleful. "The tower was demolished skilfully."

"Only in part. Two corners of the tower still stand. I thought I would demolish all of it with this blast. There is more work here."

"It will have to wait. The King wants to see you tomorrow."

"Do you know why?"

"I've heard rumours that there are criticisms at Court about some of your designs, including Drury Lane, but I've heard nothing official."

"Has Nell Gwynn complained about the theatre?"

"On the contrary. She likes your work, takes a lively interest in it."

"I didn't want it opened until our work ended, but Charles insisted."

"I think he wants to discuss one of your other designs. You have more than twenty in hand."

"Every time I think of that I feel I have assumed too much."

"You refuse none of them. No matter how they test your invention."

He couldn't, he thought. He needed work to explore, to imagine, to invent, to learn. The last was supremely vital. But he couldn't tell this to anyone, not even to Daniel or Faith, or how little he felt he truly knew. There was no magic in any of his work but a constant learning from experience, investigation, and experiment. The churches were teaching him how to design St. Paul's. Yet sometimes, he reflected, although he was supposed to lead, he needed confirmation of his judgments. In this he could trust Daniel, more than anyone else, most of the time.

Daniel sensed some of the things his friend felt, but he said, "Rembrandt was rarely satisfied. That was why he was not slovenly."

Christopher took Daniel with him to Whitehall the next day. His friend might see things he missed and knew more about the details of the Office.

Charles said, "Sir Christopher, every church is precious to us."

"Your Majesty, this is the view I seek to convey."

"But innovations are not always understood. You must remember that."

"I do, sir. There are many critics about to perform such a service."

Charles stared intently at Wren. Was he being mocked? He liked wit, but not when it was directed at him. That was a kingly privilege he reserved for himself. He said, "You do not take criticism lightly."

"Should I, Your Majesty?"

Wren was learning. But Charles was disappointed. He liked him better when the Surveyor was not a courtier. Wren must want something. He was surrounded with those who wanted something and that exhausted him.

Daniel said, "Your Majesty, in the construction of Drury Lane, we have sought to please Madame Gwynn."

"She is entertained by your efforts. But some of my Court wonder what is accomplished if they cannot be seen properly in their boxes."

Christopher said, "Your Majesty, I designed the theatre so that the players can be seen from everywhere. It was Madame Gwynn's wish."

"I know. But we will discuss this matter some other time. At least the theatre is open even if your work isn't finished. Now there are more pressing matters that concern the Royal Works."

"Complaints, Your Majesty?" Christopher asked angrily.

"Questions, Sir Christopher," Charles answered quietly. "But no one doubts your cleverness. There is much praise for the way you demolished the pillar. Your skill with gunpowder could win us many victories."

"Your Majesty, I've no taste or talent for military matters."

"Your refusal to fortify Tangier could have ruined you."

"Sir, I was an astronomer then."

"But a builder at heart. Oh, I know " Suddenly Charles had a need to justify himself to Christopher, a need he rarely felt with anyone. "I'm not without learning. From the days Newcastle tutored me, you were one of his pupils, too, I've been interested in natural philosophy and the arts. Without me, there would be no Royal Society or the rebuilding of London."

Christopher bowed and murmured, "Your Majesty, we are grateful."

"And very stubborn. Like a rock. There is concern in the parish about the placement and design of St. Mary-le-Bow. Many, including some of the largest contributors to the rebuilding, desire the church to be as it was. Even the old blind poet, Milton, has petitioned me to restore the old structure exactly as it had been. Have you read his *Paradise Lost?*"

"In part, sir. The Archbishop consulted me about its publication."

"I know. I could have stopped it, too. Are you aware that St. Mary-le-Bow is one of the city churches that is under Sheldon's jurisdiction?"

"Yes. Sir, does His Grace share your views?"

Charles almost blurted out, I have no views, but he caught himself, annoyed yet intrigued that the Surveyor provoked him; at least Wren wasn't boring. He declared, "We will examine the church now. I've ordered Milton to attend us. I'm curious as to how he will conduct himself."

"Your Majesty, have you read *Paradise Lost?*"

"That is an interesting question. When Denham mentioned it favourably, the poet sent me an inscribed copy, for he knew I respected Denham's opinions on poetry. But the royal view is that Milton must speak for himself."

Christopher hadn't seen the work at St. Mary-le-Bow recently, he was so preoccupied with St. Paul's, although it was almost within sight of the cathedral. He was disappointed but not surprised that Marshall, who was supervising the rebuilding, had not yet used his design. He had followed the principle of the Greek cross, so he could judge how it would function on a smaller scale, but Marshall still had not begun these foundations.

Moreover, when the King asked the master mason, whom he knew well, "Marshall, what are the difficulties?" the latter replied, "Several, Your Majesty. If the new building is placed on Cheapside itself, as the plan suggests, people will lose homes they possessed before the fire. The old church stood forty feet back. And there is criticism that the barrel vault will lack the beauty of the Gothic arches."

"But, Your Majesty," said Daniel, "the old building was a low, mean place, and couldn't be seen from the street."

Charles asked, "Marshall, what do you say to that?"

"I don't think it advisable to neglect the wishes of the parishioners, sir. Or there may be no money to finish the church."

Christopher said, "Then money must be raised from other sources."

"Suppose there aren't any?" asked the King.

"Sir, if Mary-le-Bow is closed in on all sides it loses its value."

Charles glanced at the master mason for his opinion.

Marshall paused and Christopher added, "I respect the master

648   Myself. Christopher Wren
```

mason's views, but I'm responsible for the design. If he wishes to assume that responsibility, I will find another master mason to work on St. Paul's."

Marshall waited for the King to assert his authority over the Surveyor, but Charles said nothing, and he didn't want to lose this lucrative contract. He said, "I respect Sir Christopher's views, but there is a strong feeling in the parish that the church should be rebuilt as it was."

"No! The previous building was a mixture of Saxon, Norman, and Gothic, but this one must have a unity that agrees with the spirit of our country."

Charles nodded; he couldn't have made a better political speech himself.

"Unless," said Christopher, "His Majesty prefers another Surveyor."

Charles thought irritably, Four years ago he could have dismissed him easily, but to remove him now could be a disaster. No one else could do so much at the same time. He was grateful that while he was pondering Milton approached, led by his wife, for the poet, at least, was a diversion.

Milton looked very old, his jaws sunken with age, yet his wife, who was young, had aged noticeably, too, Christopher observed, as if his burdens had borne her down and she had become round-shouldered and beaten before her time. Then as she told him that the King was present the poet raised his head proudly and stared straight ahead as she turned him so that he faced Charles. His wife hurried to add, "Sir, no one has a greater loyalty for His Majesty, and love for his country than he has."

"No doubt," Charles said, almost wearily, "but I was informed that other matters concern your husband today."

"You are kind, Your Majesty," said Milton. "I'm troubled by the proposed design for St. Mary-le-Bow. This is my church, I grew up within the sight of its coroneted tower and not to see that any more would be a calamity."

Christopher said, "That doesn't fit our time. I plan a steeple that can be seen from everywhere in London and which will express the presence of St. Mary-le-Bow no matter how many buildings crowd in upon it."

"One doesn't have to see to know how a thing should look."

"But a steeple should be seen. If I design this one, it will be."

Milton grumbled, "In my day master masons designed well enough."

Charles asked, "Was that the Usurper's view?"

"Sir, while you and the Lord Protector are very different kind of men, you would have been worthy of each other. Both of you are
```

skilled at conducting affairs of state. It is a talent given only to a few men."

Daniel thought, Milton must want his way very much to so obviously flatter the King, yet Charles, who was quite aware of self-seekers, was pleased, as if he were striving to compete with his greatest enemy.

Christopher wondered what the walls felt; everyone else had an opinion.

Charles said, "Milton, you are not an easy man to dissuade."

"Your Majesty, are you going to heed my views on St. Mary-le-Bow?"

"Would you heed the Surveyor General's views on *Paradise Lost?*"

"Of course not, sir!"

Marshall asked, "Your Majesty, then you favour Sir Christopher's plan?"

"I didn't say that. We will consider all views in this affair."

This was impossible, thought Christopher. "Sir, I cannot be responsible for any work that isn't my design. As you would not be responsible for any action you didn't approve of yourself. Isn't that so, Your Majesty?"

Before Charles could reply a violent blast sounded from the vicinity of St. Paul's. It shook the earth under their feet and echoed violently.

"God's Vengeance!" cried Milton. "He is punishing us for our sins!"

"It must be an earthquake!" exclaimed Marshall. "Or an invasion! Your Majesty, you must be careful of your safety!"

Charles paled but he said, "Perhaps the noise is worse than the effect."

Christopher felt betrayed. Woodruff must have used gunpowder without his permission. He said, "Your Majesty, it sounds to me like an explosive charge at St. Paul's. May I attend at once? To see what has occurred?"

Charles nodded and Christopher ran toward the ruins, followed closely by Daniel, who was afraid but who couldn't allow his friend to go alone. Then, more slowly, Charles mounted his horse, which had reared in terror at the sound, and trotted after them, escorted by his guard.

Marshall mumbled, "I'm needed here." Milton stated, "God is speaking!" And he ordered his cringing wife to see what was happening.

Christopher arrived at the ruins, Daniel with him, and found an angry mob milling around Woodruff, Sancroft, and a group of workmen. When Woodruff saw Christopher he exclaimed hysterically, "Since you left me in charge of the demolishing, I put

X*

another mine in one of the other pillars. But I used a larger quantity of powder. As a special favour to you, I wanted to demolish all of the roof and tower that remained. But perhaps I wasn't as exact as you, or I didn't fortify the mouth of the mine enough. When the mine exploded, many stones shot out."

"Recklessly!" a middle-aged woman screamed. She led a group of other women of the same age and station and she added, "We were working in the bookseller's shop across the churchyard, when stones crashed through our balcony door and penetrated where we work and threatened our lives."

Christopher asked, "Was anybody hurt?"

By now the King had arrived but he didn't dismount and his guard formed a protective wall around him.

"Many, Your Majesty!" the woman shouted. "Our nerves are shattered!"

"But was there any physical harm?" repeated Christopher.

"That doesn't matter. Next time we will all be destroyed. As it is, there is much anger in the neighbourhood against this work. The blasting is ungodly and should be left in God's hands. If this happens again, we cannot answer for your safety. Your Majesty, will you order it stopped?"

"I will consider it."

"But, sir," said Christopher, "The blast didn't harm anyone. Or did any damage. Not even to the tower itself. Most of it still stands."

"You heard what the women said."

"Your Majesty, powder will save much time and money and lives."

"All views will be presented to the Commission for its consideration."

Soon after the Surveyor was ordered by the Commission to halt all the blasting because of the protests of the community around St. Paul's. He argued that the work would suffer and they replied that the use of powder would cause terror and worse suffering. They added that there must not be any more explosions whatever the conditions or he would be dismissed.

Daniel expected Christopher to be outraged; instead he applied his mind to the study of demolition and decided to use a battering ram to knock down the remaining walls. He constructed a strong mast that was forty feet long, armed the bigger end with a great spike of iron, fortified with bars along the mast. Then he hung the mast in two places with rings that formed a strong tackle. Next, he placed the battering ram before the pillars of the tower and with fifteen men on each side of it, ordered them to beat the ram against the wall. He directed this himself, with Daniel as his assistant.

A whole day he beat on the wall without any apparent effect.

Sancroft said, "It will not work, the stone is too strong, too thick."

Woodruff said, "Sir Christopher, we must find another way."

The next morning he resumed the work on the fourteen foot thick wall. Hours passed and the men grew tired, complaining, querulous. Their eyes smarted from the dust; their bodies ached from the effort, and still the wall stood immovable, as it had stood for centuries.

When they had to pause to rest, Daniel asked Christopher, who was stripped to the waist, for it was hot and he had joined the men to encourage them, "As you are fond of saying, these walls were built for eternity. Do you think you can knock them down with a mere battering ram?"

"*Not by one blow. Not a wall of such bulk. But if we vibrate the ram against it incessantly, it should make a small intestine motion through all the insensible parts of the wall, and by degrees it should loosen the bonds of the mortar, and move every stone from its bed. It was why the ancients used the battering ram to besiege and beat down towns and castles.*"

Expressing this, Christopher regained his energy and enthusiasm, as if in the speaking of it, he had clarified it for himself.

Now he made it his business to vibrate the ram against the wall. The men thought he was simply suiting his humours, but he urged them to work faster, and he guided them to reach the tempo he desired. Daniel followed him, then Woodruff, and suddenly Sancroft, whose doubts had discouraged his efforts, shouted, "The wall! It moves!"

The top of the wall trembled as the ram hit it. The next time everyone pushed together and a stone fell from the wall. The ground seemed to shake but Christopher ordered them to continue, saying there was no danger, and they went on, more rapidly and strongly each time. Daniel, who kept close to Christopher, thought, The thrust of the ram had become a powerful yet beautiful thing. The entire wall shook now from the blows of the ram and as the vibrations increased, so did the trembling of the wall. Several stones fell and the pillar quivered as if it were mortally stricken.

Christopher made sure that everyone was out of danger at the end of the forty-foot mast with its great spike of iron, and then he drove it with a tremendous crash against the weakened portion of the wall where the stones had fallen and sharp cracks showed. The pillar collapsed in a spray of stone and mortar that scattered for many feet, but it did not reach the end of the ram and it brought down much of the tower and roof with it.

From then on, the workmen followed the Surveyor whole-heartedly. This lean, lithe, small-boned man had a strength they could trust. Doubts and quarrels vanished as all the walls and pillars came down before the battering ram, and Christopher felt light-footed, graceful, sure-handed.

In a few weeks the main task on the site was clearing away the debris.

This success persuaded Marshall to follow Christopher's design for St. Mary-le-Bow, despite renewed objections; Daniel continued to work on Drury Lane while the performances went on and he watched the other projects; and Christopher prepared his model for the Commission's viewing. He placed it in the Chapter House, which had been restored next to the site of old St. Paul's, and he was delighted that it was just as he had designed it.

His model was what was in his heart. This cathedral must be beautiful yet not overwhelming. It should be for the congregation, not the clergy, and express God's creation, what was seen and not seen.

He prayed that his model would convey these feelings to the Commission. While this royal body which was appointed by the King, included most of the important nobles and dignitaries in the land and stressed the combined responsibility of the Crown, City, and Church, he noticed the six members who appeared to view his model were from the clergy. Only six were needed for a quorum to conduct business, as long as the Bishop of London or the Dean of St. Paul's was present, and he was relieved that Sancroft was here.

He led the Commission to the model and saw surprise and shock on their faces. He wasn't certain the prevailing reaction was approval.

He suggested, "Perhaps, if I describe the design in detail it will be helpful." Sancroft nodded and he resumed, "The main central dome will be over the central cross. Around this will be eight smaller domes to cover the other sections and functions of the cathedral."

"What will support all this?" asked Dr. Stillingfleet, a tall, angular residentiary canon, who was the same age as Christopher.

"The large dome will rest on eight piers."

Sancroft said, "Not unlike the first design for St. Peter's, Rome."

"No! No!" Stillingfleet said impatiently and irritably, "I mean what ecclesiastical body will support a design so different from our traditions?"

Christopher suggested, "Doctor, why don't you step inside."

"Really, that isn't necessary. I can see quite clearly out here."

"But the perspective will be different inside the model."

"I'm acquainted with the inside of a cathedral."

Sancroft said, "Stillingfleet, I will step inside. If it is safe?"

"Perfectly safe, Dean," said Christopher. "I've arranged this model so you can stand inside." He guided him into the eighteen foot high model.

Sancroft marvelled at the interior. Each detail was represented exactly, carved in wood, and sufficiently large. The wood was painted to resemble stone and the roof and domes were a lead shade and there was gilding where it fitted. The Surveyor placed him so that he stood under the great dome and he found it beautiful and grand. He examined the capitals on the columns, which were precisely done, and stared down the long vistas of the cathedral which were as handsome as they were original. He was fascinated by the mind of a man who could have created such a fine perspective with a detail that was everywhere under perfect control. The model had become the cathedral itself and was lovely for its own sake. But there could be difficulties, the Dean reflected, and he must find out how the others felt. He stepped outside, the only member of the Commission to have entered the design, and he sensed objections.

Stillingfleet said the foundations of St. Paul's went back to antiquity; Dr. Turner, the Duke of York's personal Chaplain, complained that there were no side oratories in this model; the other members of the Commission thanked the Surveyor and didn't say a word about his design.

Concerned about this, when Christopher got a moment alone with Sancroft, he asked him, "Dean, do you truly like it?"

"It is indeed a noble design, fine in proportion, lucid, a beautiful and magnificent conception. But not always in the cathedral fashion."

"I'm not sure I understand."

"It has nothing in common with any previous English cathedral."

"Is that important?"

"It may be."

"I was surprised that all of the Commission were from the clergy."

"We are the ones who will have to administer the cathedral and use it. Don't you want to please us?"

"Of course I want to. But I want to please the nation, also."

"And the King, of course, and the Court."

Christopher nodded. And, he thought, himself.

A few days later while Christopher was planning the foundations of St. Paul's, as conceived in his *Great Design*, Sancroft ordered him to halt.

Stunned, Christopher cried out, "What is wrong now?"

Sancroft had come to the Chapter House to tell him this, and he stated, as he had been commanded by the other Commissioners, "There is nothing in your model that can accurately be called a proper aisle or nave or even a choir. As I warned you, it is not enough in the cathedral fashion."

"Whose fashion?" Christopher asked defiantly.

"Our church is proud of its enduring continuity with the English church throughout the centuries. All of our great cathedrals have been built in the shape of the Latin cross. We want to preserve our traditions, but your Greek cross design is Roman and your dome suggests Popery."

"I will not put a Gothic steeple on a classical cathedral."

"That is another difficulty. There is much opposition to a dome. But since I have persuaded the Commission to accept that, although reluctantly, you should accept my views. As it is, it will be hard to convince most of the clergy that a dome will not be Papist."

Christopher was angry and the Dean's objections strengthened his own resolution. He said indignantly, "This is my finest design."

"It is magnificent. But I cannot be the first Anglican Dean of St. Paul's to allow a Roman church on this site."

"Sir, on the one hand you desire to continue the medieval tradition which is Roman, on the other hand you accuse my design of being in error because it is too Roman. This is a contradiction to me."

Sancroft wished the Surveyor was more worldly. "We desire, as you do, that St. Paul's will be a lasting monument to our faith, but the Commission insists that the design must be in the true cathedral fashion, with an appropriate choir, nave, and high altar."

"Sir, the cathedral is designed for the congregation."

"Thus, the high altar should be clearly visible to the entire congregation. So we can give our message in the proper setting."

"This is a Roman concept. Does the King agree with your views?"

"These are the clergy's views. Heed them, it will save much time."

"I will take notice of any imperfections in my design, but I will not alter the essence of it. This is the best structure I can conceive."

Sancroft said nothing. But if the Surveyor assumed that this was the end of the affair, he thought, Sir Christopher was mistaken.

Christopher was sure Charles had more discernment. The King was the one who had admired the Greek cross plan so warmly; he had named it the *Great Design*. Charles was not ignorant like many of the clergy; he understood the need of a classical cathedral which would be perfectly proportioned.

No wonder Sancroft hadn't answered his question about the King. Charles was supporting his Greek cross. He asked to see him at once.

The King was at Newcastle hunting and racing. It was a month before Christopher could obtain an audience with him at Whitehall, and then only when he wrote him that the matter was urgent, that all work had halted on St. Paul's and could not resume until His Majesty was consulted.

Charles returned to London reluctantly. He disliked the city in the heat of summer and it was afflicted with hot July weather. And he had gone to Newcastle to avoid problems; he was in no mood to face a quarrel.

He ordered the Duke of York to attend them, for James had strong views on St. Paul's and was eager to express his opinions.

Christopher said, "Your Majesty, I beg you, support the *Great Design*. You admired it. You named it. Sir, you understand artistic merit and that we need a new St. Paul's as a mighty expression of your reign."

Charles smiled in agreement and just as Christopher thought, He was right to count on his support, the clergy were more conservative than the Crown, York said, "Dr. Turner tells me that you have no side oratories."

"Sir, they are not necessary."

"This is not my view. And you have made no provisions for processions."

"Sir, they are impertinent. Our religion is not using processions."

"That is not so. We have had them ever since the Restoration."

Christopher paused. It was evident that York was strongly opposed to any design that was not suited to Roman Catholic services.

Charles said wearily, having lost his interest in the heat of the day and the difference of opinion, "Sir Christopher, we must move carefully."

And offend no one, reflected Christopher, but he said, "Your Majesty, it is my hope that this design will gratify the taste of connoisseurs like yourself. Believe me, sir, it will bring great honour to your name."

Charles nodded, but said irritably, "It will be considered."

There was no one else to appeal to, for the City Commissioners were neutral. And Christopher realised, as the days passed and the clergy remained obdurate, that only the King could carry the day for him.

At dinner one night he told Faith and Daniel what was happening and yet, he felt his *Great Design* would be accepted. "Because it is a work of reason," he told them, "And the King will support me. He has taste."

Faith however, wondered if it was wise to oppose someone as

influential as Sancroft, who was also a good friend. But she didn't persist when he disagreed. He wondered why she was so preoccupied, for she retired early, although she said she felt fine, that nothing was wrong, nothing at all.

Daniel didn't think he would win. Daniel had less faith in reason.

Christopher replied, "The King esteems my Greek cross design."

"And hates a quarrel. He will do almost anything to avoid one."

"Then you think I should give in?"

"I didn't say that. Your design is admirable. I never thought a church could be so beautiful, so finely proportioned, so appropriate to man's belief in God. I not only see your design, I feel it. But you oppose the weight of centuries, and I don't want you to suffer if it is rejected."

When neither Christopher nor the clergy gave in, Sancroft offered a compromise: The Surveyor should use his pre-fire design. The Dean came to see Christopher at the studio in Scotland Yard, as a conciliatory gesture, explained his mission, and he was startled by the Surveyor's reply.

"That design was done as a compromise when we had no other choice. But I've learned much since then. It is just a fragment of what I know now."

"I liked your pre-fire design," Sancroft said defensively.

"I did, too. At that time. But today, it is impossible."

"I don't see why. You have a dome."

"And a Latin cross, and a mixture of styles, Gothic, classical, and without any unity. That is what is wrong with Winchester cathedral."

"Many admire and love Winchester."

"Which was built hundreds of years ago, piece by piece."

"That raises another difficulty. If St. Paul's is done with the Greek cross design, you will have to build it all at once, which is impossible."

That objection struck Christopher as ridiculous but he asked, "Why?"

"We want to start services as soon as possible and that can't be done with your Greek cross. In such a design the parts cannot be divided, but in the Latin cross we can begin to use sections of it for worship before the entire cathedral is finished. That could take a very long time at the rate the coal dues are coming in. Beyond my lifetime or yours."

"I intend to survive the building," Christopher said grimly.

"You may not. No cathedral in England is the work of one man."

"This one must be if it is to have the proper shape and spirit."

"But there is not enough money. We will have to go piece by piece."

Christopher turned away from Sancroft suddenly. His eyes were exhausted from staring at the *Great Design* to find an imperfection, but he had not found any. He was angry, yet Sancroft was a friend. He wanted to ask him to leave, only that would not solve anything. Yet now he believed he knew what was wrong, and he blurted out, "Again, it is a question of money."

"Let us not go backward. The future is difficult enough."

"We have already gone backward, considering the pre-fire design. You are afraid that money cannot be raised for the Greek cross design."

"It will not help our search for funds."

"Your warrant gave me the right to design."

"And reserved the right to criticise and to disapprove."

"No cathedral should be treated piece by piece."

"The sacraments are our first consideration. There must be a high altar, which doesn't exist in your present design, a Bishop's throne, stalls for the daily services within the choir, as in other cathedrals."

"Like a Roman Catholic cathedral, with an English accent."

"Isn't that true of your dome?"

Christopher was silent.

"You have to give in. Even the King will not oppose the clergy."

"It is a mistake to consider St. Paul's piece by piece. And you said it must be '*a noble, virtuous, and handsome work.*' How can you change now?"

"I must support my faith in the established manner. You have lost the day. The clergy demand the Latin cross design. They will accept no other."

"Then you are against me, too."

"I'm against a design that no one will accept."

"The King will."

Sancroft shrugged. He thought, His fellow members of the Commission were difficult, but the Surveyor was worse. And while he respected his devotion to his work, Sir Christopher was being idealistic and impractical. Now he was positive that the Greek cross design was unworkable.

After this visit Christopher, although he had promised Faith to have dinner with her—she had seen him very little lately and she had told him that she had something important she wanted to tell him—hurried over to the nearby palace of Whitehall in the hope that he could see Charles. He didn't want to put her off, but even if her views were important, they could wait a few hours. The

Greek cross design could not wait another moment. The King was the last support he had left.

Charles was in his laboratory, inspecting a secret way of opening and resealing letters without detection, when the Surveyor was announced. He was annoyed; he didn't want Wren, who was an ingenious inventor, to observe him in such activity. Yet there was such urgency in the Surveyor's request to see him—it was not like Wren to impose himself in such a hasty manner—that his curiosity got the better of his annoyance. He hid this experiment and ordered the Surveyor to be admitted, and greeted him as if Wren were a fellow natural philosopher.

But the King was taken aback by Christopher's vehemence as he declared, "Your Majesty, you said you would recommend that the Greek cross design should be accepted by the Commission."

"You are impulsive suddenly. You are not that young any more."

"Forty-two, sir." Was Charles jealous of his vitality?

"Many are dead by then. You must not be so aggressive. When you speak of St. Paul's you sound like a lover. Or is that your patron saint?"

"Sir, you appointed the Commission. They must listen to you."

"I also appointed the Royal Society. Do you always listen to me?"

"We try, Your Majesty. We appreciate your interest in natural philosophy."

"There is the endless problem of money. The cathedral must be built piece by piece. The Greek cross will not permit that. Do you ride these days? It would ease your digestion and improve your disposition."

"Your Majesty, please!" Christopher fell to his knees and pleaded, "You must not reject this noble design. I assure you that you will not regret your support and approval of the *Great Design*, as you named it."

Charles stood haughty and distrustful of so much emotion, then said coldly, "You will have to find another design. It has been decided."

Christopher was shocked and he rose to his feet, although the King had not indicated that he could, and exclaimed, "Sir, this is impossible!"

"No wonder you lost the election at Oxford. I wonder if it was wise to knight you. The Greek design will not be used. You are dismissed."

Faith had gone to bed when Christopher returned and had left word that she didn't wish to be disturbed. He realised that his failure to keep their appointment must have upset her and he wanted to make amends. But he was in one of the worst humours of his life. In his present state he might irritate her already touchy feelings. So he didn't join her.

He was so exhausted he could hardly keep his eyes open, yet he could not sleep. He sought to distract himself by examining his designs in which he was using the ideas of the Greek design, St. Mary-le-Bow, St. Stephen Walbrook, St. Mary-at-Hill, but none of them satisfied him tonight.

Whatever they were, they fulfilled him only in part.

He was forty-two; he had just had that birthday. As Charles said, he had passed the span of normal life; Matthew had died at forty-two. If he halted now, no one would be critical. He had achieved some things.

He returned to his drawings of the Greek design once more, this time to see what had gone wrong. He must have gone wrong, he thought, to arouse such opposition. But as he considered the climate of the time, the view of the cathedral as he saw it, the nature of the church, it was not possible for him in his senses to surrender a work such as this.

He had designed this house of the Lord so that God could live in it.

But they were sacrificing that, and a world of peace and beauty and proportion for a thousand pounds, or was it a halfpenny?

He shook his head in vexation. The price didn't matter.

Now they would say he was out of favour with the King, and perhaps he was. But he didn't care. He took a last look at the Greek design, before he put it away. Then, at the thought of burying it, he couldn't. He was burying part of himself. He felt so close to giving up architecture he was terrified. He felt stripped of life and honour. His favourite design was dead before it had a chance to live. He could endure almost anything but that. Christopher held the final drawing of the Greek cross design in his hand and wept.

He Has a Quality

He has a quality
It is outside of anything he does
It persists stands up even outside him
But it is all around him
It never joins
It never separates
Yet it is always there

How can a quality have so much
Be so near
And so far
And so sure
And so there and so there
And have a mind of its own
So all of its own   So all of its own

Stymean Karlen

40

He Has a Quality

WHEN FAITH AWOKE THE NEXT DAY AND DIDN'T FIND CHRISTOPHER beside her in bed she was alarmed. It was very early, a cold, frosty, windy morning, not a morning to be out, and she shivered under her blankets. He frequently came to bed quite late, many times long after she had fallen asleep, but never not at all. Something must be wrong, she felt apprehensively.

She lay there and thought, Marriage was different from what she had expected. She knew it was her duty to be submissive to her husband, but she had assumed Christopher would be different, that he would heed her views more. Instead, although he was kind and considerate, he seldom consulted her—except for household matters, which he left in her hands—and was always busy. She had anticipated that when they lived in London, they would be at Court often. But while, as Surveyor General, they resided next to Whitehall Palace so he could be easily available to the King, they were rarely at Court. It was one of her disappointments. Or, she wondered, was his absence due to something else? Most courtiers possessed a mistress. Had Christopher fallen in love with someone else?

At that idea Faith jumped out of bed and stared into her mirror. But what she saw she knew. She was not ill-favoured, pimpled, with rotten teeth, which was prevalent even among the great ladies. She still had her slim, graceful carriage, her clear complexion, although she was paler than when she had lived at Bletchington, and her features had remained fine.

But a mirror could be a false witness, she decided. She must see for herself. Faith donned her most attractive robe, which she had bought for her wedding night, and hurried into the one part of the house he might be in, the studio. When she saw him there her heart beat faster. She no longer felt like expiring. He had fallen

663

asleep at his desk, sitting in his favourite oak chair, exactly like the one he had known as a child, which he called, "*Myself*". A design of St. Paul's lay on the desk in front of him and it was strange, she thought, although he was the neatest of men, especially with his designs, this one was blotted and crumpled.

The beginning of the morning sun was in the studio warming and comforting. His books and designs, the tapestry, the oak furniture were harmonious, and yet there was a sadness in the room. It was in his expression, in the candles that had burnt out—he must have been here all night, she realised—and she hesitated to awake him.

He heard her, for suddenly he stirred and saw her standing in front of him. For an instant he felt lost, not sure where he was, and then he exclaimed, "I'm sorry! I didn't intend to miss dinner with you, but . . ."

She interrupted him, "I was worried when you didn't come to bed."

"I fell asleep here after I came back from the palace. I didn't mean to. I'm very sorry, dear, it was very thoughtless of me."

"I always find you beside me in the morning. It is a comfort. At least, I can count on you being there, even if you're not with me often."

"I've been too busy. I must work less hard. See you more."

"You won't. St. Paul's will absorb you, and your other designs."

"What did you want to tell me? You said you had important news."

"It can wait. Christopher, what happened at Whitehall?"

He shrugged and didn't reply.

Suddenly she cried out, "How can I confide in you, if you don't confide in me? You did when you courted me. Then, you even listened to me. So you said. Or were you flattering me, like so many of the courtiers?"

She looked so unhappy he forgot his own sorrow for a moment. He was touched by her concern. To some extent, he realised, he had taken her for granted. He answered. "They have rejected my Greek cross design."

"Even the King?"

"He told me that I must do a Latin cross design or none at all."

"You can't stop now. All your life St. Paul's has been in your blood."

"I'm not going to make any more models or publicly expose my designs."

"How will you proceed?"

"I'm not certain I will continue on St. Paul's. There are so many delays and difficulties it could break my heart."

She cried out, a mixture of anger and anxiety, "You must go on! You are the only one fitted to build the new cathedral. You understand what it should be better than anyone else. Did you approach the King properly?"

"I approached him honestly."

"I'm sure he appreciated that, it is so rare. Does he ever invite you to ride, to play tennis or golf? Many things are decided then. If you expressed an interest in these pursuits, he would include you."

"Faith, I'm not interested in games."

"In golf, I hear, the King has a fore-caddy to mark his ball down, and that he likes the game because he can both walk fast and saunter leisurely. And you ride excellently. You should be more attentive to his tastes."

"I'm not a courtier."

"You might be better off if you were."

"I want to please you. I will take you to Court, to anywhere you wish, but don't ask me to be a courtier. It is not my nature."

"Will you take me to Gilbert's grave?"

"Whenever you wish. But we were there recently."

"Isn't it strange that his baby clothes are the only proof that Gilbert ever lived. He was never old enough to even talk." An intense misery showed on her face and she added, "If we only had his portrait. But he wasn't even old enough to paint. Do you remember what he looked like?"

"Of course." His body ached with the memory. It hurt too much to dwell on. "He was fair. Like yourself, Faith."

"He could have become beautiful."

But who would ever know, he thought, all children were apt to be beautiful to their parents. Perhaps Faith, of all people, had known him.

She was upset suddenly, for the look she knew so well, that of preoccupation, appeared on his face. She started out, shouting, "You don't even have a decent respect for the dead!"

Too much, he thought. Mention of his dead son reminded him that he was to meet with the Privy Council to discuss the location of cemeteries. One of his strongest wishes was to prevent the burial of dead bodies within the walls of the City. During the plague and other sickly times, this had spread the illness and caused many indecencies and unnecessary deaths. But as he saw her leaving, he sensed that if he didn't act swiftly she would be even more hurt. Quickly then, he halted her by putting his arm around her affectionately and said, "Faith, what did you want to tell me last night? If it was important then, it is important now."

It was much easier to talk to Christopher when he had his arm around her. The whole of him came freely to meet her now, not just his mind. There were no diversions to distract him; there was a renewed feeling of harmony and happiness. She thought, It was much more difficult to reach him when only their minds, not their senses, touched. She said, "Christopher, I'm going to have another child."

He looked so surprised she wasn't certain he wanted one.

"Didn't you expect to have any more children?"

It wasn't that, he thought, but the doctor had warned him that this could be dangerous; her first pregnancy had been difficult and weakening. Yet he knew she desired a child more than anything else; and he did, too, if it didn't harm her. He embraced her passionately and kissed her, and said, "If it is a boy, we can call him Gilbert."

"No!" She was positive now. "We must name him Christopher!"

"I hope that is not vanity."

"You were named after your father."

He had forgotten. He felt ashamed. Everyone had referred to his father as the Dean to avoid confusion, yet his father would have been pleased with a grandchild named after him, and he told her so.

"We will name him after you and your father. Do you miss him much?"

"Sometimes. I wonder what he would say about my design for St. Paul's."

"He would support you," she said loyally.

"I'm not sure. He believed in tradition. It permeates the Church. It may be my biggest obstacle. But we mustn't talk about anything worrisome. We must celebrate. What would please you?"

"I would like to go to Drury Lane."

That was not such a bad idea, he thought, it would give him a chance to see how his design worked. He nodded and said, "You choose the play."

Since Dryden was now poet laureate and the King's favourite, Faith decided to see a revival of his heroic verse drama, *The Indian Emperor*. She wasn't sure Christopher would be interested in the conquest of Mexico by Cortez and his love for the Emperor's daughter, but she heard that the King was to attend with Madame Gwynn. It was a favourable moment, she decided, to demonstrate that her husband was not out of favour.

Christopher noticed with irritation that Faith dressed more in the manner of the Court now, in the free-and-easy style of the ladies there, with raised petticoats and lowered stays and a face patch. He liked none of this, but he didn't want to provoke her, she was in such a gay humour. He did find her low-necked bodice and full skirt of satin attractive.

Christopher seated Faith in a box in the centre of the playhouse and went below into the pit to observe the drama from there. She said that no gentleman should be seen there, and he replied that he had designed this theatre so everybody could see and hear, not just a privileged few, and he intended also to view part of the drama from the gallery above them. He was so determined that she didn't pursue the matter further.

He was pleased that Daniel had followed his plans precisely. Drury Lane was exactly as he had designed it. The stage projected to the front row of the pit and as he sat there he was gratified that he could see every performer and hear each word, although he didn't care for Dryden's grandiloquence, which he thought bombastic.

The benches were more comfortable, each one elevated above the previous one, an innovation that had been strongly opposed but which he had insisted on. He had curved them also in a semi-circle, so the sight lines were good wherever one sat. He had used this plan of elevation and a semi-circle for the entire theatre. And instead of employing the old custom of placing the royal box right over the stage, he had set side wings for the players—another innovation that had met considerable resistance—so the action could occur beyond the proscenium pillars, and put the royal box in the centre of a circle of boxes. He was gratified that even in the gallery, he could see wherever he sat or stood, and hear most of the time. And the roof was solidly constructed, without any leaks, and the light was better in the whole theatre.

The first act was over when Christopher returned to Faith. Before she could express her displeasure at his absence, the King arrived with Nell Gwynn. This justified her bringing her husband here, she thought. Everyone could see that he was still in favour; Charles sat nearby.

Christopher frowned and said, "You didn't tell me that he was coming."

"I wanted to surprise you."

"It may surprise him. I'm not sure he wants to see me." Several weeks had passed since the rejection of his design for St. Paul's, and although he had continued to conduct the business of his Office, he had stayed away from St. Paul's and had heard nothing from the King.

"You are Surveyor General. He hasn't halted your activities there."

"I doubt he will approve of the theatre. It is as different as my Greek cross design. The courtiers will be critical as the clergy."

"Then why did you do it this way?"

For a moment he almost lost his usual self-control; she should know better. But she looked so eager to help him, he said, "Faith dear, the theatre should be designed for the performers and the whole audience, not just a few nobles and ladies, who prefer to be seen rather than see."

The rest of *The Indian Emperor* bored Christopher. Faith enjoyed the audience, especially with the King and his latest mistress sitting so close. Her excitement grew when, at the end of the play, Sir Christopher and Lady Wren were summoned to His Majesty's box.

Christopher bowed to Charles, said, "Sir, your most obedient servant."

"I wonder. There are complaints about the playhouse." Charles had smiled from something Nell Gwynn had said, but now he scowled critically.

"What complaints, Your Majesty?"

"Dryden will inform you. He is the Theatre Royal's playwright." He motioned to Dryden, who was in the rear of the box, to come forward.

Christopher hadn't seen him in the shadows and he noticed that the short, fat poet laureate, who was just a year older than himself, had aged, but that his clothes were the same style and colour as the King's.

Charles added, "Dryden is an honest fellow."

Christopher smiled to himself, recalling how the ambitious poet had attached himself to whoever would aid him, contriving to support Cromwell and Charles at the same time, but he said, "Dryden, what is the trouble?"

"Sir, no one admires your designs more than I do, especially for the Sheldonian, but this is a different kind of a theatre. It is too plainly built, where Davenant's new house, Dorset Gardens, is brilliant."

"I've heard it shines like gold. But the quality of work at Drury Lane is so much better that ornate gilding would be distracting."

"You astonish me. This design will discourage the fashionable from attending. The boxes are inconspicuous. They cannot be seen properly."

"No, No, No!" Nell Gwynn said suddenly, "We can be seen! And all the actors, Charles. This playhouse has a better situation now."

Dryden bowed to her as he would to the Queen and said, "Madame Ellen Gwynn, I'm mindful of your superior knowledge of performing and that Sir Christopher is clever, but the plainness of the playhouse is distressing."

"It causes us to concentrate on the play. As you have, Dryden."

He didn't want her to be his enemy. Whatever her character, he thought, she had much influence with the King. Dryden said,

"Madame Gwynn, I respect your views. I was honoured when you were in my humble plays."

"Charles, in this playhouse everybody could see me."

"Nelly, I'm not certain I would like that," he replied.

To do her justice, Faith thought, Nell Gwynn was enticing. She was high spirited, which gave her fine complexion a rosy hue. She was even prettier than when Faith had seen her years ago, and still youthful, with her round cheeks, small chin, full mouth, and voluptuous breasts, which she displayed as if they were jewels of the Crown. But Faith wasn't sure she approved of her, although she liked her support of Christopher.

"Charles, Sir Christopher designed this playhouse in the spirit of the actors. Nothing stiff and awkward as before, but simple and graceful."

Christopher said, "Madame Gwynn, you are kind."

"What do you say, Charles? I'm right, you know."

"I know that you must have your portrait painted. In the likeness of a shepherdess, you are so concerned about your flock."

Christopher asked, "Your Majesty, is there anything else?"

Charles paused and pondered, as if not certain whether he should say what was in his mind. But when Christopher looked eager to leave, he said abruptly, "Where are your designs for St. Paul's?"

"Sir, you didn't ask for any."

"I did, indeed. I ordered you to find another design."

"Your Majesty, I cannot make another model."

"We will consider that later. Don't you wish to design the cathedral?"

Christopher was quiet. He didn't trust himself to express his passion.

"Time is growing short. Many months have passed with nothing done. We must start soon or nothing will ever be accomplished."

Faith said, "Your Majesty, my husband is devoted to your needs, but he cannot be accountable to persons who do not know half of what he knows."

"He will be accountable only to me."

Dryden asked, "Sir, are you allowing Drury Lane to stand as it is?"

Nell Gwynn said, "Charles, this theatre is a great improvement. Spacious, comfortable, light. The town talks of nothing else."

"Enough of the theatre," Charles said irritably, "It is a simple matter, compared to St. Paul's. Sir Christopher, the cathedral must be designed in the fashion the clergy desires, but modifications will be allowed."

"What modifications, sir?"

"That will be decided later."

"Sir, I cannot construct any more models."

"Your designs should be acceptable, if they follow the plan of a Latin cross." As he saw the Surveyor looking disconsolate despite this, he said, "You must not grieve. Sir Christopher, I do not want to be rid of you, as would be preferred by some of my advisers. I do not intend to destroy you by sending you to Ireland. I have too much honour to desire that."

Christopher wished Charles would leave honour out of it, it was not one of his virtues, but he said, "Sir, I appreciate your good wishes."

"The clergy has grown afraid that there will be no cathedral."

Afterwards, Faith assured Christopher that he would have his own way eventually, that Charles trusted him, the King's conduct was generous.

Christopher didn't agree; he doubted that Charles trusted anyone. But he didn't express these feelings to Faith, she looked so achieved. He was determined that nothing must disturb her pregnancy. After her first confinement, it was the risk that worried him.

That winter, while he pondered whether to create a Latin cross design for St. Paul's, he ordered Hooke to return St. Mary-at-Hill to his Greek cross plan and when the latter refused once more, he took him off the building. Hooke felt he was being conspired against, but Christopher persuaded him to continue on the construction of the Monument.

Hooke was eager to give the Monument his nature, a towering strength. "Not for my personal glory, mind you," he told Christopher, "but to remind our citizens how close London was to extinction during the fire."

Then Christopher went to one of his favourite designs, St. Stephen's Walbrook. He had put the construction in the charge of Thomas Strong, who had become a supporter since the success of the Sheldonian Theatre.

Strong was following his plan and he was pleased that his Greek cross design was working as he had imagined, and was giving this church a grace that was worthy of God. Now he could experiment with the dome and learn how it would work at St. Paul's. He was resolved not to build any more models for the cathedral, whatever the design. But St. Stephen's Walbrook could be the example of what he could do for a new St. Paul's, and this reconciled him somewhat for his disappointment over the *Great Design*.

He was resolved, too, that this must be the role of St. Mary-le-Bow. Since his meeting with the King and Milton at the site months ago, there had been no further criticism of his plans for this church.

Milton had died recently while construction had continued. Marshall was using his design now, but he disliked the way the church was wedged in between many houses. The master mason said that the avarice of the shopkeepers had forced this situation, but Christopher didn't agree with the needs of commerce. He felt the church should come first. He learned it was a view few shared. Although the church was put on Cheapside, as he insisted, and the sound of sawing timber, of hammering, was music to his ears, he realised he had to accept the cramped site. The parishioners who were paying for most of the construction preferred that things remain as they were. But he vowed to erect a steeple for St. Mary-le-Bow in the classical style that would be a pinnacle of London.

Daniel asked him to look at Temple Bar. As they approached it, he wondered why, it had been finished several years ago. Temple Bar stood as he had planned it, as the entrance to the City, where the Strand met Fleet Street. This ancient gateway to the City, which had stood for hundreds of years, was of historic importance. Here, even the King, had to obtain permission to enter the City. He disliked the way the gateway was pressed in by the buildings on each side of it and the narrow streets. What an opportunity for a beautiful, spacious London was lost here, he thought, but he was happy with his design. The four pillars of Portland stone with their large central arch gave the entrance dignity and strength. There were niches for statues of Charles I and Charles II, and two rooms above the arch. But suddenly Christopher felt ashamed of what he had built, for iron spikes had been put on Temple Bar and he saw skulls on them.

Daniel said, "The spikes were not in your original design."

"Who ordered them placed there? It was not my wish."

"The King, I've been told. As a warning to traitors."

"Is he still unsure of his throne?"

"Charles is not so much interested in governing as in surviving."

"He should have gotten over that years ago."

"He will never get over it. Once you are exiled, you never forget it."

Daniel's face grew sombre and Christopher wondered if his friend would ever feel at home in England, no matter how long he lived here. Was he never to feel rooted anywhere? Daniel did his work efficiently, rented a house on Fetter Lane, as if that was his strongest link to London, but never spoke of Anne or Sam. He didn't even know whether Daniel had a woman. Yet his friend, in contrast to the courtiers his own age, had not grown fat or grey, as they had, but retained his lean body, his fair skin, and his hair was still blonde and had darkened just a little. Christopher was pleased that he was not grey either, for Charles had gone grey under his black periwigs, and he felt it helped him preserve a kind of advantage.

"Do you know whose heads are impaled on the spikes?"

"A couple of poor wretches who were forced to make the journey from Newgate to Tyburn, where they were hung and quartered. But nobody seems to know their names or why their heads were spiked on Temple Bar."

"This is shameful. I didn't build this gateway to be a Golgotha."

Children threw stones at the two heads on the iron spikes and when they hit them, they squealed for joy. Christopher went to stop them and Daniel said, "It won't do any good. The minute we are gone, they will resume, even more energetically because you have forbidden it. I showed this to you in the hope you would speak to Charles. He could halt this practice."

"I will. I wonder how he can justify this dreadful practice."

Charles was in no mood to justify anything. The spikes on Temple Bar were a trifle beside his desperate need for money, his quarrels with Parliament over the cost of his many mistresses, their fears that he would appoint a Catholic successor, since he had no legitimate children, and his friendship with France. And there were limits to his patience. He ignored the Surveyor's complaint about the iron spikes and declared, "The delays at St. Paul's are becoming scandalous. If you don't submit some kind of a new design by spring, I will have to look elsewhere for a design."

"I beg your pardon, sir, but in the matter of Temple Bar . . ."

"You are imprudent." He was resolved, whatever the difficulties and no matter how easy going he appeared to others, to retain his perch on the throne. Above everything else, never to start out on his travels again. It was a resolution that made an iron spike of his own backbone. And it was vital to show the City, so often the seat of rebellion, what happened to anyone who threatened him. There was nothing better than a spiked head, he smiled to himself, to make that point. "If I hear any more talk of difficulties, I will not see you on any business. Is that clear?"

Christopher had never seen Charles so stern. Yet it was hard to say, "Yes, sir," and that came slowly and reluctantly.

Charles appeared satisfied. He smiled slightly and said, "Now you must sit upon your eggs and hatch something."

A few weeks later, in February, Faith gave birth to a son, whom they named Christopher. The baby was healthy, but her confinement was harsh, although he employed the housekeeper who had attended her birth.

Lucy Enfield was short, stout, elderly, with tender hands, an easy, natural manner, and was a comfort to Faith. She had served the Coghill family until Faith had grown up, and Enfields had lived on the Coghill grounds for generations. Faith and Lucy talked about family as if they were painting pictures of past times, and despite her age, she became young Christopher's nurse and a part of the household. This pleased Faith and she rejoiced in Christopher's choice of Lucy to serve her again and her baby.

Christopher was worried that Faith took a long time to recover from the birth of their son. Then, even after she was able to get out of bed, she moved slowly, lacked energy, and had no desire to go anywhere, which was not like her. It added to his concern.

He consulted Scarburgh—Sir Charles now, as Wilkins had predicted.

"Sir Charles, do you suspect anything serious?"

"We must be cautious. But don't fear, she is a virtuous woman."

Scarburgh gave Faith herbs to improve her appetite and with the coming of spring she ate better and took more interest in things, particularly in young Christopher, who, carefully tended by Lucy, was flourishing.

Unhappy though he was over Faith's slow recovery, the birth of his son gave Christopher the urge to return to a design for St. Paul's. That was also Faith's wish and when he told her that he was submitting new plans for the cathedral to the King she brightened and looked very pleased.

"You are doing him a great service," she said, fondling her son. "He will approve now. As long as it is in the form of a Latin cross."

It was the only choice he possessed. But as he worked on these plans, he shortened and broadened the length of the cross until he greatly increased the space at the crossing. And he continued to design a St. Paul's with a massive dome. These details gratified him, but as he told Daniel in confidence, they didn't truly express what he desired. "As it is now, the design is part Gothic, part classical, and part Inigo Jones."

"But not Christopher Wren?" asked Daniel.

"Not now."

"Not yet."

Christopher was puzzled.

"You can change in the construction. If they want you to compromise, they must compromise, too. But as time goes on, with the actual building, you should be able to justify whatever you do. Or alter."

Daniel's advice helped reconcile him to the task ahead, to

Y

convince Charles that these drawings were the best he could do at the moment. In this he didn't consult Sancroft, or the clergy, or the Commission, believing that if the King was persuaded, they would be persuaded.

When he felt that he had drawings which would satisfy Charles, although they didn't satisfy him, for they were a compromise, he requested another audience with the King.

Charles saw him in his bedchamber where he was dressing. This was a mark of favour, an indication of intimacy. Charles was scenting himself with an essence of roses and putting on his favourite black velvet suit which flattered his height and carriage. He was in a far better humour than he had been at their previous meeting, for he had just manoeuvred Parliament into giving him most of the money he needed and the opposite sides in the Commons into blaming the financial difficulties on each other.

"Sir," Christopher began, "I have some sketches for your viewing."

"I knew you would hatch something."

"Begging your pardon, sir, but they are a compromise."

"As are most things. But not a Greek cross, I trust."

"No, Your Majesty. Would you like to see what I've done?"

"Not as long as I have your assurance that St. Paul's will be in the plan of a Latin cross. And possess the attributes the clergy requires."

"It has, sir. But here, see for yourself."

"It isn't necessary." Charles pushed aside the drawings. "Don't bother me with details. You obtain the approval of the Commission and I will authorise a royal warrant for the construction of a new St. Paul's."

"I'm not certain I can heed all the wishes of the clergy. I can't construct a cathedral I don't believe in."

"No one says you have to."

"When the previous design was ordered, it was stated that it be *'perpetual and unchangeable.'* Sir, I cannot labour in such a vice."

"You will not have to. We will omit those words in the new warrant."

Christopher felt a load lifting off his heart. If he was not shackled by the finality of an unsuitable design, St. Paul's might still assume the character he craved. "Your Majesty, can I depend on that?"

"Don't make any speeches to the Commission, or Sancroft, or the clergy, they are masters of the sermon, but present to them your drawings of the Latin cross, with all the details they desire. If they approve, and I believe they will, you will have some freedom to design as you wish."

"Some, sir?" Christopher was sceptical, hesitant.

"Sir Christopher, you can at any time make alterations of an ornamental character in the design if you wish, without being under an obligation to submit every such change for formal approval."

"I don't understand, Your Majesty."

"Don't be a fool. Ornament gives you the opportunity to alter and improve the design visually, as long as it follows the basic principles of a Latin cross. You try my patience, sir. Have you no sense of reality?"

Christopher thought, So he must take possession of the world of St. Paul's as it was presented to him. Yet something in him wanted Charles to see his design, to show that he was keeping his word, to express gratitude, and to remain the Surveyor and not the diplomat.

This time Charles didn't refuse the drawing he handed him. But after he was gone the King crumpled the design into an unread ball of paper and tossed it into the fire, where it burned a moment and then became ashes.

Christopher, determined to include Faith in the hope that his favourable news would help her health, told her of the King's encouragement. She seemed pleased, although her lassitude remained. She was in bed, where she spent most of her time now, and her smile of satisfaction was wan.

"You feel worse," he said with a sudden burst of pessimism and fear. "I'm not sure that Scarburgh has helped you at all."

"My appetite is better," she replied weakly. "I'm glad about St. Paul's. Give me your hand, Christopher." He did, and as she clutched it, almost as if, he thought, she was clinging to life, she cried passionately, "Promise, you will not give up St. Paul's! No matter what happens!"

"Nothing will happen. Faith, you'll get better. You must."

"Promise, Christopher, promise?"

"I promise."

"Good. It is your nature and genius to start again."

Sancroft studied Christopher's Latin cross design for St. Paul's with intense care. He made sure that it contained the proper choir, nave, high altar, and other clerical details in the established fashion, and then he nodded approvingly, and said it was worthy of submission to the Commission.

Soon after, he informed the Surveyor that they approved, also.

A few days later, on May 14th, 1675, Christopher was given another royal warrant which stated: *"Charles R. Whereas we have been informed that a portion of the imposition laid on coals, which by Act of Parliament is appointed and set apart for the rebuilding of the Cathedral*

Church of St. Paul, in our capital city of London, does at present amount to a considerable sum which, although not proportionable to the greatness of the work, is notwithstanding sufficient to begin the same. And with all the materials and other assistances which may probably be expected will put a new choir in great forwardness. And whereas among divers designs which have been presented to us we have particularly pitched upon one as well because we found it very artificial, proper and useful as because it was so ordered that it might be built and finished by parts. We do therefore by these presents signify our royal approbation of the said design hereunto annexed: and do will and require you forthwith to proceed according to the said design, beginning with the east end or choir, and accomplishing the same with the present stock of money and such supplies as may probably accrue, according to the tenor of the Commission to you directed; and for so doing this shall be your warrant."

How generous a benefactor Charles was, Christopher reflected, must be left to the future. He didn't tell anyone of his private assurances, but returned to the site, for now work could begin again.

After a month of surveying the space allotted for the new St. Paul's, Christopher staked out the position of the proposed fabric. He aligned it almost the same as the old cathedral, for that was the space he had to use. He was unhappy about the rebuilt houses which crowded in around the site and which would obstruct much of the view of St. Paul's. But nothing could be done about them; they were erected already. There was enough room on the location, for his new design was shorter than the old cathedral. Much work remained to clear up debris and the foundations had to be investigated for strength and support, but there had been so many delays since the fire, that everyone, even Charles and the clergy, seemed eager for a start to be made. It was ordered for as soon as possible.

On June 21st, 1675, Christopher arranged to lay the foundation stone of the new cathedral. He knew this moment should give him great satisfaction. After almost nine years of apprehension that nothing would ever be done, of delays and indecision and too many discussions, of high hopes and bitter disappointments and unpleasant compromises, it was time to start.

He surveyed those who gathered to witness the placing of the foundation stone, Marshall, Strong, other workmen, and Daniel, and he was surprised that Charles, Dean Sancroft, and Archbishop Sheldon were absent. Faith was unable to come because of poor health, but the others had no such excuse.

Daniel said, "Many in the City object to this venture, to the time and money involved, to the dirt and dust it will cause. Most believe this will not succeed. And since Charles borrowed money from the City and then refused to repay it, they have been hostile to him. He hasn't travelled beyond Temple Bar for several years."

"Very well," said Christopher, "We will start now." He told the workmen to find a foundation stone, but none of the pieces they brought satisfied him, until Daniel handed him a smooth, flat stone. It was exactly what he wanted and as he examined it, he exclaimed, "Where did you find it?"

"Under a heap of rubble," answered Daniel. "Where I kept it hidden for this occasion. It was part of a tombstone. You can see that from what is engraved on it. That is why I saved it for your foundation stone."

"What is carved on it we must always remember. It is a good omen."

"What is it, sir?" asked Marshall, too cautious to feel optimism.

"*Resurgam.*"

"I shall rise again," Strong translated for those who didn't understand.

"Exactly so," Christopher said. "Whatever the difficulties, that must always be our motto for St. Paul's." He repeated it, to affirm his own faith.

"*Resurgam.*"

Then he put the foundation stone in place.

The Doom is There

The doom is there
When life begins
It is not
in the first pain
But in the memory
of it
That you'll never
lose
Always reminding
the pain to return
And you
    expecting it

Stymean Karlen

41

The Doom is There

THE PROBLEM WAS, CHRISTOPHER SENSED, THE DOCTORS DIDN'T know what was wrong with Faith. Scarburgh and Sydenham stood in her bedchamber arguing over her symptoms, but she had been ill for several weeks and now she was worse. He feared that her illness had become grave. She looked pale and frail between the panelled headboard and the bulbous foot-posts, she was chilled yet feverish, and still the doctors quarrelled over what was wrong.

He wondered if he could trust either one of them. He surveyed them in his search for reassurance and recalled that he had admired Scarburgh and trusted him, and so had Harvey, but now Sir Charles had little time for anybody but the King. These days Scarburgh spent more time on his toilet than his experiments; he wore a black velvet suit in imitation of the King, and walked with the stiff, stilted movements of the courtier in high heels. But he had called him because Faith wanted him. Faith had said, "Sir Charles is a gentleman, an Anglican, and the King's physician."

Sydenham, on the other hand, was dressed in the plain dark clothes of the Commonwealth and was still proud of his association with Cromwell. He was the opposite of the courtier physician, Christopher reflected, and he had answered his call only because of his friendship with Wilkins. But Sydenham had the wisdom and courage to think for himself, like Harvey, and not lean on the past, and he was observant and thorough, qualities that Christopher respected and had faith in.

Christopher joined them to learn their conclusions, although he was weary, for he had slept little lately. While it was afternoon and the September weather was moderate, a fierce fire of Scotch coal blazed in the hearth on the orders of Scarburgh. He said it was the best, warmest coal, that keeping the fire hot was vital. He had shut all the windows, too, stating that fresh air was dangerous, that a heated room was essential.

Sydenham differed. He believed strongly in the curative effects of fresh air and that the sick room should be kept at a cool temperature.

Scarburgh, when he saw Christopher approaching, announced for his benefit, "Lady Wren's condition may require another physic."

"No," said Sydenham, "Another may weaken her."

Christopher added, "And you've given her several in the past few hours, and they haven't seemed to help, but, as Sydenham says, only weakened her."

"The King believes in my physic. It has helped him often."

"But has he ever had these symptoms?"

"Of course. I've cured him of many things. His favourite enema is of antimony, sacred bitters, rock salt, beet root, and mallow leaves. If it has helped him, it should help Lady Wren."

Sydenham replied, "It can't help her if you don't know what is wrong."

"What is wrong?" Christopher cried out in his fear.

"I will save her," Scarburgh assured him. "Her youth, her faith, and our prayers will suffice. We must restore her confidence in herself."

Sydenham shook his head pessimistically. "We must diagnose first. If we don't know the condition, we don't know what to cure."

"She has vertigo, chills, fever, and a weary melancholy."

"Sir, they are symptoms, not a condition. We must go to her bedside. There alone we can learn what is her disease." He sat down by her side and began to examine her carefully. Christopher agreed with this, while Scarburgh was critical, and when Faith saw that it was Sydenham who was attending her, she turned away, crying out, "He is not pious! He is a Dissenter! Christopher, I want Sir Charles! He is an honourable man!"

She was so hysterical that Christopher had to motion to Sydenham to stop and indicate that Scarburgh proceed, although he did this with concern.

Scarburgh ordered the apothecary, who was waiting for his instructions, to prepare the prescription he had recommended, and then he had the nurse administer it. Faith took it willingly when she saw Sir Charles attending her, but she could barely drink the preparation, and instead of it easing her, she grew violently ill. Scarburgh said hurriedly, "We must give her something else. White wine, absinthe, and anise is a gentler drink. That will spare her some pain and have the same effects."

But this time she couldn't absorb the mixture, coughing it up as the nurse poured it down her throat, and afterwards she cried

out, "I cannot bear this much longer. Where's Christopher? I can't
see his face."

He sat down by her side, holding a brightly lit candle in his hand,
although the sun shone into the bedchamber and the light was good.

This appeared to revive her and as she felt his touch she whispered,
"I must take this cheerfully, for your sake, Christopher. But please!"
she begged, "don't let them touch me any more. I cannot endure
it. Do they have to stand there like ravens? Can't we have any
privacy?"

Christopher asked the doctors to allow him a few minutes alone
with his wife, and they retired into the anteroom as he requested,
although Sydenham said this was sentimental, the patient should
be thoroughly examined now and treated before it was too late,
while Scarburgh said there wasn't any urgency, but he was
disappointed in her lack of approval for his methods.

When they were alone, for the nurse and apothecary had retired,
too, Faith blurted out, "Christopher, are my hands clean?"

"Immaculate," he said consolingly.

"I hope so," she murmured. "I must go into the grave clean."

"Faith, you mustn't talk that way."

"Christopher, it is a sickly age and I'm dying. No, don't tell me
otherwise. Do you love me dying as much as you do living?"

"I love you!" He longed to repeat that over and over, but his
throat refused to function properly, he was so full of tears.

"I hope so. I'm grateful to have been loved by you."

"You will get better. Both doctors are hopeful."

"Is that why they were quarrelling so? I feel so feeble. How is
the work progressing at St. Paul's? Is it going as you wish?"

"Most of it is. Strong, whom I can trust, is responsible for the
east end, where we are starting, and he has become quite efficient."

"Is the King keeping his word?"

"I'm not sure. But I will find out. I intend to construct St.
Paul's in one piece. Then I will learn if I'm to be allowed any
latitude."

"You will be. Charles is an agreeable man and and he fancies
you. He may scold and torment you occasionally, but that is because
he admires traits in you that he doesn't possess. Are there many
workmen under you?"

Faith had a great respect for numbers, a view he didn't share,
but in the hope it would help her, he indulged it, saying, "The
two master masons are employing over sixty journeymen, and
more than a hundred labourers, who level the foundations for the
masons, prepare the mortar, and fetch the stone when it is required.
We are also using some carpenters and bricklayers, but not many
yet, and several sawyers and other craftsmen."

He paused as she seemed to be slipping off into sleep, but as the sound of his voice stopped, she roused herself and cried, "Go on!"

He had the strangest sensation that Faith was using his voice as a stimulant to keep herself alive, and he realised that she might be right, she could be dying. He was stricken with panic. With all of his knowledge of natural philosophy and anatomy he didn't know what to do. She was infected with a dangerous and pernicious disease and he hadn't the slightest idea of what it was, and he doubted the doctors did either.

"Are sufficient materials at your disposal? You do worry about that."

"So far. But we haven't had to use much stone yet. Our problems will come when I need many large, smooth blocks of quality. Then . . ." He paused, for she seemed to have fallen asleep. Or was she in a coma?

He leaned over her to listen, but he wasn't sure she was breathing and in his anxiety he hurried out to summon the doctors. Scarburgh had left to return to Whitehall Palace, to prepare for a grand ball this evening, after assuring the nurse there was nothing to worry about, but Sydenham had remained, still unsatisfied with the brevity of his examination, and he followed a desperately apprehensive Christopher into the bedchamber.

Sydenham commanded the windows to be thrown open, the fire to be dampened, and the sudden rush of cold air seemed to bring Faith back to life. But as it did, she shivered and trembled and cried out, "I'm chilled! I can't stop shaking! Christopher, please close the windows!"

Sydenham shook his head, no, but Faith was so imploring he did as she requested. The doctor shrugged and whispered to Christopher so she couldn't hear him, "It may not matter. It may be too late. If you had called me earlier, I might have had time to find out what is wrong. But now?" Sydenham shook his head dolefully. "I doubt she can be saved."

"What is wrong, Sydenham?"

"Some of the symptoms suggest scarlet fever, others smallpox."

"But you are not sure?"

"Not completely."

"There are no traces of smallpox on her skin. It is still unblemished."

"This is not an inevitable symptom."

"Christopher, may I see young Christopher?"

He looked over to the doctor who said, "Yes."

"What about infection?"

"It is not likely with the fresh air I let in. I did it as much to protect us as to help her. The baby may console her. I'll wait outside, should you need me, and I will tell the housekeeper to bring in your son."

When they were alone again, she said feebly, "Don't fear, death is a thing everyone suffers. You must marry again. Promise? You are too kind a man to remain unwed. And you must have more children. Oh, God, have mercy on me!" She was without any strength at all now, but when Lucy appeared with young Christopher and held the flourishing baby close to her, she regained a little energy and asked, "Christopher, will you miss me?"

"Faith, you must get better. You must!" He choked with emotion.

Lucy sobbed with grief, unable to contain her pain, and Faith whispered, "Don't cry. I gave my husband what he wanted. A son." She rested a minute and then she asked to look at young Christopher again.

Christopher held him now and suddenly she exclaimed, "There is a resemblance! You will finish St. Paul's? As you promised?"

"I promised. I'm building a home for us at Windsor. I wanted it to be a surprise. You must live to see it. You must! Please, Faith, please!"

She nodded and reached for his hand. He gave Lucy the infant and motioned for her to leave, and sat beside Faith to comfort her. For a few moments she was quiet, but then he felt her fingers stiffen convulsively, her breath came hard and suddenly hardly at all. He ran out of the room to fetch Sydenham, but by the time the doctor arrived Faith was dead.

Don't Cry My Child

Don't cry my child
The thunder is lonely out there
It is knocking on your door
to be let in my child

Don't cry my child
It is dark out there
The lightning is lighting its way
so the thunder can see your door my child

Don't cry my child
The thunder will stop knocking
on your door
if you let it in my child

Don't cry my child
You are frightening the poor thunder
at your door
And where will it go in the rain my child

Don't cry my child
Pity the poor thunder so lonely out there
And you so cosy and warm
And in your mamma's arms my child

Don't cry my child
We'll let the thunder in my child
It is crying now just like you my child
And I have to be a mamma to both of you

Stymean Karlen

42

Don't Cry My Child

HOLDER CONDUCTED THE FUNERAL SERVICES FOR FAITH AT ST. Martin-in-the-Fields and she was buried in the graveyard there. The church was between Scotland Yard and Temple Bar and near Charing Cross and her body was placed next to the grave of their son, Gilbert. Christopher chose this Gothic church and cemetery because it was outside of the City and had a touch of the country that Faith loved, fringed on all sides with hedges and rustic lanes. He had bought a family plot here large enough to include himself.

Susan sought to console him at the grave, but he changed the subject. He knew his sister felt responsible for his grief and shared his sorrow. She had introduced Faith to him; she had known her first. But it was too painful to talk about her now. He was astonished at how much it hurt to speak of Faith, how much he missed her; he felt so lonely, and Susan's consolation only made the pain worse. It was better, he reflected, to treasure the happy moments he had shared with Faith than to dwell on the melancholy of her passing, and to keep these feelings to himself.

After the service Susan was full of news about her husband, which was a relief to Christopher. As they walked back to Scotland Yard, she said, "We are moving to London. We have just taken a house at Amen Corner. William has been appointed a resident canon to the vacant stall at St. Paul's, and sub-dean of the Chapel Royal, in attendance to the King himself. We will see you often now. I know you miss Matthew very much. You depended on him for many practical matters. But now William can help you. You can depend on his being a friend at Court and with the clergy."

Christopher thought angrily, He depended on no one and never had. Matthew had expedited matters, not solved them. But his sister was so proud of her husband and his influence, he controlled himself and said, "This is good news. Why didn't you tell me

689

sooner? It would have pleased Faith. She was quite fond of both of you and she loved the Court."

"We weren't sure until a few days ago. Then it was too late."

Holder said suddenly, "Christopher, you must wed again. It is not seemly for a man of your disposition and character to be a widower."

Christopher was in no mood to discuss such matters. He said curtly, "I have many things to occupy myself. Enough designs for a lifetime."

"It will cure your melancholy."

The best remedy, he thought, was to be busy. He replied, "I'm visiting Windsor to survey the house I've built there. Would you like to see it?"

"Did you build it for Faith?"

"For us to live in. To keep the blood fresh and vigorous."

That night he slipped into the nursery where his son slept in the care of Lucy. As he gazed at the baby and it reminded him that Faith would never see young Christopher again, that their son would never know his mother, it was an even worse feeling than his disappointment over the design of St. Paul's, at least the cathedral was still alive. His son had a heritage of worms, however charitable the words. If death were all? But it was the other things one had to endure. He had not shed a tear since her death, but now they came in a flow he couldn't suppress.

In his agitation he awoke the child. Young Christopher stared up at him as if there was thunder in his ears and began to cry. This aroused Lucy and when she saw her master standing there, she jumped out of bed, threw her robe about her short, heavy body and took the infant into her arms.

His crying didn't stop and she said, "Sir, he misses his mother."

"Do you think he is old enough for that?"

"Six months? Yes, Sir Christopher. Her touch was his touch."

He still wasn't certain he believed her, and yet when he took the infant into his hands the baby quieted. But her hands were softer, gentler, more accustomed to touch an infant. Then, as he felt his fingers tighten around young Christopher with emotion, the baby whimpered.

My child, don't cry, he yearned to say, I will be both father and mother to you, but his voice would only thunder in his son's ears. Abruptly, with a display of feeling he didn't know he was capable of, he kissed his son and his son seemed to respond, for the infant was quiet again, and when Lucy put him back into the cradle, the baby fell asleep peacefully.

Daniel didn't want to visit Windsor in the company of the Holders. He said they didn't approve of him. Christopher stilled his protests by saying, "I need your opinion. No one else is likely to tell me the truth." The Holders had complained that they never saw Van Doorn in church on Sunday or expressed pious sentiments, but he ignored their criticism.

Everyone was polite during the trip. Christopher used the coach and four he had bought for Faith and the journey from London passed without any incident. Then, instead of taking them up the hill to the castle which dominated the landscape and where he and Susan had lived, he turned down a narrow, winding road which curved below the castle and led them to the bank of the Thames. He pointed to a spacious, two-storey brick house located on the river and asked, "Do you like it?"

Holder said, "It is rather simple for a Surveyor General." When Christopher frowned, he added hurriedly, "But it has an honest piety."

Susan said, "It doesn't resemble any of the other houses here."

"I designed the kind of home I like. Up to now, I've had to live in someone else's design. Daniel, what do you think of this fabric?"

"I like its simplicity, and that you have designed it for comfort, space, and light with a mathematical precision. It has exact proportions, a classical dignity, an imaginative setting, and a lovely garden, right on the bank of the river. And the sound of the rushing water is enchanting."

"Seth is taking care of the garden."

Susan said excitedly, "Christopher, remember when Seth warned us about the soldiers and we hid the sword of King Edward from them. I was so afraid I thought my stomach would turn inside out. Van Doorn, we had wonderful times here. Memories of my brother that no one else can share or equal."

Daniel, wanting to be friendly, said, "You must treasure them."

"We were such a pious family! Were your family pious?"

"Reasonably."

"Where do you go to church? The Dutch are Protestants, aren't they?"

"Most of them are."

Christopher interrupted, annoyed by her prying, "Susan, do you think Faith would have liked this house?"

"She would have loved it."

"It was a present for her, but it took too long and death was too quick."

Holder said, "I can testify that you were a good husband."

"I can, too," Susan said earnestly. "You were so faithful. But you will have to stop mourning, Christopher. You must return to your work."

"I am. Would you excuse us, please, while I survey the chapel with Daniel. We must see if the repairs have been done there."

A few minutes later he stood in St. George's Chapel and noted ruefully to Daniel that the cracks in the fabric had not been repaired, that most of the other defects he had seen as a boy still existed. He said, "Charles appointed May the Comptroller of the Works at Windsor Castle, but he is so busy remodelling the royal apartments in a medieval style, ornamental, elaborate, and pretty, but not serviceable for common use, that he has ignored St. George's Chapel. Its decay is not a pleasing sight."

"I hope you are taking care of yourself. You are not robust."

"Daniel, you sound like my sister."

"You've been working quite hard since your wife's death."

"It is the best medicine."

"I know you are a temperate man, but you are not invulnerable."

Christopher didn't reply. He was thinking that it was futile and foolish to go back to the past. He must make this new house part of his future.

Daniel, afraid that Christopher was angry at him, said suddenly and apologetically, "I didn't know what to say to you about the death of your wife. So, I felt, it was better to leave you alone with your grief."

"You were wise."

"Then you are not offended at me?"

"Why should I be offended?"

"I didn't come to the church. I didn't attend the services."

"I didn't expect you to. You would have been uncomfortable if you had." He took him by the arm and added, "We must return to my brother-in-law and sister. Before they envy and hate you. Holder believes he was my mentor and Susan feels that her memories of me are the important ones. What do you truly think of the house I've designed here?"

"It is charming. I would be happy and honoured to live in it."

Inspiration Alone

Inspiration
   alone
      will not enable
       the hammer
         to sing
           like the saw

Stymean Karlen

43

Inspiration Alone

THE HOUSE AT WINDSOR STAYED EMPTY AS CHRISTOPHER RETURNED to St. Paul's. Now it was as if he came back to an old friend. He resolved to absorb himself in work on the cathedral to ease the pain of Faith's death. But there were many problems. Money was still inadequate for the cost of the work. In the past year the duty imposed on coal was five thousand pounds, donations were another thousand pounds, a total that was not nearly enough, and even the continuation of this was uncertain. There was the promise of more money from the City and the Crown, but so far, none was forthcoming. Labour was underpaid and often unreliable. Craftsmen received two shillings, six pence, and unskilled labourers got one shilling, six pence, and there were frequent absences and quittings. Materials were hard to obtain or scarce or not available at all. There was much criticism of the work, especially in the City and at Court and among large segments of the clergy, who felt that the effort expended on St. Paul's detracted from the building of their own parish churches. And there were other difficulties.

Woodruff, his official assistant, died two months after Faith, and the Commission appointed John Oliver in his place. He was not Christopher's choice, although he respected the sixty-year-old surveyor's experience and honesty, but he preferred Daniel's understanding and imagination. So, unofficially, his friend became his assistant at St. Paul's, too, as the work increased in scope and intensity. Archbishop Sheldon was ill and ageing, and was unable to devote any time to St. Paul's, and Dean Sancroft's chief absorption these days was in aiding Sheldon. And there were constant problems with the weather, which was usually rainy, cold, and foggy.

Christopher's biggest difficulty was the design. The drawing that Charles approved was called the Warrant design because of the

royal warrant that authorised it, and the assumption was that the
Surveyor would conform to it, but he knew this was impossible.
The shape and pattern was a deformity he couldn't endure. The
drawing Charles had accepted contained an octagonal tower with a
Gothic steeple, a design he found acceptable for a parish church,
but a monstrosity on a classical cathedral. Inevitably, as he had
since childhood, he returned to his concept of a great central dome.

To avoid argument he decided to improvise as he went on,
although in his imagination he had a clear conception of what the
completed cathedral would be, yet not to settle on the final details
of the design until they were required. He didn't tell this to anybody.
He felt that a classical St. Paul's must be the product of one mind
and imagination, and so he planned as close to the Greek cross
design as was possible.

The foundations he prepared differed from the design that had
been approved but nobody questioned them. He sensed this was
accepted because they were almost in the same position as the
Gothic St. Paul's, and followed the Latin cross design and contained
all the required parts of the established church. He was determined
that his cathedral be more compact than the old cathedral, which
had sprawled indiscriminately, and so his foundations were shorter,
but still capable of possessing grandeur.

Work began promptly at 6 a.m. with the ringing of a bell and
Christopher came each day, while Daniel kept an eye on all the
work. Oliver suggested they build on the foundations of old St.
Paul's, but Christopher didn't trust them, for his cathedral would
be a different weight and structure.

Yet he ordered the ground to be excavated where the old
foundations had stood, starting at the west end, where there would
be a great weight.

After days of digging it became evident that the foundations of
the old cathedral had been upon a layer of very close and hard
pot-earth.

Oliver said with self-satisfaction, "As I thought, sir, the same
ground that has borne so weighty a building might reasonably be
trusted again."

Marshall and Strong stated the new foundations should be laid
on the old, for most of the cathedral's walls hadn't collapsed, even
after the fire.

Daniel added, "Sir Christopher, they could be right. The earth
is very firm and at least six feet thick. It appears quite substantial."

Christopher was tempted to agree. This pot-earth was strong and
it would be easier to start now instead of pursuing further investigations, some of which would consume much time and money,
neither of which he could afford to spare. But he had learned long

ago, that appearances were not always the reality. And this could be a potentially hazardous situation and he remembered that he was determined to build for eternity. He said, "We must search further. We cannot take anything for granted."

He dug deeper wells and found dry, loose sand under the pot-earth. This encouraged him to go on and he came to water mixed with sand and sea shells, and now he continued boring until he reached a hard beach, and still under that, until he found a natural hard clay.

Oliver exclaimed, "Sir, it is the same clay that lies under the City, the country, and the Thames, far and wide. It should support a new St. Paul's."

"Perhaps." Christopher wasn't as positive.

"Sir, it is a crust sufficiently rock-like to prevent the cathedral from being accused of having been built on sand."

Yet Christopher still wasn't satisfied.

Strong, proud of his knowledge, declared, "These sea shells indicate that the sea was where the hill is now on which St. Paul's stands."

Christopher was more interested in the present strength of the soil. "This earth must bear a heavy load on its back. We must verify the texture of the earth at all the foundations." He ordered that done.

The master masons grumbled at what they felt was excessive caution, and even Daniel wondered whether these new excavations were essential, but the Surveyor was adamant and refused to listen to their objections.

He assigned each of the four men to dig deeper at a corner of the foundations and a few days later Daniel, who was excavating the north-east corner, found an alarming weakness. He informed Christopher at once.

"The hard crust of the pot-earth is pitted with many holes. We keep finding urns, broken vessels, and pottery of many kinds. And now the odour of graves. It is strange. It could be an omen to be careful. To halt."

"No, No!" This was the last thing that Christopher could accept.

"I don't like it. Everything smells of rot and decay there."

"We will investigate further." Christopher was surprised by Daniel's apprehension; his friend acted as if he were about to violate the dead.

Oliver and the two master masons joined the Surveyor at the north-east corner and as the digging continued their apprehensions grew, too. They were approaching a vast charnel house. The workmen found new corpses buried only in shrouds who looked as if they had died as recently as the plague. Then there were those who had been buried many years ago, in coffins of metal, stone, and wood. A third layer were those who had been put here since the erection of the original St. Paul's in Norman times and they were a mixed lot.

By now most of the workmen wanted to stop, and they refused to go on until Christopher gave them double pay. And only the poorest and most adventurous of the labourers continued as the pit grew deep and large.

Christopher couldn't afford to be superstitious. St. Paul's must be built to last, he told himself, to survive even another fire or worse. And while he shuddered at what the workmen were un-covering, he was relieved that there were no rats and hadn't been since the fire.

The fourth layer was a row of Saxon graves, for they were lined with chalk stones, although some of the more eminent were en-tombed in coffins of whole stones. Below them were British graves in which were ivory and wooden pins of a hard wood, about six inches long.

Christopher thought of Faith and was shaken. These bodies had been wrapped up and pinned in woollen shrouds only, and every-thing had been consumed, except the pins, which remained whole. But he had to set the example, everyone else looked so nervous and frightened.

He motioned the workmen to go on and to encourage them, scrambled into the pit which was eighteen feet deep now. Here there were no bodies or shrouds, just Roman burial urns and the ghostly remains of a time when Romans and Britons had lived and died together.

Strong, with his knowledge of Roman history, knew most of the objects. Fascinated with what was being found, he forgot his fear and joined the Surveyor down the ladder. He enumerated, "Roman urns, lachrymatories, lamps, fragments of sacrificing vessels, all extremely well preserved."

Christopher was intrigued by a fragment of a vessel, shaped like a basin, with a carving of Charon, oar in his hand receiving a ghost.

"This must have been a Roman Temple of Diana," Strong said.

Christopher doubted this; he saw no signs of construction here, only the marks of death. And he had to build here. But would it work?

Oliver said it would if piles of timber were driven into the hole.

Christopher surveyed the eighteen-foot pit, then shook his head, No.

"Why not?" asked a puzzled Oliver. "Sir, these coffin pins have held."

"Since this gravel is like what we found at the other excavations there must be sand, some of it wet, directly underneath."

Marshall said, "But sir, it is an established fact that timber is tough and lasts well under water."

"Yes. But in this case, the timbers will be half in dry sand and half in wet sand. Not completely submerged, they will rot in time." And, he reminded himself, his endeavours were to build for eternity. "This setting isn't deep enough or right. We must go down until we find secure soil."

Oliver suggested, "Sir, we could alter the foundations."

"No. We have already established them." He was determined not to alter the basic ground plan of his design, for now it had the proportions and balance he desired. "We will have to dig down to the original clay."

"But suppose it isn't there, sir?"

"It will be there, Oliver. The composition of this earth is exactly the same as we found elsewhere in our excavations."

Yet when he began to dig deeper the next day he wasn't as sure as he sounded. He supervised this personally. He walled up the sand with timber and sank the hole to forty feet, where he came upon water and sea shells as he had before, and then a firm sea beach, and below it the hard, firm London clay, which could hold the most immense cathedral. Here, finally satisfied, he built a pier of solid masonry ten feet square, until it came to within fifteen feet of the ground, where he turned an arch that reached to the rest of the foundations. Now, he knew, the earth would hold.

It took much longer than he liked, interrupted frequently by inclement weather, and slowed by timber and masonry that was difficult to find, for he insisted on the best, and the delay and cost disturbed Sancroft.

"Was it necessary, Sir Christopher?" asked the Dean. "This excavation has cost the building fund many pounds."

"It was essential."

"I wonder. If one unexpected difficulty costs us so much in time and money, I doubt if any of us will live to see the cathedral completed."

"We must be patient."

"You must be more economical. There is very little money left."

It had taken many days of patience, reflected Christopher, and St. Paul's was still a multitude of days away from completion. What he had done was just a grain of sand. He thought of God's creation of the world and he wondered if His patience had ever wavered. Yet he resolved not to allow anything to stop him. This added to his determination to construct the cathedral in one piece. He saw it as a whole, it must be done as a whole. To build St. Paul's part by part was inconceivable. If he erected any portion independently, especially the choir, which was being built first, the Commission—if money ran out or there were other difficulties—could accept the choir as enough of a church and leave the rest of the building to the future. He had to prevent such a possibility occurring. He laid out all foundations as if they were part of the whole. Each section was interdependent on the other, with the entire structure pivoted around the dome. This dominated his thinking, and within a year of the laying of the first stone the design for the foundations was securely settled and work on the crypt began.

Christopher hadn't seen Charles since the death of Faith. The royal commands had been transmitted by others, as if, once Charles gave his assent to St. Paul's, he lost interest in the Office of the Works. But on a sunny day in July, 1676, he ordered the Surveyor to attend him.

Charles sat in the centre of the Privy Garden at Whitehall, alone except for several footmen, beside his huge sundial.

He was studying it, but when he saw the Surveyor approaching he dismissed the footmen, who retired a discreet distance away, and asked abruptly, "Sir Christopher, do you know how to work this?"

"Yes, Your Majesty." He examined it and said, "It is four p.m."

"And very hot," grumbled Charles. "I dislike London in the heat, but I have to be here on state business. I hear you built a house at Windsor."

"Yes, Your Majesty. But unfortunately, not yet occupied."

Charles thought, Whenever he was in London there were problems, but at Windsor, amid the willows, meadows, and water, the world was quiet, peaceful, unchanging, and pleasant. "I'm fond of Windsor myself, but it lacks some facilities. The location and hunting is better at Winchester. I would like you to design a palace for me there."

"Now, sir?" Christopher was surprised; there was so much else to do.

"Of course. I will not live forever."

Christopher had heard that Charles had been ill, having caught a chill playing tennis, and he did look tired and older.

"Sir Christopher, it must be on the hill overlooking Winchester."

"A graceful, classical palace, sir?"

"With a marble portico and colonnaded wings."

"And a cupola, sir?"

"Superb. Where I can see my men-of-war afloat at Spithead."

Both men smiled at the other's enthusiasm, then Christopher asked, "Sir, what about St. Paul's? It requires much attention."

"It can wait." Charles grew irritable. "In your devotion to it, you neglect other duties. You were ordered to remove the seats and pulpits from meeting houses so the Dissenters couldn't use them as places of worship, but have neglected that. Does that exceed your powers of invention?"

"I'm sorry, sir." He didn't believe the Dissenters were a threat to the Crown, and so he had put off this distasteful assignment. "I've been busy."

"See that it is done at once. And a new observatory is needed at Greenwich. You should enjoy that, as a former professor of astronomy."

"Your Majesty, I will do my best."

"Locate it on the hill where it will command the heavens."

"Sir, that is a good choice. It could be a fine observatory."

"With a touch of Wren?"

"Your Majesty, it is a science I know."

"You may do it as you please. There is also a need for a new hunting lodge at Newmarket. You must design that first. It is urgently needed. I want it to be neat and ample. I intend to spend much time there."

"As you wish, sir. Is there anything else?"

"Did you know that this sundial was given to my grandfather by a professor of astronomy at Gresham?"

"No, Your Majesty." He wondered if the King was testing him.

"I asked Evelyn, who fancies himself an authority on architecture, to define a good architect, and he quoted Vitruvius. Do you know Vitruvius?"

"Very well, sir. I've studied him carefully and used his principles."

"So has Evelyn." Charles read what he had written: "'*A good architect*,' says Vitruvius, '*should have natural ability, but should also be educated, skilful with the pencil, instructed in geometry, know much history, have followed the philosophers with attention, understand music, have some knowledge of medicine, know the opinions of jurists, and be acquainted with astronomy.*' Sir Christopher, do you agree with these precepts?"

"Yes. It is why the Royal Society was formed, sir."

"Do you qualify?"

"Your Majesty, that is not for me to say."

The Surveyor stood so patiently, refusing to be goaded, that Charles suddenly remembered the main reason he had wanted to see him. He said, more gently, "I was out of London when your wife died, and so I could not express my condolences in person, but I was grieved to hear of her passing. She possessed wit, beauty, discretion. Pray accept my profound regrets."

Christopher had never seen Charles more earnest and he was touched. And Faith would have been pleased; she had liked and admired Charles. He said, "It is kind of you, sir, to express your feelings."

"In my position that is not always possible." He stood up with a sigh. "Danby, Shaftesbury, and Buckingham are approaching, quarrelling as usual, and I'm supposed to please all of them and myself most of all. No wonder you are at Court rarely."

"Your Majesty, I try to be there as much as is necessary."

"You would serve your cause better if you were there more often. There will be a royal ball at Whitehall in September that you should attend."

Isaac Barrow's wish that he visit him at Cambridge was more appealing. The Master of Trinity College was an old friend, an esteemed mathematician.

At the college they were joined by Barrow's protege, Isaac Newton, who had succeeded him in the chair of Lucasian Professor of Mathematics.

The vigorous, strongly-built, middle-aged Barrow greeted Christopher excitedly and the preoccupied Newton warmly. He informed them that he had a vital mission to perform and that he needed their presence. Without further explanation he gathered a group of servants, armed them with stakes, and ordered everyone to follow him. As he rushed out of his house impulsively, Christopher cried after him, "Where are we going?"

"You will see. It is something I must do."

Newton followed slowly and said to Christopher, "Since you are Vice-President of the Royal Society and a member of its Council, I trust you won't think it foolish if I discuss something that concerns you, too."

Newton's lean, angular face, with its long, sharp nose and strong, pointed chin, was very serious and Christopher nodded attentively.

"I'm resolved to resign from the Society."

Newton said this as if it were such an acute necessity Christopher was startled, but he said, "I know you and Hooke have had differences of opinion, but he has them with everybody."

"Differences of opinion wouldn't drive me out. I'm not much concerned with his insinuations, although some of them are offensive."

"What is the trouble then?" Christopher increased his pace a little, for Barrow was almost out of sight on the lane ahead of them.

"I find it degrading to pay for the publication of my discoveries, which cost me so much time, and frequently so much money, to complete."

"I agree."

"The Society should make provision for inventors and discoverers."

"How do you suggest that be done?" He wished Newton would walk faster.

"The Crown should endow the Society, not just with its approval, but with money. Worthy scientists and natural philosophers should be endowed, I've no great regard for pecuniary concerns but the world differs."

"You are concerned about your weekly payments to the Royal Society?"

"Not concerned. But it shouldn't be compulsory to have to pay them."

"You wish to be excused from the weekly payments."

"They are a tribute exacted for our presence. Yet since they are obligatory and I do not desire to pay them, I must withdraw."

"Something should be arranged."

Newton said proudly, "I want no special favours."

"Hooke doesn't pay, but contributes experiments. You could do the same."

"Is it proper?"

Newton was difficult, Christopher sighed, but he was too valuable and original a mind to lose. He said carefully, "It is understood we must contribute what we can. What we are best fitted to perform. You gave us a reflecting telescope. It is a fine reward for your presence. Your experiments and discoveries will compensate for the weekly payments."

Barrow had reached an open field and he was waiting impatiently for them to join him, while his servants stood by his side with their stakes, and Newton asked Christopher, "You won't mention to Barrow what I told you?"

"Not if you don't want me to."

"I may have to resign here. Unless I enter Holy Orders, there may not be enough money to live on. Then my fellowship would be renewed, but I'm not prepared to take Holy Orders. I'm as good a theologian as any of them, but I prefer freedom of thought to subscription to any particular creed."

"Newton, Barrow is waiting."

"Let him wait. He is always in a hurry. And haste is undignified. Besides, I'm as devout as Barrow. As anyone. And certainly the clergy." Then he smiled, for the first time today. "I've petitioned the King to allow me to retain the fellowship as a layman. It is not usually done, but Charles is not as rigid as some of those in authority. And you know him well. If you spoke to him, showed him my reflecting telescope, it might persuade him to grant me the necessary funds. It is by special favour of God that I see the universe, but surely He didn't expect me to freeze. My rooms are so cold I can only sleep if I'm next to my fire and it could give me a distemper. Will you speak to the King for me?"

Christopher couldn't tell Newton that it was hard enough to obtain what he needed from the Royal purse. "Newton, I will do what I can."

"Thank you. If I have seen further than Hooke, it is by standing on the shoulders of giants. But he is so easily suspicious and hurt."

They joined Barrow, who regarded them as if they were betraying him, delaying him with their discussion, and he asked irritably, "What held you up so long? What were you talking about?"

Christopher shrugged and said, "What do you want with us here?"

"Do you know where we are?"

"This large, attractive meadow looks familiar but I'm not certain."

"Halfway between the western boundary of Neville's Court and the river Cam."

Newton, whose gait was awkward, walked about the meadow indifferently, studying it, and said, "It is not the most fertile land in Cambridge."

"Why do you think I asked you here, Isaac?"

"You know that I'm interested in the planting of fruit trees for the manufacture of cider. It could be profitable for a country gentleman, but this soil is too hard, not promising enough."

"Promising enough, for my purposes," retorted Barrow. "They won't check me now. None of them, however they try." The Master of Trinity grew angry as he told them why he had brought them here. "Sir Christopher, as Vice-Chancellor of Cambridge I called a meeting of my fellow heads of the colleges to recommend the erection of a theatre here, as you built in Oxford. It is unseemly, as it was at Oxford, to conduct the business of the university in consecrated buildings such as a church. But they refused to agree to such a structure. They said that Archbishop Sheldon paid for the theatre, that the university had no money for such a project. No matter how I argued, they rejected my plans for a theatre here."

Newton said, "I'm not surprised. They have no imagination."

Christopher said, "It is unfortunate. I've learned much since I designed the theatre at Oxford. Did they suggest an alternative?"

"They said, If I wanted to build, I should build at Trinity."

"Is that why you desired to see me?"

"Indeed. We need a new library since our old one was burnt."

"Here?" exclaimed Newton. "This is just an open field!"

"It is at the end of Neville's Court and the river is at our back. Sir Christopher, what do you think? It is feasible, isn't it?" Before the Surveyor could reply, he ordered the servants to stake out the site of the new library. The white stakes gleamed in the sun and refreshed him.

"What about the cost?" asked Newton. "You're always short of funds."

"They will be found," Barrow answered angrily, "Isaac, I invited you as a friend, not as a judge. Sir Christopher is the surveyor among us."

Barrow was clever, thought Christopher, a library could be attractive here, facing Neville's Court with the river at its back. The soil of this meadow was too hard for fruit trees, but it could be fine for a building.

"With your design, it could be Trinity College's greatest treasure."

"You will receive no fee," Newton said disgustedly. "You will have to lay the bricks yourself."

"That is not the question," said Christopher. "A library could be handsome here. However, the stakes would have to be adjusted."

"Whatever is your pleasure," Barrow said hurriedly. "This is just a start. Nothing else is final. The stakes are here to show our determination that true scholarship is not going to be halted by money-grabbing minds."

The site aroused Christopher's interest and imagination and suggested a new and beautiful counterpoise to the college. He said, "I will execute the designs without charge and if they convey the images you desire, fancy with balance and proportion, perhaps money can be accumulated for the brick and mortar. This is an intriguing project."

Barrow asked, "Should I move the stakes, Sir Christopher?"

"There is time for that. Newton will you be at the Society next week?"

"Will you talk to Charles?"

"When I can." Now he had a good reason to attend the royal ball.

"I will try to come."

"Of course he will come," Barrow said heartily. "With me, in my coach. He has new discoveries to discuss. But he refuses to publish them."

"I will publish them when I am sure I am right."

Christopher said, "With the Royal Society, I trust."

"I may. It is the best sounding board in the whole of Europe. Barrow, do you truly think you will raise the money to build a library here?"

"I must now that I have Sir Christopher's approval and aid."

Z

When the invitation to attend the royal ball arrived, Christopher accepted it. He spoke to Evelyn, Pepys, Boyle, Aubrey, and Hooke—and they agreed that Newton should be excused from the weekly payments, although Hooke was upset that the mathematician doubted his support.

Christopher told this to Newton when he came the next week, and promised to bring his fellowship and telescope to the attention of Charles. But Newton, instead of being grateful, was grumpy. He said, "I cannot accept ordination because of my doubts about the Trinity, so he must be persuaded, but you must be discreet and not offend him." Christopher was annoyed by his churlish behaviour, but fascinated with the new ideas he expressed about the nature of colours. His views, which differed widely from Hooke's, opened new vistas in the study of optics. His experiments were so clear, so logical, so masterly done, so without his usually secretive and suspicious manner, that Christopher and most of the Society agreed with him and not with Hooke.

Newton also told Christopher, "Barrow has written to many rich men for money for the library and the stakes still stand, but the students call it Barrow's folly and almost everyone thinks it is a foolish venture."

This increased Christopher's wish to design a library for Trinity. But he was so busy with other work he wasn't sure he could fulfil Barrow's demands. There was also the question of whether he could afford to do it. He doubted that Barrow would be able to pay a fee, the library could cost so much, and he wasn't certain he wanted him to.

After the meeting of the Society, he refused Evelyn's invitation to join him in a coffee house, and returned to his rooms at Scotland Yard and closeted himself in his studio to determine whether he could spare the time and money to design the library at Trinity College. He assembled all of his work. He lit a dozen candles so the light would be sufficient, and used fresh ones so they would burn a long time. And he started a brisk fire in the hearth, although it was August, but the nights were chilly.

This reminded him of the care Faith had lavished on this precious room and he was stricken with sadness. He felt better sitting in his favourite chair, *Myself*, which he had designed and built himself. As he felt the firm, upright back of oak, which kept his spine from aching, the sturdy arms which he liked to lean on in moments of reverie, the upholstered seat which bore his body comfortably, he was glad he had not followed the Court vogue for walnut furniture. This chair united him with his childhood and his father. Tears came to his eyes as he thought of how proud his father would have been to see him sitting here as Surveyor General—and surprised.

Then he caught hold of himself for there was so much to do. He turned to the parish churches first. They were the most immediate necessity and the fees he received for this work varied according to the resources of the parish and the difficulty of the design. He itemised his projects.

"St. Mary-le-Bow."
"St. Stephen's, Walbrook."
"St. Bride's, Fleet Street."
"St. Mary-at-Hill."
"St. Lawrence, Jewry."
"St. Magnus Martyr, Lower Thames Street."
"St. Benet Fink."
"St. Christopher-le-Stocks."
"St. Michael, Cornhill."
"St. Dunstan-in-the-East."
"St. Vedast, Foster Lane."
"St. Edmund King and Martyr."
"St. Nicholas, Cole Abbey."
"St. Olave, Jewry."
"St. Denis, Backchurch."
"St. Mildred, Poultry."

All these churches were in the process of construction, he reflected with satisfaction, and some were close to completion, only a few years away from his final work on their steeples. He designed the steeples last, so they would express beauty, variety, originality, and become the final and ultimate expression of his individuality and art.

Next, he reviewed the churches ordered for design but not yet started.

"St. Stephen, Coleman Street."
"St. James, Garlickhithe."
"St. Mary, Aldermanbury."
"St. Swithun, London Stone."
"St. Anne and St. Agnes, Gresham Street."
"St. Michael, Bassieshaw."

Sixteen in work, he counted, six ordered, and many more planned. Eighty-seven parish churches had been destroyed in the fire, he remembered, but surely he wouldn't be asked to rebuild all of them, Some parishes were combining, others couldn't afford a new church. He estimated that the demand would come to about fifty. He turned to the royal commissions.

"The Monument."
"The Royal Observatory at Greenwich."
"The King's hunting lodge at Newmarket."
"A new palace at Winchester."

"Repairs on the old palace of Whitehall and the Tower of London."

He felt better now that his work was organised, and he decided that he didn't need any fee for the library, but the time would be difficult.

Now if he could stress the use of an arch, he thought, perfect in balance and proportion and build for serenity rather than grandeur.

He worked on and on, ignoring his growing fatigue. Want of time must not stop him, he resolved, he must be as strong as the rock he loved.

Somewhere around dawn he fell asleep in *Myself*, and that was where Daniel found him the next morning. The candles had burned down, the fire was out, and Daniel was upset. He cried out, "I've wretched news!"

"Is something wrong? Has someone died?"

"The timber and lead that are needed for the north-east end, where we put in the special foundations, are gone. They were stolen last night."

"What about the two workmen we assigned to guard the materials?"

"They got drunk and were in a heavy slumber when work started this morning. Oliver is talking of throwing them in Newgate, or having them hung, but I said we must consult you first."

"Do you think they were involved in the robbery?"

"No. More likely, they couldn't endure the cold and had some spirits to warm them and it affected their senses. We should punish them but Newgate is too drastic. And there was other damage."

Christopher stood up, fully awake now. "Worse?"

"In some ways. The costly guy ropes of our workmen's tackle have been cut to ribbons. There is much opposition in the City to the cathedral. They feel the money you are getting on the tax of coal should go to them."

"Do you think the opposition is serious?"

"Yes. As it is, our expenditures are larger than estimated due to the special excavations. There are rumours among the workmen that there will not be enough money to pay them, not even for what they have just done."

"I must talk to the workmen." Christopher threw on his cloak.

"What are you going to do about the stealing?"

"We will build a wall around our storage place and use watch-dogs with the watchmen. And pay them enough they don't have to drink to keep warm."

As Christopher hurried out of the studio and towards his coach, Daniel exclaimed, "You must be exhausted. I can take care of whatever you decide."

The brisk air gave Christopher new vigour and now he knew how Barrow must have felt with his stakes. He held in his hand the last design he had done for the library and it was almost what he wanted.

Daniel jumped into the coach with Christopher and asked, "What is that design for?"

"A library for Trinity College at Cambridge."

"With all you have to do already? You will never complete it."

"I must. The idea is splendid."

"Christopher, you overwork yourself, and there never seems to be an end."

"I know."

"Then why don't you stop? Or, at least, go more slowly?"

"These designs are the seeds of my life, of my growth. I cannot stop."

Oh The Bud

Oh the bud
The new bud
It wasn't here
And now it is
It burst through
all the wood of the twig
Strong nerved thing
I saw you I saw you I saw you
You thought you wouldn't be seen
Oh to witness your miracle
All whole against all the green
You made me feel like a miracle too
Your destiny was mine and mine yours
That we met the instant you came to earth
And now you know your own life's purpose
Somehow you gave me mine tho I don't know what it is
Oh I know, your white flower just came through and showed me.

Stymean Karlen

44

Oh The Bud

THE THEFT HAD OTHER CONSEQUENCES. MUCH OF THE MONEY LEFT
in the depleted building fund had to be allotted to replace the stolen
materials and the damaged guy ropes, and economy had to be
practised elsewhere. Half of the workmen were dismissed because
of the shortage of funds. Four were assigned to act as watchmen
to guard the supplies and equipment, dogs were hired, and work
on St. Paul's proceeded at a reduced speed.

Christopher was distressed and he appealed to Sancroft for more
money, and the Dean promised to make a new effort to raise funds,
but the next few weeks nothing was done. It hardened Christopher's
determination to complete the cathedral. He was still able to
employ, Strong, Marshall, Oliver, and Daniel, and with them, and
his reduced force, he concentrated on laying all of the foundations
as the design clarified in his mind.

Once this was done and the walls started, particularly where he
planned to set the great central dome, he was hopeful that they
couldn't halt him. Then, even if he died, he thought, they would
have to build the cathedral with the design he had created. The
others seemed to sense his urgency and as autumn came the weather
was dry and mild, and Strong and Marshall worked very hard to
place the foundation masonry as he desired.

The Trinity College library continued to expand in his mind. He
was determined that it must be remarkable and different from
anything he had ever designed. In his spare time, which was mostly
late at night, he worked on these designs. His ideas became an
exercise in classicism, and when he decided what to do and made
six drawings, he wrote Barrow:

"*A building of this consideration deserves good care in the design and*

*able workmen to perform it, and he who takes the general management
upon himself should have the prospect of the whole, and make all the parts
inside and outside correspond together. I suppose you have good masons;
however, I would willingly take further pains to give you all the mouldings
in detail. We are scrupulous in small matters, and you must pardon us,
the architects are as great pedants as the critics and the heralds."*

He added his six drawings to this letter and sent it to Barrow with
the hope this would help the Master of Trinity raise the money.

Certainly, he thought, as he arrived at Whitehall a few nights
later for the royal ball, there appeared no want of money here.
Despite all the talk of Charles' lack of funds, it was the most lavish
entertainment he had seen.

The great hall, which had been converted into a ballroom by
Charles, was beautifully and extravagantly adorned. Whitehall,
made into a palace by Wolseley and appropriated by Henry and
used by Elizabeth, had become the expression of Charles' honour.
This ball was a magnificent and ornamental masque, an allegory
of the social pleasures of peace, but not a pastoral idyll, felt
Christopher, although this motif was favoured, for there was a
capricious and bitter reality behind these theatricals. He observed
that in the most extreme moments of the search for sensual pleasures,
there was the constant striving for self advantage—often confounded.

He was glad he had worn his most attractive brown doublet and
grey knee breeches, his fine green silk stockings and his properly
designed shoes, for he was proud that he possessed pleasing legs.
Even so, although he was comfortable in his clothes, he felt submerged by the profusion of ostentatious dress about him. The
costumes of the courtiers and the ladies filled the ballroom with a
blaze of colours. They wore, as if their honour depended on it, the
richest and most sumptuous of reds and blues, yellows and gold,
silver and greens in satins, silks, velvet, and lace. The men gave
prominence to their wigs, while the women's low circular decolletage
plunged lower and lower until it became extreme. Most of the ladies
wore face patches, while many of the courtiers, like the ladies,
painted their faces. And almost everyone was perfumed heavily,
from their scented hair to their fragrant gloves, as if neither courtier
nor lady could allow themselves to be outdone in the quality of their
smell. Yet all these extravagances, he reflected, only accentuated
the pimpled, wrinkled, blemished skin of many of those who were
thickly decorated with a face bleached by a wash, whitened with
ceruse, a white lead preparation which he despised for it could ruin
the skin, and so overdone with cosmetics that only a doll seemed
to exist under the skin.

He had put on a simple, brown wig, the same colour as his natural hair, for Charles would have been offended if he hadn't worn one. He looked about to seek a companion. There were many people here that he knew, and when Pepys caught his eye his friend joined him.

Pepys was dressed like a peacock and full of gossip and pride, for now he was Secretary to the Admiralty, with power and wealth. He exclaimed, "Everyone of consequence is here! York, Danby, Sedley, Rochester, for they divert the King, the Queen, and the King's newest favourites, the Duchess Mazarin, the Duchess of Portsmouth, and Madame Gwynn. Who do you think Charles will attend? Castlemaine is no longer his favourite."

"I presume the mistress who most fits his present mood."

"He is more constant than that. They say Mazarin is first in the King's affections. She could change much of the business at Court."

"I doubt it. He listens to many people but he follows his own counsel."

"Sir Christopher, you've known him a long time?"

"Since childhood. Did you like Newton's experiments?"

"He is a learned man, but not much of a wit. Have you ever seen him look at a woman? Or even talk about one?"

"He may have many interests of which we are not aware. But that is not our concern. No one is everywhere alike. I'm not a courtier either."

"But you could be. You have the wit for it. Evelyn says there is nothing anyone can do, that you cannot do better. You have great natural gifts. And judgment. You are much esteemed by the King."

Christopher wasn't so certain and he wondered why Pepys was flattering him. Did the Secretary of the Admiralty want a design? Before he could pursue that further, Nell Gwynn asked is she could have a moment with him. Her decolletage was the lowest he had seen so far and her pretty, pert features were painted a vivid red and white, and he was surprised by her request, yet he bowed and strolled into a corner with her.

"Sir Christopher," she said—in her excitement her voice took on a Cockney tinge, "would you design a house for me?"

He hadn't expected this, but he said, "I would be honoured."

"No! No!" she insisted. "I mean this. Charles has promised to give me a great new property in Chelsea, for our children, and to have you design it would be generous of you and would honour my situation."

She was so serious he knew he must give her a serious reply. "Madame Gwynn, I would be happy to, but I have so much to do it could take longer than you desire."

"I will be here as long as Charles lives. We have a French comedy at Court now with the presence of Mazarin and Portsmouth, but it may become a farce. They are too confident of succeeding. Charles has agreed to acknowledge my children. I've managed that. I've learned how."

She was still outspoken and fearless, he thought, traits Charles liked, they were so rare, and he was interested and that encouraged her to rush on.

"Sir Christopher, your father acknowledged you, didn't he?"

"Yes, Madame Gwynn. Naturally."

"Well, my children are Charles' natural offspring. And when he was visiting me the other day, I called to my oldest boy, '*Come hither, you little bastard.*' Charles was so shocked he said I mustn't use such words and I replied, '*I have no better name to call him by,*' so now he is going to make my son the Earl of Burford, and I'll need a new home for him."

"But the King is already unhappy that his projects have been delayed."

The Surveyor hadn't changed expression at what she had said, and curious to see if she could disturb his renowned equanimity, she added, "He'll give me preference. Mazarin and Portsmouth are Papists, but the people love me because, as I told them, '*I'm the Protestant whore.*'"

Christopher laughed as she wanted him to. She had heard that he was a sober man, not given to frivolity, but he had been always pleasant to her. Yet she was annoyed when he said, "I'm not doing any private commissions."

"You're designing a library. That is a private commission."

"Is that common knowledge?"

"Not common, but anything you design is of interest to the King. And you would be designing a home for the King's son. He would approve."

He thought, Nell Gwynn might lack learning but she had a natural wit and humour that explained why she still held Charles' interest. And while she was unpolished he liked her honesty and prettiness, and that, unlike the other mistresses of the King, she had remained unspoiled and unchanged by her rise in the world. He bowed politely and said, "Madame Gwynn, whenever you desire Burford House, I will do my best to please you."

"And please yourself. Without that, it will lack your wit."

"I'm not sure it will possess that. I've not designed any houses."

"You did at Windsor."

"I forgot." And it was still empty, he reflected ruefully.

"Charles suggested Chelsea as the location for our son's house, but I prefer Windsor. Then my boy will be close to his father and will more certainly obtain a better education. He must have what I lacked."

She paused as she saw Charles indicating he desired not her presence, but the Surveyor's. She didn't appear upset, but amused, although Christopher noticed that she lost some of her habitual gaiety.

She said, "Promise, if Mazarin or Portsmouth desire a house, you will refuse them? Please, Sir Christopher?"

"Madam, I will say that you have first call on my services. But what about the third lady who has joined the King? I don't know her."

Nell Gwynn's voice grew respectful. "She is Lady Jane Fitzwilliam. Since her parents died, Charles regards her as a ward. Her father was killed during the civil wars in the service of the King and he favours her, as a friend. She is a Londoner. Lady Fitzwilliam was born not far from where I was. But her grandfather was a sheriff and alderman of London. Do you admire her? Charles would be pleased with your interest."

"I don't know her. But she is attractive."

"I wouldn't keep Charles waiting. It is one of the few things that provokes him to anger. You will keep my commission in mind?"

"Madame Gwynn, I will indeed."

He bowed as he left her and approached the waiting King. He liked Lady Fitzwilliam's appearance even more as he saw her better. She was not an obvious beauty like the Duchess of Portsmouth with her youthful face and perfect features, or the Duchess of Mazarin, whose dark, mature beauty was striking and unusual. But he preferred her clean skin which was free of cosmetics, ceruse, and face patches. Lady Jane was petite, his own height, with a full bust, black hair, brown eyes, broad cheekbones, and a natural white and pink complexion. He realised that he had always preferred naturalness in women; all those he had loved had possessed that.

The two mistresses of Charles drifted away as if the Surveyor was of no interest to them, and Charles said, "Lady Jane, Sir Christopher."

She said, "I am honoured," and she curtsied elegantly and charmingly.

Christopher sought to equal her in politeness, while Charles said, "Lady Jane is one of the few ladies at Court who matches your learning."

She said, "Sir, you flatter me. No one could match Sir Christopher."

"You know Latin and read French and Italian like a native. You are familiar with Montaigne, Petrarch, Dante, Ovid, and even Aretino. You ride excellently and know the difference between a sweetbrier and a rose."

She blushed and Christopher thought, Charles sounds like a matchmaker. Yet Charles, of all people, must know that love was not shaped by a lady's knowledge of gardening, or riding, or even learning. But he said, "It is a privilege to meet such an accomplished lady."

His Surveyor sounded so stiff, as if he resented his efforts, Charles was annoyed. Suddenly he asked, "What did Madame Gwynn want?"

"A new house, Your Majesty. With my design."

Charles exclaimed critically, "But you have too much to do now!"

"Your Majesty, I gave her my word I would do my best to please her."

"Have you removed the seats, pulpits from the Dissenting congregations?"

"Sir, I thought other matters were more immediate."

"Like a library at Trinity? What is the urgency there? Cambridge will not vanish, at least for a few hundred years."

This was one of the reasons he wanted to build the library, but he was quiet. Charles was angry enough as it was. But he must build the library.

Lady Jane said, "Your Majesty, your patronage of learning has taught many people to read and write. Even in our remote villages."

"I'm not sure it is a good thing. Now every country squire who comes to Parliament thinks he knows as much as I do. But I have to assume the responsibility for their mistakes. And still be pleasant to them, too."

"Your Majesty, you said that Sir Christopher has no political aspirations. And thus, can be trusted."

Charles was furious, as if Lady Jane had revealed a vital secret. Then he remembered that many were watching him, no matter how they pretended to be absorbed in dancing, flirting, seducing, intriguing, for he was the centre of this universe. He said sharply, although he smiled for the benefit of those watching, "I am concerned when my Surveyor finds certain tasks disagreeable. I order a hunting lodge at Newmarket and he finds an excuse to defer it. But when he works on St. Paul's, or a library for Trinity College, nothing stops him, he is as one possessed."

"Sir, whatever is your wish, I will do with all my industry."

"I'm going to Newmarket tomorrow but my hunting lodge is not done."

"Sir, I will attend to it immediately."

"Please do. Or your devotion to other matters could be offensive."

"Sir, didn't you suggest I should attend this ball?"

"Yes."

"Why, Your Majesty?"

It was to meet Lady Jane, Charles reflected, they seemed to have the same kind of nature and it could be a good match for her, but this was not a thing he could reveal. "I wanted to see your social character. Your office requires much work with people." Wren's singular modesty vexed him even as it pleased him, for it wasn't natural. No one else, not even a humble professor like Isaac Newton who had just petitioned him for money possessed Wren's lack of vanity. "There is dissatisfaction with some of your work."

She said, "But Your Majesty, you told me that you approved of the Sheldonian Theatre and said Cambridge deserved a similar edifice. And the theatre serves exactly the purpose it was supposed to."

"Lady Jane, since when have you become an authority on building?"

"Sir, since you were kind enough to provide for my education."

"I provided too well. You have become too clever."

"Sir, I've had a good teacher. You are a master of such things."

"That is one of my difficulties. I can never resist flattery, when it is true. You see, Sir Christopher, I must indulge her. I'm indebted to her family for the services they rendered my father at great peril."

"Then, Your Majesty, you shouldn't be offended if I remember how you were praising Sir Christopher's work on the Tower a few minutes ago."

Christopher said, "I was simply repairing it."

Charles added, "But you did order your workmen to examine the staircase of St. John's Chapel. You must have felt they might find the wooden chest containing the bones of the two children at the foot of the staricase."

"Yes. If the two Princes, Edward V and Richard Duke of York, were murdered, the steps of the staircase was a likely place to inter them."

She said, "Sir Christopher, it was ingenious to think of that."

"If Richard III ordered their deaths, as is believed, he would be sufficiently superstitious to want them interred near St. John's Chapel. So their souls, in his belief at least, wouldn't be consigned to hell."

Charles said, "This is one of the reasons I ordered these remains to be interred at Westminster and that you provide a white marble coffin for the supposed bodies of the Princes you found in the Tower of London."

Christopher exclaimed, "Then you are not sure either, Your Majesty?"

"Sir Thomas More and Sir Francis Bacon agreed that the children were murdered at Richard's command, but Richard lost. Winners write history."

Neither Christopher nor Lady Jane responded. Christopher wanted to know her better; she was a lovely thing to see, and intelligent; and Faith had made him realise how vital female companionship was to him.

Lady Jane was grateful to Charles for heeding her request to meet the Surveyor; he was not aloof as she had feared. There was something in his grey eyes that was a mingling of emotion and reason, reaching out tentatively to her, yet hesitating. He was a man who had to be encouraged, she decided, but he was more appealing than the courtiers who surrounded her with flattery they seldom meant. His love of riding, of walking, and seeing for himself on his building projects had kept him from the languor of the habitual courtier. Not for him the double, soft chin of Buckingham, the sly sneer of Sedley, the peevishness of Rochester. She sensed he took pride in his lean body, his well-formed legs, his large head with its fine forehead and searching eyes. That he was determined to exist by reason, by choice, as freely as he could.

Charles said abruptly, uncomfortable in their sudden silence, "Lady Jane, what possesses you tonight? I've not ordered anyone to the Tower."

"Your Majesty, I'm grateful you are more merciful than Henry."

"Sir Christopher, she is a rare subject, she doesn't approve of the axe."

"I don't either, Your Majesty."

"You should speak to the people. I'm the one who has to restrain the people from public violence. I want to halt the practice of drowning or burning old women as witches, but there is much opposition to it both in Parliament and throughout the country. But enough of melancholy matters. Perhaps, Sir Christopher, you could show Lady Jane the parts of Whitehall that I have requested to be repaired and redesigned by you."

Charles turned away to greet Castlemaine, and Christopher said, "Lady Jane, if I may, I would be happy to heed the King's request."

"As his servant, sir?"

"As yours, Lady Jane."

He led her to the riverside terrace which the King wanted redesigned and she said, "When I was a child and my father brought me here to see the first Charles, I loved the view of St. Paul's from here. It was the City of London for me. When will we see a new cathedral on Ludgate Hill?"

"There are so many difficulties it will take many years."

"But there will be a new St. Paul's?"

"Do you doubt that, Lady Jane?"

"There are many in the City and at Court who say that St. Paul's will never be rebuilt. That it is too stupendous a work for one man."

"I know. But there will be a new St. Paul's. I'm determined on that."

She didn't answer.

"Lady Jane, don't you believe me?"

"I believe you."

He sighed with relief. Generally, he didn't care about people's views, but hers had become important. Lady Jane's white silk dress heightened her dark colouring and reminded him of Faith, for Faith had liked white, too. Was he being too hasty, he wondered, Faith had died just a year ago. But when he saw her looking uncomfortable, he asked, "May I see you again?"

She wondered if he knew she was almost as old as he was. It had been a mistake to reveal that she had visited the palace in the reign of Charles I. Yet he seemed pleased by her reference to St. Paul's.

"Have I offended you, Lady Jane? I'm sorry. I didn't intend to."

Now she knew what she wanted to know. He did care. She could tell in the way his voice had grown intense, by the admiring look in his eyes. And he might be capable of passion, even if she were not the youngest of wives, only a few years younger than himself. She was grateful that like the Duchess of Portsmouth, she had retained her youthfulness longer than usual. It had taken careful grooming and constant attention to her health.

"Lady Jane, would you like to see what has been done on St. Paul's?"

"I would be delighted."

He took her to the construction the next day and she was disappointed that so little of the work showed, although he had been building for over a year. He explained that the foundations must be carefully constructed and that haste was a vice of youth. She wondered whether this was his way of saying he knew she was only a few years younger than himself. But in the following moment he thanked her for defending him to Charles.

She replied, "I was being honest. You shouldn't have to justify yourself. What you have accomplished speaks for itself. Charles knows that, but he likes to criticise, so he can command the situation."

"That is why I can't trust him to support me when I need him the most."

"Now you sound as cynical as Charles pretends to be. I didn't think you were capable of such sentiments."

"Without some cynicism, reality would be unbearable. Often, I think, if a new St. Paul's is going to stand here some day, it will be not so much because I have withstood opposition as survived it."

"You will, Sir Christopher, it is your nature."

He wondered why women he liked felt inclined to advise him. Was that a weakness in himself, he reflected, or a need to use their intelligence? In any event, he wanted to see her again and soon and he said so.

She asked, "Despite all the work you must do? When will you have time?"

"Lady Jane, I will make the time."

"Are you going ahead with the library at Trinity College?"

"If Barrow approves of my designs." A look of shame appeared on his face and he exclaimed, "I forgot one of my reasons for attending the ball!"

She teased, "It wasn't to meet me?"

"Of course! But I had promised Professor Newton to speak on his behalf to the King. When I met you, it went out of my head completely."

"I can't believe that."

"You enchanted me. But Charles is at Newmarket now."

"You could go there. To survey the grounds on which you are to place the hunting lodge. Charles will be pleased and more amenable to reason."

"A very good idea. Lady Jane, may I call on you when I return?"

"So I can view another of your designs, Sir Christopher?"

"To do whatever you wish." He excused himself for a minute to consult with Daniel, who told him that nothing had been stolen since the dogs had been obtained, but that they were running out of lead and timber.

As Christopher rode into Newmarket several days later, he tried to put St. Paul's out of his mind. Perhaps Charles was right, perhaps he was mad to devote so much of himself to the cathedral, and he wanted some time away from London to settle his thoughts about Jane. He missed her, he knew that now, and he desired more children and they would not have many years for that, he thought, she was almost as old as he was. And the lovely autumn countryside heightened his longings for feminine affection.

Newmarket was a beautiful mixture of reds, browns, and greens as he arrived at the King's old hunting lodge. The footmen said the King was at the races, but that he would be back soon. He didn't mind; he wanted to examine the site of the new hunting lodge before Charles returned. The air was crisp and clean and increased his feeling of vitality. There was none of the smoke, haze, and fog that so often hung over London from the many coal fires, and he understood why Charles liked Newmarket so much.

Just as the sun was setting in a blaze of vivid colours, Charles came back from the races. When he saw the small form of his Surveyor studying the soil, the vista, the scrubby vegetation, he ordered his servants and courtiers who were attending him to wait at the old hunting lodge and he approached Christopher, curious and pleased. So Sir Christopher had kept his word after all. But he had to taunt him, to have an advantage, and he asked, "Did you stop off first at Cambridge to work on your library?"

"No, Your Majesty, your requests come first."

"Newmarket has the sweetest air in England, it is hard to believe it is in the same country as London. That is why I want the hunting lodge here."

"Like Versailles, sir? It started out as a hunting lodge, but it has become a grand palace. I viewed it when that was starting."

"What do you think, Sir Christopher?"

Charles must be in a good humour, he thought, and he said, "A palace and a hunting lodge serve different functions and shouldn't be mixed. It is the quiet simplicity of this country that is beautiful and appealing."

"You may be right. But it must be large, with spacious rooms, to match my height, the heath and the rolling countryside. I don't understand why you wish to locate it here. The trees and vegetation grow poorly."

"That can be remedied, sir. This location commands the best view, is accessible to the heath you like to walk on, yet it is secluded from the noise of the coaches on the country road. And the soil is strong."

"Perhaps. Have you recovered from the Court ball?"

"Very well, sir."

"Some of my courtiers are still tired, but I wasn't. Did you enjoy the company of Lady Jane? She has an excellent inheritance and a fine house."

"It was flattering of you, sir, to introduce me to her."

"Is that all?" Charles disliked being obvious, but Sir Christopher was devious when it came to women. "She is much like your first wife."

"Thank you, sir. Faith liked and admired you. She was pleased by your interest in our affairs. But I don't want to outlive another wife."

"You needn't. Lady Jane enjoys splendid health. She loves to ride. She comes here often. But she is not fond of hawking. Are you?"

"I like to ride, Your Majesty. As you do."

"I love the feel of the saddle. This afternoon my horse won the main race when I was in the saddle. I swear, it was a remarkable feeling."

Christopher doubted he would ever find the King in a better mood, and so he ventured to say, although hesitantly, "Sir, there is one other matter, if I may, that I would like to bring to Your Majesty's attention."

"St. Paul's? I hear there is the usual shortage of funds. Wren, I came here to escape the problems of London, not to be pursued by them."

"Sir, it is not St. Paul's, although the need is dire there. It is Professor Newton. If you would see his reflecting telescope, you would understand how worthy he is of your assistance."

"I'm not an astronomer and have no wish to be."

"But sir, you have shown a regard for natural philosophy that no other monarch has. If Newton could be established securely at Cambridge, with your endowment, it could add lustre to your reign."

"So that is why you came to Newmarket."

"No, sir. My duty to you brought me here. My office is to design a hunting lodge that fulfils your needs. But Newton is a friend to knowledge and if he should leave Cambridge the loss would be great."

Charles grew stern but he said, "We are not savages. Tell him to send me his telescope. Possibly it will be an interesting diversion."

"And his fellowship, Your Majesty?"

"That depends." He strode off to join the waiting courtiers and to resume the life he loved so much, dancing, feasting, hawking, revelling.

The following morning Jane appeared for the hawking. Christopher wasn't surprised to see her, although he had a feeling she was at his heels; he felt like riding, too, and he preferred her company to any one here.

It was a day without imperfections and as they joined the King's party, Christopher thought, There was nothing so becoming a good complexion as the wind in their faces. Soon, when the others charged furiously after Charles to be in on the kill, they deliberately fell behind. They heard the guns go off, but they sounded remote. The murmur of the wind was what they listened to, and when they came to a gentle brook they dismounted.

It was the first time he felt truly alone with her. They sat on a large rock and the sun shone on their faces and they seemed joined together by their warming blood. The sound of the hawking faded in the distance and he thought, Jane didn't need to be a Queen, nature bestowed its own homage on her. His hand touched hers and now they sat side by side, hands lightly clasped, seeing in each other what was unique.

He noticed her nose was short, pert, that her feet, even in her riding boots, were pretty, that her breast was rising and falling with her emotion, and that her brown eyes were like fresh buds about to bloom.

She saw that his senses were so acute he heard the dropping of a leaf, that his body leaned towards her, as if to be reborn. He had such nice lips, she thought, full, but not too full, and she yearned to put her fingers to them, and suddenly she did.

He kissed the tips of her fingers, then fondled them, and inevitably their mouths met as if that was the most natural act of all. There was neither pursuit nor flight in either of them and she didn't protest or demand, but looked joyful. Nothing mattered in this instant but each other.

It was so natural to Christopher that he found himself saying without planning to, "Jane, will you marry me?"

She yearned to say Yes; she had felt this way since she had met him; but he mustn't know this, it would lessen her worth in his eyes. So she appeared to hesitate, to look perplexed.

"You're beautiful," he whispered. "And we could be happy together. My dear, the life I want for myself and my children must include you. Jane, you want children, too, don't you?"

His voice had grown apprehensive and she assured him that she did, although she wasn't certain she could, she was almost forty.

"Then why are you hesitating, Jane dear?"

"I've had sudden proposals from courtiers, but you're not a courtier."

"That is why you must believe me. Unless you don't care for me?"

"I do! But we have known each other such a short time."

"It is enough. I mustn't wait any more. And if the expression in your eyes is honest you don't want to either."

By the time they returned to Newmarket that evening they decided to marry early next year. Jane felt that was fitting. She pointed out that Faith had been dead only about a year and that they should wait a little. They told Charles, who was gratified. The King had promised her mother to take care of her, and now he had. He insisted that they marry in the Chapel Royal at Whitehall Palace, and promised to attend.

The next morning Charles was puzzled when he found Christopher burying dead rabbits underneath the scrubby vegetation at the site of the new hunting lodge. Normally, what was not eaten was regarded as vermin and fed to the hawks, but the Surveyor said to the King, "Sir, I have a better use for the carcasses. They will nourish the trees and the flowers. The rabbit meat will give the roses a beautiful bloom next year.''

Charles disagreed, but Christopher was so insistent he didn't stop him.

All work halted on St. Paul's when heavy snow blanketed London that winter. It was the most severe weather in many years and opponents of St. Paul's stated it was the heavy hand of a disapproving God, but Christopher couldn't believe that. Materials were low, in some instances unavailable, but he kept the watchmen on duty to guard what supplies were there and what was already built. When Sancroft said there were no more funds for this, he paid the watchmen out of his own pocket. At least, he felt, as long as he provided activity at St. Paul's life still existed in the cathedral.

If God Were My Neighbour

If God were my neighbour
Could I befriend Him
In a neighbourly way
No I could not
He would know more
about me
Than I would know about
Myself
That is what is wrong
With my neighbour
     He thinks He is God

Stymean Karlen

45

If God Were My Neighbour

HOLDER MARRIED CHRISTOPHER AND JANE IN THE ROYAL CHAPEL at Whitehall Palace in the presence of Charles. He knew he was an eloquent preacher, and he performed the ceremony with as musical an elocution as piety permitted. He felt he must be impressive, conscious of his importance as sub-dean of the Chapel Royal and newly appointed sub-almoner to the King.

Susan was proud of her husband and brother. Much of the Court was in attendance and it was a royal occasion. She felt sad when she thought of Faith, but she was pleased with his new wife. Jane's family was even better situated than Faith's; Lord Fitzwilliam's influence remained in the person of his daughter. She could tell from the presence of Charles.

Christopher recalled how his uncle had wed the Princess Mary to William of Orange here years ago. Then there were shouts of rebellion on the streets outside. None of this was occurring now, yet it reminded him that Charles was out of favour with much of the country and there was new talk of rebellion. But as he saw Jane at his side, radiant in white, he tried to dismiss this from his mind. It was February 24, 1677; he had kept his word to Jane; he had waited almost a year and a half after Faith's death to wed her. And she looked so happy he felt it was wrong to worry.

Jane was grateful he had heeded her wishes and as Charles congratulated them, she felt she had directed her accomplishments to a worthy end.

That evening, when they were alone at Scotland Yard, he said to her, "As soon as the weather improves, we will occupy the house at Windsor."

"Windsor is lovely in the spring," she replied, and she was glad that there she wouldn't be sleeping in someone else's bed.

It was odd, he reflected, he had built it for one bride and finished it for another. He said, "It is my own design. I think you will like it. The bedrooms are spacious, look out on the river, and the air is fine."

"Christopher dear, I like anything you design."

"You must be more discerning than that." Yet he was pleased. As they prepared for bed he steeled himself not to think of Faith, but only Jane.

She was resolved to please him from the start, and the best way was to give him children. More than one, so he would be well remembered. When, just before they were to join together, he suggested, "Perhaps I should use a sheath, Faith, and decide later about children," she put her fingers to his lips, although she was hurt for he had called her Faith, and said, "No, Christopher, we must have children as soon as possible."

"And call her Jane."

"I thought you wanted another son."

"I have a son. I would enjoy a daughter. Like yourself."

She gave herself willingly then, and so did he.

Christopher thought the winter would never end and it was April before all of the snow and cold were gone from London. Everyone said it was the severest winter in the memory of man, but he was more interested in resuming the construction of St. Paul's and his other projects in the City. He made many designs and there was progress on the hunting lodge. There was no snow at Newmarket, and Charles was in a great hurry to use it.

With the coming of spring Jane told him triumphantly that she was pregnant. He kissed her lovingly and begged her to be careful. Over half of the infants failed to survive birth, and many of the mothers suffered the same fate, and she was older than most. They had never discussed her age and he gave no indication that he knew it, but she sensed he did, he was so cautious. She nodded, still determined to be as young a wife as he needed. Jane didn't tell him that she had prayed to become pregnant. She thanked God. Until now, she had not been sure she could.

The news of another child helped him as labour resumed on St. Paul's and there was a further consolation. Although work was going on at half the speed he desired because of the continuing shortage of materials and funds, all the foundation masonry was laid. That was a relief, for even if he didn't finish the cathedral himself, which was a possibility he had to consider, whoever did, would have to follow his design.

That encouraged him to leave the site with Daniel for his periodic tour of the City churches. They walked along Cheapside and he was pleased that much of London was rebuilt. In the ten years since the reconstruction of the City had begun, many traces of the fire had vanished. While his design for a new London had been ignored and faults of the old city had been restored with a rebuilding of the crooked, winding, narrow lanes and alleys, he noted with satisfaction that as Surveyor General he had improved the construction of the new buildings. He had reduced the danger of plague and fire. The use of timber in houses had been abolished. All new structures, on his orders, too, had to be constructed of stone or brick. Even the details were regulated; the height of the rooms, the level of the basements and streets, the thickness and strength of the walls.

As Christopher noted these things, he said, "London is still a closely built city, but it is safer to live in. It has moved out of the middle ages. It is no longer a medieval city. It is a large step forward."

"Not a complete step," replied Daniel, as mobs on Cheapside pressed in on them. "London is just as noisy and crowded as it ever was. Even more so, I think. The city gets more overcrowded each day. There are more of everything, hackney coaches, private coaches, luggage carts, pack-horses, sedan chairs, dung carts, brewer's drays, herds of cattle, and droves of turkeys. Often I yearn for the peace and quiet of the country. You are fortunate you have a house at Windsor you can retreat to."

"Have you ever thought of settling down? Of marrying? Of raising a family?" As Christopher asked, he realised he didn't know whether Daniel saw any women, or had a mistress, or what his purpose was.

Daniel changed the subject. "Are you going ahead with Trinity?"

"Yes. Barrow is delighted with my designs and says it fulfils his intention exactly. I wish everyone was so co-operative."

"Why shouldn't he be co-operative? He's not paying you anything."

"He may. The new designs raised a large sum of money and in a few weeks the foundations will be started." What was Daniel truly interested in, he wondered, he doubted it was surveying. Daniel did what he was told, but he offered nothing original. This was not the friend he had known with affection and pride. Was Daniel disappointed in love? Had his friend cared deeply for Anne, even though she had used him badly? He heard hawkers shouting, "Dumplins! Tarts! Pippins!" just as they had done many years ago. It took him down the bright vital streets of memory when Daniel had led him into the City for his first experience of it. He had never forgotten that and suddenly he said, "Remember our first journey here and the watermen shouting, 'Oars! Do you want any oars!' And it sounded like 'Whores! Do you want any whores!'"

Daniel grinned in a way Christopher hadn't seen in a long time. "And the whores who tried to entice us in St. Paul's. Do you remember them?"

"Of course I do. They were only twice our age."

"You were afraid, weren't you?"

"Weren't you?"

Daniel hesitated, then smiled again and said, "Yes. But I wasn't going to admit it before you did. I was taking you, remember?"

"Very well. You gave me my first good view of St. Paul's. We loved London so much then, with all its faults. Sometimes, I still feel that way, but I'm not sure that you do, Daniel."

"It is a fine city to be successful in, especially if you are one of those who have something to say about what is being done. But I'm just an employee, who opens his mouth occasionally and wipes the dust off the chair."

"Daniel, you are far more than that. Especially to me."

The two men faced each other, ignoring the shouts of the hawkers, the pedestrians jostling them, the conveyances jamming Cheapside.

It was more intricate than he could express, thought Daniel; he trusted Christopher's affection, for the most part, but in some things he wasn't certain the Surveyor would be sympathetic. Christopher came from such an Anglican family and now was building all these churches and there was so much fear of Rome about, he couldn't discuss his Catholic mistress, Maria. And he didn't want to speak about the painting he had returned to in his free time, for he wasn't sure of its worth. He said, "You'll be late."

"Not much. I hope you will never be formal with me."

"Even if horns are put on me?"

"Daniel, can I be of any help to you?"

"You have, giving me this position as your unofficial assistant."

Christopher sighed. It was growing late. But he had to say, "If you have any difficulties, will you come to me first? Promise?"

Suddenly Daniel wanted to weep. His experience with Rembrandt and Spinoza flooded over him, the loss of his paintings, his break with his family, his departure from Amsterdam, his resolution not to look back, not to care, and yet Christopher, with all his genius and position, stood with him, faithful and reasonable. He whispered, "I promise."

Christopher's perplexed look disappeared and he took Daniel by the arm affectionately and led him to St. Mary-le-Bow and asked his opinion.

"The church is almost finished," said Daniel, "But, as you feared, choked by the buildings around it. Yet the elevation is good and should bear the noble steeple you plan for it. When the parishioners raise the money. They are complaining that you have made no provision for rituals."

"What do you think?"

"I find rituals absurd, antiquated, but I'm not qualified to judge."

"Do you feel the same way about Jewish synagogues?"

"Yes. If man must try to talk to God, I believe he should address Him directly, not through an intermediary and with a vast ceremony."

"That is the heart of the matter. This is what I hoped the Reformation accomplished. But many of the Anglican clergy love an elaborate ceremony just as much as the Roman priests. When I reduce it to a minimum they accuse me of being sacrilegious. But devoutness is a personal matter. It is why I dislike pews. *The church should not be so filled with pews that the poor only have room enough to stand in the alleys. For the gospel is preached equally to them. There should be no pews but benches, but there is no stemming the tide of profit and the advantage for the pew-keepers."*

"Do you ever wish you didn't have to build all these City churches?"

"No! No! It is better that I design them. I know what I am doing, my method is good, I have clear notions, and if God must have a building in which we worship Him, it is better that He be housed intelligently."

At St. Stephen's, Walbrook the workmen were waiting for the arrival of the Surveyor to remove the scaffolding about the dome. Strong was supposed to supervise this job, but like the workmen, he was afraid the dome would collapse when the scaffolding was dismantled. When Daniel saw their fear and hesitation, he said, "Sir Christopher, I will do it," but his friend replied, "Mr. Van Doorn, we will do it." As they stepped forward to take down the remaining timbers, Strong was shamed into action.

He ordered the workmen to do that job, but he watched fearfully, while all the labourers except those taking down the scaffolding, waited outside, still afraid the dome would collapse. Instead, when the last piece of wood was pulled down and the dome remained securely in place, as designed, Strong looked triumphant, Christopher felt regenerated, and Daniel was more aware of what his friend desired and planned for St. Paul's.

St. Lawrence, Jewry was almost completed except for some of the interior and that pleased Christopher, for John Wilkins had been rector of this church, and his old friend would have been happy with its proportions.

Daniel stayed outside while Christopher went inside to continue his survey, for he remembered that this church had been named because this was where the Jewish part of London had been, until the Jewish population had been massacred. He couldn't go in. He had to be faithful to his past.

Daniel liked St. Mary-at-Hill, for he felt partially responsible for its design, since he had been instrumental in taking it out of Hooke's hands and returning it to Christopher's conception.

Christopher was gratified that this church was finished as he had planned it, a modest, comfortable edifice with a simple, square exterior. He was glad he had put a dome here, too, it gave the interior the style and symmetry essential for this building and proved again it could succeed.

Christopher didn't try to see all of the parish churches in the City of London that he had designed — there were twenty-five now — but after viewing those which required his immediate attention, he took Daniel to a coffee house. He chose a corner where they could talk undisturbed.

Daniel was concerned that the steeples were taking such a long time to construct, and Christopher said, "It is my doing. I design the churches for the ease and convenience of the congregations, but I want the steeples to be beautiful, varied, my personal expression of my faith in God. Even if London cannot be designed as attractively and intelligently as it should be, the horizon can express the eloquence and aspirations of our London."

"But if you know what you want, why do they take so long?"

"Bow Church tower, done as I plan it, will cost over seven thousand pounds, while the building itself will come to only eight thousand pounds. That disturbs parishioners. They want only what is necessary. But they will scrape up money for the steeple some-how, for they believe it will place Bow Church second in importance only to St. Paul's."

At a meeting of the Royal Society a week later, Newton informed Christopher, "I presented a reflecting telescope to the King."

"What did he say?"

"His steward took it. The King was at Newmarket."

"Have you heard anything about your fellowship to Cambridge?"

"Not a word. It will be impossible for me to go on this way much longer," he stated irascibly. "I do not eat properly and I cannot afford the proper fuel for my fires. I am devoted to natural philosophy but my body has a reverence for food and heat. Will you speak to the King again?"

"If I can. I haven't seen him lately myself."

"Then make it a point to," Newton said irritably. "I have a tender nature, but I cannot conduct my experiments if I lack human comforts."

After this meeting with Newton, Hooke wanted to show him how he had completed the design for the Monument, which was to be dedicated in a few days. Christopher, occupied with so much else, had not viewed the work on the Monument for a year, and he desired to see what had been done. Yet as they strolled from the rooms of the Society at Gresham and toward the column on Fish Hill street, Hooke talked about Newton.

He complained, "More than half of the members of the Society are failing to pay their weekly dues, and Newton puts us at a serious inconvenience."

"Because he has been excused from those dues?"

"We are short of funds. As Curator, I know that better than anyone else."

"What troubles you about Newton now?"

"Someone sent him a prism from abroad, a rarity in England, and it came to the Customs House and he claimed it. The officers asked him to set a value on it so they could decide the duty on it. Newton, valuing the prism by his own idea of its use and excellence, said, '*The value is so great I cannot ascertain it.*' They pressed him again to set some estimate on it, but he still replied, '*I cannot say what it is worth, for the value is inestimable.*' The Customs House officers took him at his word, and made him pay an exorbitant duty for the prism, which he might have taken away cheaply, only paying a rate according to the weight of the glass."

"It is priceless to him. That is his privilege."

"Not to me. He told the officers to charge us for the duty on the prism, since he intends to use it at the meetings of the Society."

"In natural philosophy Newton ennobles much of what he does. We must find money for the prism somewhere."

"Out of your pocket? The Society has none to spare." They walked by buildings he had designed as City Surveyor and he said proudly, "The City heeded my plan for the rebuilding of London. I've widened many streets."

"Not enough, I'm afraid. The congestion grows worse daily and the way London expands the crowding could become impossible some day."

"You have never appreciated me."

"You are prodigiously inventive and a fine surveyor. But London, which we both want to endure, is still too flimsy, too haphazard. Instead of imposing our will on London, it has imposed its will on us, and since that will is without reason or order, so is the city."

Hooke subsided into silence until they reached the Monument.

The scaffolding was gone and Christopher saw that Hooke had followed his design. The Doric column was supported on a pedestal 28 feet square and 40 feet high, the shaft was 15 feet thick and 202 feet high, and 202 feet from where the fire had begun on Pudding Lane. Then he frowned. The phoenix rising from the top was not there.

He said this as they looked upward and Hooke replied, "It was abandoned on the grounds that no one would understand what the stone bird was."

"Do we always have to lead people by the hand? Can't they imagine?"

"The Lord Mayor and the City aldermen said it would cost too much."

Christopher tried to hide his disappointment—he had set his heart on a phoenix rising out of the ashes—and he said, "Then we should place a statue of Charles there. He fought the fire bravely."

"The City authorities are unhappy about the expense of the Monument."

"The hunting lodge costs more."

"That is the King's money. This is the City's. I've designed an urn for the top." Christopher wasn't listening to him, staring unhappily at the Monument, and Hooke went on impatiently and loudly, "However, the King is praised highly. Listen to the inscription on the south side."

He read from one of the documents he was carrying:

"Charles the Second, son of Charles the Martyr, King of Great Britain, France, and Ireland, Defender of the Faith, a most generous prince, commiserating the deplorable state of things, while the ruins were yet smoking, provided for the comfort of the citizens and the ornaments of his city, remitted their taxes, and referred the petitions of the inhabitants to the Parliament, who immediately passed an Act that public works should be restored to greater beauty, with public money, to be raised by an imposition on coals; that churches, and the cathedral of St. Paul, should be rebuilt from their foundations, with all magnificence; that bridges, gates, and prisons should be made new, the sewers cleaned, the streets made straight and regular, and those too narrow made wider. Every house should be built with party walls, and all in front raised of equal height, and those walls of square stone or brick, and that no man should delay building beyond the space of seven years. Anniversary prayers were enjoined; and to perpetuate the memory hereof in posterity, they caused this column to be erected . . ."

Christopher interrupted, "It sounds reasonably accurate."

"That's not all. On the west side they are putting the names of the city officials responsible for the Monument, but I'm sorry to say, not your name."

"That isn't important. The design is. And the reason for erecting it."

"The inscription on the north side will be about the fire." He quoted:

"In the year of 1666, the second day of September, eastward from hence, at the distance of two hundred and two feet, a most terrible fire broke out, which, driven by a high wind, not only wasted the adjacent parts, but also remote places, with incredible noise and fury. It consumed eighty-nine churches, the City gates, Guildhall, many public structures, hospitals, schools, libraries, a vast number of stately edifices, thirteen thousand two hundred dwelling houses, four hundred streets . . ."

Hooke paused and stated proudly, "I drew up these figures myself."

Christopher was hearing the crackle of the flames; Hooke hardly at all.

"The ruins of the City were four hundred and thirty-six acres."

"I know."

"But I wrote most of this." Hooke was inexorable as he read on:

" . . . the fire burned from the Tower by the Thames side to the Temple Church, and from the north-east along the city wall to Holborn Bridge."

Hooke paused and said, "Did you know that only seven or eight died?"

"So I was told. But the suffering was great."

"I mentioned that." Hooke rushed on:

"The destruction was sudden, for in a small space of time the city was reduced to nothing. Three days after, when this fatal fire had baffled all human counsels and endeavours, in the opinion of all, it stopped as if it were by a command from Heaven, and was on every side extinguished."

What about the fire breaks that were created and the lives risked fighting the blaze? thought Christopher, but Hooke was so pleased with what he had written and read he merely nodded and said, "It should suffice."

"That is not all!" exclaimed Hooke, halting Christopher's departure. "There is still the west side inscription, but this has caused trouble."

Hooke's tone grew so vehement Christopher listened carefully.

"This pillar was set up in perpetual remembrance of the most dreadful burning of this Protestant city, begun and carried on by the treachery and malice of the Popish faction, in the beginning of September, 1666, in order to the effecting their horrid plot for the extirpating the Protestant religion and English liberties, and to introduce Popery and slavery."

Christopher was outraged by this falsehood and he cried out, "This isn't true! Everyone knows the fire was started by accident!"

2A

"Many differ and believe the fire was started by Popish incendiaries."

"This is slanderous and it will only inflame the populace."

"That is what the King says. He has forbidden this to be used. But he may not win. There is much passion against Popery in the country and especially in London, and this could explode at any time."

Christopher shook his head sadly and said, "This isn't why I designed the Monument. These words are a profanation of what I've done."

"They haven't been used yet. It depends on what happens in the City."

Early in the autumn Christopher and Jane were invited to Newmarket by Charles to celebrate the completion of his hunting lodge. Christopher questioned the wisdom of her going, she was growing large with child, but she said she wouldn't miss this occasion for anything. They travelled in his coach and four, which had been Faith's, and he ordered the driver to go carefully, and as the sun lighted the hedges on the Newmarket road Jane's complexion improved so markedly that his anxiety vanished.

Charles was hunting when they arrived, which gave Christopher time to survey the hunting lodge. It was as he had specified. No liberties had been taken with the design. He thought, The King should be satisfied.

He was standing outside the lodge while Jane was resting inside, when Nell Gwynn approached him. She was accompanied by Buckingham and Rochester.

He congratulated her on the King's patent appointing her oldest son the Earl of Burford, a peer of the realm with a seat in the House of Lords.

"But I'm disappointed," she said. "Charles wants me to use a house in London. For his convenience. Would you consider a design in the city?"

"As I said, Madame Gwynn, wherever you desire."

"Nelly," Buckingham said suddenly, "he is just a builder of churches."

She replied, "He will give it his own distinction."

Christopher noticed that Buckingham, once considered the best looking man in the realm, had grown fatter and more dissolute.

Buckingham said, "Because he knows the King almost as long as I do, he takes advantage of that, as if he understands him. I prefer Rochester's view of Charles. It is more accurate. Friend, recite it."

The slim, saturnine, younger Rochester shrugged indifferently, but said:

"Here lies our sovereign Lord the King,
Whose word no man relies on;
Who never said a foolish thing,
And never did a wise one."

Christopher said, "It is one view."

"A very amusing one," said a clear, resonant voice.

They all turned to face the speaker, although they knew who it was.

Charles stood amid flowers which bloomed profusely near a grove of flourishing trees—where he had buried the rabbits, Christopher remembered—and his grin matched Buckingham's and Rochester's.

Charles would never allow anyone to outdo him in worldliness, thought Christopher, even at his own expense. It was, perhaps, his one ideal.

"Rochester, that is almost as witty as Buckingham's view of my brother and myself. How does it go? It is immodest of me to quote it."

"York would see things if he could, the King could if he would."

Charles smiled and said, "Buckingham, that has served you well."

"Sir, I'm always flattered by your interest in what I say."

"Yes, Your Majesty," added Rochester. "Did the hunting go well?"

"At first, only vermin—a few foxes and rabbits. But I persisted and bagged some woodcock and partridge, and the riding was good."

Nell Gwynn interrupted, annoyed by these diversions, "Charles, don't you want to inspect the hunting lodge with your Surveyor?"

"Indeed, Nell, a fine idea. Sir Christopher, where is Lady Jane?"

"Resting, Your Majesty. But she will want to hear your views."

He went to call her and returned soon after with her, while Charles waited with a patience that was rare for him, and then greeted her warmly.

Charles led them into the lodge but in his absorption with Jane, he forgot to bend his head and bumped it. Buckingham snickered and Rochester grinned and Charles said angrily, *"The rooms are too low!"*

Christopher replied, *"Sir, I think they are high enough."*

Charles stooped to Christopher's height, then crept about the room, and said, *"Yes, Sir Christopher, I think they are high enough."*

Everybody laughed, even Christopher, except Jane, who looked hurt.

Charles, who was enjoying this as much as anyone, said suddenly, "Lady Jane, never fear, your ingenious husband can support you in many ways."

"What do you mean, Your Majesty?"

"Sir Christopher proposed to the silk stocking weavers of London a way to weave seven pairs of stockings at once, or was it nine?"

Christopher said, "Sir, it had to be an odd number."

"I was told you were offered four hundred pounds by some weavers, but other weavers begged you not to go ahead with your invention, that it would make them poor, and so you broke the model of your engine before them."

"Uncontrolled making of the silk stockings would have hurt too many people. Your Majesty, did you enjoy Newton's telescope?"

"You are a persistent man. You might finish St. Paul's after all."

"Sir, you instructed me to submit his telescope to you."

"There is nothing more to say."

"But, Your Majesty . . ."

Charles cut him short. "I've been studying a map of America with Sir William Penn. I have properties there that you could design."

Christopher was silent. He had no wish to go to the colonies.

The hush that fell was ominous. It was not like Charles to be silent long, and Buckingham and Rochester excused themselves, which was granted curtly, and this was too much for Nell Gwynn.

She cried out, "Charles, you took me to Cambridge yourself, and the professors entertained us royally and even wrote verses in my honour."

"They had one eye for your beauty and one for my favour."

"Professor Newton attended. You said you liked his telescope."

"So I do."

Jane added, "Sir, it was your wish my husband design the observatory at Greenwich. Would you deny the use of it to him or to Newton?"

"Of course not."

Nell Gwynn said, "Then why do you deny Newton his post at Cambridge?"

"I've denied him nothing!" Charles roared with unusual violence. "He still retains his Fellowship as a layman and a Lucasian professor."

Suddenly he realised what he had admitted and he burst into laughter. "Nell, you are an intriguing one, you've gotten your way after all."

Christopher cried out, "Sir, then you've granted Newton's petition?"

"Weeks ago. Hasn't he been notified?"

"Apparently not, sir."

"I will have my steward confirm it."

Christopher couldn't resist saying now, "Sir, did you notice how.

the flowers and trees have flourished where the dead rabbits were buried?"

"So you have some vanity after all!" Charles exclaimed triumphantly.

"Not vanity, Your Majesty," said Jane, "But a desire to please you."

Charles said, "Sir Christopher, I noticed your gardening. Some of these flowers are taller than those rooms."

Nine months after their marriage Jane gave birth to a girl, whom Christopher insisted on naming after her. Although it was a long, hard pregnancy, she survived it in moderately good health and he was relieved.

Dr. Sydenham, who attended her, suggested she wait a few months before attempting to have any more children. At her age, he told them, some convalescence was preferable, and his decision was accepted.

Neither of them mentioned what her age was. They were happy that everybody was healthy: Mother Jane, Baby Jane, Young Christopher, and Lucy Enfield, who was taking care of both children.

Almost a year passed before Christopher agreed to Jane's wish to have another child. She had recovered her strength, and she said she could spend the vital months at the end of her pregnancy in their home in Windsor, which she loved, and his agreement added to her happiness. It was as if, after many years of not expecting to have any children, the possibility of having two was a gift from God. Soon she was pregnant.

At the same time work continued on St. Paul's with frequent delays, stoppages, and a complete halt during the winter, but there were some signs of progress as the north and south walls began to rise above the ground. Other parish churches were finished and more were ordered and now he had designed thirty. The royal observatory at Greenwich was done and he was pleased with its design, location, and usefulness. Barrow had died suddenly and unexpectedly, but the building of the library at Trinity College went on with a design that Christopher treasured, although the pace was as slow as St. Paul's. To his relief the Monument had been dedicated without the malicious inscription—because of Charles' intervention—but Hooke believed it would be put on eventually. Nell Gwynn had acquired a house on Pall Mall without being able to use his design, but he didn't mind, since houses, for the most part, didn't stimulate his imagination. Repairs were being made on

Whitehall, at Charles' request, and the King had approved of his plans for a new palace at Winchester, which was the King's favourite building enterprise. Everything appeared to be progressing without any special difficulties when he was urgently summoned by Charles.

It was mid-October and the King's steward informed the Surveyor that his presence was required in Charles' bedchamber the next morning.

Jane was excited by this summons, but Christopher was pessimistic.

She said, "It must concern Winchester. He must have raised the money for work to start on it at once. You know it is his favourite project."

"Start it with winter coming on? I doubt that. It is not like Charles to want to see me so privately. I wonder what has gone wrong?"

"Christopher, you mustn't always expect the worst."

"I don't. But the times are difficult and grow worse every day."

"Yet Charles was relaxed and cheerful at Windsor this summer."

"It may have been the calm before the storm. The country is split between those who support Charles and those who don't. The fear of Rome spreads alarmingly and it could lead to disaster."

Christopher went into the next room to complete his toilet and she gazed at the bouquet of flowers he had brought her from Windsor on her return several weeks ago. They were blooming and she grew reflective. August and September had been marvellous months at Windsor, she thought, the weather warm and dry, the days beautiful, and although Christopher hadn't been there as much as she liked, he had been there more than usual, sometimes a few days at a time. Then he gardened with his old retainer, Seth, and played with the children, helping Young Christopher to walk better, and taking a special delight in fondling Baby Jane, who seemed to give him as much pleasure as anybody did. He got down on the floor with her as she crawled about and he loved her company. Neither of them went hunting or hawking with Charles, who was also at Windsor with his Court, although he made it evident that the Wrens were welcome. Pepys and Evelyn came several times, and stopped by to see them in their house on the river. Daniel, too, visited Christopher to discuss how the work in London was going.

Then, she noticed, her husband displayed an affection for Daniel he gave only to her and their children, yet she knew she mustn't be jealous—they had shared so much. She liked Daniel's manners and appearance; he was always so clean and attractive; but she was curious about his family, for he was far more than an assistant to Christopher. Daniel never talked about them, and she didn't even know which church he went to, or if he went. She wondered if he were a Dissenter or a Puritan or worse, in her view, a Papist, although that seemed unlikely with his Dutch background.

This was on her mind when Christopher returned to say good bye and she blurted out, "Did you know Daniel Van Doorn's family?"

"Jane, dear, what has that to do with my visit this morning?"

"Does the King approve of him?"

"Charles has never said otherwise."

"Did your first wife like him?"

"I think Faith did, except when she was jealous of memories she couldn't share. But no two people have the same memories."

"We were so happy at Windsor, weren't we, Christopher dear?"

"Jane, who is being pessimistic now?" He kissed her, then asked, "Have you decided what Charles wants me for?"

"Whatever it is, heed him. With all his difficulties, he is your friend."

Christopher was startled to see guards patrolling the approaches to the palace, cannons set up at strategic places, and that heavily armed footmen ushered him into Whitehall. He was well known at the palace with all the repairs he was supervising, and he was escorted quickly to the bedchamber.

Charles wore a scarlet night gown with a blue velvet robe over it that reached to the floor and accentuated his height, but Christopher was taken aback by the gravity of his expression. Yet he greeted him with a smile and said, "I'm glad you are prompt, there is much for you to do."

"Is Winchester ready, sir?" Christopher had heard there wasn't enough money for it and that Parliament had refused to vote more for the King.

"I wish it were only that." Charles sighed heavily. "I asked you to attend me in the privacy of my bedchamber where no one can observe or overhear us. No matter where else I am in the palace, I am plagued with petitioners seeking something. Have you heard of Titus Oates?"

"Sir, the unfrocked clergyman who is spreading the wild rumours?"

"Yes. This clerical adventurer, once a Separatist, then an Anglican, and finally a supposed Catholic priest, now accuses Rome of a terrible Popish plot. This ill-speaking, ill-looking fellow, with his low brow, short neck, thick body claims there is an international conspiracy by the Pope, his prelates, the King of France, and a multitude of English Catholics to assassinate me, put my brother on the throne, and impose Catholicism on England by fire and sword. Do you believe him?"

"No, sir. Do you, Your Majesty?"

"His tales are absurd. But already there are tales of murderers searching for me with foot-long knives and silver bullets. And now that the magistrate that Oates first told his wild stories to, Sir Edmund Bury Godfrey, has been found murdered, more and more people believe Oates."

"Sir, they want to believe him. He fits their own prejudices."

"Now there are rumours of new fires and plagues, of midnight uprisings, of invasions from abroad, of rebellion in Scotland and Ireland. Mobs roam the streets of London searching for priests, Catholics, and hidden arms. It is a dreadful time for Catholics, it is impossible to protect them."

"I didn't expect this Popish plot to be taken seriously, sir."

"Neither did I. But the hysteria grows worse every day."

"What about the Church, sir? Do they support this frenzy?"

"Many of the clergy do, but not your friend, Sancroft. When Sheldon died last year and I wanted to raise Sancroft to the vacant see of Canterbury, he protested that he wasn't fit for such an important post."

"I know, sir. He declined a bishopric so, as Dean of St. Paul's, he could personally supervise the rebuilding of St. Paul's."

"He told me. Fool. He will never live to see that completed."

Christopher was silent. There was a brisk fire in the grate with the King's favourite Scotch coal, and he saw several of his pet dogs lying by the hearth, and the great canopied bed, imported from France, looked unslept in, and he wondered which mistress was honoured last night. He felt it wasn't Nell Gwynn; Charles appeared too grave for that. He heard clocks chiming the quarter hour. This irritated him; he told himself, Time wasn't only to measure, but to use. Almost everyone was saying that St. Paul's would never be finished in his lifetime and that sickened him.

"Sir Christopher, you don't share my view of the cathedral, do you?"

"Your Majesty, how could I and continue to work on it?"

"You may live to see it done, but I doubt I will. Perhaps Sancroft feels that way, too, for he is Archbishop of Canterbury now. Of course, he had no choice, for I had already given his Deanery to somebody else."

"Your Majesty, do you think St. Paul's will be harmed?"

"Not at all. Now it will be regarded as a Protestant stronghold."

"Sir, it was kind of you to aid Professor Newton."

"Oh, that!" Charles thought, This was a trifle compared to the problems he was facing. He didn't believe that Titus Oates was acting on his own. He was convinced the real plot wasn't Popish, but a conspiracy by his enemies in Parliament, led by Shaftesbury, which wanted his bastard son, the Protestant Duke of Monmouth, to succeed to the throne instead of his Catholic brother, James. It infuriated him, for it scandalised his views of legitimacy, but he was determined to avoid the mistakes his father had made. If he possessed the support of Christopher Wren, an avowed Anglican, builder of thirty Established churches and the Cathedral of London, son and nephew of ministers who had suffered for their faith, he would not be accused of Popish inclinations. And it would help him survive. He said, "I have something else for you to do, Sir Christopher."

"At your service, sir."

"Parliament is to meet to hear Oates and there are rumours of a new gunpowder plot. As Chief Surveyor, I want you to search the cellars under the House of Lords and make sure no gunpowder is stored there."

"Sir, no Catholic would attempt that, it would lead to their massacre."

"That is why some of those supporting Oates might think it clever to plant gunpowder there. You must be sure there are no Guy Fawkes under the House of Lords, particularly of Protestant persuasion, of any persuasion."

Christopher realised England was a powder keg and one spark wrongly applied and the entire country could explode. "I will do my best, sir."

"And tell no one, except me, what you are doing or what you find."

"Your Majesty, when is Parliament meeting?"

"In three days. I want you to search the cellars just before it sits. Today, I have something else for you to do. The House of Lords insists that all communication between the Spanish Ambassador's house and that of his neighbour, Mr. Weld, be secured, on the grounds that they have been passing secret messages between them. And they have designated you to see that this is carried out. They believe you can be trusted."

"Sir, do they truly think the Catholics are planning an uprising?"

"Yes. I may have to send my brother out of the country to assure his safety. But if that is necessary, I'll send my son Monmouth away, too."

"Your Majesty, is there anything else?"

"The declaration of indulgence I recommended to Parliament to make Catholicism acceptable in return for the same indulgence for Dissenters was fought hardest by the Dissenters. They were Protestants first. My proposal failed. Would you run again for Parliament?"

"Sir, I have so much to do. And I'm too logical for Parliament."

Charles retorted, "Parliament considers an eclipse of the sun a portent of disaster."

"That can be explained. Sir, it is due to natural causes."

"The country isn't interested in explanations, they desire victims."

"Your Majesty, I trust you will be careful."

"Thanks for your solicitude. In your case, I believe you mean it." Despite his cynicism, he was touched; they had known each other a long time.

Christopher blushed, as if he had expressed emotion that was supposed to be hidden. But he did like Charles, whatever his flaws, and he did mean it.

"I have provided for a Protestant succession, should my brother fail. I was the one who insisted on York's daughter marrying the present William of Orange. James was against the idea of his daughter marrying a Protestant, but it was essential to retain the support of the country."

Once again Christopher sensed that Charles had to justify his acts to him, not a trait the self-possessed King showed to others. Then he thought of a Catholic church which persecuted to save souls, and a Protestant faith which hated any kind of non-conformity and he felt sick. It caused him to ask, "Sir, do you think these religious wars will ever end?"

"I doubt it. I take no pleasure in being virtuous by punishing other people for their opinions, but many do."

"Your Majesty, how should I proceed with the Spanish Ambassador?"

"Firmly, but gently. And express my regrets."

"Mine, too, sir. It is idiocy."

"It has just begun, I fear. Men are ready to believe anything. Especially since the gunpowder plot and the plague and fire. If you find anything under the House of Lords, report back to me privately."

Christopher asked Daniel to assist him on these two tasks. They were so unpleasant to him that he had to have someone he trusted.

Daniel refused at first; he abhorred what Christopher had to do. But finally, when his friend begged him to help, something he rarely did, Daniel agreed to act as his assistant, although his anger remained.

"Why didn't you refuse Charles?" Daniel asked, as they started out.

"I couldn't. He asked me to do it for the same reason I asked you. He wanted someone he could trust, who would perform these acts sensibly."

"But there is no sense in any of this! Shaftesbury's brisk boys from Wapping roam the streets of London attacking every Catholic they find."

"Then it is better we bring a note of moderation to this witch hunt."

"That is Charles' excuse for doing nothing, but it isn't ours."

"Daniel, what would you do instead? Fight the mobs and start a new civil war? You know how terrible the last one was."

"You are safe, Christopher, but not everyone else is."

Daniel's words mocked Christopher and he was troubled by them as they reached their destination. He felt Daniel was being too personal, when today, of all times, it was essential to be impersonal. Was it possible, he wondered, that Daniel was as partisan as everybody else? His friend had said nothing since, but carried the padlocks as if they were a cross.

A small crowd loitered before the adjoining houses of the Spanish Ambassador and his supposed spy, Mr. Weld, but he was relieved that there was no violence, although the hostile crowd was disappointed there were no soldiers to arrest the suspects. He assured himself, It was better for a rational man like himself to do these difficult acts; he would do them without offence. He felt Daniel saw him as a tacit supporter of the mobs searching for Papists to hate, when he was no more like them than Daniel.

He knocked on the door of the Spanish Ambassador and asked to see His Excellency, Count Egmont, who came at once, as if the Count was warned to expect him. Christopher explained his mission with the utmost politeness, and Count Egmont replied with equal civility and gave permission for the necessary things to be done on the side of his house which faced Mr. Weld's, adding, "I do not wish to embarrass His Majesty."

He treated Mr. Weld with the same courtesy and the English Catholic agreed willingly to have his door that faced Count Egmont padlocked.

Mr. Weld looked relieved, saying, "With the present loss of wits in London, I will be safer, not from Spain, but from the Protestant mobs."

Christopher padlocked the doors and the crowd cheered. "So," Daniel said sarcastically, "The thirty thousand pilgrims who are coming from Spain to join the forty thousand who are to rise in London against the government, could be thwarted. This is stupid. These padlocks prove nothing."

"Perhaps," said Christopher, "But this act strengthens the King's hand, and he supports our views. And Parliament will feel more secure."

The crowd dispersed as they walked away, while Mr. Weld locked his other doors himself, and the Spanish Ambassador slipped out of his river exit and was rowed up the Thames to thank Charles for his protection.

Christopher handed over the keys to the Clerk of Parliament, who criticised him for not barring the doors with iron, too.

Two hours before Parliament was scheduled to assemble to hear Titus Oates reveal the names of all the conspirators in the Popish plot, Christopher led a party of ten soldiers and ten workmen toward the cellar where the gunpowder plot had been located by Guy Fawkes. Daniel was by his side, curious about what they would find. He didn't expect another gunpowder plot, but he was interested in seeing the spot where Guy Fawkes had expected to blow up Parliament, and with it, the English government.

They entered through the Old Palace Yard and Christopher pointed out to Daniel the place where Geoffrey Chaucer, in his office as Clerk of the King's Works, had lived, and the ground, a little further on, where Walter Raleigh had died by the headsman's axe. Christopher regarded that ground as if it was besmirched and he hurried past it as fast as he could.

The building that housed the Lords was an ancient Gothic edifice, of unknown origins, an oblong ninety feet in length and thirty in width. Christopher, who knew it well from his days at Westminster, although he had never been in the cellar, which was forbidden to all visitors, guided his party along an enclosed Gothic corridor to a heavy wooden door with metal bars and a huge padlock on it. He unlocked it with another key the Clerk of Parliament had given him, but it took several soldiers to push it open, it was so heavy, rusty, and unused. The workmen carried lanterns and torches and the soldiers were strongly armed with muskets and spears.

Christopher thought unhappily, What am I doing here? This is a military exercise. He disliked swords and spears; he felt steel could be put to better use. But the task had to be done, and perhaps Charles was right, it was better done by him than a disordered mind. The door opened on a circular row of stone steps leading down to the vault and as everyone hesitated, for there were many superstitions about this cellar—that the ghost of Guy Fawkes strode here nightly in its gory, bloody, disembowelled splendour, searching for those who had betrayed him, the headless body of Walter Raleigh by his side—Christopher took the brightest lantern from one of the workmen and started down the stairs, Daniel right behind him.

Thirty-six barrels of gunpowder had been found with Guy Fawkes, who had stayed to light the fuse at the proper moment. Christopher heard a scurrying of feet at the bottom of the steps and held his lantern high, while even the soldiers cringed, afraid of spirits, and he saw rats run across the floor and into holes. He sighed with relief; they were not the bluish-black rats that he was convinced had spread the plague, although few agreed with his view. It was eerie to tread the cobblestones of the cellar by the light of lantern and torch. The stone spiral stair ended in a pile of rubble, broken boards, cracked stones, nails, and melted lead.

Daniel went straight to where Guy Fawkes had been caught. It was in a corner of the cellar by a small window with prison-like bars, so tightly constructed together, a rat could hardly squeeze through them, and the daylight seeped into the cellar in tiny, box-like fragments. It was empty.

"There is no one here!" exclaimed Christopher. "Not a living soul!"

"Did you expect to find anybody?" Daniel asked sceptically.

"I didn't know what the vault would yield." The soldiers and workmen formed a small group behind the Surveyor and his assistant, waiting for further orders, and Christopher added, "This cellar is in a very ruinous condition. It should be repaired before it collapses."

Daniel said, "Don't tell them, or you will have to do it yourself."

"Someone will have to do it. These iron pillars are rusted, we are very near the river and water must have seeped in, the stone is corroded."

He paused, noticing an arch where Guy Fawkes was supposed to have set the gunpowder. He tapped the stone wall and as he thought, there was a hollow sound. He ordered the workmen to knock down this wall and after a few minutes of labour with their pickaxes, they came face to face with a small crypt. There were several skeletons here, but all identification was gone. The workmen quarrelled over who they were with such savagery Christopher quieted them with a stern admonition. It didn't matter, he reflected, it was impossible even to tell the sex, and he recalled with a sudden poignant sadness that the remains of the gentle and witty Elizabeth Claypole had lain in state above his head. Yet, not many years later, the body of her father had been dug up and his head set up at the end of nearby Westminster Hall. One of the workmen picked up the jawbone of one of the skeletons and asked, "Sir, did they bury Fawkes here?"

"No," said Christopher, and remembered the wife, whose husband, captured by the enemy during the civil war, had had his head struck off in the town marketplace, and put there, where his wife had rescued it, washed his face, combed his hair, and ringed it with lighted religious candles.

He ordered the two skeletons to be put into the crypt. He boarded it up, and then, feeling as if he was coming out of a tomb, he sealed up the vault with the strongest padlock he could find. And before he reported his survey to Charles, he had to pause a moment by the fountain in the Old Palace Yard and watch the water and sun playing on the grey stone. Now refreshed, he asked Daniel to pay the workmen, and accompanied by the soldiers he turned toward Whitehall Palace, very much aware that he could see Westminster School out of the corner of his eye. It reminded him that he hadn't talked to Busby for years, although Busby was still Head Master. But he was on the King's business, and perhaps his report would ease the hysteria against the Catholics. He hurried on to see Charles.

The King was pleased with his Surveyor's news and he conveyed it to Parliament at once. However, it didn't appease their fears of a Popish plot as Charles and Christopher hoped. When Oates appeared before Parliament later that day, the majority of the members encouraged him so openly he uttered even wilder accusations. He declared that the Catholics, especially the Jesuits, intended to set fire to London, to raise the Irish Catholics in rebellion, and conquer England with the aid of the Irish and French, and then massacre all the Protestants and murder the King.

In vain Charles replied that no man in his right mind would be so foolish as to assassinate him to put his brother on the throne.

At this meeting of Parliament, as far as the majority were concerned, whatever Oates said was gospel, whoever he accused was arrested at once. His declaration that he was the saviour of the nation was hailed as a voice from above. An ancient stone, unearthed at Oatlands, inscribed with the words: "*Oats shall save this land from destruction,*" was accepted as proof of his godly mission. Parliament insisted, over Charles' protests, that Oates be given living quarters at Whitehall, where he could protect the King, and awarded him £1,200 and a strongly armed guard.

When Sir Edmund Bury Godfrey was buried ten days later he was a Protestant martyr and Oates was regarded as an English Joan of Arc. It was a day of national mourning, and seventy-two clergymen paraded before the bier and the funeral services were conducted by an Anglican minister who used this occasion to rant against the Papists and the conspiracies of Rome. He was loudly cheered and hailed as a servant of God.

This troubled Christopher. He had tried to ignore the fear and hysteria that continued to spread like a plague by devoting himself to his work, particularly St. Paul's. He was eager to finish a portion of the walls before winter set in and halted all building. But it was hard to get the workmen to toil. Most of them were more eager to hang Papists than to lay bricks. Daniel assisted him, but he felt his friend's disapproval. Many Catholics were beaten to death simply because they were Catholics, and he couldn't excuse this to Daniel. Most of the church were behind Oates, which he couldn't justify either. So little that was personal was said between them, and then only what was essential to accomplish the task at hand, Christopher feared this rift would never be healed.

Then, at the Society despite the rule that politics and religion were never mentioned, the only subject discussed was the Popish plot. Most of the members believed Oates, a few wondered, and only Christopher felt he was lying. Pepys said Oates was unfair to York, accusing him of complicity in the plot, but he believed that other Catholics were implicated. Boyle stated he was an authority on theology and uttered a polemic against Romanism; Newton said piety and philosophy should be preserved distinct from each other, but that he knew more divinity than all of them put together; Hooke declared it was nobler to suffer for natural philosophy, not a dread of hell, and to bear the ills they had.

This contention was too much for Christopher and as presiding officer he cut short the meeting. But Evelyn persuaded him to hear Dr. Tillotson preach before the Commons at St. Margaret's about the Popish plot.

Evelyn said, "It is November 5th, the anniversary of the gun-powder plot, and Dr. Tillotson is a friend of yours. You respect his views and nature."

"I do." The Dean of Canterbury and the new residentiary at St. Paul's combined a logical, clear mind with a benevolent nature and was a fellow of the society and his sermons were tolerant and fair-minded.

Yet Dr. Tillotson's usually pleasant face was stern as he preached: "*The Papists are now arriving at that impudence, as to deny there ever was such as the gunpowder conspiracy. Yet I myself have letters written by Sir Everard Digby, one of the traitors, in which he gloried that he was to suffer for it. The Romanists are exceedingly bold and busy everywhere, and we must find out the depth of their conspiracy.*"

Evelyn nodded, but Christopher looked pained.

Evelyn declared, "So you see, even an accomplished cleric like Dr. Tillotson, the best humoured of men, believes that Oates tells the truth."

"But he is not infallable. It is one of the things we oppose in the Catholic church." The congregation looked uplifted, as if they had been urged to wage a divine war against Catholics, and that idea appalled him and he was silent, for he felt hopelessly in the minority.

Soon after Catholic peers were sent to the Tower as traitors on Oates' word, quickly tried, condemned, and executed. The charges were treason, but the real charge, Christopher thought bitterly, was a difference of opinion.

Parliament passed a bill excluding all Catholics from sitting in either House, and declared that all Papists should be disarmed, banished ten miles from London and confined to their homes, that masses were idolatry and an unseemly interference with English rights.

Jane said this was a sensible precaution in view of what was learned of the treasonable activities of the Papists, and when he replied, "That is nonsense," she was hurt, as if he doubted her sanity. But the sensation of the child growing in her prevented her from showing how she felt, and he didn't pursue the matter. She was in good health and he was determined to keep her free from aggravation. From then on, he didn't discuss with her the spreading reign of terror against the Catholics. Even Charles was unable to restrain it, although he was strongly opposed to it.

Christopher reflected sadly, He had lived through many unhappy times, but this was one of the worst, there was so much unreason about.

Early the following April he was puzzled when Daniel failed to appear at his studio for their appointment at ten in the morning. It was not like Daniel to be late, although his friend had been restless and touchy lately, and this meeting was important. Daniel had agreed to survey the materials and money available for St. Paul's, so he could judge when work would resume, if it could resume. The winter had been very severe and while building had ceased, some workmen had been kept on duty at the site to guard the masonry boarded over to protect it from the weather, and the temporary gutters to draw off the rainwater, snow, and melting ice. But even so, he knew, some brickwork would have to be relaid, other damages would be found and other repairs would be necessary.

Had Daniel found something so bad he didn't want to tell him? Was there a quarrel again over how much could be done, how many workmen could be rehired? When Daniel didn't appear by noon, the questions piled up in Christopher's mind and his anxiety increased. Daniel had never failed to keep an appointment. Was his friend in trouble himself?

Jane was planning to visit Windsor the moment the weather was warm enough and the flowers began to bloom, and she was so cheerful he didn't want to trouble her. But she insisted on knowing where he was going, and so he told her, "To St. Paul's to see what is wrong?"

"Do you think the mobs have attacked the cathedral?"

"I don't know. Most of the clergy supports Oates, but Sancroft doesn't."

"Be careful, Christopher." Her eyes filled with tears at the idea of anything unpleasant happening to him. "The brisk boys from Wapping could mistake you for a Papist. Or maybe there is trouble at St. Paul's. Use your official coach with the insignia of your office on it and go armed. I hear that the ladies who go out these days carry pistols in their muffs."

Christopher, to please Jane, heeded her advice and took a squad of soldiers from the palace as an escort. He had a strong feeling that he might need them. Yet he didn't experience any difficulties on the drive to St. Paul's. The Strand and Fleet Street had their usual large number of vehicles, chiefly hackney coaches, and there were spiked heads on Temple Bar which made him wince, but his soldiers cleared the way efficiently.

At the site he sought out Oliver, who was supervising the mending of the stone wall about the masonry, but no construction was going on. The Assistant Surveyor said he was waiting for instructions, since he wasn't sure there would be money to pay the workmen, but he was pleased that what had been done before the coming of winter had not been damaged.

"Oliver, have you seen Mr. Van Doorn?" asked Christopher.

"He was here yesterday and surveyed everything in your name. He didn't leave until he had a complete report for you. But I haven't heard anything about him today. Sir, have you tried his house on Fetter Lane?"

"No. Thank you, Oliver. We will resume construction tomorrow."

"Will there be money, sir? The workmen will not start unless they are paid in advance. Many of them were not paid fully last year."

"Hire those who will work and I'll speak to the Commissioners about the building fund. There was a good sum of money raised several years ago."

At the moment he could hardly look at the site. His dreams of quick progress had become a hauntingly slow rebuilding. Nearly four years had passed since the first stone was laid, yet the cathedral still hadn't taken shape. No wonder, he thought sadly, there were so many jibes about St. Paul's. The choir walls, which he had been ordered to build first, so services could start as soon as possible, didn't even extend waist high. But now he must find out what had happened to Daniel. He hurried toward Fetter Lane, filled with a new and immediate sense of urgency.

Daniel's house was a few doors north of where he had lived with

Anne, one of the buildings that had escaped both the plague and the fire. Most of Fetter Lane had been rebuilt. There was an empty lot where the house he had inherited had stood, but all the debris had been cleared away.

He had no time for memories, for he saw an angry mob in front of Daniel's house, and they were screaming imprecations. He ordered the soldiers to push back the mob, glad he had listened to Jane, for the mob was vicious, and they did so, while the mob retreated slowly, still muttering threats.

And then, as he stood before the front door and it began to drizzle, a window was flung open on the ground floor and Daniel appeared in it.

Christopher asked, "May I come in?"

"It could be dangerous. They will brand you as they have branded me."

"I'll worry about that some other time. What is wrong?"

"They say I'm a Papist sympathiser. Because of Maria."

"Maria?"

"My friend. She is staying here at the moment, for safety."

"Daniel, I'm getting wet out here. It's beginning to rain hard."

"You'll be accused of being a Papist sympathiser. It will hurt you."

"Let me in. I'm used to criticism."

Daniel did so, still reluctantly, and it took time, for his door was heavily bolted. Christopher, who had never been in this home, saw many evidences of comfort. Daniel took him into his reception room and he liked that the floor was well laid, the tapestries hanging on the walls were finely done, the furniture was a splendid carved oak, and there was a portrait of a lovely young woman over the fireplace. As he looked around he heard footsteps behind him and he turned and saw a replica of the woman on the wall approaching him. She was even lovelier in person, he noted, with an abundance of black hair, a fair, creamy skin, a great regularity of features, but surprisingly, with bright blue eyes. An interesting mixture of physical traits, he thought, as Daniel introduced him to Maria Snowden.

Christopher bowed and observed that she wore a cross around her neck and that she was dressed all in black, as if in mourning.

Daniel, seeing his friend's eyes widen at the sight of the cross, said, "Maria is a Catholic. Her grandfather was Spanish, he was one of those washed ashore in Ireland with the wreck of the Armada, and he wed an Irish girl. Their oldest son came to London to earn a living and he married an English woman, and Maria was born here, where her father earned his living as a goldsmith. Until a few days ago."

"He was murdered, Sir Christopher," she whispered tearfully.

"Yesterday. So I came here for safety. But somebody on the street found out."

"He was killed," said Daniel, "Because they found a Roman crucifix in their house on Shoe Lane. We've been unable to go out because this mob is threatening her, too."

"I thought they were persecuting only priests and peers."

"Not any more," Daniel said angrily. "There is talk of chopping off the pretty head of Portsmouth because she is Catholic and French, and now Nell Gwynn is truly '*The Protestant Whore*'. Because of her religion she has become the mob's favourite, the image of Protestant virtue and womanhood."

"I'll have this mob dispersed."

"It won't help. The moment your soldiers are gone they will be back."

"Then you must live elsewhere until this insanity disappears."

"It won't disappear. Not for a long time."

Yet Maria felt that Sir Christopher should talk to the mob, perhaps they would listen to him. He went outside and asked to meet with the leader and two men came forward from the mob which the soldiers had forced back to the other side of Fetter Lane. The first one stated, "I'm Praise-God Barebone and this is my son, Dr. Nicholas Barebone!"

Christopher was startled. He had assumed that this gloomy Puritan, who had ruled Fetter Lane for the Commonwealth, was dead. He had heard about this crotchety, fanatical supporter of Prynne, who had thought Cromwell too tender of conscience in his treatment of the Cavaliers.

Praise-God Barebone wore leather clothes that were Elizabethan. He was very old, slight and gaunt, with a long, straggly beard, and spit-flecked lips, but the mob heeded his every word as if it were the gospel, and so, evidently, sensed Christopher, did his short, corpulent, grinning son.

"I'm Sir Christopher Wren, Surveyor, here on the King's business."

"I know," said Praise-God Barebone. "You risk much giving aid and comfort to Papists. No one will support St. Paul's after that."

"But Mr. Van Doorn is not a Catholic. He is of Dutch ancestry."

"His mistress is. And he regards her with a carnal eye and they live in sin. This woman has a bad character and must be cast out."

His son said, "I own much property here and on the Strand and the presence of a Catholic will destroy its value. People will move out. She must suffer the vengeance of God."

The mob edged closer to Praise-God Barebone to hear his words and he intoned, "Out of Christian compassion, she must be driven out. I reside on Three-Leg Alley, just off Fetter Lane, and I rebuilt my house at great expense after the fire and I don't intend to have it violated now."

"Hear! Hear!" exclaimed the crowd.

The wizened, gaunt old man smelled so from his rage Christopher backed away, and Praise-God Barebone, sensing that, said suddenly, "Old men have more moisture than heat. Your friend is cast into a deep pit by the devil and his hot cloven hoof and he must push it away and pull himself out."

"What do you want?" asked Christopher. "Or expect?"

"The whore!" shrieked the women in the mob. "We must examine her! She has bewitched the man with her Romanism!"

"You see, Sir Christopher," said Dr. Barebone, "my father is merciful."

"Yes," Praise-God Barebone said fearfully. "The Papists surround us with apparitions, and threaten good Christians like myself with assassination, and if they were in power they would burn me as a heretic."

Christopher said, "When the King returned you were not punished for your dissent. And you could have been. The regicides were executed."

"I must strike a blow against the devil. Papal Rome is an image of Pagan Rome and we must never allow either to return to Protestant England."

"But Mr. Van Doorn is your neighbour."

"Not my neighbour!"

"Nor ours!" echoed the crowd.

"Surveyor, I warn you, if you persist in defending Romanism, your work will suffer, the City will not contribute to the rebuilding of St. Paul's. Many of us feel already that the dome you plan will make it a Roman church."

Christopher turned away in disgust. The more he was threatened, the less he could give in. He commanded the soldiers to disperse the mob, but without violence, and then he returned to the house and Daniel and Maria.

He said, "You can't stay here. There is no mercy in them. I will leave a guard here to protect the property, but you won't be safe. Daniel, you and Miss Snowden must stay with me until things quiet down."

"It won't be fair to your wife. She's expecting another child."

"I'll decide that. It will give you and Miss Snowden time to find a refuge. Is there anything you want to take with you?"

"My paintings. Oh, I'll never be a Rembrandt," Daniel snapped when he saw Christopher's surprise. "But it is my expression of life."

"I'm glad you're painting again. Surveying doesn't satisfy you."

"And he is prolific," said Maria. "Daniel overflows with ideas."

"That is the difficulty," said Daniel, "Painting isn't ideas. I'm competent, but my pictures will never be as moving as the ones I lost."

Yet he carefully wrapped his paintings while Maria put on a large, broad-brimmed hat which hid her face, and then Christopher escorted them into his coach and told two soldiers to guard the house until relieved. There was no sign of the mob but as the coach started down Fetter Lane, women ran out of the alleys in which they were hiding and screamed, "Tear off the whore's hat, let us see her face! The devil will fetch her to us yet!" Children, some of them not much older than Young Christopher, pelted the coach with stones and mud, one hit the window and glass shattered at their feet and suddenly Maria was holding Daniel and sobbing painfully.

Daniel felt that Lady Jane was unhappy about his and Maria's presence, that she didn't approve of Maria, although she treated both guests politely. Maria wore plain black and white linen and was demure, yet Christopher was very much aware that under the puritanical clothes, there was an enticing, nubile young woman, while his wife was fat with child.

After a week at Scotland Yard Daniel told Christopher that he and Maria were going to seek refuge in Amsterdam. They were reviewing his report on the state of St. Paul's in the studio, where Daniel felt most at home, and Christopher was thinking, it was discouraging—there was such a shortage of materials, money, hope, workmen. The only abundance was problems. But at Daniel's sudden announcement he looked up from his newest design for St. Paul's, which was still evolving in his mind, and said, "For one who says he doesn't believe in God, you strongly support one who does."

"I don't want to die alone. And we love each other."

"You are fortunate. She is a lovely young lady."

"And a Catholic."

"Daniel, do you hold that against her, too?"

"Of course not! But that is why we haven't married."

"Does she know that you are Jewish?"

"Yes. She says she loves me anyway. But that she can't marry me. She is afraid of hell and eternal fire. Catholics do believe in that."

"Did you tell Praise-God Barebone that you are Jewish?"

"I tried when he accused me of being a Papist. But he refused to believe me. He said I didn't look like a Jew."

Christopher smiled but didn't speak.

Then Daniel asked, "Did you ever see Anne again?"

"No. Did you?"

"Never. But I thought . . ." Daniel caught hold of himself.

"That she might just come back to Fetter Lane?"

"It was possible. Maria and I are leaving for Amsterdam tomorrow. I've made arrangements to go on a ship that my father used to own."

"Why so soon?"

"I don't want anything to change my mind. In the Netherlands, with all its imperfections, Maria and I should be allowed to live in peace."

This time, Christopher had a feeling that Daniel would not return. Yet he couldn't disagree with his friend's decision. He did insist on taking them to the ship in his coach so no one would molest them.

Then it was the moment to say good-bye and Maria blurted out, "I'm sorry, Sir Christopher, I'm to blame for his leaving, I'm . . ." and Daniel halted her and said, "No! No! Nobody is to blame. I've outlived my usefulness here," thinking, For many years I've been in the shadow of Christopher, but in Amsterdam I may be my own man. "But we mustn't complain. We've had many good days."

"Some of the best!" Christopher cried. "If you ever need me!"

"If you ever need me!" repeated Daniel.

"I always have," said Christopher.

"No more. Your designs are the finest I've seen and your drawings would please even Rembrandt."

He had not yet recovered from the shock of Daniel's departure when Evelyn informed him that Pepys had been confined to the Tower.

Evelyn added, "*On a charge of Popery, felony, piracy, and treason.*"

"Will this madness never end?"

"The charge also concerns misdemeanours in the conduct of his office as Secretary of the Admiralty. He is accused of betraying naval secrets to the French, and of planning to overthrow the Protestant religion."

"But he is as devout a Protestant as there is."

"I know. I believe he is unjustly charged. Pepys was a supporter of Cromwell, although few are aware of that, and he has kept that hidden. I believe he was put in the Tower because of his friendship with York. Will you visit him with me?"

"I will be honoured."

Pepys was grateful for their visit and philosophical about his imprisonment. But he was troubled that he needed a hundred pounds to pay for his legal fees and to defray the expenses of his hearing. Evelyn thought their friend had been quite extravagant to be in such a predicament, but when Christopher offered to loan Pepys all of the money he was shamed into giving half. Then he was sorry that he had been soft, yet proud that he had been generous. Now he was convinced that Oates was a vain, insolent liar, and he told Christopher so.

It was a rewarding day for Evelyn when Christopher invited him to be godfather to his newly born son. The child was named William and there was just one distressing note, Lady Jane was absent due to ill health, and Christopher was preoccupied and anxious. Later that week, Evelyn found out why. Lady Jane died as a result of her second pregnancy.

Most of the time during the childbirth she was unconscious but there was one moment when she recovered consciousness and whispered to Christopher, "I'm in a wretched state. I cannot delight you," and the last words he remembered her uttering was a prayer for her soul and that he would live to finish St. Paul's.

Charles' condolences were heartfelt, but they didn't help. Christopher sat in his favourite chair, *Myself*, thinking of Jane buried next to Faith in St. Martin's-in-the-Fields. He had done everything he knew to preserve her health and yet she had died. It was quiet in Scotland Yard, Lucy had taken the three children to Windsor for their health, and he tried to be reflective but it was difficult. Holder and Tillotson had raised enough money for construction to start again on St. Paul's, using the threat of the Popish plot to inspire their congregations to give to the building fund. Holder told him proudly, "Anti-Romanism is the best weapon it has."

He remembered also what Charles had said to him recently.

"They will respect me yet. I have dissolved Parliament, and I will go on dissolving it until the country is convinced I can rule without it. Take my advice, work on what is wanted. Once the Popish plot is forgotten, there will be no money for St. Paul's. If I were you, I would concentrate on the City churches, Winchester Palace, even Trinity, for the City is hostile to the rebuilding of the cathedral and I won't be here forever."

"Your Majesty, we are almost the same age."

"But different men, Sir Christopher, with different responsibilities."

He stood up abruptly and walked to the window, but that didn't ease him, for there was no view of London. Then he strode to the nearby river bank and stared at the City and saw only an empty space where St. Paul's should have been. Yet there were silhouettes of several of his steeples on the horizon and he felt a little better as he realised that there could be much more eventually. So many he had cared for had faded into the past but his designs were still here. No one else was by the waterside and as he looked down the Thames where it curved south of him, he visualised a dome of great beauty and serenity. He owed that to Jane and Faith and so many others, and most of all, he felt, to himself. He choked back his tears and returned to his studio to continue his evolving designs for St. Paul's.

You May Note My Days But

You may note my days but
Start with my last day first
That day will be my best
My tendency was toward growth
Unnoticed by me at first
But later it compelled me
I will have a rich wise death

Stymean Karlen

46

You May Note My Days But

THE NEXT FIVE YEARS NOTHING MATTERED BUT WORK. ENGLAND became earth and landscape, design and construction, brick and stone, and a national studio in which to work. St. Paul's and the library at Trinity College continued to grow at the same slow pace, but as he planned them, and now there were a dozen of his steeples on the horizon of London and forty churches that he was building according to his own designs. Then there were the new commissions. He was building a royal hospital at Chelsea; he had built a chapel at Emmanuel College in Cambridge and a Tower for Christ's Church at Oxford— commissions that gratified him; and he was working hard on the most pressing task of all, a grand palace at Winchester for Charles.

Parliament was dissolved for the last time in 1681 by the King, and from then on Charles ruled the country without interference. He avoided assassination and adulation with equal equanimity and discredited the Popish plot, but while the persecution of the Catholics ceased their rights were not restored and they were not allowed to hold office.

Christopher sought to see his three children every day no matter how busy he was elsewhere; the only exceptions were the days he spent out of London. They had increased since work had started in 1683 at Winchester for the palace, and his appointment as Comptroller of the Works for Windsor after the death of Hugh May. Between the needs for repair on the castle, which he had wanted to do since childhood, and Charles' passion for Winchester, he was away from London more than he liked. He was chosen President of the Royal Society in 1681 and 1682, and he resigned from this office only after the demands of the surveyorship became incessant. Yet he attended meetings when he could, vitally interested in the controversy occurring between Hooke and Newton over planetry motion.

And now there was an urgent summons from Charles to attend him at once. Again the King desired to see him in the royal bedchamber, where this most accessible of monarchs was least accessible to others. It must be an affair of importance, thought Christopher, and he hurried to obey.

He arrived at Whitehall Palace late in the afternoon and Charles was still dressing for supper and the festivities that were to happen afterwards on this Sunday evening, but he was ushered in immediately.

Charles was putting on his royal blue robe over his red gown. The King must be preparing to visit one of his mistresses, reflected Christopher, Charles was so elegant. Then he noticed the King wore loose slippers.

"My heel is sore," Charles said, noticing Christopher's puzzled glance, and ordered his attendants to leave him alone with his Surveyor.

His lined face showed marked signs of age and Christopher recalled the rumours that the King had been ill lately.

"I want a fixed date when the palace at Winchester will be finished."

"Sir, I told you last summer that it will take another year."

"That is too long. I don't want it to become another St. Paul's."

"Sir, I . . . !" Christopher halted, striving to control his temper.

"I know it is not your fault. Nonetheless, ten years have passed since work began on St. Paul's and hardly anything can be seen of what is done."

"Sir, one more year at Winchester and it will be ready for you."

"That is not quick enough." Charles limped over to the window of his bedchamber which looked out on the river southward and added, "Here is a fine view of the City, yet while I can see many buildings that have been rebuilt since the fire, there is no sign of a cathedral."

"There will be, Your Majesty." Christopher's tone grew strong.

"But I doubt I will see it. I summoned you because I want you to resume work at Winchester now, and not wait for spring."

"Sir, it is only February 1st and the winter is very severe."

"It is said that 1685 is the most severe winter in years. But so was 1684 and 1683. I wonder if this is a portent of evil times to come."

"Weather goes in cycles, sir. The Society has learned that."

"Did Professor Newton thank you?"

"No, Your Majesty."

Charles smiled cynically.

"It wasn't necessary. Sir, it will be very difficult to get anyone to work on Winchester in this freezing weather. They will want extra pay."

"I'm aware of the cold. Whitehall should be renovated. Even with the best coal it isn't warm enough. I'm almost always chilled these days. I want a report from you tomorrow on a date when Winchester will be completed."

"Sir, I'll do my best."

"You always have." Then, as if afraid his Surveyor would take advantage of the compliment, he changed the subject. "Did you know that I had given the land for the hospital at Chelsea to Madame Gwynn?"

"She told me, sir."

"Did she tell you also that when she heard about the proposal for a hospital there and that you would design it, she said, '*Charles, I will return it to you for such a purpose*,' and interested me in the scheme."

"Madame Gwynn didn't mention that, but she is very kind, sir."

"She appreciates your courtesy and gifts. Have you ever contemplated marrying again?"

"No, Your Majesty, two deaths are enough."

"Surely you don't blame yourself."

"Not actually, but I have enough to occupy myself, what with my work and three growing children." But he was pleased with Charles' concern. The King's interest was more than politeness and it warmed him. "Your Majesty, you have your heart set on living at Winchester, don't you?"

Charles didn't reply. He should be allowed his dreams, too, even if he was King. The Court thought his wish to build a palace at Winchester was because he liked the climate, its nearness to the sea, but it was more than that. At Winchester he might regain his vitality, or, at least, not feel like an ageing man. The air from the sea, the sunshine should pump blood into his tired veins. Whitehall and Windsor were inherited palaces, but Winchester would be his own, it would express what he loved in life. It would be his Versailles. The design resembled Louis' grand palace; it was French in tone, with a dome that was Wren's choice. He had agreed to a great cupola when the Surveyor had said it would be seen from far out at sea. He saw grey clouds growing in the west and he shivered, anticipating snow. He didn't feel well, despite what he said. He wished he dared to discuss his health with Wren, the Surveyor had so much common sense, but it might give him an advantage that could be costly. Yet, intrigued and attracted by this man's nature, as he was so often, he blurted out, "Sir Christopher, have you ever failed?"

Christopher laughed, relieved. He had feared that he had offended Charles. "Many times, sir. Even now, perhaps."

"With St. Paul's?"

"No, not yet." Christopher's usually amiable features grew stern.

"At Winchester?"

"Please God, I hope not!"

They both laughed.

"But sir, while I learned much about anatomy I was unable to preserve the lives of Faith or Jane. We know so little about our own bodies."

"I'm discovering that every day."

"And where do you think you have failed, Your Majesty?"

For an instant, Charles wanted to strike down the questioner. This was presumptuous, insolent, or was it, with the Surveyor's character? Maybe he could trust him; Wren had no opportunistic motives. He said suddenly, "We shouldn't have fought the Dutch at all. And I've wondered whether the plague or the fire could have been avoided."

"So have I, sir. We must be very careful."

"I've tried to learn from the past." He felt the velvet curtains of his bedchamber and added, "There were many days in my travels when I knew far less. It has caused me to move cautiously on occasion."

"Your Majesty, could the inscription on the Monument blaming the Catholics for the fire be removed? It was put on a few years ago, in 1681."

"I regret that as much as you do, but in this I'm powerless. The City insisted on it in return for my evicting Oates from Whitehall. I'm convinced he lied, but so far, I've been unable to prove it."

"Your Majesty, there are people waiting for you in the anteroom."

"Scarburgh, Sancroft, and Evelyn." Charles laughed. "The first wants to assure me that I will live a long time when he cannot even measure my blood, the second yearns for my soul and the third covets my praise."

"All of them are your devoted servants, sir."

"No doubt. You know them well. What do you want, Sir Christopher?"

"Your good health, Your Majesty."

"I wish I had it to give." Charles remembered the child he had known, and said, "You were always intelligent, even as a boy. Don't deny it. Too much modesty is immodest. And a building can affect eternity."

"As a King can, sir?"

"That is more questionable, but the country is at peace now. Many want me to fight the French or Spanish, but peace is better. Our trade prospers, our colonies in America expand, the Carolinas and New York increase our commerce greatly. Elizabeth took from the Spaniards but we earn it. The only colony that has failed is the one you refused me years ago, Tangier."

"Sir, the country is grateful for the peace."

"*I hope so. I'm weary of travelling and I'm resolved to go abroad no more. But when I'm dead and gone, I do not know what my brother will do. I'm much afraid that when he comes to wear the crown he will be obliged to travel again. And yet I will take care to leave my kingdoms to him in peace, wishing he may keep them so. But this has all my fears, little of my hopes and less of my reason.*"

"You must be tired, sir, to be so pessimistic."

"Ailing, which is worse. This severe cold gives me an aching pain in my side, and I have a chill from Whitehall. But tell no one."

"Not even Dr. Scarburgh, sir?"

"He least of all. At Winchester I can see the sea. I love the ocean. It is never the same two days running, when most people are never different from year to year. You will report on it tomorrow. There will be money for the workmen. I will expect you here at the same time."

"Sir, the shell is ready and we will put in the marble pilings soon."

"Good. Did you ever repair the cellar under the House of Lords?"

"As best I could, sir. But a new building should be erected."

"Later." Charles reached for Christopher's hand and pressed it with unexpected affection, and stated emotionally, "I appreciate your services. Then he put his arm around his Surveyor's shoulder and added, "I will be happy when my house in Winchester is covered with lead."

Afterwards, while Christopher was speaking to Scarburgh, Sancroft, and Evelyn, who were still waiting in the anteroom for Charles, the King entered regally, without any trace of a limp. They approached him to beg an audience and he announced, "Another time. My guests are waiting."

Dr. Scarburgh said, "Your Majesty, you asked me to attend you."

"I feel better, Sir Charles. And you have not cured my sore heel."

"You should rest, sir. It is my professional responsibility."

"And mine is to govern. I trust all of you will join us at the party this evening." Then he was gone, sauntering away gracefully.

Dr. Scarburgh said doefully, "His Majesty risks his health. He insists on seeing his mistresses as much as possible, when he should be resting. He had a superb constitution, vigorous and robust, but he has aged."

Archbishop Sancroft nodded in agreement and said, "It is his constant dissipations. I came here tonight in the hope he would observe our Anglican services, but while it is Sunday, he ignores them."

"Some say," ventured Evelyn, "that he prefers Romanism."

"It is possible," said Sancroft. "It may be one of the reasons he was so critical of Oates and the Catholic persecutions."

"So were you, Your Grace," Christopher reminded the Archbishop.

"I was on principle. Oates was a liar. I'm not sure Charles shared that view. I cannot attend his party tonight. Not on a Sunday."

"Neither can I," grumbled Scarburgh. "I'm desired elsewhere."

When they were gone, Evelyn confided in Christopher, "I wonder about the Archbishop. He is reputed to be a timid, mild man, but in some things he is strong-minded. The Thames is frozen over now and when I suggested to the Archbishop, whom I visited this noon in his palace at Lambeth, that we drive across the river from Lambeth, he was delighted with the idea."

Christopher said, "He is much more resolute and bold than he is given credit for. Come Evelyn, let us attend the festivities."

The party was occurring in the great gallery where he had met Jane and at first he was stricken with nostalgia, but when he saw the gaiety his spirits improved. But Evelyn was censorious, "*I cannot forget this inexpressible luxury, profaneness, gaming, and dissoluteness, and the total forgetfulness of God. It is Sunday evening, yet the King sits and toys with his concubines, Portsmouth, Cleveland, and Mazarin, and a French boy sings love songs. While in this glorious gallery twenty of our great courtiers and other dissolute persons are at basset around a large table, a bank of at least £2,000 in gold before them. I am astonished.*"

Christopher was seeing another side of Charles. A few minutes later the King was in a splendid humour, discussing poetry with Dryden, music with Purcell, and the theatre with Wycherley. Then Nell Gwynn called over to him, "Charles, I hope I shall have your company tonight!"

Charles didn't reply but smiled and said to the three artists, "The great aim of an ally is to engage you in a war, and then to give you as little aid as they can, so you bleed while they prosper. Don't you agree?" They did, and he added, "Yet London seems to have fallen into an easy quiet. When I enter it, I'm even cheered, and blessed. It is a pleasant change."

Christopher's attention was diverted by Pepys, who joined him and Evelyn. Although Pepys had grown quite stout, he was in a fine humour, for he had been freed from the Tower after eight months of imprisonment and last year he had resumed his post of Secretary of the Admiralty and had been chosen President of the Royal Society.

He beamed at them, for they had voted for him, and said, "Charles is in good spirits. I like that."

"But I do not see York," said Evelyn, "although he is back in favour."

"That has made him pious," said Pepys. "He is sure of his succession now. Evelyn, what are you doing here? At this impious Court?"

"I was invited by the King to discuss his gardens at Winchester. He asked me to plan them. I'm an expert. But he spent so much time with Sir Christopher, he had none for me. Or perhaps, he is not interested."

Christopher said, "Evelyn, he is interested, but tonight is a different occasion. He wants to glory in it before it is too late."

"What did he discuss in your audience with him?"

"Winchester."

"Was that all?"

Pepys was listening intently, too, and Christopher said, "I don't see the Queen. Doesn't she usually attend these functions?"

"When she feels it is her duty to the King," said Pepys. "She is still in love with him in spite of the way he has treated her."

"He treats her with courtesy," said Evelyn. "It is his indulgences with his mistresses that offend the righteous."

Christopher's attention was on the beautiful ladies he saw in the great gallery, and their enticing figures in velvet and satin. He had known no women since Jane, and he was possessed with yearning for feminine company. Pepys and Evelyn gossiped about who was in favour, and he searched the female faces as if to find one that appealed to him. But most were painted an inch thick, or wore black face patches, or had a skin that was bleached white with ceruse or had other blemishes. He thought, He could love both fair and dark, both country bred and city born, but he could not love the artificial complexions and false appearances. Then he heard a loud murmur run through the gallery as Charles left suddenly. It was not yet nine in the evening, an extraordinary early time for the King to retire.

Pepys said, "Charles must be ill."

Evelyn said, "Unless he has found a new concubine."

Charles had grown pale, Christopher noticed, just before he had gone and could be in pain. Yet the party went on as if nothing was amiss. Pepys and Evelyn argued over which mistress was the King's present favourite. Pepys believed it was Nell Gwynn, while Evelyn felt it was Portsmouth, for she was the youngest looking. They paused only when Christopher said that he had to go, also, that he had much work to do tonight.

Pepys exclaimed, "But you have earned your place, Sir Christopher!"

"Possibly," said Evelyn, "he has private affairs. A lady to see."

"My daughter. I haven't seen her today. Jane is almost eight and a delight, and looks like her mother." And he wanted his report for the King to be ready. Perhaps Charles was right, there wasn't much time.

Yet when he returned to the palace the next afternoon to keep his appointment with Charles, he was surprised to hear that the King was seriously ill. It was a bitterly cold day and even the anteroom, with the fires blazing fiercely, was chilly and he could imagine how uncomfortable was the royal bedchamber with its exposure on the river. Many courtiers were there, eager to see Charles, and when Christopher saw Dr. Scarburgh emerging from the bedchamber, he approached him and asked how the King was.

"It is hard to say. He has had a seizure. But he takes it bravely."

"Is he seeing anyone, Sir Charles? I have the final plans for his palace at Winchester which he asked to see urgently."

"He is seeing no one except his doctors and his brother and his Queen. I must return to him. I came out here for a breath of fresh air."

Christopher wished he could help, but no one asked his advice.

He came back the following day in the hope he could be of service, but as he sat in the anteroom he was ignored except by Scarburgh, who was eager to tell him how Scarburgh was leading the fourteen doctors treating Charles.

Scarburgh was proud of what he was doing, as if this proved that he was truly blessed, that he was not Sir Charles Scarburgh in vain.

"First," Scarburgh told Christopher in a moment of rest from his labours, "we bled the King for his blood is weak, then we cupped him, and gave him an emetic, a purgative, another emetic. We're doing everything possible. The enema contains antimony, sacred bitters, mallow leaves, rock salt, beet root, violets, fennel seed, saffron, and aloes. We have also forced strong purgatives down his throat, applied sneezing powders to his nose, burning plasters to his body, and raised a blister on his head to draw out poisons."

What he needed most of all, Christopher reflected sadly, rest, fresh air, warmth and love, were missing. He said, "Isn't that too much?"

"Not at all. When he awoke this morning he told me, '*I rejoice greatly in what you have done, Sir Charles, for I know I am still alive, since I feel the pain so keenly.*' But I forbid him to speak, for he must save his strength, although he replied, '*Such a command could kill weaker monarchs.*'"

Scarburgh hurried back to the bedchamber to administer more purges and emetics, and that went on day after day. There were moments when the King managed to be cheerful, to jest, as was his nature, but most of the time he could not hide the pain. Then the remedies resumed, doing more harm than good, Christopher was certain now, but no one heeded him. The fourteen doctors were virtuous men and the most learned in the realm.

Regularly, with Scarburgh in command, they gave Charles cathartics mixed with barley water, absinthe and anise, and extracts of thistle leaves, rue, mint, and angelica. They applied plaster of Burgandy pitch to his body and pigeon dung to his feet. But when Charles grew weak, Scarburgh said it was an emergency and gave him forty drops of an extract from a human skull.

He told Christopher, "To allay his convulsions."

The days became a vast drug as Christopher realised that Charles was dying and the desperate doctors were only making matters worse. He arrived at the palace Thursday night—just five days since the party, which was hard to accept, Charles was so vital then—wanting to speak to him once more. After all, he thought, he had known Charles longer than anybody, even Buckingham or York, who was a year younger, and in his own way, better, for he had wanted less. But the doctors wouldn't allow him in.

Scarburgh did pause in his duties as the King's physician to tell Christopher what he had done, so the Surveyor would recognise how important he was. "He has had such an ill-fated night that finally, I gave him bezoar stone, but his strength is exhausted to such a degree that the whole assembly of physicians have lost all hope and become despondent."

"Possibly, if you allowed him to rest."

Scarburgh went on as if he hadn't heard him. "Still, so as not to appear that we are failing in our duty in any detail, we have brought into play the most active cordial. We have forced down his throat a combination of Raleigh's antidote, which contains an enormous amount of herbs and animal extracts. But Archbishop Sancroft is here. The King is in his hands now."

"Could I speak to Charles? I have good news about the palace at Winchester. It could be finished this summer. That would please him."

"It is not in my hands." Scarburgh returned to the bedchamber, to see if there were any medicines he had forgotten to use.

A little later Sancroft and his bishops emerged from the bed-chamber looking disconsolate. But when the Archbishop of Canterbury saw the Surveyor sitting in the anteroom quietly and patiently, he excused himself from the others and approached Christopher.

"It is no use," said Sancroft. "He is seeing only those he has to see. His brother, the Queen, and I'm afraid, a Catholic priest. I begged him to accept the last rites of our Protestant communion, he is the head of our Church, but he refused, although he thanked me for my entreaties."

"Did he say anything else?"

"The Queen asked his pardon and he replied, '*Poor woman, she asks my pardon, I beg hers with all my heart,*' and he begged his brother to forgive him if he had sometimes seemed unkind, and not to let Nelly starve."

Christopher turned to go. The clocks continued to chime every quarter of an hour, which was Charles' design, and he smelled the little spaniels lying in the bedchamber, for their odour was strong and all the windows were closed to prevent the King from catching a chill. There was nothing he could do, he realised, and there hadn't been from the beginning.

Sancroft said mournfully, "I fear Charles will die in the arms of the Catholic church and that we are in for a Papist reign. It is too bad."

Charles died a few hours later, on Friday morning, just six days after the party he had given on February 1st. A post-mortem was taken of his body, some thought he was poisoned, but if he was, Christopher reflected, it was by his physicians. The funeral was simple, for as Sancroft had suspected, Charles had died in the Catholic faith. The last rites for the King had been given by Father Huddleston, an elderly Catholic priest whom York had kept close for just such an eventuality.

It was an act that Sancroft, Scarburgh, Evelyn, and Pepys found hard to forgive, but Christopher hoped that a completed Winchester Palace would be a fitting monument to the King. He had known Charles all of his remembered life and some of that was buried with him. He realised that Charles would have laughed at tears, or made a cynical or amusing remark, but his eyes were full of them as he recalled how affectionately Charles had put an arm around his shoulder. And had said with his last conscious breath, "*I'm sorry, friends, to cause you such inconvenience, to be so long dying.*"

One Plus One Plus One Plus One is How

One plus one plus one plus one is how
   you add up to what
populates the universe
   A tree has a faith and will not be
overlooked
   A bird has an instinct that can see
you including it
   A rose has a petal that senses your
observance of it
   A cloud a human a brook a frog a day
were born to know you mean them
   One plus one plus one plus one will
prove it

Stymean Karlen

47

One Plus One Plus One Plus One is How

King James ended all work at Winchester. He knew Wren wouldn't mind, for he intended to divert those funds to St. Paul's, and show the nation he was a devout supporter of piety. He ordered Wren to meet him on Ludgate Hill.

Spring was approaching, work was about to resume on the cathedral, and Christopher was glad he arrived early, for the King was prompt, too.

James rode up on horseback, followed by a large entourage of guards, as if he didn't trust the loyalty of the people, although his accession to the throne, so bitterly opposed during the days of the Popish plot, had been accepted by quiet, but genuine rejoicing. Thanks to Charles, thought Christopher, and now the country wanted peace. Behind the King were his closest advisers, Father Edward Petrie, a lean, sombre priest, and Lord Chief Justice Jeffreys, whose heavy, square face wore a scowl. They dismounted with the King and joined him in his examination of St. Paul's.

"Hardly anything is done!" exclaimed Jeffreys. "Your Majesty, do you truly believe this construction should be continued?"

"Of course!" said James. "It will reflect the vigour of my reign. Wren, I will give you whatever help you need."

"Thank you, Your Majesty. I'm sure you will not regret it."

"But you must adapt your design more to the Roman style, since you favour a dome like St. Peter's. And be sure there are oratories. The sooner services can be conducted here the better for all of our souls."

James stood as if he intended to master St. Paul's by his presence, and in some ways, Christopher felt, the new King was imposing. He was tall like Charles, with the same long features, but James was fair where Charles had been dark and awkward where his brother had been graceful. His face was dominated by a long, stiff nose, a petulant

775

mouth, a stubborn chin, and he affected a large yellow wig to express his light complexion.

"When I reconvene Parliament, I will order them to extend and increase the coal dues for St. Paul's. We mustn't allow our piety to suffer."

"Sir, what about Winchester? All work has stopped there, but if it were resumed it would be habitable by summer, as was your brother's wish."

"No!"

"But, Your Majesty . . ."

"I do not enjoy your questions. The matter is closed."

Christopher was disappointed. He wanted to carry out Charles' wishes for Winchester, but from the rigidity of James' expression he realised this was not the time to insist. He turned back to St. Paul's. The walls on the north and south fronts rose one storey above the ground, where much work had been done, and he asked the King to view them.

James did so superficially, then said critically, "You're not very fast. Twenty years have passed since the fire."

Nineteen to be exact, Christopher wanted to remind him, but James was stern, so he said, "Your Majesty, the crypt is virtually finished and the church floor progresses. Would you like to see the crypt?"

James looked at it briefly, drew back distastefully, retreating up the newly laid stone steps to the ground floor, stating, "It is too dark."

"Sir, the dimness of the London atmosphere makes it hard to get much contrast of light and shade, but the twilight effect can be striking."

"Perhaps. You must be sure to have wide side aisles in this cathedral."

Our Anglican faith doesn't have processions, Christopher almost replied, but he said, "They will be as wide as necessary, Your Majesty."

"Make sure of that, Wren."

Father Petrie added, "Sir, the church must contain oratories."

James added, "We must follow our old traditions. If you want my favour, Wren. I intend to appoint a new commission to support my views."

Christopher didn't leave with the King, who was riding to the Monument for the purpose of erasing the inscription that attributed the fire to Popish incendiaries. He agreed with his decision, but he was concerned about James' reasons. There were rumours the King meant to restore Catholicism as the state religion, and once that was done he was converting St. Paul's into a Catholic cathedral. This was an idea that Christopher couldn't accept. He was building St. Paul's so ritual would be reduced, so the congregations would be an integral part of the services, and not be segregated from the clergy. He was resolved not to allow the design he had evolved to be altered. He didn't want to bar Catholics from worship, but St. Paul's was his church; he was an Anglican, he told himself, not because of inheritance, but because of preference.

He recalled Charles' advice that he run for Parliament to support St. Paul's, and when James called for a new Parliament—there had been none the last four years of Charles' reign—he stood for a constituency from Plympton in Devonshire. Both the Whigs who were anti-Catholic and the Tories who supported the Crown desired his support and he was elected.

He was one of those who voted James the money the King requested, in the hope that some of the funds would be used for St. Paul's. He disliked the constant bickering of the Parliament, the lack of attention to the business at hand, the frequent changes of mind, the corruption, but he did like voting funds that might be for St. Paul's.

James, as he promised and to show he was the most pious person in the kingdom, arranged for the funds allotted for St. Paul's to be increased. The King ordered them to be raised from £6,000 a year to £18,000. A munificent gesture, Christopher thought joyfully, far more than he expected, and enough to satisfy his financial needs. But there was a difficulty. The increase in the building funds was not to be available until the beginning of 1687, almost two years away. His mood changed to pessimism; so much that was discouraging could happen in the interval.

At the site there were new difficulties. Marshall and Strong, whom he had come to depend on, had died, and while Strong was succeeded by his brother, many adjustments had to be made. Other vital employees passed away, Oliver was growing old and frail, no one had taken Daniel's place and he missed him as much as ever. He sent out calls for surveyors and he hoped he would find several able young ones, for youth had become vital as he realised that the building of the cathedral would take many more years. He might even need an assistant who could outlive him, although this was not a prospect he relished. He was going on fifty-three, and while he felt fine and had not had a sick day in years, so few lived past fifty he was very much aware of his own mortality. Yet he was pleased that his body still responded to all the necessary physical situations.

He stood in the Chapter House on the site a few days after

he had sat as a member of Parliament, and as he looked outside he was afflicted with more pessimism. It was pouring with an intensity that was terrifying, the wind lashing the rain against the construction with a torrential fury that threatened everything in its path. It had rained incessantly for a week, often with gale force, and while he had built an elaborate and efficient drainage system for the fabric, there was so much water on the site he wondered how much longer that could endure.

And all labour, once again, had ceased. But what he feared most was an accident that would require extra funds. He felt there was no one to turn to for aid; the old Commission had lost interest in St. Paul's, it was taking too long for their patience; the Protestant City authorities were hostile, especially now that the Catholic King was supporting it; Sancroft and most of the clergy were busy elsewhere defending their Church against the encroachments of James' Catholicism; while James was concentrating on enlarging his Catholic chapels in his favourite palace, St. James.

The neglect had just one advantage, his mind ran on, it allowed him to clarify his design so it was becoming, with the passage of time, more like the Greek cross plan and less like the Warrant, although the Latin cross ground plan remained. What he had learned in the building of St. Stephen, Walbrook, St. Mary-le-Bow, and other city churches—over forty now bore his design—was helping him greatly in the evolution of St. Paul's.

His reverie ended abruptly as he heard a knock on the door. He looked out and saw with relief that the rain had subsided suddenly. He decided that it must be Oliver, informing him that work could resume.

He opened the door and saw a drenched Oliver, looking stricken as his assistant cried out, "Sir, the pipes in the drainage system have broken. Part of the foundations have caved in and formed a deep trench, and the water is seeping into the crypt. Cracks are appearing in the stone facing and in many places mortar is oozing out of the joints."

Christopher, as if part of him had anticipated this, hurried to the damaged drainage system without another word, led by a frightened Oliver.

It was even worse than he expected. He was grateful the rain had stopped, a few more hours of downpour and the damage could have been beyond repair, and even now, he wasn't sure. There were only a few workmen on the site because of the rain and they were serving as watchmen, but he ordered them to follow him. Holding the lantern himself, he was the first one into the crypt where the masonry had cracked and the leakage was most severe, although Oliver warned him it could be dangerous. But the walls had held.

They should, he assured himself, He was building for eternity.

After he inspected the damage he returned to the drainage system where the water pipes had broken. This was the most immediate repair. He told Oliver to fetch every mason, carpenter, and bricklayer that could be found, and waded into the ditch to investigate the break. Then, without pause, as the workmen assisted him, he laboured all night to repair the damage. By morning, while others held the torches, lanterns, and candles, for he did much of the work himself, the drainage system was fixed. He was glad of his skill with tools—he could do most of the things the workmen could do—and it was a relief and a release to be working rather than waiting.

But he didn't pause to rest. The skies were still grey, and while he was grateful it hadn't rained the last few hours, he couldn't take that for granted. He returned to the crypt and the repairs that were needed there. He worked all that day and night to fix the cracks in the masonry with the help of the masons, bricklayers, and carpenters Oliver obtained. Christopher felt better when he saw that the foundations had not caved in as Oliver had said, but the crust of the pot earth, which was less thick here than elsewhere on the site. But fortunately, he thought, because of the precautions he had taken years ago, this earth was not sand, but substantial soil, and everything was repairable and permanent damage had been avoided.

Yet while Oliver, who slept the second day of the emergency, was afraid the Surveyor would collapse—Sir Christopher laboured forty-eight hours without a halt, fearless of danger—he couldn't stop until he was certain everything was in order again. There were many moments when he felt exhausted, that he couldn't move another step, but always, as he realised what could happen if he didn't persist, he managed to continue.

Later however, when he reached his home in Scotland Yard, he couldn't sleep. He lost track of the time and it didn't matter, he told himself, as long as St. Paul's was in good health. There was still daylight in the sky and he was relieved that it hadn't rained any more. He walked into his studio and sat in his favourite chair, and as he felt the sturdy back of *Myself*, and leaned on its arms he felt refreshed.

He had a new problem to solve. He wasn't sure the cracks in the masonry in the crypt were from the water; they could be from the weight that was growing on them. Yet he couldn't displace them, the work was too far on its way. The only remedy was to make sure that the great piers could hold the most massive weight for centuries to come without strain. Or perhaps lighten the load. Then there was the question of money. He had promised the workmen who had been summoned for the emergency that they would receive double pay, and he could imagine the outraged protests from the building fund. If it wasn't available from that source, he would have to give it to them out of his own pocket. As it was, the two hundred pounds he was paid each year as Surveyor was not enough to live on.

He said to himself aloud for consolation, "I'm fortunate to have other commissions, and at least, Charles paid me regularly as Chief Surveyor."

"What is that, father?"

He saw his eight-year-old daughter, Jane, standing in the doorway. She looked very pretty, with her dark brown hair and pert features that reminded him of her mother, and her hair tied with pink ribbons, and when she saw his pleasure at the sight of her, she ran up to him and hugged him.

"Shouldn't you be in bed, Jane dear?" he asked. She was not robust, although she had a fine complexion and possessed his grey eyes.

"It is still daylight. I haven't seen you for several days, but Lucy said you were in London, working on the cathedral. So when I noticed that the hangings were open and I know you like the light . . ."

"You decided I was here."

She nodded proudly, then said softly, "I missed you, father."

"I missed you, too. Come, sit here, with me, on *Myself*."

"*Myself?* What is that?" She looked bewildered.

"It is what I call this chair. I had one like it when I was about your age and lived in Windsor at the Deanery. Everyone else preferred the big chairs because mine was too small for them, but it was fine for me."

"May I sit in *Myself* now?"

"Of course, dear." He got up and she sat in it like a Queen. And as he admired her and she glowed with happiness, he thought, Jane was the most gifted of his children. Young Christopher, who was eleven, was a student at Eton because of its closeness to their house at Windsor, and while his oldest child was attractive, usually amiable, he was without much curiosity or reverence for knowledge, and his youngest child, William, had difficulty in learning. But Jane was like himself at her age. She loved to read, she took instructions quickly. Nothing delighted her more than to spend a day in his studio while he worked on his designs, reading history and the poets, even Homer and Horace. She knew Latin as well as he had at eight, and he liked her taste. And she had one gift he had lacked, she was musical. She had a sweet voice and she was studying singing and the harpsichord with Purcell, keeper of the King's keyboard and wind instruments and composer for the King's violins. Evelyn, who was proud of his knowledge of music, thought Henry

Purcell too young, not yet thirty; he preferred the Italian masters who had tutored his children. But Christopher liked that Purcell was English. It was fine to be guided by Italian art, he believed; he was, too, but better to be your own man.

Suddenly Jane, afraid she was losing his attention as she saw the absent-minded look in his eyes, pulled him close to her.

As his daughter held him tight and kissed him and gave her love fully, he realised he desired very much to be loved, that he didn't want to resist, but it must be truly felt and trusted. And this was so true of Jane. He wasn't even certain about Young Christopher, who could be devious and difficult, or William, who tended to be sullen and to retreat within himself, but Jane gave of herself whole-heartedly, without restraint.

"Father," she said abruptly, "you told me there are many things I should learn. When are you going to teach me?"

"Your tutor is a learned man, a graduate of Pembroke Hall, Cambridge."

"But he has no imagination. When I talk to my flowers, he says I'm talking to myself. Did my mother cry when I was born?"

"She laughed, dear. She was very happy. We both wanted a girl."

"You did." She was surprised. "I thought boys were wanted. I think Lucy feels that way. She favours Christopher."

"Lucy was close to Christopher's mother. But she loves you, too."

"Not like you do." She snuggled into his arms, preferring their warmth to the oak chair. "You listen to me, whatever I say. When you are home."

He had a stab of regret. He had been home too little since her mother had died. He must spend more time with his children, especially Jane, who was so responsive. He asked, "Would you like to see St. Paul's?"

"Father!" She slid off his lap, her eyes glowing, and cried out, "You will take me yourself?"

"Myself."

She hugged him with an abandon she had never exhibited before and skipped joyously around the studio and shouted, "Can I count the stones?"

"There are a great many of them."

"Father, I'm a good counter."

It was odd, he thought, of all his children, she seemed the only one who had inherited his gift for mathematics. But it was of no use to her as a female, except as a pastime. It was too bad, he said to himself, and then as he held her in his arms and kissed her tenderly he was glad she was a girl; it would have been too difficult to express this emotion to his sons; it would appear unmanly. "Dear, we will both count the stones."

At St. Paul's the next day, after he arranged to give the workmen who had responded to the emergency the extra pay out of his own pocket and he was relieved to see that fair weather was continuing, he showed his daughter the entire construction. She was fascinated with it, and she asked, "How do you count the stones, Father?"

"I don't. There are too many. Although I wish I could."

"Do you feel like you are putting every stone into it?"

"Sometimes, dear."

She nodded and wanted to see the crypt. The interior didn't frighten her, but it puzzled her and she asked, "Why is it so necessary?"

"Important people will be buried here."

"Will you be one of them, father?"

"Jane!" Then he laughed, she was so serious and concerned. "Of course not! I'm just the surveyor. Archbishops will be buried here, and Kings perhaps, statesmen, generals, admirals, and painters and poets, I hope."

"Why?"

"This is the custom."

"Many things are the custom. When you were my age was that true?"

"Even more so, dear."

"I wouldn't like to be put in this crypt. I would like to see the sun when I'm buried."

"Jane, that is a long way off. You mustn't talk like that."

"My mother died young. Father, did yours?"

"Yes." He sighed and explained, "I never knew mine either. It is another thing we have in common. It is strange."

"Did you love my mother?"

"Very much. As I love you. But we mustn't talk of the past. You have a bright future ahead of you." He took her up to the church floor and she wanted to climb up the huge scaffold masts which were being built to support the rising walls, but he said, "No, it is not fitting."

"Have you ever climbed them?"

"When I had to."

Her attention was diverted by a blade of grass growing through the cathedral floor and it filled her with wonder. He ordered it removed and the crack patched, but she looked at him as if he were committing a brutal act although he explained that the grass had no place here. She felt it had a place anywhere. The child was so sad he suggested that she view some of the other things he had designed and that made her happy again, even while she felt that her father was using this to distract her.

Jane didn't care much for the Monument, the height made her

dizzy and she thought the column monotonous. The child was intrigued by the shape of the steeple on St. Mary-le-Bow, and it didn't make her giddy when she gazed at it, although she thought it was taller than the Monument.

"You are right, it is." He was pleased with her powers of observation. "234 feet to 202 feet. Now I will show you a church with a dome."

She liked the dome of St. Stephen, Walbrook. It reminded her of a round, smooth apple. But she was excited when he took her to Oxford and Cambridge; she had heard much about his designs at the universities.

The child's favourite fabric at Oxford was not the Sheldonian Theatre as he expected, she said it was pressed in, irregular, but she loved the bell tower he had built for Christ Church. Known as the Tom Tower, it was one of his rare designs in the Gothic fashion and she was fascinated by its rhythmical construction. She begged to hear the bells rung and when her father had this done she regarded him as a worker of miracles.

At Cambridge he showed her his chapel at Emmanuel College, for that was finished, and again she was intrigued by her father's sense of order and proportion. She counted, "Five windows, three windows, five windows over five arches, three arches, five arches." He was amused and pleased with her love of numbers. But what gratified her at Emmanuel enchanted her at Trinity. The library interior wasn't done yet, but the exterior was, and she preferred that there was no break in the front as there was at Emmanuel. She gasped in wonder and cried out, "Father, this is the most beautiful building I have ever seen!"

"You exaggerate, dear," he replied, but he was happy with her feeling. He had taken great pains with his plans for this fabric. After St. Paul's, it was his favourite design. While the work had gone more slowly than he liked and there were many delays because of money, he hadn't made any compromises with his design. This was his idea of balance between the horizontal and vertical view of the library. "But I'm glad you like it."

"I love it."

"You forgot to count."

"No, I didn't. It has eleven arches and eleven windows."

"Yes, dear." Christopher saw Newton, who was a Professor at Trinity, approaching, sunk in reverie. His stockings were untied, his surplice was half off, his shoes were down at their heels, he wore no wig and Christopher, whose hair was still brown, noticed that the much younger Newton's was grey. Newton held papers in his hand but he wasn't looking anywhere but inwards. For a moment Christopher was tempted not to halt him, but Newton was facing the front of the library now and he wondered what the mathematician thought about it—if he thought about it.

Newton wasn't surprised by the appearance of Christopher, but annoyed by the inconvenience of the interruption. Yet when he was introduced to Jane, while he didn't smile—Christopher couldn't remember the last time he had seen Newton smile—he bowed and said, "I'm honoured, Mistress Wren."

She curtsied and said, "Sir, my father built this."

"I know. It has a unity of creation worthy of the universe."

Christopher was surprised. Newton rarely praised anything. He said, "I've wondered if you ever saw it."

"I teach here. Of course I see it. When it is necessary to see. I'm devoted to this garden and I cannot endure to see a weed in it. Although, often, I wonder why I teach. So few want to hear me, and fewer understand me, that frequently I read to the walls. It is not a virtuous feeling."

Jane ventured, "Sir, don't you think the library is beautiful?"

"Child, it is useful, which has its own beauty. Books are rare and they must be treated respectfully. They must be honoured and housed like princes. Books have minds of their own. Do you read much?"

"Yes, sir, as much as I can."

"Good. Wren, I have a problem. Hooke still disputes my findings on celestial motion and gravity. I do not think it worthy of the Society. I doubt I should continue as a member. I cannot waste my time in quarrels."

"I think I have a remedy. Come to the next meeting and you will see."

There Christopher proposed: "*Since there is a serious difference of opinion between Mr. Hooke and Mr. Newton concerning planetary motions I am offering a book worth forty shillings to whoever will give us a convincing proof that their theories are correct.*"

Edmund Halley, the young astronomer and protégé of Newton, who had become a member of the Society at the age of twenty-two, stood up and said, "I propose we put a limit of time on this." Not yet thirty, lean, dark, very active physically, he added, "Our esteemed colleague, Professor Newton, already has put many of his findings in writing, so we do not have to take his word for them, as we have to do with Mr. Hooke."

"I will have my findings written!" Hooke shouted, flushing angrily.

Christopher wasn't sure that Newton was listening. The professor sat in the rear of the meeting room as if Hooke's emotionalism was vulgar.

Pepys said, "As President, I recommend that we allow the gentlemen one year to put their findings in writing that will be available to us."

"That isn't necessary," said Hooke. "I will have mine much sooner."

"Regardless, a year is more sensible. Do you agree, Mr. Newton?"

Newton shrugged, as if it were a matter of indifference to him, but Halley said, "Mr. Pepys, I'm sure he does. He has confidence that his principles will be acceptable to the other members of the Society and that you will do him the honour of publishing them."

"I don't know whether they should be published," Newton said abruptly. "That may cause confusion. I consider the account of the creation in Genesis is adapted to the judgment of the vulgar, but it has given great concern in certain quarters and the consequences may cause me suffering."

"Nonetheless," said Evelyn, "While I differ with Professor Newton's theological observations, we should hear his philosophical ones. And if he prefers, regard them confidentially. They do have a place here."

Halley said, "Perhaps, Newton, if I work on your manuscript and notes, your observations can be ready for publication next year."

"Nonsense," Newton replied indignantly, "I don't need any help. I can do the work myself. My Latin is as good as anyone's. If I'm reluctant to make known my discoveries, it is because I don't wish to publish anything that will be taken as an attack on Christianity."

"Then write a preface to that effect, sir."

"How, Halley? I do not wish to support Atheism."

"When you complete your treatise about our system, say that your principles are such as might work with a belief in the Deity."

"Nothing will rejoice me more than to find it useful for that purpose."

Christopher said, "You will prepare your proof for us at your leisure?"

"I do not need leisure," Newton snapped. "My principles have been in my mind for years. I will move without delay. Which I doubt Hooke will."

Hooke jumped furiously to his feet and sneered, "The whole world will look with admiration on my findings, not Newton's. Wren's forty shillings brings the argument to reality. I was the first to discover the rotation of Jupiter, as I have been in so many things." In his emotion he became giddy and he had to sit down to keep from fainting.

Christopher observed sadly, Hooke, always pale, had grown ashen, and his misshapen body had become more bent and deformed with age. While he believed that Newton was right and Hooke was wrong, he felt sorry for his friend. He was one of the very few who could endure his suspicious, jealous temper, but then Newton was the same way. And Hooke's ability to anticipate discoveries was phenomenal. He said, "When the Society was founded, it was the hope that all kinds of views could be presented. We mustn't forget it is still our purpose, no matter what else happens."

"Agreed!" cried the others. "We will wait a year, but no longer!"

Christopher thought of his daughter's wonder at the sight of the blade of grass forcing its growth through the strength of St. Paul's, and he hoped he would feel the same way at Newton or Hooke's discoveries, whoever won the precious forty shilling book.

Lord Prove That You Know Me

Lord prove that you know me
You should know how

If I were you Lord I would know how
Shall I tell you

I wouldn't profane you
by knowing more than I should

Lord prove that you know me
I await it

Then Lord I will tell you
I am you Lord in doubt about myself

Stymean Karlen

48

Lord Prove That You Know Me

SEVERAL WEEKS LATER, IN JUNE, 1685, THE DUKE OF MONMOUTH, Charles' oldest son, invaded England with a small army. While he was illegitimate, he hoped to arouse the country to put him on the throne as the Protestant King. When he failed and he was captured the nation's support swung in favour of James. Much of London turned out to see Monmouth beheaded on Tower Hill, then to witness the pillorying of Oates, who was whipped at the end of a cart from Newgate to Aldgate. And the words on the Monument that accused the Papists of starting the fire were erased from it.

Christopher was glad about the Monument, but Monmouth's fate saddened him. He was disgusted with the London mob, who reviled Oates with the same passion they had heeded him. But what troubled him most was James' revenge on those who had followed Monmouth. Jeffreys hung hundreds of them on the authority of the King, and many more were sold as slaves to the planters of Jamaica and Barbadoes. The tales he heard of Jeffreys' "Bloody Assize", especially against the peasants of the west country, where Plympton was, made his blood run cold, the suffering was terrible.

Yet when Parliament met in November, James rewarded Jeffreys' reign of terror with the highest post in the land, Lord Chancellor. The weather was dry, which helped Christopher's work on St. Paul's and the city churches and James hadn't interfered, but he was sick at heart over what was happening to his beloved country. The dispute between Newton and Hooke became a waiting for the philosophers to submit proof in writing of their principles, but James assumed he didn't need proof of anything he was doing. The King made it clear that he intended to govern by divine right, and that his realm would become as Catholic as he was.

This forced Parliament, which had agreed with James in the spring, to resist his wishes and in his anger and spite he dismissed them.

Christopher voted against the King; he couldn't approve of a policy that could eventually change St. Paul's into a St. Peter's. He expected to be discharged from his post as Chief Surveyor, or at least to be severely reprimanded. Instead, there was a constant stream of orders.

James' attitude was: Only Wren could give him the estimate of the cost of the new stables he was building at St. James' Palace; design the next planting in the gardens at Hampton Court; soothe the complaints from Winchester, where the stoppage had caused great inconvenience and expense; and build a Catholic chapel for his Queen. These assignments annoyed Christopher, but he did them conscientiously, except the chapel, which he avoided by saying there was a shortage of the kind of stone it needed.

Then it was 1686 and a year after the date set by the Society for the award of the forty shilling book. Newton came reluctantly, as if only Halley's will propelled him, but he held a manuscript in his hand.

Evelyn, Aubrey, Dryden, Scarburgh, Holder, and more recent members, Denis Papin, William Penn, Robert Pitt, and Benjamin von Munchausen were present. After Pepys, as President, called the meeting to order and everyone was attentive, Hooke took the floor with passion.

He said, "I appreciate the members' concern with this question, but I've been ill. But whatever Newton has written is in my head."

Christopher asked, "Are we going to talk about gravitation?"

"Of course. I know how it exists."

Halley interrupted, "Yet Mr. Hooke, it is Professor Newton who has proven it with evidence in his manuscript. As he will demonstrate."

"I'm not sure that I should," said Newton.

Newton looked so uncomfortable that Christopher wondered if his reluctance to publish his findings were due to an intense craving for privacy. Or was it that he was never sure? Or suspicious that his findings would be stolen or claimed by someone else? Or that the vital thing was to find out and the rest was unimportant? Yet there was vanity in him, and ambition, and a concern with what the world thought of him.

Halley said, "In this book, the *Principia*, Newton proves that gravity is universal, that it governs celestial motion as well as our own."

Newton explained what he had written, and as Christopher listened the surveyor realised that the evidence was on his side. Hooke's vehement protest that he had given Newton the first hint of his findings were an admission that Hooke, too, accepted Newton's conclusions as correct.

Newton stated, "The nature of this force which causes the apple to fall to the ground is the same as that which causes the moon to move around the earth, and the planets to maintain their orbits about the sun. I have verified their positions and the proof is in this manuscript."

Hooke said, "Until it is published how can we be sure?"

"You can be sure. I've directed my whole energy to these principles."

"Newton, I wrote you years ago about these ideas."

"But you lacked the mathematical ability to prove it."

"I was first."

"But I was right." Newton turned to the others. "As early as 1665 and 1666, before I knew Hooke, I came to these conclusions. It is one thing to watch an apple falling from a tree and another to know why. It is not enough to be hit on the head, a head must contain something in it which can speculate. I have all the proper calculations in this manuscript."

"And you took them from me. I demand that justice be done."

"You were helpful, but many were. Without the earlier findings of Sir Christopher, I might never have discovered the laws of motion."

"In this I agree," said Hooke. "Wren, you could have discovered and revealed all this if you had devoted yourself to astronomy, rather than allowing yourself to be distracted by architecture, an inferior art."

"But Newton has," replied Christopher, "and I believe he is right."

Newton said, "I have expressed my indebtedness in *Principia*." He read:

"By the same (the first two laws of motion), together with the third law, Sir Christopher Wren, Dr. Wallis and Mr. Huygens, the greatest geometers of our times, did determine the rules of the collision and mutual rebound of hard bodies, and communicated their discoveries to the Royal Society, agreeing among themselves as to those rules. Sir Christopher Wren confirmed the truth of the theory before the Royal Society, by the experiments of suspended balls. He established that bodies absolutely hard return one from another with the same velocity with which they meet."

He paused, then added, *"Without this, and other of Sir Christopher's findings, I doubt I would have found the laws of motion and gravitation."*

"It is kind of you to express this, Newton," said Christopher. "But this is the way of learning. It doesn't begin just in one mind, but is the product of many minds even though it is usually resolved by one."

Halley said, "I move that the book be awarded to Professor Newton."

The vote was overwhelmingly in favour of that, although Hooke declared, "I'm being robbed of the fruits of my labour."

Newton said, "I do not have to publish. It will not alter anything."

Hooke smiled, as if to say that was so, but Halley reminded Newton, "It will help others to learn."

Christopher said, "I propose that the Society publish the *Principia*."

"I agree," said Pepys, "in principle. But it will have to wait. We have just done a publication of Willoughby's four volumes on *The History of Fishes*, and we are in debt and we cannot undertake anything new now."

Newton said determinedly, "I will not publish it at my own charge."

Evelyn suggested, "Perhaps it should be done privately."

"No," Halley said positively, "Publicly."

Hooke said, "Or be deferred until we are sure of its conclusions."

Pepys was annoyed. He considered himself a connoisseur of books and since his elevation to the Chair of the Society, he had no intention of allowing Hooke to spoil it. If it was in his power to promote natural philosophy and his own reputation he would. "We must find other means."

Halley declared, "I will do it myself."

"At your own expense?" Pepys asked with surprise.

"If it will contain the imprimatur of the Royal Society."

Hooke pointed out, "That will require the King's permission. Every publication must be licensed and many are not. James' views are rigid."

Pepys said hopefully, "But he has been attentive to mine. Because of his interest in the Navy. I will speak to him on behalf of the *Principia*."

Newton said, "Let Sir Christopher consider what is fit for the press."

"I would be honoured," Christopher replied, "But Halley is more suitable. He is better acquainted with the contents and a skilled astronomer."

He suggested this as a motion and it was carried with Hooke abstaining. Then he proposed that the *Principia* be published with the authorisation of the Society. This was approved unanimously, even Hooke assenting, although grudgingly. After further discussion, the following resolution was drawn up: "*The Council of the Royal Society orders that Mr. Newton's book be printed and that E. Halley shall undertake the business of looking after it, and printing it at his own charge, which he engages to do.*"

This settled, Newton asked about the prize—the forty shilling book.

"Oh, yes," said Christopher, and handed him a copy of *Paradise Lost*.

Newton looked puzzled while Evelyn exclaimed, "Forty shillings for that? Milton wrote for the Regicides. A most unworthy fellow."

Pepys said, "I have a copy for which I paid only three shillings."

Christopher said, "This was a presentation copy for Charles, with Milton's signature, and specially bound. This copy is very rare."

Newton examined the book with the crowned monogram of Charles stamped in gold on the panels of the back and said, "But I hear he uses the Ptolemaic system, that his universe is Pre-Copernican. His ignorance can hardly be considered advantageous to his poem and his argument."

"It has many fine and splendid poetic conceptions of the universe."

"I do not have much inclination for the fine arts."

"If you don't want the book I will give it to someone else."

"I do. It is the Society's affirmation of my place as a philosopher. Wren, I've never understood how someone as gifted as you are in astronomy and mathematics can waste his time on earthly matters such as buildings when there are so many heavenly matters to be explored."

They were alone now, for the others, Hooke too, were carefully examining the contents of the manuscript of the *Principia*, which Halley held.

"Each of us must live under his own oak tree."

"And you take even less pains than I do to secure for yourself the credit for your various inventions and discoveries."

Perhaps, he thought, that was because Hooke had to be first, Newton had to be right, but he had to know. However, he said, "My work engages me. I enjoy using my natural curiosity. That is enough."

"Wren, I'm not a prophet. I've had no experiences that are not common to other men. If I observe an apple rather than eat it, others could."

"Then you may enjoy *Paradise Lost* after all. There is a vivid human imagination in it. It has greatness in it, as your work does."

Newton, instead of looking pleased was almost sad as he replied, "*It may be so, but it is the facts and experiments that interest me. I do not know what will appear to the world, but to myself I seem to be only like a boy playing on the seashore, and diverting myself in now and then finding a smoother pebble or prettier shell than ordinary, while the great ocean of truth lies all undiscovered before me.*"

Christopher tried to use Newton's words to guide him in the

difficult months that followed the Society's decision to publish the *Principia*, and to be consoled by the latter's discoveries. This was essential, for the civil quarrels increased daily in bitterness. The various religious sects insisted they possessed God's truth and that the other faiths were liars. No matter where he turned it was impossible to avoid the sectarian battles which were splitting the nation. Yet he had to push ahead with St. Paul's. He revised his plans for the part of the site where the masonry had cracked so less weight would be borne by the great piers, yet so the space under the dome would have a harmonious repose. He also began the vaulting of the choir, the first portion of the cathedral that was to be roofed and finished, so that services could be held. But while the work on St. Paul's improved, the world grew worse. 1686 was a sad year, he thought, except for the cathedral and the *Principia*.

Early the next spring he was surprised and pleased when Newton visited him in the studio at Scotland Yard and gave him a copy of his book. There was more dissension in the land and the study of natural philosophy seemed an even greater blessing than before. And he was touched by Newton's gift. The mathematician was not one to bestow affection lightly.

"This is a first copy. I wanted you to have one before anyone else."

"I am honoured. May I examine the book?"

"Please do. It is not as finely bound or inscribed as that copy of *Paradise Lost* you gave me, but it is printed in readable type."

Christopher saw that the book was a small quarto of 500 pages, the price nine shillings. The text was in Latin, as were all learned books, the title page said: *Philosphise Naturalis Principia Mathematica.* Rather formal, he reflected, for a book that revolutionised man's view of the universe. The inscription stated: "*The author is Lucasian Professor of Mathematics at Trinity College, Cambridge, and a Fellow of the Royal Society*". Beneath, in large letters, was the word, *Imprimatur*, and under that he saw the name of Pepys, as President of the Royal Society, and the date, July 5th, 1687. He was startled, it was only April 25th, 1687.

Newton saw Christopher's puzzled look and said, "That is the date of publication, but Halley printed the books in advance, before the licensing authorities could change their minds and censor it. As it is, with the current troubles, I'm surprised it hasn't been suppressed."

"What troubles?" There were so many these days it was impossible to tell what Newton was referring to.

"Didn't you hear how James imposed his own candidate on Oxford as Dean of Christ Church, even though he has no qualifications for the post except that the King prefers him because he is a Catholic?"

"I heard. It is a foolish decision. That is a position which demands the highest academic abilities, not a sectarian point of view."

"James is trying to do the same thing at Cambridge."

"I'm not surprised."

"But we are not going to allow it."

Christopher was surprised, especially by Newton's vehemence.

"If we allow one Catholic priest to enter, there will be more, and eventually the Protestant nature of the university will be destroyed."

"That is true."

"I'm one of a group that is to appear at Westminster Hall this afternoon before the Privy Council to defend our view. Will you attend?"

"I don't know."

"You're probably right. It could harm your position with the King."

"That isn't why I'm hesitating. I have another appointment."

"Your presence could be consoling."

And possibly, and more importantly, assert his own point of view. He said, "I will come. I hope you win."

"We must win. Eventually. We are right. And God is on our side."

Christopher wasn't so sure, but he went with Newton to Westminster Hall.

Jeffreys conducted the hearing with the spite of a Prynne, Christopher thought, and Newton reminded him of his uncle, Bishop Matthew Wren, in the strength of his defence. He observed wryly, The more history changed, the more it was the same. The Lord Chancellor was determined to impose his will on Cambridge, which was the King's will, and Newton, who was the most outspoken of the delegates supporting the University's position, was just as determined in his defence. Jeffreys harangued Newton, sought to browbeat him, his voice turned cruel, threatening, but the professor refused to be silenced, even after Jeffreys dismissed the Vice-Chancellor of Cambridge—the nominal leader of the delegation—from his post.

When the Lord Chancellor stated that as a former student at Trinity, he knew more about the College than they did, Newton rose from his seat.

He ignored Jeffreys' order to sit down and said, "You may establish such a claim, sir, but as of 1662, you were still my junior by a year."

"You are insolent, Professor."

"And you are in error, sir. It is not a diploma to a monk that we resist. That is a simple, trivial matter. What we are defending are the rights of the University not to be subverted by religion."

"If you are not careful you will be put out of the University."

"If you are not careful, sir, there will be no University."

Christopher had never seen Newton so resolute, so willing to face the world, it was a side of him that he had not seen before and he was amazed.

Jeffreys shouted, "You are dismissed! All of you!" He commanded the council chamber to be cleared, and Christopher joined Newton on the way out to express his support and to see how his friend felt.

Newton glowed as if his emergence into public life revitalised him, and as they stood in the Old Palace Yard, he said, "Jeffreys is a brute and James' mind is empty of intellectual concepts, but they won't dare attack the University if we continue to resist. That ground is dangerous." He adjusted his simple wig, brushed his plain clothes. "And Cambridge will resist. James is not a Cromwell. He will back down if opposed."

"But suppose the King doesn't?"

"Would you have us behave differently? Should we surrender?"

"No. What you've done is the only course possible."

"Yes. As long as I teach, neither religion nor the other rights of the University must be invaded. Otherwise, it is no longer a university."

"Have you read *Paradise Lost?*"

"Some of it. Milton's views of the universe disturb me."

"They are the expression of his vision and imagination."

"But the universe is too important to be treated erroneously."

James' response to Cambridge's defiance was to dissolve Parliament, to turn Magdalen, Oxford, into a Catholic seminary, but when the rest of that University became rebellious he avoided any further clash with Cambridge. He pretended that his dispute was not important but the nation's reaction was that Cambridge's victory was of great importance.

Yet Christopher felt this was not the end of the conflict between the King and the country, but just the start. The next twelve months the burning question became: Who was going to rule? Everywhere Christopher looked he saw James putting Catholics into positions of authority in the army and state and Church as the King had done at Oxford. What inflamed the people even more was Louis XIV's persecution of the Huguenots. Hundreds of thousands of these French Protestants escaped into England, bringing with them bitter tales of Catholic cruelty. This added to the country's apprehensions and when James marched an army of 13,000— mainly Catholic peasants recruited from Ireland—on to Hounslow Heath in an obvious effort to intimidate London, the heart of Protestantism, the fear he would impose Catholicism on the entire nation increased intensely.

Then, just a year after Newton opposed James' attempt to dictate to Cambridge, on April 25th, 1688, the King attacked the Church of England.

Christopher learned about this when he was summoned urgently to Lambeth Palace by Sancroft. The usually mild-mannered Archbishop of Canterbury was deeply agitated as he told the surveyor about the King's latest decree.

"James has ordered all the clergy of our Church of England to read from their pulpits what he calls *A Declaration of Indulgence*. It opens all positions to Catholics and Dissenters without the consent of the country. And we are supposed to announce it, to proclaim it. And we cannot. We do not oppose the rights of Catholics and Dissenters to worship, but we do oppose being forced to break the law. It is another way he seeks to humiliate us. We must resist him. By any means that are in our power."

"How, Your Grace?"

"With passive resistance. But I need your help."

"Your Grace, I'm not a public speaker and Parliament is dissolved."

"No, No! We must be more practical. Can you make the choir adequate for services by the end of May, when we have been ordered to read this Declaration of Indulgence from our pulpits?"

"Sir, to concur with James' command?"

"Of course not! I want services to be conducted in St. Paul's, the cathedral church of London, and his decree ignored. It will express our resistance better than anything else we can do. Will the choir be ready?"

"Your Grace, it is some years away from completion."

"Isn't anything done?" Sancroft was exasperated with such slowness. "I was right when I told Charles I would not live to see it completed."

Christopher longed to retort angrily, I can build only as fast as the resources you provide allow me and most of the time they are niggardly. But he controlled his temper and said, "Your Grace, the floor is done, some of the walls and part of the vaulting. The roof will have to be temporary, but the rest is permanent. I will try to make it usable."

"Make every endeavour. It is most important."

The next few weeks Christopher extended a temporary wooden roof across the vaulting and a day before the Declaration of Indulgence was supposed to be read it was almost done.

He came to the site on Saturday to supervise the setting of the final bricks in place and wondered if St. Paul's was haunted by evil things. Apprentice boys from the City were hurling bricks at the workmen, shouting, "You're making our church into a St. Peter's! We know why you want a dome!" And the workmen were hurling bricks back. But he needed those bricks to finish. He ran into the courtyard between the two sides, although he was afraid, for the apprentice boys looked angry enough to tear him to pieces, and held up his hands for quiet and order. His workmen stopped when they saw him, but the apprentice boys kept hurling bricks at him. Attempting to ignore that, praying that their aim would be poor, he began to pick up the bricks scattered at his feet and to carry them back to the spot where they were being used. Startled by his apparent indifference, the attackers halted, not sure what to do.

In this pause he turned back toward them and announced, "This is a Protestant church and I am determined that it will remain one."

The leader of the apprentice boys, a well dressed older man, who reminded him of Sir Richard Wiseman, who had been killed during the attack on Westminster Abbey many years ago, asked, "Is that why you plan a dome?"

"St. Stephen, Walbrook has a dome and the services are Anglican."

"That's so!" several of the boys shouted.

One of them added, "I go there myself!"

The leader snapped, "That proves nothing. How can we be sure you won't say one thing and do another and read the Declaration anyhow?"

"Come tomorrow and see for yourself." He addressed the youngsters, some not much older than his children. "Unless you are afraid."

"Of what?" sneered the leader, fondling the small sword he wore.

"Of ignoring the Declaration."

The apprentice boys wavered.

Christopher walked into the middle of them and said, "Help me put the bricks where they belong. The services will be in our Anglican faith. There will be no Declaration read here. I promise you."

"How can I trust you?" asked the leader.

"Because I will be here and I'm bringing my own children. Now are you going to help me with the bricks?" He said this with such assurance, although it wasn't what he felt, that most of the apprentice boys joined him in this task and by late afternoon the choir was ready.

Even so, as he sat in it the next day with Lucy and his three children, and he saw some of the apprentice boys in the congregation, he hoped his trust wasn't misplaced. He expected the Archbishop to conduct the services; he was surprised to see Holder appear in the pulpit instead.

Yet that was fitting, he thought, Holder was a resident canon of St. Paul's and sub-dean of the Chapel Royal. His proximity to both the palace and the cathedral made him a worthy choice. He was disappointed that Susan was absent; ordinarily his sister would be sitting here very proud of her husband. His children were pleased that they knew the preacher. Even his youngest, the nine-year-old William, who rarely seemed interested, listened as he saw that it was his Uncle William who was giving the sermon, while the eleven-year-old Jane was attentive, and the thirteen-year-old Christopher was quiet, which was unusual.

Holder's sermons stated, "God punished the Reformed church of Judah because it sinned, but when it repented God delivered that church from its suffering. And today, our English Reformed Church, whenever it is insulted or persecuted, as now, must defend itself. Rest assured, with God's help."

Christopher seldom had seen a congregation that listened so intently. But there was no mention of the King's Declaration of Indulgence. Not a person left until the end and then it was with satisfaction, and some of the apprentice boys came up to the surveyor and congratulated him.

"Why?" asked Holder, who was talking to Christopher and the children, who were in the care of Lucy Enfield. He felt he deserved the praise.

"They weren't sure you would ignore the Declaration."

"I had to," insisted Holder. "It is a matter of principle."

Jane asked, "Uncle William, where is Aunt Susan? I miss her."

"She is not feeling well, child. But I'm sure she misses you, too."

Holder excused himself for Dr. Stillingfleet, the Dean of St. Paul's, approached with Dr. Tillotson, the Dean of Canterbury, to congratulate him and he didn't want them to be distracted by childish remarks.

Jane asked, "Father, does this mean that St. Paul's is open now?"

Christopher answered, "Not really, dear. This was a special occasion."

"I knew that," said Young Christopher. "Didn't I, Lucy?"

Lucy said, "Yes, and I'm sure Jane did, too."

Jane asked suddenly, gathering courage from her father's presence—she was happy that he hadn't left them like Uncle William did when older people appeared—"Lucy, you knew my mother, didn't you?"

"I was honoured to know her, dear. I prayed a lot when she fell ill."

"Do I look like her?"

"Good Lord, yes!" Then Lucy looked guilty, for they were still in St. Paul's. "Just as Young Christopher looks like his mother."

William mumbled, "I look like my father."

"Of course you do," said Christopher, and took his hand. "William, would you like to see the rest of the cathedral?"

"No." The child pulled away, wishing he had something to eat. The surveyor asked, "Would you, Christopher?"

He shrugged and asked, "Why didn't they read the Declaration?"

"Son, because the church is against it."

"But the King is for it."

Jane cut in, "The King is wrong. Father said so."

Young Christopher said, "Won't he hurt us?"

"I don't know," said his father. "But we must obey our consciences."

The children argued whether they could touch their consciences. Jane said it was in her heart, Christopher insisted that it was in this church, and William grumbled that he didn't know what it meant. Lucy wanted to quiet them, afraid this was sacrilegious, but their father was curious how it would end. William grew sulky as his older brother ignored him, while Jane became tired of arguing when Christopher was insistent.

"Besides," she said to her attentive father, "I want to see the cathedral again since you told me how much more is done. Please?"

She was the light coming through the dark windows, her father thought, but Christopher was bored with the unfinished building, while William said his stomach hurt and cried that he wanted to go home.

"Jane, I'll show it to you another time," the surveyor said. "We must go now. The health of all of you is precious to me." He felt this was a useful day after all, at least St. Paul's was truly begun.

When James heard that his Declaration was ignored by most of the clergy and conspicuously in St. Paul's, he was furious. What made it worst in his view was that the country agreed with the Church of England. And what upset him more than anything else was the petition they presented to him.

It stated that their objection to the Declaration of Indulgence was not on the grounds of faith, but on legal grounds.

One phrase, in particular, infuriated him. It said: "*The Declaration having been founded on such a dispensing power as might at pleasure set aside all laws ecclesiastical, it appears to us illegal. It is a point of such consequence we cannot make ourselves parties to it as the reading of it in church during the time of Divine Services would have done."*

James felt this taunted him and incited to rebellion.

He ordered the seven leading bishops of the Church of England to be tried on the charge of publishing a seditious libel and to be sent to the Tower.

Led by Sancroft, they met at Lambeth Palace to await their arrest and to act as one. As the barge arrived to convey them to the Tower, a vast crowd assembled at the dock to exhibit their support and devotion to their Church. Christopher watched anxiously from the other side of the Thames, most of the seven bishops were friends of his. He recalled the others whom he had seen take this journey, and that Laud hadn't returned and his uncle hadn't come back for eighteen years.

Sancroft guided his bishops to the barge and as they stepped into it the great multitude knelt for his blessing. When the Archbishop gave that the thousands standing further down the shore waded into the river as the barge passed and begged for his blessing, too. Much of London had turned out to express their fidelity to the Church of England and they lined the banks of the Thames all the way to the Tower and Traitor's Gate.

Christopher heard a low but persistent hum as many prayed. Then his eyes widened as they followed the barge down the river, for St. Paul's came into his view, the first time he saw a glimpse of it on the London horizon since the old cathedral had burnt down over twenty-two years ago. The gap in time astonished him, and in some ways stunned him; he hadn't realised it was so long; in emotional time it seemed like only yesterday. His eyes embraced the scaffolding that rose on the skyline like the masts of a tall sailing ship. And suddenly it lifted his heart. This was the expression of what the bishops were prepared to sacrifice themselves for, even their lives. He continued to stare at it, telling himself, There must always be a view of St. Paul's on the London horizon. That was the city brought to a logical conclusion. And in his vision the dome emerged and fastened itself on the sky, as if it were always there, always there.

The trial of the seven bishops was watched by all of London and when the jury retired to consider their verdict few slept. At the judgment of "Not Guilty", the entire City, rich and poor, Anglicans and Dissenters, Whigs and Tories, went wild with joy. London was illuminated everywhere with candles as a symbol of their liberation. The favourite number was seven, with the tallest central one representing the Archbishop. The bells in the newly constructed City parish churches rang continuously.

Christopher wasn't able to join the festivities. His sister died the day the bishops were acquitted, and the next day, on Holder's wish, she was buried in the crypt of St. Paul's. He put her in the north-east corner which was finished, still not sure what had killed her. But now, he felt sadly, the stone held Susan to its breast and that was fitting, for St. Paul's had been in her blood, too, and now she was a part of it.

Holder stared at her tomb as if he couldn't believe her death, looking old and frail and every one of his seventy-two years. As the last stone was fixed in place with Susan under it, he cried out, "I should have been the one to go first! She was always nursing me, and now she is dead. I'm not even certain of what. It was so sudden, so abrupt, Christopher. Do you think God punished me for disobeying the King?"

"No, William," said Christopher, yearning for the days Holder had tutored him and hardly anyone he knew died.

Holder asked, "Are the bishops free?"

"Yes. Can't you hear the way the bells keep ringing?"

"Strange, I thought it was for Susan. Will the walls hold?"

Christopher gazed at the newly finished pillars and arches that were to sustain the great dome and said, "Everything here is secure."

Holder shook his head in wonder. "I used to doubt you would ever finish, but now that the crypt is in use, it is indeed a cathedral."

"I don't favour cemeteries in the city, but this is different."

"Very different." Holder sighed, and then he added positively, "Once St. Paul's is totally finished, many will be buried here. That is why it must remain our church."

Only Jane came to the funeral with Christopher, for the older boy had caught a cold from the younger, and Lucy said it wouldn't be safe. But the simple truth was that Jane brought him a love that consoled him for many sorrows. She filled his heart with such affection he was beginning to believe he could not do without it. As they left St. Paul's, he reached for her hand and as it came to him, he thought gratefully, It was always there. It and St. Paul's, he repeated to himself. He could feel her fingers clutching his, as if to never let go.

I Have Taken Myself

I have taken myself
  To Freedom
    And I have learned
      How to be Freedom
      Whatever tries
        to stop me
          or take me
            out of my path
            of Freedom
            I will pull
                from its socket
                the hand
                  that tried

Stymean Karlen

49

I Have Taken Myself

◆HIS WORK ABSORBED HIM THE NEXT FEW MONTHS. THERE WERE FIVE new city churches to design—the total was fifty now—and more steeples, which were done last. The parishes were determined to show the King that he could not extinguish their faith. And while the extra funds James had promised St. Paul's were not forthcoming, the Church authorities made sure the Surveyor had sufficient money and materials to continue his work on the cathedral. Since Holder's sermon and his defiance of James' *Declaration of Indulgence*, St. Paul's had become a symbol of Protestant resistance to the King's tyranny. Lucy gave ten pounds to the building fund; Christopher donated half of his yearly salary, the seven bishops, Holder, and many other clergymen, gave what they could spare; contributions came from all over the country.

There was no such need at Chelsea Hospital, where he polished the portico and completed the elegant chapel—that was a royal design. He found much to do on the interior of the library at Trinity, which was as vital to him as the exterior. And it was his way of demonstrating that he supported Newton and the university. There were no more attacks on Cambridge's freedom, but the divisions in the land grew wider and deeper and more difficult to bridge.

The Queen gave birth to a son, but instead of the nation celebrating the arrival of an heir to the throne, which was customary, this event added to the general apprehension. Christopher heard much talk that England was destined for a Catholic dynasty. Most of his workmen were convinced of that and declared they would refuse to work before they accepted such a situation. The site was also full of rumours that many important lords had invited William of Orange to save England from Popery.

When Oliver mentioned this to the Surveyor, he replied, "It is possible. William is married to James' oldest daughter, Mary, and they are both Protestants. They have a legitimacy that Monmouth lacked."

Oliver looked around to be sure he wasn't heard—he was certain James' Catholic spies were everywhere—then he whispered, "I won't mind. Even if William is a Dutchman. His wife is English. Sir, do you think we will be able to continue working on the cathedral? It goes fine now."

"We must. This is the rock of our faith that must not break. Tell that to the workmen, if it is necessary. To make St. Paul's a great and noble church is our best way of resisting the attacks on our faith."

"Yes, sir. But how can you keep so many things in your head? St. Paul's, alone, is such a complex task. And now that you have given out the contracts for the west front, which includes the portico, the western towers, and the western parts of the chapels and vestibule, it would overwhelm most men. I wonder that you can sleep."

Christopher smiled and shrugged. He had just worked out in his mind, after much pondering, the final design for the west front. It contained traces of Inigo Jones' plan, but essentially it was his own. However, his assistant looked so worried, he asked, "Have you found any good young surveyors? As we have been looking for?"

"Not yet, sir. And so much effort is still ahead of us."

"Much?" Christopher couldn't resist jesting, relieved that the work was going well. "The timber scaffolding for the crypt vaulting and the choir floor are down without any damage. The brickwork that forms the crypt vaulting and the choir floor is in place. Soon too, we should be able to start on the permanent lower roof of the choir with the best oak timber, and on the transepts. Oliver, we mustn't lose heart."

Oliver nodded, thinking, He didn't expect to survive the building of St. Paul's, but the Surveyor might, Sir Christopher was so persistent.

Christopher asked, "Are you concerned about the political situation?"

"Everybody is, sir. No one knows which way the wind will blow."

Late in October the state of the wind became a national question.

A meeting of the Royal Society was arranged to consider a new device invented by Sir Christopher Wren for planting corn and to hear a further report on celestial motion by Professor Isaac Newton. But the moment the new President of the Society, Lord Vaughan, called the meeting to order, Pepys said, "It is reported that the Prince of Orange and his Dutch fleet have set sail from the Hague with the intention of invading us. If the wind blows from the east they could be off our coast soon."

"Good," said Newton. He put his paper away.

"It is about time," said Halley.

Christopher asked, "Will our fleet oppose them?"

Halley said, "No one seems to know."

"I hope not," said Newton. "Our Navy is Protestant, too."

Hooke, who stood by the window, grumbled, "The wind changes. It has turned Papist and become westerly. If it blows any harder it will become a gale and disperse the Dutch fleet. That would be unfortunate."

Pepys said, "I think the Navy will support James. He has improved the ships and the service. He has listened to my views."

"He has treated you well," said Evelyn. "But not everyone has been so fortunate. There is much distress in the country over his latest acts. Many are in expectation of the Dutch fleet."

"Are you, Evelyn?"

"I'm for whatever is right for our beloved country and blessed faith."

"Are you, Wren?" Pepys repeated. "I know how Newton and Hooke feel. It is the first time I've seen them in agreement in years. But you don't run with the herd. Are you for James or William and Mary?"

"The Society was formed to avoid quarrels over politics and religion."

"That is no answer, sir!" Pepys was exasperated.

"It is the answer. I will not be able to put a dome on St. Paul's by guesswork and I would prefer not to have my fate decided by the wind."

Newton said, "Wren, I respect your planting instrument which will plough and harrow equally. I once considered being a farmer, but these are unusual times. James has put our Protestant faith in great danger."

Pepys said, "You do not understand James. He means well."

"It is only his faith that is wrong, is that it?" Newton asked.

"The *Principia* was licensed. He respects natural philosophy. He has asked me to inquire of the learned minds of the Society if they could devise a quick method of forecasting the direction of the wind in advance."

"If I could, I would not tell him."

"Neither would I," declared Hooke.

"The wind will not alter anything," said Christopher. "The country's mind is made up. Only a change of James' mind can remedy matters."

Pepys said, "Perhaps you will have that opportunity. The King has told me to invite you to a ball that he is giving next week."

Evelyn asked in astonishment, "At this time when the country is on the verge of invasion and civil war?"

"He is determined to show he is not afraid. You are invited, too."

"But we are not, are we?" Hooke complained bitterly.

"You do not serve him," said Pepys. "We do. The King's party is to celebrate his birthday and the birth of the heir to the throne. Will you attend, Sir Christopher? You are still his Chief Surveyor."

Not as firmly as Pepys assumed, he thought. After James had attacked the bishops, he had considered resigning as the King's Surveyor, but when he mentioned this to Sancroft the Archbishop replied, "You must not quit now. You will do our faith more good as His Majesty's Surveyor. Another could design our churches as Catholic chapels."

"Wren, will you attend?" Pepys asked. "Or do you desert him, too?"

"I desert no one. But it may be that James deserts us."

Christopher approached the ball at Whitehall with mixed feelings. He was curious yet wary, not sure what to expect. The Dutch fleet was said to be still at sea, but no one seemed to know where it was. The wind had turned easterly again and the last sight of the fleet was when it was blown past the white cliffs of Dover. Then, Christopher had heard, many had stood and waved a greeting to it, but the Dutch fleet had sailed on.

He walked from Scotland Yard, leaving Jane and William in the care of Lucy—Christopher was back in Eton. A hard frost had settled on London, although it was early for such weather. There hadn't been any work on St. Paul's the last few days, which was blamed on the cold, but he felt it was as if the cathedral waited to see what was going to happen, too.

At the palace there were more soldiers than footmen, but he was admitted without any difficulty and was ushered into the great gallery.

The ball was decorated lavishly with royal emblems everywhere and James and his Queen, the beautiful Mary of Modena, sat on the throne so they were above everyone else. James assumed his most stately posture, while his much younger second wife held herself proudly, as if to say—At last I've justified my position, I've given him an heir to the throne.

Christopher saw Pepys and Evelyn, but most of the other faces were different from the days of Charles. There were no more mistresses at James' Court. They were gone or dead, like Nell Gwynn, who had died last year. James, in his new righteousness, had dismissed even his own mistress from the Court, although he found her absence a terrible ordeal.

Father Petrie and Jeffreys, the Lord Chancellor, stood on each side of the King so their influence would be obvious, but Christopher's attention was attracted by the presence of the Princess Anne, James' youngest daughter, and third in succession to the throne. Her husband was with her, and the bulky, clumsy Prince George, a blue-eyed, fair-haired, hearty Dane, was attentive to her. Yet Christopher noticed that Anne still looked uncomfortable. Perhaps it was because of her ordinary appearance, he thought, her projecting teeth, her prominent eyeballs, her round features which tended to overweight, her heavy, awkward body, which was severely corseted. Or possibly, his mind ran on, it was because Anne remained a staunch Protestant, and thus, was a thorn in her father's flesh.

Then he saw the Princess Anne's inevitable companion, the pretty, slim and strong-willed Lady Sarah Churchill, whose husband, the recently created Lord John Churchill, commanded James' army.

He approached Anne first, which pleased her. She liked his manners and that his father and uncle had been pillars of the Church of England. But before she could acknowledge his bow and ask him in which direction he thought the wind would blow—he should know, she felt, as past President of the Royal Society—her father wanted to speak to his Surveyor.

Christopher turned to obey this command and noticed that James was dressed as elegantly as Charles ever had been, in crimson and gold.

James was proud of his wide lace cuffs and cravat, which he knew blended splendidly with his three-foot yellow wig that framed his long, pointed face in a fashion that fitted his kingly nature. He was determined that everything would be proper at his Court. Tonight, he felt with satisfaction, there were no whores here any more, not even his own.

Yet with all of James' efforts to impress with his presence, as he addressed his surveyor he stuttered with the fumbling thick speech which afflicted him when he was nervous or upset. "Wren, you are expert in natural philosophy. Can you judge the nature and purpose of the wind?"

"Sometimes, Your Majesty, but not always."

"I hear so many conflicting reports of the wind, I don't know what to believe. Yet the fate of the nation could rest on it. Although Churchill assures me his army can repel any Dutch invasion. What do you think?"

Christopher was surprised by this question. "Sir, I'm no soldier."

"You handle stone strongly. Could you fortify London if necessary?"

2C*

"Your Majesty, I have no experience in military matters."

"I remember. You refused my brother's wish to fortify Tangier." Have you made provisions for the oratories in St. Paul's as I ordered?"

"Not yet, Your Majesty, there were other things we had to do first."

"Such as using the choir to defy me?"

Christopher was silent, recalling a remark of Charles, "*The redness of my brother's face frightens many people.*" James' face was very red now.

"Wren, you do me an injustice. I always remember and never forget."

"Sir, I'm at your service."

"Why have you avoided designing the chapel for the Queen? Don't answer, I know. I'm a better navigator than you think. I could dismiss you for failing to obey my command to construct the chapel."

Christopher bowed formally and said, "Sir, that is your privilege."

"Come, come, don't be so formal." James stood up to show he could be forgiving. "The Crown needs men like you. Wren, why do so many of your fellows oppose me? I mean them no harm. I am as English as anyone."

But so righteous, thought Christopher. He said, "Your Majesty, could you look into the matter of the extra funds for St. Paul's which you promised us several years ago?"

"Promised? What blasphemy is this?" James was indignant, and fancied himself a God of wrath. "After what the bishops did? Vicious men! Wren, my Queen worries about the bird huts in St. James' Park and asks me to dispatch you to repair them, much paint is needed on Whitehall and many locks are broken. Do you want to be confined to such duties? Orange, with this strong east wind, could be blown all the way to the colonies."

Before Christopher could respond to this change of mood a messenger rushed in. The horseman ran straight to the King and shouted to him, "They are coming, Your Majesty. The Dutch Prince has landed at Torbay. Two days ago, on Guy Fawkes Day. I've ridden ever since with the news. They arrived before nightfall, when the wind subsided."

James was furious. Father Petrie had to stop him from venting his rage on the unhappy messenger. "Didn't anyone try to repel them?"

"No. They were welcomed, Your Majesty. Begging your pardon."

Christopher saw consternation on the King's face. He turned and whispered to his wife, who retired at once, looking panic-stricken. Then he addressed the silent Court. "The rebels will be put down with all the forces at my command." But when James instinctively crossed himself, Christopher thought, Such a gesture could cost him an army. "I will hang every one of them. The English ones, too. I will destroy all the rebels."

James motioned for Father Petrie and Jeffreys to follow him as he left, but they paused to speak to the Surveyor. Jeffreys sneered, "After your support of Newton and the bishops, you are fortunate to be invited here. If I were the King, you would no longer be my Surveyor."

"Patience, Jeffreys," said Father Petrie. "We must be compassionate. Wren is afflicted with original sin, as are all of us."

"Original vice," Jeffreys muttered. "James is too patient for me."

Petrie said, "Wren, you are a learned man, you know that the King is God's appointed ruler. Your Church affirms that, too. Why don't you come to terms with the inevitable? For the good of your soul."

"Father, I appreciate your solicitude," Christopher replied, "But I must leave the welfare of my soul in other hands."

A footman from the King demanded their presence at once, and this time they obeyed, for the footman said that the King was very angry.

On the way out Christopher met Pepys and Evelyn. Everyone was leaving, as if the plague had struck, and he was sorry he had been unable to talk to the Princess Anne, she had seemed eager for him to do so, but she and her husband and the Churchills were gone now, too.

At the street Evelyn and Pepys had their own coaches waiting, but Christopher said he intended to walk home.

Evelyn asked, "You're not afraid?"

"No. And it's such a short distance."

"I would be. The rabble could mistake you for a Papist, coming from Whitehall Palace these days."

Christopher sighed and said, "Will this religious fighting ever end?"

Evelyn said abruptly, "Why should it when our faith is threatened?"

Pepys added, "I still don't think the nation will support the Prince. His army is small while the royal army is large. And the people are tired of fighting, of civil war. I believe they will back James."

Christopher said, "I wonder why the King wanted us here tonight?"

Pepys said, "As long as we are here, we are considered his supporters."

William of Orange didn't march on London as Christopher

expected. Instead, the Prince turned deep into Devon where the opposition to James was strongest because of Jeffreys' "Bloody Assize", and moved at a snail-like pace toward London, often just a few miles a day. Then Christopher realised why. The Prince was forcing the King to assume responsibility for civil war, or retreat, while he gained strength. And gradually, as more and more of James' supporters went over to William of Orange, Christopher realised the subtlety of the invader's strategy.

Later in November there was a new summons to come to Whitehall. It surprised Christopher; he thought James was with his troops at Salisbury. And when he was led into the King's audience chamber, he was startled by his agitation. Without any preamble or explanation, James said, "Wren, you are a good friend of Compton, the Bishop of London, aren't you?"

"I think so, sir. He has been a good friend of St. Paul's."

"I want you to speak to him. As soon as possible."

"What about, Your Majesty?"

"Bishop Compton was my daughter Anne's tutor and he still has great influence with her. I wouldn't want him to sway her in the wrong way."

"But sir, you were the one who suspended him from his office two years ago."

For an instant the Surveyor thought he was going to be ordered to the Tower, James was so angry. His cheeks flushed, his hand shook, but then he caught hold of himself, and stuttering with his thick speech, he said, "I pardoned Compton recently. I allowed him to resume his duties."

"Your Majesty, I'm sure the Bishop is grateful."

"I don't know. I'm not convinced that the country realises I have its best interests at heart. That I know what is right for the nation."

"Sir, what would you like me to say to Bishop Compton?"

"I wouldn't want him to persuade my daughter to support the rebels. Wren, you have children, don't you?"

"I have, Your Majesty."

"Would you like them to desert you?"

The thought made Christopher shudder.

"And a daughter, too, I believe?"

"A lovely girl of eleven, sir. She already has a good notion of design."

"Would you be happy if she were raised in a faith apart from your own?"

"I would accept it, Your Majesty."

"You are evading the question." James strode over to the window and gazed down the river to the scaffolding of St. Paul's in the distance. "Wren, I can't help St. Paul's, if you don't help me."

"Your Majesty, what do you want me to do?"

"Convince the Bishop to persuade my daughter to support me. As you would wish your own daughter to do. If Anne betrays me, I'm lost."

"But, Your Majesty, I can't . . ."

James wasn't listening. He had regained his self control and he cut him short and declared, "My children must not desert me." Before Christopher could say another word or refuse this mission, as was his intention, James ordered him to hurry on this assignment or it would be too late.

He wondered if he should warn Compton of the King's feelings and finally, believing that justified a visit, he went to see the Bishop the next day at his residence close to St. Paul's. This morning, with James' implied threats, the scaffolds reminded him more of a skeleton than a Church, but he was resolved now to warn his friend. But Compton was gone, and no one would tell the Surveyor where the Bishop was.

He asked Holder, who often assisted Compton, and his brother-in-law shook his head wearily and said, "I've heard rumours, but Sancroft should know. Have you become an emissary of the King?"

"James wants me to be, but that's not why I want to see the Bishop."

At Lambeth Palace the Archbishop of Canterbury, possibly his oldest and best friend in the Church, greeted him sadly. Sancroft was distressed by the landing of William of Orange. He said, "Much as I dislike James, he is our rightful monarch. But Compton, who was a soldier in the civil war, differs. I think he likes the idea of a war. He has persuaded the Princess Anne to desert her father and to join the northern insurgents in Nottingham. Compton has taken her to them himself."

"I didn't intend to change the Bishop's mind, I wanted to warn him."

"Maybe it is the King who should be warned. I hear that Lady Churchill is with the Princess Anne, which means that her husband will be the next to desert the King. Without Churchill's military skill, he cannot win."

Later that day Christopher heard that Churchill, the Commander of the King's army, had gone over to the Prince of Orange. And now the exodus of other soldiers and officials from James' cause became overwhelming.

Meanwhile, William still advanced slowly, as if he intended to avoid an armed clash with James' army at Salisbury in the hope it would continue to disintegrate. No building was occurring these early days of December and there was much confusion around the palace. Many times Christopher heard the clatter of cavalry and the rumble of cannons moving about Whitehall. He thought of moving Jane and William to Windsor, which might be safer. Yet he didn't want to lose sight of Jane, especially in such difficult times, and he couldn't treat one child differently from the other. So he told Lucy to keep the children off the street, even in daylight, and that their play should be confined to their garden.

Then one morning while he was working on a design for the dome of St. Paul's in his studio at Scotland Yard he had an unexpected visitor. It was a trusted steward of the King, who informed him that James wanted to see his Surveyor secretly. He added, "No one knows the King is here."

It was December 9th, 1688, and from everything that Christopher had seen and heard the King's situation had worsened enormously, and yet he felt he had to obey. He was still the King's Chief Surveyor and in that capacity he could not desert him, whatever others had done.

As the steward led him into the palace without being observed, he said, "His Majesty doesn't want his presence at Whitehall known. Not yet."

"I understand." He followed the steward into the royal bed-chamber.

James was half in his military dress, half in his travelling clothes, as if he couldn't make up his mind what to do next. He was in the middle of a serious difference of opinion with Jeffreys and Petrie. But his favourite advisers hushed when they saw the Surveyor.

Christopher bowed and asked, "Your Majesty, you desire my presence?"

"I desire my Chief Surveyor. I hear you are a skilful engineer."

"When it is necessary, I hope, sir."

"It is very necessary now, Wren. Could you fortify the palace?"

"Whitehall, sir? The Tower could be defended for a time, perhaps, it was built as a fortress, but the palace is too exposed and weak."

"What about the City? London itself?"

"The Roman wall is very old and frail, more of a boundary than a fortification, sir. And the citizens would not support such a stand."

Jeffreys said, "Sir, that is what I advised. Your only hope is to fight outside of London, where the population is more friendly, or . . ."

The Lord Chancellor didn't dare finish what he was thinking, but

Petrie did. "In France, sir, you will find help to recover your kingdom."

"Then you think it is already gone!" That horrified James.

"For the moment, sir," said Petrie. "I'm surprised you called this man. He is Church of England to the bone. He is their Surveyor, not yours. And never has been your man, whatever he says."

Christopher replied, "I'm Surveyor to the King of England. But I'm also Surveyor to St. Paul's. And they should serve the same ends."

"Nonsense!" Jeffreys snapped, "The man talks in riddles. Your Majesty, you see how little Wren helped with Compton. You should have dismissed him when I suggested. It may be too late now."

James said, "His dismissal would have aroused his Church as much as the bishops'. It wasn't politic. But I thought Wren would speak to Compton."

Christopher said, "Sir, you should have talked to your daughter yourself."

"God help me! I'm a ruined man! My own daughters have deserted me!"

Christopher moved toward the door, although the King hadn't dismissed him but had sunk on his bed sobbing incoherently until Petrie shouted in his ear, "Your Majesty, you must prepare to leave before it is too late! Your wife and son are about to go now and you must follow them."

"Yes." James rose wearily and as he saw the Surveyor he cried out, "I never thought my children would betray me! I cannot fight that! Mary is even worse than Anne, for her husband leads the rebellion and she supports him. Go, Wren, while I'm still merciful." He put on his armour and sword and said, "I must not allow them to assassinate me. I will ask the Lord's blessing." With one hand he dismissed Christopher, and with the other he ordered Father Petrie to hear his confession.

Jeffreys walked to the door with Christopher and said, "I told him it was impossible to fortify this old palace. But when he makes up his mind nothing can change it. Time is running out on him, but he still expects the Virgin Mary to save him."

The Queen fled to France that night with her son and the next day the King tried to follow her. But, disguised as a priest, he insisted on saying his devotions in public, and he was captured and returned to Whitehall. However, William was resolved not to enter London until James was gone. He sent his Dutch soldiers to escort James to Rochester. He had promised his wife that no harm would come to her father in return for her support. So, on William's orders, there were no guards at the rear of the house where James was confined. When the King took the hint and escaped to France, Christopher observed that most people sighed with relief. Bloodshed, for the most part, was avoided. Jeffreys was captured and was only saved from an enraged mob by being put in the Tower, while Petrie joined James in France, where the exile still considered himself King of England and was encouraged in this belief by Louis XIV.

Christopher took Jane to observe the entrance of the Prince of Orange into London. They watched at Scotland Yard, just before the entrance to Whitehall, and as William rode past Jane was excited.

She liked the streets gay with orange ribbons, the flags flying from the towers, the many mounted lords riding ahead of the royal carriage, the Dutch soldiers protecting the person of the Prince of Orange, the crowds cheering him as if he were their saviour. Then Jane cried out in her disappointment, "Father, I don't see his wife, The Princess Mary!"

"Jane, she will come later. It wasn't thought fitting now, since it was her father who was deposed."

"The Prince is so yellow-faced, thin. But I hear that his wife is pretty. Do you think they love each other?"

"They say she loves him. I'm not sure he feels the same way about her."

"She doesn't love her father."

"What makes you say that?"

"She has taken the throne away from him. I would never do that to you."

But he was not James. He thought, Once the French heard James' ideas they would understand why James had been driven out.

"I love you, Father."

"I love you, Jane."

You Cannot Teach Me

You cannot teach me
That the smallest
Particle is not
Considered by the
ETERNAL

You cannot teach me
That the smallest
Particle
Was not first the
ETERNAL

Stymean Karlen

50

You Cannot Teach Me

HAMPTON COURT SPREAD ACROSS THE LANDSCAPE OF RICHMOND LIKE Henry in Holbein's portrait of him, swaggering and domineering. This was fitting, reflected Christopher, it had been Henry's favourite palace. And as he approached it in his coach and four the following spring, he glanced at Jane who sat beside him, interested in her view of the journey.

Lucy had dressed her in a pink and white court gown, which heightened the charm of her pert features, dark brown hair, deep grey eyes, and revealed the suggestion of young, budding breasts. Jane was very much the young lady now, he thought proudly, going on twelve and as tall as he was. While he had doubts about the warmth of the King's welcome, although both William and Mary were securely on the throne now, Jane was so eager with anticipation he was glad that he had obeyed the Queen's request.

Mary had said to him at Whitehall Palace, "Sir Christopher, we would like you to attend us at Hampton Court. It will be for dinner. Bring your little girl, too. I prefer girls, and she will brighten the palace and distract me when you discuss business with the King after dinner. I miss children, I have none, but you are fortunate, you have three."

At the Anne Boleyn gate he said to Jane, "Henry loved this palace. He brought all his Queens here, except the first, Anne Boleyn, Jane Seymour, Catherine Howard, Anne of Cleeves, and Catherine Parr. After he took it away from Wolsey. It is the most Tudor of all the palaces."

"Who designed it, Father?"

"They are not sure who the surveyor was, or surveyors. It was probably built by several and a number of master masons and carpenters. In Henry's day the Chief Surveyor in the Office of the Works was a craftsman like a master carpenter or a master mason.

Wolsey began Hampton Court but Henry enlarged it, at least as it stands now, with all of its sprawling grandeur."

"It has so many bricks. Did the King and Queen come by coach?"

"By royal barge. They were rowed up the river from Whitehall."

Two grooms waited at the Anne Boleyn gate to take care of their coach and coachman and there was a steward to escort them to the royal chambers. Dinner had started in the Presence Chamber and the King and Queen were at the table already. As the Wrens were brought before them and bowed, William replied stiffly but Mary smiled graciously and naturally.

It was a small royal dinner, Christopher noted, William sitting at the head of the table with the two sisters, Queen Mary and the Princess Anne, on each side of him. George, the Prince of Denmark, was next to Mary, while Lady Churchill was by the side of Anne. A few courtiers were scattered about and the Wrens were seated at the end of the long table.

Christopher didn't mind, he could observe better there, while Jane was so absorbed it didn't matter to her either. William was yellow-faced as his daughter had said, a little, thin, sharp-featured, middle-aged man, who was prematurely aged. Mary, on the other hand, was attractive and youthful. Twelve years younger than her husband, she had a soft, dark loveliness, with a fine regularity of features and an excellent carriage that was more like her Uncle Charles than her father, James.

There was no conversation at the table. Despite a repast that disappointed Christopher, overboiled beef, roast fowl which was burnt, Rhenish claret instead of English ale, and butter-basted turnips that had no taste, almost everyone devoured the meal ravenously, particularly Anne and George. But perhaps the solemnity was due to William, he thought, for the King ate quickly, single-mindedly, as if eating required all of his energy and emotion. Or possibly, his mind ran on, it was an excuse not to talk. Jane was too excited to care, sipping a little wine with his permission and nibbling indifferently on the roast fowl, but not caring about any-thing but the people around her. But there were seven desserts, ranging from tarts, fruit, and cheese to various pies, and when they were served the mood lightened and there were even a few smiles and jokes.

Finally the dinner ended and William wanted to talk to Christopher, while Mary asked Jane to join her.

Christopher waited for the King to speak. Their previous en-counters at Whitehall had been stiff, formal, as if William didn't trust him and hadn't decided whether to retain him or to dismiss him. So he had gone on with the work in hand, particularly St. Paul's and the City churches, which were only indirectly subject to the royal influence.

William walked over to the window which looked out on the gardens to the east, indicating to the others that he didn't want to be disturbed, and said slowly, with a thick Dutch accent, "You supported James Stuart."

"Your Majesty, I am Surveyor to the Crown, as I was for his brother."

"You did not resign." William stated that as an accusation.

"Your Majesty, I was appointed by Charles."

"But you did serve James Stuart."

"Sir, should I have deserted him, as so many did?"

William frowned, as if annoyed with this reply, then said, "Your good friend, the Archbishop of Canterbury, refuses to acknowledge me."

Christopher had been surprised by Sancroft's refusal to take the oath of allegiance to the new King, but he couldn't quarrel with him over it, he had too much respect for the Archbishop's sincerity. He said, "Sir, that is his responsibility, not mine."

"But you are close to him. How can I be sure you can be trusted?"

"Sir, as a member of Parliament from New Windsor, I voted for your succession to the throne in the Convention Parliament that was called to consider that. As did my friend, Newton, representing Cambridge."

"I know." William thought coldly, That didn't prove loyalty. Many voted that way, willing to forsake principle for expediency.

"Sir, it was my own decision. But if you wish me to resign I will submit it to you whenever you wish. Is that why you invited me here?"

William appeared to be thinking and he didn't reply. He believed it was wiser to say nothing than to say a foolish thing.

"Your Majesty, why did you invite my daughter? To humiliate us?"

"That was the Queen's idea. She likes children. Because she hasn't any. Why do you think I shouldn't put a Dutch surveyor in your place?"

"Because this is England, sir."

"You think Dutch stone and craftsmanship worse than yours?"

"Different, Your Majesty. My best friend was Dutch."

"Where is he now?" William regarded him cynically.

"He returned to Amsterdam a few years ago. Until then, Daniel Van Doorn was my first assistant. Sir, does the name mean anything to you?"

"Wren, there are a thousand Van Doorns in the Netherlands."

"Your Majesty, he was a friend of Rembrandt and Spinoza."

"A renegade Jew," William said contemptuously, "and a ruined painter, too Dutch for his own good. Van Doorn has poor references. Is that all you have to say for yourself, Wren? So far, it is not impressive."

"Sir, my work speaks for itself."

"A cathedral that was started twenty-three years ago and isn't even half finished. That is not much of a recommendation."

"Sir, it was begun fourteen years ago, in 1675, not 1666."

"That doesn't matter. The way it is going it will never be finished."

Christopher thought ruefully, At least, if he was dismissed as Chief Surveyor he would have more time to work on St. Paul's, unless the King interfered there, too. But he felt sad as he asked, "Is that all, sir?"

"What else do you expect! You stay with James to the last moment, you are seen in his quarters before he flees, no doubt planning his escape."

"Sir, that is a lie. He asked me to fortify the palace and London and I said it was impossible, the nation's mind was made up in your favour."

"That may be, but your loyalty is questionable. I order you to halt all your duties for the Crown until a final decision is reached."

Christopher cried out angrily, "I've always been loyal to the Crown!"

"Is that why your best friend, the Archbishop, refuses to acknowledge me as King? Obviously, you belong to that part of the Church of England which will not accept me as their monarch. You should be dismissed now."

"Sir, if I am one of those who do not support you, why was it that I attended the marriage of your father and mother?"

William exclaimed, "You couldn't have! You're not that old!"

"Sir, I will be sixty in three years."

"And I will be forty next year. You don't look it."

"And it was my uncle, Bishop Matthew Wren, who officiated, sir."

William thought, It was better to be silent, then he couldn't say the wrong thing. That was James Stuart's difficulty; he didn't know when to hold his tongue. "Why didn't you tell me sooner?"

"Your Majesty, no one ever questioned my loyalty before."

"It is your judgment that is questioned, not your loyalty."

Christopher didn't correct him, but said, "Sir, I was honoured to attend the wedding of your parents. It was one of the great occasions of my life."

William turned back from the window which grew misty with

rain, looking for a fire to warm his chilled body, it was as damp here as it was in Holland, and asked, "Was it a happy ceremony?"

"I was only going on nine, sir, but I thought so. The mob on the street outside shouted for Strafford's blood. but your parents looked proud, and my uncle said it was one of the noble moments of his life."

"I never knew my father. He died before I was born and my mother when I was ten. I've wondered about my father all my life."

"Sir, my mother died, too, before I knew her. When I was an infant."

William shook his head in sympathy and sighed, "I can understand. Do you remember what my father looked like? Paintings are so flattering."

"As I recall, sir, a moderate sized man, fair, slim, good eyes. His colouring reminded me of my friend, Daniel, it was so similar."

"Naturally. They were both Dutch. Do I resemble him in any way?"

"Sir, you are about the same height and have the same colouring."

"Except mine is soured by my military campaigns. My body is worn out before its time, I've spent so many harsh winters in the saddle. I'm racked with chills and stricken with asthmatic attacks. That is why I want this palace rebuilt. Do you think it is practical, Wren? Can it be done quickly? The Queen thinks it will help my health to live here."

"Sir, are you asking me as your Chief Surveyor?"

"It is your duty."

"But a few minutes ago, sir, you said . . ."

"I didn't know if I could trust you. I still don't. But my wife does. It was her idea to invite you and your daughter here and to look at the palace. Besides, I change my mind occasionally. That was James Stuart's trouble. He never did. Remember, however, you work for me, no one else."

"What about my other designs? St. Paul's, the churches, Trinity?"

"You'll have time, but Hampton Court comes first. The damp air at Whitehall will kill me. I want a palace to rival any owned by Louis, but quieter in style. I understand you've seen the Louvre and Versailles."

"Sir, only when the French were starting Versailles and the Louvre was being rebuilt. I didn't agree with everything I saw there."

"Who does? We will look at Hampton Court Palace tomorrow."

"Thank you, sir. I trust you will allow me to show you St. Paul's and what has been accomplished. In a few years there should be a choir."

"I'm too busy!" William was even more abrupt than before, as if he regretted his brief display of emotion. "Discuss that with the Queen!"

The Queen was talking to Jane when Christopher returned from his meeting with the King and she said, "Sir Christopher, I found out an interesting thing from your daughter. She said that I had to do what I did to my father, that he forced me to betray him."

"Your Highness," interrupted Jane, "forgive me, but I didn't say betray, but oppose. You had to for the sake of our country and Church."

"Would you oppose your father if he was wrong?"

"Your Highness, I'm not a Queen."

"That is not an answer, Mistress Jane."

"That is the way I feel, Your Highness. But you had to do what you did."

Mary turned to Christopher and asked, "Was Hampton Court approved?"

"It was a close thing, Your Majesty, but I believe so now."

"The King doesn't know you like I do. My grandfather, Clarendon, was fond of your work, he said you would not corrupt your duties, and your cousin, who was his secretary, was devoted to your interests. When I was Jane's age I heard many favourable things about you. And now I see your churches everywhere and many other works. Your record is impressive."

"Your Majesty, you are kind. May I pay my respects to Princess Anne?"

"She has left. She hasn't felt well lately. You are a fortunate man, you have a charming daughter. It is a joy I have missed."

"Your Majesty, perhaps in time."

"God has decided otherwise. You will be shown to your quarters."

The Queen's Lady in Waiting, Mistress Grace Fenton, told Jane that her bedchamber had been occupied by Anne Boleyn and Catherine Howard, both of whom had been beheaded, and Jane was frightened. Her father said there was no such thing as ghosts but she wasn't sure. Finally, when she fell asleep she dreamed of the two Queens striking each other with broadswords. She awoke with a start and ran in her bare feet to the window. It was almost dawn, there was some light in the sky, and she saw a lone bird on the branch of a tree and she was fascinated by the ease with which it balanced itself. She wondered if the bird had to learn that or knew how by instinct. Her father didn't like the word inspiration; he said his designs were the result of constant thinking and hard work. But she was sure it was more than that. No one else made designs like his. St. Paul's was so big and he made so many sketches. He always had ideas. He didn't believe that God sent down his designs to him from above. He told her, The vital thing was to be on the right track and then he could always find a solution. The bird flew off and she felt as if she had lost a friend, and she hoped the two Queens had liked birds. She heard the lady in waiting, who was sleeping on a couch in a corner of the large bedchamber, stir restlessly, and she tiptoed back to bed. She wished Mistress Fenton didn't snore, it could upset a future husband.

William met his Surveyor the next morning on the broad walk before the east front of Hampton Court. He stated he desired the entire old Tudor palace pulled down, except possibly, the great hall. His instructions were emphatic. Wren must do the east front first and he expected the new foundations to begin within a few weeks. The King repeated that it must outdo anything designed for Louis, since Hampton Court possessed an even more intelligent location than Versailles, with the west front on the Thames, and it was closer to its capital than was the French palace. Then William was gone, as abruptly as he had come and spoken.

As they rode back to London later that afternoon, Christopher asked Jane, "What do you think of the King and Queen?"

"She is nicer than he is. I'm not sure he likes you."

"I don't think he likes many people, dear. He has had a hard life."

"Father, are you going to rebuild the palace for him?"

"If he doesn't change his mind. Or fall ill. Winchester is almost done, the time it will take just to pull down Hampton Court would be sufficient to complete Winchester, but James wasn't interested and I doubt William and Mary are either. It is not their conception. Each monarch prefers to express his own taste. That is why it is vital that St. Paul's is built by one brain. So it reflects a unified point of view."

They rode through fields of grass as green as Jane had ever seen and she said, "Father, last night I thought I saw Anne Boleyn and Catherine Howard. Do you think it is possible?"

"No. Did you see anything else?"

"A beautiful bird. It balanced itself like a blade of grass."

The first plans Christopher submitted to William were rejected, but the King ordered him to demolish the east front anyhow. After his plans were rejected again, the King said that the Surveyor's third designs might do.

Christopher felt William did this more to assert his authority than because the previous images were flat and insipid, as the King stated, but he went ahead with his new designs. He doubted William would ever be a patron of the arts, his ideas for Hampton Court were conventional—the concept which still dominated his thinking was Versailles, with a mixture of the Louvre—and neither of these styles fitted Christopher's plans.

Gradually, as the old east front came down piece by piece he planned a facade of simplicity yet strength, seeking to achieve the proper effect of balance and symmetry. Then he designed an inner court of brick and stone to equal any at Oxford and Cambridge.

It was more pleasing to work on the designs for the interior of the library at Trinity College. When they satisfied him, he invited his favourite sculptor and wood carver, Grinling Gibbons, to discuss the fittings.

The Dutch-born artist arrived promptly at the studio on Scotland Yard, and Christopher greeted him warmly. Gibbons had gained weight since the day Evelyn had introduced the artist to him, thought Christopher, but at forty he remained a handsome man, with broad, regular features, alert brown eyes, and hands that possessed both vigour and subtlety. He motioned to Gibbons to join him and showed him the designs he was working on.

Gibbons examined them with great care and said wonderingly, "Sir, you intend the interior to match the grace and quality of the exterior."

He hadn't told anyone except Jane that the two storeys of columns and arches were what he had desired originally for St. Paul's in his Greek cross design. He said, "Those who use this library must have the best in ease and quiet. The library I used at Westminster School was a barbarity. It must not be repeated at Trinity or at any library I design."

"Sir Christopher, these designs are beautiful as drawings. They are so expressive, so firm yet flexible. They are works of art. You have such skilled hands I've wondered why you didn't become a painter or an etcher."

"I've a friend who is better and Rembrandt said he wasn't good enough."

"That's not fair. Rembrandt judged everybody by himself."

"Besides, I prefer to build. I'm a mathematician, too, and an engineer, and I want to construct things for use as well as for viewing."

"Sir, you have even made sketches for the reading tables and stools!"

"I want everything to match."

"It could be very expensive."

"The value is in the use of the library, not its cost. Notice, there are no main tables, they are all equal in quality." When he saw a puzzled look appear on Gibbons' face as the carver glanced at the design for the floor, he added, "The floor is dropped to the springing of the lower arches, so the bookstacks can be set above the windows and the readers can enjoy an excellent light from above. And the central aisle is of stone because it will be quieter and less dusty than wood."

"Sir, you have anticipated everything."

"I have tried. I want it to be a library to be enjoyed when used."

"But I have wondered about the exterior, sir." Gibbons thought the surveyor had used his powers of invention to their fullest in the long, rectangular design of the interior of the library, but he wasn't as certain about the exterior, for it was without adornment. "You have not asked me to embellish the outer fabric."

"*No! Elaboration on the exterior would be an impertinence!*"

Gibbons flushed and backed away. He felt his art was being attacked.

Christopher, when he saw his hurt, said quickly, "I didn't ask you here to criticise you, but to consult you. Your carvings are the cleverest I know. I hope you will furnish the fittings for the library."

"How?"

"As suits your gifts and the library. Every inch here matters. I've taken immense pains with this interior, as I'm sure you will. Quickness is not needed here, only . . ."

Gibbons filled in the surveyor's thought, " . . . perfection."

"As much as is possible."

"You honour me, Sir Christopher."

"No more than your gifts do. I wish I had a surveyor of your quality to work with me. Oliver means well, but he is ageing, approaching eighty, and growing frail. He is still capable of following and administering orders, but he is without any views or vitality of his own."

Gibbons, who had started out, eager to put his ideas for the library in effect, paused and asked, "Are you really interested in other views?"

"Naturally. I'm not infallible. Most of my designs are the result of much trial and error. I'm always experimenting. Even with St. Paul's. Do you know of some one, Gibbons? You have an odd smile on your face."

"Sir, there is one right under your nose who might do very well?"

"Where?" Christopher felt the carver meant a person he knew.

"In your own office."

Gibbons sounded so sure Christopher asked eagerly, "Who is gifted?"

"Yes. Nicholas Hawksmoor."

"My clerk? He has been with me almost ten years, since he was eighteen. He worked for me at Winchester and Chelsea. He keeps good accounts, knows the cost of materials, but this has little to do with design."

"He also draws accurately and vigorously. And with his own mind."

"Does Oliver know?"

"Oliver is jealous. He doesn't want anyone to supplant him in your affection and esteem. He has kept this knowledge from you."

And I've been so preoccupied, so self-absorbed I've not noticed, thought Christopher wryly. But perhaps the carver was being too enthusiastic, too much the friend, too easily influenced. He came out of his brief reverie and said, "It would be better if I talked to Hawksmoor himself. If you could ask him to bring me some of his drawings it would be appreciated."

Christopher was determined to be critical. Surveying required the highest standards. The next day Nicholas Hawksmoor came to the studio with a sheaf of his drawings as the Chief Surveyor had ordered. As he handed them to Christopher with an air of expected suffering, the Surveyor realised that this young man's personality handicapped him. Hawksmoor was so lean he was scrawny, with a thin upper lip and a thicker lower lip which overhung his mouth and locked him in. His features were tight and compressed, yet his drawings possessed ease and fluidity. Christopher liked the ideas expressed. He saw delicate designs and lively sketches. He wondered why Hawksmoor appeared to be so withdrawn and melancholy.

The clerk waited to be dismissed. It was a waste to submit his work to the Surveyor, nothing would result. He was too different in taste. He was not a mathematician or an engineer, and he liked to indulge his fancy in spite of his innate pessimism, and they were of a different generation.

Christopher asked, "Hawksmoor, how long have you been drawing?"

"For years. May I have them, sir. They are my only copies."

"Of course." Christopher gave them back to him.

There was a pause and then Hawksmoor, although he told himself that he was a fool to ask, said, "Sir, are they impossible?"

"What are, Hawksmoor?"

"My drawings, sir."

"It depends on what you intend to do with them. How long have you wanted to be a surveyor?"

"As long as I can remember." For the first time passion came into Hawksmoor's voice. "That is why I sought your favour and esteem."

"By becoming my clerk? Keeping accounts? It is not the easiest way."

"I had nothing else to recommend me but my capabilities."

"As a trained clerk? That is not enough."

"Is that all, sir?"

Christopher's impulse was to dismiss Hawksmoor, the clerk looked so abject and hopeless. But while some of his drawings were crude in style, most of them revealed a keen eye and a strong, accurate hand and he liked Hawksmoor's audacity and dramatic effects. He said, "I find your work useful and promising. Could you visit Hampton Court with me?"

"As your clerk, sir?"

"As a possible assistant surveyor, if you are interested."

Hawksmoor smiled, although it took some effort, and he said, "Would you like to keep these drawings, Sir Christopher? I have many more."

"No. One must start afresh, to fit the demands of each commission."

Almost all of the east front of the old Hampton Court Palace was down when they arrived at Richmond. Christopher had come on this warm, clear summer day because he was told that the royal family were in residence and he wanted Hawksmoor to be present when he consulted the King.

But only the Queen was there. She was pleased to see the Surveyor, and while she acknowledged Hawksmoor's presence only with a curt nod of her head, she was happy to look at Christopher's designs for the park block. Mary made it evident she could not consider Hawksmoor's opinions, since he had not been born a gentleman and his dour manner didn't improve matters. She was surprised that the Surveyor intended to use him on Hampton Court.

This strengthened Christopher's determination to give Hawksmoor a chance to prove he was qualified. He said, "Your Majesty, we will be able to lay the foundations for the new block soon, but I wanted to consult with the King before I did so, to be sure he would be satisfied."

"He is in Amsterdam, deciding with Marshall Schomberg on how they can best resist James' invasion of Ireland. Over two thousand Protestants who have supported us have been condemned to death, and most of the other Protestants have retreated to the north, to Londonderry, where they have sworn to resist the Catholic soldiers of my father to the end. I must oppose him now, for our country and Church."

"I will go ahead, Your Majesty, and perhaps by next year, when the fighting is over, this block will be habitable for you and the King."

"I doubt the religious wars will ever be over, Sir Christopher. They haven't shown any signs of abating in my time."

Or in mine, he thought grimly. "Your Majesty, if you will excuse us, Mr. Hawksmoor and I will examine the site and the building materials."

She assented and he introduced Hawksmoor to the master mason and the workmen as his Deputy Surveyor at Hampton Court Palace.

Hawksmoor looked apprehensive yet gratified and mumbled, "Thanks."

Now definitely, Hawksmoor was no longer the clerk, thought Christopher, but he remembered the Queen's parting words also. "Whatever you do must be approved by the King when he returns from his armies." Yet Mary didn't know when William would be back and he doubted that anyone did.

Hawksmoor was checking the materials and the men with a growing authority and Christopher was pleased with the affectionate yet careful way the Deputy Surveyor was handling the bricks.

He picked up a small piece of Portland stone that had arrived for the foundations and he thought, How perfect, how rare.

By His Ignorance

By his ignorance
He showed me
The Wisdom

Stymean Karlen

51

By His Ignorance

"SIR, I WOULD LIKE YOU TO MEET THE NEW COMPTROLLER OF THE Royal Works."

Christopher turned away from his survey of St. Paul's to greet Oliver and his guest.

"Sir Christopher Wren."

"Mr. William Talman."

They bowed politely to each other to acknowledge Oliver's introduction. Then Talman waited for the Surveyor to speak, as befitted his position.

It was April, 1690, work was about to resume on the site, and the Surveyor was examining the west front where construction was to start. This was an important moment, but the Comptroller was important, too.

He looked at him carefully and saw a tall, slender man of forty, with a fair skin, dark red hair, and light brown eyes, framed in the elegant dress of the courtier. He knew the new Comptroller by reputation: a gentleman architect who had built several country houses for the nobility, but who was more renowned for his politics than his designs. Talman was a member of the Whig party, which was favoured by the King, and was a superb drinker of toasts to the Glorious Revolution of 1688. This was typical of many in William's service, but it didn't recommend him as the Comptroller, the second most vital post in the Office of the Works. He wondered if William was using this as a way of controlling him.

He asked, "Is this your first view of our work here?"

"I've passed St. Paul's a few times, but I haven't had time to stop and see what is being done. But now that His Majesty has honoured me, it is my duty to see how his guineas are spent."

"Mr. Talman, every penny, every pound is checked."

"But there must be some waste, Sir Christopher. There always is."

"It is the building fund that supports St. Paul's, not the royal purse."

"But His Majesty has the power to regulate the amount of the coal tax that is allotted to the rebuilding of the cathedral."

"Come," Christopher said pleasantly, "you must see the work for yourself."

Talman's eyes widened at the scope of the construction. Carpenters were stripping off the boards and other temporary coverings that had been built over the partially completed work to protect it from the rigours of winter. There was a vast accumulation of materials and a multitude of workmen sorting and moving them for use. New scaffolding masts were going up by the sides of the old ones. Tackles were being installed for raising the dressed blocks to the men on the walls, and there were small wooden platforms, gibbets shaped like gallows, for the smaller blocks of stone.

Talman said, "Interesting, but you have so many workmen."

Christopher said, "Sawyers, plumbers, carpenters, masons, carvers, joiners, painters, smiths, clerks. All part of the work."

"And there is so much confusion."

"Everyone has their own task to do."

"Are they all necessary?"

"All!" Christopher said emphatically.

"What about those waiting?"

"There is a reason."

"Sitting down?" Talman was very sceptical.

"Is it more efficient to wait standing?"

"But they are waiting, and that is costly. You can't deny that."

"It is more costly if they aren't here when the stone arrives."

Oliver added, "We expect some large blocks from Portland. If they aren't ready to work on them, it holds up other work on St. Paul's."

Christopher explained the design for the west front and that the stone was for it, and Talman nodded indifferently and said, "The King is concerned about the excessive cost of St. Paul's and the excessive time it is taking."

"What is your remedy?" asked Christopher, prepared to fight back.

Talman said, "That is your problem. Mine is to watch over the expenditures and report on them to the King. As your colleague."

More like a rival than a colleague, thought Christopher.

Talman said, "Besides, why is Portland stone so important?"

"Is that why blocks were diverted from St. Paul's to Hampton Court?"

"That's not so."

"We have an assistant on the Isle of Portland who receives our order for stone weekly. So that blocks of the required size and right texture with the best weather-resisting quality can be quarried, to prevent waste and the wrong stone being sent. The transportation cost is high. Two twenty-ton blocks, which are vital for the west front of St. Paul's, ended at Hampton Court although they were shipped here."

"Who said that?"

"It doesn't matter. We need those blocks of stone at the cathedral."

"There are other considerations. Hampton Court is vital to the King."

"But I'm the Surveyor there and I will decide what stone it needs."

"It must have been Hawksmoor who told you. He will ruin Hampton Court with his bungling. Be wise, Sir Christopher, dismiss him."

Christopher sensed Talman would object to anyone who stood in his way, and his way led to the post of Chief Surveyor. He had no intention of getting rid of Hawksmoor. His deputy was doing the work at Hampton Court so efficiently he had given him another commission. The King, after buying Nottingham House in Kensington, had ordered Christopher to enlarge and remodel it into a palace, and he had assigned most of the work to his deputy. The only new design he was doing himself was the new College of Physicians on nearby Warwick Lane, within sight of St. Paul's.

It was next door to where Daniel's father had lived and it awoke many memories. And while the College was squeezed in by other buildings, his design had a high, handsome front and an imposing tower and dome. He gave special attention to the acoustics in the demonstration and lecture rooms and fitted in his other work in his spare time.

Talman was sure the Surveyor was using this silence to contrive an attack on him and he said, "With war going on against the French and the Irish there is a serious shortage of timber and stone."

Before Christopher could reply, he was interrupted by an agitated Hawksmoor, who rushed to his side, crying out, "Sir, the twenty-ton block you re-ordered has come, but they are having great difficulty moving it at the dock. We need your help to decide what is to be done next."

Christopher said, "Mr. Talman, will you excuse me? Mr. Oliver can show you whatever else you would like to see." Without waiting for an answer, he hurried away with Hawksmoor, it was clear he was needed urgently.

They ran down the narrow, winding street from Ludgate Hill which led to Paul's Wharf on the Thames, pushing their way past many carts, drays, pack horses, chickens, wagons, coaches, pigs, cattle, and pedestrians. There was hardly space for their bodies, Christopher saw ruefully, yet the huge block of stone had to be conveyed up the hill, as quickly as possible.

At Paul's Wharf the great twenty-ton block of Portland stone had fallen in such a way it had cracked the dock. Yet the piece was undamaged, he saw with relief, and just what he needed for the start of the west front.

Hawksmoor said hurriedly, "Sir, we took all the necessary precautions. The ship from Portland carried only one hundred and fifty tons of stone, the limit you set, and this block was unloaded at Redriff, below the shipping in the Pool and London Bridge, and brought from there on a lighter, then transferred here by crane, but something broke."

Christopher checked and discovered that the operator of the crane was at fault. The next question was what would support such a massive weight. He chose a low cart with thick ash planks fastened securely with iron and four sturdy wheels. Two teams of horses were attached to it and a squad of workmen to guide the vehicle and to keep the block from swaying or falling. Christopher supervised the loading of the stone on to the wagon and verified each detail until the block was in place.

Talman arrived to see what the excitement was about and said, "That wasn't such a crisis after all." He was surprised the Surveyor intended to remain with the wagon. "Do you expect any more difficulties?"

"You never know. This is the largest stone we have conveyed so far."

"This is a busy place. I see so many things that you have unloaded here. Lime, chalk, gravel, sand, timber, lead, tools, ropes."

"The river is the quickest and cheapest means of conveyance. Our roads are still barbarous and travel on them takes too long."

Hawksmoor asked, "Sir Christopher, should we begin?"

The sky was growing grey with the feel of rain in the air and Christopher glanced at it apprehensively and hesitated.

Talman said critically, "Sir, are you afraid of the weather?"

"Indeed. It will make streets slippery for the horses. When they will need the very best footing for such a load. Especially uphill."

"But if you postpone it all those men waiting at the site will have to be paid, although they have not performed any work."

"That is a consideration."

"That will not please the King."

Christopher didn't reply.

"I would be afraid if I were supervising it."

Christopher, annoyed by Talman's goading, did something that was rare for him. He made his decision on impulse. He ordered the workmen to proceed with the twenty-ton block although it was starting to rain and the congestion was heavy and he decided to take the direct route.

He guided the men, for he knew it by heart. From Paul's Wharf they went on to Thames Street, where the fire had spread first and burnt so fiercely; past St. Benet's, the Welsh church where Inigo Jones was buried and which he had rebuilt a few years ago; then up St. Benet's Hill. But he was very much aware this was only a start. There was still the hill to St. Paul's and its incline was steep. A squad of workmen moved ahead of the load to clear the way through the swarm of pedestrians and vehicles and as the cart inched ahead his hopes revived. Perhaps he hadn't been impulsive but rational, he told himself, and they would reach the churchyard before nightfall. Pedestrians jeered at them for supporting, "Paul's Folly" but he didn't reply. The cathedral didn't need any justifications. It must be the focal point on London's horizon. This added to his energy, and without thinking, he found himself pulling the horses with the workmen.

The Comptroller, who had been walking beside him, wanting to find out how this would end, gazed at him in amazement. No surveyor with sense soiled his hands. And even Hawksmoor, accustomed to Wren's deep, personal involvement in his work, was startled and shaken.

They were halfway up the narrow, busy street that led to St. Paul's when he felt the risk was too much. Other wagons jostled them; his own horses were slipping more than was safe. Then, as he feared, the lead horse in the first team fell, broke his leg, and took the whole team with him. For a moment Christopher expected the entire load to collapse and shatter the block of stone into a thousand pieces. But Hawksmoor, at great danger to himself, grabbed the second team to keep them pulling on the load so the wagon would not roll out of control, and many workmen followed his example. His quick act kept the load stationary and upright.

Christopher put thick wedges under the rear wheels to brace them—this was a standard piece of equipment for all teams pulling supplies up the hill—and Hawksmoor and the workmen were able to let go.

Hawksmoor felt as if his arms were about to come out of his sockets but the Surveyor's smile of appreciation was a reward he cherished. He was grateful for Wren's support, although he was unable to put it in words, but if the Surveyor could soil his hands, so could he.

It was raining hard now and Christopher decided that further work today was too difficult and dangerous. After he was sure the

cart was secure, he ordered the horses unharnessed, set up a guard
of workmen around the stone and said they would resume the work
tomorrow with other means.

Hawksmoor asked his permission to remain with the workmen,
who were rebellious until the Surveyor assured them they would
receive double pay.

Christopher granted Hawksmoor's request, but Talman was
indignant about the double pay, saying, "The King will not consent
to it."

"Sir," Christopher reminded him patiently, "much of the building
fund comes from private donations. I will take the extra pay out of
that."

"You could have gone on." Talman stood under a roof to
keep from getting wet. "Only one horse had to be destroyed."

"I will not jeopardise the workmen's safety."

"Are you returning to Whitehall?"

"I'm remaining here. I must find a better way to bring up the
stone."

But as they walked back to Talman's coach, which was waiting
for him in the churchyard, the Comptroller, still wondering why
this Portland stone was so important for St. Paul's, asked the
Surveyor.

Christopher didn't answer until they were at the site and within
sight of the walls, which finally, were higher than he could reach.
Then he said, "It is time for the cathedral to start rising."

"Your level is still quite low. And the Portland stone is expensive."

"It is the best. And easily available, for the quarries are owned
by the Crown. This fine, white freestone can be cut freely into
slabs, and unlike most freestone it is ideal for the outer walls of St.
Paul's. It weathers splendidly and can be dressed so it has a smooth
surface that will not crumble or blister no matter how long it is
exposed to heat or cold."

"Have you any idea how much you will need?"

Christopher sighed. "An exact estimate is impossible, but it could
amount to over fifty thousand tons of Portland stone, twenty-five
thousand tons of other kinds, and many wagonloads of bricks, lead,
iron, timber, sand, copper, slate and lime. But why do you ask?"

"It is such an expense. And the King is interested in saving
money."

"For the war?"

"How did you know?"

"That requires no prescience. This excuse was used before to
hinder the building of St. Paul's. It is one of the Crown's favourite
reasons."

"This time it could be serious."

"Mr. Talman, it is always serious. Now if you will excuse me . . ."

The Comptroller bowed politely and stepped into his elegant coach. As he rode back to Whitehall to frame his report to William, he thought, Wren was an old and arrogant man, with little time left to succeed with St. Paul's, while if he was patient and clever, much could be accomplished. He sank back into his luxurious upholstery, pleased with the way he had conducted his visit. As Comptroller, he could veto much of the funds.

The next morning, after a night of study on the site, Christopher devised a system of trolleys and pulleys to pull the twenty-ton block up the rest of the way. He hadn't slept all night, creating these devices, but he didn't mind, his ideas excited him enough to restore his energy.

Hawksmoor and the workmen were relieved by a fresh crew and he was satisfied that the stone was secure, although there were complaints that it blocked the street and threats to remove it, by force, if necessary.

He gave Oliver a list of materials he needed to move the stone and his assistant said, "Sir, there is a scarcity of nails."

"Nails? I bought enough for several years."

"They are valuable and easily stolen. I believe the workmen did it."

"We are already under attack for spending more money than we should."

"I know. But the thefts continue. Of other things, too, lead, timber, guy ropes. I may have trouble supplying many things you need. Despite our watchmen and our dogs, sir, crime is increasing in London these days."

"I'm glad I stored nails at St. Mary-le-Bow and St. Stephen, Walbrook, for an emergency. Have them picked up at once."

"Do you want me to continue to order stone from Portland?"

"Oliver, that is more essential than ever. As long as the six ships in our service can bring the stone to us from Portland we must utilise them. And prove their usefulness."

Now he felt it was even more urgent to bring the block up the hill. To reduce it in size was to ruin it. He must have blocks of stone of this dimension on the site to build St. Paul's as he had conceived it.

But it took another day before he could resume his effort to bring the block into the churchyard. Then he threw a great sling around it and attached that to trolleys drawn on pulleys by many horses and workmen. When he had everything in place he gave the order to pull. The great stone didn't budge. He had a horrible feeling that he would never get this huge block, so essential to his designs, up this dreadful hill. He had not told anyone, but he had found a deep fissure in the cart, convincing him that they would not suffice for such heavy transport. Yet this process he was trying now, he realised, would have to be repeated many times if the walls were to grow higher. After several more efforts to move the stone failed, he felt that all his wonderful and beautiful plans were floundering on this cruel incline.

Finally, as the workmen sweated and the horses strained and the ropes creaked and there was still no movement, Christopher put his hand to the ropes himself. Knowing himself small, weighing barely one hundred and thirty pounds, wiry but not unusually strong, with a good grip but not beyond firmness, going on fifty-eight, although he didn't feel like a slave to his age, he had to conquer this stubborn stone and hill. His effort almost pulled him to his knees, but it also aroused the workmen to greater effort. Hawksmoor and Oliver, who were assisting him in his supervision, joined him on the ropes—even the frail, aged Oliver—and the renewed urgency in all of them moved the rock an inch. Christopher had never known an inch could be so important. Encouraged, they moved the block another inch, several, and then a foot at a time. The ropes were fully stretched and taut and all their hands seemed possessed with a new strength and the horses dug in and Christopher realised that they must all pull in unison, as one. He told them this and they followed his instructions and by the end of the day they moved the block a hundred feet.

As they returned to the site after stationing a guard around the stone, Oliver said, trembling from his efforts, "It is such a little bit. It will take us such a long time to reach the churchyard."

Christopher said, "But now we know it can be done."

It took a week to reach the churchyard but when Christopher saw the block before the west front he felt it was worth the effort. Now others would know how to do it, without damage to the stone or themselves.

He was exhausted. He had tried to sleep at the site, feeling that his presence was necessary, but he had tossed restlessly most of the time.

He arrived at his home after an absence of a week and he felt stripped to the bone. It was just before Jane and William were to go to bed and when she saw her father, she cried in her joy, but then she noticed the lines on his face, and she exclaimed, "Father, are you ill?"

"Overtired, that is all."

"Is it St. Paul's?"

"Yes. Some extra work that had to be done."

"Isn't there always extra work?"

"Most of the time. But it is growing." He was disappointed that William was interested only in the small carved wooden frigate that Grinling Gibbons had constructed for the child as a toy to sail on his pond at Windsor. At ten his youngest son was still having as much trouble learning as his daughter found it easy. "William, do you like it?"

"It has no guns. Why not?"

"Not all ships have guns, son."

"The King's do." William ran off to try it in a bucket of water.

Jane however, was eager to stay with him. "Father, I haven't seen you for a long time. Seven days. May I watch you work?"

"Not tonight, dear. I have too much work to do."

After both children were in bed he walked into his studio but for once his mind refused to obey his will. He sat down on *Myself*, but instead of thinking of a new design his mind turned to the days he was a boy at Windsor and had met Inigo Jones and dreamed of building without believing it could come true. He bowed his head and uttered a silent prayer that he could sustain himself until he finished St. Paul's. Any other hands would mar it or deface it. So many were talking about his age, he was beginning to wonder about it himself. Was he growing old after all? Yet he had gotten the stone up the hill. In a way, he smiled to himself, with his bare hands. That made him feel better and he fell asleep soundly for the first time in many days.

A few days later a part of the new building at Hampton Court collapsed and killed two workmen. Appalled, Christopher drove out to the palace to find out why it happened and came on Hawksmoor and Talman examining the damage. It was a corner of the east front and the Comptroller blamed the Deputy. Christopher noticed that the Portland stone he had ordered put here had not been used, but a cheaper, inferior stone had been substituted. Probably to fill someone's pocket, he thought angrily, and very likely Talman's, the Comptroller denounced Hawksmoor so vehemently.

Hawksmoor stood in stubborn silence.

"It is as I said," Talman declared. "The Deputy made a fatal error."

Christopher replied, "Whoever put the wrong stone here made an error."

"What stone?" asked Hawksmoor. "Sir Christopher, I ordered the mason to use what you designed, Portland stone of the best quality."

2D

"It wasn't used. Mr. Talman, what happened to the Portland stone that was sent here? I don't see any on the site."

"There wasn't any sent here."

"Our account books show two twenty-ton blocks intended for St. Paul's continued up the river on a barge and were delivered at Hampton Court. And smaller blocks were sent here for the east front. They were signed for and acknowledged. Mr. Talman, someone is stealing stone."

"I don't know anything about that."

Hawksmoor said, "But you are quick to blame someone else. Sir, it was pouring when the men fell. I had ordered all work to stop because of the risk but after I left work resumed on orders of the Comptroller."

"That is not true!" Talman shouted. "Hawksmoor is no gentleman!"

Christopher turned to the Master Mason, Thomas Hill, who had the masonry contract at Hampton Court because he had found this middle-aged man trustworthy at St. Paul's and asked him what had happened.

"The Comptroller ordered work to proceed, although Mr. Hawksmoor and I had left, thinking everything was shut down. The workmen told me that Mr. Talman said to stop in midday was a waste of money, and that he threatened to fire them if they didn't continue, although they warned him that it could be dangerous. But he didn't listen, Sir Christopher."

"Mr. Talman, were you trying to save one shilling, six pence a day?"

"Every shilling counts, Wren. Those men weren't energetic anyhow."

"Mr. Talman, from now on, keep your hands off my designs. And if you don't, I will give orders that you be barred from all the royal sites."

"The King will never stand for that."

"I will not have anyone contravening my orders."

"Not even His Majesty?"

"No one. Not when lives are at stake."

"I will speak to the King. As soon as I can."

"Please do. Mr. Hill, didn't you notice the difference in the stone?"

"Yes, sir. But Mr. Talman insisted I use it. He said it was the King's wish and since he is Comptroller, I thought it was your wish, too."

Talman demanded an inquiry to investigate negligence in Wren's work at Hampton Court. But the King was in Ireland to oppose the invasion of James Stuart, and the Queen, as Regent, heard his complaint. She asked the Surveyor to be present and when they met at Whitehall, she praised his work at Kensington and she didn't want to talk about Hampton Court.

"Sir Christopher, I'm especially pleased with your alterations at Kensington. The new courtyard and the King's staircase are splendid."

He didn't tell her they were mainly Hawksmoor's work but listened.

Talman couldn't endure what he considered her evasion. He blurted out, "Your Majesty, aren't you going to review Hampton Court?"

"I have. When I asked the King to commission Sir Christopher to redesign it. You are foolish to question his integrity. You are only jeopardising your own reputation. I have the report on who ordered the men to work. Do not take advantage of the King's absence."

"Your Highness, I'm only trying to account for all the expenditures."

"You have. Sir Christopher, when do you think the choir of St. Paul's will be ready for divine services?"

"In a few years, Your Majesty. It depends on the difficulties. Some materials are not easy to obtain and the war adds to the delays."

"If I can help you, I will. Mr. Talman, is there anything else you wish to say? Your views give me no pleasure."

He bowed stiffly, angry that he had wasted his energy. He must wait until the King returned; William should be more sympathetic; the King had no emotional connections with Wren and his family, as the Queen did. He said, "Your Majesty, I am always at your service."

"Then save the money elsewhere." She dismissed Talman and said, "Sir Christopher, I'm looking forward to the day you finish the choir of St. Paul's. It will be an honour to be the first Queen of England to use it."

Christopher was celebrating William's decisive victory over James in Ireland at the battle of the Boyne on July 1st, when he heard of a new threat to the cathedral. The day before, on June 30th, the English fleet was defeated by the French at Beachy Head and driven from the Channel. Six stone ships from Portland were sunk by the French and they blockaded the Channel. Now no ships from Portland could reach London and he was forced to look elsewhere for stone. Some was available from quarries at Taynton, Oxford, and Headington, but was not right for the exterior of St.

Paul's. Work on the walls had to halt completely. Yet he couldn't shut down the site in the middle of summer. He feared that if he did it would become the established pattern. He decided to focus on whatever work was possible. He turned to the lower roof of the choir which required great beams of oak of the best quality. But when he looked for such timber, he learned that the best oak was confiscated by the Navy and what little was left was costly and its price was rising. Unable to accept this situation, he thought of the one friend at Court who might be able to help him, and appealed to the Queen for assistance.

The Surveyor's request for royal timber worried Mary. William had commanded her, as Regent—he was still away at the head of the army—to use the finest timber to repair and to rebuild the severely damaged warships. But the idea of work ceasing on the cathedral distressed her, too. Perhaps she cherished St. Paul's more than William did, she thought, but it was her way of proving that she supported the Anglican faith, and thus, her opposition to her father was wise and inevitable.

She asked the Surveyor to attend her at Hampton Court and informed him, "I possess land near Windsor which my father left me. It contains a grove of fine oak trees. Sir Christopher, how many would you need?"

"Twenty or thirty. I can't be sure, Your Majesty, until I see their size and fibre and whether they can provide the lengths I need."

"I believe there are forty in the grove. Do not take them all. As it is our forests dwindle too much in our time. Make twenty do."

"I will try, Your Majesty. It will help keep St. Paul's alive."

"Consider it my contribution to the building fund. But you must cut them down and transport them yourself."

The grove was near Runnymede where the *Magna Carta* had been signed and *Cooper's Hill*, the site of Sir John Denham's best known work, and he hoped that the poet's restless soul had found peace. Christopher took Hawksmoor with him and the Deputy was astonished by the amount of detail the Surveyor felt was essential. He was more concerned about the fibre of the trees than their appearance. He examined each oak to be sure it was neither hollow nor rotten, but possessed a hard and solid trunk and good sap. Then he waited until autumn to cut down the trees, so there would be no fresh sap running in them and the wood would be as dry as possible. He told a puzzled Deputy, "Now the wood is less likely to warp, twist, swell, or shrink. And it must be cut in the direction which the fibres run for the wood to have its greatest strength. We must also be sure that the trees are tall enough for the long beams of the choir roof."

Such an accumulation of knowledge stunned Hawksmoor, but he listened carefully, for some day he, too, might have to cut down a great forest.

Moreover, the Surveyor chose his trees so that those left standing formed a grove that could still be cherished. Finally, when all was decided, he moved back to the road where the wagons and the horses waited for the trees to be felled. As he watched, aware of Hawksmoor's interest in his feelings, he said, "These oaks are a treasure. I want to take only what is absolutely necessary for St. Paul's. They grow sadly scarce these days. We must not lose them on the landscape."

"Yes, now a man can ride miles outside of London without seeing a single grove of oaks. Sir, when I was a boy that wasn't so."

"This was where I was a boy. I spent many happy hours here."

"Sir, was the time as confusing as it is now?"

"More so. Affairs were out of order between Cromwell and Charles."

"Sir, you knew them both, didn't you?"

"After a fashion. I'm not an authority on either man."

"Did you like Cromwell?"

"He wasn't a man to like, but I respected his ability and he had a high regard for learning and he encouraged it when I was at Oxford. But we mustn't look back. We have a great task ahead of us at St. Paul's."

Hawksmoor understood this better when it came time to convey the wood to London. After the huge beams were loaded on to the wagons it took a double team of horses to move them. Then the Surveyor insisted on accompanying the first one, guiding it through narrow, winding village streets, where the extraordinary length of the beams caused many difficulties. But they were the size he had to have for the roof of the choir and so he persisted with a patience that amazed Hawksmoor. And the Surveyor had estimated correctly what weight the wagon would take.

When the journey was over and the timber was safely in the churchyard, Christopher said, "Mr. Hawksmoor, you can supervise the next trip."

After a long pause, Hawksmoor said, "You still trust me, sir?"

"I always have. By Talman's ignorance, we know him."

Hawksmoor hoped he could follow the Surveyor's footsteps. When he supervised the second trip he did exactly what Sir Christopher had done. He also wore a feather in his hat, for once he didn't have a look of resignation, but rode upon his horse as if he belonged there, and even cried out on several occasions, "Make way for the Royal oak!"

I See My Future

I see my future
Only in your vision

Thank you for finding
Whatever
I have ever lost
And keeping it

Creating with it
a future for me
Almost here

Stymean Karlen

52

I See My Future

JANE ARRANGED EVERYTHING.

"With Lucy and Seth's help," she reminded her father, when he praised her for the skill with which she was managing this party for his sixtieth birthday. They were standing in their drawing room a few minutes before the guests were expected and he was delighted with her maturity and poise.

Although, with his passion for accuracy, Christopher had to add, "But you know, dear, you are being premature. I won't be sixty for six weeks, on the twentieth of October. You mustn't make me older than I am."

"I didn't want to lose this chance to celebrate your happiness about St. Paul's. Tomorrow, you said, you expect building to return to normal for the first time in two years. Since you moved that block of stone."

"Yes, with the victory of our Navy at La Hogue the blockade has been lifted and the first stone ship is expected at Paul's Wharf tomorrow."

"That is why today is fitting for a party. But I had to say on the invitations that it was for your birthday, to get the guests to come."

He nodded, wanting to be obedient to her wishes as she desired.

"Father, you did give me permission to be your hostess. As the King would expect, if he had no wife but a daughter my age. Now don't be nervous. I'm going to the studio to see that Lucy and Seth have put everything in order. You do like having the party there, don't you?"

"Most heartily. It's my favourite room. When are our guests expected?"

"Any moment." Jane started to run toward the studio in her eagerness, then remembered, she was a young lady of fifteen and she must not disgrace her father. And so, as she left the drawing room with the dignity of a Queen, she whispered to him, "Don't be anxious. Everybody will come."

He smiled to himself and took a last glance into the mirror to be sure he looked as well as Jane wished. He had dressed carefully, chiefly to please her. He wore a new brown wig, white silk stockings, a blue doublet, grey breeches, and a fine lace collar. Considering his age, he thought, what he saw in the glass was reassuring. His hair was still brown, his eyes were clear and he didn't need spectacles, although there were a few lines about them, his skin was good, with no patches of smallpox which scarred so many, and his body was straight, compact, and agile. He could climb a scaffold with any of the workmen and his natural senses were keen.

Age was a state of mind, he decided, as he joined her.

The studio was decorated like the King's gallery with red and blue hangings, silver candlesticks, and a harpsichord in the corner. Lucy and Seth were still arranging the chairs so there would be room for everyone to sit or walk about as it suited them. Two servants were helping them—Christopher and Jane could not think of Lucy and Seth as anything but part of the family—yet Seth insisted on doing everything.

Christopher was delighted that his daughter had included Seth; the gardener was the only person alive who knew him from his childhood. He was amused that Seth was not reconciled to his age. The gardener, who was in his seventies, regarded his years as a nuisance to be ignored. He felt he still had as good a hand with a rose as anyone, that he could carve his name on the bark of a tree more firmly than his master's boys, even Young Christopher, who was a sturdy seventeen now.

Everything appeared ready for the party and he was glad he hadn't altered the way Faith had furnished the studio. There was a small fire in the hearth, although it was a mild September day. All his papers and designs were on the shelves and in the closets and the table he worked on was filled with refreshments and Jane sat in *Myself* as if it were a throne.

Then suddenly, she cried out, "Do you think anybody will come?"

He recalled a day much like this years ago when Faith had expressed the same anxiety as they had awaited a visit from Charles, and he knew he must put such memories aside, they hurt too much. One of the reasons he treasured Jane was that she was the future. So much of her life could still be ahead of her, and he must do his best to preserve it.

He turned to face his first guest, whom Jane was greeting, and he was surprised. It was Hooke. His friend hadn't been feeling well lately and he was more stooped than ever, but when he saw Christopher's instinctive smile of pleasure he pushed his shoulders back with a great effort, although they were still misshapen and he clutched the outstretched hand.

"I couldn't miss your father's birthday, Mistress Jane," he growled. "We are almost the same age. I went to Westminster with him. And Oxford."

"I know, Mr. Hooke. He has told me about it often."

"Has he?" Hooke grinned. "And how we were the best students?"

"Sir, he never talks about himself or his own accomplishments."

"Christopher, how many buildings have you designed? Do you have any idea of the number? I know how many I've done."

"I've lost track."

Jane said proudly, "I've counted them. Forty-one churches are done, seven are almost finished, and four are just beginning. And many other buildings. I have a record of twenty-two. And St. Paul's, of course."

"I haven't finished that yet, Jane dear."

"You will, Father."

Holder entered, looking old and careworn. But when he saw his niece he brightened and asked where the boys were.

"Uncle, William is playing in his room and Christopher is at Cambridge, although he said he would try to come in for the birthday party."

Holder said to Christopher, "I've been very tired lately. I wouldn't have come myself if it weren't a special occasion. Do you expect the choir of St. Paul's to be open soon? I would like to live to see that event."

"It depends on how much wood, stone, and money is available."

Holder sighed. "You've been shut down for two years. It is sad."

"Not shut down, Uncle," said Jane, "But working at half-speed."

"It is almost the same. At that rate it will take centuries."

Christopher said, "I intend to finish the choir as quickly as possible."

"It is too bad the cathedral has gone out of fashion at Court."

"Not with the Queen."

"But many of her notions are ignored by William. It is contrary to his inclinations to support anything as English as St. Paul's."

Aubrey joined them. Christopher had heard he was in financial trouble, but today he was cheerful, for he expected a book he had written on antiquities to be published, and he congratulated Christopher on his birthday.

"Actually, it isn't. I'm not yet sixty."

"You will be. You will live a long time. Your humours are favourable."

Pepys and Evelyn followed Aubrey. Pepys kissed Jane's hand, which delighted her, while Evelyn bowed to her as if she were a Queen and said, "Such a lovely young lady would be an honour to the greatest in England. It is kind of you to invite us. Your father should be the happiest of men."

Jane blushed and Christopher recalled that Evelyn had lost a daughter of nineteen to smallpox and still mourned her. He shuddered at the idea of this happening to Jane and he sought to absorb himself in his friends.

Pepys had been removed from his office at the Admiralty because of his closeness to James, and after another sojourn in the Tower, was in retirement. His round, fat features were heavier and he wore a long reddish-brown wig to match his cloak and colouring, while Evelyn disdained a wig and his long white hair was beautifully curled and he carried himself erectly although he was in his seventies. Pepys was fascinated by the studio and the Surveyor's accumulation of books and papers. He was proud of his own library, one of the best in England, and he wanted to examine everything. Christopher asked Jane, who knew where all his work was, to show Mr. Pepys around and she did it with grace and pride.

Evelyn asked, "Do you truly expect the stone ships to arrive?"

"I've been assured they are on their way. One is expected tomorrow."

"We've regained control of the seas but the French are still afloat. If any of their captains has the skill of a Drake it could be sunk."

"They must get through. The stone is essential."

"Perhaps the Queen can persuade the King to give your ships an escort."

"I requested that and she said she will do what she can."

"The weather is poor for shipping. It is exceedingly wet with a long and tempestuous north-east wind. Many boats are wrecked. I've been asked to take the office of President of the Society, but I declined again."

"We would be honoured. We would benefit from your presence in the Chair."

"I'm too old. Your daughter is well fashioned, almost a grown woman." Holder, Aubrey, and Hooke were discussing the war against the French and wondering if it would ever end. "I trust that you are more fortunate than I was. It is a sickly time. There is much smallpox about."

Newton and Halley arrived and the former, who was edgy although

Halley was animated, said, "I would not have come for anybody else's birthday. I have had such a loss of appetite and want of sleep I have no stability or consistency of mind. Cambridge and the Crown, despite my support, will not guarantee a permanent situation and I cannot find another post here."

"Since the publication of the *Principia*," said Halley, "the Professor has expected an improvement in his fortunes, but it hasn't occurred."

There was so much solemnity in the studio Christopher suggested that Jane perform on her harpsichord. Pepys, who loved music, thought it a fine idea, especially since she decided to play a piece by her music master, Purcell. She performed with such a gentle touch that when she finished all the guests applauded, even the glum Newton.

Pepys said, "What a lovely selection! It is a mighty pretty piece and Mistress Jane plays like an angel. She is a young lady of many gifts."

Evelyn said, "Accomplished and exceedingly modest. Like her father."

Jane asked Lucy to bring coffee and cake for the gentlemen and Seth added wine.

Evelyn said, "Mistress Jane, don't be in too great a hurry to grow up. Treasure your youth while you still possess it. Women, even of honour, tend to become too interested in fashion and self-advantage."

Aubrey said, "She will be splendid. She is a most gracious hostess."

"And virtuous," said Holder.

"She can even read a design like a surveyor," said Hooke.

Instead of being happy at this praise, Jane was uncomfortable. Like myself, reflected Christopher and he hurried to rescue her, "I want to thank all of you for visiting us. May I propose a toast to the Royal Society which brought us together and has united us in learning."

Everyone was drinking to this when Young Christopher strode in. He was out of breath, his fine complexion ruddy from his exertion, and he said apologetically, "Father, I'm sorry to be late, but the roads are bad."

Christopher nodded, knowing that Young Christopher was late often. He introduced his attractive, fair-haired son, who was the tallest one in the family, to the guests while his uncle embraced him and regarded him proudly.

Aubrey asked, "Young man, where have you ridden from in such haste?"

"Cambridge, sir. I am at Pembroke."

Newton asked brusquely, "Do you ever use the library at Trinity?"

"Sir, I . . ." The son faltered, not knowing what to say.

Christopher cut in, "My son's work takes him elsewhere."

"That is too bad. The library is a model of order and serenity. I use if often, Sir Christopher. I am grateful for its space and light."

"And I am grateful that it is finally finished."

Newton persisted, "Master Christopher, what is your vocation?"

"I don't know yet, sir. Perhaps, to help my father some day."

Christopher was surprised. His son had never expressed that before, or a strong desire for any vocation. He knew him hardly at all.

Jane said suddenly, "Gentlemen, may I propose another toast?" She felt daring, but she prayed that no one would object, for this was of great importance. "To celebrate yet another great occasion."

Christopher sensed what she was going to suggest but before he could say anything, Pepys exclaimed, "Of course, Mistress Wren! What is it?"

"To St. Paul's! May it continue to grow like a mighty oak tree!"

All the glasses went up as one. Hooke stood by Newton and agreed with him for once. Even Holder, who was abstemious, was drinking, and so were his son and daughter, which pleased Christopher—he hadn't known his son cared—and in the rear of the studio Seth and Lucy smiled proudly.

Then Hooke, as the first to come, had to be the first to go. He bowed to Jane, although he winced from pain, and said, "You are fortunate. Sir Christopher always knows you are there, few others do." He left quickly.

Newton asked, "Do you remember when the library was proposed to you?"

"Yes. Very well."

"At that time I didn't think you would finish it."

Evelyn said, "Poor Sancroft. Removed as Archbishop because he refused to take the oath to William. I saw him before he died earlier this year. Sir Christopher, he was fond of you. When he learned that he was failing, his main regret was that he would not see a completed St. Paul's."

"Sancroft was foolish," declared Newton. "He left the King no choice. I have supported William from the start, but my petitions for permanency are ignored. Yet it was good of you to invite me, Sir Christopher, and I'm sure that everyone shares that view."

There was a murmur of assent and then all the guests were gone. But Christopher, in spite of his friends' appreciation, which he believed, was unhappy. His son had not congratulated him on his birthday or the probable resumption of full time work on St. Paul's, but was in a corner with Jane, apparently confiding in her. He felt that with all of his vaunted wisdom he had failed with his son. He wondered why.

Seth, seeing his master's concern, stepped forward and said to Christopher, "Sir, he is a little afraid of you."

"Of me?" Christopher was startled. "Seth, why should he fear me?"

"He feels he cannot live up to what you expect of him."

To Know How Many Surfaces One Needs

To know how many surfaces one needs
for one's work
Can take a lifetime to find out
Constancy and endless explorations
observing this
Can perfect many things
As well as provide space
      For the discovered truth

Stymean Karlen

53

To Know How Many Surfaces One Needs

Now St. Paul's should grow beyond any man's reach. Now no one should be able to stop it. Now all of its many surfaces should be constructed.

Christopher repeated these hopes to himself as he stood on Paul's Wharf the day after the party and waited eagerly and anxiously. No matter how cheerful a face he maintained for the world, it had been a difficult time. There had been no shipments of Portland stone for over two years because of the French blockade, and he had managed to keep St. Paul's alive only by contriving to work on the roof of the choir. That, too, had been difficult, with the scarcity of sound oak, and he had been forced to allot it with great care, which had caused the workmen to move more slowly than he liked. But the wooden part of the choir roof was complete. And, he told himself, another large step had been taken.

The wind was from the north-west, which troubled him. This could mean stormy seas in the Channel, but the sky was still clear, although clouds were spreading from the west and there was the feel of rain in the air. Christopher, Jane, and Hawksmoor were beside him and he noticed they were eager, too, yet apprehensive. He had invited his oldest son to join him and Christopher had accepted. Somewhat hesitantly, he felt, yet willingly, while Jane had asked to come, and Hawksmoor was along as his deputy.

He knew he mustn't call his son Young Christopher any more, or even think of him in such terms, but he didn't want to push him either.

Hawksmoor asked suddenly, "Sir, do you think Oliver failed after all?"

Oliver had insisted on going to Portland when the blockade was lifted with the purpose of guiding the first stone ship back to London. His assistant had been indignant when he expressed concern that such an arduous venture was risky. Oliver had replied, "Sir, the sea air will do me good, refresh my mind, and I want to make sure the correct stones are shipped and arrive here, not elsewhere." And because he didn't want to be outdone by Hawksmoor, thought Christopher, and was resolved to show he was as good an English sailor as anyone, despite his age.

So he had given Oliver a list of the stone needed by each master mason, grateful for his help. Too often, even with the most careful precautions, the wrong stone arrived and he wanted to avoid such waste.

His son said pessimistically, "I don't see any large ships at all."

"They don't come up this far," Jane said. "Because of London Bridge. But there are some sailing ships in the Pool below it. Look!"

She pointed to many tall masts further down the Thames.

This pleased Christopher; it indicated the blockade was truly broken.

She cried out, "Father, there are some lighters coming!"

He saw several loaded ones approaching under London Bridge and he was excited. Then his spirits fell. Their cargoes were saltpetre for gunpowder, spices to preserve meat and to season it, raw silk, tea and coffee. He had learned from much watching at Paul's Wharf how to tell the cargoes from a distance. But he felt better when he saw coal barges unloading on the wharf below them, for the sea coal from Newcastle was the first thing sunk by the French, and this was a hopeful sign.

His son said, not to be outdone by Jane in knowledge, "Father, doesn't that mean there will be coal dues again and money for St. Paul's?"

"Yes, Christopher, if the King doesn't take it all for the war."

Hawksmoor added, "Master Wren, whenever the colliers are held up it is a disaster for St. Paul's. Bad weather, the French blockade, wrecked cargoes mean less money for the cathedral, and sometimes, none."

"Yet at Cambridge the students joke about how long it is taking."

Christopher said, "They joke about it everywhere. But they are wrong."

"That is what I said, Father. I almost had a duel over St. Paul's."

"You did? Did Seth know?" Could his son protect himself properly?

"Yes. But I swore him to secrecy. Finally, my opponent apologised."

Christopher didn't know whether to scold him or to embrace him. He asked, "What do the students think of the library at Trinity?"

"They say it is the cleanest, most comfortable building in Cambridge."

"How do you feel about it, son?"

He shrugged, blurted out, "It is attractive."

Jane jumped up and down in her excitement and shouted, "It is coming, father, a stone ship. And I can see Mr. Oliver at the front."

Actually, it was a lighter but he did perceive the slight, frail figure of his elderly assistant in front and it was turning into Paul's Wharf. And there was stone in it, he could tell by the way the lighter rode low in the water. He glanced around to be sure the loading crew and the wagons were ready. They were leaning on their tools. It was not easy to recruit such crews, for most of them were vagabonds, poor labourers who drifted from one menial job to another. Then the current took hold of the lighter and for a terrible moment he was afraid it was going to hit the wharf and smash the stone to pieces. He ran to the edge of the dock, Hawksmoor behind him, and grabbed a pole to hold off the charging lighter until the current subsided. His son was by his side with another pole and the three of them were able to dock the lighter safely.

Once it was tied up Christopher jumped aboard to examine the cargo.

Oliver apologised for this near disaster. "We have an inexperienced, skeleton crew, sir. The best seamen have been pressed into the Navy."

"You brought the stone I ordered?"

"All but the twenty- and ten-ton blocks. The sailors refused to take them, they said it was too risky, that it made the ship easy to sink."

"Are many seamen being pressed into the service?"

"Enough to halt the shipments, sir. What are you going to do?"

"Speak to the King. I'm having an audience with him next week." When Oliver still looked concerned, he added, "Don't worry, the Queen assured me that she will be there and she is a friend of the cathedral's."

"Will Talman be present?"

"Possibly. But I will fight him all the way. Oliver, I'm grateful that you went. For once, there isn't any useless stone aboard. That would have been discouraging after all the effort we went to." He paused at what he saw, then exclaimed, "This stone is red!"

"It is stained with the blood of seamen from a French attack. I didn't want to tell you, it will worry you, sir, but while the blockade has been broken, the French warships still prey on our shipping. And stone ships are so slow they are easy targets for warships."

"But why should they want to sink them now?" asked Jane. "Mr. Oliver, they have nothing to do with the war."

"We are the enemy. That is enough. Sir Christopher, if we don't get a naval escort for the stone ships, I don't think they will venture forth. We lost a half dozen seamen to French cannon before one of our frigates drove them off. Four good Weymouth men, two from Brighton. We buried them at sea. We were lucky the stone wasn't shattered. It was as if it had nine lives. Sir, much blood goes into the cathedral."

Too much, thought Christopher, all the natural philosophy in the world couldn't remedy that. Yet St. Paul's had to survive, so much else had gone into it. And it was as much the fibre of the land as the land itself.

"Sir, if you can't persuade the Crown to give us a naval escort this may be the only shipment of Portland stone you will get until the war ends. And the war goes on for years. I trust I've convinced you."

Christopher needed no convincing. He saw blood on other stones and the lighter crew talked about the cannon holes they had seen in the stone ship and how close it had come to going adrift even after it had been rescued by an English frigate. He thought wryly, His audience with the King grew more important each moment. But he must maintain a calmness, no matter how concerned he was inside. He ordered everyone off the dock but the loading crew and then supervised them as they took the stone from the lighter to the wagons. He still remembered how the crane had broken two years ago and he was determined to avoid that recurring.

Grey clouds appeared on the horizon but he felt he must get the blocks to the cathedral as soon as possible. If for no other reason, he thought, to hearten the workmen, especially the masons, who were so essential and who did most of the work. He supervised the conveying of the stone every step of the way, past the carts and coaches that crowded the familiar route. He had chosen his strongest wagons and horses and he took the shortest way instead of the easiest, so he would reach the site in time for some work to be done today. His breaking up the shipment into several loads made this possible and when the wagons arrived at the churchyard and the waiting masons saw the Portland stone they cheered.

His son was surprised by all the things his father did personally; he was Sir Christopher Wren, Chief Surveyor of the Office of the Works.

At the site he asked him, "Why do you have to do so much?" His father even was supervising the fetching of the stone to the masons and the preparation of the mortar. "I didn't know the masonry was so vital."

"It is essential, son. The construction of St. Paul's, in spite of all the bricks, lead, wood, and other materials, is largely masonry work, slow and laborious in execution, but also the flesh of the fabric."

"That isn't what I meant. I was speaking about all you do yourself. Do you have to? Must you guide so much of the work yourself?"

"I have to supervise most things the first time they are done. To set the example and to show how they should be done correctly."

But he allowed Oliver and Hawksmoor to assist him as the newly arrived Portland stone was apportioned to the masons. Most of it was going to the masonry of the choir. Once that was completed and was ready for divine worship he felt that nothing could halt him. The great drive in him now was to roof the choir. He was tired of waiting; he felt out of excuses. Yet by the time he was scheduled to see the King and Queen most of the Portland stone was used and there was only enough for a few days.

The audience was at Hampton Court, for the King desired to discuss it with his Surveyor. The Queen and the Comptroller were with him and a few advisers, but as he ordered the Surveyor to examine the construction with him, he dismissed everyone but the Queen and the Comptroller. The Park Block was half done yet William looked discontented with what he saw.

William appeared more tired and thinner, but his skin was better, as if the years in the field had helped his sallow complexion. The Queen was quiet, waiting for her husband to speak first, while the Comptroller was dressed in the height of fashion, to accentuate his good looks.

William said abruptly, "Wren, I'm disappointed with the lack of progress here. You are almost as slow as you are at St. Paul's."

"The difficulties are the same, sir. We had no stone from Portland for two years because of the French blockade, and even now, only one ship has arrived. And with sailors being pressed into the Navy the crews are poor."

"Can't you use other stone? England is supposed to be rich in quarries."

"Sir, Taynton stone is of a high quality but wrong for exteriors and Derbyshire freestone, while it endures the fiercest fire, is brittle."

"The Comptroller also informs me that expenses increase each year."

"Sir, the price of materials continues to rise with the war."

"Nonetheless, Hampton Court must continue."

"And St. Paul's, Your Majesty?"

William walked away suddenly, and indicated that only the Surveyor should follow him. At the fountain he said, "I have several other tasks for you, Wren. I want you to submit an estimate of repairs on the Tower. It needs renovation badly. So does St.

George's Chapel at Windsor. That should please you. You grew up there, didn't you?"

"Yes, Your Majesty. How did you know?"

"The Queen considers that important. But not Talman." Then William, with an apparent change of mood, summoned the Queen and the Comptroller, and said to Talman, "You've been telling me how unhappy you are with the Surveyor's work. I would like him to hear your grievances."

"Your Majesty, I think only of serving you."

"It is the strangest thing," murmured the King. "No one ever thinks of himself. Or of their own interest. Except possibly, myself."

"I do, sir," said Christopher. "I am part of every brick and stone I put in Hampton Court and St. Paul's. And I suspect you are the same when you are in the field and think of each life that is in your care."

William turned away from the east front as if he didn't want it to divert him, back to the memories of many wars and battles. Ever since he had become the ruler of the Netherlands he had been fighting the French desire to dominate Europe. He had been forced to spill blood like the masons spilled mortar. And now, as ruler of England, the struggles only intensified. Yet Hampton Court and St. Paul's could outlive all of them.

Mary said quietly, "May I suggest something that will serve you?"

The fact is, he felt like retorting, nobody did but himself. Yet she meant well and possibly, genuinely loved him. He wondered if he loved anyone, even himself. It was his duty to preserve the Netherlands, England, Ireland, and Scotland in the Protestant faith, not for the love of God as the Churches said, but as a responsibility he couldn't evade. Perhaps that was why Wren was persistent. He asked, "Mary, what will serve me?"

"A strong St. Paul's and a splendid Hampton Court. I've seen Sir Christopher's designs for the fountain court and for the King's staircase and I believe you will approve. Their style is superb."

"But this gentleman," said William, indicating Talman, "states that we cannot afford St. Paul's and since it isn't absolutely necessary . . ."

"It is, William. Its completion should unite the nation behind you."

"Wren, what is needed for speedier work?"

"Naval help, sir, to convoy the stone ships."

"Anything else?"

Talman said, "We are having great difficulty as it is, Your Majesty, preserving our Navy. It will cost us much if we grant his demands."

William asked, "Wren, how much money?"

"I don't know, sir. But I know that my plans for St. Paul's are not a waste of money or time. I don't seek rare or precious materials, but those which are substantial and trustworthy. It would be extravagant of me to lower the standards, to use materials that are shoddy and second-rate. That would be the waste. It is my duty and responsibility to preserve God in the proper house, as it was my uncle's to marry your parents. I must support St. Paul's as he supported your dynasty."

Wren was cleverer than Talman realised, William thought grimly. He said, "Since it is the Queen's wish, the stone ships will be convoyed."

She asked, "And their sailors will not be pressed into the service?"

"Agreed. But don't bring it up again, Mary. If you've mentioned St. Paul's once, you've done it a dozen times. Wren, I want you to take down Rubens' paintings on the ceiling of the Banqueting House and have them cleaned. They are one of the few works of art this country possesses."

Convoys were assigned to the stone ships and now there was enough Portland stone for both St. Paul's and Hampton Court. There were no emergencies the next year as Christopher continued to concentrate on the choir, while he worked also on Hampton Court, the Tower, the Rubens paintings, the new palace at Kensington, and repairing St. George's Chapel, and a dozen of the City churches and their steeples. During that time he was able to cover the choir roof with lead, a vital step, and by the autumn of 1694—two years after he had appealed to William for help—the roof of the choir was done. He knew it would be several more years before the choir would be ready for divine services, for that needed many fittings, but as the scaffolding was dismantled and the entire shape of the choir could be seen for the first time he felt joyful and achieved.

As soon as the choir was suitable for viewing he journeyed to Hampton Court to invite the King and Queen to see it. William was in Holland but Mary was at the palace and she was pleased to see the Surveyor.

She said, "I will be happy to visit St. Paul's to celebrate the completion of the roofing of the choir. But not now. It will be more appropriate for me to view it in the presence of the King. So I must wait until he returns from the Netherlands."

"When will that be, Your Majesty?" Christopher asked. They were in her audience chamber and she did look vitally interested.

"I'm not sure," she said. But when she saw his disappointment, she added, "However, I have another project which should please you."

2E

He waited, expecting another chore like the Tower or Rubens' paintings.

"I've decided to convert the King's House at Greenwich into a hospital for old and disabled seamen. Like Chelsea. And we want you to design it. On a grand scale. To rival St. Paul's. We must establish that the King and I are as concerned with the welfare of our subjects as any monarch our nation has known and I require your aid, Sir Christopher."

She was as serious as he had ever seen her, and beautiful in her intensity. "Your Majesty," he asked, "when should I submit my designs?"

"At once. With grandeur. They must be a monument to our King's reign."

He returned several weeks later with designs which rivalled anything he had done in scope. He used the King Charles II block that Webb had built as a start, but recalling his earlier experiences at Greenwich, he set his work sufficiently back from the river.

He was surprised and delighted that the Queen accepted his designs without question and stated that actual work should start shortly.

William arrived in London soon afterwards and a charter was granted in his name and the Queen's for the building of a Royal Hospital at Greenwich under the direct supervision of Sir Christopher Wren.

Christopher was repeating to himself the key words in the charter, *"We order you to build a fabric with great magnificence at Greenwich,"* and waiting for William and Mary to visit St. Paul's when she fell ill.

Many came to see the choir and he remembered Evelyn's comment: "*I wanted to see the finished stone work. Some exceptions might perhaps be taken as to the placing columns on pilasters at the east tribunal, but as to the rest it is a piece of architecture without reproach.*" He cherished Evelyn's comment, even his criticism; he knew his friend had to question something, to prove that Evelyn was an authority.

He hoped that the King and Queen would approve. But her illness grew worse and on December 28th Mary died unexpectedly of the smallpox.

Christopher was stunned and stricken. He knew he had lost a good friend and a devoted patron. He sent his condolences to William and some weeks later he received an acknowledgement but no invitation to see the King.

The winter was severe, the Thames froze over, the smallpox increased, and he sent his children to stay at Windsor in the care of Lucy and Seth.

With the coming of spring he was ordered to resume work on Hampton Court and to continue his plans for the hospital at Greenwich, which the King announced was a memorial to his devoted spouse, Queen Mary II.

Christopher was prepared for the placing of the fittings in the choir when he discovered there wasn't enough money. William, with Mary's death, lost interest in St. Paul's and there were no contributions from the Crown. The City authorities, now that most of their parish churches were finished, felt there was no longer a need for piety. There was still money from the coal dues, but much of that was going to the cost of the war. There were donations from the clergy and private citizens, often substantial and amounting to thousands of pounds yearly, but they were not enough either. The increase in construction, the drive to roof the choir, and the rising cost of everything caused the yearly expenses to jump from £10,000 a year to £19,000. Christopher sensed they faced a profound crisis. Yet St. Paul's was so close to being usable that it was inconceivable to him that work would be halted now. The Commissioners found only one solution, to borrow. At Christopher's suggestion the leading contractors agreed to wait for their payments and to regard them as loans, giving the cathedral the privilege of paying them when it would be convenient. But the contractors only assented to this arrangement when Christopher first lent the building fund a thousand pounds of his own money. He was grateful for the pay he received as Surveyor for the Crown and his outside commissions, although he hadn't taken any fee for the library at Trinity and didn't intend to for Greenwich. He felt the loan was an inevitable decision and he returned to working on St. Paul's with renewed vigour. Now, more than ever, he was toiling for himself, too.

This added to his resolve not to allow anything to stand in the way of divine services. The next three years he worked with a single-mindedness that surpassed even his previous efforts and con-centration. He was determined to have the choir ready by 1697. The fittings became the crucial task at St. Paul's during this time. While the north and south fronts rose steadily with the regular shipment of stone from Portland, and the entire fabric took the shape of a cathedral, it was the carvings of Grinling Gibbons and the wrought iron work of Jean Tijou that became the essence of the moment. Their work delighted Christopher and nourished him.

There was a grave problem with the organ. Christopher wanted it placed on the north side of the choir, so there would be an uninterrupted view of St. Paul's from the great doors on the western end to the beautiful choir on the eastern end. But the builder of the organ, Father Bernard Smith, insisted it must be installed over the dome end of the choir where it would obscure the view. The organ builder was supported by the Commissioners and the clergy, who were more interested in the organ's prominence than in the proper placing. So, once again, the Surveyor was forced to adjust.

This time he designed two altars to cover the organ pipes, which he regarded as excrescences. He knew, without pride or vanity, that what distinguished the choir and the cathedral was the design, which harmonised the proportion, balance, and symmetry into an universal unity.

The finely-carved, richly-worked fittings were finished just as it was announced that on December 2nd, 1697, the choir of St. Paul's would be opened for divine services. It was also to be a ceremony of national thanksgiving for the Peace of Ryswick. William had signed this treaty with France, ending the long drawn out war, confirming his victory over Louis XIV, and establishing him firmly and permanently on the English throne. The City and cathedral authorities invited the King to lead the international group of notables who were attending the celebration.

The day before this opening Christopher took his oldest son and daughter with him for a final look at the cathedral before the opening ceremonies. He left his youngest son home, for William was indisposed, which was just as well, he thought, for William seemed to prefer Lucy's company, and the presence of Christopher and Jane was enough to make him happy.

It was a brisk, clear, winter afternoon and he felt they were the most appropriate partners for this venture. His son had left Pembroke without graduating and had asked for a post in his office. And since he appeared to have some talent for drawing and figures, he had been appointed assistant deputy engrosser. Christopher thought that Jane, although younger, was better qualified, but such a situation was impossible for a female, and her brother had become more serious minded and was revealing a taste for antiquities and a new devotion for St. Paul's.

At the cathedral many women were scouring the marble pavement to make it clean and bright for the thanksgiving services and the opening, and there was frenzied activity and commotion inside to be sure that the glory of God would shine forth, but Christopher didn't go within. Tomorrow, he thought, would be time enough. He wanted his children to see St. Paul's as a whole, or as much of a whole as was possible. But that wasn't to be done, he realised, standing on Ludgate Hill. Scaffolding masts surrounded the walls, there were supplies and sheds everywhere, and a vast round void where the dome was to go. And the closer they were to the walls, the lower they looked. Suddenly, so he could raise the structure in his own view as well as in his children's, he moved away.

Jane followed him and said, "Father, the further we go away, the higher the walls go up." She backed off but she was still displeased with the view. "Too many things block it, St. Paul's looks lower than it is."

"Come," said her father, "we will see it from a better vantage point." He led his children down the hill to Paul's Wharf.

His son grumbled, "All you can see from here are the scaffolding masts. They just might as well be a fleet of ships, lying in the Pool below. The buildings block any decent view." He wondered why his father was grinning.

Christopher ordered the wharf crew to row him and his children across the Thames. The two men did this naturally, as if they had done it many times before, and put them off at a flight of stone steps on the south river bank. Christopher left the oarsmen to watch the boat and took his children to a small house directly across from St. Paul's. Their eyes opened in wonder. The view of the cathedral from here was superb.

He said, "I come here when I want to see St. Paul's best."

His son said, "Now the walls rise above the buildings in between."

"From here," said Jane, "there is nothing in between. St. Paul's looks much taller. Most of the second order is finished and it is higher than anyone can reach. Now I see what you intend, Father. When the double orders are done, there will be the dome and the west front elevations."

"Yes, there will be twin towers on the west front."

"So far, good."

"You approve, dear?"

"Don't tease me, father. You know that I do."

"And you, son?"

"One gets a clear notion of the cathedral here and what you intend."

"I come here often to observe and even stay over occasionally. To see it at dawn and at nightfall, in light and shadow. But although the Globe Theatre of Shakespeare's plays was near this part of Bankside, most of it is public brothels and a refuge for those who are evading the law."

His son asked, "Aren't you afraid?"

"No. I dress plainly. I wear no jewels or ornaments worth stealing. I think they've become accustomed to me. Or they think I'm crazy, a small, elderly man staring at an unfinished building across the river."

"You're not old!" Jane denied indignantly. "You still climb the scaffolds with the younger men, although Mr. Hawksmoor doesn't go up."

Yes, he thought, and afterwards the pulse in his wrist was as regular and strong as ever. But he was sixty-five and one of these days, he said to himself, he would have to stop. And the scaffolds would grow loftier as the walls continued to rise. By the time they reached the dome such climbing ventures might be impossible. Then his son had a puzzled look on his face and he asked, "Christopher, what is wrong?"

"I can hardly see the walls behind the scaffolds. I'm not sure how they will look on the horizon."

Jane said, "I can see them. They will be the glory of England. The dome will dominate the horizon. I can visualise it in my imagination."

"Yet it mustn't override anything else. Everything in St. Paul's must go together, from the roof being the right size, the door in the right place, the walls of the right dimensions, all in proportion."

"People always talk about the Portland stone you're putting in it, but I'm fascinated by the bricks. Have you ever tried to count them?"

"It would be impossible, but there are thousands and thousands already in the fabric and there will be many more."

"And look at your city churches! You can see many of them from here."

His son said, "Now I understand why you devoted so much time and care to their steeples. No two of them are alike. You never repeat yourself."

As he saw the pleasure in his children's eyes, he was glad he had endured. This gave him as much gratification as anything he experienced.

Jane asked, "Is the King coming tomorrow?"

"Nobody knows. Some say he is still afraid of assassination, others say he wants to appear as the victor over Louis. But no one is sure."

"He is not your friend."

"Few kings are. Or can afford to be. Charles might have been, if he wasn't King, but their situation makes them suspicious."

"Professor Newton is suspicious and he isn't King."

"He has his own domain and he feels he has to protect it. We must go before it gets dark. We have much to do to prepare for tomorrow."

The King didn't come to the thanksgiving services—the reason given was the threat of assassination by the Jacobite supporters of

James—but Christopher felt it was because of his indifference to St. Paul's.

As the Surveyor sat in the completed choir with Christopher, Jane, and Holder, he was happy with his company, particularly the presence of Holder.

His brother-in-law, in his eighty-first year, was not well and had gotten out of bed to attend this blessed ceremony. There were so many times Holder hadn't expected this day to arrive he couldn't miss it now.

Then, while no church bell had been installed in St. Paul's yet, the air filled with the tolling of bells. Christopher realised they were the bells of St. Mary-le-Bow, St. Stephen's, Walbrook, St. Benet's, and other churches he had built and he was grateful for them. They were rejoicing.

Important personages were present for the divine services: the Lord Mayor and the aldermen, peers, admirals, generals, ambassadors, bishops, but Christopher, while he knew many of those in attendance and some of them were his friends, was thinking of two messages he carried.

The letter opened, "Now that you have a Dutch King . . ." Then he knew who it was and his heart leaped from joy at the thought that Daniel remembered.

". . . it is fitting that I write you. But I would have anyhow, to congratulate you on the completion and opening of the choir. Only you know what perseverance and devotion this accomplishment required, but I am grateful that in a small way I know, too, and experienced some of this with you. And now the world knows what I've known a long time, that Christopher Wren finishes what he starts. It must be a great joy for you and it should be.

For myself, Maria and I manage. My father left me sufficient to provide for my needs and I paint and design scenery for the stage. The rich burghers like masques and Maria is good with a needle and helps with the costumes and is complimented often on her good taste. We have not wed due to her faith, but the world thinks so, for we live on the Joden Breestraat in Amsterdam, near where Rembrandt resided. She has a little chapel in our house, which I designed, and why not, I assisted the best church builder I know. Meanwhile, I worship the universe and trust it will preserve me in good health and my dear friend, Christopher.

Your obedient servant,
Daniel Van Doorn."

The other message was an official one from Parliament. The

Commons felt that St. Paul's was being built too slowly and, dissatisfied with the rate of progress, informed him of the following in writing. *"Until St. Paul's is finished, the Surveyor shall hereafter be given only half of his salary, one hundred pounds per annum. And then, when the cathedral is done, it will be considered whether he can have his arrears."*

He smiled to himself, thinking, If they assumed he would resign his post they were fools. But for a moment he was angry and it showed.

Holder sensed what irritated him. He whispered, "Parliament cut your salary on Talman's advice and with the King's consent. The Commons feels that will spur you to quicker and harder activity. They don't understand the obstacles you have had to overcome. But we, the clergy, have a remedy for their stupidity."

"What is it?" Holder, despite his age and frailty, was animated.

"We circumvented them and their impious reverence for money. The Church is giving you the post of Surveyor of Westminster Abbey. At one hundred pounds per annum. You will not suffer at all. But have a new honour."

"I have the good fortune to have friends."

"You have the good fortune to be Christopher Wren."

Surely that was not unique, he reflected, yet Holder looked elevated as he said that and added, "I'm proud that I contributed to your education. I may be remembered most for that. It was an act of grace."

Dr. Compton, the Bishop of London, and an old friend of both of them, appeared in the pulpit he had designed and Gibbons had carved. It was the final sermon of the divine services and as Compton preached of the glory of God, he prayed that St. Paul's would ennoble what it touched.

He was standing outside a few minutes later when his son said, "It is too bad the King didn't come. It could hurt St. Paul's."

"It doesn't matter. We have suffered far worse neglect and endured."

"But you are his Surveyor, too!"

"As I was for Charles and James. And they contributed to St. Paul's."

"I don't think so. The Crown hasn't helped it much. It was built on the coals from Newcastle and with your blood and energy."

"Let us hope it lasts, son. Particularly my energy." He turned away, looking for Jane, curious about what she was feeling.

She stood on the steps outside the west front where the dignitaries emerged in their glittering costumes and sparkling jewels. He saw many peers and bishops pass her; he heard Dutch and French and Spanish accents. But Jane was looking past all of them and staring at the fabric of St. Paul's as if it were flesh, and when she saw him, excited and happy, she exclaimed, "Father, now St. Paul's can rise and rise as if it grows of its own accord. The ground will nourish it and the sun and the rain."

"Yes." He sighed. "Perhaps God can live here."

"It could become the most beautiful thing in London. It could make me forget what is base, cruel, and inhuman on this earth."

Jane said that with passion but he loved the gentleness on her face.

He squeezed her hand to show that he approved and then he said, "You and Christopher wait here. I want to go back into St. Paul's for a moment."

His son, taken aback, asked, "Father, have you lost something?"

"Possibly." Now that everyone was gone but the watchman, he slipped into the choir and knelt before the altar, a slight figure against the high curve of the choir, and prayed. It was a very private plea to God. "Please," the words formed in him, "in Your infinite mercy give me the strength and sustenance and years to complete Your House."

I Form

I Form
With each thing that forms
Still unborn

I Begin
With each thing that begins
Just born

I cannot say I die
With each thing that dies
I never learned how to end

My nature never deceived me
It must be that
death has a different meaning

Stymean Karlen

54

I Form

"FATHER, THERE IS A MESSAGE FROM MR. EVELYN. HE WANTS TO know if you will attend today's meeting of the Royal Society with him."

Christopher looked up from his drawing board and said, "I'm too busy, Jane. Tell him I may be able to go to the next meeting, but not today's."

She nodded and retired to convey his reply to Evelyn's messenger, who waited outside. Evelyn was visiting Whitehall Palace and he was prepared to stop by on his way to Gresham if the Surveyor would join him.

He returned to the designs he was pondering, but for the moment it was difficult to concentrate; he was thinking of the changes in the Society. Many of his friends had died or were too old to attend and the last few years he had gone to the meetings less and less. Moreover, there was still so much to do on St. Paul's, yet he was oppressed with the feeling there was so little time. And what he was seeking to design now was in some ways the most difficult task of all: to conceive a dome that would satisfy him both externally and internally. He was still exploring but details had clarified since the choir was achieved. It was a month after the opening of St. Paul's and these hours at the studio were precious. There was no better place to work. Jane was always prepared to serve him and she understood his intentions, and his son was supposed to help him, too, although he was absent now, which was not unusual. Jane was back and he asked, "Do you know where my earlier designs for the dome are?"

"Yes. I've kept a file here of everything that you've done."

She brought them to him at once, knowing just where they were.

He studied the most recent first, and suddenly he was annoyed, which was rare for him, and asked, "What are Hawksmoor's sketches doing here?"

"I don't know, Father. But he has access to them as your assistant."

"I want to give him every opportunity I can, but that doesn't include doing my work for me. As he has done here. He must be told."

"What should I write your office?"

"*That his function is not to assist the Surveyor in drawing designs, but in copying them.*" He had no intention of inviting Hawksmoor's ideas or anyone else's; he wasn't that old yet.

"Should I put this in your name?"

"Of course! It is my decision!"

"He could be offended."

"That would be unfortunate. But St. Paul's is my design, no one else's. He has asked to design churches and steeples and that is fitting, and I intend to encourage his wish when suitable opportunities occur."

"Father?" Jane halted self-consciously, which was not like her.

At twenty-one she was poised and gifted in whatever she did, and while she would never be a beauty—her features were too wide, too square for that, like his own—her complexion was excellent and her face possessed character. He wondered if she had ever been in love. "What is it, Jane?"

"St. Dunstan's in the East waits for a steeple and I've thought of something that might be appropriate."

His impulse was to say No at once, but she was so serious he couldn't be abrupt. In some ways her devotion to his work was as intense as his own. "Why St. Dunstan's?"

"The structure of the church suggests a straight, high spire."

"Is that all?"

"I also think it should be in the Gothic fashion."

"Why?"

"I know you don't favour it, but it is appropriate to the structure of the church itself. I would rest it on four arches. It might be a difficult piece of engineering but I believe it can be done."

He was intrigued by her suggestion. Although St. Dunstan's in the East had been damaged by the fire, its walls had survived because of the efforts of the students from Westminster School. And because of his passionate belief that a structure should be all of a piece a Gothic steeple and spire should be fitting for the Gothic walls and masonry.

"Do you see what I mean, father?"

"Your suggestions are sensible. Put them down. That is always the best way. Then we can judge if your ideas are suitable yet beautiful."

"Thank you."

"That doesn't mean I will accept them, but I will examine them carefully." He paused, then added, "Jane, since you've had no mother, I felt I must be many things to you. I believe, if she were here, she would be asking you, 'Aren't you interested in any young men? You are twenty-one.'"

"You told me that my mother didn't marry until she was much older."

"She regretted that."

"She didn't regret marrying you, did she?"

"Jane, you were the result! But you should think of having a family."

"I have a family. All these designs."

"Christopher has several young ladies he attends and courts."

"He likes to play the gallant, the courtier. He is different from me."

Jane looked so vexed, a state he couldn't endure, he changed the subject. "Does Lucy think William is any better?"

"Not much, father. Do you think his illness is permanent?"

"*It may be. Poor Billy continues in his indisposition, and I fear is lost to me and the world, to my great discomfort and to our future sorrow.*"

"Can't the doctors do anything?"

"When I take him to the doctors they say he will grow out of it, only he hasn't so far. A building problem can be solved, but the longer I live the less I think the doctors know what they are talking about."

Jane nodded, and returned to the steeple she wanted for St. Dunstan's. No man she had met knew as much as her father or could talk so cleverly when he wanted to, yet he never sought to deceive her with flattery. And most of them, she felt, courted her because of her father's position. She disliked that, although her brother made much of being the son of the Chief Surveyor.

He arrived at the studio an hour later and found his father and sister working on different designs. Jane was better with a pencil than he was, he thought, but he was more worldly. He was determined to marry well, after he sowed a few wild oats.

Christopher saw his son but he continued working. He was close to what he desired for the dome of St. Paul's. For years he had realised that a single fabric would not be as effective internally as it would be externally. So he had decided long ago that two envelopes would be needed, an exterior one which would express the grandeur and proportions of the total St. Paul's, and an interior fabric which would convey the majesty and serenity of the space within the cathedral. What concerned him most was the structural relationship between the two domes. He had experimented with many possibilities ever since he had submitted his Greek cross design and gradually a likely solution had evolved. Now he believed he had the answer for which he was searching: an intermediate cone between the two domes, which in a sense, was a third dome, supporting yet uniting the outer and inner fabric. If that was possible, he told himself, and he was almost certain it was, the next step was to find the best material for what would not be one structure but three. The more he thought about this concept, the more logical and sensible it became.

He sensed that his son wished to talk to him, but he was so engrossed he didn't want to be interrupted and he ignored Young Christopher's presence.

He was thinking with gratification, These days it was unlikely his designs for a dome would be thwarted. Almost everyone who had opposed his Greek cross design and insisted on the Warrant design were gone. Moreover, the present Commissioners could not close down the construction of St. Paul's on him now. His determination to build the cathedral as a whole instead of putting it up piece by piece had worked. Although the choir was functioning, it could not function properly until St. Paul's was complete. The part of the cathedral which led to the choir was open to the sky, a void where the dome was to be. By now he was far away from the design that had been accepted, for while he still followed the Latin cross plan, his St. Paul's possessed the dimensions and style he desired.

His son's impatience got the better of his judgment. He knew his father's preoccupied manner very well and that it could last a long time, and he blurted out, "I have something I want to discuss with you."

"Can't you see that I'm busy with St. Paul's!" He was estimating the materials he would need for the two domes, for he had decided to consider the intermediate structure a support rather than a dome.

His son replied, "But now that St. Paul's is open and is performing as a church with divine services, you shouldn't be in a rush."

Jane understood better, Christopher thought, but he didn't try to explain. "Son, what is so urgent?"

"I want to go abroad, but . . ."

"You want my permission and aid?"

"I will do whatever you wish, but you have said many times that your journey to France taught you much. Now that I have the same opportunity I thought you would approve. And I have a travelling companion."

"Do I know him?"

"Yes. Edward Strong's son. Strong is your favourite mason."

Christopher felt he couldn't refuse what he had desired himself. He said, "If that is your wish," and his son embraced him, crying out, "I'm the happiest of men! What are you doing, Father? You look pleased with it? Is it a dome? I know it matters to you. Have you found a solution?"

"Possibly." He showed him what he was doing.

"It looks satisfactory to me," said his son, after a quick look.

"It needs more than one look," said Christopher. "You never know what unexpected difficulty you can encounter."

Jane joined them, drawn by her brother's excitement and her father's gratification, and she said, "There are many things to consider in a dome. How it will wear? How it will sound? How it will look?"

"Father will solve them," he said confidently. "He always does."

"Not always," answered Christopher, but before he could try to impress on his son that surveying wasn't as easy as that, Lucy stood in the doorway, shouting, "Fire! Master! Fire!"

"St. Paul's?" It was the thing he feared more than anything else, there was so much wood and other inflammable material on the site.

He started toward St. Paul's and Lucy cried, "No! No! It's closer! Whitehall is ablaze and it spreads so fast it could reach us!"

All of them ran into King Street but it was already too late to put out the fire, Christopher realised, or to save the palace. The old, rambling sprawl of Tudor buildings were being consumed before anything could be done to save them. The flames were moving west from the privy stairs where he had seen Anne and the riverside terraces which he had renovated, and were destroying everything in their path. Then the fire spread south, engulfing the Great Hall and the chapel, and ran along the stone gallery and even enveloped parts of the privy garden. He felt stricken and stupefied, for there was nothing he could do to help. Palace servants fought bravely to douse the flames but their efforts were in vain. All the royal apartments were being burnt to a cinder. He was grateful for the empty ground between the burning buildings and the Banqueting House, it was a fire break, and he prayed that this work of art be spared.

Jane watched in a mixture of fascination and horror, but Lucy was still afraid the flames would reach them and his son shared her view, but Christopher said, "I doubt it. The fire is being blown away from us."

By the next day Whitehall Palace was a charred ruin, but the Banqueting House and the buildings at Scotland Yard had escaped the flames.

Christopher hurried to St. Paul's to make sure that the strict precautions he had ordered at the cathedral to prevent a similar occurrence were being obeyed. Oliver, who was still supervising in spite of his age, assured him that everybody was being very careful.

But as he saw the carpenters erecting new scaffolds he was concerned, for the wood was exposed and vulnerable, and St. Paul's was cluttered with sheds. He placed water and sand where it would be easily available if needed. Then he cautioned the workmen to take all the necessary precautions to avoid fire, even if it meant a longer time to finish their work.

Hawksmoor reminded him that this could bring complaints from the Comptroller's Office, and he replied that such matters should be referred to him and he would judge what the labour should cost.

Oliver had another concern. Portland stone ordered for St. Paul's had been shipped to Hampton Court again. Hawksmoor said that he knew nothing about it, that it must have been done by Talman, who was at Hampton Court often, and Christopher said he would look into this matter.

The opportunity came quickly. William moved to Hampton Court after the burning of Whitehall, and he ordered his Surveyor to attend him there.

He saw Christopher in his private dining room after he had eaten. He ignored the pleasantries and asked abruptly, "Why was work halted here?"

Talman stood behind William, smiling slyly, having dined with the King, and Christopher replied, "Sir, I was told to stop when the Queen died."

"But Mr. Talman continued."

"Your Majesty, I have the order in writing commanding us to halt. Do you wish to see it?"

"Never mind." In his concentration on fighting the French and James Stuart, he had forgotten that he had ordered all work on Hampton Court to be stopped with his wife's death. Rebuilding this palace had been mostly her idea anyhow; but now, perhaps, it was sensible. He grumbled, "With the destruction of Whitehall, work here is more essential than ever. Wren, what you have done at Kensington Palace has made it more habitable, but it is too near London for my comfort, too close to the Court and too damp. When can these apartments be finished?"

"Sir, it depends on the amount of money, labour, and materials that are allotted. If they are sufficient, only a couple of years."

"That is too long. I don't have that much time."

"What about Winchester, sir? If you are in such a hurry, it could be completed in less time. Everything is finished but the roof."

"I'm not interested in Winchester. That was Charles' idea. Talman claims he can have Hampton Court ready for full occupancy in a few months."

"Sir, he doesn't take all the factors into consideration."

William asked impatiently, "What factors, Wren?"

"He is concerned chiefly with cost, sir. It is not enough."

"I will decide what is enough."

"Very well, Your Majesty. But I would appreciate if you would remind Mr. Talman that he must not confiscate stone intended for St. Paul's."

William turned to the Comptroller, asked, "Is this true, Talman?"

"Sir, the stone was needed here. And I knew you wanted work to resume at Hampton Court. I was only anticipating your wishes."

"On the contrary, sir," said Christopher. "He used the Portland stone for the garden, which is a waste. A different stone should be used there."

Talman retorted contemptuously, "As if it matters."

"It does matter, especially for one so concerned with money."

"No one will distinguish the difference."

"They will when the cracks show."

William, who had become stooped and gaunt from his wars, picked up the papers he had been studying when the Surveyor had been admitted. As he saw the sneer on Talman's face and the Surveyor's defiance, he snapped, "Enough of your altercations! Wren, I expect you to resume work on Hampton Court at once!"

"Sir, what about the stone intended for St. Paul's?"

"I'm at the helm! I will steer! I will decide!" He started to read his papers to indicate that the Surveyor was dismissed, but when Christopher didn't move, he stated, "You are fortunate that St. Paul's is not finished. If it were, I'm not sure we would have any further need of your services."

"What about Greenwich, sir?"

"Now that we have laid the foundation stone and have your designs there are others who can complete it. Talman has experience as a surveyor and Hawksmoor, your assistant at Kensington, has substantial knowledge and knows what I want. The stone is your problem, I have enough of my own."

"Then I should continue my work on Hampton Court and Greenwich, sir?"

"At my pleasure. No wonder St. Paul's takes so long, you are so cautious."

Christopher didn't feel cautious at all. He seethed inside; he was angry enough to resign, but he didn't want to jeopardise St. Paul's. So, instead of showing his feelings, he bowed and said, "Sir, is that all?"

"One more thing. Talman has a complaint from the Treasury."

The Comptroller said, "The Treasury requested the Chief Surveyor to repair the tennis courts at Hampton Court Palace. As Keeper of His Majesty's Tennis Courts it is his responsibility. But he has refused."

Christopher added, "Your Majesty, I did only because I am unacquainted with tennis play. Someone who knows the game should do this."

"You are Surveyor of the Works. It is your duty to take care of all the royal establishments. Tennis courts, too. Although I don't play either. It doesn't suit my legs."

This reminded William that he had forgotten to take off his riding boots in his haste to eat and in his desire to avoid pain. Only now it hurt more to wear them than to remove them. He motioned to his groom to pull off his boots. But when the young man did such a grimace of anguish appeared on William's face, Christopher realised he suffered severely from the gout, and perhaps, much worse. There were many rumours that the King was ailing and this was what gave him such a rude disposition. When Christopher saw the King's swollen legs, which formed a grotesque contrast to his shrunken, wasted body, he felt sorry for him instead of being angry at him for his curt behaviour. And as William hobbled painfully and awkwardly into his bedchamber he doubted that the King had many years to live.

It was a relief to return to St. Paul's. There was peace at the moment, although there was talk of war resuming with France and James Stuart, and Christopher concentrated on obtaining stone for the next few years. He ordered more from Portland than he needed for the present, and when most of it arrived of the size and quantity he requested, he felt there should not be any more pauses in the construction of the cathedral.

His son was travelling on the continent, but Jane was still by his side and seeking a solution to the steeple of St. Dunstan's. He liked the direction of her designs and yet, so far, they were not quite right.

Hampton Court and Greenwich continued the next year without any more criticism from William, and while stone intended for St. Paul's was diverted to Richmond, Christopher tried to make the best of it by using it properly there. The Fountain Court and the King's staircase were developing as elegantly and symmetrically in the building as they were in his designs. And while he had followed William's instructions and the Park Block was more sober and sedate than he liked, he was pleased that the interior was comfortable and spacious and that it was finished.

Late in February, 1699, he stood inside the cathedral with Jane by his side—her role as his unofficial assistant had become accepted without ever being discussed—and sought to sort out in his own mind the various parts that were being constructed and their progress.

The finest accomplishment of the past year, he reflected, was the completion of the Morning Prayer chapel. It had opened a month ago and he and Jane had attended the first services. He remembered this occasion with pleasure. The start of the daily recital of morning prayers was quiet, modest; the congregation was mostly workmen; it was without the pomp that had accompanied the opening of the choir. He hadn't missed the many dignitaries, but he had missed Holder, who had died a month after the first divine services. Then he realised what a struggle it had been for his brother-in-law to come. So many old friends were vanishing he felt it was better not to look back. And he rarely saw those that were left.

He was supposed to conserve his energy now, he was told, he was going on sixty-eight. But he felt fine, although his muscles ached occasionally when he climbed heights. Moreover, it was impossible to retire, his mind ran on, no matter how often it was suggested and that was frequent.

Oliver had fallen ill after twenty-five years of devoted service and he had to lean more and more on Hawksmoor. By now Hawksmoor had shown that he was a fine draftsman, conscientious and pain-staking and accurate, but his sullenness and melancholy troubled Christopher. He felt it could appear in his designs. But what truly appalled him was the thought of leaving the completion of St. Paul's to anyone else.

"Is something wrong?" Jane asked, her father looked so serious.

"I was thinking about the Morning Prayer chapel and other things."

"Do you think you devoted too much time and energy to finishing it?"

"Not at all. The choir is too grand for daily services. The Morning Prayer chapel is essential. As long as St. Paul's is open each day for services, it is alive. And it continues to rise. Almost all the double orders and the supports for the dome are done. If nothing goes wrong, we should be able to start on the dome in a year or two."

"Father, do you still expect something to go wrong?"

"I would like to think not, but experience has taught me to be wary. When you do many things at the same time, one act of carelessness could be a disaster. I'm always saying to myself, If it works, if it holds, if it is finished, although in my heart I believe everything will succeed. If I'm superstitious it is to protect myself against disappointment."

"I'm surprised that you speak of a dome. I thought you had decided on two envelopes, with an intermediate cone in between them."

"I have. But in my mind I always think of the covering and the ceiling of the fabric as one dome rather than a separate unity." He frowned.

"What is wrong now?"

"Father Smith is still rearranging the pipes of the organ. He is determined that it should dominate the view and I'm determined that it should be heard rather than seen. So far, neither of us have won."

Jane was concerned about her father's pessimism. In her eyes the main portion of St. Paul's was finished except for the dome and the west front. She said, "Father, I know that much of your life is bound up in St. Paul's, but don't you worry about it too much."

"No more than is necessary, dear."

He walked to the shed where the main supply of Portland stone was stored to see if the supply was sufficient for the next year. It was, he saw with satisfaction. Perhaps Jane was right, everything essential was done except the dome and the west front and they should be accomplished soon. She was saying, "Nothing should stop you now, Father," when he heard a cry he dreaded, "Fire!" Then he smelled smoke and knew it was real.

He rushed outside, followed by Jane, and to his horror he saw that the smoke was coming from the inside of the cathedral. They ran down the nave to the shed in the north-east corner of St. Paul's, which was a mass of flames. It was a short distance from the choir screen and a great wooden partition which rose to the ceiling. If either caught fire, he knew in this instant, the entire cathedral could be doomed.

He was grateful that at the cry of "Fire!" all the workmen discarded their tools and hurried to the blaze as he had ordered, and that he had put sand, water, and many buckets nearby. The workmen threw water and sand on the burning shed. But that was futile, he realised, the shed was gone; the vital thing was to save the rest of St. Paul's. Only it might be too late. Sparks settled on the dry timbers of the partition and suddenly they were ablaze. He felt sick. But then, as always, he couldn't surrender, even to the most feared enemy of all. He pulled off his coat and beat at the burning wood; Jane followed his example, using the lovely cloak he had bought her for her birthday; the workmen joined them, some using their bare hands, and then he knew it was not enough. He called for axes and when they came, brought on the run, he ordered all wood near the flames and anything that was inflammable to be demolished and removed. It meant the destruction of scaffolding that had taken much time and effort to construct but he was inflexible. By now he was in control of his senses again and recalling how he had fought the Great Fire. The workmen were doing everything he asked of them, and apprentices and shopkeepers from the neighbourhood hurriedly joined their struggle to save the cathedral.

Gradually he built a fire break around the blazing shed. No one minded singed hands, blackened faces, burnt clothes; only St. Paul's mattered. When the choir screen caught fire he had it destroyed. Great craft had gone into it but he was ruthless. There were moments when it was hard to breathe, but there was no retreating. Led by the Surveyor, while his daughter conveyed his orders to the many groups fighting the blaze, the fire-fighters battled as if there was nothing else to do but contain the flames or allow St. Paul's to die.

Finally there was a complete fire break around the blazing shed and the tide began to turn. Christopher concentrated on the other parts of the cathedral that had caught fire and eventually all that was burning was extinguished or removed. But he didn't halt until each ember was doused with water and sand and he was sure that St. Paul's was safe.

He was shocked to learn that the blaze had begun in the shed because a joiner had left his glue pot heating while going outside to smoke his pipe, which was forbidden on the premises. Then the paper designs had caught fire and soon after the shed was aflame.

Jane whispered through soot-covered lips that he had won, but he thought it was a costly victory. A large portion of the masonry was cracked, blackened, stained, broken. The marble pavement was in a similar condition and there was terrible damage elsewhere. He realised that while he had preserved St. Paul's, completion had been pushed back a long time.

He had hoped to finish the cathedral shortly, but now he knew that was impossible. He learned it would take at least two years to repair the damage. Much wood was needed and most of it was difficult to obtain. He was glad there was no shortage of stone, thanks to his foresight in storing an ample supply, but more would be required to replace the injured masonry and that meant a large increase in expenditures.

The rest of that year he didn't tell anyone of his discouragement, even Jane. He sought to save money wherever he could, as long as it didn't affect the quality of the work, and kept his fears to himself.

He was approaching a new century and he believed it should be greeted affirmatively. Yet when 1700 arrived, it brought another difficulty.

Parliament asked—before deciding on how much of the new coal dues were to go to St. Paul's—for an estimate from the Surveyor of the cost of completing the fabric of the cathedral.

Christopher, forming his judgment on regular work at St. Paul's, said the total would be £175,000. To be exact, he added in a footnote to this estimate, £178,282.

Shocked, the Parliament which had chided him for his slow progress and had cut his salary in half to prod him to faster and greater activity, ordered him to slow down to save money. And they reduced the money the building fund was to receive from the coal dues to a third of the former amount.

In many ways this was the worst blow of all, for it forced him to work at a reduced rate, a situation he had vowed never to allow to happen again. And there was no one to appeal to. The King wouldn't even discuss St. Paul's with him; William was interested only in the designs he had suggested.

So while Christopher continued to work on the foundations of the dome, he put off the final steps to conserve his limited resources for the two western towers. Once they were up, he felt, the entire ground plan would be established; then surely, they could not deny him the dome.

Work limped along at St. Paul's through 1700, but early the next year, when there was a call for a new Parliament he was elected a member from Weymouth. But his voice was drowned out in the clatter of other matters. Hardly anyone wanted to discuss the cathedral, that was a part of the past.

By 1702 he doubted he would live to see what he had striven so many years to achieve. He was going on seventy, he had already outlived most of his contemporaries. It was hard to remember his other achievements in this battle that never seemed to end. Sceptics sneered that the cathedral would take a hundred years. Jokes were common that to be truly lazy one had to be a St. Paul's workman. That three were needed to do the work of one: one worked, one watched, and one criticised.

Then William died suddenly as a result of a fall from a horse. The Surveyor heard the news with mixed feelings. This King had not been a friend of St. Paul's, yet he had served England to the best of his ability.

Christopher's hopes for St. Paul's revived a little when Anne ascended the throne, for she had visited the choir while a princess. But then war began again with France and the energies and the expenditures of the nation were diverted once more to feed and fuel the Army and Navy, and he was sure the cathedral would remain neglected. Yet unless the pace of the work was doubled, he saw no prospect of living long enough to finish it.

He was striving to overcome his discouragement which had afflicted him ever since the fire at St. Paul's, when Jane ran into the studio. She was unusually flushed, but perhaps it was her excitement, he thought, she was very excited. He put down what he felt could be the final designs for the dome, an interruption he rarely permitted. But he loved her enthusiasms. Christopher was a nice young man, but not unusual, while poor Billy was too sickly to amount to anything, but Jane was Jane, like no one else he knew, yet very much his daughter, with her gift for design.

"What is it, dear? Is the news really that good?"

"I think so. Queen Anne has ordered November 12th to be declared a national day of thanksgiving to honour the victories of Lord Marlborough."

"Why are you so pleased? You are not infatuated with war."

"The Queen has commanded also that this day is to be celebrated with divine services at St. Paul's and she has promised to attend."

The preparations were elaborate and a great crowd assembled around the cathedral to greet the Queen, who arrived in the royal coach drawn by six horses, a fanfare of trumpets, and many yeomen of the guard.

Christopher stood on the marble steps before the unfinished west front and watched the Queen's approach, with his daughter and oldest son. In spite of his wish to be restrained, he was almost as excited as his children. He had marked his seventieth birthday two weeks ago and time had gone by so swiftly, it was inconceivable to him that ten years had passed since the party Jane had given for him. Yet his daughter was quite grown-up at twenty-six, and Christopher was talking about getting married. He remembered Anne as a little girl, as he had remembered her older sister, Mary, for his cousin Matthew had been their grandfather's secretary, and then no one had expected either of the girls to be a queen.

The most important dignitaries in the realm were present and many from abroad, but Christopher had eyes only for the Queen, as if the future of St. Paul's depended on her. Anne had gained so much weight with her many pregnancies he realised she had lost what little good looks she had possessed. He recalled that she had twelve miscarriages and only one child had survived beyond an early age, and even that one, whom she had adored, had died young. No wonder there was sadness in her eyes, he thought, to lose one child was a calamity and she had lost twelve. He forgot the splendour of her jewels, her high hair, her royal emblems, her stout, shapeless body, and felt the mother she had longed to be.

At the end of the services, which included music from the organ and the royal choir, some of which caused Jane to wince, it was so bad, her father was summoned by the Queen and ordered to bring his children with him.

Anne stood in front of the dais and canopy which had been placed before the altar for her presence, surrounded by the Archbishop of Canterbury, the Bishop of London, the Dean of St. Paul's, all quite different men from those who had begun this venture with him, reflected Christopher, although he knew these three clerics, too. When she saw the slight, trim figure of her Chief Surveyor she motioned for the others to leave, she desired to speak to him privately—but for his children to join them.

He bowed and introduced his children, thinking, He had never seen St. Paul's so clean, so scrubbed, and all traces of the fire were gone.

Anne said, "Sir Christopher, you are fortunate to have all your children." Her voice was slow but distinct and had a note of conviction it had lacked in the past. "I have lost all of mine." Her eyes filled with tears and for an instant he thought she was going to cry. But then, as if aware that everybody watched her now and her days of obscurity were over, she regained her self-control and added, "I want to talk about St. Paul's."

"Your Majesty, the cathedral is honoured by your presence."

"And I am honoured by yours, Sir Christopher. I know your gifts. They are all about me. We must finish St. Paul's as finely as it is begun."

"Your interest, Your Majesty, is most helpful."

"More than interest. We have ordered the coal dues for the cathedral to be doubled and their payment extended from 1708 for another eight years. That should give you more than enough time and money to finish."

At first he thought she was poking fun at him, but her plain, heavy features were solemn and he realised she was serious. This was beyond his expectations. Finally it appeared likely that he wouldn't have to worry about money. Perhaps he might finish it after all as he had conceived it.

Jane smiled so hard that tears came to her eyes and even his son was joyous and Christopher said, "Your Majesty, you make us very happy."

"We have had enough of procrastinations. No one understands our faith better than I do and the need of our country to support it."

For an instant he felt her support was an expression of opposition to her father's claim to the throne, then he decided that idea was spiteful.

"Ever since I can remember I have watched St. Paul's grow. It always has been the heart of London for me. As it must be for you, Sir Christopher."

The Queen's support heartened him and he returned to the cathedral with renewed vigour. A few days later he was informed officially of the improved financial situation and that Talman had been dismissed as Comptroller and that Mr. John Vanburgh, play-wright and gentleman of fashion, had been appointed in his place, and would be subject to all the Surveyor's wishes.

He didn't shut down this year with the coming of winter, but made the necessary provisions to work inside. He was in a rare good humour.

A month later he told Jane after much pondering, "Dear, I've decided to use your design for St. Dunstan's." She had entered as he contemplated two splendid towers and a magnificent dome and he hoped that the Queen would live to see that sight. It should take five years perhaps, but no more. He was surprised that Jane wasn't overwhelmed with pleasure about St. Dunstan's, but nodded wearily and sat down. "Dear, aren't you feeling well?"

"I'm tired. It may be a touch of the ague."

"You are too young for that."

"I will feel better after I rest."

He put her to bed and called the three best physicians he knew. The first doctor said Jane had scarlet fever and that it could appear at any season, the second, who was one of the fourteen who had attended Charles, suggested the same remedies for her, although he wasn't sure what was wrong, the third was certain that she had smallpox. But none could cure her. He refused to allow the second physician to inflict the torment Charles had endured and no other remedies were offered.

Less than seven weeks after he had experienced one of the happiest days of his life, Jane died. She was in a coma the last few hours and that was one of the worst blows of all. Not to be able to talk with her, to feel her animate hand in his was the cruellest act of nature. It was December 28th, the same day that Queen Mary had died of smallpox eight years ago.

He buried Jane in the crypt of St. Paul's next to his sister and brother-in-law. Then, as she was placed in the vault, he couldn't stop crying. He put his hands to his face to hide the tears from his son, but Christopher was crying, too, and Lucy looked as if she would never smile again and he wondered if he ever could. So many he had loved had died but none like this. By now he believed that Jane had died of smallpox. But he kept thinking, All his intelligence, all his learning, all his wit, all his skills had been nothing before the foulness which had infected her. Many important personages, including Queen Anne, had expressed their condolences, but for once he couldn't respond. Still another one he loved would not see the cathedral he built, and to her it had meant so much, it had been such a joy. He wanted to love his children the same, but Jane was Jane, and somehow, he felt, life had failed her.

His son dried his eyes, wishing he knew what to say—his sister had a quick word for everything—and read the inscription his father had written in Latin to be placed on her tomb:

"Like her father, fond of learning, dutiful, kind, home loving, an expert musician."

Unnatural, unnatural, Christopher sobbed to himself, Jane was confined in a small room when she should be so greatly alive. As the funeral party turned to go from the crypt he had designed and built, but he had never intended for his own use, he knew that part of his heart went into the grave with her. And Jane had never expected to die.

I Wave My Hands In Greeting

I wave my hands in greeting
Whenever I can
It is such a friendly thing
to do

Then everything around knows
I am part of everything around
But I must depend on the breeze

Sometimes I wait so long
It seems
I have been motionless for a year

If the Highest on High
would grant a wish to a tree

I would ask
Could I wave my hands in greeting
Whenever I wished
without having to depend
                    on the breeze

Stymean Karlen

55

I Wave My Hands In Greeting

Two years later work stopped at St. Paul's again. Christopher arrived at the site on a pleasant, mild day in August, an ideal day for working and putting into practice his new and final plans for the fabric of the dome—which he had come to supervise—and he was shocked that no one was working. Most of the workmen had gone home and the few that remained were storing materials as if this delay might last some time. It was a sorry sight and he wondered what had happened. There was no sign of a disaster. The scaffolding that rose hundreds of feet into the sky and shrouded the beginnings of the dome was intact. The double orders gleamed in the sun and looked as he desired. He paused before the west front, despite his impatience to find out what was wrong, to admire and enjoy it. Then, to see it better, he backed away as Jane had preferred. He liked the way he had used the giant columns and counted them as Jane had loved to do: twelve on the first storey, eight on the second. That was fine and suitable, for the lessening of the columns on top drew the eyes to the apex of the cathedral which would culminate in the dome and the lantern upon it.

He saw no trace of his son, who had taken Jane's place as his unofficial assistant, or Thomas Bateman, who had been appointed to Oliver's post when his deputy had died. Just as he was about to go inside St. Paul's to see if anything had gone wrong there, Hawksmoor hurried toward him and stated sombrely, "Sir, all activity has been halted on orders of Queen Anne."

"What is the excuse this time?" Christopher asked wearily.

"Marlborough is about to meet the French and Bavarians in a crucial battle and the Queen has commanded all construction in the country to be suspended until the result is known. If we should lose, all the coal dues will have to go to refit the army and raise new troops."

"Is it known where this battle is to take place?"

"They say the armies are facing each other at a small town on the Danube. Called Blenheim. I've never heard of it, sir."

"Neither have I. Do you know if the battle has started yet?"

"It may be over for all I know. How are you feeling, sir?"

"Fine! I'm working as I always did. Greenwich flourishes, and I've finished the steeple on St. Dunstan's, although many said it wouldn't hold."

"It is beautiful, sir. It captures the church's Gothic look."

"It was my daughter's conception. I've encountered many delays during my years on Ludgate Hill, but this is one I didn't expect."

"Anne fears that if Marlborough loses, her throne will be shaky."

"I doubt that. The nation has had enough of civil wars."

"And we are having trouble with the stone ships again. Four have been captured by the French in the past few months and a storm sank another."

"We are so close, I can't believe we will fail now. We need only another year of Portland stone, then two years of uninterrupted work. To be halted now would be cruel and inhuman." He shivered; they were Jane's words.

"Sir, you can't be so unfortunate. You've overcome worse obstacles."

"There have been moments, building St. Paul's, I have felt like Job."

"Things have gone well with Anne, sir. Except with Hampton Court."

"I expected it to end with the death of William, just as construction of Winchester ended with the death of Charles. But Greenwich grows splendidly and for a change we have no difficulties there. It is one of my favourite designs. Hawksmoor, why do you think it has gone smoothly?"

"Patriotism, sir. With so many wounded the nation feels it is useful. I want to thank you for recommending me as the designer for the new City churches and appointing me your deputy at Greenwich. You are very kind."

"Not at all," Christopher said brusquely, embarrassed by Hawksmoor's gratitude. "You are the best man for the work. Come, we mustn't stop, whatever the others do. We must see what is needed inside."

Hawksmoor trailed him through the great west door of St. Paul's. He was surprised by his brisk stride—Wren was in his seventies, although the Surveyor didn't look it—and he had difficulty keeping up with him.

He thought, Much of genius was energy and Wren still had this gift in abundance. The length of the nave delighted him. He glanced up at the roof and while it was higher than he would have designed it, he felt the grandeur and the symmetrical saucer domes that covered it. He was intrigued by the skill and beauty with which Gibbons had endowed the choir stalls; it was clever of the Surveyor to choose him and give him a free hand. Wren was good at picking deputies, he reflected, and he didn't intend to alter that. He loved the huge arches, which like the details inside the nearly finished St. Paul's, were in proportion and balance with everything else. And the dome, if it worked, would be incomparable.

They paused at the crossing where the huge columns rose, prepared to support the inner envelope, and Hawksmoor, while he had stood here often, had to look once more. His mind ran on, Whatever the Surveyor had desired with his Greek cross design, Wren had achieved a classical beauty here. St. Paul's might not be a perfect structure, but then man wasn't either. Considering the difficulties, the manifold differences of opinion, it was remarkable it was as unified as it was. Yet even now, the cathedral's final face could depend on the whim of one person. He knew there was still much opposition to some of the Surveyor's ideas: to the shape of the dome, the materials in it, the windows in it. He wondered how Wren could be so patient, yet so stubborn. He would have quit long ago.

Hawksmoor felt Wren read his mind, for the Surveyor said to him, as they examined the scaffolds which, at the moment, were deserted, "The clergy want me to put windows in the dome like a Gothic cathedral. But they are wrong, they will have to be repaired often, which is hard and risky."

"Yet you must have light there for the steps leading to the lantern."

"I will use openings that you won't see but they will give light."

Hawksmoor believed him; the Surveyor was ingenious. Wren thrived on such problems, where other surveyors sought simpler, more obvious solutions. "Then you don't feel that this delay is serious, sir?"

"All delays are serious. London must never be allowed to do without St. Paul's. They might come to accept that. Nothing is so sad as a site where there is work to be done and no one to do it." He turned to go and saw his son running toward them excitedly. It was not like him to show such enthusiasm; his twenty-nine year old son considered that unworldly.

"Father, I've been looking for you everywhere. Where have you been?"

"Right here. What is wrong?"

"Wrong? We've won. The news just arrived and I wanted to be the first to tell you. Our Lord Duke of Marlborough has had a

2F

great victory at Blenheim. I'm thinking of volunteering. To be one
of his aides."

"I hear he has more than he needs now."

Hawksmoor asked, "Mr. Wren, have you ever been in a battle?"

"No, but our Lord Duke is a great soldier. He always wins."

Christopher said, "I hope you lay aside your design for the army.
It is neither safe nor pertinent, but a dirty, tedious business. Do
you have any news about St. Paul's? Surely we should be able to
resume now?"

"No, but I have something else to discuss with you. Mr.
Hawksmoor, would you excuse us?"

"Christopher, I have important matters to review with Mr.
Hawksmoor."

"Father, this is vitally important. Please?"

His son was so imploring Christopher motioned to his deputy to
excuse them, but as Hawksmoor started off he added, "Find out if
the men can be called back tomorrow." Then he turned to listen to
his anxious son.

"I'm considering a proposal of marriage and I would like your
approval."

Christopher was startled. His son courted many. "Who is it?"

"Mary Musard. She is slight, dark, pretty, not as clever as Jane,
but pleasant mannered, good tempered, and part of the Court."
When his father looked perplexed, he added, "You know her family.
Her father is Philip Musard, jeweller to Queen Anne, and she is a
lady in waiting."

"You seem to have made up your mind."

His son wavered, thinking, He couldn't afford to support a wife
and family in the style he desired on what he earned as his father's
assistant. Yet while his father wasn't wealthy, there was no lack of
means. The large old house on Scotland Yard contained sixteen
rooms besides cellars and stables, and there were two carriages and
four servants now to maintain the household. Lucy devoted herself
only to Billy, who would probably remain an invalid, while Seth
pottered about the gardens of Windsor, too old to do anything else,
although he would miss him when Seth was gone.

"Son, why are you hesitating?"

"I want your permission."

"But how can I give it until I meet Mistress Musard."

"You will like her."

"It is more important that you do. Are you worried about your
means?"

His son nodded reluctantly yet emphatically.

"There will be enough for you to live on comfortably. It is one
of the reasons I have been frugal. And now that there will not be a

dowry for Jane, whatever I possess will be yours, except for funds to take care of Billy. You will look after him when I am gone?"

"Father, you have many years ahead of you."

"At seventy-two? It is not likely."

"Your good friend, Evelyn, is still alive, and he is eighty-three."

"But Hooke is gone, and Pepys. Even the members of the Society are of a different generation now. Do be careful. You and William are all I have."

"Then you approve? Consent?"

Christopher took his son's arm affectionately, a rare gesture for him. And as he led him out, deciding that in this situation he must put his family first, even before St. Paul's, he said, "I trust your judgment. We must celebrate. There is a coffee house nearby that I favour, but I haven't been there for some time. Let us indulge ourselves."

The son was amazed by the way his father held on to him. The young man knew it was not from physical weakness; the Surveyor still climbed scaffolds and his long, slender fingers were still strong and his grip firm. The son wondered, Did his father care that much?

Work resumed the day after the news of Blenheim and a month later the Queen held another service of national thanksgiving at St. Paul's. She complimented Sir Christopher on the amount of progress he had made on the cathedral, and she praised the growth of the west front. It was almost done, although the scaffolding remained, and she was pleased with it.

From the moment Christopher met Mary Musard he thought her very pretty indeed. Her dark, vibrant beauty reminded him of Daniel's Maria. She also had excellent manners and a lovely figure. But he wasn't sure whether she was intelligent. He knew many husbands preferred their wives to be without wit or intelligence— they felt such traits handicapped women—it was enough they adorned the clothes they wore, supervised their households, and furnished them with healthy children, preferably sons. But he hoped his son desired more, as he had. He couldn't tell, for his son had a coy expression on his face, as if being with Mary was a constant flirtation. He noticed, too, that Mary gave more attention to her appearance than to her conversation. But she was overjoyed when his son told her that they would wed in St. Paul's when the cathedral was finished. That was a splendid idea, Christopher agreed, except he doubted if St. Paul's would be done in the next year or two.

This added to his effort not to allow anything to distract from that aim. Whatever else he did, even his supervision of Greenwich, his repairs for Westminster Abbey and Windsor and Westminster School, the few steeples still being completed on the City churches, he put after St. Paul's. He felt so close to his goal he wanted to work night as well as day. He considered sleeping there, then realised it would not speed matters, and he needed the privacy of his studio to concentrate on the final details.

He was preparing for the final effort on St. Paul's when the Duchess of Marlborough asked to see him at Kensington Palace. The high panelled chamber, which he had renovated for William and Mary, was empty except for the beautiful Sarah Churchill, whose sharp features were decisive. She spoke directly, not one to be reticent, "Have you heard about the great house my husband, the Duke, is planning?"

"I have, Madam. I'm sure it will be worthy of his victories."

"That is our intention. The Queen gave him the land as a reward for his great victory at Blenheim and we desire a grand palace to rival any in the world. We are calling it Blenheim. Would you consider it?"

"Madam, I'm very busy at St. Paul's."

"Aren't you always? You've been building there since I can remember."

"It is almost done, but I really have little time for anything else."

"Sir, you may have a point. Blenheim will take years. And you are not a young man. But you could submit some designs."

"Madam, I've not done any country houses. It's not work I favour."

She was indignant, "This is to be a palace. The greatest of all."

"I'm honoured that you want to consider my views."

"You are the Chief Surveyor for the Crown. Anne thinks highly of you. But your age concerns me. Sir Christopher, how old are you?"

"Madam, I think our conversation serves no purpose. If you're in a mood to interrogate, I suggest you approach someone else. There are other architects who are available. Nicholas Hawksmoor, for one."

"What about John Vanbrugh?"

"He is a playwright, Madam!"

"He is also Comptroller and in the last few years has had experience with building projects. He knows how to save money. That is vital. This is not a royal or clerical work where money can be squandered."

Christopher knew that Sarah Churchill had one of the sharpest tongues at Court and never hesitated to use it, even with the Queen, but he was in no mood to suffer it. "Madam, would you excuse me? I'm certain you will find a suitable surveyor for the execution of your plans."

"Aren't you interested?" she flushed and was surprised.

Not really, he wanted to reply, but she was influential with Anne and he didn't want to do anything which would offend the Queen, at least until the dome was on securely and the lantern was in place. He asked politely, more from duty than from desire, "Madam, what are your views?"

She seldom respected surveyors and she liked to say so, but occasionally they were necessary, and Wren might have an idea or two worth using. She stated, "I want Blenheim to be a great baroque palace, prodigious in scope, to match the Duke's reputation, and to outdo anything built so far."

He thought her concept overdone and the opposite of what he believed in architecture, but he asked, "What does the Queen think?"

"It was her suggestion that I speak to you. Do you like my ideas?"

"They are quite grand. Blenheim could take many years to build."

"That is not your concern. But you must make your contracts cheaper, not like St. Paul's, and build more quickly than you usually do. Then, if other matters are satisfactory, my husband will consider you."

He bowed and as he left he said, "And I will consider your proposal."

Christopher was not surprised to hear soon after that Vanbrugh was commissioned to design Blenheim. There were many rumours why she hadn't chosen him, the most noted surveyor in the land. And he was standing in the north choir aisle with Hawksmoor when he heard two workmen talking about some of these rumours. The workmen, who were repairing the high altar, didn't see them. Generally he would have ignored their gossip—he knew it went on all the time—but at the mention of the Duchess he was curious. He motioned to Hawksmoor, who was uncomfortable, to be quiet and listened.

The first workman said, "I hear the Duchess said she had no fancy for Wren, but since he was an old servant he had to be considered, yet that she decided against him as soon as he spoke."

The other workman replied, "Because, I was told, she said the poor old man is much imposed upon by his workmen."

"I wish I could impose upon him. He watches every shilling that is spent. You might think it is going into his pocket."

"She also keeps talking about the poor old man having to be

carried up and down here in a basket. Do you think he is too old?"

"I don't know, but since we began on the dome he never wants to stop."

"Yes," said the second, "Maybe he was the one who said No first."

After the workmen were gone Hawksmoor said apologetically, "Sir, the Duchess likes to talk. I would ignore her."

"*Poor old man*," Christopher repeated. Then he smiled. "I'm glad I thought of the basket to take us up to the dome. Otherwise, we would all be exhausted. I hope Vanbrugh is fortunate in this commission, but I'm well out of it. I had no intention of building Blenheim for her, but if she wishes to make it sound as if she refused me, I won't argue."

Hawksmoor asked excitedly, "Then it was you who refused her?"

"Not refused. I never accepted. I am too old. For Sarah Churchill."

The first giant step toward constructing the dome was taken the next spring. It was the only portion of the fabric which was not finished, except for the west towers and they were rising rapidly. After a winter of more pondering and experimenting Christopher decided to form the inner envelope as a hemisphere of bricks. But first, he had to devise a way of doing it. The workmen needed the kind of footing which would give them perfect balance so they would avoid falling while the bricks were put in precisely. He realised that the usual upright scaffolds would not be safe or efficient. So he created a system of circular ledges around the inner dome which were braced by a framework of wood. This made it possible for the workmen to stand under the ceiling without fear of falling and to form it into a smooth and perfect hemisphere. Then he climbed the structure himself to verify that it was as he wished. But as he glanced down to the crossing below him, he had a moment of dizziness which alarmed him. He was troubled by the knowledge that he could no longer trust himself at such heights, but he was too close to his destination to pause for regrets.

As the work progressed steadily that year he tied a mighty iron chain around the envelope to keep it from spreading. The inner dome became a ceiling composed of a massive and secure wall of layers of bricks.

Then, without pause, he started the middle envelope—or the second dome, as his son preferred to call it—and constructed a great cone of bricks whose main function was to support the outer dome and the lantern.

By now his son felt it was a mistake for his marriage to wait until the completion of St. Paul's. But it wasn't his fault, he assured himself, his father was slower than he had expected. The Surveyor was too painstaking to suit him and his plans. When it was evident early in 1706 that there was still several years of work ahead, the son asked his father if the ceremony could be held now. Christopher said that was a good idea and arranged for a Sunday that would be suitable.

It was a small wedding, with only the immediate families present. The inner dome was done now and there was a complete ceiling over their heads and Christopher tried not to think of his daughter lying under their feet. But this was what he had desired for Jane, and as his son and Mary Musard were married he prayed that they would be more fortunate.

Then he approached Mary's parents to express his congratulations. Her father was the dominant figure in the family, a dark, elegant, middle-aged man, who dressed like a courtier, and who was favoured by the Queen because of his taste in jewels. Mrs. Musard was a Londoner, who had lived within the sound of Bow Bells most of her life, a stocky, round-faced woman with reddish-brown hair and a freckled complexion.

They had met several times before, but they were formal with each other. Christopher knew that the Musards were pleased with the marriage—they considered his son a catch—and he hoped the boy would not disappoint them. His son was intelligent enough, thought Christopher, but didn't always apply himself. Yet he had provided him with a home of his own, a coach and four, a servant, and an independent income, although the son was still receiving an income in the Office of the Works. There were moments when he felt that his son wanted to follow in his footsteps, and this seemed to be one of them. Well, he reflected, he would give him the chance, but he couldn't favour him, much as he wanted him to succeed.

There was a moment of pleasantries and then the happy couple left for their honeymoon and Christopher excused himself.

"Of course," said Mr. Musard. "There is still much to be done here."

"It isn't that," replied Christopher, "but I've been working so hard lately that I've had to go to bed early. Extra work was necessary to prepare the cathedral for this ceremony. But they look very happy."

"Yes," said Mrs. Musard, "We are honoured to have our daughter wed in such a magnificent edifice. I was a little girl when the old St. Paul's collapsed after the great fire. Sir, you have performed wonders."

"Thank you, Mrs. Musard, you are very kind," Christopher replied. "But as Mr. Musard said, St. Paul's is not yet done."

They complimented each other on how fortunate they were and said adieu.

When the inner and middle envelopes of the dome were finished by the following summer, Christopher felt the end was within reach. The only major work still to be done on St. Paul's was the outer envelope of the dome, the roof. But that was vital to him. This part of the cathedral was his signature on the skyline of London. On a clear day it would be seen for miles. It would rise above anything else on the horizon. For many, perhaps most of his countrymen, it would be London.

These thoughts ran through his mind as he stood before the completed west towers while the workmen prepared for the last great step. He itemised the details. He had all of them solved but one. Yet that one troubled him. He had to be sure that the oak framework was secure and the usual method of doing this was with nails. Only nails exposed to the elements would rust, and the roof was the most exposed part of the fabric; it would have to take directly the worst onslaughts of the weather. Such rust would weaken the fabric. But he was building for eternity. He must find another way to fasten the timbers or a better way to protect the nails.

He was so absorbed in this problem it was a minute before he realised a messenger was informing him that his presence was required at a meeting of the building committee. From the tone of the summons, he sensed criticism or a complaint. But of what, he wondered. Nothing in the design could be altered now, it was all done, except for the roof.

He entered the meeting room of the Chapter House and saw that the new Dean of St. Paul's, Dr. Henry Godolphin, occupied the chair, and was surrounded by five members of the committee who were his friends. He knew each of the clergymen, although none were close to him. All of them had become part of the committee only in the last few years. And they had met rarely, and then just to approve the use of the building funds. But this occasion, he sensed, was different.

No one asked him to sit and Dean Godolphin scowled at him.

Since he had become involved with St. Paul's, Christopher reflected, he had known four Deans of the cathedral—Sancroft, Stillingfleet, Tillotson, and Sherlock, and all had been supporters of his, although in different ways—but not this one, Godolphin, appointed a few months ago and brother of the Queen's Treasurer, was making it clear that he was going to have a dominating voice in everything concerning St. Paul's. He glared at the Surveyor, a black-haired, heavy-browed, dark-complexioned man of forty, who obviously intended to be Archbishop some day.

Dean Godolphin said, sounding like both interrogator and judge, "The building fund informs me that you have ordered lead for the roof."

"Yes, sir. We are almost ready to cover it."

"We don't approve of lead. The building committee has decided that copper is more suitable for the roof."

What committee, Christopher wondered, no one had said a word but Godolphin. None of the other Deans had told him what materials to use, whatever the occasional differences of opinion. But all his old friends in the clergy were dead or very old and no longer active. He had a start of fear that at this moment when he was so close to realising a dream of a lifetime it was going to be snatched away from him. Yet he sought to use reason. He said, "I respect your views, but lead is more suitable."

"That is not our view. As we said."

"I have already decided on it and ordered it."

"Cancel the order. Copper is a good English Protestant covering. And it is easy to obtain. We possess the best copper works in the world."

So there was money involved, thought Christopher, this could be a difficult situation indeed. But while Godolphin looked adamant and so did the others, he said, "Dean, I respect your views, but it is essential that the outer fabric be right."

"That is why we want copper for the roof. It is more durable."

"Copper may be durable, but lead is more suitable."

"I don't see why."

"Lead blends beautifully with the rest of the fabric and the surroundings, but copper will tarnish or blemish and develop a green or black look."

"You are very sure."

"Dean, I have seen it happen to other roofs." Observation, as he had learned years ago in natural philosophy, was the final test. "I am sure."

"But we are the ones who will have to use and maintain the fabric. I propose that copper be used for the roof instead of lead."

The Dean put it in the form of a motion and the committee agreed.

"Sir, I cannot use copper."

"And we will not allow lead. I will tell the building fund not to pay for what you ordered. And I'm asking the government to support our views. There will be no more lead poured on our roof. Wren, it is our building, not yours, although you act as if you possess it."

Perhaps it was that St. Paul's possessed him, but he said, "Just as

I would not tell you how to preach, you should not tell me how to design." He could adjust to some changes, but not to a defacement of the dome. Copper would convert the roof into a cheap bauble and be a disgrace. He strode out with his head held high, although he was despondent.

The next day, as he feared, there was an order from the Queen to halt the use of lead on the outer envelope of the dome. In response, he asked for an audience. She granted it quickly, which gave him some hope.

But when he appealed to her to revoke the order, she replied, "Sir Christopher, I'm sorry you are so agitated, you know I'm sympathetic to your designs, but this is a matter which concerns the whole country. Dean Godolphin is bringing this affair before Parliament and they will decide on what material should cover the roof of St. Paul's."

He left her presence wishing he could be the ruler just this once, and an absolute one at that. The idea of a hundred different minds in Parliament deciding on the final fabric revolted him. Yet he felt impotent. Dean Godolphin had many political allies and he had none.

February, 1708, the year Christopher hoped to finish the cathedral, the House of Commons voted that the roof of St. Paul's must be covered with copper, an act which filled him with sorrow. He told no one of his feelings, not even his son, who felt he was too stubborn, or Hawksmoor, who had been asked by Vanbrugh to assist him at Blenheim and who had accepted. He thought bitterly, He was supposed to be the first surveyor in the land, his buildings were everywhere, there were almost a hundred in existence, the spires of fifty churches he had designed, each one different from the other, dominated the London skyline, and the single design he desired most was about to be taken away from him. Christopher had devised a method of using nails without risk of their rusting, but that seemed like a waste now; there appeared to be no choice but to resign. He couldn't suppress his judgment; it was the best part of him. Copper was wrong, he repeated to himself, just as various stone and many kinds of timber had been wrong. He was framing a letter of resignation in his mind when he heard that the House of Lords had refused to approve the use of copper. Not because they were against it, but because they were angry at the Commons for going ahead without consulting them or asking their approval. In the row which developed over the matter of procedure and power, of which House was more important and right, the issue of copper for the roof of St. Paul's was forgotten. When Parliament was dissolved in April, quite abruptly, Dean Godolphin's effort on behalf of the copper industry had failed.

With St. Paul's so close to completion, the mood of the country was to finish it, and the obvious choice again became Sir Christopher Wren.

Queen Anne notified him of this decision and added that a meeting of the building committee had been called to express her approval. They met at her command—Dean Godolphin did not attend— and the committee ordered the Surveyor to proceed with the roof without further delay.

Christopher ordered twice as much lead as he expected to use and doubled the number of workmen on the site, resolved to finish St. Paul's before another delay could occur. He knew exactly what he wanted to do with the nails and he covered them with folded lead sheets so they were protected from the elements and yet were able to securely bind the timber framework. When the outer envelope was roofed with lead late that year and it was time to set the last stone on the lantern on the top of the cathedral he was gratified, for his design of St. Paul's was complete.

Hawksmoor told him, "The dome can be seen from a great distance. I can see the fabric clearly from Greenwich, and the shape is perfect, sir."

"Thank you." The lead preserved the colour that Christopher had visualised, and he was convinced it would endure. "It should work."

It was his son's suggestion that the last stone be placed in the lantern on October 20th. It was Christopher's seventy-sixth birthday, and he told him that it was appropriate, for this act signified that the entire design was done and that St. Paul's was finished.

Christopher didn't argue; he was very pleased by his son's feeling.

The ceremony was in the Surveyor's hands, this was still a building act, and he arranged it with the utmost simplicity, as the first stone had been laid thirty-three years ago. No dignitaries were invited, but those who were working on the cathedral, the men who had covered the roof and placed the lantern—it was their triumph, he thought, as much as his—and the Dean of St. Paul's and the Bishop of London. Godolphin didn't come, on the excuse that he was busy elsewhere on the Church's business. But Compton joined them, although the aged Bishop of London, once a vigorous man, able soldier and horseman, was feeble and had to be supported by his servant. Yet Christopher was happy to see him, for no one who had started this long journey with him thirty-three years before was here, and Compton had travelled much of the way with him and had sustained him in many moments of difficulty. Even Evelyn, hardy as he had been, had passed away two years ago at the age of eighty-six. The one close friend from the Society who remained had become Sir Isaac Newton, President of the Society and Master of the Mint. The shy, retiring scholar now was worldly and political. Sir Isaac had sent his regrets when Christopher invited him.

Perhaps that was better, the Surveyor decided, while he waited for the ceremony to start. Newton had never shown any interest in St. Paul's.

The master mason handed him the last stone, the basket was ready to ascend to the lofty heights of the lantern, but he saw a look of anxiety appear on his son's face. He asked, "What is wrong, Christopher?"

"It is very high. Don't you think a younger man should take it up?"

For a second he was hurt, then he realised that his son's concern was genuine and he asked, "Can you think of someone more appropriate?"

His son bit his lips as if he had an answer but couldn't say it.

Christopher sensed what his son desired. He handed him the perfectly fashioned stone and said, "You are right. The lantern is very high and one could get dizzy. You put it in place."

The son doubted that his father felt dizzy, for Christopher's eyes were bright with anticipation and he stood erect, but in this moment the son felt very close to his father and said, "I am honoured."

"We all are. But be careful. As you said, it is quite high."

"I know. Three hundred and sixty-five feet. Was that calculated?"

"Christopher dear, everything I do in surveying is calculated. A foot for each day in the year. The height has been in my mind for a long time."

The basket went up and up until his son was a tiny figure in the sky and then the stone was in place and the small group who stood there applauded, and Christopher bowed his head and said to himself, "Thank You, God." Little had he dreamed when he had recommended a new St. Paul's forty-two years ago that it would be so difficult and take so long.

He felt someone touch him on the shoulder. It couldn't be his son, and Hawksmoor wouldn't do this, it was too familiar, and Compton was too feeble, having retired to the Chapter House to rest. But the touch felt personal. He swung around, annoyed at being distracted—he didn't want to be diverted at this precious moment—yet he was also curious.

The visitor was tall, slender, straight, white-haired, but without a wig, and for an instant he didn't recognise him. Then the elderly man smiled and that was unmistakable and they fell into each other's arms.

"I had to come, Christopher. I had to see what you wrought."

"What God wrought."

"As you wish. It is even more exciting than I anticipated."

"Does it work for you? Does it make sense? Do you understand now why it had to be a dome? A grey one? Of lead?"

"I never questioned your conception even when I couldn't visualise it like you could."

"You were being loyal. A good friend."

"That was not the reason. I knew that what you attempted you would achieve." Daniel backed away to see the cathedral better: the double order of columns, the west towers, the great front elevation, the stately circle of windows, the vast curve of the design, and the apex, the magnificent and superbly formed dome. "I had to come. I had to see what you had done. In many ways St. Paul's has been one of the most important parts of my life, too. It helped save me during the plague, I'll never forget how we fought the fire, and fought just as hard to get a new St. Paul's started. I'm glad I helped a little."

"Greatly. You did whatever I asked. However difficult or dangerous."

Daniel changed the subject. "How are you, Christopher? You look well."

"I feel fine. With time one acquires a few wrinkles, grey hair, a pound or two, but I can still climb a scaffold. How are you, Daniel?"

"Ambulatory."

"And things in Amsterdam?"

"Peaceful. As I wrote you, I paint and design masques."

"Your letter meant a great deal to me. I still have it. And Maria . . . ?" He paused, afraid to ask further.

Daniel grinned, almost boyish in this instant. "She is splendid. We didn't marry due to her religious views, but we are happy with each other."

"Any children?"

"No. We thought it better not to. But you have three, don't you?"

"Two now," Christopher said sadly. "My daughter lies here, in the crypt below. We were close. It is the one reason I might be willing to be buried here." For a moment the Surveyor sounded as if he were smothered in her ashes, then he returned to the present. "My youngest boy, Billy, is an invalid, but my oldest child, Christopher, assists me in my work and is the one who has just put the last stone in place."

"You must be proud of him."

"I can't complain. He is a good son. And now he has made me a grandfather and there is another Christopher Wren, the fourth. That was my own father's name, too."

After a long pause, Daniel added, "I visited St. Peter's in Rome."

"I've never seen it. I've not been out of England since you left."

"I like St. Paul's better."

"Daniel, I do not compete but I appreciate what you mean."

"At first, I was afraid to look here, I heard so much about your difficulties. I was worried that they had perverted your ideas."

"It was tried." Christopher smiled and glanced upwards again. His son was starting down and everyone was watching him intently. But he saw something else: the dome was saying something to him, not in words, but he could feel the expression of its surfaces, so many varied and different surfaces and materials. His buildings were alive for him, and in his imagination he talked to them, and this one more than any other, for he had spent so many of his days here. He felt it was waving a greeting to him; it didn't have to speak, the intention was there. Yet nothing moved. A breeze had sprung up but the dome was motionless.

Daniel said, "Every bit of the fabric is right."

"I hope so. I want it to be worthy of God. It is His House."

"I'm not sure that London is. It has changed."

"It is always changing. What it was yesterday is different today and will be another thing tomorrow. Especially for those who come back to it."

"And you've built so much of it."

"As much as I could." He loved London. With all its imperfections, with all its difficulties it had given him so much. He took Daniel by the arm and said, "I want to introduce you to my son and show you the inside of St. Paul's. Where, I pray, all men will feel reverence."

"Then is it truly finished?"

"Yes. As I designed it."

They walked toward the west front and Christopher realised that in every direction he looked he saw his steeples. There was St. Mary-le-Bow to the east, St. Benet's to the south and St. Bride's to the west. Whoever saw London, he thought, should see the steeples, silhouetted against the sky.

"You are fortunate, Christopher. You have finished what you started. I'm always trying to begin. Even now, at seventy-six."

"I'm trying, too. I never feel finished as long as I can begin again. I can't believe my age."

"You don't look it."

"I don't feel it. Not today."

"Christopher, I am glad I came back."

"So am I." He put his arm through Daniel's to express his affection and felt that they had come a long way. His son approached, looking more fulfilled than he had ever seen him, Daniel was here, and with the dome in place St. Paul's waved its hand in greeting to London and their future.

56

Aftermath

CHRISTOPHER CONTINUED TO WORK AS HE ALWAYS DID. AND SINCE he had finished St. Paul's, he petitioned for a return of the salary which had been taken away from him years ago. He sent it to the Queen, who referred it to the Commissioners, who referred it to the Archbishop of Canterbury, who passed it on to Parliament, where, after more arguments and delays, the Attorney-General ruled that since St. Paul's was *officially done*, the Surveyor should be given his back pay. It averaged two pounds a week.

He designed a wrought iron fence for the cathedral; Dean Godolphin insisted on cast iron. The latter also insisted on a balustrade which he said was unnecessary. And as the Commissioners rejected Christopher's views on these matters, they rejected his plans for the ceiling of the dome. They said that the artists he wanted were neither English nor Protestant.

Anne died in 1714 and the new ruler, the German George I, the fifth he had served as Surveyor, had no interest in St. Paul's or Christopher Wren. Four years later he was dismissed from his life appointment in the forty-ninth year of his surveyorship and the eighty-fifth of his life. He didn't argue but wrote in his papers, *"And there arose a King who knew not Joseph,"* and added, *"Now Fortune commands me to apply myself more closely to Philosophy."*

He pursued inquiries and experiments, he visited St. Paul's regularly, without animosity to anyone, although he was amused when he learned that Sarah Churchill had fallen out with Vanbrugh, and at the age of ninety he designed two church steeples. When he died in 1723 he was buried next to his daughter in St. Paul's and his son Christopher wrote on his simple tomb:

"Below is laid the builder of this Church and City, Christopher Wren, who lived above ninety years, not for himself but for the public good.

Reader if you seek a monument, look about you."

Acknowledgements

IT IS A GREAT PLEASURE TO ACKNOWLEDGE THE HELP GIVEN ME BY the following individuals in the construction and completion of *Myself, Christopher Wren*.

Three editors gave generously of their time and skill: Robin Denniston and Maureen Rissik of Hodder and Stoughton, and Patricia B. Soliman of Coward, McCann and Geoghegan.

Equally helpful, each in their unique way, were Peter Giddy of Hatchard's, Ted Gregory of Selfridge's, and Bob Crayford of St. Paul's Cathedral.

Then there were three librarians and libraries who contributed much to the making of this book. They were Douglas Matthews and the staff of the London Library; R. H. Millward and the staff of the Victoria Library, Westminster City Libraries; and H. E. Shufro and the staff of the Mercantile Library of New York.

I am grateful especially to Stymean Karlen for her poetry, which illuminates Christopher Wren.

> David Weiss
> London
> May 5, 1973.

Sources

Abernethy, Cecil, *Mr. Pepys of Seething Lane*, 1957.

Ashley, Maurice, *Oliver Cromwell and the Puritan Revolution*, 1958; *The Stuarts in Love*, 1964.

Bedford, John, *London's Burning*, 1966.

Bell, Malcom, *Rembrandt Van Rijn*, 1901.

Bell, Walter G., *The Great Fire of London in 1666*, 1923; *The Great Plague in London, 1665*, 1951.

Belt, G. F., *The Order of the Garter*, 1886.

Bigham, Clive, *The Chief Minister of England*, 1923.

Boas, F., *With Milton and the Cavaliers*, 1905.

Bolton, Glorney, *Sir Christopher Wren*, 1956.

Bowen, Catherine Drinker, *The Lion and the Throne*, 1956.

Bray, William, *Diary of John Evelyn*, (Edited by) 1879; *Diary of Samuel Pepys*, (Edited by) 1890; *Memoirs of John Evelyn*, (Edited by) 1827.

Bresford, J., *Gossip of the Seventeenth and Eighteenth Centuries*, 1924.

Bridenbaugh, Carl, *Vexed and Troubled Englishmen (1590–1642)*, 1968.

Briggs, M. S., *Baroque Architecture*, 1913; *Christopher Wren*, 1951; *Wren, the Incomparable*, 1953.

Brisbane, F. A., *If Stones Could Speak*, 1929.

Bryant, Arthur, *King Charles II*, 1931; *Restoration England*, 1960; *Samuel Pepys*, 1933; *Samuel Pepys, The Man in the Making*, 1967.

Buchan, John, *Cromwell*, 1934.

Burke, Bernard, *The Book of Orders of Knighthood*, 1858.

Burrows, Montagu, *Worthies of All Souls*, 1874.

Carleton, J. D., *Westminster School*, 1965.

Carpenter, E., *A House of Kings—The Official History of Westminster Abbey*, (Edited by) 1966.

Cecil, Evelyn, *A History of Gardening in England*, 1910.

Chapman, Hester, *The Tragedy of Charles II (1630–60)*, 1964.

Chauvois, Louis, *William Harvey, His Life and Times*, 1957.

Cheyney, E. P., *Readings in English History Drawn from Original Sources*, (Edited by) 1908.

Church, Richard, *London, Flower of Cities All*, 1966.

Chute, Marchette, *Ben Jonson of Westminster*, 1954.

Clarendon Edition, *Diary and Correspondence of Samuel Pepys*.

Connoisseur, The, *The Stuart Period (1603–1714)*, 1957.

Cook, G. H., *Old St. Paul's Cathedral*, 1955.

Cranston, Maurice, *John Locke*, 1957.

Dasant, A. I., *The Private Life of Charles the Second*, 1927.

Davies, Godfrey, *The Restoration of Charles II (1658–1660)*, 1955.

Dewhurst, Kenneth, *Dr. Thomas Syndeham*, 1966.

Dick, O. L., *Aubrey's Brief Lives* (Edited by), 1950.

Dimont, M. I., *Jews, God, and History*, 1964.

Dobbs, Brian, *Drury Lane (1661–1971)*, 1972.

Dorr, J. C. R., *Cathedral Pilgrimage*, 1896.

Downes, Kerry, *Christopher Wren*, 1971; *English Baroque Architecture*, 1966; *Hawksmoor*, 1959.

Drinkwater, John, *Mr. Charles, King of England*, 1926; *Pepys, His Life and Character*, 1930.

Dugdale, George, *Whitehall Through the Centuries*, 1950.

Dugdale, Sir William, *The History of St. Paul's Cathedral*, 1818.

Durant, Will and Ariel, *The Age of Louis XIV*, 1963; *The Age of Reason Begins*, 1961.

Dutton, Ralph, *The Age of Wren*, 1951; *London Homes*, 1952.

Eckstein, Gustav, *The Body Has A Head*, 1971.

Edwards, H. S., *Old and New Paris*, 1893.

Edwards, W., *Notes on British History*, 1959.

Elmes, James, *Sir Christopher Wren*, 1852.

Elsna, Helen, *Catherine of Braganza*, 1967.

Forshall, F. H., *Westminster School: Past and Present*, 1884.

Franklin, K. J., *William Harvey—Englishman*, 1961.

French, J. M., *The Life Records of John Milton*, 1956.

Ghomso, Thomas, *History of the Royal Society*, 1819.

Gloag, John, *English Furniture*, 1965.

Gotch, J. A., *Architecture of the Renaissance in England*, 1894; *Inigo Jones*, 1928.

Graeme, Bruch, *The Story of Windsor Castle*, 1937.

Graetz, H. L., *History of the Jews*, 1892.

Green, David, *Queen Anne*, 1970.

Green, J. R., *A Short History of the English People*, 1960.

Guthrie, Douglas, *A History of Medicine*, 1945.

Haak, R., *Rembrandt, His Life, Work and Times*, 1969.

Haggard, H. W., *Devils, Drugs, and Doctors*, 1929; *The Lame, the Halt, and the Blind*, 1932; *Mystery, Magic, and Medicine*, 1933.

Hall, E. R., & M. B., *The Correspondence of Henry Oldenburg*, (Edited by) 1971.

Halliday, F. E., *An Illustrated Cultural History of England*, 1967.

Hamilton, Anthony, *Count Gramont at the Court of Charles II*, 1965.

Hanford, J. H., *A Restoration Reader*, 1854.

Harvey, William, *The Circulation of the Blood*, 1963.

Hayes, John, *London—A Pictoral History*, 1969.

Hibbard, H., *Bernini*, 1965.

Hibbert, Christopher, *Charles I*, 1968; *London, The Biography of a City*, 1969.

Higham, F. M. G., *Charles I*, 1932.

Hill, Christopher, *God's Englishman, Oliver Cromwell and the English Revolution*, 1970.

Hobhouse, Christopher, *Oxford*, 1962.

Huizinga, J. H., *Dutch Civilization in the 17th Century*, 1968.

Hutton, Charles, and Shaw, George, and Pearson, Richard, *The Philosophical Transactions of the Royal Society*, 1809.

Jenkins, Elizabeth, *Elizabeth the Great*, 1959.

Jenkinson, W., *London Churches Before the Great Fire*, 1917.

Jesse, J. H., *Memoirs of the Court of England*, 1855.

Keynes, Geoffrey, *Life of William Harvey*, 1966; *The Personality of William Harvey*, 1949.

Kronenberger, Louis, *Kings and Desperate Men*, 1942.

Lang, Jane, *Rebuilding St. Paul's*, 1956.

Ley, Willy, *Watchers of the Skies*, 1963.

Lindsey, J., *Wren, His Work and Times*, 1951.

Loffont, R., *Paris and Its People* (Edited by), 1958.

Loftie, W. J., *Westminster Abbey*, 1914.

Lord, G., *Andrew Marvell* (Edited by), 1968.

Macaulay, Thomas B., *History of England*, 1861.

Mallet, C. E., *A History of the University of Oxford*, 1964.

Masson, David, *The Life of John Milton*, 1880.

Mathew, David, *The Age of Charles I*, 1951.

Maurois, Andre, *An Illustrated History of England*, 1963; *The Miracle of England*, 1937.

McKenny, Ruth and Branstein, Richard, *Here's England*, 1951.

Mee, Arthur, *Oxfordshire*, 1965.

Miles, Hamish, *Portraits and Anecdotes*, 1965.

Milman, H. H., *Annals of St. Paul's Cathedral*, 1868.

Milman, Lena, *Sir Christopher Wren*, 1908.

Mitchell, H. J. and Leys, M. D. R., *A History of the English People*, 1950; *A History of London Life*, 1958.

Mitchell, S. Weir, *Some Recently discovered letters by William Harvey*, 1912.

Mitford, Nancy, *The Sun King*, 1968.

Moorhouse, S. H., *Samuel Pepys*, 1909.

More, L. T., *The Life and Works of the Honorable Robert Boyle*, 1944.

Moreshead, Sir Owen, *Windsor Castle*, 1951.

Muir, Erskine, *Oxford*.

Muller, Joseph-Emile, *Rembrandt, His Life and His Work*, 1964.

Nethercot, A. H., *Abraham Cowley*, 1931.

Norrie, Ian, *The Book of the City*, 1961.

Osman, Charles, *Castles*, 1926.

Palme, Per, *Triumph of Peace*, 1957.

Payne, J. F., *Thomas Syndeham*, 1900.

Peterson, R. T., *Sir John Digby*, 1956.

Pevsner, Nikolaus, *The Buildings of England*, 1962.

Phillimore, Lucy, *Sir Christopher Wren, His Family and His Times*, 1881.

Pilkington, Roger, *Robert Boyle*, 1959.

Pollock, Sir Frederick, *Spinoza, His Life and Philosophy*, 1912.

Ponsonby, Arthur, *John Evelyn*, 1933.

Powers, D'Arcy, *William Harvey*, 1897.

Priestly, Harold, *London, The Years of Change*, 1966.

Quennell, M., and C. H. B., *A History of Everyday Things in England*, 1960.

Ralph, James, *A Critical Review of the Public Buildings in and about London*, 1734.

Rasmussen, S. E., *Experiencing Architecture*, 1960; *London: The Unique City*, 1961.

Record of the Royal Society of London, 1940.

Reddaway, T. F., *Rebuilding London after the Great Fire*, 1940.

Richardson, A. E., and Gill, C. L., *London Houses from 1660 to 1820*, 1911.

Ritchie, R. L. G., *France: A Companion to French Studies*, 1958.

Robinson, E. F., *The Early History of the Coffee-House in England*, 1893.

Rosenberg, Jakob, *Rembrandt, His Life and Work*, 1964.

Ross, Ivan, *The Great Rebellion (1642-1660)*, 1966.

Ross, Sutherland, *The Plague and the Fire of London*, 1965.

Roth, Cecil, *Anglo-Jewish Letters*, 1938; *Essays and Portraits in Anglo-Jewish History*, 1962; *History of the Jews in England*, 1941.

Rousseau, Pierre, *Man's Conquest of the Stars*, 1959.

Rowse, A. L., *The English Spirit*, 1945; *The Tower of London*, 1972.

Royston, O. M., and Harrison, Molly, *How They Lived (1485-1700)*, 1963.

Rubenstein, Stanley, *Historians of London*, 1968.

Rukeyser, Muriel, *The Traces of Thomas Harriot*, 1971.

Rye, W. B., *England as seen by Foreigners in the days of Elizabeth and James I*, 1865.

Saillens, Emile, *John Milton*, 1964.

Sallman, R. R., *Civil War and Commonwealth*.

Sargeaunt, John, *Annals of Westminster School*, 1898.

Saunders, Beatrice, *The Age of Candlelight*, 1959; *John Evelyn and His Times*, 1970.

Saunders, Hilary St. George, *Westminster Hall*, 1951.

Shepherd, C. W., *Everyone's St. Paul's*, 1966.

Shepperd, E., *Memorials of St. James' Palace*, 1894; *The Old Royal Palace of Whitehall*, 1902.

Sitwell, Sacheverell, *British Architects and Craftsmen*, 1948; *The Netherlands*, 1948.

Steegman, John, *Cambridge*, 1943.

Steinberg, S. H., *A New Dictionary of British History*, 1963.

Stephenson, H. T., *Shakespeare's London*, 1905.

Stokes, Hugh, *Sir Anthony Van Dyck*, 1905.

Stow, W., *Remarks on London and Westminster*, 1722.

Summerson, John, *Architecture in Britain (1530–1830)*, 1953; *Inigo Jones*, 1966; *Sir Christopher Wren*, 1953.

Tanner, I. E., *History and Treasures of Westminster Abbey*, 1953.

Taylor, V. E., *Samuel Pepys*, 1967.

Terry, Benjamin, *A History of England*, 1901.

Thiel, Rudolf, *And There Was Light*, 1957.

Thomson, G. M., *Sir Francis Drake*, 1972.

Thornbury, Walter, *London Old and New*, 1897.

Trease, Geoffrey, *Samuel Pepys and his world*, 1972.

Trevelyan, G. M., *The English Revolution 1688*; *England under the Stuarts*; *A History of England*, 1952; *Illustrated English Social History*, 1966.

Trevor-Roper, H. R., *Essays in British History*, 1964.

Walcott, M., *Memorials of Westminster*, 1851.

Ward, Charles, E., *The Life of John Dryden*, 1961.

Ward, John, *Lives of the Professors of Gresham College*, 1740.

Ward, R. A., *The Architecture of the Renaissance in France*, 1911.

Warner, Townsend, *A Brief Survey of British History*, 1951.

Waugh, Norah, *The Cut of Men's Clothes (1600–1900)*, 1964.

Weaver, Lawrence, *Sir Christopher Wren*, 1951.

Wedgwood, C. V., *A Coffin for King Charles*, 1964; *Oliver Cromwell*; *The King's Peace (1637–1641)*, 1955; *The King's War (1641–1647)*, 1968; *The Trial of Charles I*, 1964.

Welch, Joseph, *Queen's Scholars, Westminster*, 1852.

Whinney, Margaret, *Wren*, 1971.

Whistler, L., *The Imagination of Sir John Vanbrugh*, 1954; *Sir John Vanbrugh, Architect and Dramatist*, 1938.

White, Christopher, *Rembrandt and his world*, 1964.

Wilcox, Turner, *The Dictionary of Costume*, 1969.

Wildeblood, Joan, and Peter Brinson, *The Polite World*, 1965.

Willis, R., *Benedict de Spinoza, His Life, Correspondence, Ethics*, 1870.

Wilson, John, *Nell Gwynn*.

Wilson-Whitaker, G., *Sir Christopher Wren, His Life and Times*, 1932.

Wittkower, Rudolf, *Bernini—Bust of Louis XIV*, 1951; With F. Saxl, *British Art and the Mediterranean*, 1948.

Wolley, A. R., *Oxford University and City*, 1951.

Wren, C., *Parentalia*, 1750.

Young, Elizabeth and Wayland, *Old English Churches*, 1956.

Zagorin, Perez, *The Court and the Country*, 1969.

Ziegler, Gilette, *The Court of Versailles*, 1962.